BROKEN DOVE

THE FANTASYLAND SERIES
BOOK FOUR

KRISTEN ASHLEY

A LOVE IS EVERYTHING SAGA BY

KRISTEN

NEW YORK TIMES BESTSELLING AUTHOR

ASHLEY

FANTASYLAND BOOK FOUR

BROKEN DOVE

Broken Dove

This book is a work of fiction. Any reference to historical events, real people, or real places are used fictitiously. Other names, characters, places, and incidents are products of the author's imagination. Any resemblance to actual events, locales, or persons, living or dead, is coincidental.

Cover Image: Pixel Mischief Designs

Every girl's gotta have her girl that no matter what time passes,
No matter the distance,
When they are again together, all that fades away.
And every girl's gotta have the girl who gives her peace.
Calm. Contentment.
But likes her fantasy.
That girl for me is Elizabeth "Bethy" Bullard.
So this book is for her.

PROLOGUE
NOT HIS PLANS

Apollo Ulfr saw the dancing lights against his closed eyelids before he felt the presence in the room.

He rolled out of the bed, grabbing the knife from underneath his pillow as he did so. Crouching by the bed, scanning the room even as his eyes became accustomed to the dark, suddenly he felt it and knew it was her.

The witch.

Valentine Rousseau.

Annoyed, seeing as it was the dead of night, he was naked, had not long before sent the Beniessienne whore to her own bed and he'd already told the witch his plans (and these were not the plans he'd shared with her, hence the whore who had left), and last, he was in Fleuridia to collect his children from boarding school so he could put them in a safe place before darkness settled on the land, he straightened, doing so speaking.

"Witch, I told you the time and place you were to bring her to me, and this is not—"

She interrupted him, her voice, as usual, wry, but there was an underlying urgency to it that made his skin prickle.

"If you want to meet the Ilsa of my world, I suggest you change your plans."

Through the dark, Apollo narrowed his eyes on her slim shadow.

"And this means...?" he prompted when she said no more.

"This means, the Apollo of my world has found her."

When last they spoke, she'd explained what that meant.

The Apollo Ulfr of the other world, his twin, was not a good man.

And he'd harmed Ilsa. Because of this, she was evading him.

Now his twin had found her.

Gods damn it. He'd waited bloody years to have his wife back. He wasn't going to let the other bloody him in a parallel universe take her away.

Without delay, Apollo bent to collect his clothes from the floor, commanding, "You'll take me to her."

"Is that a question?" she asked in reply.

Yanking up his breeches, he cut his gaze to her shadow. "No, it's bloody not."

Thankfully, the maddening witch, who could be sly and perverse, instantly lifted her elegant hands with her long, slim fingers tipped in scarlet-painted nails, and he saw the green mist start to light the room.

"Bring your weapons," she warned.

Bloody hell.

Ilsa.

"Of course," he murmured, having yanked on his shirt, he pulled on his boots and moved quickly to the chair where he'd thrown his cape and saber.

"All of them, Apollo," she went on.

Bloody hell.

He didn't respond.

He swung his cape around, quickly buckling it on its slant across his chest. He did the same with the scabbard that held his saber. He donned his knife belt, shoved his blade into the sheath and moved to the wardrobe. Bending low, he pulled the knives out of the box at the bottom and shoved them in his boots, one on each side.

The green mist had encompassed the room and he and the witch were both fading by the time he moved to her.

Although he didn't fall, he felt the ground give way beneath his feet and all faded to black.

When he felt solid beneath him again and their environs came into sharp focus, at what Apollo saw, his blood coursed scalding through his veins, he opened his mouth...

And he *roared.*

I

TENDERNESS AND PAIN

F*ive minutes earlier...*

I RAN up the steps as fast as I could, one of my hands carrying my keys (always ready, *always*), the other hand in my purse, digging into the side pocket where I kept my phone.

The asshole had found me.

Three years on the run and he'd found me.

Damn it!

Oh well. Fuck it. I'd planned for this.

It was go time.

I made it to the shabby landing where my apartment was located and sprinted down the hall, my breath coming fast, my heart beating hard, my skin cold.

But my head was clear.

I'd been preparing for this.

He wasn't going to get me again.

Not again.

Quickly, I shoved my key into the lock and turned. Repeat with the dead-bolt. I opened the door, dashed inside and slammed it shut.

It was a crap door. But not crap locks since I'd sweet-talked my creepy, ogling landlord with a lot of batting of lashes and broken promises to give me a significant upgrade.

Now I was counting on those good locks to give me time.

My apartment was not in a great area of town, as most of them weren't these last three years. Cheap and not my style.

I liked nice things. I was a label whore. I wanted a good life.

It was a flaw in my nature that cost me a lot.

Too much.

In other words, everything.

Also, my apartments were chosen so the landlords wouldn't blink when I jumped the lease seeing as they probably lost tenants regularly for a variety of shitty life reasons that the people who were forced to live in these shitty places always had.

Then again, this apartment was rented like all my apartments were, on a fake ID. So even if a landlord wanted to find me after I jumped the lease three, six, nine months early, he wouldn't know who to look for.

I turned the lock, threw the deadbolt home and engaged the chain.

Then I ran to my bedroom. Having pulled out my phone, my thumb moved over the screen to hit a contact I had programmed in as A-ICE so it was top of the heap.

I made it to my bedroom as I hit go on the phone.

Three years ago, I'd never phone the police. Pol had taught me not to do that.

For the three years I'd been on the run, I didn't get them involved either since I'd learned that lesson well.

Now, I'd need them to clean up the mess (maybe).

I made it to the safe in my closet before I heard, "Nine one one, what's your emergency?"

"My husband—" I started, jabbing the first two digits of the code into the keypad on the safe but hitting the third wrong when I jumped because I heard a loud thump on my front door.

I shook my head and closed my eyes hard.

Focus, Ilsa. Focus, I told myself, opening my eyes and clearing the code on the safe.

"Ma'am?" the 911 operator called. "Your emergency?"

"My husband found me," I told her, hitting the correct digits and the release button and gratefully hearing the whirs of the door opening on the safe. "His name is Pol Ulfr. Apollo Ulfr. He's a drug dealer in Portland, Oregon. He's abusive and I've been running from him for three years. Now he's caught me. I'm in apartment 3D at twenty-six, sixty-one Rampart Street."

I heard another thud on the door.

Therefore, I added, "And he's right outside my door."

I reached into the safe and wrapped my hand around the grip as I kept speaking.

"I've got a gun. You need to send someone soon. If he gets to me first, I'll use it."

"Ma'am, do not arm yourself. I'm dispatching officers immediately to your location," the 911 operator told me, but I ignored this.

She didn't know. She didn't have a clue. And I hoped to God she never would.

Instead of sharing that, I warned her, "He'll have men. At least one. And trust me, badges and uniforms will not stop them from getting what they want."

And they wanted me.

Or at least Pol did.

But with the loyalty his men showed him, they'd go down in a hail of gunfire before they'd give up doing whatever they had to do to get Pol what he wanted.

"They're en route now," the operator continued. "So find a safe place and please—"

Another thud on the door which included some splintering wood.

They'd be through soon.

Thus, there was no safe place. Not in this apartment.

Not anywhere.

Unless I made it safe.

I darted to a corner of the room and hunkered down, eyes aimed through the dark at the door, saying, "Gotta go now."

"Ma'am—"

"Bah-bye," I whispered, hit end call, dropped my phone on the floor and shrugged my purse off.

I then lifted the gun to point it at the door.

Shit.

The outside door crashed open.

Shit!

I checked to make certain the safety was off.

It was off.

Could I do this?

I sucked in breath through my nose.

I could do this.

But only because I had to.

I moved my finger to the trigger.

I heard the thumping feet. Running. One man, not several.

Pol wouldn't be running. That wasn't Pol's style. He sauntered, he didn't run. Not unless he was on a state-of-the art treadmill while making drug deals on his Bluetooth.

Then again, he'd been deprived of his favorite toy for three years. He didn't treat that toy nice, far from it. But it was still his favorite, he'd want it back and he got what he wanted.

Always.

I sucked in another breath, then whispered, "Not tonight."

A shadow came through the door.

My throat closed and I froze.

I'd planned for this. Damn it, I'd planned. I'd been psyching myself up for this exact moment for years.

Why was he getting closer, and I wasn't pulling the stupid trigger?

"Stop, I've got a gun!" I shouted my warning.

He didn't stop and was almost on me when my finger remembered my plans and squeezed.

I jumped at the loud sound of the gunshot, heard a surprised, pained grunt and the shadow was reeling back.

Oh God.

I'd shot a man. Crap! I'd shot a man!

God, how I *hated* Pol.

But I saw now that man wasn't Pol. I knew it because I could feel it and see it. Pol was taller than that staggering shadow, not as bulky.

And he was right behind that shadow when it fell back.

I knew this because I heard his hated but nevertheless deep, attractive voice that I *so* never wanted to hear again clip, "Jesus, what the fuck?"

I wasn't prepared for him to be so close.

So I wasn't prepared when his hand snaked out catching mine that held the gun at the wrist, twisting so hard the pain shot up my arm, shoulder and even my neck, making my ear tingle.

I'd planned. I really had.

But I'd also planned before.

And Pol, fucking, fucking *Pol* always got the best of me.

In order to focus on not getting some part of my arm broken, I had to twist my body with it and my fingers let loose around the grip of the gun.

Pol let me go, caught the gun and clearly flipped it to hold it by the barrel because the next thing I knew, the butt was coming down hard on the flesh under my cheekbone.

Freaking *ouch*.

I fell to one hand at my side, the other one instinctively going up to my cheekbone as agony radiated through my cheek and eye, causing black spots to form in my vision.

Shit, I'd forgotten.

If you told me I'd ever forget how this felt, I wouldn't believe you.

But three years without it, I'd forgotten how fucking much *it hurt.*

New thing, though, even though the spots were still flickering behind my eyes, the rest of my vision was turning an eerie, emerald green.

Weird and probably not good.

"You shot Manny. Jesus, Ilsa, you stupid *cunt,*" Pol barked from close, and as usual, he didn't hesitate.

I felt his foot connect with my ribs so hard, it lifted me straight up and turned me so my back slammed against the wall.

I came down hard on my side just in time to hear a terrifying masculine roar.

Not a shout.

Not a bellow.

An animalistic (but still human) *roar* of unadulterated *rage.*

At first, I thought it was coming from Pol and I stiffened in order to brace for the next blow.

But when it didn't come, as I lifted my eyes, that eerie green light was so bright it was illuminating the room so I could now see everything clearly.

Still, I blinked and shoved up to my forearm, the pain in my face and ribs completely forgotten because I was pretty certain, as clear as things were in that strange light, I wasn't seeing correctly.

This was because I was seeing the impossible.

And the impossible was that there were two Pols.

One was the Pol I was used to. Tall. Powerfully built. Fit. Hair well-groomed. Tailored slacks and shirt making him look classy and hot (if you didn't know what an asshole he was, that was).

The other was a different Pol.

Still tall and powerfully built, he was, however, more fit. *Clearly* more fit. Like, by *a lot.* He made the other Pol look like Pol Lite. This new Pol was a Pol Powerhouse.

His dark hair was also not well-groomed but in need of a cut and it looked like he just got out of bed. And he wasn't wearing classy, tailored clothes. He wasn't even wearing jeans and a t-shirt.

I blinked again.

Good God, he was wearing what looked like breeches, tall boots that went up to his knees, a lace-up-the-collar shirt, and a freaking *cape* of all things.

Yes. A cape!

Apparently, being pistol whipped made you hallucinate. But there it was. The vision before me was Pol in a dude-from-a-romance-novel-cover outfit *hammering* the normal Pol with his fists, the mighty, nauseating thud of flesh against flesh thumping through the room.

Holy cow.

The Pol I knew was down on a knee. But he suddenly twisted away from the romance-novel-cover Pol and began to lift his hand that was still carrying my gun.

That was when I heard an attractive, cultured, insanely bored-sounding female say, "Apollo, *chéri*, the other you holds a deadly weapon."

I was about to take my eyes away from the two Pols to look where the woman's voice was coming from but didn't when I heard what I could swear was the hiss of steel.

Yep. I was right. It was the hiss of steel. I knew this because the romance-novel-cover Pol was now wielding a sword.

A freaking *sword*!

What the hell!

Then I pressed myself back into the wall when, with a practiced, economical, cool-as-shit (if it wasn't scary-as-all-get-out and seriously gross besides) slice going around almost in a full circle, the romance-novel-cover Pol *cut off* the regular Pol's hand.

Yes.

Cut off his hand!

I made a noise in my throat as I swallowed hard against the vomit that surged up and Pol emitted a violent rumble of fury and pain, clutching his still-there hand to his now stumped wrist.

Okay. I wasn't hallucinating.

I was unconscious and having a very sick disgusting dream.

Still, even knowing this, I didn't wake up which I really wished I would.

But no. The dream continued and the romance-novel-cover Pol with his big sword came around for another pass. I closed my eyes and shrunk back further, pressing into the wall behind me like I wanted it to absorb me because it looked like he intended to cut Pol's head off.

I heard a thud of a body hitting floor (though not a second thud which would indicate a head hitting the floor) and I again swallowed bile and terror as police sirens sounded in the distance.

I didn't know if this was good or bad. I could explain my need for a gun, and I'd do my time if a jury of my peers thought I deserved it.

I couldn't explain a beheading.

"We must leave *tout de suite*." The woman said and she didn't sound bored anymore. She didn't sound freaked like I was (in a big fucking way). But there was a hint of urgency to her voice.

I opened my eyes just in time to be lifted up in romance-novel-cover Pol's arms.

Uh-oh.

This wasn't what unconscious felt like. I'd been that way often in my life and not just due to sleeping. I knew what it felt like. And this was not it.

His arms around my middle back and behind my knees caged me iron tight to his broad chest as he peered down at me, straightened and turned, walking to the middle of the room and stopping.

I would have protested. I *should* have protested.

I didn't protest.

This was because I was looking in Pol's eyes.

But this was not Pol.

I'd seen a myriad of looks in Pol's eyes. Love. Hate. Fury. Annoyance. Passion. Humor. I could go on (and on).

This man in his weird clothes did not have any of the looks Pol had given me over the way-too-many years we were together.

He was gazing at me with a tenderness that was so acute I swear it looked like he was in pain.

And not a little of it, the tenderness *or* the pain.

"You're not Pol," I whispered.

"No. I am not," he replied, steel threading through his tone, his voice Pol's voice and yet...*not.*

His arms held me close as all around us went black.

The loss of the green didn't concern me. This guy concerned me. This guy who wore weird clothes, knew how to wield a sword and didn't hesitate using it and looked at me like I was his reason for breathing concerned me.

So I kept talking.

"You're not a hallucination."

Some of the tenderness leaked from his eyes but only so amusement could replace it, and this was far from unattractive.

"I'm not that either, my dove."

My dove?

What the hell?

"Do I have a brain injury?" I asked, figuring this was the only explanation, and his eyes dropped to my cheek.

The tenderness and humor vanished before his gaze came back to mine.

"We shall see."

That wasn't a good answer.

I mean, I was uncertain about a reality where some dude had beat the shit out of Pol, cut off his hand and maybe his head, but only because there'd be a lot of explaining to do with the police. And I didn't care what that said about me. Perhaps dismemberment was a wee bit harsh a punishment for all of Pol's transgressions. But only a *wee* bit.

I wasn't uncertain about not wanting to have a brain injury. Pol had inflicted a lot of damage over the years (broken wrist, broken ribs, concussions, contusions, sprained ankles, etc.) but he'd never put me into a coma.

Before I could come to terms with any of this, new Pol was gently lying me down on a bed and it was a fluffy bed that felt great (thus I knew it wasn't my lumpy bed in my apartment that didn't feel great).

He muttered to the room at large, "Light," which I took as an order to the unknown woman I sensed still with us because within seconds weak light lit the room.

I didn't get the chance to process this new impossibility of me being on a comfy bed because he sat by my side and lifted his hand to rest it on my cheek. The flat of his thumb was just below the still stinging, tightening (thus swelling) flesh where Pol hit me with the butt of the gun.

Oh, and he'd bent deep, his face was close to mine and that sweet look was on it again.

"What did you endure prior to our arrival, Ilsa?" he asked, his voice low, deep, warm and chock full of concern.

And near as sweet as his look.

Right. Time to reassess. I was all geared up to defend myself when Pol found me, so geared up I was ready to go down fighting (if I had to, though obviously this was not my preference). I'd even shot Manny, who was a dufus and a pathologically mean one and those two things didn't go well together, but I still didn't want to shoot him (or anyone).

I was not prepared for whatever the hell was currently happening.

Therefore, I answered, "Uh..."

"Do I need to call a physician?" he asked.

I knew the answer to that. It might have been years and that pistol whip hurt like a mother, but this was tame in comparison to what Pol could do to me.

"No, thanks," I answered then stupidly got chatty. "I'm good. I've had way worse. Thanks to, uh...*you*, he didn't get the chance to get started so I'll be all right."

This was the wrong thing to say, and I knew it instantly.

His adoring look fled. His jade-green eyes got hot, his strong jaw went hard, and a muscle ticked straight up that jaw into his cheek.

Oh boy.

There it was. That was the Pol I knew, and I shrank back into the pillow as my body prepared to flee.

He saw it, and I was guessing, like Pol, he didn't miss much. Or, with the shine of intelligence that Pol did not have emanating from his eyes, not exactly like Pol, perhaps he didn't miss *anything*.

"I would not harm you, Ilsa," he gritted from between clenched teeth.

"Uh-huh," I mumbled unconvincingly, as anyone would, seeing as I was staring at the wrath in his eyes and listening to him talk between his teeth.

The pads of his fingers pressed surprisingly gently into my cheek, and he dipped his face closer.

"Never," he whispered, his tone fierce and still angry but something struck me.

This was not just a word. It also wasn't a promise.

It was a vow.

What the hell was happening?

I knew what wasn't happening. I wasn't in my bed. There were no police sirens sounding. And the green was gone. Giving that a millisecond of reflection, that green was not right.

Nothing was right.

So, considering nothing was right, I knew I had to get this new Pol out of my face so I could take stock and make a new plan.

Therefore, I breathed, "Okeydokey."

His head tipped slightly to the side and his dark brows twitched.

"Okeydokey?" he asked.

Oh boy.

Why did his deep voice saying that ridiculous word low and bemused make my mouth get dry at the same time it made me want to smile in a moment that was so far from smile-worthy, it was not funny.

Shit!

I didn't know who this guy was or what was happening. What I did know was that I'd been here before. I'd looked at that handsome face with those fabulous lips and that head of rich, dark, thick hair. I'd looked into those amazing eyes that were pure jade. No joke. They were a milky, translucent green that was so beautiful, once you caught sight of it you never wanted to look away. All of this on a tall, commanding body that made my knees weak, and my nipples get hard.

Years ago, I'd looked at all that was him and I'd made the biggest mistake in my life.

And that was *not* going to happen again, even if I was currently comatose from a pistol-whipping brain injury and not experiencing any of this at all.

His hand at my cheek slid down to my neck. I focused on him when it did, and he spoke.

"I don't know this word, my dove."

Who didn't know the word "okeydokey?"

I didn't ask that.

I explained. Quickly.

"It means okay. Fine. Good. All right. In this case, I believe you."

"If you do, why do you press yourself against the pillows still?" he asked.

"Habit?" I said the word as a question as well as an answer and it was another mistake.

His face started to darken again with anger, so I lifted up a hand, palm toward him and kept babbling.

"Okay, don't go all freaky on me again. It's cool. I'm good. I'll relax." I forced myself to relax (slightly) and pointed it out by indicating myself with a sweep of the hand. "See. Relaxed. I'm chilling. It's all good. I'm fine."

"You lie," he said softly. "You lie with very strange words, but you still lie."

God!

I needed to get myself together. Although he said that softly, my guess would be he didn't like liars (because no one liked liars) and I needed to keep him calm, not rile him up.

"I—" I started to try and cover my lie, but he cut me off.

"You don't know where you are or who I am. You've been kicked and sustained a blow to your face. And you've witnessed—"

I closed my eyes tight and requested, "Please, let's not do a blow by blow."

His fingers gave my neck a squeeze and I opened my eyes. "I needed to disarm him, Ilsa," he explained, his voice still soft.

"By cutting off his hand?" I asked and his brows drew together.

It was a scary look.

Uh-oh.

"You concern yourself with his welfare?" he asked back.

"I actually don't care what happens to Pol. I just don't want to *see* it happen. And that was some sick shit, but cutting off his head—"

He interrupted me, his brows still drawn, his look no less scary. "I did not take his head."

He didn't?

Well, I guessed that was why I didn't hear a head hit the floor.

I thought on this a nanosecond and decided to take it as good news.

"And if he gets attention for his wound and it's cauterized, he'll not lose his life due to losing his hand," the new Pol went on.

I decided to take that as good news too, simply because I was a human being, and it was required of me.

The new Pol then finished, "I hit him on the side of his head with the flat of my saber. He lost consciousness, but not his life."

Well, there you go.

"Okeydokey," I replied, his eyes lit, and his mouth quirked.

Oh boy.

That look wasn't scary. It was something else altogether.

"Could I interrupt at this juncture, *chéri*, and suggest you get a cool compress, ice if it's available, raw meat if it's not?" The polished female voice came at us, and I was glad of it because new Pol lifted a few inches away and turned his head to peer into the shadows.

I looked beyond him and saw, through not very good lighting, a willowy redhead in a fabulous green dress and way more fabulous green slingback platform pumps, top to toe as slick and urbane as her voice would lead you to believe.

"Her cheek is swelling. It may not be too late for the ice to contain some of it," she continued, and the new Pol was up in a flash.

"I'll see to this immediately," he stated, moving swiftly, his cape swinging out dramatically behind him (which unusually, but awesomely, was set at a slant along his back—over one shoulder, under the other) and then it swung again when he stopped and turned back to me. "Rest. I will return shortly," he ordered then he looked at the redhead and kept at it. "See to her until I return."

After issuing his commands, he disappeared into the shadows, and I heard a door open and close.

My eyes shifted to the woman.

When they did, I saw her move into the shadows, but she came back into the circle of weak light pulling an elegant armchair with her, positioning it close to the bed.

Without a word, she again disappeared into the shadows. I stared in the direction she disappeared, my focus on her and what might come next in this bizarreness, only vaguely noting that I was on a somewhat large bed with an arched footboard that had light-colored padding on it, which was just as elegant as the armchair. I also noted the coverlet I was lying on was quilted, it was satin (satin!), and it looked in the dim light like it might be some shade of blue.

She reappeared carrying two wineglasses filled with red wine. And they were not just any wineglasses. Like the chair, footboard and coverlet, they were elegant—finely etched and gracefully blown.

I knew nice things. I had champagne tastes and studied the finer things in life with great energy and rapt attention. Pol was just like me and lived a life where he was certain to get them for himself, and, by extension, for me.

So I knew everything around me was most definitely *not* my shabby, cheap, furnished apartment in a crappy neighborhood.

I just didn't know where I was.

Or how I got there.

She set one glass of wine on a nightstand by the bed and seated herself probably like a ballerina would take a load off (not that I'd ever seen that, but still). She slowly crossed her legs and her knees dropped to the side but her back and shoulders stayed straight so she looked like she was posing for a picture, not relaxing for a chat.

"Fleuridian wine," she murmured, tipping her head slightly to the glass on the nightstand all the while lifting hers close to her lips. "Have some. It's superb."

I'd never heard of Fleuridian wine.

I didn't ask. I also didn't reach for the wineglass.

I held her eyes.

She took a sip of wine not releasing my gaze.

Then her hand slowly fell so she could rest it against the arm of the chair, and she continued to hold my eyes.

Finally, she announced, "I am Valentine Rousseau. Like you, I'm not of this world. I live in New Orleans. And I'm a witch."

I stared at her, feeling my lips part and thinking one word.

Fabulous.

2

DEEP TO EXTREMES

"Not of this world?" I asked quietly when she didn't continue.

She nodded her head but said, "I would advise, beautiful Ilsa, that you listen closely and quickly come to terms with all I'm about to tell you. I have little time before Ulfr gets back. He'll want to make certain you're seen to, but he'll not want to be separated from you for long."

I ignored that and repeated, "Not of this world?" Then I kept at it without giving her a chance to respond. "What is this world? And you're a witch? What does that mean?"

"We'll start at the beginning," she offered.

"That'd be a good idea," I replied, pushing myself up in the bed so my shoulders were against the headboard, and I managed to do this only flinching a little bit at the pain.

She watched me as I moved and her eyes narrowed slightly, like I'd surprised her.

But she didn't mention that.

She started from the beginning which should have been a blessing, but it turned out to be somewhat of a curse. Or, if not a curse in the strictest sense, it was definitely bizarre, confusing and maybe not so good.

"I am a witch from a long line of witches," she began. "And when I say that, *chérie*, my people have practiced the craft in New Orleans for centuries, and before that we practiced in France. Before that Rome. And before *that*...Egypt."

Visions of faces forming out of sandstorms and massive armies of huge-ass beetles crawling all over the place *à la* the movie *The Mummy* collided in my head even as I blinked in shock at what she was saying.

Then I made the best decision I'd made in a long time. I reached out to the wineglass, nabbed it and took a big, old sip.

As I did so, Valentine continued, "Therefore, the craft being passed through my line for millennia, I am powerful. *Very*. This power gives me the ability to move between worlds, which is very difficult and consumes an enormous amount of magic. And with the strength born in me through countless generations of witches, I can not only move myself at will and as often as I like, I can also move others."

Move between worlds.

Oh boy.

I was already ready for her to be done, but alas, she kept going.

"And you will see, of course, looking around you, that you are no longer in our world. You're in a parallel universe. Specifically, Fleuridia, my favorite of the countries in the Northlands. Though, saying that, I have no favorite in the Southlands." She gave a delicate shudder that was barely a movement but said it all about whatever the freaking Southlands were. Then she finished. "And you will have noted that in this parallel universe, we have twins, as you've already met your husband's."

Okay.

Seriously.

How hard had Pol hit me with that gun?

"I see you don't believe me," she stated, telling me I was not hiding my reaction in the slightest. "And this is what I wish for you to come to terms with quickly, for I speak the truth."

When she quit talking, I held her eyes and laid it out.

"Let me get this straight. Twenty minutes ago, I was running from my husband, a *really* not very good husband I've been running from for years. He caught me, started to do what he does best, that being inflicting pain. Then you and that other Pol show up, coming from another dimension. The other Pol wears romance novel guy clothes, and he also doesn't hesitate in cutting off the Pol of my dimension's hand and whacking him upside the head with the flat of his sword. After that, you spirited us to wherever-we-are-now which is someplace that has twins of people in our dimension, very comfortable beds and really lovely wineglasses."

"We are not in another dimension, *chérie*," she corrected. "We are in a *parallel universe*."

"There's a difference?" I asked.

"Oh yes," she answered. "There's only one parallel universe but there are many different dimensions, and you don't want to go to any of those." Her lip curled in a refined sneer that, no matter how freaked I was, I had to admit was all kinds of cool. "The creatures there..." she trailed off as she shook her head.

"Well, thanks for not taking me to another dimension," I muttered and sucked back another healthy sip of wine.

She leaned slightly forward, again catching my eyes and her smooth voice was deadly serious when she stated, "Ilsa, this is not a jest. This is not a hallucination. This is not a dream. This is real. All you will experience in the coming days and weeks will seem very strange to you and you must prepare for it, accept it and adapt to it. Quickly. That said, you are here now, you're safe, and you're not going back. But with what is to come, it's important that you adjust swiftly to your new circumstances."

That didn't sound great. None of it did, to be honest. But that *really* didn't.

"With what's to come?" I inquired when she didn't explain.

She threw out her hand not holding her wineglass. "That's not for now. What you must understand for now is that you're safe here, you must learn to trust in that, and," she leaned deeper toward me, "the man who just left this room is not the Pol you know. He's Apollo Ulfr of the House of Ulfr of the ice country of the north, Lunwyn."

"Pol is also Apollo Ulfr of the, um...House of Ulfr, I guess, but from the rain city of Portland," I joked, perhaps getting a little hysterical (and who would blame me).

"Again, this is not amusing." Her voice held a vein of impatience. "This is real. And you must understand these two men are not the same man," she stressed.

"I got that," I mumbled and took another sip of wine.

"*Chérie,*" more leaning and her eyes got kind of scary, "they...are *not*...the same man."

She was freaking me out and to freak out while freaking out didn't feel all that great.

So the only thing I could do was whisper, "Okeydokey."

She studied me a moment before she sat back. "It will be difficult, with what you've endured at the hand of the other Apollo, to remember that. But don't forget it."

"You've made your point," I assured her.

"I haven't," she disagreed. "You see, in each world the same people reside, yet they aren't the same."

"You've already told me that," I reminded her, wondering how she could forget considering we were still talking about it.

"No, beautiful Ilsa, you're too dazed by all that's occurred to put it together. If there are two Apollos, then there are two Ilsas."

Uh-oh.

More not good.

She wasn't done.

"Alas, the Ilsa of this world is no longer *of* this world. She has passed."

Oh my God.

The other me was dead?

That sucked!

Valentine still wasn't done, and she had a whopper of a grand finale.

"And she was the wife of the Apollo of this world."

Oh boy.

"Holy crap," I whispered.

"Indeed," she replied.

"I don't get it," I told her. "What does that mean?"

It hit me. My eyes flew to the shadows where I heard the door open and close when Apollo left then I looked back to her.

"Shit, does he think she's me? Or I'm her? Or..." I threw out a hand, "whatever?"

"He does not. He's aware of the twins. He knows you are not her. But that didn't stop him from acquiring my services to find you and bring you to him. I am far from inexpensive, *chérie,* and I warned him of your plight in our world and that you might not receive him very well. But he was very determined."

None of this was good. It was weird. Bizarre. Unbelievable. *Fantastical.*

And it wasn't getting any better.

"I'm not certain that's good," I shared my understatement.

"I agree. I don't know how the other Ilsa died. I don't know when she died. I do know it has been some time. And I also know that in that time, his grief has not faded. Not at all."

That tenderness I saw in his eyes.

And the pain.

Yep. This wasn't getting any better.

"I'm not her," I whispered.

"I am aware of that," she replied, not in a whisper.

We held each other's eyes. When I couldn't take it anymore, I sucked back another healthy sip of wine, straightened my shoulders against the headboard and again looked at her.

"So, I'm in a parallel universe, safe from Pol, which is good normally but now it's better because he's going to be seriously pissed he no longer has a hand, as anyone would be, but Pol will take that to his usual extremes. And extremes of his extremes, my guess, would be catastrophic. And I'm with *another* Pol, who's not Pol but Apollo, and he brought me here to replace his dead wife."

She shook her head again.

"Do not mistake that man for a man who would allow grief to dull his intellect," she warned. "He was driven to have you here, but he is also very aware that you are not the woman he loved and lost. I do not know his intentions in having you here. I know only that he is a man of character. A man of honor. A very brave man. And last, one who feels deeply. Deeper than most. I would even go so far as to say deep *to extremes*, even if he rarely shows it."

I was thinking that was good and bad. The other Pol felt deep to extremes and his extremes were no good.

But the Pol I knew had no problems showing it. It was me who had a problem with the way he showed it.

This was a lot to take in, but I was beginning to find it hard to concentrate. Either due to the blow to the face or my adrenaline crashing, suddenly I was fading.

Valentine saw it and I felt the wineglass sliding out of my hand.

I blinked up at her, drowsiness coming on so quickly it wasn't right, and I knew it was no adrenaline crash.

My eyes dropped to the wineglass.

"Settle, *ma chérie*," she murmured, pressing on my shoulder so I had no choice but to slide back down the bed.

"You drugged me," I accused.

She didn't deny it.

Instead, she said, "Sleep is good. Tomorrow, you'll be rested, and you can better understand all that's happening and acclimatize to your surroundings."

"You drugged me," I repeated, my words now slightly slurred, whatever she gave me working fast.

"It's for the best."

Someone drugging you without your knowledge was not for the best. Maybe *their* best, but not yours.

"You—"

"Sleep," she whispered.

"But..."

I heard her sigh, but I said no more, because against my will, I did as I was told and slept.

I REGAINED consciousness in a sluggish way when my body was moved.

I was still mostly out of it, but I could tell the person in bed with me wasn't just joining me there. He was changing positions and taking me with him.

I didn't know how we were before, but when he settled, I was tucked close to his side, my cheek on his shoulder. As I struggled with consciousness, his fingers wrapped around my wrist and tugged my arm across his flat stomach.

I felt warm, soft skin over firm muscle pretty much everywhere.

Crap.

It was too bad I didn't have it in me to protest. But I was so lethargic, I couldn't move.

But I could speak.

"Pol?" I murmured and his arm holding me to him tightened as his hand at my wrist slid up my arm to curve around me.

"No," he grunted forcefully.

"Apollo," I whispered.

That got me a double arm squeeze.

"Yes," he replied, gently this time. "Sleep, my dove."

Oh boy.

Carefully, my voice as drowsy and vague as my brain, I said softly, "I don't think I'm your dove."

His reply was immediate. "You are my dove."

"I—"

Another squeeze of the arms, this could not be mistaken for anything but a "shut up squeeze," before he said, "A dove has great beauty, but is easily broken."

That was nice and all, poetic even, though a wee bit scary, and last, all true.

However.

"But—"

"She was 'my beauty,'" he whispered, an ache in his voice that made my stomach hurt and my throat tingle and bad, no matter how out of it I was.

He knew I knew.

And he knew I was not her.

At that ache, I didn't know why I did it, but it was me who cuddled closer as I whispered back, "I'm sorry."

On my words, his body stilled for a brief moment before he turned into me and gathered me even closer as he murmured, "As am I."

"Why are you—?"

He cut me off again with, "I could not save her."

Oh boy.

He kept going. "But I can save you."

Oh boy.

"Apollo—"

"Sleep."

"I—"

"We will talk later. Now, sleep."

I had a mind to ask about the sleeping arrangements. I also had a mind to thank him for saving me from Pol. Even if the way he did it was over the top and grisly, he still did it. I further had a mind to explore this parallel universe thing a bit more seeing as I was groggy, but I was still obviously there with him so there was a there to be.

Even if I had a mind to all this, I unfortunately blinked a blink that malfunctioned so that when my lids lowered, they stayed that way.

3
BE CAREFUL WHAT YOU WISH FOR

I felt the sunlight against my eyelids, so I opened them.

When I did, I saw a sea of satin sheets that were deep lilac in color, covered in a quilted satin bedspread that was pool blue. Beyond that, a vast expanse of room that led to a wall on which there were four sets of arched French doors all covered in wispy, pure-white sheers. The woodwork was painted an antique white. The walls a cool pale blue.

Between sets of doors two and three was a French provincial table on which was a large, etched glass vase out of which burst a thick, fluffy array of hydrangea blooms, the majority of them a delicate blue with one deep purple and one rich cream stuck in as a striking, but beautiful, contrast.

It was a room I'd never seen before. Yet I'd woken up in it.

I pushed up in bed, muttering, "What the—?"

Then it all came back to me.

Parallel universe.

The bad seed Pol's good guy (maybe) twin.

And a witch from New Orleans.

"Shit," I whispered, feeling the tightness in my face, the ache at my ribs, both very real. And also feeling the bed soft beneath me, the sheets luxurious against my hand, knowing it had all happened.

It had happened.

I looked around the room.

As I'd semi-noted last night, I was in a large bed, bigger than a queen, but not as big as a king. The intricately carved and arched head and footboard were both padded and buttoned in a creamy material, the wood around it painted antique white.

There were two nightstands, both French provincial, the carving also ornate.

On them—I leaned to my side carefully to look closer—there was what looked like extravagant *gas* lamps, their bases shining silver, their globes milky, frilled and beautifully engraved. My half-drunk wineglass was still there, and in the bright sunlight streaming through the curtains, that glass was even more extraordinary.

I pushed up and continued my study of the room.

An enormous antique white wardrobe with four doors, more carving and an arched top. A long, low dresser with nine drawers, the three in the middle narrower than the six at the sides, all their fronts having undulating curves.

There was another bouquet of hydrangeas on the top, this one carrying a majority of creamy white blooms with a couple of pale-blue ones added for contrast. On either side, milky globed lamps, taller than the ones on the nightstands but still matching them.

The dresser also held an elegant decanter half-full of wine, with two empty wineglasses, all sitting on a silver tray with a frilled lip.

I turned my head and saw in the far corner a squat, baroque dressing table with a three-sided mirror and a stool in front with a cushion padded in buttoned lilac velvet. The top was void—not a bottle, not a vase, but the piece needed no adornment. Still, it was clear it was unused.

I turned my head the other way and saw a pale-blue velvet covered chaise lounge with an arch to the side of the back and sweeping arms at top and foot that sat at a diagonal, aimed for a view out the French doors. In front of the doors at the other side was a seating arrangement of two armchairs, including the one Valentine had sat in, which had clearly been moved back. A table sat between them with another, smaller vase filled with purple hydrangea blooms.

The wood floors were covered in rugs with intricate but elusive designs, made so by their muted colors of blues, purples, creams and grays.

And set in the walls were more milky-globed sconces intermingled with black framed, cream matted pencil sketches of women all wearing fabulous, chic but old-fashioned gowns from evening wear to day wear to outdoor gear (I knew the last because they were wearing hats and peeking from around parasols).

The room was lavish, yet classy. Opulent, however still tasteful. It was more of everything I'd ever seen of this style of décor—more intricacy in the carving, the sweeping lines more delicate, the colors lusher. In fact, it was totally over-the-top. But weirdly, it managed to be gracious, not garish.

I concluded my perusal of the space thinking, *Okay, this might not be so bad,* the appearance of gas lamps and the understanding that Apollo was handy with a sword and Valentine had to explain that a gun was a deadly weapon and what these might mean notwithstanding.

I was about to throw the bedclothes back, get out of bed and find a bathroom (which I hoped they had) and take a look at my face, which felt worse than normal, when the door flew open.

My head jerked that way and I saw Apollo striding in.

He was still in romance novel hero clothes.

But these were better.

Dark-brown breeches that fit really well and by that I meant like a freaking *glove*. They left pretty much nothing to the imagination and what they did leave to the imagination, the parts that didn't told you the rest of it could be nothing but *perfection*.

And again, this proved he was all Pol because, at least looks-wise, Pol was all that, top to toe. It was just everything else that made him a jackass.

I stopped thinking of Pol and followed Apollo's breeches to his dark-brown boots that were kind of shiny like someone attempted to take care of them, but they weren't worn as a fashion statement. They were just *worn*.

Up my eyes went and I saw topping these was a cream shirt, full-sleeved and the collar was clearly meant to go up high on his neck and cover his throat, possibly with one of those poofy neck cloth thingies, but he wore the collar open at the throat, exposing the strong column of it, creating a miracle. Because at the sight of his throat, I forgot about his breeches.

I tore my eyes from his neck to look at his face.

Yep, this was Pol Powerhouse.

Or Apollo Powerhouse.

Pol didn't hold a candle to this guy.

I watched his gaze slide through me and he turned his head toward the door he'd just walked through.

I looked down at the pillow beside me that was dented seeing as his head had rested on it through the night, wondering distractedly how late it was and how long he'd been gone seeing as he was dressed and had already gone about facing the day.

Then I looked back his way to see that he was in the room, and he wasn't the only one.

A troop of women came with him. I stopped counting at six (and *maybe* was half done) when he started talking.

Or more accurately *commanding*, his gaze on one woman. "She'll need to be bathed and dressed. Take measurements in order that you can commence creating her apparel without delay. You'll have one week to provide her with a wardrobe that will see her through travel, on land and at sea."

Uh.

What?

He wasn't done.

"Send a missive to Lunwyn urgently. They'll need to prepare for her arrival. We make haste to Lunwyn so inform them that they have two months."

Wait.

It took two months to get to Lunwyn?

Two months?

He turned to me, took two steps toward the bed, but stopped, which put him at about ten feet away.

His eyes were blank when they fell on me, something I thought was weird, but I didn't have a lot of time to think on how weird it was because he continued talking immediately.

"Obviously, I was not prepared for your arrival and in your current condition," he looked to my cheek then back to my eyes, "the children shouldn't see you."

All the air compressed out of my lungs, and due to lack of oxygen they started burning.

Children?

He seemed not to notice my response for he went on.

"Indeed, I had planned carefully for how you would be introduced to them. Therefore, you may be traveling separately from us so I can take that time to prepare them. We mustn't delay in being away, however, for the witches are conniving with Baldur and whatever strike they intend to make is possibly imminent. We need to make haste in all of us arriving at the Ulfr estate in Lunwyn where I can leave you with the children in safety and rejoin Frey, Tor and the Dax."

Clearly, he thought Valentine was a lot more forthcoming during our conversation last night because I had no clue what he was talking about, but he seemed to think I did.

But I didn't ask.

I was still stuck on *children*.

Therefore, I wheezed, "Children?"

"Yes," he replied matter-of-factly.

"*Your* children?" I pushed out.

He stopped looking blank in order to look mildly impatient. "Yes. My children. Christophe and Élan."

Christophe and Élan.

A boy and a girl.

Or maybe two boys (I'd never heard the name Élan).

It didn't matter.

Children.

Apollo of this world and his dead Ilsa had children.

Two of them.

Two of them.

Suddenly, I was certain I was going to throw up, but luckily, he spoke again so I had something to focus on and could swallow it down.

"These women are lady's maids and seamstresses. They will attend you."

I didn't need lady's maids and seamstresses. I didn't even need a bathroom anymore.

I needed Valentine. Like *now*.

So I asked, "Where's Valentine?"

"I do not know. She disappeared in the night, as is her wont."

Disappeared?

Why?

Shit!

"Uh...I think she left a lot out last night," I informed him.

"I'm late being away to the children's school. You and I will talk later. But I'll warn you now, I'll have little time. There's much to be done before we embark on our journey, so think on your questions and use that time wisely," he stated and turned to leave.

Wait.

Hang on a second.

Who was this guy? And where was the guy who was all affectionate and kind and concerned and fierce?

"Wait!" I called when he'd almost made the door.

He turned back to me, definitely impatient now. "Ilsa, as I said, I'm late being away. I should have left half an hour ago."

"I..." I hesitated and tipped my head to the side. "Are you okay?"

His impatience fled, the blank mask slid over his face, and he answered, "I will be, if you leave me to go collect my children."

"Right," I said softly. "Of course."

He didn't acknowledge that. Not with a nod of his head, a lift of his chin or anything.

He just turned and walked out the door, and without pause, the troop of women rushed forward and descended on me.

It was late evening.

After Apollo took off, I'd been measured for clothing and then led to a room down the hall, which fortunately had a screen painted with a lovely landscape with people picnicking on it, behind which, unfortunately, there was a chamber pot.

I wasn't fired up about the chamber pot business, but it was something that didn't include me tiptoeing through the tulips (or whatever) to answer nature's call, so I used it.

The room also had a fabulous porcelain bath with silver claw feet and high sides.

It was safe to say, I was fired up about *that.*

The girls left and I was allowed to take a bath alone, but I noted there was no plumbing, although there was a drain. Still, the water was warm, the shampoo smelled of citrus, the soap of lavender, and the washcloth was slightly rough in a loofah kind of way.

When I got out, I grabbed the towel they left me on a dainty stool by the bath. It wasn't terrycloth but it was soft and absorbent and a fabulous shade of blue.

They'd also left a robe. It was silk, there was a fair bit of delicate lace, and it was butter yellow.

Okay, it was safe to say I was getting fired up more and more.

The women came back (three of them) and brushed my hair until it was almost dry then arranged it in a soft ponytail at my nape. They gave me light makeup, taking care with my bruised cheek (the room with the tub also had an oval mirror with scalloped edges on the wall; I looked in it and saw my cheek was not good, but still, as bad as it hurt, I'd had worse).

They also gave me undies (no bra, just a pair of white lace panties and they were like panties in my world except a *whole lot better*).

Then they helped me put on a dress that didn't fit, it was a hint too big, but it was lovely all the same. A gossamer fabric over a phenomenal crêpe de chine, both the color of a bruised peach. It had a scoop neck that showed some serious cleavage, a gathered bodice that led to an empire waist, and the skirts swept down to my feet, the back of it ending in a small kickass train.

After I got the dress on, they gave me four different pairs of slippers that I tried (they were all beautiful, two embroidered, one with a flat bow at the toe and one just plain satin). But none of them fit, (three too small, one too big) so I went barefoot.

And last, they brought me breakfast, which was croissants, jam, fruit, and thankfully, coffee.

Then they left.

I tried talking to them, but they spoke what sounded like French and I might know what *tout de suite* and *chérie* meant, but I took Spanish in high school so the rest of it was lost on me.

Since Apollo had spoken to one of them in English, which I would assume he'd know she'd understand, I tried to ask for her to come back as she'd disappeared with the women with the measuring tape.

This got me smiles, head tilts, brows drawing and shrugs, so I was thinking they were in the same boat as me and had no clue.

Thus, I gave up.

After I ate, I wandered to the French doors and pulled a set open.

Then I took a step back and winced.

I didn't wince from pain.

I winced because the rolling countryside was a green so green, a green so extraordinarily beautiful, it was difficult to witness.

In fact, it was so beautiful, it appeared unnatural.

I blinked several times and cautiously moved out onto the balcony.

The view was a unlike any other I'd seen, and I'd traveled with Pol, broadly.

But I'd never seen anything like what I was seeing then. That verdant green. The winding, creamy lane that was flanked on both sides by a riot of wild-flowers so bright, their stark juxtaposition against that green was unreal.

And that green seemed to go on and on, cut only by a steeple topping a church made of mellow rust stone, and opposite that some ways away, a large patch of bushy rows of what appeared to be lavender.

But in the distance, the green darkened in what appeared to be a forest that climbed partly up some jagged-topped mountains, their stone a severe gray which was lightened by deep grooves that scored nearly down to the tree line, the grooves filled with snow.

It was phenomenal. Amazing.

Otherworldly.

"My God," I breathed, finally believing without a doubt I was in a parallel universe.

There was nothing like this in my world and I couldn't make this up in a dream. No one could make this up in a dream, it was just that phenomenal.

I determined to take a walk and see it close up but decided to do that the next day (if we weren't "away" by then). After the activity of the morning, my ribs were killing me, my face didn't feel all that great, and I didn't speak French (or whatever) so I couldn't ask the girls if they had ibuprofen or aspirin.

Instead, I drank in the view until it dissolved in front of me as two names laid siege to my brain.

Christophe and Élan.

I closed my eyes tight and sucked in a deep breath, the kind I'd practiced over and over again the last eleven years Pol had been in my life. And in pulling in that breath, as I'd learned to do and do it well, I controlled the emotion I couldn't allow myself to feel.

I opened my eyes, and having it under control, I allowed my mind to go there.

Christophe and Élan.

I would never name my kids those names.

But Pol would. He'd totally name our kids names like that. And Pol, being

Pol, even if I'd picked out my own names, would name them whatever the hell he wanted.

Unfortunately, he'd lost his mind about something I no longer remembered—but when he did, the reasons were never really important—and beat the crap out of me when I was seven months pregnant, and thus, I lost our boy.

And I'd miscarried in my sixth month and lost our girl.

These had bought me the only long blocks of time with Pol that hadn't included him losing it frequently. Being the biggest asshole I'd ever met in my life, even he wasn't that big of an asshole to blame me for losing our son after he'd beat the crap out of me and I'd eventually hit the ground and rolled down the six brick stairs that led to our fabulous pool.

So he'd treated me like crystal for months after that.

Until he'd stopped doing it.

And even Pol had loved me enough in his way to revert right back to that tender care when we found out I was pregnant again, giving me the first hint since he showed me the true Pol four months after we were married that maybe he could change, and we could make a go of it.

Further, he knew I was crushed when I got so far along with our baby girl and lost her, so he kept doing it.

Until he'd stopped doing it again, forever shattering any illusion that he could change, and we could make a go of it.

A year after that, carefully timed, carefully planned, I'd escaped.

Now I was here.

My eyes were open, but I didn't see the view to beat all views.

I saw nothing but heard the Apollo of this world saying he would be preparing his children to meet me, something that would be difficult for me to do.

For if he was Pol of this world, and I was his Ilsa, then his children...

I shook my head and took another deep, steadying breath.

Letting it out, I decided that couldn't be. There had to be differences between the worlds and obviously there were. For the Apollo and Ilsa of this world had kids, and Pol and I did not.

His kids were not what our kids would have been.

No way.

I'd paid a very heavy price for my self-indulgence, materialism and avarice. No god in any universe would make me pay *that* kind of price.

I turned my mind from that and started to wonder when Apollo's children's mother died, if they were young and didn't remember her or if they did.

And if they did, I didn't think it was that hot of an idea for them to meet me.

In fact, it would be cruel. He'd been blank and impatient that morning and the night before he'd more than once been seriously scary, so I was guessing he had it in him to be cruel. But I couldn't find it in me to believe the man I'd met the night before would be cruel to his own children.

I had to turn my mind away from these thoughts and my future. No answers came from worrying and wondering. I'd learned that a long time ago. Answers came from seeing and doing.

I just had to wait.

I left the balcony and took a tour of the house, which was a long tour since it was a huge-ass house.

And the entirety of it was much like the room I slept in, elegant to almost cartoon-like extremes, but nevertheless strangely tasteful and absolutely gorgeous.

A maid found me (and not the English-speaking one, unfortunately) and guided me to a dining room decorated in yellows and blues. There, I got a light lunch of salad with flakes of tuna, quarters of hard-boiled egg, crisp bacon bits and olives in a light oil-based dressing flavored in lemon with a heavenly roll on the side, this served with wine, of which I partook a lot.

Which led me to going back to my room and taking a nap.

After I got up, worried the children might be there and not wanting them to see me, but still needing to speak to Apollo, I went in search of him. Surreptitiously I left my room, careful not to turn corners or enter rooms if I heard anyone.

I didn't hear anyone, but I did run into one of the maids who helped me that morning.

When I said, "Mr. Ulfr...here?" while pointing at the floor, she replied, shaking her head, "*Monsieur* Ulfr, *non*."

I put my fingers to my mouth and arched them out, asking, "Does anyone here speak English?"

A head tilt and then, "*Je suis désolée. Je ne comprends pas.*"

I guessed at what that meant (or some of it) and nodded.

She smiled and took off.

I watched her go, wondering at her reaction to me, as in, she had none. She was friendly but that was it.

This made me wonder if Apollo had told them about me, if everyone knew about this parallel universe, or if they'd never met the other Ilsa.

I put that on my list of things to ask Apollo in the short time he'd told me I'd have to ask questions.

Though, I was hoping I could talk him into a longer session since I had a lot of questions, they were all important and it was difficult to prioritize them.

Dinner was as delicious as lunch, if far more heavy, and after it ended and time went on, dusk fell and he nor the children returned, I started to get antsy.

Then panicked.

I was in a different world, wearing different clothes I wasn't used to (and I wasn't letting my mind go to the possibility they were the other me's), no shoes and I couldn't communicate with anyone around me.

The only person I knew, I didn't really know, and he'd been weird with me that morning. The only other person I knew had disappeared.

I'd spent three years on the run and hiding. Being careful of every move I made, every person I met, keeping track of every lie I told, always looking over my shoulder, never letting my guard down.

Valentine told me I was safe here. And there were beautiful things, good food and great beauty here.

But having that hurried, borderline unfriendly chat with Apollo this morning and then nothing, I wasn't feeling all that safe here.

On that thought, I heard what sounded like horse's hooves beating on stone and my heart slid up into my throat.

This was for a variety of reasons.

One was, there were horse's hooves on stone. I was getting the sense that this universe was not as advanced as ours and all evidence was suggesting this was very true.

Two was, this might herald Apollo being home which might mean Christophe and Élan were with him, and I suddenly didn't want to meet Christophe and Élan, not by mistake, not at all.

Not now.

Not ever.

I was sitting in a chair in the library, looking through a picture book that had pretty enough pictures but captions in another language when I heard boots coming down the hall.

Setting the book aside, I stood and faced the door, pulling in a deep breath, turning my head this way and that, looking for escape.

There was one door, and the boots were approaching it.

But my deep breathing didn't work this time. My heart swelled in my throat, cutting off my breath.

I heard one set of boots, but the children still might be with him.

His children.

His children with Ilsa.

His children that could have been mine.

He strode through the door, his dark-brown cape flying behind him. He took six steps in and stopped, his cape swaying forward, enveloping him briefly as if it was a living thing giving him an embrace, before it settled.

His eyes roamed me top to toe swiftly then they locked on mine, and he announced, "I've left the children at the house in Benies. Since they're prepared to travel and you must wait for your garments to be completed, and," he threw out a hand, "anything else you need to acquire, they will be away by ship tomorrow and I'll be with them. I've men in Benies. They're trained, talented, loyal and trustworthy. They will arrive in the morning, and when you're ready, they'll take you through Fleuridia and the Vale, you'll board a ship there and sail the rest of the way to Lunwyn under their guard."

I would?

Alas, I thought this question. I did not ask it out loud nor did I say anything fast enough to get it in before he went on.

"Now, do you have any questions?" he asked.

Did I have any questions?

Was he insane?

"Well...yes," I answered then all the questions I had crashed into my brain. There were a lot of them, and I couldn't get a lock on a single one, so I quit talking.

The impatience hit his handsome face.

"Ilsa, I have little time. I wish to be back to Benies before the children go to bed and it's an hour's ride."

I caught a thought and shared, "I...well, I have a slight problem. No one here understands me. I don't speak the language."

His head cocked sharply to the side. "You don't speak Fleuridian?"

"Uh...no."

He righted his head and declared, "Valentine speaks Fleuridian."

She did?

It must be full-on French then. Or she spent a lot of time here.

"Well, I don't," I replied.

His eyes flashed before he continued, "Ilsa's father was from Fleuridia. She was fluent in both Fleuridian and the language of the Vale."

I had no idea what he was talking about, but I thought it important to cautiously and thoughtfully point something out.

So, gently, I said, "I'm not her."

His eyes swept me again before locking on mine, whereupon he stated roughly, "This, I know," in a way that felt not-so-vaguely like an insult.

It was *so* not-so-vaguely that in delivering that line, it felt like he'd delivered a blow.

A blow that made my head twitch, but he either didn't catch it or decided to ignore it and he kept talking.

"This matters not. My men speak the language of the Vale, which is spoken throughout the Northlands, except in Fleuridia."

"Oh...well, okay," I murmured.

"You have other questions?" he prompted, raising a dark, thick eyebrow, every line of his body indicating he wanted to be anywhere but there.

"About a million of them," I told him, and he pulled in a sharp, annoyed breath through his nostrils.

"I don't have time for a million questions, Ilsa," he stated.

I took a step toward him and stopped but lifted a hand. "Apollo, I'm kind of at a loss here. Your world is not like my world, like, in *any* way. Sure, we have tuna, and you have tuna—"

Another sharp cock of the head accompanied by his brows snapping together and he cut me off to ask, "Tuna?"

Right, they didn't call it tuna.

Moving on.

I lifted my hand higher and circled it, "It doesn't matter. What I'm saying is, things are very different here and I've been thrown in the deep end—"

Another brow draw but this one was ominous.

"You'd have me send my children on a journey such as this without me accompanying them?"

"No," I replied quickly. "But just pointing out, I don't know what kind of journey that is seeing as I don't know *anything*."

He jerked up his chin and said, "I will talk with my men. They'll explain things to you."

"But—"

"You'll be safe with them."

"Okay, but—"

"And I'll have time to explain things to the children, prepare them for your arrival."

"And that would be—"

"Now, if there's nothing more," he stated, his body moving as if he was preparing to leave.

Yes.

He was barely letting me get a word in edgewise and preparing to leave!

So much for Valentine saying he wouldn't want to be separated from me.

I took two more quick steps toward him, calling swiftly, "Wait!"

He settled but he didn't look happy about it.

"Ilsa—"

"You can't just bring me here and then leave me here."

"You'd rather be with a man who kicks you?" he asked curtly.

"No, of course not. That's not what I'm—"

"You're safe from him here. You'll be safe from what's happening here with my men. Then you'll be home with the children, and you can settle."

Oh shit.

"Maybe we can talk about that," I hurried to say.

"We shall. I'll meet your sleigh in the village outside my estate and we'll have a discussion before you meet the children."

My sleigh?

"Now, I'm away," he murmured, turning to leave, his cape swinging out behind him, and it was cool, that cape and how it moved with him, and weirdly hot at the same time.

But I couldn't think about how cool and hot his cape was because I was beginning to lose my temper.

"Apollo!" I cried, taking two more steps toward him.

But he turned back, his cape wrapping around him, his eyes leveling on me.

When I saw what was in his eyes, I quit moving, quit talking and stared.

He didn't stare.

He spoke.

And when he did, his voice was a low, angry rumble that felt like it shook the room.

"You know of her and yet you seem not to understand how difficult this is for me."

I was following, but I wasn't.

I mean, *he* was the one who brought *me* here.

"Of course I understand," I said quietly, "but that doesn't mean—"

Again, he didn't let me finish.

"Just gazing on you, it feels like brands searing into my eyes."

Oh God.

That sucked. Seriously sucked. That had to kill, and I felt for him. I really, *really* did.

But still.

"I understand that." I kept my tone low and gentle. "But—"

"You look like her. You sound like her. You even smell like her."

That sucked too.

Big time.

I pressed my lips together.

"But you are not her," he finished.

"I'm sorry," I whispered. "But *you* brought me here and you knew I wouldn't be her. And right now it seems urgent things are happening. Things I don't understand in a world I don't understand and you're responsible for bringing me into this world. Now you're leaving me alone in it without even giving me time to ask questions, the answers to which might help me to know how to conduct myself, what I'm dealing with, both giving me a hint of peace of mind."

"And I explained, my men will answer."

"Okay, that's great, but we have things to talk about regarding my future here and—"

He was back to interrupting me and he did it by saying, "And I explained that as well. We will talk when you reach Lunwyn before you come to the estate."

Was he crazy?

My understanding was that would be two freaking months from now.

"I'd like to do it now," I requested carefully.

"And I don't have time now," he denied me, not carefully.

I took in a deep breath and held his eyes.

Then I shared, "It's important, Apollo."

"It's important for me to get back to my children and make haste in getting them to safety. Your future here is secure. That's all you need to know," he paused, "for now. Now, I'm away."

Was he serious?

He turned and started toward the door.

He was serious.

"Wait!" I called, going after him.

He didn't wait.

He kept going.

I kept following, crying, "Apollo! Hang on a second!"

His legs were longer than mine so I had to jog to catch up.

This I did at the front door.

And when I did it, I made a mistake.

I said his name and wrapped my fingers around his bicep.

The instant I did, he pulled it forcefully from my touch, rearing back. And with my history, he did it appearing like he was preparing to strike.

Instinctively, I lifted a hand in front of my face, palm toward him, and backed up, tripping on my train but managing to right myself before I went down. I yanked it from under me and took another step back, my eyes glued to him, my body prepared for anything.

I stopped moving back, suddenly breathing heavily. When I noticed he was not preparing to strike, I dropped my hand to press it to my chest.

Through all this, his eyes were also glued to me, but I couldn't read them.

And for some reason, we stood in the preposterously elegant foyer of his preposterously fabulous country house situated in the preposterously beautiful countryside of a parallel universe and we stared into each other's eyes, not speaking. His thoughts were cloaked. Mine, I doubted, were the same.

Then he shared his thoughts.

And if his earlier comment was an insult that landed an invisible blow, this one delivered a kill shot.

"Be careful what you wish for," he whispered, his eyes locked to mine as I drew in breath. "You might get it." He put his hand to the doorknob and finished, "And not want it."

Then he was gone.

4

I WAS USED TO IT

It was safe to say I was pissed.

It was the next morning after Apollo dealt his death blow.

I was in another gown that was very pretty but didn't fit me. I was bathed, watered and fed. And a maid who didn't speak my language had just come to my room, gesturing in a way I knew I was being summoned for something.

I'd heard horses' hooves on the stone outside so I figured my guard was there.

But I didn't care.

I hadn't slept. Not a wink.

This was because, at first, I was hurt.

No.

Wounded. Wounded was the word to describe it.

Wounded *deeply.*

I didn't know why. I just knew I was.

Deeply.

Then I started to think on things, and I got mad.

Sure, one could say I didn't want to go back to Pol and endure a life with him, walking on eggshells, taking my beatings whenever whatever was in his head would snap and he'd lose it. Then planning my escape and escaping, only to be found, beaten, dragged back and starting the process all over again and doing all this not-very-fun stuff until the day I died.

That didn't work for me. As in *really* didn't work.

But I'd been transported by a freaking *witch* to a freaking *parallel universe* by a man grieving his wife who was my twin. Then he got me, held me in his arms as I slept (and seriously, what was *that* all about) and for some reason decided he didn't want me (not that I wanted him, either, for God's sake). And finally, he threw me to the proverbial wolves.

Not that there were wolves, as such. The staff seemed nice, smiling, friendly, solicitous, and it wasn't like I was in a prison with nowhere to sleep but on cold stone and nothing to eat but moldy bread and fetid water.

But still!

So, needless to say, this all meant I didn't sleep. Which didn't help with me being pissed.

But I did force a smile at the maid and followed her, though I did it stomping and even that pissed me off because I still was barefoot so my stomping wasn't very effective.

I saw him when I was halfway down the stairs, and not surprisingly, he was tall, blond, built and preposterously good-looking.

He was also wearing romance novel guy clothes.

Exhausted and in a bad mood, this annoyed me more.

As I descended the stairs, his eyes lifted to me, and his mouth dropped open.

He knew the other Ilsa.

Whatever.

He snapped his mouth shut and wiped his face blank.

I'd seen that before.

Again.

Whatever.

I stomped to four feet away from him and stopped.

"I take it you're my guard," I guessed.

His eyes moved over my face, lingering on the bruise at my cheek (whatever!) before stopping on mine. "Yes, madam, myself and the seven men outside."

Seven men?

That seemed like a lot which didn't bode good things.

I didn't share these musings with him.

I introduced myself, of a sort. "I take it you know I'm Ilsa."

"I do," he replied.

"And you are?" I asked.

"Derrik," he answered.

"It's a pleasure to meet you," I snapped.

His eyes lit and his lips twitched.

I found this a bizarre reaction, so I asked, "Is that funny?"

"Yes, seeing as you said kind words you so obviously didn't mean and I'm not entirely certain what I've done in the last three seconds to earn your ire, having done nothing but stand here and greet you," he shared.

Crap.

He *hadn't* done anything. I was being rude.

I wasn't averse to being rude if a situation warranted it, say, a telemarketer called during dinner...or *ever*.

But mostly I was averse to being rude.

Therefore, I decided to explain.

"I'm annoyed," I told him. "Not at you," I added hurriedly. "At your master, or leader...or...whoever."

He dipped his chin and looked at me from under his brow, his voice gentling. "I am of the House of Lazarus. I trained under the House of Ulfr. Apollo and I grew close, shared a bond that was strong enough that, when I would have returned to my own House, I elected to stay with him and command his men in his stead when he's absent. I'm not in line for the Head of my House therefore it's a good position." He grinned and lifted his chin, not letting go of my gaze. "And the women of the House of Ulfr are more pleasing to look at and not one of them is my cousin or sister."

At his words, I felt my own lips twitching and surmised, "So you're his second in command."

"Yes," he affirmed.

I decided to take this as good, Apollo leaving his second in command. I was guessing by the way this guy's shoulders looked in his shirt, his thighs looked in his breeches, and the casual way he carried that sword at a slant in his back, he was no pushover.

So at least the jerk gave me something.

"Do you speak French, or...um, Fleuridian?" I asked.

"Haltingly, but I can make myself understood," he paused, "eventually."

"That's not much of an interpreter," I mumbled, looking at my feet.

"I'm not an interpreter, madam, I'm charged with your safety," he returned, and I looked back at him to see he looked peeved.

"Sorry," I said quietly. "I just don't speak *any* Fleuridian, and it seems I'm going to be here a while so I was kind of hoping you or one of your guys could help out."

The peeved look faded and he replied, "One of the...*guys* can help. In fact, three of them can."

Finally, good news.

I smiled.

His gaze dropped to my mouth and pain chased its way through them before he shuttered it from me.

Yes, he knew Ilsa.

"You know who I am," I whispered.

"I do," he agreed, and his eyes may have been shuttered, but he couldn't quite mask the vein of grief in his voice.

"Does it hurt you to look at me?" I asked. "If so, I can—" I started to offer, beginning to take a step back, but he lifted a hand, palm up toward me.

"I cared for her. She meant much to me. Her loss is still felt by all who knew her. But you are not her. Apollo told all the men who you are and where you're from. He warned us how this would feel. We're prepared."

I took this as indication the other Ilsa was beloved by his men and thus, obviously, had been around to meet them.

More questions flooded my brain but now was not the time to ask them.

Then again, I was thinking there would never be a time. Not with this lot.

"Prepared or not, I'll try to keep myself to myself," I told him.

"That's not nec—"

"Please," I said softly. "I can imagine how this feels for you. If you'd do me the kindness of trying to imagine how it feels for me, simply standing here talking and breathing causing people to re-experience grief. It doesn't feel nice, and not to be rude or anything, I'd rather not be around it."

He took in a short breath and nodded.

"Can you tell me one thing before I leave you be?" I asked.

"Of course," he answered.

"The staff in this house," I swept a hand out, "did they know her?"

"Apollo acquired this house after she left us, madam," he shared.

I nodded.

That I also decided to take as good, not to mention indication that the clothes I was wearing were most likely not hers.

Then, feeling awkward, I stammered, "I'll, uh...I don't know how long what needs to happen will take or what I need to...well, *acquire*, but I'm assuming someone will be able to communicate to you when I'm ready for us to leave."

"Yes, they'll tell us, and I'll share it with you so you have plenty of time to prepare."

I nodded.

He took a step back, indicating the door behind him with his hand. "The men are outside. Would you give them the honor of meeting them?"

I shook my head. "Not now. Please?"

"Of course," he replied, his voice gentle.

"Thank you." I swallowed. "I'll just..." Another sweep of my arm, indicating the stairs.

But I trailed off because I had no clue what I'd just do.

I hadn't looked at all of the books in the library, but the ones I looked at were in a language I couldn't read. There was no TV. There was nothing around us but what appeared to be a barn, a small square building with smoke coming out the top and nothing else. Not even a formal garden to wander through.

I was alone with nothing to do. Those who I could speak to knew and loved the other me so I couldn't be around them without causing them pain. The ones who didn't know her didn't understand me.

I didn't have anything to do or anyone to share my time with.

This was sad and it sucked.

It had always sucked.

But there was one thing about it.

I was used to it.

"I'll just...be going," I finished.

Derrik nodded.

I gave him a small smile.

Then I went.

I WAS LYING on the lounge in my preposterously fabulous bedroom lamenting my plight as I'd been doing all day, when I heard it.

It was dark, late, I was fatigued, but I couldn't sleep because I was sad, pissed and worried.

But the noise sounded like what I guessed a horse and carriage would sound like on a stone road and I was curious to see if I was right. Not to mention, curious at what a horse and carriage looked like.

So I pushed myself up and made my way to the French doors.

I was wearing a nightgown, of which I now had three, all my own (I knew this because I'd tried them all on and they all fit). It was a satin the deep purple hue of blackberries and it fell to my ankles. It also had a panel of same-color lace that started narrow under my arm and got wider as it followed the length of the gown to the hem.

In other words, it was the shit.

That said, it was bedroom-only wear, the curtains were sheer and several of the lamps in the room had been lit, giving the entire room a soft glow that would mean, if you were outside, you could see in.

Therefore, I approached the French doors carefully, coming at them from the side, pulling the sheers open a few inches and peering out.

The outside was ablaze too (or as ablaze as you could get without electricity). I could see a woman alighting from a black, covered carriage, the man in rough clothing the wardrobe people for a movie would dress a peasant in at the seat in front, not bothering to help her down.

But I didn't have time for the man.

I was staring at the woman.

She had dark hair swept up in an elaborate updo of big curls. I could only see her profile, but I could tell her makeup was far from light. In fact, it was borderline gaudy. Her gown was ostentatious, if seemingly well-made. It wasn't borderline over the top, it just *was*. And her cleavage was, no other word for it, indecent. Last, she was wearing a lot of jewelry which pushed gaudy to tawdry.

Regardless of all this, she was beautiful. Beyond beautiful. *Breathtaking*. Her looks so lush, her curves so abundant, she was a knockout.

What the hell? Who was she?

She moved to the curving steps that led up to the house just as a tall, broad-shouldered man I'd never seen before with burnished, dark-red hair came out of the house and walked down the steps. Not surprisingly, he was in romance hero clothes. I couldn't see his face, just the top of his head, and he approached her directly.

I watched them have a conversation, her gesturing, him shaking his head.

Her head tipped to the side, she smiled a coquettish smile and said something that made him dig in his pocket. He pulled out a small pouch, opened it and got something out, placing it in her upturned palm which she instantly closed.

My breath stuttered.

Holy cow.

Her gaze lifted to my window, her face wistful, and I stopped breathing altogether when her eyes met mine. The wistfulness left her expression and a knowing catty smile curved her mouth.

She lifted her hand and gave me a finger wave.

I quickly stepped away from the window and deep breathed.

"Holy cow," I whispered.

Here and in my world, hell, anywhere, I knew what she was.

I knew.

She was a prostitute, and she was here for Apollo.

She'd also been here before and the activities they'd engaged in, she'd liked (a woman didn't get wistful for nothing).

And they'd done them in this room.

I shook my head and moved farther into the room, aiming my feet toward the dresser which had the decanter now filled with fresh wine. I pulled out the heavy crystal stopper and poured myself a heavier dose.

I stoppered the decanter, lifted the wine to my lips and took a sip (Valentine was right, Fleuridian wine really was superb), staring unseeing at the hydrangea blooms.

It shouldn't surprise me. Apollo was a man. He'd have to get himself some.

But a prostitute?

And he'd put me in the bed he'd had her in?

"Good God," I breathed, shaking my head and moving to the dressing table across the room.

I sat on the stool and stared at my reflection.

God had given me much even if he'd taken more away. But one of the few bounties that was mine to keep was my hair. It was auburn, had soft curls, some of them ringlets. It wasn't kinky or coarse, it was thick but silky.

I'd always loved my hair.

God had also given me lovely skin, only a sprinkling of freckles across my nose that Pol wasn't very fond of and asked (okay, demanded) I cover them up with foundation before we went out.

I did so he wouldn't get angry, but I'd always thought they were cute.

So had my dad. He'd thought they were adorable. It was one of the few things he liked about me, or about anyone or, truth be told, *anything*.

What he hadn't thought was adorable was me hooking up with a drug dealer.

He didn't think that was adorable at all.

Mom either. Then again, Mom thought whatever Dad thought seeing as doing that was a lot less hassle.

I closed my eyes, shook my head, took a deep breath and opened them, taking another sip of wine.

I had nice enough features, I thought. I straight, slim nose. A decent jawline. Defined cheekbones. Dark-brown eyes that had a lovely shape.

I was tall-ish, standing at five eight. I had ass. I had breasts. They weren't well-above average, but you couldn't miss that they existed. I also had a slim waist, so my booty and breasts both were more pronounced.

My second favorite feature was my legs. I had good legs.

Not that you could see them in the clothes of this world, but still.

I didn't look anything like the lush beauty who came to call for Apollo.

In other words, he didn't fuck anyone who might remind him of his Ilsa.

I got that. I *so* did.

But...*a prostitute?*

Evidence was suggesting the Apollo of this world wasn't all that hot either.

In fact, evidence was suggesting Apollo of this world was a self-indulgent jerk.

And I knew all about that.

Boy did I.

So I stared at myself, coming out of my pity party and beginning to think this was good.

This place was amazing, the clothes were great, the food was fabulous, the people seemed friendly. Sure, there wasn't electricity or cars or movie theaters, but if I got my head out of my ass, I might find it was fun to explore a world like this.

Further, I was safe from Pol. He'd *never* get to me here.

And Apollo wanted nothing to do with me.

Eleven years ago, at twenty-two years old, working in an exclusive department store, I'd met Pol and made mistake after mistake after mistake that destroyed my life. I'd been seduced by his good looks, the wads of cash always in his pockets, his easy smile and his taking me on the town in his Corvette (which he traded up to a Porsche, then up to a Maserati and finally an Aston Martin—things were always good in the drug trade).

I'd wanted that life and I'd got it (minus the drug trade part, of course, though I'd got that too). I thought, it coming with all the outward lusciousness that was Pol, I'd have everything I ever wanted. A handsome, wealthy, powerful man and the life he could give me.

And I got nothing.

But now I had a second chance. A second chance to make a life all my own. It came in a bizarre way that I would never in my wildest dreams imagine would be real.

But I had it.

"So I'm going to take it," I vowed to my reflection in the mirror.

My eyes stared back and me and they were determined.

And hopeful.

I liked that look on me. I hadn't seen it in so long, I wasn't certain I'd ever seen it.

But now I was seeing it.

So I was going to go for it.

5
Making Me Feel Free

I'd lost control of the horse under me. He was pounding through the wildflowers behind the house, his movements jarring my ribs and that hurt.

But I wasn't focusing on that. I figured he knew what he was doing. He was just taking me along for the ride.

No, I was focusing on the wind in my hair, the sun shining on my skin and the beauty all around me.

Pierre, who was teaching me how to ride, was running after us, shouting in French. But his voice was fading away as the horse and I galloped through the flowers.

It was two days after the prostitute had come to call.

Two glorious days.

And I was on a horse because it occurred to me that, seeing as they didn't have cars here and I didn't know how to ride, I should learn. So I'd spoken (okay, gestured) to the maids.

With a lot of smiles and laughter at my machinations, I finally got the message across and had been introduced to Pierre. I didn't know what he did at the house, but it didn't matter. While I smiled and laughed at his gesticulations, he agreed to teach me how to ride. But I only understood this when he led me to the stables, showed me how to saddle a horse and then he showed me how to get on. It continued from there.

I also knew all the maids' names. I further knew how to say horse in French (*cheval*). I'd remembered *bonjour* and *merci*, which I started using (making the staff smile happily and nod enthusiastically) and I learned *bonne nuit.* Sure, it wasn't much, but it was something.

Further, I'd taken a walk down the wildflower-flanked lane, almost to the church, which was a lot further than it looked, so I'd stopped and turned back. Nevertheless, if the view was something from my balcony, it was much better up close.

This meant I had slippers that fit me (six pairs and they were all *awesome* and fit like they were made for me—because they were!). I also had dresses that fit me (and they were even more amazing than the ones I'd been wearing).

And I'd taken the time to thoroughly peruse the shelves in the library. When I did, I found several books in English. Two were all poetry (which I'd tried but it wasn't my gig). One was a gothic drama (which I was reading, and it was pretty good).

But the most important book I found was a history of the Houses of Lunwyn.

This I read with great interest.

It didn't have Apollo's name in it, so I was guessing it was dated. But it did have a rather long forward that gave a lot of history of Lunwyn (including dragons and elves!) as well as an explanation that a "House" in Lunwyn was a line of aristocracy. Some were richer than others, some held more land, some more power (power went hand in hand with money and land, by the way), but all of them had been around for centuries.

Reading it, I'd learned the Ulfr House was very powerful, and according to the book, very respected. This wasn't exactly a surprise (perhaps the respected part was, considering the head of it was a jerk). I could tell Apollo of this world had some serious cabbage and my guess was money in any world meant power.

Further, the day before, after my fittings, the maids had excitedly given me a newspaper that was in English. It was dated, but it shared the joyous news that the beloved Black Prince Noctorno of Hawkvale and ruler of Bellebryn, and his bride, Cora, the Gracious (kickass nickname) had successfully delivered upon "the Vale" another heir to the throne, Prince Hayden.

Good news for the Vale, as the birth of a child always was, but an heir to the throne meant a whole country got to celebrate (and they did, with festivities planned for a week).

And last, I was having my second horseback riding lesson, and although not doing well with it, it was fun.

I knew I should pull back on the reins and call "whoa," but I just couldn't. It didn't feel good on my ribs but that didn't mean it didn't feel *good.*

So instead, I held on, endured the pain, bent forward over the horse's back, allowed the beauty all around me to fly by and let my mind go.

That was, I did this until I heard the beat of horse's hooves behind me.

I turned to look and saw one of Apollo's men racing after me.

In the last two days I'd seen all of Apollo's men, though I hadn't spoken a word to one of them (still, not to be rude, if they caught my eye, I smiled, and they usually smiled back). I did this on purpose and took great pains in doing it. I was building happy mojo and a reminder of the other Ilsa, and mostly Apollo, might be a blow to that effort.

I wasn't ready. We'd be "away" sometime probably soon, and since I'd be traveling with them, I'd have no choice but to do it then.

So I'd do it then.

But this one (dark hair and features that told me he could very well be related to Apollo) clearly thought I was in trouble and was coming to my rescue.

That was nice and all but the only thing I could think was, *Crap*.

I pulled back on the reins. The horse slowed but not fast enough. I knew this because suddenly the dude chasing me was right beside me.

I gasped aloud when he wasn't beside me but *on my horse with me*.

Somehow, in the blink of an eye, he was seated behind me, his arm snaking across my belly to hold me to him. He pulled the reins from my hand and yanked back. I also felt his thighs squeeze the horse and it slowed to a stop.

Without delay, he swung off, and once he had his feet on the ground, he reached up to me. His hands spanned my waist, and he pulled me down with him. He was gentle but that didn't mean I didn't hit the ground with a thud that sent pain through my midsection, enough to make me wince.

I heard incoming hooves beating but I couldn't turn to look because he was addressing me.

"Are you all right?"

I looked up at him.

A strong brow, much like Apollo's, and his hair was exactly the same as Apollo's, though cut shorter (however, it was not short).

But his eyes were a rich chocolate brown.

Pol had a big family, this I knew, though I'd never met a one of them. They didn't like drug dealers either, apparently. Then again, Pol had shown signs of going to the dark side early on in life. I knew this because, in a rare moment of honesty, he'd shared he had a juvie record and by the time I'd met him he'd long since been disowned.

This made our wedding a lonely affair that I'd lied to myself was just fine. I had him and he was all I needed (that was a lie too, then and more so much later).

Looking into the kind, intelligent eyes of the man with me, I wished I'd met some of Pol's family.

They might have warned me.

Then again, I wouldn't have listened.

"Fine. I just got my ribs jarred a little," I answered, his head cocked, and I quickly went on. "Thanks for coming to my rescue."

"My apologies, madam. I was too rough pulling you from the steed," he replied. "You'd lost control and I didn't want you on him by yourself with me on the ground. When a horse senses it has control, it can take advantage."

I shook my head. "It wasn't you who hurt me. It's...before I got here, to this world, I mean, I..." I trailed off when his eyes dropped to the fading bruise on my cheekbone.

I heard some "whoas" around me and knew we were being joined by several someones, but again he spoke so I couldn't look.

"Of course, Apollo had told us."

Great.

"It's okay," I assured him as I felt others joining us.

"It is not. And it's also not a good idea for you to be on the back of a horse in your state. Especially if you don't know how to ride, precisely due to what just happened. You could have been injured worse."

"You need to use your legs."

This was another voice and I looked to my left to see burnished-haired hot romance novel guy who spoke with the prostitute and the boy I'd noticed around the last couple of days. Though, he wasn't exactly a boy, more like a boy-man. I was guessing he was sixteen or seventeen years old. He had dark-blond hair and dark-blue eyes, and I knew he'd grow up to be a looker because he already was one.

"And your mouth," the voice went on, that voice coming from the boy-man.

"My mouth?" I asked.

One side of his lips twitched up. "To say, 'whoa,'" he instructed then continued. "It'd also be a good idea to use your reins."

I pressed my lips together but didn't succeed in suppressing my smile before I replied, "I'll remember that next time."

"Her ribs are injured," the man who saved me informed the burnished-haired man.

"Then why is she on a horse?" the burnished-haired man asked him then his annoyed gaze slid to me. "Especially if she doesn't know how to ride one."

Jeez.

"This is a good question," the man who saved me noted, and I looked to him.

"I've never ridden a horse. Never even been around one, really, until yesterday," I explained, and his eyes widened in immediate shock.

"You jest," the burnished-haired man drew my attention and he, too, looked shocked.

"We don't have horses where I'm from. I mean, we do," I said the last quickly because their shock had turned to what appeared to be alarmed astonishment. "But only rich people have them. Or, if you love horses enough, you sacrifice other things so you can keep them or pay to ride them."

"The poor walk?" the boy-man asked in disgusted disbelief.

"Well, no," I answered. "Pretty much everyone has cars."

The boy-man blinked. The other two narrowed their gazes on me in puzzlement.

I lifted my hands and curled my fingers around a non-existent steering wheel, shifting them side-to-side like I was steering. "Automobiles. With four wheels and an engine. It goes on its own power. It doesn't need a horse."

The three of them watched my hands then they lifted their eyes to stare at me.

"You have to see it to understand it," I muttered, dropping my hands.

The dark-haired one turned to the burnished-haired one and announced, "We cannot be away if madam has injured ribs and doesn't know how to ride a horse."

Uh-oh.

This wasn't good. I was thinking Apollo wouldn't like that.

So I cried quickly, "Oh no!" I took a step deeper into our huddle and lifted a hand. "Don't let me delay our departure."

The dark-haired guy looked down at me. "You winced solely being pulled off the back of a horse," he reminded me.

I shook my head but said, "Yeah, I did. But I'm good. Really. It's okay."

"It is not," he returned.

"Our progress would be slowed if she rides injured, especially if she can't handle her own steed," the burnished-haired guy said, and I looked to him.

"I'll keep up," I promised.

His blue eyes moved to me. "And break your neck?"

"I'll try to keep up without doing that," I offered.

He stared at me a moment then looked at his comrade. "I'll speak with Derrik. She'll need lessons and time for her injury to heal. We'll send word to Apollo we'll be delayed for two weeks."

Oh boy.

"Really," I stated hurriedly. "I'm fine. I can practice horse riding while on our, um...journey."

This gained me the dark-haired man's eyes. "On day one, after our ride, you'll be nothing but aches and pains. The next morning, your body will protest at your simplest movement. You cannot take that while injured."

"How about I give it a try," I suggested, not wanting to delay because I really didn't think Apollo would like it.

Sure, he wouldn't get word we'd be late for two months, but then he'd have two whole weeks to stew on it and that probably wasn't a good thing.

I came out of these thoughts when I noticed no one was speaking. They were all staring at me again.

Finally, the dark-haired man offered his big, calloused hand. "I'm Achilles of the House of Ulfr. Cousin to Apollo."

Yep. I was right. Family.

I took his hand and murmured, "Achilles."

"I am Draven of the House of Sinclair," the burnished-haired guy said, and I let Achilles go to take Draven's hand.

"Hey," I said, and his eyes lit with humor.

"I'm Aleksander, of the House of Lazarus," the boy-man said, grinning at me and offering his hand. I took it and he finished, "Alek."

"Nice to meet you, Alek," I said on a squeeze and let him go.

"You'll walk back, not ride," Achilles decreed, and my gaze went back to him. "We'll talk tomorrow to see how you feel. And when you're well enough, Hans will instruct you on riding. He's our most talented horseman."

"Really, that's not—" I started, but he moved closer to me. Not by a lot, it wasn't an aggressive move, it was one designed to get my attention.

And it got my attention.

But the serious look in his eye, a look accompanied by not a small amount of kindness was what *really* got my attention.

"I have known those who life has taught to keep themselves isolated," he stated quietly. "It is always folly and never ends well. No matter what experiences we have, we must keep ourselves open to having more. Don't you agree?"

I pulled in a breath and nodded because he was right.

"The men are anxious to meet you and it would serve you well to meet them," he informed me. "We act as your guard as a duty, and we very much understand duty. But we do that duty out of allegiance to Apollo and the House of Ulfr." He held my gaze but dipped his face an inch closer to me and his voice got lower when he concluded, "If the men were to meet you, madam, and you were to allow them to get to know you, I have no doubt they would act as your guard for much different reasons."

"The Ilsa of your world," I whispered, totally getting him.

"No, the madam who puts herself on the back of a horse while injured, determined to learn something new to her world. And the woman who takes a hand in greeting while looking steadfastly in your eyes, hers hesitant but unwavering. And last, the woman who would do her best to embrace a new world very foreign to her even when circumstances are not in her favor. I know all of this having officially met you moments ago and watching but for two days. What I want to know is what more there is to know."

Okay, maybe I didn't totally get him.

And when he was done speaking, I was holding my breath and doing this because tears were stinging my eyes seeing as all he said was so nice.

Since he'd shut up and no one was saying anything, I realized it was up to me to break the silence.

"I was having a pity party," I shared. "I thought I'd gotten over it but maybe I was hanging on to some of it."

While I was talking, he'd moved slightly back, and his brows had drawn together.

When I stopped talking, he asked, "A pity what?"

"A pity party," I replied. "I was feeling sorry for myself and being self-indulgent. It's a weakness."

"It's my experience that a weakness understood is no weakness," Draven put in at this point, and I looked to him. "If you know you have it, even if you can't control it, you can make allowances for it. It is those who ignore or don't understand their weaknesses who are wasted by them."

I blinked.

Then I blurted, "Are you all philosopher soldiers, or what?"

This got me a smile from Achilles, a chuckle from Draven and a burst of laughter from Alek, and I had to admit, all three felt good.

"Come," Achilles said, offering me his arm even as he tipped his head toward our horses, his eyes on Alek. "I'll accompany you to the house."

I caught his eyes when he looked back at me, took his arm and whispered, "I'd like that."

He lifted his chin.

Alek jogged around us to the horses.

Draven grinned at me before he turned to his mount.

And Achilles tucked me close to his side and guided us forward.

"It grows late, madam, we must get you in your carriage in order to be back at the country house for dinner."

My heart plummeted, I turned, grabbed Derrik's arm and leaned toward him, catching his eyes and begging, "No. Please? Can't we stay in Benies for dinner?"

He stared down his nose at me.

Suffice it to say, I freaking *loved* Benies.

Pol had taken me to Munich, London, Barcelona and Athens. We'd vacationed on beaches in the Bahamas, Antigua and Montserrat. I'd seen a lot, all of it amazing, including in this world where I saw even more during the long carriage ride into the city in order to "acquire" the things I needed (these, I found out, being jewelry, perfume, makeup, hair stuff, shawls and the like, and let's just say that shopping in a parallel universe was *the bomb*).

But I'd never seen anything like Benies.

There weren't any skyscrapers and there was nothing like an Eiffel Tower or ruins, but it was still beyond the beyond.

Some of the buildings were painted a rich cream but most of them were painted in pastel colors and almost all of them had some magnificently dramatic black wrought iron work, either on balconies or on verandas or just decorating the fronts of windows.

And all of the buildings had flowers everywhere, blooming out of window boxes and pots on sills and steps and on flowering shrubbery.

In fact, shrubbery was a thing here, clipped in a variety of amazing shapes in front of houses or along boulevards or in small city parks. Anything from simple cones to fleur de lis to swans to entire people. I'd seen some fancy clip work in my time, but nothing like this.

So it wasn't about architecture. It was about colors and embellishments, each building, shop or home seeming to try to best the one next to it, this making it all magnificent.

And then there was the hustle and bustle. So much was happening, people everywhere.

And their clothes! Mine were good, but the women around me, their gloves, their hats, the feathers in their hair, the delicate shawls around their shoulders, the frilly parasols they used, their jewelry blinking in the sun.

Unbelievable.

Breathtaking.

And there were also cafés with outdoor seating, big striped awnings with scalloped edges, white-aproned, black-breeches-wearing waiters with hair parted down the middle and oiled to their scalps and crazy-ass mustaches scurrying to take and bring orders.

And there were the patisseries with such concoctions in their windows, my mouth watered just looking at them. Derrik noticed, took me in one and bought me the best éclair and cream puff (yes, both, I couldn't choose) I'd ever had *in my life*.

And there were also coffee houses.

And elegant restaurants (not yet opened, Derrik explained the formal restaurants only opened for dinner).

And the shops!

Shops carrying miles of bolts of fabrics in every color and pattern you could think of. Or big baskets of yarn. Or huge barrels of amazing-smelling spices. Jewelry. Ribbons. China. Crystal. Shelves and shelves of wine. Or with cases of dozens upon dozens of cheeses with sausages hanging from the ceiling.

Last, there was the Marhac Sea, a vast expanse of water that looked like an ocean that stretched the length of the city on the southern end, the sun blinking off the tranquil waters, the water itself giving the city's air a crisp, clean freshness. Plus, there was the cry of the seagulls screaming to anyone who lived landlocked that they were on *vacation.*

I loved it. I couldn't get enough, take enough in. I wanted to stay there for days, not hours.

Of course, the shopping bit started out weird seeing as Derrik instructed me to get "anything you fancy," and since I was using Apollo's money, I didn't want to get anything at all.

Achilles, who had come with us, noticed and gave me a good talking to so I decided to get a few things to appease them.

Laures and Hans also came with.

Laures had dark hair, seeing as he was of the House of Ulfr, and dark-brown eyes, like Achilles. But he was shorter (by a bit), also broader (by a bit) and he had a small half-moon scar around his mouth where a dimple would be that made his normal hotness hotter.

He and Hans (very blond, ice-blue eyes, slimmer than the others but taller), also noticed my hesitancy and did something about it.

And what they did cracked me right the hell up, seeing as they were genuinely trying to help me find things I liked, but both had very bad taste so everything they showed me was heinous and I wouldn't buy it in this world or *any* world.

I knew they were doing this so we could move along as shopping was clearly not one of their favorite pastimes. And they eventually caught on that I was playing with them when I dragged my heels in shops, hemmed and hawed on decisions about the various things they presented for me to hurry up and buy so we could get the fuck out and move on.

We all got into the joke and Hans and Laures began choosing a variety of intentionally hideous or gaudy things for me, none of which they bought for me, all of which made me laugh until my sides hurt.

Derrik shut this down (after the fifth shop) and told us to stay focused, though he did it with a smile.

All the men also noticed that I was wide-eyed with wonder, and enjoying myself immensely, so it was *them* who started dragging their heels or leading me down various avenues to show me fountains or statues or buildings of note.

Giving me a great day.

It had been a whole week since I'd been transported to this world.

Now, I knew all the men. They dined with me in the evenings (every one of them, as a courtesy at first, I guessed, but I was hoping it was their preference now). One, two or most of them would always be at the breakfast table in the morning, coming or going or lounging with me and chatting while I ate.

There was Derrik, Achilles, Draven, Alek, Hans and Laures. There was also Remi and Gaston.

Hans had started my horseback riding lessons.

Laures, Gaston and Remi were teaching me to speak Fleuridian.

Achilles was teaching me a one-on-one board game called ricken that was a lot like chess but far more violent. In other words, every piece had a weapon, and when you took it, you snapped the weapon off. Apparently "servants" mended the pieces when you were done playing, though I didn't know how since they started out exquisitely carved and didn't look mended.

I asked and Achilles didn't know how either, so I was getting what "servants" got up to didn't concern their masters, just as long as they got up to it.

By the way, I sucked at ricken.

Also by the way, Achilles thought this was hysterically funny, as did Draven and Hans, who often watched, shook their heads and grinned at me with every move I made (you will note, they shook their heads and grinned, but they didn't give me any advice).

But all the men were teaching me tuble, a card game that was a game of chance. We played it in the evenings after dinner. And I was good at that.

They were also teaching me how to cheat, which apparently you were *supposed* to do.

I was *great* at that.

And now they were giving me Benies.

Needless to say, the last few days had been better than the first few by, like, *a lot.*

This one the best of all.

And I didn't want it to end.

So I had a feeling my eyes were beseeching when I looked up at Derrik and awaited his reply.

He continued to look down his nose at me with his clear blue eyes and I held my breath.

Then he murmured, "We'll take you to dine at *Le Pont de L'eau*."

I leaned back, clapped my hands and cried, "Yay!"

He smiled indulgently at me.

"Bloody brilliant," Laures muttered. "Best veal in Benies."

"Forget the veal, best whiskey in Benies," Hans, also muttering, put in.

They were already moving to the elegant, shiny black carriage that brought me here (I rode alone, they rode their horses beside it) as I felt Derrik's hand on my elbow.

When I looked back to him, it slid down the inside of my forearm and his big hand curled around mine bringing it up and tucking it close to the side of his chest. And hence, tucking *me* close to his side as he directed us to the carriage.

It felt nice holding hands and being tucked beside a protective hot guy in a beautiful city in a parallel universe, so I went with it.

"Also the best views, madam, of Benies and the Marhac Sea," he said softly, his eyes on me. "It's right on the water and elevated four stories."

"Yay," I replied softly back, and his dancing eyes danced brighter.

I grinned at him then smiled at the carriage where Achilles was standing, holding open the door and also smiling at me.

Yes, this was the best day here by far.

And they kept getting better.

~

Achilles

"OH MY GOD, NO!"

Achilles heard Ilsa's voice as he approached the door to the kitchen, seeing Derrik standing in it leaning against the jamb, his back to Achilles.

He stopped behind Derrik but to his side, looking in and seeing Ilsa sitting on a stool and leaning on her forearms on the battered kitchen table, listening, or more to the point, watching with rapt attention as one of the maids acted something out.

There were a few halting words spoken, as Ilsa was picking up Fleuridian by the day, but mostly it was wild gesticulations, a parody of a mime that was already a parody so he could see within seconds it was amusing.

He watched as all the other maids standing around as well as Ilsa burst out laughing, Ilsa doing it banging her fist on the table and dropping her forehead to it.

She threw her head back suddenly and cried out, "That's *too* funny!"

All the maids nodded and smiled at her with big smiles even though they probably didn't know what she was saying. Or maybe they did, picking up the language of the Vale through Ilsa.

Achilles turned his head to look at Derrik who was watching this, or more likely, watching Ilsa with even more rapt attention than Ilsa had been watching the story mimed out.

"Hans says her seat on a horse is secure," Achilles noted in a quiet voice.

Derrik started and turned his head to catch Achilles' eyes.

"He's reported this to me."

"We were to be away three weeks ago," Achilles reminded him.

"She's enjoying herself," Derrik replied, and Achilles took in a short breath.

Then he got closer, and his voice dipped lower. "It's our charge to get her to safety."

"She has eight guards and Apollo explained he's relatively certain the witch from the other world watches over her," Derrik returned.

"Relatively certain is not certain and his orders are to get her to Ulfr grounds as soon as possible," Achilles retorted.

Derrik held his eyes.

Then he lifted his chin.

After that, he turned his attention back to the kitchen and muttered, "We'll leave the day after tomorrow. Tomorrow, we take madam back to Benies one last time. She's enjoyed her days there."

He was right. She had. All four of them.

Achilles stifled a sigh but not his misgivings.

He would have to keep a sharp eye.

His gaze moved to the kitchen, and he saw Ilsa was looking at them.

She lifted her hand and gave them an enthusiastic wave.

And, damn it all, along with Derrik, he lifted his hand and waved back.

Laures

LAURES TURNED his steed and dug his heels in so the horse was at a gallop.

When he did, he saw Maddie—what they now called Ilsa instead of "madam" so they didn't have to address her formally nor call her by her twin's name. Her skirts were lifted in one hand, her parasol in the other bobbing over her head, her feet taking her across the arena toward him, her glorious hair streaming out behind her.

At the sight, he forgot the pain the blows he took from his competitor's blunt sword caused and he grinned.

She came to a teetering halt beside him as he pulled up his reins and she lifted her free hand high, palm facing him, while crying, "You won!"

He had.

How he got entered in the games they'd happened on, he didn't know. Then again, as they rode over Fleuridia, they'd stayed for a fayre in Aisles they were not scheduled to attend. And also, after they crossed into Hawkvale, they'd been roped into attending a sheep shearing festival in Drinton upon which they had no time to waste. But they did.

"Don't leave me hanging!" she exclaimed.

"Pardon?" he asked.

She shook her hand in the air. "High five!"

He stared down at her having no idea what she was on about.

She dropped her parasol unheeded to the ground, reached out, grabbed his gloved hand from his thigh and moved it to smack it against her hand.

"High five," she declared. She moved her hand low, palm facing up and slapped his hand against it again. "Low five." She turned her hand sideways, slapped his hand against it one more time and stated, "To the side." Lastly, she curled her hand around his, the juncture of her thumb connected to his, her fingers curled around, and she pumped their hands back and forth, saying excitedly, "You *the man*!"

It was one of her world things, of which they'd been learning many, some of them amusing, all of them fantastical.

He grinned at her again.

"You won!" Alek yelled, and Laures looked up, still holding Maddie's hand, to see all the men had gathered around. "That means you'll have to enter the arena tomorrow for the championship!"

He would indeed.

"I'll send Apollo a missive and tell him we'll be at least another week," Hans muttered, breaking off from the huddle and striding away.

Laures looked from Hans to Maddie and bent deep. He let go of her hand but wrapped his arm around her waist and pulled her on his horse before him.

"Fancy a victory lap, sweets?" he asked.

She'd turned her head, and he watched her eyes light as she nodded happily.

He bent deep into her, dug his heels in his horse's flanks and took off.

When he did, the peel of Maddie's laughter rang through the arena, and as it did, it warmed Laures's heart.

Then again, anytime Maddie laughed, it warmed his heart.

Achilles

"So, as you can guess from the end of the story, it wasn't all that great, living in my world," Maddie murmured her understatement, her eyes on the ground, her fingers tugging at blades of grass and distractedly tossing them away.

She was lying on the soft turf on her side but up on an elbow, head in her hand, legs curled around, the toes of blue satin slippers peeking out from beneath her lavender skirts. The detritus of their luncheon was spread across the blanket some feet away from their trio.

Derrik sat on his arse across from her, legs bent at the knees, weight back on his hands behind him.

Achilles sat with his back against a tree trunk, one knee up. He'd laid his wrist on his knee, hand dangling. His other leg was stretched out.

Both men's eyes were on Maddie.

The sun was shining, and they had stopped riding to take lunch. They were two days' journey from the port city in Hawkvale where they'd board the ship to Lunwyn. The other men were inspecting the steeds in preparation to ride on.

The men's belongings being few (save weapons, which they carried on their persons), Maddie's much more abundant belongings were separated amongst the saddlebags of their nine horses.

They should have taken a carriage, but Apollo instructed they not. A carriage was much slower going. It would delay their return by some time.

In the end, however, their return had been delayed by a lot longer than a carriage would have done it. And Achilles had no doubt that Apollo's wish for them to arrive at Karsvall without delay going unheeded would not make his cousin happy.

Achilles wasn't thinking about this.

He was thinking about what Maddie had just told them, the sun and wine at lunch perhaps loosening her tongue.

However, it was more likely that she had just become comfortable enough with them to share. It was impossible on a long ride such as theirs not to bond with those around you, spending day in and day out with them. And they'd had quite a number of days together, and adventures.

But with Maddie, the way she was, the sadness constantly lurking in her eyes, the joy she allowed to show openly coating it, it was impossible not to bond.

There was something about her that made a man wish to watch over her. There was something else about her that made a man wish to get to know her, prod under a veneer Achilles was certain she thought was a shield but didn't understand it was flimsy. It made a man wish to dig deeper and discover what lay beneath.

And she'd just gifted them with some of what lay beneath. Her story of how she got there, running from her husband and why, being found beaten and Apollo and the witch with the green magic from the other world saving her.

That was the end of her story.

But what she'd shared was enough.

Achilles tore his gaze away from Maddie, feeling his mouth tight, and looked at Derrik. With one glance, he knew Derrik was feeling what he was feeling.

Maybe more.

He turned back to Maddie. "You're here now, little bug, safe from that."

She lifted her lovely brown eyes to him, eyes he'd looked in a million times before he'd even met her. Yet not.

And looking in them now, he knew definitely not.

It had been jarring at first, Maddie looking like Ilsa, but they got used to it. And then the Ilsa they saw in Maddie had faded away and it was just her.

Now, after that story, it was only her.

"I know," she whispered.

She said, *I know*.

She meant, *Thank you.*

He grinned at her, pushed away from the tree and bent close to kiss the side of her head.

When he pulled away, she tipped her head and grinned back.

"Thank you for trusting that to us," he said gently.

"Thank you for being trustworthy enough to get it," she replied.

He winked.

Her eyes twinkled.

"If you lazy cusses are done being lazy, we need to be away," Remi called from his horse thirty feet away.

Achilles pushed up to gain his feet and when he did, Derrik was there, offering Maddie his hand.

"Let's get you up," Derrik muttered, his tone tender.

She took Derrik's hand, and he pulled her up, unnecessarily sliding his other hand partly around her waist to steady her when she gained her feet.

Achilles looked over Maddie's head and saw Laures. His cousin's gaze was on Maddie and Derrik. He felt Achilles looking at him, caught Achilles' eyes and shook his head.

Achilles shook his back and moved behind Derrik and Maddie as Derrik led her to her mount.

~

Derrik

"I'm a ramblin' wreck from Georgia Tech and a helluvan engineer," Maddie sang, swaying her tankard side by side as Derrik and all the other men sat watching and grinning.

Suddenly, she slammed the tankard down and leaned toward them.

"Actually, I'm not. I went to the University of Oregon, and I didn't study engineering." She shook her head. "*Nooooo.* I studied medieval history but don't let that fool you." She leaned deeper. "It's *hard.*" She leaned back and announced, "But it also doesn't put bread on the table. Thus, I should have listened to my father and studied something that could actually lead to a job."

Derrik had no idea what she was talking about.

What he did know was that Maddie was so deep in her cups she'd wake up tomorrow and still be swimming in them.

"That said, in my world, you're supposed to sing that song when you're drunk," she went on. Abruptly her eyes rolled up, the irises shot back and forth, and Derrik grew alarmed before she looked back at the men and remarked, "Or maybe it's just me who sings that song when I'm drunk. I hope that doesn't offend anyone from Georgia Tech." Suddenly she shrugged and emitted a soft giggle. "Though, it doesn't matter. It's safe to say none of them are here."

At that, she burst out laughing, as did all the men, even though they had no earthly clue what she was on about.

Then again, Maddie's laughter was infectious, and it was thus because it was clear she hadn't done it very often.

Not until the last four months.

And she made it clear in those four months she was grateful to have it back, which was something that heartened every single man at that table.

Derrik included.

It was as if he'd given a gift he didn't know he was giving, but it was treasured beyond compare. And that was far from a bad feeling.

She pressed her hand flat to the table and looked around, her body swaying in a circle, noting, "Ships rock, like, *a lot*."

Thus, giving him the sign she was done for the night.

He got up and moved toward her, murmuring, "Let's get you to your cabin."

They were through the Vale and had boarded a galleon, halfway through their journey at sea to Lunwyn.

They were also off schedule. Their arrival would be two months later than when Apollo wanted them at the Ulfr stronghold of Karsvall.

But as Maddie took in her new world, and enjoyed every minute of it with abandon, he, nor any of the men including, eventually, Achilles, had the heart to rush her. So they'd stopped at games (and entered), festivals, fayres, cafés, shops, altars, churches, museums and anything else that caught Maddie's eye, teaching her all they could about her new world as they did.

Apollo, Derrik knew, would not be best pleased.

But experiencing his world through Maddie's eyes, listening to her stories of her own world as they rode and noting just how significant the differences were, and sharing in her excitement and laughter, he didn't care.

He'd explain to Apollo, and if his friend didn't understand, it didn't matter.

It was done.

He helped Maddie off her stool as she looked up at him with her inebriated, but warm and exceedingly beautiful brown eyes, and she declared, "We should play tuble."

"You need to be to your bed, Maddie," he told her. "Not playing card games. In your state, you'll fumble the cheat and pay the price."

"But—" she began as he moved to push her gently toward the passageway.

"Bed," he ordered.

"It's annoying when you boys go macho," she muttered.

He had no idea what she meant, but this happened frequently, to him and all the men.

Sometimes they asked. Sometimes they didn't. And sometimes when she answered, they still had no idea what she was talking about.

But whenever they asked, if they understood it or not, it was always interesting.

She didn't protest further, looked around him as he guided her away, waved and called her goodnights.

She got the same in return.

He moved her into the passageway.

"This ship is a lot bigger than I would have expected," she remarked as he pressed his fingers into the small of her back to move her before him.

"Mm," he answered.

"It's also way cool. I'm pretty much expecting Captain Jack Sparrow to jump out at any given time," she went on.

He grinned, shook his head but said nothing.

She kept talking.

"And this would not be unwelcome. Johnny Depp is *hot.*"

Derrik stayed silent except for his chuckle.

They made the door of her cabin. There, she stopped and turned to him, lifting her eyes to his.

He no longer saw the Ilsa he'd known for years. The Ilsa his closest friend adored. The Ilsa who made them laugh in a dry way, not an exuberant one. Whose intelligence matched her husband's, therefore she frequently challenged him and all of them to battles of wits, amusingly and wholeheartedly, just as she frequently won those battles (even against her husband).

No. Now he only saw Maddie, who was not one thing like Ilsa, except in looks.

She tipped her head to the side and shared, "I know I'm drunk."

Derrik smiled down at her and replied, "You're not drunk, Maddie. You're *drunk.*"

She smiled up at him, the smile lighting up her whole face, and he felt his heart thump harder.

"Okay, I know I'm *drunk,*" she agreed.

He shook his head, still smiling.

"And when you're drunk, the truth comes out," she informed him.

He turned his eyes to the ceiling and joked, "Gods, deliver me."

She smacked his chest, and he looked down at her just as she said, "I'm being serious, Derrik."

He rearranged his features and promised, "You have my full attention, Maddie."

She rolled her eyes.

When she rolled them back, her face sobered and she held his gaze.

Then she said, "Apollo wished for my return, my *twin's* return, really, but in being that he sought bringing me here. And he got it. Or, I guess, me. And then he didn't want it, *it* being, well...*me*. And that sucks. It hurt, and then being here all alone scared me. And depressed me. Because I'd been alone a long time. A *really* long time. Losing my parents because they turned their backs on me when I picked the wrong husband. Running from him because he hurt me."

She sucked in a deep breath even as Derrik pulled in a shallow one at her words.

"But I know we're getting closer to Lunwyn," she continued. "So I wanted to make sure I said thank you, to you and all the guys for turning a bad situation into a good one." She smiled a smile that wasn't her normal smile. It was smaller, slightly forlorn, but still warm. "No, a *great* one. And I'm starting with you."

His heart didn't thump harder at that.

It warmed.

"You're more than welcome, Maddie," Derrik replied quietly.

Her smile got bigger, and she whispered, "You're the bomb."

He'd heard that before, repeatedly. So he knew it was good.

"And you are very sweet," he returned.

"I am," she agreed cheekily and finished, "When I'm not beating your ass in tuble, that is."

At that, he tilted his head back and laughed, and when he again looked at her, he saw she was doing it with him.

She sobered again and said softly, "Thank you, Derrik."

His heart warmed further, and he lifted his chin.

She gave him another smile and a wink before she turned to her door.

He turned to the passageway but something she said registered, therefore he stopped and turned back.

"Maddie, just to say," he called, and she stuck her head out the door. "Apollo left before you to get his children to safety. You should not take that as him not wanting you here."

The forlorn went back into her face as she shook her head and returned, "Oh, he doesn't want me."

Derrik turned fully to her and started, "That isn't—"

But she interrupted him.

"It is, Derrik. He said it to my face. 'Be careful what you wish for, you might get it. And not want it.' That's what he said. Word for word. I think that says pretty clear he doesn't want me, don't you?"

Derrik didn't answer. This was because he was concentrating on the blood roaring in his ears.

"Anyway, I've sorted it all out," she carried on. "I've been thinking on it, and I have a plan. I'll have a word with him when we get there, and it'll all be good."

He still said nothing.

"'Night," she called.

"Goodnight, Maddie," he forced out.

She gave him a small wave and shut her cabin door.

Derrik stared at it for long moments, his hands fisted, her words ringing in his head.

Then he moved in order to a get to a place where there was ale.

And whiskey.

Ilsa

It was freaking *cold* in Lunwyn.

Freezing.

So I was glad when we made the inn, or more aptly, *inside* the inn, where a fire was roaring and Derrik got me a room, ordering, "Get the fire going in her chamber immediately," and the innkeeper's son scurried off.

This was, of course, as the innkeeper stared at me in shock.

Clearly, he knew or had seen Ilsa.

I smiled at him and dipped my eyes.

"She'll need wine, some cheese, bread, fruit, a hot bath and a lady's maid," Derrik kept going.

The innkeeper snapped his fingers and his wife (who was also staring at me), started then she took off too.

"I'll escort her to her room. There will be a guard in the hall and outside the inn. Seven men. After I take her to her room, I ride to Karsvall," Derrik went on.

The innkeeper nodded.

"Her key?" Derrik prompted.

The innkeeper jumped, turned and grabbed a skeleton key with a massive heart at its top. He turned back to Derrik and handed him the key.

"Best in the house, top floor, end of the hall to the right," the innkeeper told Derrik.

Derrik nodded, put his hand to my elbow and moved me to the stairs.

I moved with him, trying not to cry.

It was over.

My time with the guys was over.

No more ricken. No more tuble.

No more games that were like jousts, but they didn't have lances and charge each other. They had blunt swords and beat each other off their horses. At first, I thought this was a little brutal. But then I noticed Laures was really good at it and everyone around me in the arena (with actual bleachers and enormous colorful pendants flying from posts all around) was really into it. So I got into it too. In a big way.

Also, no more delicious, herbed, roasted meat on a stick bought from venders at fayres.

And no more watching girls dancing with streaming ribbons and fluffy skirts at festivals.

Further, no more telling Alek made-up pirate stories while we lay on our backs on the deck of the ship, rough wool blankets under us, another one pulled up to our chins, as we stared up at the stars.

We were in Lunwyn, met by someone the men didn't introduce me to who gave us a trunk with more stuff for me. This included boots, heavier clothing and capes, hats and gloves—the last three all made of fur or lined hides.

And off the horse I was, put in a sleigh (a sleigh! And a cool one!) with my trunk at the back and we'd ridden for three days across the icy landscape.

I had to admit, it was just as beautiful as the graceful exquisiteness of Fleuridia and the sumptuous splendor of Hawkvale.

It was just covered in snow and ice.

And freezing cold.

Now it was done, and I'd had four months to come up with my plan, which I'd done.

It scared me but it also excited me.

A new beginning.

A new life.

A new me.

All of it mine. All of it made by my hand, my decisions, my work.

Or it would be.

I was terrified.

And I couldn't wait.

But after we climbed the stairs, Derrik opened the door and handed me the key, I knew I'd miss the guys.

Badly.

I pulled in a very deep breath and got control as I let it go.

Then I looked up at him.

"Thank you again for everything, honey," I whispered.

"Maddie, I'll see you again in a few hours," he replied, not whispering.

He wouldn't.

I was going to take a bath, eat, drink wine, speak with Apollo (who Derrik was off to announce our arrival to and bring back to the inn for our chat).

Then I was going to leave.

I didn't say that. Maybe because of that time my father said it to me with such finality when I announced I was going to marry Pol. He was telling me I couldn't because Pol was a criminal. I was telling him I was twenty-three and I could do what I wanted. Then I'd never seen Dad again, except for when I was forced to go back and he'd shut the door in my face (twice), but I didn't figure those counted.

Yeah, maybe this was why I hated good-byes.

So I didn't intend to say them.

I was just going to go.

I'd write them letters later (maybe).

"I'll see you this evening," Derrik murmured and moved to leave.

But I called his name, and he turned back.

"Thank you," I repeated.

"Maddie—"

I shook my head, lifted my hand and felt so much emotion I couldn't speak in a normal voice. Therefore, what I had to say came out trembling and low.

But I forced it to come out.

"You know about him," I stated, and Derrik's jaw went hard.

Over the months, the dinners, the long rides, the sitting in pubs or on the grass or out under the stars and talking, I'd told him. At first a little. Then a lot. He and Achilles, both of them, I'd told all about Pol.

He knew.

"I haven't felt free in eleven years," I whispered.

A muscle jumped in his cheek and his eyes bored into mine.

"Thank you for making me feel free," I finished.

Then I swept into the room, closed the door and told myself one day I'd forget the love and tenderness that suffused Derrik's face at my words.

But I was lying.

6

NOT YOUR BIGGEST FAN

Apollo

Apollo drummed his fingers on the top of his desk, scowling at the papers there as his secretary droned on.

But he wasn't listening to a word the man said.

He was staring at the stack of missives that reported the frequent delays—and the reasons behind them—of Derrik's party arriving in Lunwyn.

From the last letter, he estimated they were to arrive any day.

And he had a damned war to plan. For the gods' sakes, he had no time to sit around waiting for a troop of guards watching over a single woman to frolic through three countries, taking double the time it should to make the journey simply because a female from another world wanted to watch Laures win a challenge.

"My lord, did you hear me?" Jeremiah, his secretary, called.

Apollo lifted his head and transferred his scowl to the man.

Jeremiah caught it and nervously lifted a finger to push his half-spectacles up the bridge of his nose.

"As I said, decline all invitations and my calendar is to be kept clear for the foreseeable future," Apollo stated.

Jeremiah, nor anyone but rulers, a few select generals and trusted soldiers, knew that any day, at any time, darkness could descend, sweeping across the land, black magic and dragons at war, lives at stake, men taking up arms, no one safe.

This being the whole bloody reason he had no time to sit in his study waiting for some woman from another world to enjoy the new one she found herself in.

Jeremiah's eyes got wide. "But there are hunts and gales you attend every year."

"I won't be attending them this year," Apollo returned.

"But—"

"Send my apologies," Apollo ordered. "And Achilles will be arriving imminently. He'll look after my affairs while I'm away. As soon as the party I'm awaiting arrives, I'll be leaving for Bellebryn."

"But—"

Apollo interrupted him by raising his hand as he heard running feet outside the door.

He trained his eyes to the door seconds before it was thrown open.

His young servant Nathaniel ran in and came to a swaying halt, snowflakes in his sandy-blond hair, his boy's short cloak still on.

"You said to say the minute I saw riders and I saw a rider, sir. It's Derrik returned," he announced.

Bloody hell.

Finally.

"Go to Torment, saddle him and bring him to the front. Then get warm," Apollo commanded and looked at Jeremiah. "Leave me."

Jeremiah's eyes got wide. "But sir, we have hours of—"

Apollo stood, leaned into both his fists in his desk and rumbled, "*Leave me.*"

Jeremiah nodded, quickly gathered the large stacks of papers he had in his lap, and the ones on the edge of Apollo's desk, and also the ones in the chair he'd pulled close. He shoved them in the gaping, battered case, grabbed it and hurried out.

Nathaniel was already gone.

Jeremiah closed the door behind him.

Apollo moved to the window that had a view to the front of the house and looked out, seeing Derrik on his horse galloping into view up the pine-lined lane as he did so.

He took a breath in through his nose. This did not calm his temper so he took in another one. This, too, failed, so he stopped trying.

When Derrik halted at the steps in front of the house, Apollo turned away from the window and moved to his desk. He stopped beside it and leaned his thigh against its edge. He then crossed his arms on his chest and his boots at the ankle.

He stared at the door, and as he did so, he didn't bother himself with taking deep breaths to remain calm.

Moments later, it opened without a knock and Derrik came through, his cloak and hair dusted with snow, the former swirling around him.

He was taking off his gloves but doing this with his eyes to Apollo.

"Close the door," Apollo ordered.

Derrik kicked it closed with a boot, took two strides into the room and stopped, gaze still locked with Apollo's.

"You're late," Apollo uttered a vast understatement.

Derrik said nothing.

"By two bloody months," Apollo went on.

Derrik still said nothing.

"War is pending," Apollo reminded him.

Derrik remained silent.

Apollo held on to the frayed threads of his control and invited, "Would you like to explain why you're late?"

Derrik finally spoke. "I believe that was explained in our missives."

"Indeed," Apollo bit out.

Games. Fayres. And Ilsa of the other world wanting to eat some fish cooked in a thick crust of salt, this descending, for some mad reason, into a two-day cooking war where she tried to best a local chef in the preparation of seafood.

She'd won, Remi had reported with apparent jubilation, with some dish that included salmon wrapped in pastry dough.

At the reminder, Apollo clenched his teeth.

He unclenched them to ask, "Is she at The Swan?"

"*She* is," Derrik answered, and Apollo didn't understand the emphasis on *she*.

He also didn't care.

He pushed from the desk, dropped his arms and murmured, "Then I'm away to The Swan."

"If you don't want her, I'll have her."

At Derrik's words, Apollo stopped dead and pierced his friend with his eyes.

"Pardon?" he whispered.

He wanted to believe he didn't understand his friend.

But he had a feeling he understood his friend.

He watched as Derrik planted his feet apart and his fists to his hips.

Oh yes.

He understood his friend.

"If you don't want her, I'll take her," he repeated.

By the gods, he had to jest.

"Are you talking about my wife?" Apollo asked low.

"She's not your wife," Derrik returned.

"She's my wife," Apollo bit out.

"She's not your bloody wife," Derrik clipped.

"Gods, man!" Apollo exploded, coming to the end of his patience and swinging out a hand. "You know she is just as she isn't."

"No, Lo. I just know she *isn't*," Derrik returned.

Apollo felt his eyes narrow. "Are you deranged?"

"Not in the slightest. She told me you told her that you didn't want her. If that's the case, I'll take her. We'll be away this eve. We'll go to the Vale, Fleuridia, somewhere you don't know where we are but also somewhere far away from you so you'll never see her with me."

Suddenly, Apollo's palms itched, his skin prickled, and through this he warned, "I suggest you stop talking."

Derrik shook his head.

"I won't. You left her alone, forlorn and frightened. She will not be alone, she'll not be frightened, and she'll *never* be forlorn. Not with me," Derrik stated.

Apollo held his friend's eyes—his *closest* friend—and a sick feeling snaked up his throat.

Because of this, his voice was deadly quiet when he asked, "In saying this, are you saying that you held feelings for Ilsa?"

"Don't be daft," Derrik spit out. "In saying this, I'm telling you I have feelings for Maddie."

Apollo's head jerked. "Who the bloody hell is Maddie?"

"She's our Ilsa," Derrik replied.

Apollo crossed his arms on his chest and inquired, "*Our* Ilsa?"

"Me and the men. Maddie is our Ilsa. We called her madam out of respect and because it was too difficult to call her Ilsa remembering the one before her. Through that, she became Maddie."

This intimacy, this shared history, no matter how recent, struck Apollo in his gut and the poison again started to rise in his throat.

He didn't have time for this discussion or these feelings. He needed to end both right now, get to Ilsa, speak with her, get her to Karsvall and get on his way.

"You speak of my wife, so you knew my response before you made your pronouncement," he declared. "You'll not take her. She isn't yours to have. She's mine."

"She isn't. She's Maddie. And she's free to do what she wishes with whom she wishes it," Derrik returned.

His meaning clear, it was another blow and more poison choked him.

"Careful, brother," Apollo whispered.

"I understand you," Derrik told him, his voice gentling. "I understand what you're feeling."

"You have no bloody idea," Apollo gritted.

"I do," Derrik retorted.

"Then, if you did, you'd know, your closest friend, a brother of the horse if not of blood, walking into your study telling you he'd take the woman who's the spitting image of your dead wife to the Vale, to Fleuridia, to *his bed*, is beyond the pale. You could take her to the stars, you would still lie awake at night knowing I was lying awake at night tormented in the knowledge that she was pressed to your side. And you'd do that knowing in your gut that was the worst betrayal imaginable."

Apollo watched Derrik flinch, but he didn't back down.

He bit off, "You can't not want her and still have her, Lo."

"I can do whatever I gods damn want, Rik," Apollo returned. "I paid for her to be here. She's *my* wife. *I'll* see to her, and *I'll* protect her."

"How? By doing the same thing that toad of a husband of hers did to her in the other world?" Derrik shot back. "But abusing her through neglect rather than with your fists?"

His vision darkened and Apollo strode forward. Derrik prepared as he did so, bracing, ready for a confrontation.

He didn't get one.

Apollo moved by him and threw open the door.

He turned in it and leveled his gaze on his friend.

"Think on this," he ordered.

"I have, for four months," Derrik replied.

"Then think longer," Apollo ground out, slammed the door and stormed down the hall.

He paced the secluded room he'd demanded for this meeting, its fire warm in the grate, but Apollo didn't feel warm.

I'm sorry.

He heard her whispered words, her voice had been sleepy, but those words were heartfelt.

And he felt her soft body burrowing into his.

I'm sorry.

He stopped pacing and closed his eyes.

But when he did, he saw her eyes, scared, confused and holding pain, peering deep into his.

You're not a hallucination.

He opened his eyes and muttered to himself, "Where the bloody hell is she?"

He was at The Swan.

He'd managed to drive Torment, his roan, through the snow and into the town with his mind consumed with finding reasons not to murder his closest friend.

But he'd been at the inn for twenty minutes, waiting for *her*, and thus he was having difficulty controlling his thoughts.

Thoughts he'd kept tightly leashed since that morning he slid away from her somnolent body and understood he'd made a colossal mistake.

Not saving her from her husband, that was not his mistake. But he could have arranged that without seeing her.

No, his mistake was seeing her.

Touching her.

Hearing her.

Smelling her.

Understanding instantly that she was not his Ilsa.

But the Ilsa she was was dangerous.

Something he now knew categorically considering his conversation with Derrik.

Therefore, when he should have been planning for an attack, he was making other plans.

And those plans included him negotiating the purchase of a chalet, a large one, a luxurious one, but one that was miles away from any of his estates.

And he'd already opened an account and deposited enough money in it that she could live and do so with every desire met but without her ever having the need to come to him and ask for a thing.

And live far away and well taken care of she would do, after they dealt with whatever was coming.

Unfortunately, until that time, for her safety she needed to be at Karsvall, with his men and with the witch who was watching over all of them.

Also with his children.

He'd explained all about Ilsa carefully to Christophe and Élan and watched closely after he did so.

His daughter had been a year and a half when her mother had died. She was now six. She didn't remember her mother, though she was excited about meeting Ilsa, as she was excited about everything under the sun.

It didn't take much with his Élan. The flight of a sparrow could brighten her day.

Where she got that, he had no idea. It wasn't from him.

It also wasn't from her mother.

His Ilsa was quick to smile, droll with words, and so gods damned smart, it was, at times, alarming.

But she was not a dreamer. She did not anticipate excitement around every corner. She did not rush out to meet life, like her daughter.

Christophe, on the other hand, had been four when Ilsa was lost to him. He was now eight, almost nine.

He remembered her. Those memories were elusive due to his age, but he'd carried a locket with his mother's tiny portrait in it since he'd found it on Apollo's dresser when he was five.

He was never without it.

He was also not excited to meet Ilsa. He tried to hide it from his father and sister.

But he failed.

This concerned Apollo but he intended to have a word with Achilles about it.

Achilles would keep an eye on things.

On this thought, the door opened and Ilsa moved into the room.

Apollo clenched his teeth and braced inwardly at the sight of her.

She looked exactly like his wife. She sounded like her. She even smelled like her.

But she didn't move like her. Not her gait. Not a tilt of her head. Not a movement of her hands.

Nothing.

Her eyes came to him, and those eyes were not his beauty's eyes.

His Ilsa had lived a life full of abundance and serenity. When she was a child, she broke her toe, but that was the biggest difficulty she faced until she faced the difficulty that ended her days on this earth. They met young, fell in love young and married young. They had a marriage full of promise and passion, laughter and contentment. His Ilsa had a good life from her first breath, but not to the last one.

No, six months she suffered from her illness. Actually longer, though they didn't catch it at first.

Then she took her last breath and that breath, as had the ones before it for months, had been pained.

But this Ilsa, what lurked behind her eyes was so deep he could mine it for centuries and never get to the bottom of it.

He also didn't know, if he made that effort, if he would find riches...or despair.

What he knew, what he'd come to understand in their brief time together, and what he must guard against was the overwhelming desire he felt to find a shovel and start digging.

"Thank you for coming so quickly," she said, taking him from his contemplations, and he knew by her expression she might not know his exact thoughts, but she suspected they were of her twin.

She was right as well as wrong.

There was also pain in her eyes, perhaps for her, perhaps for him, maybe even both. Further, there was sorrow, and that was probably for him.

But she also looked angry.

And that was a surprise.

"I didn't know you would be here so fast," she carried on. "I had something to eat, some wine and a bath. If I'd have known, I would have delayed the bath."

He most assuredly did not need her talking about having a bath. It brought thoughts of her pressing close to him when she was in his arms in his bed in Fleuridia, and when she did that, she'd been fully clothed in her world's garments. Thoughts of that, and worse, thoughts of her naked, were thoughts he did not need.

Therefore, to end them, he stated, "I should have given you some time to refresh yourself. But now we're both here, we should proceed."

She nodded, took a step into the room and began talking.

And when she did, Apollo couldn't believe what he was hearing.

"You're right. We should proceed so we can move on. And I'd like to start by thanking you for the guard and the clothes and, well...everything."

"It's my duty to—" he started, but she spoke over him.

"And I'll ask that you allow me to keep them when I leave."

He blinked. Slowly.

She carried on.

"I'll also ask for a loan. A small one and I'll leave it up to you how much it is because you'll know better than me how much it should be to get me to where I need to go so I can do what I need to do. But it'll need to be enough to get me back to the Vale, maybe Fleuridia, and help me to get set up."

She lifted a hand and quickly continued.

"I want to assure you that it's pretty obvious in your world you've got a wad, or about seven of them, of cash, but still, I'm not taking advantage. I'll keep track, and when I have a job, I'll start to pay you back."

"When you have a job?" Apollo repeated her words in a question because he was not sure of every word she'd said, but he thought he was sure of her meaning.

He just couldn't believe it.

"Yes," she confirmed.

"A job in Fleuridia or the Vale," he stated.

"Yes. It's pretty here but it's also pretty cold and, uh...well, kind of close to you," she replied.

Apollo said nothing.

But he felt a number of things and none of them were good.

"I'd actually like to be on my way tonight," she informed him. "Is that too much of a rush for you? To get me a loan, I mean. That is, if you agree to the loan. If you don't, I understand. I'll ask Achilles. Or Derrik."

He had something to say to that.

"You'll not be seeing Derrik for some time," Apollo declared and watched her head give a small jerk.

"Sorry?" she asked.

"You and Derrik will not be in each other's company for some time," he stated.

"Um...I...well, I know. As I said, I'm going, like, tonight. And I'm not good at good-byes so if I could ask one more thing of you and that is for you to tell all the guys I said *adieu* and thank them," she put her hand to her chest, "from the bottom of my heart for being so cool, I'd appreciate it." Her head twitched again, and she clarified. "I mean, I won't see Derrik again unless I have to ask him for money. After that, I probably won't see him at all."

She said this and she didn't like saying it. There were many ways she was surprising him, but that message was clear.

She would miss the men, and specifically Derrik.

Apollo felt his skin start to prickle again.

"You won't see him again not because you're leaving to go somewhere to get *set up*." he said, attempting to keep the annoyance out of his tone. "You won't see him again because I'm not allowing it."

Her back shot straight and she whispered, "You won't allow it?"

"No," he replied.

"But—"

"You'll also not be going anywhere but Karsvall."

"I—"

"And you'll not be working at all. An Ulfr woman does not work."

She blinked.

Then she stared.

"And you may not be of this world, but you're an Ulfr," he finished.

"How can I make money if I don't work?" she asked.

"If you need anything, you ask for it. It will be provided for you," he answered.

"But—"

"Now," he interrupted again. "As for the children—"

It was she who interrupted this time, and she did it by snapping, "Hang on a ding-donged second."

"Ilsa—"

"No." She kept snapping and now she did it advancing, her hand up, finger pointing at him and jabbing the air. "*You* listen to me now and stop cutting me off. It's rude." She stopped moving and dropped her hand. "You can't tell me what I can and can't do. Where I can go and who I can see."

She stopped talking so he requested, "May I speak?"

"Only if you don't piss me off when you do it," she allowed, and he really didn't want to find her amusing.

But, damn it all, he did.

He just didn't let it show.

"I'm afraid what I'm about to say will do that...if I take your meaning as I've learned what those words mean from Finnie, Cora and Circe."

Her head tipped to the side. "Finnie, Cora and Circe?"

"Women here from your world married to men from mine."

Her eyes got huge and that wasn't amusing.

It was endearing.

Gods, but he'd made a colossal mistake bringing her here.

"*What?*" she cried.

He drew in breath and explained, "Finnie, the Ice Princess of Lunwyn, Cora, the Gracious, Princess of Hawkvale, and Circe, the warrior Queen of Korwahk, are all from your world."

Her eyes got even bigger.

Thus, more endearing.

Bloody hell.

"Cora, the Gracious is of my people?" she breathed.

"You've heard of her," Apollo deduced.

She threw out a hand and exclaimed, "Hell yeah! Everyone raves about her in the Vale."

"She's much loved," Apollo agreed.

"Totally," she stated. "Holy cow. She's from home?"

Apollo crossed his arms on his chest. "Your home, as is hers, is here now, Ilsa."

"Well, yeah. I know," she replied immediately. "But you know what I mean."

"My point is, it would be good to stop thinking of the other world as home."

She said nothing but the excited surprise drifted from her delicate features as she held his gaze.

He tried not to think that he rather enjoyed the excited surprise lighting her features and reverted to their previous subject.

"As I was saying, I'm afraid I'll anger you with what I have to say, but in this world, you are a woman, you are my charge, and you are an Ulfr. Further, you're aristocracy by birth as well as marriage. Your father in Fleuridia was a count. Therefore, all around, you are an aristocrat and must behave in this world as one."

Her tone was cautious when she asked, "I can assume it's widely known your wife has passed?"

"It is," he affirmed tersely.

"So everyone will know she's not me. And anyway, if I'm not here then I don't have to behave in any way that's expected of me."

"I have decided to explain your..." he paused, "appearance by saying you're a distant cousin of Ilsa's with an uncanny resemblance to her but you grew up in the Vale, thus you don't know how to speak Fleuridian. You've come to be sheltered here due to your parents' untimely demise and your unwed status, seeing as your husband also met an untimely end."

She took another step to him and stopped, saying, "But don't you see, Apollo? If I just go, no explanations have to be made."

"You're not going, Ilsa," he denied.

She mimicked him, crossing her arms on her chest. "I'm not staying, Apollo."

He was losing patience, not that he had much in the first place.

"It's not safe," he told her curtly.

"I was on the run from Pol for three years. Yes, this world is different, but I think I can take care of myself."

"I'll remind you that you were on the run, and he found you. When first I laid eyes on you, you were not doing so well at keeping yourself safe."

She clamped her mouth shut and he knew his point was made.

So he moved on.

"It's my duty—" he began to continue but she interrupted him.

"I'm not a duty. I'm a person."

"I'm aware of that."

"And I can work. I *can* take care of myself. And if I can't, frankly, that's none of your business. I'll deal with that too."

He tried a new tactic and asked, "And how will you feed yourself?"

"I haven't decided yet, but it isn't like you don't have restaurants, pubs. I'll get a job as a waitress."

His brows shot together, and when she saw it, for some reason, she took a step back.

But he ignored that.

"A *barmaid*?" he asked, his voice dripping with derision, and at the sound of it, her spine straightened so quickly, it was wonder he didn't hear it snap.

"Yes," she hissed. "A *barmaid*," she mimicked his tone then defended her questionable choice of profession. "It's honest work."

"You're an Ulfr," he reminded her.

"Yes, that's my last name given to me by a man I now detest so it's a name I don't want. And the other man who has that name, I don't like all that much. So I'll be going back to my maiden name and no one will even know I'm an Ulfr. Which is okay by me because the time that I was," she leaned in, "*all* of it," she stressed, her meaning clear, "I didn't like all that much."

He didn't like her meaning. Not at all.

And he didn't hesitate to take issue with it.

"Did you suffer at my men's hands?" he asked.

"No, they were awesome. Every last one. But *you* haven't been all that great."

"Well, you can rest in the knowledge, my dove, that you won't have to concern yourself with me," he returned. "I'll be away to Bellebryn the minute I drop you at Karsvall."

"That's fabulous news," she replied sarcastically. "But even if I don't have to concern myself with you, I *do* have to concern myself with your children."

This time he didn't understand her meaning, but he knew he didn't like it.

Therefore, he whispered, "Careful, Ilsa."

"You know, I've lived for over a decade being careful," she started conversationally then leaned in again and hissed, "And I'm *sick of it.* I've also been controlled by a man for over a decade and I'm," she leaned in further, "*sick of that too.*"

He uncrossed an arm to throw it toward her, sweeping it up to indicate her body, and crossing it again before he stated, "You wear fine garments. You slept in the best cabin on the ship, your passage paid by me. You slept in the finest inns and ate the finest foods that could be found during your journey. I know. I ordered it and my men follow orders precisely. You look well, healthy and rested. Everything that has been done for you since you came to this world has been done with your protection, safety and comfort in mind. And you can talk for the next four days and not convince me you have not been *very* comfortable for the last *four months* all at my expense."

"You brought me here, asshole," she fired back. "And left me there." She swept an arm out in the general direction of the Winter Sea to the north, not Fleuridia, which was to the south, and she kept talking. "And, just saying, that's how it all starts, all the good stuff with my *comfort* in mind. Then all the bad shit goes down that isn't comfortable at all."

His waning patience began to fade faster.

"I am not him, Ilsa," he growled.

"No, but you throwing all that in my face says that you believe I'm beholden to you for giving me clothes and food and safe passage. Well, get this through your head, hot guy, you're off the hook. Just let me go, you'll never see me again and I won't cost you another dime."

"And for you to leave, you need the garments I purchased for you and a loan," he reminded her, her head jerked, and her eyes narrowed to a glare.

He had her.

He almost smiled.

Then she proved he didn't.

"I'll walk out of here naked, I don't give a damn."

He lifted one of his brows. "And die in the elements?"

"At least that'll be my choice," she snapped, uncrossing her arms and planting her hands on her hips.

Apollo drew in breath through his nose.

This was going too far. He had to rein it in.

He let his breath out, and in order to control their discussion, forcing calm, he stated, "We have an issue, you and I."

"You think?" she asked sardonically.

"Let me finish," he demanded quietly.

She took her hands from her hips and crossed them on her chest again.

He resumed speaking.

"You can't see past him. I'm having difficulty seeing past her."

Ilsa said nothing but a flash in her eyes indicated she agreed.

"Dark times are ahead for us all. It would take some time to explain this to you fully, but I will try to do what I can now."

When he said no more, she nodded for him to go on, and he did so.

"I know that magic is not practiced openly in your world. You may or may not know that it is here. And there are those who have amassed great amounts of power. One, in the Vale, so much she is considered a she-god."

Her eyes widened at these words, and he really wished she'd cease doing that.

With difficulty, he ignored it and kept speaking.

"And the ones of concern do not use their magic for good. Now, they have aligned themselves with a deposed ruler who no doubt has vengeance on his mind. They have also kidnapped the Cora of this world, who is not a good woman, but cold to her bones, selfish and deceitful. This is not a noble brew. They mean ill and they have the power to rain misfortune on the land, the kind of misfortune that has not ever been experienced in our world. The kind of misfortune anyone would hope would *never* be experienced in this world or any other."

"Holy cow," she breathed.

"Yes," he agreed. "For this reason, you are not safe here without protection. You are also not safe in your world. But I would feel better and more in control of your safety if you were in my world. After we're through this tense period, we can again discuss what your future in this world will be. But for now, I'm asking you to allow me to see to your safety. It would mean much to me to know I've kept you safe from him and kept you safe here as well."

He could see by the warmth that crept into her eyes and the softness that had settled about her mouth that she was going to concede, and he relaxed.

Then she didn't concede.

"I cannot go to Karsvall," she informed him.

"Ilsa—"

"I can't be around your children."

He took in another breath, and guessing at her hesitancy, he explained, "They've been told of you. They understand."

She held his eyes a moment before she looked to the side.

He watched her profile and suddenly it struck him with a bolt that electrified his entire frame.

He didn't know what she was thinking.

He couldn't predict what would come out of her mouth. He couldn't read the flashes in her eyes. He could barely guess at the expressions on her face.

Not like he could with his Ilsa.

She was new.

He understood she was new; he just didn't understand she was *new*.

Entirely new.

Gods.

She looked back at him, right in his eyes, but her voice was so quiet he could barely hear her when she said, "I lost two babies. A boy," she pulled in a soft breath, "and a girl."

His gut twisted.

Oh yes, she was new.

And now he knew he'd mined some of those depths that lurked behind her eyes.

He just wished he did not know what he'd unearthed.

But more, far more, he wished those losses were not buried in her soul.

"Logically," she continued in her quiet voice, "I understand that they are not mine. Irrationally, I've tried to convince myself that they aren't what I could have had in my world. But I know with the way things are with our worlds that *they are*."

"Ilsa—"

Her eyes swam with tears, and she whispered, "I can't do it. I..." She swallowed and admitted, "It would kill me."

It was then he found his mouth saying, "Tonight you stay at The Swan and rest. Tomorrow, we're away to Bellebryn."

She blinked before she breathed, "What?"

"Tomorrow, we're away to Bellebryn."

"Tomorrow...Bellebryn..." She shook her head sharply then asked, "What do you mean *we*?"

"We means you and me."

Her entire frame visibly locked tight.

"But I can't...you can't..." She threw out her hands. "We don't even *like* each other."

"I don't know you enough not to like you, Ilsa," he pointed out.

"Well, you weren't fired up to *get* to know me," she returned, the fire back in her eyes. "And the way you communicated that, I'm not *your* biggest fan."

He fought his lips twitching, failed in that endeavor and her eyes narrowed on his mouth.

He felt her eyes there and he felt them elsewhere as well.

Bloody hell.

Bellebryn with Ilsa was not a good plan.

But to save her the heartache of meeting Christophe and Élan, it was his only one.

However, she would make the choice.

"You have two choices, my dove," he shared. "Karsvall with the children or Bellebryn with me." He began to move to the door. "You have until the morning to make the choice. I'm here at sunrise. I either take you back to my home or I take you with me." He stopped with his hand on the doorknob, his eyes on her. "I'll come prepared either way."

"I...you...we can't...that's..." she spluttered.

"Until the morning," he said as his farewell, opened the door, moved through it and closed it behind him.

He expected her to follow him, calling his name and pleading or spitting fire.

If he was honest, he wasn't expecting it. He was hoping for either one, he didn't care which. Though he was leaning toward spitting fire.

She didn't do either.

He fought back the disappointment he knew it was unhealthy to feel, grabbed his cloak from the hook by the door and lifted his chin to Henri, the innkeeper. When Henri gave him a wave, Apollo moved out into the cold and buckled on his cloak as he headed to the stables where he'd put Torment to keep him out of the chill.

He led Torment out, mounted him and clicked his tongue against his teeth, leaning forward digging in his heels, and Torment shot through the snow.

He rode home knowing he should be thinking about a variety of things, making plans, prioritizing conversations.

But he didn't ride home thinking about any of that.

He did it wondering what her answer on the morrow would be.

As Apollo rode toward his stables, he saw Achilles strolling out of them.

He reined in Torment close to his cousin and swung off, leading the horse to his brethren.

Achilles looked beyond him, then back at Apollo.

"Maddie is not with you," he noted, and Apollo felt his mouth tighten at the familiar name they called Ilsa.

He forced it to relax in order to say, "Indeed. She's to stay at The Swan this eve. Dispatch fresh guards to relieve the ones at the inn."

Achilles nodded but watched him closely, his cousin's eyes, Apollo knew, not missing anything.

"This is a change in plans," he remarked.

"As has been everything when it comes to Ilsa of the other world since her arrival," Apollo returned and lifted a brow. "Four months, Achilles?"

His cousin's lips twitched.

Apollo found nothing amusing. "You know the dangers that lurk and thus the haste that should have been made."

"She's difficult to deny," Achilles replied.

Apollo was already concerned about that. The steadfast Achilles falling to her charms made him more so.

"I'm sensing this," Apollo told him and then shared, "Derrik and I had words."

"I was afraid of that," Achilles murmured.

Yes. Achilles didn't miss much.

"He will not be in her company for some time," Apollo stated.

Again, Achilles watched him closely, but he said nothing, only nodded.

"As you noted, plans have changed," Apollo told him. "She has some concerns about being around Christophe and Élan. I've given her the choice to come with me to Bellebryn tomorrow or come here."

He ignored Achilles' look of surprise and carried on.

"She has until sunrise to make her decision. When I leave, if I don't return, you'll know she chose to come with me. You're to stay here, as is Derrik. Dispatch Remi, Laures, Hans and Draven to follow us to Bellebryn. I'll act as her guard on the journey. They'll look after her in Bellebryn."

"Four months ago," Achilles started carefully, "you did not seem keen to spend time with her, cousin."

"She and I have had a discussion that has changed my mind."

Achilles blew out a breath and Apollo knew what that meant.

"It's not that way," he assured him.

"It wasn't that way for Derrik either, in the beginning. And you should know it wasn't that way for Laures or Remi as well. For Derrik, it took about a week. Remi and Laures fell not long after. And I have suspicions about Hans *and* Gaston."

It was worse than he thought but not worse than he could imagine. Not after spending time with her, in the beginning *and* at the inn.

Still, he whispered an irritated, "Bloody hell."

"The good news is, they'll be an excellent guard. They'd lay down their lives for her," Achilles offered.

"They lust after my wife," Apollo bit out and watched Achilles tilt his head to the side.

"Is she?" he asked quietly.

And the second time that day, Apollo found his mouth speaking for him before his mind engaged.

"She will be."

Achilles blinked and asked, "What?"

Warming to this thought, he explained, "The story being shared as people will see Ilsa and wonder is that she is a distant cousin of my Ilsa's, widowed, and her parents have recently been lost. She's come to Lunwyn for my protection. And it's custom, is it not, for a widowed man to take to wife a widowed woman who is in the family, however removed, in order to provide her succor and protection?"

"By the gods, cousin," Achilles whispered. "It is, but it will be lost on no soul for miles around and throughout the Houses that Maddie is the image of your departed wife."

"A happenstance that will likely not be questioned considering I did not hide my feelings for my wife or the ones I held after she was lost. Therefore, it would not be a leap that I would be drawn to one who looks just like her."

"Too true, but this is mad, Lo." Achilles was still whispering. "Once the troubles are over and Maddie takes her place at your side, everyone will know she's a replacement of the one you cared so deeply for and lost."

Having just made this decision, he'd obviously not thought of that, and it caused not a small amount of unease.

But he had made this decision. And Apollo Ulfr was many things, one of them decisive.

Therefore, he asked his cousin, "Have I ever cared what people thought?"

"No, but has it occurred to you that Maddie might?' his cousin asked him.

It, of course, hadn't, and this idea, too, troubled him.

But time never stopped, and people accustomed themselves to a variety of things, given enough of it. They would accustom themselves to the new Ilsa. And if she was discomfited by it in the meantime, he'd just keep her close and not take her out in society.

He explained his decision by saying, "She's been in the company of her guard for four months, Lees, and five have fallen. Derrik so deeply, he confronted me and asked to take her away."

"Gods," Achilles muttered, shock on his face, but not surprise.

The shock was that Derrik would confront him. The lack of surprise was that Achilles knew it might happen.

"Precisely," Apollo said tersely. "She's extremely spirited. She's also exquisitely beautiful. And I know you have not missed there are other things about her which would pull at any man."

"Have they pulled at you?" Achilles asked quietly.

Apollo didn't answer.

Instead, he stated, "For her protection, I must take her as wife."

Achilles remained silent.

Apollo did not.

"Therefore, if she chooses to stay here, I bid you to keep her protected from the attentions that might come at her, as well as see to my affairs and keep an eye on Christophe and Élan. Élan will have no issue with her. Christophe may have difficulties coping."

Achilles nodded.

Apollo continued, "If she is to stay here, when I deliver her in the morning, I will collect Derrik and take him with me."

Achilles nodded again.

Apollo went on, "Upon my return, we'll see to a quiet wedding."

Achilles didn't nod at that. He held Apollo's gaze and said nothing.

Apollo ignored the reservations in his cousin's eyes and kept speaking.

"If she comes with me, dispatch the guard as I instructed, however not the men I chose. You choose who to send but send four of them. I'll wed her along the way."

Again, Apollo didn't nod.

Instead, he advised, "I urge you to take some time to consider this, cousin."

"I have no choice but to sleep on it," Apollo replied.

He watched his cousin take in a breath and let it out.

Then he again watched his cousin nod. This did not surprise Apollo. They'd grown up together, alongside Laures, Draven and Derrik. Achilles knew when Apollo's mind was made up, there was no changing it.

And Achilles would champion it, if not in word at that moment, when the time came, he'd do it in word and deed. For Apollo, and he was in no doubt, also for Ilsa.

Therefore, Apollo nodded back and ended the conversation by leading Torment into the stables.

His fist on his cock pumping, his eyes closed, the vision of her running her tongue up the underside was in his brain.

Her face, he knew.

But he'd never had that tongue.

Or those eyes.

Eyes that were burning on him now, burning on him and through him even if only in his imagination.

Fathomless.

A mystery.

His mystery.

On this thought and the small enigmatic smile she gave him before she rolled her tongue around the tip, his head pressed back into the pillows and Apollo stifled his own groan as he spent himself on his stomach.

Slowly opening his eyes to the dark of his room, he milked the last beads from his shaft as she continued to steal his thoughts.

Then he reached to his nightstand, opened the drawer and pulled out a handkerchief. He wiped up his seed and tossed the cloth aside. He then yanked the covers over him and turned to his side, stretching out his arm to curl around the pillow and pull it to him.

Tonight, a pillow.

Tomorrow, something else entirely.

He'd lied to his cousin.

He didn't intend to sleep on anything.

He intended to sleep *with* something.

Yes, he'd made a colossal mistake.

One he just no longer had any intention to rectify by sending her away.

On that thought, Apollo closed his eyes and faded to sleep.

AT SUNRISE THE NEXT DAY, with his gloved hand on a lead to a horse that was hitched to the sleigh prepared to take Ilsa forward or back, Apollo saw her standing on the steps of the inn.

She was wearing a fur cape, holding a fur cap in her hand, her auburn hair shining in the sun and her eyes were aimed at him.

He pulled back on Torment, halting close and looking down at her.

She looked up, and before he could speak, she snapped, "Bellebryn."

Then, without delay, she stomped through the snow to the sleigh.

Knowing he was cursed and not caring in the slightest, when she did, Apollo smiled.

7

Away to Bed

I was learning something new.

That was, you could not stomp out your anger when a man had your hand tucked in the crook of his arm and was leading you up some stairs behind an innkeeper.

You also couldn't do it when you were in the presence of an aristocrat, even if you weren't one yourself (officially), because that wasn't the done thing.

But I already knew you couldn't throw a hissy fit in public, it was rude—in this world, my world or *any* world—no matter how much reason you had to do it.

That said, I was going to do it when we reached *our* room.

Yes, *our* room.

The first day gliding over the frosty tundra with Apollo had gone relatively well. This mostly had to do with Apollo riding beside me through the snow and not attempting conversation.

On my way through Lunwyn the first time, as the men rode close to my sleigh and we chatted, for the most part, my attention had been taken from the landscape.

Without that diversion, I was able to more fully take in the beauty of what was around me. The rolling plains covered in soft snow twinkling in the sun. The vistas dotted with green pines tufted with white. The small villages we passed, sleepy and closed away from the cold, smoke drifting lazily from chimneys coming out of roofs covered in marshmallow blankets.

As the glorious white horse with its smoky gray mane (the contrast to Apollo's fantastic beast, which was smoky gray with an unusual white mane) pulled my dark-green lacquered sleigh, I could give it my full attention. And I saw it was far more beautiful than I'd noted on the way in.

This annoyed me. It was silly and even childish, but I didn't want to like anything that came with Apollo. And considering the latest turn of events, after a wonderful four months that had been the happiest maybe in my life, I was feeling okay with being silly and childish.

One of the worst parts of this turn of events was that it included being in the presence of Apollo.

He was worse than I imagined, and he was pretty bad before.

Sure, there were reasons I couldn't go forth and start my new life, free to be whatever I felt like being. I mean, malevolent magic was imminent, and I didn't want to seem like a wuss, but I didn't think it was the smartest decision to go it alone in a whole new world when bad witches and vengeful deposed rulers were plotting to unleash misfortune on the land.

And he'd been cool (okay, I had to admit, he'd been relatively kind) when I explained about Christophe and Élan.

But mostly he was dictatorial, haughty and arrogant, and it *really* annoyed me when he interrupted me like what I had to say wasn't as important as what he had to say.

I'd slept on it and come to the decision that being with him would be easier to deal with than being around his children. And I decided this because I decided at the same time to ignore him as much as I could when I was with him.

I could ignore a dictatorial, haughty, arrogant grown man (maybe). I couldn't ignore kids (definitely).

Decision made, I put it into practice when we stopped briefly for lunch, and he tried to engage me in conversation. Without a peep, I turned my eyes away, chomped into the roasted pork sandwich one of his servants (no doubt, I didn't see Apollo in a kitchen slapping together sandwiches) had provided (which was delicious, by the way) and ignored him.

The good part about this was it worked. He quit trying to talk to me from the moment I looked away from him.

The bad part about this was that, when my eyes slid through him moments later, he was leaning against the side of the sleigh, his gaze to the ground, his mouth curved up, and I knew it was *me* he found amusing.

That annoyed me also, so I decided to ignore that too.

Off we went maybe ten minutes later, and he kept apace with my sleigh, but he said nothing further.

He also said nothing when he guided us into a larger village, this one beside a lovely streaming creek that had glistening black rocks at its banks. He took us straight to a building that had a shingle hanging from it that said "Rock Creek Inn" (not original, but apt), where we stopped.

He also said nothing when he wrapped his reins around a post in front of the inn and came back to me, offering his arm as I dismounted from the sleigh. I was, of course, a now consummate sleigh-driver seeing as Gaston gave me a lesson when we got to Lunwyn, and I'd been in charge of my sleigh ever since. Though, truthfully, it wasn't much to brag about since it wasn't all that hard.

I took his arm but did it with my face turned away and I didn't even glance at him because I didn't want to see if this amused him due to the fact that I knew that would annoy me.

He did curve his fingers around my hand in the crook of his elbow, but I ignored that too. Since my hand had rabbit fur-lined gloves on it, I could even pretend his hand wasn't there.

This was what I did.

He then took us into the inn, right to the desk, and instantly asked the innkeeper for his best room.

That would be one room, singular.

It was not your standard Holiday Inn, but it had more than one room, I was sure. And I seriously doubted Apollo intended to sleep in my sleigh. Further, the only other time we'd stayed under the same roof overnight, for some insane reason, he'd slept in bed with me.

So he either intended to share a room with me or find somewhere else warm to lie his head (or not lie his head, considering who had shared his bed in Fleuridia before me—it was doubtful he got much rest when he was paying for the time of the person he was with).

Therefore, I was seething but controlling it.

We'd have words in *our* room.

Which was right where the innkeeper took us, opening the door for us to the room at the very end of the hall on the second floor.

He turned to Apollo, handed him the iron key with a big cross at the top and said, "I'll have a boy up to start a fire soon's I can, yer lordship. Would you be requiring any wine, ale or tea to warm you after yer ride?"

I felt Apollo's eyes on me. I didn't look at him but I did take this as a sign he was asking me if I wanted any of these things.

"Wine, please," I requested, forcing my tone to sound calm and wishing I could order tequila. Alas, I'd asked the guys and also copiously tasted the various spirits available in this world and tequila wasn't among them.

"Of course, milady," he muttered.

He glanced at Apollo and when Apollo grunted, "Wine will be fine," the man nodded, skirted us with difficulty (due to the fact that Apollo hadn't let me go so we were taking up the hallway, nor, might I add, did he move us out of the poor man's way when he was obviously sucking in his gut to slide by us) and scurried away.

Apollo led me into the room.

The minute he closed the door, I pulled my hand from his elbow and took three paces into the room, sucking in a deep breath.

I turned to him but made a show of glancing around the room, taking it all in before I lifted my gaze to his.

When my eyes hit him, I noticed he was in the process of rearranging his face. And what he was arranging it from was amusement. What he changed it to when my eyes caught his was fake courteous inquiry.

I ignored that and remarked, "This is a lovely room."

Apollo looked around and I knew what he saw since I'd just looked at it.

A bed, double at most, with a quilted bedspread and two fluffy pillows, the pillows being the only good things in room.

The rest included a thick braided rug on the floor that appeared like it needed to be taken out and beaten and this needed to be done about twelve months ago. There was not a thing on the walls, not even a chipped mirror. There was a table and two chairs by the window. The table was nicked and scratched. The chairs looked like their comfort level was set at "torture chamber." And over the windows, heavy drab curtains of a nondescript color because whatever color they were originally faded to nothing two decades ago.

His eyes came to mine and his face was studiously blank when he replied, "Indeed."

"I'll enjoy my brief sojourn here," I shared, ignored the blank look slipping as his eyes flashed with humor and inquired, "Would you care to share where you'll be sleeping?"

He held my gaze and answered, "In here."

I cocked my head to the side. "So I'm to sleep in the sleigh?"

"Not unless you fancy your digits being amputated tomorrow due to frost bite," he replied.

"No, I don't fancy that," I informed him, taking great pains to keep my tone neutral. "So, will it be you or me sleeping on the floor?"

"Neither."

I took in another deep breath, found calm on the exhale, and asked, "Would you care to explain?"

He did care to explain because he immediately did that.

"I need to get to Bellebryn without delay. You need a constantly vigilant guard. As you're coming with me, I'm your guard. Therefore, I'm keeping you safe."

"By sleeping with me?" I snapped, at his answer completely failing to keep my tone neutral.

"I can hardly keep you safe if I can't keep my eye on you."

"The guys managed to keep me safe on the journey here without any of them sleeping with me," I pointed out, and his eyes flashed in a different way at my remark.

I'd seen that flash before. It was the way I'd seen them flash the day before when we were talking about Derrik.

"There were eight of them," he stated, cutting into my thoughts. "With eight of them, they could keep watch inside and out. There's only one of me and I'll be unable to keep an eye on you if you're in a different room and I can't actually *see* you."

That was logical and totally irrational at the same time.

"Am I in imminent danger of being kidnapped?" I queried.

"I've no idea what the imminent danger is. I just know it's imminent so I'm not taking any chances."

Unfortunately, that was just logical which I found annoying. I wouldn't know, of course, but I would guess malevolent witches with the power of gods were more than a vague threat to pretty much everybody, so it was probably good to be prepared.

"Perhaps," I began to suggest, "we can request a room with two beds."

His head tipped slightly to the side, and he asked, "Is this something available in your world?"

"Yes," I replied with the sinking feeling that it wasn't available in this one.

He confirmed that sinking feeling.

"Well, it isn't available here."

Fabulous.

"Apollo—"

He cut me off. "We sleep together Ilsa."

I clenched my teeth.

Forcing myself to release them, I drew in another deep breath and tried again.

"Okay, maybe we can request a room with a bigger bed."

"You've stayed in inns on your journey, no?"

I had. Many of them. And all of them (albeit most of them cleaner and nicer) had beds like this. We'd happened onto bigger hotels and lodges along our journey that had way nicer rooms and much bigger beds but not in a village of this size.

Drat.

He assumed my answer was what it was even not verbalized and continued.

"It will also be warmer."

It most definitely would be that considering he was a big guy, I wasn't exactly tiny, and us sharing that bed would mean personal mattress space would be at a minimum.

Or possibly non-existent.

Shit.

I couldn't reply as there was a knock on the door, and seeing as Apollo was standing in front of it, he turned and opened it.

A boy of about ten was standing outside. He looked up at Apollo and dipped his chin. When Apollo moved out of his way, he rushed in, his arms laden with split wood, a bucket dangling from one hand.

"Milady," he muttered to me and didn't wait for my greeting. He dropped to his knees by the fireplace and started work immediately.

Apollo didn't get the door closed before a girl was at it, carrying a tray with a dark bottle on it, the top sealed with blue wax, and there were two simple wineglasses on it.

"The table," Apollo muttered to her.

She bobbed a mini-curtsy, strode in two feet, gave me a mini-curtsy too, and then she moved to the table, making light work of depositing her tray and getting out of there.

Before she left, however, Apollo ordered, "Water so Lady Ulfr can refresh."

The girl nodded briefly and took off.

Hmm.

The "Lady Ulfr" bit was something new (the guys had referred to me to staff as "madam"). I didn't know how to feel about it but decided to ignore it. I ignored it mostly because what I did know how I felt about it was that it irked me at the same time I had to admit (against my will) it was kind of cool.

I also ignored the bobbing a curtsy, something that had happened frequently along my journey from Fleuridia to Lunwyn that I had not yet gotten used to.

Instead, I noted, as I'd noted repeatedly along my journey, staff at inns didn't get tips.

Staff at hotels and lodges did.

I found this slightly irritating since all of them—but by the looks of them especially the ones who worked at inns—could use the money.

Apollo moved to the wine, and had it uncorked and glasses filled by the time the boy got the fire roaring and was backing away from it.

"Bring fuel," Apollo commanded, and the boy's gaze lifted to him. "Enough for the evening. We've a long journey and need to be rested on the morrow. We don't need to constantly be calling for wood."

The boy gave a nod, a truncated bow and took off, closing the door behind him.

Apollo handed me a wineglass and I took it, asking, "Do you not know the word please?"

He held my gaze over the rim of his wineglass as he took a sip.

When he was done and had dropped his hand, he answered, "I do."

"Can I ask why you don't use it?" I pushed.

His body moved in a way that it was hardly moving at all, but I could tell he was settling in, which I thought was a little weird, and it did this as he asked, "And what have I done to vex you, Ilsa?"

I took a sip of my own wine that was so far from the quality of Fleuridian wine it was not funny and thus I had to fight against making a face and replied, "I'm not vexed."

"You've spoken one word to me all day, that being first thing this morning. Until we arrived at the inn. Then we make our room, and you also make it clear nothing I do pleases you. Can you explain why?"

I threw an arm out and told him, "They're servants but they're people. You order them around like they're slaves and beneath your notice."

"They have many duties to see to from dawn until dusk, likely earlier and later, I would imagine. They don't have time for courtesy and conversation."

"Everyone has time for courtesy," I returned and added, "Achilles said please." Thinking on it, I included, "So did Remi. As did Derrik, after, of course, I mentioned it to him."

This last was true. Way back in Fleuridia, I'd had to give Derrik a talking to.

That got another eye flash and the annoyed response of, "Well, I'm not Achilles, Remi *or* Derrik."

"I'm *well* aware of that," I replied.

"And none of them are Heads of Houses," he noted.

"So the Head of a House has carte blanche to be discourteous and bossy?" I asked.

His eyes narrowed and he asked back, "Am I to be treated to your surly disposition the entirety of our journey?"

"Probably," I retorted.

"When you're not pretending I don't exist, of course," he continued.

"Of course," I agreed flippantly.

"Excellent," he muttered and threw back a healthy gulp of wine before putting his glass on the table. He looked back to me and spoke on, but his face belied his words. "Please continue. It amuses me."

"I aim to please," I murmured.

"I doubt that," he returned.

Suddenly, I wished I'd never said anything and just ignored him completely. So we slept in the same bed. So what? We'd done it before. I would be asleep. I could ignore him there too.

"Perhaps we can stop talking," I requested.

"Excellent idea," he agreed and instantly moved to the door. "If you'd like dinner, meet me downstairs after you've had a moment to refresh."

I was hungry and I needed to eat and to do that I needed him and his money, so it was exasperating but I had to say, "I'll be down in a few minutes."

He said nothing. Just opened the door, went through it, turned, dipped his chin at me and closed it behind him.

I stared at the door thinking that maybe I should have sucked it up and went to Karsvall.

Imaginary children's laughter peeled through my brain.

No, I wouldn't have been able to suck it up and go to Karsvall.

I took another sip of my wine, and when I was done, I muttered, sounding like a spoiled child, "Stupid malevolent witches and deposed rulers, ruining everything."

But they damn well had.

My plans for me and my future.

My brief but brilliant feeling of freedom.

Now, I was back where I started, my life not my own but controlled by a rich and powerful man.

There was a knock at the door, so I called, "Come in."

The girl came in carrying a pitcher with what thankfully looked like clean drying cloths folded over her forearm.

She moved directly to the nightstand and set it down.

And as she left, I was sure to thank her.

Dinner was not the greatest.

We went to a pub down the street and the not-the-greatest-part wasn't the food.

Unsurprisingly, without asking me my preference, Apollo ordered by stating, "Wine, red. And patty pie for the both of us."

I had no clue what patty pie was, but it didn't sound all that great.

And during my time with the guys, they always asked the waiters to explain my choices so that I could make them.

Not Apollo.

Oh no.

After our to-do at the inn, I wisely decided to let this go, and luckily patty pie turned out to be us each receiving our own small casserole dish filled with fluffy mashed potatoes topped with melted cheese that looked really good. Under this I discovered corn, carrots and peas in a thick delicious brown gravy. This was poured over a patty of ground beef flavored with onion. In other words, a sort of shepherd's pie but with a meat crust.

I dug in, finding it was way yummy, and I did this ignoring Apollo and also ignoring the looks we were getting.

This also happened in the less fine establishments when I was with the boys. My guess was that it mostly had to do with the fact that, even though our clothing was travel-worn, it was all better quality than what most of the populace was wearing.

In other words, no matter what country you were in, we could just say that in this world there was definitely a line between the haves and have-nots.

Here, this included Apollo wearing a dark-brown, thick, wool turtleneck sweater that was knit exquisitely and fit his broad shoulders and wide chest perfectly. This topped tight-fitting dark-brown wool breeches and (mostly) shined, obviously fine-quality boots. The cloak he unbuckled and tossed carelessly on an unused chair at our table had, on the outside, a dark-tanned hide, and the inside was a silky lustrous dark-brown-to-black fur.

I was wearing a soft green cashmere to-the-floor dress that skimmed my figure perfectly, had a scooped neckline and bell sleeves (which were kind of annoying when trying to eat, but lovely besides), the edges of both having very pretty, delicate pointelle stitching. It also had a thin belt knitted of the same cashmere but with silver threads in that I'd tied so it hung low on my hips.

On my feet, I had on low-heeled but high-rising (to the mid-thigh) buff-colored suede boots lined in cream fur. My cape had a high collar, the hide on the outside a fawn color, the fur on the inside thick luscious cream. I'd taken my cape off, too, but I'd been more careful placing it beside Apollo's on the chair.

It must be said, of all my clothes in this world, the ones for Lunwyn were the best.

But as we silently drank our wine and ate our food, me avoiding Apollo's eyes, him I didn't know since I wasn't looking at him, I noticed that here, the attention we were getting wasn't the fact that we were of the obviously-rare-in-these-parts upper-crust.

No.

As I surreptitiously glanced around, I realized it was something else.

When I caught eyes on me, before they looked away, I saw surprise in some faces. Extreme curiosity in others. Unease in a few.

And I knew.

We were a day away from her home, but I had a not-vague feeling that they knew who Apollo was, and worse, they'd seen him with the other Ilsa. An Ilsa who was supposed to be dead.

An Ilsa who looked exactly like me.

I had not noticed this on the way into Lunwyn. Then again, the men kept me sheltered and there were so many of them about, all of them big, it would have been difficult to note looks like this.

Or maybe I was so engaged with them, I just didn't notice.

But with both Apollo and I giving each other the silent treatment, I had nothing to do but notice.

My meal finished, I saw his hand raise the wine bottle to my glass and he poured.

I took in a deep breath, and with it calm and control. Only then did I lift my gaze to Apollo.

He was also done with his food. As I watched, he refreshed his glass and set the bottle down. Then he twisted his chair a bit from the table and sat back. After that, he stretched his long legs out in front of him and crossed his feet at the ankle. He nabbed his wineglass, held it before him in both hands and tipped his chin down.

Then he settled.

He appeared to be contemplating his boots.

And it appeared this contemplation was brooding.

Hmm.

He must have felt my attention because, before I could look away, he turned his head to me.

"The men, they call you Maddie," he announced.

I briefly considered ignoring him, but for reasons unknown to me, I didn't.

"Yes," I confirmed.

"I explained the story we're telling about you being here," he stated, and I fought looking around to see if anyone was close enough to hear as I nodded. "Obviously, you'll need a name that's not Ilsa. Is this what you wish to be called?"

Instantly and strangely, his question lightened something in my chest. It was as if my lungs were twisted but I'd lived with it so long, I didn't even notice it was making it hard for me to breathe.

And just as instantly as that relief settled through my chest, it occurred to me why.

Right there, in that restaurant and for the foreseeable future, I was back where I started, depending on and thus controlled by a handsome, wealthy, powerful man.

But that didn't mean my life wasn't new.

I'd never given much thought to my name, after, of course, I grew up. It was unusual and growing up with an unusual name, kids sometimes being mean, well, it sucked.

After that, it was just a name. A name my parents gave to me, and after I screwed up royally and married Pol, it was the only thing I had left of them.

But I'd screwed up royally. And when it finally dawned on me that I was in a very bad situation and it was getting worse, I'd left Pol.

And my father had told me not to come crying back to him when I figured it out.

Of course, when I figured it out and needed safe haven, I went crying back to him.

Literally.

He shut the door in my face.

Twice.

And he, and Mom, had hung up on me. And they'd done it so many times, I'd lost count.

Who did that to their daughter?

I'd fucked up, definitely.

But to shut me out forever just because I fell in love with the wrong man and made a stupid, headstrong decision at the age of twenty-three?

"Ilsa?" Apollo prompted.

I jumped, coming out of my thoughts and looking to him.

"Do you have the name Madeleine in this world?" I asked.

"Yes," he answered.

"Then that's who I'll be. Madeleine. Maddie," I declared.

His brows drew slightly together, and his gaze grew more intense as I did it.

I knew why.

It was a declaration. Firm. Definite. Inflexible.

It didn't exactly need to be that strong a declaration.

But it absolutely was.

Once I'd made it, I wanted to cheer. To get up and dance. For some reason, it felt like I'd slithered out of old tired worn-out skin and been born anew, and I had so much energy and excitement bubbling inside me it was hard to keep my seat.

"Madeleine," he murmured, again capturing my attention, and his rich deep voice smoothing over that beautiful name sent a shiver sliding up my back.

Crap.

Maybe I should have picked Agnes.

On that thought, he surprised me by remarking, "You've noted they knew her here."

I rolled my lips together and nodded.

"She was here often. I've also been to this village more than once over the years," he continued and that confused me.

It confused me because it inferred she had been here without him.

Pol never let me go anywhere without him.

Apollo was not Pol, but it wasn't easy getting places here and it wasn't like this village was around the corner and she could just hop in a sleigh, come here for tea and be back for dinner.

Since he seemed okay talking about her, I ventured, "Did she come from around here?"

"We lived most of the year at Karsvall."

That didn't un-confuse me.

"Are you saying she'd travel without you?"

"Frequently," he replied, and that surprised me.

He looked away, took a sip from his wine and again contemplated his boots but he kept talking.

"I've many enterprises, and due to them, travel widely. Sometimes, she would come with me. Sometimes, she'd stay here. Usually, when she stayed here, it was because there was someone in need of her care. And she would travel from Karsvall somewhat broadly in order to do that, a days' ride away. Even three days' ride."

Curiosity at his words pushed me to ask, "Someone in her care?"

He again looked at me. "She was a physician."

Oh boy.

Dear, departed, pined-for, beloved, fabulous Ilsa was a doctor in this world.

I had a Bachelor of Arts degree with a major in medieval history. My last job was as a salesperson in the handbag and accessories department of an exclusive department store. Other than that, I hadn't worked or done much of anything for nearly twelve years.

I felt something lodge in my throat and forced around it, "That's...um, impressive."

He looked back to his boots and murmured, "She was, indeed, that."

I took a sip of wine and looked anywhere but him, not liking what I was feeling. Also not entirely understanding it, but definitely knowing I didn't like it. It wasn't pain, but it still felt like an ache.

He seemed unwilling to move in order to, say, go back to the hotel and put me out of the misery of this conversation.

And I felt uncomfortable sitting there staring at the floor, so I asked conversationally, "Is it usual for a woman in this world to be a doctor?"

"No," he told his boots. "A midwife, yes. An herbalist. A plant healer. Even an apothecary. But a physician, no."

I nodded even if he wasn't looking at me.

He said nothing.

"Uh...just saying, I thought you mentioned Ulfr women didn't work," I noted.

"I'll amend that," he again told his boots. "She worked, and she was dedicated to her work, but she didn't get paid."

A doctor who didn't seek payment?

I thought it but I didn't ask it.

He didn't share further.

I took another sip of my wine, thinking of Ilsa gallivanting across the snow, doing good deeds as I leaned back in my chair and tried not to focus on anyone giving me strange looks, on Apollo, on *anything* (including Ilsa doing good deeds) and I worried my lip.

Eventually, I couldn't take it anymore, so I looked back to him and saw his profile had set back to broody.

He was thinking of his dear, departed, pined-for, beloved, fabulous, *benevolent* Ilsa.

Shit, maybe I should have sucked it up and gone to spend time with his kids.

Pulling it together, I decided a change of subject was in order.

To do that, I asked, "What are your enterprises?"

"Oil," he answered his boots immediately, then turned his head and looked at me. "The House of Ulfr owns vast tracks of land. Under some of it oil was found. The oil used in lamps."

"Oh," I mumbled, thinking, if this was the case, although it might not be as highly sought after in his world as in mine, it still was probably still highly sought after.

No wonder he seemed loaded.

"And other land has gas," he carried on.

Yes, loaded.

He continued, "We're behind Fleuridia in equipping buildings and homes with gas lights and heat, but we're quickly catching up. The House of Ulfr also owns controlling interest in the largest firm that's doing that work."

Totally loaded.

"We have electricity in my world," I offered.

He nodded and looked away, saying, "Yes. Finnie explained this to me. It's an intriguing concept, and after we fought to unite Lunwyn with Middleland, I set researchers on harnessing it."

"That was smart," I muttered lamely.

I'd already learned from the guys of the recent war in which Apollo and all his men fought to reunite the countries of Lunwyn and Middleland that had been split by a now-deceased king in order to give his twin sons land to rule.

Luckily, their side won.

"I also own a mine here that produces Sjofn ice diamonds as well as import jewels from Korwahk, have them cut and sell them to jewelers throughout the Northlands," Apollo informed me. "Further, the House of Ulfr owns a variety of farms that raise mink, ermine, sable, rabbit, cattle, and the like. They sell the meat and tan the hides to provide fur and leather to clothiers."

He stopped talking, so I observed, "With all that going on, you must be very busy."

"I am," he agreed.

"So, I guess me and malevolent witches are really kind of a pain in your ass," I noted, trying to inject a badly needed dose of humor into the conversation.

I swiftly got his eyes, and they weren't flashing with amusement.

"Malevolent witches, yes. You, no. Not when you're being as you are now. When you're being churlish, yes."

Suddenly, I felt like a bitch, and it didn't feel good.

"Apollo—"

Before I could say more (not that I had any clue what to say), he straightened in his chair, turned to me but tipped his head to the table.

"You're finished?"

"Yes," I said softly.

"Then we're away to bed."

Away to bed.

Crap.

He stood and reached toward the chair that held our capes.

I stood as well, starting, "Maybe we should—"

His eyes came to mine as he moved around the table holding my cape. "I'll escort you to the hotel and give you time to prepare for bed. I'll join you after you've had time to settle."

All right then.

That sounded like a plan.

"Okeydokey," I whispered and again watched his eyes flash, this one I'd not seen before.

I didn't get a chance to get a lock on it before he was behind me and settling my cape on my shoulders.

I pushed my hands through the slits as he buckled on his cloak, and I waited as he threw some coins on the table.

He then offered his arm, and I took it. Like Derrik, he didn't hesitate to pull me closer, tucking his arm with my hand to his side. Unlike Derrik, he did this in a perfunctory way, even if he did curl his warm fingers over mine.

Then we were "away" into the night on the swept-of-snow wooden walkways that served as sidewalks in this village.

That would be, away to bed.

Again.

Crap.

8

NO RECRIMINATIONS

"I'll...uh, see you in a bit," I said at the door to Apollo, who had unlocked it and thrown it open, sticking his head in to take a cursory look around, but he did this and was now standing at its side.

"You will," he replied, pocketing the key. "Lock up behind you."

I nodded then watched as he turned and strode away.

He was out of sight down the stairs before I went into the room, closed the door and locked it behind me.

"Okay, what the fuck is the matter with me?" I asked the empty room.

Of course, I received no answer.

What I did was notice that the fire was dancing merrily in its grate, a large iron grid sitting in front of it with lips that curled into the stone so no sparks would fly out. There were big stacks of split logs, plenty of fuel for his lordship to keep the fire burning all night and not bother calling a servant to do it for him.

I also noticed that our trunks had been hauled up which meant I had my nightgown.

I didn't go to the nightgown.

I went to the nightstand closest to me, opened the drawer and found what I always found when at an inn in Lunwyn or Hawkvale. A supply of rudimentary matches.

I lit the lamp by the bed then moved to the opposite side and lit that one as well.

I walked to the fire, carefully removed the grid, tossed the used matchsticks in, fed it more logs and returned the grid.

I stood back and stared at it.

I had no idea how long Apollo would give me to get changed so I knew I should get a move on.

But as I stared into the flames, I didn't get a move on.

Instead, my mind was filled with other things and one of those other things was the fact that I kind of forgot why I was so pissed at him.

He'd saved me from Pol.

His reasons for doing this were because the wife he obviously adored had died and he wanted her back. Clearly being a man of action, when he found the impossible—that there was something he could do about that—he'd done something about it. This was slightly unbalanced, but I could get that.

But then he made the heartbreaking realization, in having me, he couldn't get her back.

Sure, he was a jerk about informing me of that, but I could kind of get that too.

Then he'd understandably taken off to get his children to safety and get away from me, the woman it hurt to even look at. But he'd left me in a beautiful house in a beautiful country with kind people. He'd given me gorgeous clothes. He'd provided me with a guard of great guys who saw me here, and in doing so gave me the best time of my life.

Now, he was forced to endure my presence and he was doing it as a kindness to me so I wouldn't have to be around the this-world children I couldn't have in mine.

So he was arrogant and autocratic. He was the head of an aristocratic line in this world. What did I know of how they behaved? He was the only one I knew. Hell, others might even be worse than him.

And, truth be told, if I thought about it (which I hadn't until then), his men said something about him.

Actually, if I *really* thought about it, Apollo had often displayed a sense of humor and he definitely displayed a sense of duty. He was clearly intelligent. He was also generous. There were reasons he inspired loyalty from those men, especially the ones from different Houses. They didn't have to stay with him.

And he'd been displaying those reasons since the night I met him.

Chiefly, him traveling to another world to save me from Pol.

Okay, so this world was living under the threat of misfortune raining down on it through witchy she-gods.

But the misfortune Pol had rained down on me was pretty danged bad and it threatened to last a lifetime.

Now I was safe from that.

Forever.

Because of Apollo.

What did I have to be a bitch about?

I pulled off my fabulous fur cape (another reason not to be a bitch, seriously, it was awesome), moving to the table to throw it over a chair, thinking I was going to have to sort myself out.

This wasn't easy on either of us. There was no reason to make it harder.

I tossed my cape over the chair and was about to move to my trunk when I noticed on the table that the wine and glasses were gone. In their place were a teapot and two teacups.

My head tipped to the side as I stared at it.

It wasn't unusual for the finer establishments to have a pot of tea or a bottle of brandy waiting for you in your room when you came up from dinner.

But usually, you ordered it.

Maybe when Apollo was downstairs without me, he'd ordered it.

The thing was that the teapot and cups were made of fine china, embellished with gold engravings around which were beautiful emerald-green designs. In my experience of that world, this was not something an inn like this would have.

"Maybe they pull out the good stuff when the gentry come to call," I murmured, reaching out a hand to lift the top off the teapot.

I did this because I was curious. I didn't intend to drink it. I needed to get to sleep, and fast, hopefully before Apollo showed, and the tea here had caffeine in it.

But the top dropped with a clatter to the table when I released it in surprise as a soft glow emanated from the pot.

"What the...?" I whispered, leaning in and peering closer.

Yep. There it was. A soft glow.

A *pretty* soft glow.

"How weird," I murmured, unafraid because I'd spent over four months in that world and I'd seen some amazing stuff, all of it beautiful, so at that point glowing tea didn't faze me.

I hooked my fingers around the delicate handle, lifted it to my nose and took a sniff.

"Wow," I breathed.

It smelled *divine*. Like peppermint mixed with licorice and vanilla.

It was clear this was herbal tea and I wondered if they provided it to soothe you and help you get to sleep. Or if Apollo had ordered it for that reason.

The one thing I knew: that smell was certainly soothing.

And I could use some soothing. I could also use some warm in my belly. The fire was great, but I'd learned in my time in Lunwyn that I wouldn't be warm and toasty until I was under the covers.

I put the top back on the pot and poured a cup, grinning in fascination as I noted the glitter dancing in the tea.

No wonder it glowed.

I took a cautious sip and closed my eyes slowly.

Bliss.

I then took a not-cautious sip, enjoyed it immensely and put the cup down. I moved to the bed, pulled up my skirts and tugged off my boots. I was also wearing tights of a fine, soft cream wool. I pulled those down too.

And felt them slide magnificently across every inch of my skin.

Although that hadn't happened the times I'd done it before, I wasn't surprised. The wool of my tights wasn't cashmere, but its softness was close. And it was warm, so it wasn't a surprise the coolness of the room hitting my legs when I lost that warmth made me tremble.

I went to my trunk, unlocked it and threw it open, tossing the tights inside and grabbing a nightgown that I'd laid on top.

It was unfortunate at this juncture with the sleeping arrangements that all my nightgowns were awesome, as in awesomely *sexy*. But I was hoping to be under the covers before Apollo saw one.

I went back to the table and nabbed the cup, taking two more quick sips as I walked back to the bed. I tossed the nightgown on the bed to free my hands to take off my dress, but when I'd done that, I didn't take off the dress.

I wrapped both hands around the warm cup and drank more of that heavenly tea.

Then more.

And I did this because I suddenly wasn't sipping tea.

I was *experiencing* it, an explosion on my taste buds and a warmth that spread through me from inside to out.

My eyelids got heavy as I took another sip and became vaguely conscious of every inch of my skin. This was because it was tingling in a way I *really* liked. I took one hand from the cup and wrapped it around my belly to hold myself as I experienced it.

"Fabulous," I whispered, lifting the cup and drinking in more.

Suddenly, my legs were restless, moving without me telling them to. My knees went back and forth, rubbing my thighs together, the friction warming them and sliding up between my legs, an area I noted just then was drenched with wet.

"Oh God," I breathed, looking into the glittering dregs of the tea.

This wasn't right.

My hand moved from my waist over to my belly and down and I couldn't stop it.

God, I had to touch myself, *now*.

I swallowed and put the cup down. Lifting my other hand to my hair, I pulled out the ribbon that held it in a ponytail at the nape of my neck. The fall of my hair drifting across my back was vague through the cashmere of my dress, but I still felt it sear through me, making my nipples hard. So hard they were aching.

"Oh *God*," I whispered, knowing something in that tea was making me feel this way.

But it was too late.

My hand at my belly moved down to cover the juncture of my legs.

Apollo was coming back at any moment, but I had to touch myself.

I *had* to.

Or better, find someone to touch me.

Oh yes.

Find someone to touch me.

It had been years.

Years.

On that thought, I moved my hands to the sides of my skirts, clenched them into the material and pulled up.

A soft knock came at the door.

My eyes went to the door and my mind filled with Apollo in his turtleneck and breeches.

Especially those *breeches.*

Blood rushed to my breasts and more wet saturated between my legs.

"Ils...Madeleine?" his deep voice sounded outside the door.

I was across the room in a flash.

I turned the lock, threw open the door and reached out a hand. I clenched it in his sweater and yanked him into the room.

"Bloody hell, what—?"

I knew I should stop. I knew it.

I just couldn't.

I ran my hands over his sweater at his chest, the feel of the soft, thick wool and the hint of hardness beneath it, swear to God, I nearly climaxed on the spot.

My knees did get weak, and I had to lean into him, my hand darting up and curling around the back of his neck.

I put pressure on and tipped my head back to see him looking across the room. I distractedly noticed he'd put a hand to my waist, but his body was tight and unmoving as I unsuccessfully tried to pull his head down to me at the same time I pressed deep into his body.

Finally, what seemed like took years, his chin dipped, and his unbelievable jade eyes looked into mine.

"Madeleine, my dove, did you drink that tea?" he asked gently, but his tone also sounded wary, urgent and alarmed.

"It's delicious," I whispered, going up on my toes, burrowing close to his body, putting more pressure on his neck, my other hand sliding down his chest with a specific aim.

He caught that wrist and yanked my hand back up his chest and pressed it there.

"Listen to me," he said, now sounding only urgent.

"Okay," I replied and successfully got my nose on his jaw.

I ran it the length and felt his fingers around my wrist tighten. I took that as a good sign so when I came back down his jaw, I used my lips.

He pulled back and shook me carefully. "Maddie, look at me and listen."

"Come closer," I begged.

"I need to gag you and tie you to the bed," he declared.

Oh God.

Awesome.

"*Yes,*" I breathed, pressing close to him again.

His eyes flashed, the pads of his fingers at my waist and those around my wrist dug in and he said, "No, my dove, not for that. For your own good. You've had adela tea and the effects won't wear off for some time. I need to leave you alone. And so you don't get into trouble, I need to tie you down."

"I'm okay with the tying down bit, not okay with the leaving bit," I told him.

"I must."

"You mustn't."

"Maddie, I must."

I shook my head and pressed closer. "Please, don't leave."

"But I must," he repeated.

I ignored that and pulled him with me as I took a step back, urging, "Come to bed."

"I can't."

I slid my hand to his jaw and got up on tiptoe, begging, "*Please.*"

He moved both of his hands to my face and dipped his close, but his hold on me was firm so I couldn't get to his mouth. I knew this because I tried.

"My poppy, focus on my eyes, listen to me."

"I'm listening," I assured him. "But I can listen better in bed."

"We get in that bed, neither of us will be talking."

"I'm down with that too," I shared.

"I think I understand what you mean by that, and if I do, I can also assure you won't be *down with that* in the morning."

"I will," I replied quickly. "I promise. *Swear.*"

"Maddie—"

I got up on my toes as close to him as I could.

He moved that inch away, which sucked.

I tried a different tactic and whispered, "It's been over three years."

"Gods," he rumbled, the sound of that single word going through me in a way that I had to stifle a moan of pleasure.

"I need you, baby," I pleaded.

"This isn't right, my dove. You don't know it now, but you'll thank me in the morning."

"It's right. It's *so* right." I pushed closer. "It's been years, honey. I need your hands on me. Your mouth on me."

"Maddie—" he started, the sound like a groan, spurring me on.

I held his eyes and framed his face with my hands as he was mine and whispered, "I need you."

"You don't, my dove. It's the tea," he whispered back.

I stared at him, my breasts heavy, my breaths shallow, my sex saturated, every inch of my skin sensitized, and I thought, *Fuck it.*

I let him go and stepped back so he let me go.

I watched his hands fall to the sides and I took in all that was him.

There was a lot.

And all of it was good.

Then I pounced.

I landed on him with arms around his shoulders and curled my legs around his hips. Automatically, his hands went to my ass to catch me, and a whimper slid up my throat at his touch as I slammed my mouth down on his.

His hand slid up my back and into my hair and that was good.

Until he turned his head away, breaking the contact of our lips.

He shoved his face in my neck and muttered, "Gods damn it."

I hoped that was capitulation and I had hope since he was walking me to the bed.

He put me down on it, but once he'd done that, he captured both of my hands and yanked them over my head. Holding them in one of his, his other went to his belt.

I had a feeling I knew what this meant, and it was not that he was giving me what I wanted, but that he was going to use his belt to tie me to the bed and then take off.

"You're leaving me?" I gasped, seeking confirmation.

"For your own good, poppy," he confirmed.

I shook my head. "Then don't tie me down. If you have to go, go. But I *need* my hands."

He took my meaning. I knew this when his eyes darkened and went over my head as his lips murmured, "I should have gagged her first."

I struggled on the bed. "If you're going to leave me like this, I *need* my hands, Apollo."

I was writhing uncontrollably on the bed, and he was watching me.

God, his eyes.

That mouth.

God.

"If I can't have you, let me have my hands." I sounded desperate and imploring, mostly because I was.

Something had to give and soon.

I licked my lips and watched a muscle tick up his cheek and it was *hot.*

So hot, I moaned.

At my moan, his voice gruff, he demanded, "You're in no shape but still, swear it. Swear it to me now, Madeleine. No recriminations tomorrow."

Oh my God.

Was he...?

I wasn't going to waste time asking.

I shook my head frantically. "None, nope, not a one. It'll all be good tomorrow. *All* good."

His gaze burned into mine and it did this, like, *forever.*

So long, I couldn't take a moment longer and breathed, "*Baby.*"

His eyes shifted to my mouth. "This word goes through me like a knife."

"Is that good?" I asked.

His eyes came back to mine.

Then he let me go and exited the bed.

Shit.

He moved to the door.

Shit!

He stopped at it, locked it and moved to the table.

Oh God.

Yes.

I pushed up to my knees, yanking my skirts out from under them so I could walk on them across the bed. I stopped at its edge.

He poured a cup of tea, and just the delicate cup in his big hand turned me on beyond reason (not that I wasn't already there) and nearly sent me over the edge.

I did a full-body tremble when he put the cup to his mouth and threw his head back, downing it.

Oh God.

Yes.

He put the cup down and turned to me.

God, oh God, he was *beautiful.*

I stood on my knees on the bed, the insides of my thighs quivering, and stared at him.

He stared back.

"You're beautiful, Apollo," I whispered.

I watched him run his tongue over his lower lip.

At the sight, my sex convulsed, and I whimpered.

At my sound, Apollo lunged.

Finally.

I was on my back in the bed, Apollo on me, and he felt so good, so damned *good.*

What was better was his mouth on mine and his tongue in my mouth.

That wasn't good, that was *awesome.*

But I wanted more, and he'd made me wait long enough, I was going to get it.

I slid my hands in his sweater and yanked up. He broke contact with my mouth to arch back, lifting his arms. I tugged his sweater off and tossed it away.

He came back to me, lips to lips, tongues tangling, and I moaned into his mouth as I bucked. He let me move him, but I suspected only because he knew I'd move with him, and I did. He rolled to his back, me on top and then it was me breaking contact with our lips.

But my lips didn't break contact with him. They slid down his neck, over to his corded throat, down his chest, the ridges of his stomach to the waistband of his breeches.

There, I broke away but only to lift up to straddling him. I clenched my fingers in my dress and tugged it off, the cashmere dragging over my skin in a way that made my nipples ache *and* my clit pulse.

"Gods," he grunted.

I was wearing nothing but green satin panties and a cream satin bustier with green ribbons, and my guess from his tone, he liked it.

I looked down at him staring up at me, his face dark, his eyes hot, feeling my lips curl in a little smile that made him say, "*Gods,*" again but in a groan this time.

I felt that groan shoot straight between my legs and knew it was time to get a move on.

So I did, slithering off the bed. I grabbed him behind his knee and lifted up his calf. Straddling it, I yanked off his boot, then his sock. On to the next foot then I was moving to him. He'd already unbuttoned his breeches and I curled my fingers in his waistband, tugging down. Apollo helped by bucking his hips from the bed and they were off.

I tossed them behind me and entered the bed, crawling up him on all fours, my eyes on my goal.

And *what* a goal. His cock was hard, thick and long, the veins distended in a way that demanded the trace of a tip of a tongue. So big. So swollen. So beautiful.

I had to have it.

I didn't delay. Wrapping my hand around it, putting my lips to the tip then taking him so deep, I felt him in the back of my throat, my gag reflex g-o-n-e, *gone.*

"By the bloody *gods,*" he rumbled, sliding the fingers of both hands into my hair and curling them around my scalp.

I slid him out but didn't take him back in.

He lifted his hips and surged back in.

Yes.

Oh, fuck yes.

I took his thrusts, whimpering and moaning against his cock, my body trembling, my clit throbbing, and suddenly I felt him knife up. His hands went under my arms, and he hauled me up his body.

"Baby, I wasn't—" I started to protest.

But he rolled me to my back, dragged my panties down my legs and moved around so he was on all fours over me, backwards.

Yes.

Oh, *fuck* yes.

I lifted my hands and curled my fingers around his ass, using it to pull my head and shoulders off the bed as he spread my thighs. Then his mouth was there. *Right there.* Just as I slid the tip of his cock between my lips, and he surged in.

He fucked my mouth as his mouth ravaged my sex, and I was done. I was there.

I exploded, moaning against his cock, clutching his ass, taking his thrusts. It was so huge, it engulfed me, and my hips jerked against his mouth.

Still coming, he pulled out and I found myself yanked further in the bed. Then he was covering me. One of his arms hooked behind my knee, jerking it up. His hips fell between mine, I felt him hitch a knee high for leverage and I knew this was going to be good.

Through this, all I could see were his extraordinary jade-green eyes burning into mine.

But he was there. Right there. I could feel him. But he wasn't giving himself to me.

Instead, he was staring at me like he was waiting for the answer to a question.

I gave him the only answer I had.

"Please," I whispered, and he drove inside.

My neck arched back, and my three free limbs surrounded him and squeezed tight.

He buried his face in my neck and groaned, "Maddie."

Then he thrust, and thrust, and *thrust,* deep, hard, fast, rough, God, so hard, so freaking deep and so *amazingly* rough.

His mouth came to mine, and I breathed, "Don't come too fast. I'm not close to done."

"My poppy, I drank the tea to keep up with you. I'll stay hard all night."

Excellent.

I felt my mouth smile and had no idea my eyes did the same.

Then they closed because he was kissing me, as hard, deep and rough as he was fucking me.

It was brilliant. So brilliant, I slid over the edge again and cried out when my latest orgasm shook me, the noise driving down his throat.

Moments later, he grunted his release down mine.

I was running my tongue down the side of his neck when he rolled us and pulled me up his body, positioning me in a way I knew what he wanted.

"But...you're inside me," I gasped just as his big hands closed on my hips and he yanked me down on his mouth.

My head flew back.

He fed on me ravenously as I ran my hands over my body, grinding into his mouth.

Suddenly, it was too much. I couldn't take anything but what he was doing between my legs. The air on my skin was burning into me, my hair swaying down my back was driving me mad.

I lifted both arms and pulled my hair up, holding it at the back of my head, seeking maximum contact with Apollo's talented lips and tongue even as one of his hands at my hips yanked me deeper.

I sensed something, looked over my shoulder and saw his other hand wrapped around his glorious cock, pumping.

Oh God.

Seriously.

How hot was that?

It was so hot, I cried out again, arching back, coming.

Excruciatingly.

Exquisitely.

He pulled me off and I was on my belly in the bed. I felt his knee nudging my legs apart, and still in the throes of my most recent climax, I helped, spreading them wider. Then he was between my legs yanking up my hips.

He pounded in.

When he filled me, my head flew back, my hair drifting over my skin and I whimpered, "*Yes*," as I started to push up to my hands.

I didn't get very far as, still thrusting, I felt his hand in the middle of my back, pushing me down.

"No, Maddie, I just want your beautiful arse."

I could do that. I *so* could.

I gave him my ass, tipping it high.

He took it, fucking me, and I felt his wet thumb gliding between my cheeks and then it pressed inside the sensitive sweet spot.

Phenomenal.

I moaned as it overwhelmed me yet again, bucking back into him violently even as he pounded deep inside me and pressed his thumb in my ass.

"Beautiful, my poppy. Bloody hell, *magnificent*," he growled, surged inside, and I heard his grunts turn into a rumble before I heard his shuddering groan and just hearing it, another orgasm rolled over the one I was still having.

Hazy, still turned on, coming down, and even doing that, it building back up, Apollo pulled out. He gently rolled me to my back and covered me again, instantly sliding back inside and gliding slowly, his gaze holding mine, his lips a breath away.

"More?" he whispered.

"You up for it?" I whispered back.

I felt his lips touch mine and they were smiling, as were his eyes.

And in all the fabulous we'd just shared, that might have been the best part.

"Absolutely," he murmured.

"Then yes," I breathed and wrapped my legs around his hips. "More." I wrapped my arms around his shoulders. "Please." And I slid my tongue along his lips.

He slanted his head, those lips took mine, his tongue took mine and he gave me more.

~

Some time later, I was on top, Apollo inside me. I was sliding up slowly and down even slower, my face in his neck, my eyelids drooping.

I needed sleep. Like, *bad.*

But I had something to say.

Sliding down, filling myself full of him, my sex drenched with him and me, I pressed my face in his neck, slid my hand up the other side and brushed my thumb along his stubbled jaw.

"Thank you for not leaving me," I whispered.

He had one hand resting lightly, almost casually on my ass. Paradoxically, he had one arm wrapped tightly, even possessively across my middle back.

At my words, both convulsed.

Powerfully.

I had no time to assess this reaction.

Because his voice said low and sweet, "Sleep, Maddie," and my mind took that moment in a vague way to realize all throughout the night he'd called me nothing but Maddie, Madeleine, my dove or my poppy.

And this vague thought made my insides warm.

That was when I fell was asleep.

9
Heart Mighty as Goliath

Apollo did not sleep.

Maddie on top of him, her knees high and pressed tight to his sides taking some of her weight, his body gladly supported the rest of it.

Drifting his fingers through the silken weight, he smelled the citrus of her hair, the lavender scent of her skin, both mixed with the aroma of sweat and sex.

He stared at the dark ceiling thinking he'd never smelled anything more beautiful.

And it was not Ilsa's smell. After she bathed, Ilsa's skin smelled of roses, her hair of mint.

Maddie shifted slightly and he naturally slid out of her. When he did, his seed mingled with her juices glided from her, drifting between the juncture of his thighs, their essence mixed, the most intimate parts of them joined, he stared at the ceiling thinking he'd never felt anything sweeter.

Further, he was struggling with why this would be so, considering the depth of love he had for his wife. Not to mention, the depth of passion they shared in their bed.

However, he'd never had anything with Ilsa like he'd had with Madeleine last night.

It was, of course, the adela tea.

But now he was no longer under the influence of adela tea and still these thoughts assailed him.

And last, he was thinking he'd made yet another colossal mistake.

He should have gagged her, tied her to the bed and left her.

But he didn't.

Instead, he took advantage.

Coming unraveled by her entreaty, allured by her beauty and her touch, aroused by her sharing that she'd take care of herself if he left...gods, aroused by it all, he'd taken advantage.

He couldn't even blame it on losing control. It was slipping but he hadn't lost it.

No, he wanted her.

He wanted her before she pressed to him and begged, and he definitely wanted her during.

He'd made her swear no recriminations, but she was under the influence of adela tea. He knew the effects of that brew. She didn't know what she was saying but he knew she'd say anything to get what the tea made her need.

And he'd given it to her, and in doing so, he took.

He had no trust of hers to break. If he had, he'd broken it in Fleuridia before he left her. But if he'd gained any since their reunion (which was doubtful), last night, he'd have shattered it.

When her eyes opened later that morning, the effects of the tea abated, she'd know it.

And she'd hate him for it.

He sighed, closing his eyes and ceasing running his fingers through her hair so he could wrap his arms around her, certain this was all he'd get. When she woke, she'd be lost to him.

For good.

There would be no winning her. It had only been a day and in that day, her adorable stubbornness, even her exasperating peevishness, he realized he wanted to win her more than he had before. And in her adorable stubbornness and exasperating peevishness, Apollo also realized the challenge of doing this was even more difficult than he'd earlier suspected.

Which made him wish to best it all the more.

Now it would be impossible.

Surprising him at the intensity of it, this knowledge felt like a weight crushing his chest.

But he'd had a broken dove in his hand, and instead of setting about mending it, from near on the moment he brought her to his world, he'd done nothing but tighten his grip, fracturing her further.

He opened his eyes, sliding his hands over her soft skin, and in her sleep, she pressed her face deeper into his neck, arched her torso into his slightly then relaxed on an unconscious fluttering sigh he felt in his gut.

And that was when he saw the flash of green that streaked across the room.

A warning shot.

Bloody hell.

He knew what that meant, and he knew why she was coming.

It was she who left the tea.

His frame tightened and he gently slid Madeleine off his body. He rolled away from her and found his feet on the floor by the side of the bed. He had his breeches on with all the buttons done up when the green mist started swirling in the room. He'd pulled his sweater on and was standing with his hands on his hips when she formed three feet in front of him.

"You'll speak quietly," he commanded immediately. "Madeleine is sleeping."

The witch looked to the bed then to Apollo.

"Madeleine?" she asked, thankfully her voice was soft.

"Her name in this world," he explained.

"Madeleine." She said it like she was tasting it on her tongue. "I approve of this name," she shared.

He didn't respond to that because he didn't care if she approved or not. Maddie approved of it. Indeed, she'd claimed it with a vivacity that was vaguely troubling.

But it meant something to her, so it was hers and it didn't matter what the witch thought of it.

"The adela tea," he stated and felt her eyes grow intense on him.

He saw her shadow give a delicate shrug. "You were taking too long."

He was right in what he'd deduced when she fired her warning shot, indicating she was coming. Valentine had left the adela tea for Maddie to find. And drink.

He felt the skin around his neck get tight and his voice was a growl when he said, "That was sly and scheming."

He saw her head tip to the side. "Are you arguing the results?"

He didn't respond to that.

Instead, he said, "You have not made the road Madeleine must travel any easier."

"Oh, *chéri*," she purred. "I don't know about that."

He fought back the urge to lean into her threateningly. "In times like these, a woman like that, you play?"

"It wasn't me playing last night, Ulfr..." she hesitated and finished, "*for five hours.*"

He continued to struggle with his anger as he clipped, "You watched?"

"It was gravely annoying, your gentlemanly behavior."

He ground his teeth.

"But," she went on, "your capitulation was spectacular."

He came close to losing his struggle and warned, "I would leave me now, witch."

"Calm, *chéri*," she urged. "I only watched until you tackled her. As magnificent as that was, I left you to your enjoyment of each other and waited the duration the effects the adela tea normally lasts. And considering your obvious," she swept a hand his way, "*virility*, I gave it even more time. Only then did I check to be certain I could come to visit. By the time I did, cuddling had commenced."

At least she gave them that.

He decided to move on.

"And the reason for you coming to call?" he prompted.

She ceased playing and did not hesitate in her caustic reply.

"The reason I've come to call is to warn you to stop messing about and claim her." He drew in a quiet breath and her voice was lower when she warned, "If you don't, I will."

Apollo felt his entire body get tight and his tone was dangerous when he asked, "Pardon?"

She threw out a shadowy hand. "I allowed you to have her because I thought I knew the man you were, Ulfr. A heart as mighty as Goliath. And yet, when I check in on her, she's with Hans. She's with Remi. She's with *Derrik*." She put significant stress on Derrik's name and continued. "Who, I might add, followed you and he's in the room across the hall, and just a warning, *chéri*, he heard your activities with..." she paused, "Madeleine last night and he's not best pleased."

Apollo's eyes cut to the opposite wall and the witch kept talking.

"What she was not, in the times I checked, was with you."

He looked back to her as she went on.

"I let you have her because I thought you'd mend our little dove's broken wings. You have not. You haven't even tried. And if you don't, I'll take her back with me and make her safe. The Apollo of my world will suffer much more than a severed hand if he gets anywhere near her."

"You will not..." he drew in a sharp breath and finished, "take her."

Valentine grew silent.

Apollo didn't.

"You will not again meddle in our affairs," he ordered.

Valentine remained silent.

"And you will cease your devious machinations against her," he concluded.

"The sharing of adela tea with a partner is a beautiful experience, creating memories to cherish and a closeness unsurpassed. It is not a *devious machination*."

"Only if you care about and trust the partner you're sharing it with," he returned. "It is if it's taken without your knowledge or given against your will."

"I think you mistake how she feels about you," she shared.

"I think you've not been paying close enough attention as you spy, for I'm very aware of how she feels about me, and I do not think you are."

"No, *chéri*," she whispered. "You're very aware of how she struggles to find her footing in a new world, with a new life, around people who care about her and don't abuse her or neglect her, something she has not had since her birth. Indeed, *mon loup*, you're bearing the brunt of that. But with a heart as mighty as Goliath, I'm counting on you to persevere."

That heart she spoke of felt tight at her words and he grunted, "Explain."

"I think that should come from our *colombe*, don't you?"

Apollo said nothing.

He sensed her body relaxing as she asked, "Would you like to hear news from Bellebryn?"

"You have it?" he asked back.

"Of course, *chéri*."

"Then share it," he demanded shortly.

He heard the smile in her voice even as she said, "It's not good. Or, I should say, there isn't much to it. The scouting party returned, all intact fortunately, without finding any of their targets, unfortunately."

"So the she-god Minerva, Baldur and the others remain hidden," Apollo muttered, frustrated, not to mention concerned.

"They do," she confirmed. "The Drakkar immediately wanted to send another scouting party, led by him, but I had a word and he's changed his mind."

This, he didn't understand.

"Frey and his men are very good at these kinds of missions, witch."

She shook her head and retorted, "During their situation, Frey was separated from his love due to injury and knew he would return to her. But you will note that Dax Lahn nor Noctorno volunteered for such a mission. When they were separated from their loves, they had no way of knowing they would be reunited. They are not so eager to be separated again." She paused and this pause was heavy. When she spoke again, her voice was the same. "I would suggest you learn from that."

Apollo said nothing. He knew all about the affairs of Frey, The Drakkar the witch referred to, and his Finnie, Dax Lahn and his Circe and Prince Noctorno and his Cora.

Starting the war with Middleland, Frey had been gravely injured and taken by the elves to their world under the ice to be healed. Finnie did not know he lived on and that was her torture. But Frey always knew he'd go back to her.

Lahn's Circe had spirited herself back to the other world. Lahn had sent a man to search for a way to bring her back, knowing for months, and feeling the accompanying anguish as they were separated, that he might not find that way.

And Minerva had torn apart Tor and Cora. As she had united their souls at birth, it was a cruelty unimaginable and brought on physical pain to endure as well as emotional. Both struggled with the agony for weeks, both desperately searching their worlds to find a way to reunite before they bested that challenge.

And he'd lost his Ilsa therefore he knew what that felt like, well worse than the others because there was no way on any world to get her back.

His focus turned to the bed, and before he could form a thought or force his heart to start beating without that tightness shrouding it, the witch spoke again. He looked back to her.

"You are aware that Lavinia and I are concerned that there are too many coincidences linked to our foes and the couples united over the worlds. Dax Lahn and Noctorno take that into account, I would assume, with every breath. I urge you to remember that in your dealings with Madeleine."

He *was* aware and he was in agreement that there seemed to be far too much linking the couples who found each other, spanning universes, and the ones who they feared conspired against the peace and prosperity that both the Northlands and the Southlands currently enjoyed.

They had their own strengths, however. The most powerful witch in Lunwyn, Lavinia, was aligned with their fight and had formed a closeness with Valentine, who had, for a fee (and not coincidentally, part of that substantial fee included a sack of the now priceless adela tea) agreed to help.

They were a formidable pair.

It would remain to be seen if they were more formidable than their foe.

"I have taken pains to keep her safe," Apollo reminded her.

"For a day. The rest of the time, your men have," she reminded him.

He didn't reply, for he had none as she was right.

Dawn began to force its way around the curtains, but the room was still mostly in shadows as she stated, "Now I will leave you." She turned and motioned to the door. "You have things to see to across the hall."

The green mist was forming but Apollo still addressed her. "I have a bath and breakfast to see to for Maddie. Then I'll address the issue across the hall."

The mist illuminated the room and her, and he saw her cat's smile before she purred, "There's my Goliath."

He had no idea what she was talking about and no intention to ask. Even if he did, he would have no chance as she faded away.

When she did, Apollo walked to the windows. Pulling a curtain back slightly, he assessed the sun's rays and noted they were deeper into the dawn than he suspected.

With a sigh, he dropped the curtains and moved to the fire. Pulling back the screen, he fed it more fuel, stirring it until it was blazing.

He then returned the screen and walked to the bed, sat on it and wrapped his hand around the side of Maddie's neck.

"Madeleine, my dove, wake," he whispered, giving her a squeeze.

He watched her eyes blink and again before she turned only her head on the pillow and stared somnolently up at him.

And it wasn't lost on him he saw nothing but Maddie.

Nothing.

As he felt nothing but her last night. Her mouth on his cock. Her sex convulsing around him. Her eyes burning into him. Her little, inscrutable smile making his shaft ache.

He also tasted nothing but her either. Heard nothing but her whimpers, moans and cries. Her pleas for more. Or harder. Or faster.

Nothing.

But her.

He felt his cock twitch.

"Is it morning already?" her sleepy voice asked, taking him from his heated thoughts, and he gave her another squeeze.

"Alas, it is, poppy, and you must arise as we must be away."

She blinked again.

Adorable.

Gods, how he wished he had this for the next hour, the next day, as long as he could have it.

Not have it taken away when consciousness fully came to her, and she understood the advantage he'd taken.

"I'll call for a bath, breakfast," he told her softly. "I'm sorry but you must prepare for us to be on our way. You can sleep in the sleigh."

She lifted up on her forearm and asked, "If I'm asleep, how can I steer the sleigh?"

She wouldn't have to. So she could rest, he'd be in it with her, if she allowed that, and he'd do it.

Torment would not like being hitched to the sleigh, but his horse would suffer that indignity for him. And with two horses dragging the load, they'd make better time.

"Leave that to me. Now, rouse yourself. I'll give you time and be back."

She blinked yet again, and her head tipped to the side, but thankfully, understanding of his selfishness did not dawn and she nodded.

He bent and brushed his mouth against hers. Pulling away, he saw her eyes and the skin around her mouth were soft and he felt that softness gather around his heart, memorizing her look because he was sure that was all he'd have.

"Rouse, poppy," he murmured.

She nodded and he left her in the bed.

He went to his socks and boots, pulling them on. He then moved to leave the room, glancing at her in bed.

She was up on her arse, the covers pulled up to her chest, the curls and ringlets of her hair tousled, gloriously framing her exquisite face and falling over her shoulders and down her chest.

She was gazing around, looking bemused.

That was adorable too.

But it would likely not last long.

A stone weighing in his gut, he unlocked the door and moved out of the room. His eyes cut through the door opposite, but he walked down the hall and found a servant. He ordered a hot bath and breakfast for Maddie and one for himself in another chamber, bidding them to bring him fresh clothes from his trunk in their room.

He ended with, "And I want a boy in the hall. If the man in the room opposite approaches my door, I want to know immediately."

The servant nodded and hurried away.

As he watched her go, he thought distractedly that he should have thanked her.

Then he thought no more of that and went about his business.

The morning preparations took some time as the water needed to heat, and it was time that seemed to crawl. There was little to fill it that took his mind from the unpleasantness he was sure to encounter imminently.

Twice.

So he thought of nothing but his upcoming confrontations, except when he went to the stables and ordered the sleigh hitched and trunks brought down.

But eventually, bathed and fed, he moved back up the stairs. He saw the young boy who'd started their fire yesterday standing outside his and Maddie's door.

He lifted his chin to the boy.

The boy dipped his and dashed by him to the stairs.

Apollo went to the door opposite.

He knocked quietly, and within seconds, Derrik opened the door.

His clothes were rumpled, his hair in disarray, his eyes rimmed red.

He had not slept.

When he saw Apollo, his face went hard, and his eyes went sharp.

"That didn't take long, brother," he clipped.

Yes.

He'd heard.

"We need words," Apollo told him. "And not in the hall."

"Is there something to say?" Derrik asked acidly.

"Yes," Apollo answered. He made a show of twisting at the waist and looking meaningfully at the door behind him before he turned his attention back to his friend. "But not in the hall."

Derrik looked to the door as well before he hesitated and finally backed into the room.

Apollo followed him, closing the door behind him.

He noted the lamps still burning but the fire was just embers in its grate. He also noted the bed was disheveled but had not been slept in.

He then turned his gaze to Derrik.

"Would you like to explain what you're doing here?" he asked, his voice low.

On his words, Derrik's brows shot up, but his reply was to query, "Would you like to explain why your rough, long and *loud* bedplay with gods damned *Maddie* could be heard throughout the gods damned *village*?"

"We'll not be discussing that," Apollo told him.

"We won't?" Derrik fired back.

"No," Apollo said firmly.

Derrik studied him.

Then he stated conversationally, "Gods, man, if I didn't think I'd murder you on sight, I would have gone over solely to warn you that your activities might break the bed or send you through the floor." His tone degenerated when he added, "Or, perhaps, commend you on your bloody stamina."

Apollo said nothing.

Derrik's eyes narrowed. "How many times did you have her?"

Apollo remained silent.

"I counted twelve of hers, just nine of yours. If I were to tell the men, you'd be legend."

Apollo kept his silence and Derrik lost his patience.

And his gallantry.

"By the sounds you made when she could not be heard, I can assume she has much talent with her mouth."

Apollo ceased remaining silent.

"Careful, brother," he warned.

He leaned in toward Apollo and his voice went snide. "By the sounds *she* made when *you* could not be heard, it's a definite you share the same talent. Tell me, *brother*, does she taste as sweet as she promises?"

Apollo's entire body grew tight for the second time that day. But this time, he didn't keep as close a grasp on the threads that held his temper.

Derrik was a man, Valentine a woman. If Derrik did something that deserved it, Apollo would not hesitate to give it.

"Careful," he growled.

"She isn't Ilsa," Derrik bit out.

Apollo blinked.

Understanding hit him.

He crossed his arms on his chest and said quietly, "Gods, brother, I know that."

At that, Derrik's head jerked.

"You—" he began.

"Lost my wife years ago," Apollo interrupted him to say. "And came to terms with that only four months ago. The woman in my bed is Madeleine."

"Madeleine?"

"The name she's chosen for this world. A name chosen from what you and the men gave her," Apollo explained and when Derrik didn't reply, he shared, "She's rather fond of it."

Derrik looked to the wall behind Apollo, the hardness moving out of his face. Then he looked back.

"I'm in love with her," he admitted, his voice gruff, his admission dredged from somewhere deep.

"I'm sorry," Apollo replied and said no more for there was no more to say.

His friend may love Madeleine and Apollo may love his friend.

But he could not have her.

Derrik's face grew hard again, and he demanded, "Convince me you care for her."

"That's not yours to have," Apollo returned, and Derrik's jaw got tight before Apollo finished, "It's hers."

At that, Derrik's jaw went slack.

Apollo cared deeply for his friend, but even so, he had no time for this. "I'll remind you, she's alone over there."

Derrik's back went straight. "If you hurt her—"

Apollo didn't let him finish. "It will be my hurt to salve."

Derrik kept trying. "She's not—"

At that, Apollo spoke quickly, reining in his temper. A temper that had to do with the fact that Derrik more than likely knew much of what Maddie was and was not, whereas Apollo knew very little of both, and he didn't like that. He further didn't like the fact that it was *he* who'd orchestrated it.

"She may have shared her mysteries with you, but they are her mysteries to share. They are also now mine to discover."

They locked eyes and neither man spoke for some time.

Apollo grew impatient with it, and he was about to break it before Derrik did.

And he did it to announce, "I'll be leaving Karsvall and returning to the Lazarus seat."

Apollo's gut got tight at this loss, but he nodded and requested, "I understand your need to do so, but I'll ask that you continue to see to the safety of my children at Karsvall until Madeleine and my return."

Derrik flipped out a hand even as he didn't quite successfully stifle his flinch at the words "Madeleine and my" and he muttered, "Of course."

Again, the men locked eyes. But needing to face whatever Maddie cared to make him endure, Apollo broke it and moved to the door.

He opened it, stood in it and looked back to his friend.

"I understand your need to break from Ulfr, Derrik, but when that happens, know you will be missed and welcomed back should that desire return to your heart."

Derrik made no move or noise. He just held Apollo's eyes.

So be it.

Apollo moved to leave him, but Derrik finally spoke.

"Take care of her."

Again, he looked directly into Derrik's eyes, and when he said the words, Derrik knew him well enough to know what they were.

And what they were was a vow.

"I will."

He left it at that and walked out of the door, closing it behind him.

In the step it took him to reach his own, he pulled in a deep breath and braced.

Then he opened the door and entered the room, eyes glued to Madeleine sitting at the table, a bowl of untouched porridge in front of her.

She was wearing a very becoming dress the color of the inside of a blood orange. He had her side, but he could still see the deep cowl that dropped down her chest, likely exposing skin behind it. The sleeves were knitted to fit tight at her arms and her long skirt was belled out on the floor around her chair. Her hair, as it had been yesterday, was pulled back at her nape in a satin ribbon the color of a mushroom.

Normally, she would have been a vision.

But she had one hand wrapped around a forgotten cup of coffee and her other elbow was on the table. Her head was turned to the window, but her back was bowed so she could hold it in her hand.

He felt his throat begin to close at witnessing her pose of defeat.

He closed the door, and when she heard it, she jumped. As he took two paces in the room, slowly, she turned her gaze to him.

He halted when he saw her beautiful eyes swimming with tears.

Gods, *gods*, he'd damaged her worse than he thought.

"Madel—" he started.

But she spoke over him.

Her voice trembling, she whispered, "I'm sorry."

That was not what he expected to hear.

"Pardon?"

"So, so sorry." She kept whispering.

"Madeleine."

She shook her head. "So, so, so, so, *so* sorry, Apollo."

She was sorry?

"My dove—"

"I'm selfish," she stated, and he stared. "It's a weakness. Selfish and self-indulgent and thoughtless and stupid."

Not liking her words, he took a step toward her, but she sat back in her chair and lifted her hand his way.

"That tea was..." she started when he stopped moving. "I don't know what it was. But you were trying to be nice. Trying to take care of me. Trying to be gentle. And I pushed it because I wanted something and..."

Suddenly, she looked away, her neck twisting so deep, he only had the back of her ear and head before she twisted back, and he saw the tears chasing down her cheeks.

"As usual, I got what I wanted, damn the consequences," she whispered brokenly and continued in her tortured voice. "Hurting you in the process."

He remained where he was, distant, as caution dictated he do in her state, and asked, "Poppy, how on earth did you hurt me?"

"I look like her." She informed him, her voice now agonized, and he finally understood. "I look like her and you miss her. I threw myself at you, and first, you're a guy. What are you going to do? Turn down a sure thing?" She shook her head. "No. No way. But one who looks exactly like your—"

At that, he was done.

He moved to her, pulled her from her chair and wrapped his arms around her, pressing her to his body. He glided a hand up her neck, her hair sliding over, and he twisted his fist in it, pulling back gently even as he slid his cheek along hers so he had his lips at her ear.

"I did not make love to my wife last night, Madeleine. I made love to you," he said there.

"Well, yes...I know. I was there, but—"

His hand tightened in her hair slightly and he raised his head to capture her eyes.

"No buts."

She looked deep in his eyes, hers still wet, and came to a conclusion.

The wrong one.

"You're just being nice."

"Mad—"

"Like you've been nice all along."

"Maddie—"

"Since the beginning. Except that one time when you weren't nice but that was understandable."

"My dove, will you cease speaking so I can—"

"And I've been a bitch."

Apollo shut his mouth.

She had to let it out?

He'd allow that.

And he knew she had to let it out because she didn't stop.

"A silly, childish, selfish, thoughtless *bitch*."

Apollo said nothing.

"And that's not nice, but last night was *way* not nice. It was cruel. I'm cruel!"

Her voice was rising but Apollo held his silence.

"I'm a silly, childish, selfish, thoughtless, *cruel...bitch*!"

Apollo remained silent and Madeleine fell into the same.

After some time, her eyeballs rolled this way and that. Finally, they stuck on him.

"Um...why are you holding me in your arms?" she asked hesitantly.

"Because you were weeping and saying foolish things and I wished to comfort you and assure you that you were being foolish. However, you wouldn't be quiet and allow me to speak so I couldn't assure you that you were being foolish so that left just my holding you in an effort to comfort you."

She stared at him a moment before she queried, "You want to comfort me?"

He gave her a squeeze and answered, "Yes."

"But I'm a selfish, thoughtless, cruel bitch," she reminded him, and with effort he successfully fought back his chuckle.

After he accomplished that, he stated, "My dove, the more time I spend with you, the more I learn about you and the more I come to understand there's much to learn. What I have learned is that you are amusing. You are spirited. You can be charming. You can also be disagreeable. You can further be vexing. You're annoyingly very good during an argument. But that simply means you're quick-witted, which is not a bad thing, unless one finds themselves in an argument with you."

She blinked endearingly and he finished.

"What you are not is a selfish, thoughtless or cruel."

She studied him closely as if his face would tell her the veracity of his words and she must have read it wrong because her eyes again clouded.

"But, Apollo," she started softly, pain beginning to thread its way back into her voice. "I look like—"

He gave her another squeeze and dipped his face close.

His voice was threaded with steel when he declared. "Ilsa is gone, Madeleine. And you are here. You look like her, indeed. But you are *not* her."

"But you said looking at me felt like brands searing into your eyes."

Bloody hell, she remembered his exact words.

"And that, my dove," he whispered, "was *me* being selfish, thoughtless and cruel. But when I spoke those words to you, I genuinely was, and you..." He shook his head. "You had drunk adela tea and were not in control of yourself. That is not selfish, thoughtless or cruel. That is simply what was."

"Adela tea?" she inquired.

"I'll explain later," he said.

Her eyes suddenly narrowed, and he nearly smiled.

There she was.

"Did you order it?" she asked.

"Valentine connives," he answered, and her eyes grew huge, and at that, he *did* smile.

"She was here?" she queried.

"Twice," he affirmed.

"*Twice?*" Her voice was pitched high, and he felt his smile widen.

"Twice. I'll explain that later too."

She held his gaze, the astonishment left hers and dark started seeping in again, but through it she asked, her voice now almost timid. "So you don't hate me?"

He gathered her closer and whispered, "No, my poppy, I don't hate you."

The darkness receded and her body started to calm in his hold, but she wasn't done with her interrogation.

"Your poppy?"

His hand still in her hair pulled the tail over her shoulder and up between their faces. Sliding his thumb and finger together through the soft strands until he captured one like he was searching for, he held it and looked back to her.

"The color of poppies," he said softly and then went on to say openly. "Ilsa did not have poppies in her hair."

The skin around her mouth grew soft and she asked, "Did she spend much time outside?"

"She was not fond of the out of doors."

"I am," she whispered, again it was shyly and this time he knew why.

She was sharing something of herself with him and she was concerned how he'd take her doing it.

He dropped her hair and wrapped both arms around her, again pulling her close.

"This pleases me," he whispered back.

Her eyes dropped to his mouth and her little white teeth came out to worry her lip.

As elated as he was that this scene was what it was rather than what he feared it would be, with her focus on his mouth, he knew it had to end and it had to end immediately, or they would not be to their sleigh for hours.

Tonight, after they talked, they would take time getting to know each other without adela tea.

Now, unfortunately, they had to be on their way.
“We must be away, my dove,” he reminded her.
She lifted her gaze to his.
“Okeydokey.”
And at that word, Apollo knew all was well, and again, he smiled.

10

HOW HE TREASURED IT

I felt warm and cozy, except my nose, which was cold but there was something tickling it. I also felt motion all around me. Finally, the sun bright against my eyelids slid through my burgeoning consciousness, and for a second, things didn't seem right.

Then I remembered.

I was out in the cold elements of Lunwyn in a sleigh with Apollo.

More precisely, I was in Apollo's sleigh *with* Apollo, a huge fur blanket over our laps, wrapped up tight in my cloak (the same one as yesterday, after my emotional upheavals of the morning I didn't have it in me to dig out one that matched my outfit better—and by the way, I had *four*). I was snuggled up to Apollo, my arm resting across his stomach, my cheek to his chest and what was tickling my nose was the fur inside *his* cloak.

Oh God.

I was snuggled up to Apollo.

Crap.

I didn't move or open my eyes. Instead, I faked still sleeping.

I did this because I couldn't face him, not yet. I had to get my shit together before I attempted that.

He'd been cool this morning, actually really sweet and very understanding. I'd spent the time since he left the room torturing myself about what I'd done, but the way he'd acted, the things he'd said totally made me feel better.

About that.

But this did not negate the fact that he'd been kind to me (in his way) since I'd gotten there, and I'd been a bitch to him.

And it definitely did not negate the fact that last night I'd fucked his brains out, he'd fucked my brains out, and this all commenced when I threw myself at him.

It was clear this all came about because I drank that tea.

But still.

It was embarrassing.

He, however, seemed not to have a problem with this. Not at all. It was almost like it didn't happen. Then again, men could often separate life from sex. It happened, you moved on. And maybe some women could too.

But I couldn't.

And definitely not what we did last night.

God, I burned with humiliation just thinking about it.

I'd had one lover before Pol. And then there was Pol, and he was good in bed, actually great. We never had a problem with that. In fact, that was one of the reasons why, in the beginning, I held on to hope. If he could be that generous, and sometimes even sweet and tender in bed, I thought he could, and would, eventually bring that into our everyday lives.

I'd even talked to him about it. Until I did it too often, it started to annoy him, and for obvious reasons I did my best not to annoy Pol.

But he took care of me every time, and once, the time I liked to think was when we created our daughter, he took care of me twice in one go.

That was, he took care of me until I started having to fake it because I couldn't stand his hands on me, and if he knew, *that* would really annoy him.

However, I'd never had anything like what I had with Apollo last night. The hunger. The heat.

The freedom.

I didn't think of anything I did. I wasn't in my head at all. I just went for it.

Actually, the truth of it was, Apollo led it and I went along for the ride, totally about him and what he was doing to my body. No hang ups. Nothing but him and me and what I could make him feel and what he was making me feel.

I'd done things with him I'd never done with Pol, never even considered doing with *anybody*.

At the time, I didn't care.

Now, it mortified me.

Because I barely knew him.

I didn't know about the sexual strictures on this world, but considering women still covered their ankles, I really, *really* hoped he understood all about whatever that tea was so he didn't think I was a big floozy.

"Maddie, are you awake?"

I made a mental note that I sucked at fake sleeping and realized the heaviness around my back was his arm holding me to him when it tightened.

"Poppy, you've stirred. Are you awake?"

"Yeah," I muttered.

"Come here, dove," he muttered back, and I didn't know how much more "here" I could get, but I still shifted up, tipped my head back and gave him my eyes.

He looked down at me with tenderness in his.

I'd seen that before, but it had been so long, and it was so beautiful, I felt my breath leave my lungs.

"How are you feeling?" he asked gently.

The truth of it was, I ached, and I was still kind of fatigued. Fucking someone's brains out took it out of you.

I didn't share that.

"Fine," I told him.

"Are you hungry?" he inquired.

I was. I didn't have breakfast. I mean, it was served to me, but I didn't eat it.

"I could eat," I answered.

"Good," he murmured and looked ahead.

I did too, again realizing that his arm was around my back, and it hadn't moved. He was still holding me to him and doing it in a way that he wasn't going to let go.

I decided this likely had to do with the fact that cuddling together was a whole lot warmer than sitting apart.

We were riding through pines that were set far apart but he steered the horses closer to one and he did this speaking.

"I'll take care of the horses. You unpack the sandwiches, yes?"

"Okeydokey," I mumbled, and his arm gave me a squeeze and didn't let go so I was fit more snuggly to his body.

Okay.

What?

He pulled back on the reins and the horses stopped. Taking me with him, he leaned forward and draped them on a hook in front of us then turned to me, still holding me close.

I looked up at him just in time for his gloved hand to cup my jaw and his head to descend. He brushed his lips against my parted-in-surprise ones and murmured, "I'll be back."

He lifted up to kiss my forehead and moved out from under the fur to leave the sleigh.

Okay.

What?

Right, well, he'd been way cool this morning, holding me and comforting me while I cried and freaked out. He'd also been solicitous as we left the inn, offering his arm, pulling me close when I took it and wrapping his hand over mine at his elbow, walking that way the whole way through the inn and out of it as he led me to the sleigh. I made not a peep when I saw both the horses hitched to it and I still didn't when he climbed into the sleigh with me.

We took off, and our wild-ass sex-a-thon, no sleep and my crying jag all crashed into me, and I was out within fifteen minutes of our being on our way.

Now was now and he wasn't being way cool.

He was being way sweet.

And affectionate.

Way affectionate.

He'd gone to the back of the sleigh, and I watched him move to the front, feedbags for the horses in his hands, and decided I better hop to it because he'd be back soon and expecting his sandwich.

I bent to the corner of the sleigh where there was a basket from which Apollo had produced our lunch yesterday. As I did that, I saw something out of the corner of my eye.

I looked over the side of the sleigh and saw a cute bunny with gray fur and a white tail hopping toward me.

He was so adorable, I stopped and smiled.

He stopped, lifted up on his hind feet and made a bunch of noises.

He made a bunch of noises, but in my head, I heard, "Lady, you have any lettuce?"

I went still and stared at the bunny.

He looked to the right then back at me and made more noises.

But in my head, I heard. "Lady, I asked, do you have any lettuce?"

"Is that bunny talking to me?" I breathed to no one.

Except, of course, the bunny.

He made more noises, a lot of them, but in my head, I heard, "Of course I'm talking to you. Who else would I be talking to? Now, do you have any lettuce?"

"Oh my God," I whispered then shot to my feet, turned and ran out of the sleigh, into the snow, passing Apollo who was coming back.

"Maddie, what's amiss?" he called.

But I kept running, with difficulty seeing as the snow was halfway up my calves. Still, I kept doing it mainly because a *freaking* bunny was talking *in my head.*

"Madeleine!" Apollo shouted.

I kept on running.

Then I stopped because an arm flashed around my middle, and I was yanked back into a hard body.

"Maddie, what did you see?" Apollo demanded to know, his mouth at my ear and he was dragging me back to the sleigh.

I didn't want to go to the sleigh. The cute little bunny who could speak in my mind was at that sleigh.

So I pushed at his arm, struggling against his hold as he kept dragging me.

He stopped and I went with him as he bent into the sleigh for something.

I heard steel hiss and then I was shaken gently, and again at my ear, "What did you see?"

I twisted in his arm and looked up at his wary face.

"Does that tea make you hallucinate?" I asked.

His brows shot together. "Pardon?"

I put my hands to his chest and pressed in, lifting up on my toes in the snow.

"That tea, Apollo, *that tea*. Does it make you hallucinate?"

"For males and females, it significantly increases sex drive and even more significantly enhances arousal. For men, it increases blood flow and stamina," he finally answered.

That was interesting, very interesting actually, but it didn't answer my question.

Then he answered my question, "I've never heard it known to cause hallucinations."

Crap!

Suddenly his face was in my face. "Maddie, my dove, *what did you see*?"

"A bunny."

His head jerked back. "What?"

"I saw a bunny," I told him.

He stared down at me like he wanted to take my temperature, or more likely admit me for a full battery of psychological tests (if they did that sort of thing in this world).

Then, cautiously, he asked, "You fear rabbits?"

"No," I answered. "I fear rabbits," I got up on my toes again, "that *talk in my head*."

All of a sudden, he relaxed, his eyes lit with amusement and his face got soft.

He also kept hold of me even as he twisted and tossed his sword on the seat of the sleigh.

Then he came back to me, lifted his hand to the side of my neck and dipped his face close again.

"All right, poppy, I believe all three of the other women from your world had this same reaction, and unfortunately, I didn't think to mention it to you. Though, I must admit to some surprise that it did not happen along your journey."

"This same reaction to what?" I asked and didn't wait for him to answer. I asked another question. "What didn't happen along my journey?"

"This same reaction to the fact that, in our world, animals can talk to you."

"*What?*" I breathed, my eyes getting wide, and in return, his eyes warmed but held their humor.

"They talk to you."

I said nothing. Just stared at him.

"Not all of them," he kept the information flowing, "But many. And both genders don't understand the same creatures. For instance, I as a man can understand the likes of horses, wolves and snakes. You as a woman will be able to understand the likes of rabbits, cats and mice."

Okay, in thinking about it, the talking animals thing wasn't a big surprise, though it still freaked me out. I'd quit feeling surprised at a lot of what went on around me since getting to this world. Sure, when a bunny sounded in my head, I felt immediate shock. But knowing it was something of this world that was, well...that.

Still, at learning this nuance of it, my brows snapped together, and I asked, "Why do the guys get all the cool animals? I mean, rabbits are cute and I've no doubt cats are interesting, but who really cares what a mouse has to say? No offense to mice, of course," I hastened to say, just in case any were around and could hear me. "Now, I don't like snakes all that much, but I bet I'd be interested in what one has to say."

For a moment, he just studied me.

Then he threw back his head, his hand at my neck sliding down to join his other arm around me, both convulsed, and he burst out laughing.

I'd never seen him laugh.

It was fascinating.

And shockingly, it was nothing like Pol.

Sure, it kind of sounded like Pol's laughter. But Pol never laughed with that rich genuineness that seemed to pour over your skin in a warm and happy way like Apollo did.

He sobered, kind of, his big body still shaking because he was chuckling, and he kept me held close as he looked down at me.

"If we come across a snake, I'll act as interpreter," he offered.

I hoped we didn't run across a snake since I didn't lie, I really didn't like them much, but I still said, "Cool."

He smiled down at me.

I stared up at him.

God, he was beautiful.

And I didn't know how it was, but even looking exactly like him, he was beautiful in a way that was nothing like Pol.

"Now, are you over your fright? Can we eat?" he asked.

I was over my fright. I was still freaking out that animals could talk to me in this world, but I wasn't tempted to go dashing through the snow anymore.

"We can eat," I murmured.

He let me go but only to guide me into the sleigh.

I went after the basket. When I turned with our sandwiches, he'd put his sword back in its scabbard and was sitting on the seat under the furs, the edge thrown back for me.

I handed him his, sat, and he threw the fur over me.

I unwrapped the muslin cloth from around my sandwich and bit in.

Cold beef nowhere near as flavorful as what Apollo's staff provided. And there was nothing to it, no condiments, just mostly grisly beef and kind of stale bread.

Ugh.

"We'll be in Vasterhague just after sundown. Unlike last night, we'll have choice and I'll take you for a fine meal."

My eyes slid to him to see his on me and my guess from his comment was he knew I didn't like the sandwich much.

"This is fine," I assured him, lifting my sandwich stupidly to indicate I was talking about it, something he had to know.

"This is rubbish," he returned, grinning at me and biting into his.

I gave him a hesitant grin back and returned my attention to my food, which was to say away from him.

And I kept my attention away from him. But after I'd eaten half the sandwich, it occurred to me that yesterday I'd ignored him all day. And today I was trying not to be a bitch, stupid, selfish, childish or silly, but still, right then, I was ignoring him again. Of course, I had different reasons, but it still wasn't cool.

So I lifted my eyes to the landscape and asked him, "Is there anything else crazy like animals talking to you that I should know about this world?"

"Do you know of our dragons and elves?"

I slid my gaze to him, chewing and nodding.

"And I know you know of our magic," he went on.

I kept chewing and nodding.

His beautiful eyes held mine and they were back to tender. "Truth be told, poppy, from what I've learned from Finnie, our world is much simpler than your world. Your world seems very complicated. And from her descriptions, and I do not intend to offend you with these words, but my world seems less rushed than your world, the land less molested, the air less drab and heavy, and thus all of it more attractive."

I looked to the landscape. Outside of bunny tracks, the snow was untouched. The pine trees stark green against its white and the so-very-blue of the sky, the tufts of snow on the trees' branches thick and fluffy. The air was serene. There was no noise. No airplanes overhead, no railroad tracks, no cars or roads or billboard signs. It actually looked like a Christmas card, or the vision of a holiday animated movie come to life, not anything real.

Yet it was.

And it was extraordinary.

"I think you're right," I agreed and took another bite of sandwich.

At this point, I saw his used piece of muslin fly through the air and land in the opened basket.

I turned my eyes to him and saw him reaching for the wineskin of water hanging from another hook on the front of the sleigh. Stupidly, I watched him sit back, tip his head and drink from it. And even more stupidly, since I could see his throat above his turtleneck working as he drank, and I'd had my lips (and tongue) on that throat and I'd liked it, I became fascinated.

His turtleneck today was a forest green, no less spectacular than the one the day before, except for the fact that the color did amazing things to his eyes.

His breeches, I'd noticed that morning, were another dark brown, but this pair had a wide, darker brown swatch of leather stitched to the entirety of the inseam, even the crotch.

Which, at the thought, brought to mind a part of him I paid a good deal of attention to last night, and that part wasn't his throat. And he'd used that part brilliantly on me multiple times.

All these thoughts made my breasts swell, my breathing turned shallow, and my mind blanked of everything but him.

Which meant, when he dipped his chin and his gaze moved to me, he caught the look on my face. A look I knew communicated thoughts I wasn't hiding when his eyes instantly grew dark, and his hand flashed out to hook around the back of my neck and pull me to him.

His darkened eyes and his hand on me pulling me close made my clit throb, and I was so focused on that heady feeling, as he leaned into me, his lips brushing mine then his cheek sliding against mine so his mouth was at my ear, I didn't move a muscle.

Then in my ear, he growled, "You must cease looking at me this way, poppy. If you don't, I'll cover the floor of this sleigh with this fur and take you in the cold."

Oh God.

I wanted that.

Oh *God*, what was happening?

"And out of necessity, it would be hurried," he continued. "I'm much looking forward to reacquainting myself with your taste and that beautiful arse of yours tonight and taking my time doing it. So the sooner we get to Vasterhague, the more time we'll have."

Okay.

What was happening?

He lifted away from me, and the heat had not left his eyes so I continued to stare stupidly into them.

"Yes?" he prompted.

"Uh...yes," I forced out. "Okay."

"Okay," he whispered, leaned in, touched his mouth first to one eye, then the other, and that was so sweet, my belly melted. He pulled back and went on, "Finish your sandwich, poppy. I'll see to the horses, and we'll be away."

At that, I forced myself to nod.

He smiled at me.

I bit my lip.

Then I watched his shoulders as he exited the sleigh.

He had great shoulders. Broad. Powerful. And I knew, under all those clothes, exquisitely muscled.

Oh God.

I turned my attention to my sandwich and found after a couple of bites, my dry mouth couldn't take more. I wrapped it up in the muslin, tossed it in and closed the basket. By this time, Apollo was done with the horses and moving back to the sleigh so I situated myself farther across the seat so I wouldn't be sitting too close to him.

Distance was good. I could get my head sorted if he wasn't close. Cuddling was bad. I mean, in many circumstances, it was good, way good. But, at this juncture, it was also bad. *Way* bad.

He got in the sleigh, grabbed the reins and sat, pulling the furs over his lap. He clicked his teeth, snapped the reins and off we went.

Okay, getting my head together...apparently Apollo thought last night we'd broken the seal. So instead of it happening and him being way cool about it and putting it behind us, he thought our relationship had changed.

And I could not say I wasn't down with that.

In fact, after last night and the way he'd been today, I was *so* down with that.

But I knew I shouldn't be.

Things with us were weird and complicated. He told me he'd made love to me last night, not his dead wife, and I believed him. I believed him because the way he said it, the way he was behaving with me made me believe him. But more, I remembered every minute of last night and he'd not once slipped and called me Ilsa or "my beauty."

He'd only used the names he had for me.

So it was just me for him.

And as for him, not once, not even once did I think of Pol.

So it was just him for me.

But still.

We'd been in each other's presence, I counted, six times. And if you counted our uncomfortable meal last night, we'd only had one semi-kind-of-date and that date went far from well.

This shift wasn't right.

Or, if not exactly right, it was too fast.

The sleigh slid over the snow, and I worried my lip as it did. Then I pressed my lips together when his arm moved along the back of my seat, curled around me and pulled me across the seat and into him. Without delay, once he got me close, he curved me closer.

Oh boy.

"Apollo?" I called.

"Yes, dove," he muttered.

God, really, him calling me "dove" was all kinds of lovely.

"Um...are we, have we...?"

Just suck it up and talk to him about it, Ils...fuck, Madeleine!

I took in a deep breath and asked, "Has the state of play between us changed?"

His deep voice sounded puzzled when he asked back, "The state of play?"

I pulled up courage and tipped my head back to look at him to see him already looking down at me.

Yes, puzzled.

"You seem, I mean..." I drew in breath. "You're being very affectionate."

His head tipped to the side. "This troubles you?"

"We were, uh...kind of fighting yesterday, and of course, the day before, and, well, dinner wasn't all that—"

His eyes started dancing so I shut up, and thus he could say, "We weren't fighting last night."

We absolutely weren't.

"No," I agreed breathily.

"And I much enjoyed last night."

I'd got that. Still, it felt nice him confirming it.

"Good." I was still talking breathily.

He pulled me closer and up a bit so we were nearly face to face. That was, nearly face to face with our faces about an inch away.

"Adela tea," he began, his voice deeper than normal and warmer than normal and that was a double whammy. "Comes from adela trees. Have the gods of my world been explained to you?"

I nodded. I knew all about their gods and the fact that they had a bunch of them. "Gaston told me about them."

He nodded in return. "Then you know that Adele is the goddess of love. And she created those trees. The bark of those trees, if taken and infused with water, is what makes adela tea. These trees have many uses and are sacred. The tea is one of those uses. It is understood the goddess Adele created it to enhance the physical connection along with the emotional connection, if one is to be had, between lovers. It works as I explained before, but it also breaks down inhibitions."

Oh, it certainly did that.

His arm gave me a squeeze before he kept explaining. "Even if we don't realize it, things in our head can build barriers to sharing in a variety of ways, including during bedplay. With those swept away, lovers can understand each other better. What pleasures them. Where to touch that feels best. Smells, noises, tastes that enhance gratification."

It certainly did that, too.

Apollo wasn't done.

"And, through future relations, once had, the understanding of all this will never be lost, even if the tea isn't consumed. Therefore, it continues to make relations all that more intense, deeper, a beautiful experience every time you engage in it."

Oh boy.

That sounded *awesome*.

He kept going.

"And if there is an emotional connection, or one that is building, all this serves to enhance that as well, most precisely, trust."

His face got closer to mine so he was now only half an inch away and my breath caught.

"Amongst the other things, I feel that is what it's done for us, my poppy. You must admit, regardless of the unusual circumstances that brought us together, we would not argue with such passion if there was not some emotional connection on which to feed that passion."

This made sense, of course, but there *was* the history that came before, for both of us, which could actually be the cause of said "passion."

So, I started to protest, "But—"

He knew what my protest would be because his eyes grew slightly hard and he declared, "It is not about him for you, and it is not about her for me. We both know this. They were not there last night."

"No, they weren't," I whispered, and the hardness slid out of his eyes.

"They were between us, Maddie. *Were*. Last night, with the tea, with the way you gave yourself to me so freely, so magnificently, and how I treasure that, now they're gone."

Okay.

Shit.

How he treasured it?

I liked that.

Like, a lot.

Still.

"Okay, I get that," I said. "But if that's the case, if we're, um...enhancing relations, maybe we should take that slowly."

His head gave a slight jerk then his hand slid up to cup the back of my head. He shoved my face in his neck just as he burst out laughing.

I wasn't exactly sure what was funny.

Before I could ask, his fingers twisted carefully in my ponytail, he tugged back a bit and his mouth hit mine for a hard, closed-mouth kiss before he moved a breath away.

"Do you think, dove, that you could give me the abundance and beauty of last night then make me wait to have you again?"

Hmm.

"I'll answer that," he said, his eyes still lit with humor. "You can't."

"Uh...okay."

"And Madeleine, with the way you've been looking at me, it's quite clear you don't want to."

I had to admit, he might not be wrong about that.

I began to worry my lip.

His eyes dropped to it and then I watched them smile.

That smile faded to warmth when he stated, "I'll make you a promise. Tonight, we'll go slower, and I'll be more gentle. How's that?"

Apollo being slow and gentle.

Crap.

My clit was pulsing again.

"Uh...okay."

He smiled, leaned in and touched his mouth to mine again and finally sat back, his hand sliding out of my hair to round my back and hold me close, yes...*again*.

Okay.

Did I just agree to start a sexual relationship...no, to *continue* one alongside beginning a relationship-relationship with the Apollo of this world?

I think I did.

Okay.

Right.

Shit.

11

IN THERE

I watched the door close behind Apollo, and dazedly, I turned and looked down at my trunks.

Trunks.

Yes, three.

I'd come in with only one as well as the things we brought from Fleuridia. Only one had been brought up to the room yesterday. And I had not studied what was packed behind us under the silken green tarp of our sleigh.

But now, to my surprise, I had three.

We were in Vasterhague.

Vasterhague was much bigger than the village we'd stayed in the night before. In fact, it was as big as a small city.

When the boys were bringing me into Lunwyn, we'd stayed there, and they'd told me a lot about it.

But as he drove the sleigh, moving our conversation to something that was much more comfortable, Apollo told me about it too. And as I needed more comfortable conversation and since he seemed keen to share with me, I didn't tell him I knew a lot of what he had to say.

And that was that Vasterhague was kind of a cosmopolitan trading post. Situated equidistant from two large port cities, it had large warehouses at its outer edges where merchandise from ships was delivered and then disseminated. Because of this, there was a great deal of activity, merchants going there to sell their wares, buyers going there to make deals, delivery sleighs going there to pick up shipments. And naturally, a variety of other things had grown up around it.

Outside of the warehouses, and the four long rows of massive greenhouses built a bit away from the city, the rest looked like any other sleepy village I'd seen in Lunwyn. There were buildings that were taller, larger and grander, but the feel was rustic simplicity. Perhaps more elegant than the other villages, but still rustic.

Thus welcoming.

Draven had explained the greenhouses (as did Apollo) and their existence made sense. In this frozen landscape, they were essential. They held fruit trees and berry vines and vegetable patches that were forced to grow during the long time of the year (three quarters of it!) that Lunwyn was under snow.

Apollo had gone on to tell me what Draven did not. And that was that the greenhouses of Vasterhague were a smaller collection. Across Lunwyn, there were acres of them dotted across the land (and he, not surprisingly, ran two such "enterprises"). Many of the richer citizens with larger homes and enough money to have servants also had their own small (and large) greenhouses to supply their homes (as well as those dwelling around them).

"I have greenhouses at all my homes," he'd said.

This comment made me look at him and ask, "How many homes do you have?"

"Four, in Lunwyn," he told the landscape then looked down at me. "As well as apartments in Bellebryn, the house where you stayed in Fleuridia, a town-home in Benies and then there's my castle in Hawkvale."

Uh.

Castle?

"You own a castle?" I asked, and for some reason this question made his brows draw together.

"Yes, of course. Did you not stay in it as you journeyed through the Vale?"

"Uh...no," I answered.

This made his mouth get tight and he looked back to the snowy plain as he murmured, "Curious, as it was on your way."

He said "curious," but I was getting the feeling it wasn't curious to him. It was, instead, annoying. I just didn't know why.

I also didn't know why the guys didn't take me there, thus I definitely found it curious.

Though, since he found it annoying, I didn't press about it.

Upon entering the city, Apollo had informed me of something else the boys had not. This was pointing out the large warehouse (from what I could tell, the largest of the lot) that was his.

"That looks like it could hold a lot of jewels and furs," I noted, staring at it as we slid down the snow encrusted lane that took us deeper into the city.

"I may not have mentioned that I also trade in lumber," he replied on a murmur, a comment that made me again look at him.

"So in other words, you're loaded."

He looked from the lane to me. "Loaded?"

"Loaded," I repeated. "As in, with wealth."

He grinned and gave me yet another squeeze as he looked back at the lane and confirmed, "Indeed. I'm *loaded.*"

The dry, self-effacing way he said this made me giggle which meant he gave me another squeeze.

I took in the hustle and bustle of the city (definitely more activity there than in the sleepy villages) as Apollo took us directly to Treeburn Lodge, where Derrik and the guys had taken me the last time I was here. It was by far the biggest, and most elegant (but still rustic) of all the hotels that I'd noticed in Vasterhague. I also knew it had bigger, way nicer rooms than the room we had last night.

It also had bigger, way more comfortable beds.

The minute that thought hit my head, I pushed it back. I needed to get through the next minute, then the next and not do it hyperventilating or possibly having a spontaneous orgasm.

When we checked in, Apollo asked for what Derrik asked for, their "suite." This, since I'd stayed in it before, was a suite because it had a small sitting room, a large bedroom, a small bathing room and an even smaller room that held the dread chamber pot. But at least the latter gave the feel of a bathroom, which wasn't much, but it was something.

He also asked that "Lady Madeleine" have wine to drink and water to refresh and "all our trunks" should be delivered with haste to our room.

I liked "Lady Madeleine," it was pretty awesome. But it was a crapshoot if I liked that better than "Lady Ulfr."

On this thought, I knew I was in trouble because it wasn't just Apollo taking this fast, my brain was taking it Mach three.

Apollo escorted me to our room, poured the wine for me when it came (but not a glass for himself), explained he'd be "preparing for dinner" somewhere else, and when the trunks were delivered, he also explained them.

"The garments you were met with in Lunwyn were for your journey through this land. But a wardrobe befitting a lady of my House was created for you, this including apparel for a variety of occasions as well as that to wear during travel and in different countries." He indicated the trunks with a sweep of his hand. "As we're going to Bellebryn, these additional trunks include wardrobes that are suitable there and in the Vale as well as more of a selection for you while you're here."

He came to me as I stared up at him and he lifted a hand to curl around my neck, dipping his face close.

"Tonight, I'll take you to The Boar. Don't be mistaken by the name. It started as a simple pub that served excellent fare. But over the years, its reputation has spread wide. It's since grown and it is now a place where many travel long distances to go. People hold weddings there. Special occasions are celebrated there." He paused. "And you dress when you go there."

I had an idea what this meant, it was nice of him to warn me, and I was glad for two more trunks because, although my Lunwynian clothes were fab, they were not what you would wear when you needed to "dress."

Apollo clarified what he meant even further by stating, "You don't need to prepare as if you were going to a gale or a ball, but travel-wear is also not appropriate."

I knew what a "gale" was, the boys had told me. It was, in essence, a ball, so that meant I didn't know why he made the distinction.

I also didn't ask.

I just nodded and mumbled, "Gotcha."

He smiled, bent and touched his mouth to mine and only moved a hint away when he said, "I'll give you time and then we'll dine."

I nodded again.

His hand at my neck gave me a squeeze and he took off.

And as I said, after he left, I looked down at my trunks, plural, marveling at another show of his generosity.

But mostly freaking out, because essentially, we were having our first bona-fide date.

"Holy hell," I murmured.

With nothing for it, I got down to it.

Setting my wineglass aside, I dropped to my knees and opened the first new trunk.

That one was filled with clothes for Bellebryn. I knew this because they were lighter-weight material, and they were in the style of what women wore in the Vale.

I wanted to explore but I didn't. I had a date to get ready for, and I had to admit, I was excited.

But I was also anxious. Near-to-panic anxious.

Therefore, I needed to take my mind off my panic and what better way to do that than get myself gussied up?

I threw that trunk closed and opened the next one.

He was right. Quickly, but breathlessly pulling clothes from the trunk, I found its carefully packed contents not only included a variety of gowns that were much like what I was wearing, lovely, but warm and functional. It also included another cape. This one was with black-dyed hide on the outside, thick long silvery fur with a smattering of black hairs on the inside. And last, it included four ball gowns—*four*—all four of them graceful, sophisticated, beautifully cut and stunning.

But it was the three dresses that were not the normal daywear/travel-wear that I turned my attention to.

And I homed in on one.

It was again a sweater dress, the square neckline, bodice and upper sleeves knitted in a fabulous, paler than pale lilac. But under the breasts and down over the hips, coming to a point in the front and back, as well as from elbow to wrist on the sleeves, was a deep purple, to-die-for supple suede. On the sides, mid-thigh to hem, and from the point of the suede that stopped at my heels at the back, flowing in a short but elegant train, was more of the lilac sweater material.

It was kind of rock 'n' roll meets Lunwyn, edgy but elegant.

I loved it.

Sucking back some wine, I used the water to "refresh." Then I did my makeup for evening, deeper and smokier.

After that, I put on the dress.

It fit like a glove, but you couldn't see that the cleavage was as low as it was when it wasn't on. And the way the knit and suede clung to my figure, the way it was cut, the design—it highlighted everything a woman wanted to highlight, breasts, ass, collarbone, even legs.

"Holy cow," I breathed, turning this way and that to check out every inch in the free-standing, full-length mirror.

Yes, I loved that dress.

But I didn't have three years to admire myself in it. I needed to be ready by the time Apollo returned.

So I moved on to my hair.

In Fleuridia, when I had lady's maids, they often did my hair in soft, but intricate updos that really rocked.

I didn't have that talent with hair, alas. But fiddling with it using my small kit of hairbobs that I'd bought in Benies and had been supplemented by the stuff Apollo gave me in Lunwyn, I pulled it loosely away from my face and fastened it in a (not so bad, if I did say so myself), messy, sexy bun at the side of my neck behind my ear.

With this, I slid on a pair of smoke-gray suede boots.

I was hurrying through last minute preparations, spritzing with perfume, shoving hairpins with purple stones in my hair, at the same time inserting silver chandelier earrings with purple beads in my earlobes when a knock came at the door.

My heart flew to my throat, my eyes to the mirror and the doorknob turned.

Crap, I was going to throw up.

I turned to the door when it opened, and Apollo entered.

No. I wasn't going to throw up.

I was going to have that spontaneous orgasm I'd been fearing all afternoon.

This was because he had on a green shirt that was deeper than forest green. I didn't know what that color was. I just knew it looked really, *really* good on him. The collar came up high on his neck, but he didn't have a neck cloth like I'd seen on men in the Vale. It was open there, exposing the strong column of his throat—something of the many, *many* things that made up all that was Apollo that I especially liked.

With this, he was wearing a black jacket with black leather swatches at the shoulders and tight black trousers tucked into tall, black boots.

His hair, which was almost always disheveled, was now swept away from his face, but the ends curled around his neck and ears in a way that made your hands itch to touch them.

In other words, he looked *hot.*

"You'll meet me downstairs," he commanded, his voice terse, and my gaze shot from those curls around his ears to his (for some reason) stormy eyes.

"Wh-what?" I stammered.

"If you wish to eat, you'll meet me downstairs."

Confused, I asked, "Why?"

"Because if I walk one more step into this room, we will not be leaving it."

Every inch of my skin started tingling like I'd just sipped some adela tea.

Oh boy.

I was taking it he liked my dress too.

"Right. I'll meet you downstairs," I whispered.

His eyes slid down my body, and I swear it felt like his hands did it. I was trembling by the time he dipped his head to me in a way that was gallant, which was a way I liked a whole lot, then he moved out the door.

I stared at it again then turned back to look at myself in the mirror.

Yes. Definitely yes.

I loved this dress.

Smiling, I walked to my new cloak, threw it over my shoulders and headed to the door.

If Vasterhague was cosmopolitan but rustic (which it was), The Boar was just plain old cosmopolitan.

Actually, it was cosmopolitan elegance.

No kidding, it could be picked up inch for inch and transported to Benies, it was that classy. In fact, if women wore ball gowns, it would not be lost on the décor.

Luckily, they didn't. They wore much what I wore.

But mine was the best.

The chandelier-sporting, white-tablecloth, silver, china, crystal-laden-table-filled, peach-walls-with-crown-molding interior of The Boar was so amazing that it even managed to capture my attention.

Attention that was diverted to other things seeing as it wasn't exactly close to our lodge, and we'd had to ride there on Apollo's horse.

And to ride there on Apollo's horse meant him lifting me up to sit sidesaddle and him mounting behind me, his arm then snaking around my waist, pulling me deep, holding me close to his body, my behind snug in his crotch.

Sitting with him that way felt nice.

Scary nice.

Which felt scary good.

God.

Further making this somewhat short journey epic was him doing it the entire time with his lips at my ear, pointing out different shops or cafés I might later peruse should "we" find ourselves in Vasterhague with time to enjoy it.

His deep voice sounding intimately in my ear, the smell of him in my nostrils (he wore cologne that night, it was subtle but it had hints of cedar and musk, and mingled with his natural smell that was all man, it did a number on me), his arm tight around my belly, by the time we made it to the restaurant (what I guessed was around ten blocks) at his horse's slow canter, I was in a state.

Luckily, the restaurant took my mind off that state, and I was able to behave with decorum while having my cape taken away, being led to the table where Apollo pulled out my chair, being seated and handed a menu as Apollo ordered, "Bring us a bottle of Belle St. Michel and ask our waiter to give Lady Madeleine time with the menu."

The maître d' bowed and moved away.

I didn't look at the menu.

I looked at him.

"What's Belle St. Michel?" I asked.

His eyes went from his menu to me. "Do you have white wine with bubbles in your world?"

"Champagne?"

"Indeed." He nodded. "Belle St. Michel is champagne from a region in Fleuridia."

I grinned at my menu, thinking, *Fabulous. Fleuridian champagne. This night just kept getting better and better.*

"That pleases you?" he queried, and I knew he caught my grin.

I looked back at him. "I like Fleuridian wine."

At that, his lips tipped up and he looked down to his menu, murmuring, "A lady with excellent taste."

It was meant as a compliment, but it struck me, and not in a good way.

Because I was that lady.

I was exactly that lady. The kind of lady who knew just how excellent the quality was of my boots and cape. My dress. This restaurant. Fine wine. I knew all that and more very well, in this world and my own.

I worried my lip with my teeth, perused the menu and became aware of eyes on me. Peeking around, I saw Apollo and I getting furtive glances, the patrons here too well-mannered to stare outright.

They knew him here. And Ilsa.

Fabulous.

Oh well.

Whatever. It wasn't the first, it wouldn't be the last, and because of that, I'd have to get used to it.

I might as well start now.

The wine came and I set my menu aside to watch it being served.

And I saw there was no taste testing exercise to go through here. The waiter just put down delicately etched, flat-bowled champagne glasses in front of Apollo and me, popped the cork and poured.

He then took orders. This time, Apollo allowed me to order for myself.

And then the waiter was away and I was alone with Apollo and champagne.

I went after the champagne and took a sip.

Beauty.

"What you expected?" Apollo asked.

My attention went to him to see he was asking this with his gaze on me over the rim of his wineglass, and like everything about him, that was hot.

He took a sip as I answered, "Better."

His eyes smiled as he swallowed and set the glass aside.

It was then, it hit me that our date had commenced, and I felt my palms start to get wet.

But here I was, in a new world, and I knew one thing. I had no choice but to make the best of the situation.

In fact, I'd been doing that from the beginning.

And one could say that, so far, with a few minor blips that were mostly my fault, I hadn't done too badly.

I set my glass aside, linked my hands in my lap and sought an easy subject of conversation.

I decided on, "What's your horse's name?"

He sat back in his chair and leveled his eyes on me.

Again, a simple movement, a simple posture.

And totally hot.

"Torment," he answered.

I blinked because, although that was a kickass name, it was also a strange one.

"Really?"

"Yes."

I didn't know what to say.

"His sister guides your sleigh," Apollo continued.

"What's her name?" I inquired.

"Anguish."

I blinked again.

Then I threw out a hand. "Those are, well...interesting names."

"They were born of the same mare at the same time. Rare and dangerous," he told me. "Usually, if a mare produces twins, one or both of the foals or the mare will perish during birth. If a foal was to survive, it would be small and sickly and not last long. Unusually, Torment and Anguish both were strong healthy foals, if still small." He reached to his glass and took a sip, finishing his story as he put the glass back to the table. "However, they killed their mother at birth."

"Oh my God," I whispered.

"She was Ilsa's. They were born within a week of her dying."

Shit.

Well, there you go. The reason for their names.

I decided not to reply.

"Surprisingly," he carried on. "They grew healthy and strong. A miracle. One built on tragedy but one nonetheless."

"Yes, a miracle," I murmured, reaching for my own wineglass and looking away when I took a sip.

"We must speak of them."

At his words, I turned back to him, not understanding. "Sorry?"

"They existed. We can't pretend they did not. Burying memories, treasured or detested, is unhealthy," he explained.

He was talking of Ilsa and Pol and he was doing it matter-of-factly.

He was also right, of course.

I still wasn't fired up to share about Pol during our kind of first date.

Apollo leaned into me, and he said softly, "Reliving unhappy memories is always unpleasant, Maddie. I'm simply saying that it's likely I'll refer to her because she was once in my life and to know me, you must know of my life. She's also the mother of my children and will always be a part of my life in some way because of that." His voice dropped even softer, and his gaze held mine, his intense but warm, when he went on, "And last, I loved her deeply, so she simply always will be a part of me."

I nodded as this was true, but he wasn't done.

"I'm also saying if you feel the need to release your memories, unhappy or otherwise, and need someone to tell them to, and in the case of the unhappy ones, if you need someone to help take them from you, I'm here."

God, that was sweet.

Seriously, could this guy get better?

"Thanks," I whispered, though I added, "But can it not be now?"

"Absolutely, it can not be now. It can be never. It's your decision whether you wish to share...or not."

Yep.

This guy could get better.

And then he got even better, and he did that by sitting back and changing the subject, which at that point was exactly what I needed.

"I have yet to tell you of Valentine's visits."

I nodded, and since I wanted to know about that, I put my elbows to the table and leaned into them, placing my chin in my palms and curling my fingers up my cheeks.

When I did, his eyes melted to tender, and my belly melted at the view.

But what he said didn't make me feel warm and squishy.

"I must ask, dove, that if she visits you, you tell me. This is again your choice, but it is my preference to know if she meddles."

That surprised me. "Is she not a nice person?"

"I am not unskilled in reading people. This witch, however, I cannot say. She seems to have a rather robust protective bent to you. Yet she left you the tea without you understanding its potency or effects. It led to us sharing something beautiful, but this is not done. Indeed, it's frowned upon and there have even been men and women brought up on charges when they've used it on those who were unsuspecting."

"It's used as a date rape drug," I deduced quietly.

"Explain this," he ordered.

I lifted my chin from my palms and did just that.

"In my world, men and women go on dates before marriage. It's a kind of wooing, I guess. Courtship. A getting-to-know-each-other period. Sometimes, this leads to a union, marriage or the like. Sometimes, it doesn't work out and you move on. Also in my world, there are drugs that are used to make women—they're mostly used on women—unconscious or unable to defend themselves so the men they're dating can take advantage. They're called date rape drugs because, when it all boils down, even if there's no violence or struggle, that's only because the woman has been incapacitated. So it's still rape. Using adela tea like that is not the same, but it kind of is."

He nodded once, sharply, and concurred, "It is."

I sat back, reached for my wineglass and took a sip, replacing it to the table, mumbling, "So I guess that's the second time she drugged me without my knowledge."

"Your first night in our world," he stated, and I looked at him again.

"Yes."

He looked away but did it appearing annoyed, and I'd know why when he murmured, "I'd wondered why you slipped into sleep so easily after your trauma."

"That was why," I affirmed.

He looked back to me. "This is precisely why I wish for you to inform me if she comes to you. In word and deed, she seems to have your best interests at heart. But it all depends on the person and their actions if their best interests are also yours, no?"

He was *so* right.

I nodded my agreement.

He again leaned toward me and gentled his tone when he requested, "And please, from now on, don't touch, accept or consume anything unless you're certain it was provided to you by me. Can you do that?"

"Yes," I said softly.

His lips curved up and he whispered, "Thank you, poppy."

Okay.

Totally.

This guy kept getting so much better I was beginning to wonder if he was even real.

"We must discuss something else sensitive before our food is served so it can have both our attention and then we can go on to enjoy the evening unhindered by such discourse."

Oh boy.

So far this date wasn't much for the easy conversation.

"Okay," I said slowly.

"Last night was just you and me," he declared.

I felt my brows draw together in confusion but agreed to the obvious. "Yes."

"What I'm saying is, considering what you shared with me was the length of time since you were last active before yesterday eve, I would doubt you're taking pennyrium and not once did I wear a sheath."

I shook my head, still confused. "I don't—"

"To protect against conception."

Holy shit.

My entire body grew still.

Apollo obviously didn't notice because he kept talking.

"Prior to leaving Vasterhague, we will procure you some pennyrium, and tonight, I'll wear a sheath."

I had no idea what pennyrium was. I could guess what a sheath was. And that last was nice and all, but my heart was racing and my mind was reeling.

I tried to count the times he came inside me the night before and I couldn't. There were too many. At least five. Maybe more.

Shit!

I hadn't thought of that. Upon waking, I'd only thought about him being hurt and angry. Then I'd, of course, fallen asleep. After that, it was all about him being sweet and affectionate and getting ready for our date.

Shit.

Shit!

"Maddie," he called.

I forced myself to focus on him. "Um...I would say that all this is good, Apollo. Nice. I like it." I indicated him, me and the table with a circling hand, and when I was done, I dropped that hand to rest on the table. "But pregnancy at this point is definitely taking things too freaking quickly," I shared.

"Agreed," he said slowly, reaching out a hand, capturing mine and holding it tight. "And I'll share that pennyrium didn't agree with Ilsa and we wished time together after we were wed before Christophe was born. The sheath gave us that time as well as time between Christophe and Élan. It is often used and quite dependable. If you can take pennyrium, it's even better."

"What's pennyrium?" I asked.

"A powder you take once a day that protects you from conceiving. One must be careful using it, for if you wish to conceive, even if you cease consuming the powder, it can take some time to leave the system and long-term usage can make conception difficult. But it's effective."

"Okay, let's get me some of that," I said swiftly.

His hand tightened around mine and his lips twitched. "I'll see to that without delay."

I nodded enthusiastically.

He pressed his lips together, his eyes lit with humor then he pulled our hands to his mouth and touched my knuckles to his lips.

I quit freaking about all the unprotected sex we had, and my heart flipped.

He kept my hand to his lips and his voice was so quiet, so gentle, I had to lean further forward to hear him when he asked a very big question with two simple words, "Your children?"

"Can we not talk about that now?" I whispered.

"Of course, poppy," he replied.

I thanked him with my eyes as I tried to force my body to relax.

"Ulfr!"

His name called jovially made me jump and turn my head to see a man in much the same clothing as Apollo (but with a neck cloth and his shirt was blue) coming to our table. He was also stout, had a bit of white at the temples of his black hair and my guess was he was shorter than Apollo by about three inches and older than Apollo by about ten years.

He was smiling at Apollo, but his smile went weird when his eyes hit me.

"Danforth," Apollo said, giving my fingers a squeeze and letting them go.

He stood and offered his hand, the man taking it and gripping hard at the same time he clapped Apollo on the shoulder a half a dozen times in a way that a lesser man would fall to his knee.

Apollo didn't budge, if you didn't count his jaw going hard.

I took this as him not liking the greeting much, and/or the man.

Then suddenly, he let Apollo go and turned to me with a sharp movement and something a creepy bit more than curiosity in his eyes.

"And who might this be?" he asked.

It was then I remembered who I looked like and my insides froze.

"This is Madeleine, Lady Ulfr," Apollo said, and the man's eyes cut immediately back to him as his body gave a visible start.

"Lady Ulfr?" he said in a weighty tone that I didn't quite understand but I also didn't think boded well. And I didn't think this boded well not because I looked exactly like the no-longer-with-us Lady Ulfr but for another reason. I just didn't know what that reason was.

"Lady Ulfr," Apollo repeated in a firm way that brooked no return questioning.

"I had...well," the man threw both hands out, "I'd heard that a cousin of Ilsa's was journeying to Karsvall from the Vale but...but..." His attention returned to me. It was assessing in a way that made me feel uncomfortable even as he finished, "This is indeed good news."

Good news?

"It is," Apollo agreed, and the man looked back at him.

"For you, my man." He looked again at me. "And for you, madam." He then lifted his hand in a flourish toward his head and gave me a short bow.

I didn't know what to do with that, so when he straightened, I inclined my head.

He held out his hand, palm up, and murmured, "It is surely a pleasure to meet you, Madeleine, Lady Ulfr."

I placed my fingers in his and replied, "And you, sir."

His fingers wrapped around mine for a short squeeze then he let me go.

Thankfully, the waiter showed at that point with our appetizers.

"Ulfr." Danforth clapped Apollo on the back and it was a wonder Apollo's shoulder didn't jerk forward at the strength of the blow. "I'll leave you to your meal, your lady and your," he glanced meaningfully at the champagne, "celebrations."

"My gratitude," Apollo replied, his words short, his tone tight.

The man turned to me. "Pleasure."

"Yes," I agreed, feeling weird about what was happening and stupid because I had no clue how to act in this situation as "Lady Ulfr."

He swept away and Apollo sat down as the waiter set our plates in front of us.

And as Apollo sat, he muttered, "Bloody hell."

The waiter bowed and moved away, and I leaned in immediately.

"What was that?" I asked in a low voice.

Apollo moved his angry gaze that was directed to his plate to me and he rearranged his features instantly.

He was hiding something.

Not good.

"I'll explain later, dove," he murmured.

Oh no. He wasn't getting to me with that sweet, lovely "dove" business.

"Apollo, what was that?" I repeated.

His eyes grew intense on mine and he also repeated, "I'll explain later, Maddie."

Telling myself he was not Pol, not Pol, *not Pol*, I still couldn't stop myself from thinking about a Pol who dealt drugs for a living and thus kept a variety of things from me. Not that I wanted to know, but it still didn't feel nice, as secrets never did.

A Pol who decided what house we lived in without much input from me (as in, *none*). A Pol who also decided what car I would drive, ditto the input. And with this kind of thing, I could go on (and on).

And he was a Pol who had a variety of things on his mind, stressors in his life (seeing as he was a drug dealer, one high up the food chain, but one nonetheless) and he didn't share those concerns with me through anything but his fists.

Apollo was not Pol.

But I'd learned through Pol that I didn't like things kept from me.

I would not want to know Pol's dealings. What I did know, I didn't like. What I did know was another reason to leave him. And he knew that. So he didn't give it to me outright, and in the end he just didn't give me anything but good sex and bad times.

And maybe he didn't because he knew, if it was out in the open, I'd betray him to the police. Or I'd hate him and do it for more reasons other than the fact that he made me keep secrets too. Secrets that I detested. The biggest one being that I lived in fear of him, and every second of every day I had to live a lie and hide that.

But that was moot now.

I understood Apollo was not Pol.

But I wasn't going to start a relationship with a man who held anything back from me.

I leaned deeper into the table and enunciated clearly, "Apollo...what... was...*that*?"

He studied me, he did it for a long time and he did it with conflicted eyes.

Then he made his decision.

And for some reason, his decision at that very second meant everything to me.

Absolutely everything.

Because I knew, if he made the wrong one, the damage would be irrevocable.

"In this country," he began slowly, and when he did, I knew he'd made the right one, so I pulled in a soft, relieved breath. "At times, it is customary, when a man is unattached, usually widowed, for him to take a wife who has been the same. This could, of course, be a natural coupling where they meet, find each other agreeable and wed. Other times, a man will take this wife, a relative not of blood, say, his cousin's widowed bride..."

He hesitated.

I braced and I was glad I did when he carried on.

"Or a relation of his dead wife, in order to provide her a home the likes to which she has become accustomed. It happens mostly only amongst those who are members of a House, and it happens with women who sometimes have children, but also if she is alone, or perhaps a man who has children and thus they have no mother. And it usually happens in order that the female, who is unlikely to be able to provide herself with an income, is able to live amongst those of her own in comfort and with protection."

I let out my breath in a whoosh, having a feeling I knew where this was going and not sure how I felt about it.

"In any case, amongst the Houses where a man intends to take a woman as wife, if that intention is understood and agreed between the parties, that union being inevitable, prior to that she will begin to be addressed as a lady of that House. In this case," he held my eyes, "you being addressed as Lady Ulfr."

Yes, I knew where it was going.

"And who in your House am I marrying?" I asked instantly.

"Me," he replied just as instantly.

I stared at him for long moments.

He let me.

Then I stated, "So you just told that man we're engaged."

"Yes," he confirmed.

Holy cow!

"Are we engaged?" I asked.

"Yes," he answered immediately and decisively.

I sucked in a sharp breath and on the exhale, noted, "I think this is pretty much the definition of moving too fast, Apollo."

Apollo said nothing.

"Did I miss your proposal?" I queried.

"The words weren't uttered," he replied. "But I think your answer was 'please.'"

I blinked and asked, "What?"

He suddenly leaned forward, his hand shooting out and clasping mine.

This was not an affectionate gesture.

It was a claiming one.

And his eyes were burning into mine.

Oh shit.

"When I covered you last night, before I took you, you said 'please.'"

I remembered that. Hell, I'd never forget it.

But seriously?

I felt my eyes get big. "That's a marriage proposal?"

"It'll do for us."

Oh my God!

Maybe he *didn't* keep getting better.

I leaned in too and hissed, "Apollo, that's insane."

"I was unsheathed."

Crap!

"And you took me repeatedly," he went on.

Crap!

I knew what he was saying. He was saying unprotected sex often equals pregnancy. And pregnancy also often equals marriage. Obviously even in this world.

I didn't need to deal with that right then. That was too big for me to deal with. And I decided in that moment I couldn't worry about something when I didn't know if there was anything to worry about. Instead, I would deal with it only when I knew that there was something to deal with.

Now, I needed to deal with the matter at hand.

"Apollo—"

"And I'm having you again tonight."

Here we go. Back to arrogant Apollo.

"*Repeatedly*," he went on.

I felt my heart thump just as my clit pulsed and I tried to pull my hand from his, but his tightened on mine and I failed.

"And the next night and the next. I think you understand me," he stated.

I glared at him.

"And we're traveling together and sleeping in the same room."

"For protection," I snapped.

"Until last night, yes."

"And yesterday, you called me Lady Ulfr to the staff at the inn and that was *before* what happened last night."

"Indeed, as my intention was to take you to wife then too."

Oh my God!

Was this happening?

"This is crazy," I declared.

"No, it isn't," he disagreed.

I leaned deeper and bit out, "It so totally is."

"And you'd be contented with allowing me to bring you to this world, bring you from yours where you lived in fear and on the run, and let you carry forth working as a barmaid?" he asked curtly. "Subsisting from coin to coin. Forcing down food much worse than our sandwiches today because you could afford no better. A woman who understands and appreciates the finest champagne, reduced to that and me forcing it on you?"

"It isn't about champagne," I snapped, his comment hitting way too close to the bone. "And it wouldn't be you forcing it on me. It would be my choice."

"It would be me forcing it on you, Maddie. Taking you from the other world, that was not your choice. That was mine. You have grand ideas of how you would exist on this world, but you have no idea how those who work in inns or pubs or elsewhere survive. I'm sure there is contentment and even happiness. But you're not simply a woman who appreciates the finest champagne. You're a woman who deserves it."

At that unexpected and unbelievably nice compliment, I clamped my mouth shut as I felt my heart seize.

"And my first wife was a physician. She had her life, I had mine, and we successfully managed to have both of those together. Do you not think it's a better idea to be fed, comfortable and safe while you decide how you'd like to spend your time in your new world? And then be the same while you go about doing it?"

My heart burst into action and was beating so fast, it scared the hell out of me, so I focused on that and on his words and didn't answer.

He didn't seem to mind and kept talking.

"You may wish to go from gale to gale, ball to ball, hunt to hunt and wear fine clothes and jewels, and I would not care, glad simply to have you on my arm. Or you may wish to study a profession and then put it to practice, and I would not care, but only if you share your days with me when they are at an end. You may instead wish to bake the best cakes in all of Lunwyn, and I wouldn't care, for I'd get to eat them. Hell, you could desire to learn something of my financial interests and become involved, and I would welcome it."

Totally.

Seriously.

Completely.

Was this guy for real?

His hand tightened in mine. "In other words, I don't care what you do. The only thing I care about is that you're safe and happy while doing it. You've not shared with me, but you know that I know that you've had a life where you were not either. Not in the slightest. I didn't bring you here to give you the same ugliness but in a different way, slaving in a pub to feed yourself. I brought you here to give you," his hand jerked mine, "*better*."

Oh my God.

Suddenly, the vision of him was swimming and this was because my eyes had filled with tears.

His hand gentled around mine and his voice was gentle too when he whispered, "Poppy."

"Now *that*," I started, my voice trembling, "was a marriage proposal."

Apollo made no reply, and I looked away as I grabbed my napkin to dab my eyes, hoping (even though it was doubtful), that no one was watching.

And as I did, Apollo again tugged my hand across the table, and I felt his lips brush my knuckles.

I closed my eyes tight.

He put our hands to the table but gave mine a gentle squeeze.

"Is that a yes, my dove?"

I drew in a calming breath and on its heels another one. With tears under control, if not the beating of my heart, I lifted my eyes to him.

"This is going very fast," I reiterated.

"Yes," he agreed, not letting go of my hand or my gaze.

"It's scary."

"Yes," he agreed again, and I watched in fascination as his beautiful jade eyes turned hard and determined. "And this, my poppy, will be the last thing on this world or any other that you fear."

Oh...my...*God*.

My stomach dropped and I forgot how to breathe.

"Now, is it a yes?" he repeated.

With effort, I pulled myself together and asked, "Can I have some time to think about it?"

"Yes," he answered, and I felt myself relax. "But only if, when that time is up, the answer is yes."

I stared at him.

Then I couldn't help it.

I burst out laughing.

When I was done, he was still holding my hand, but he was doing it smiling at me.

And God, *God*, he was beautiful.

"I'll just say that it's only been a day where things have been cool between us and you're already doing a bang-up job getting in there," I told him.

His eyes changed to something else altogether and he replied, "I don't understand your language, dove, since, last night, I already got *in there*."

My nipples grew hard.

Oh crap.

"Well, in my world," I hurried to explain, "'in there' means..." I faltered then started giggling as I shared, "Well, pretty much what you said it means."

His eyes lit with amusement, and he turned our hands, using his thumb to stroke the skin of the inside of my wrist.

"How about we cease discussing this, I give you the time you desire, and we start that time by enjoying our meal?" he suggested quietly.

"Okay," I answered just as quietly.

His thumb gave my wrist one last stroke (which, by the way, felt unbelievably nice) then he let my hand go.

He picked up his fork.

I did too.

Then I looked at him and called, "Apollo?"

He gave me his gaze, warm with inquiry, one brow lifted.

Yes.

Beautiful.

"Even though you knew I might lose it," I started. "Thank you for telling me anyway." My voice dipped when I shared, "That means a lot, honey."

His regard grew intense on me and I knew he wanted more.

But he didn't ask for more.

He said, "You're welcome, poppy."

He didn't push it and for that I was grateful.

And, just to say, also for that, he got deeper *in there.*

12
HEDGE CLIPPERS

We were walking down the hall toward our room at the lodge, my hand not in the bend of Apollo's arm but held in his, lifted up and pressed close to his chest.

The rest of the "date" had gone well. Really well. No bizarre marriage proposals. No in-depth discussions of birth control. Instead, great food, excellent champagne and the continued discovery that Apollo could be good company.

I was right. He had a great sense of humor. And I knew I was right because I made him laugh often during dinner. I also found I liked doing it. A whole lot. Mostly because I knew he'd struggled with the loss of his wife for a long time, and his rich laughter and quick smiles made me feel like I'd scaled mountains.

In fact, it was actually Apollo who led the conversation to calmer waters, asking about my world, and laughing about such things as reality television shows and treadmills.

"Why on earth would someone run on a machine and not through a meadow...or run at all unless they had to which would not be a positive happenstance?" he'd asked while chuckling.

I'd had no answer because I didn't have one and also because I was laughing too.

He'd also told me a bit more about his world, mostly about the Houses, explaining I was right about Danforth. He was of Apollo's ilk, and he wasn't Apollo's favorite person.

"There is nothing genuine about that man. But then, there are many in the lesser Houses where this is the case. Always scheming to better their positions or attempting to hide their weaknesses."

That didn't make me feel great about socializing with the upper crust, but I'd learned that knowing what you were facing was a lot better than not, so I was grateful to know it.

In other words, the date had gone great. And Apollo had been wonderful.

But now the date was over.

So now my mind was in a battle. The battle I knew was totally irrational of the panic I felt that I was about to get me some and it was highly likely it was going to be good, but that good was not under the influence of magical tea created by a goddess. This was fighting against extreme excitement that I was going to get me some and it was highly likely it was going to be good.

I had, of course, noted in all our discussions of adela tea, Apollo had not explained one of its effects was making you an excellent lover. So, my guess was, if you were crap in bed before adela tea, you were the same but more pronounced with it.

And the opposite was true.

So Apollo was far from crap in bed. *Way* far.

In other words, in my internal battle, the excitement was winning.

My heart started beating faster when Apollo pulled the key from his pocket, unlocked the door, returned the key and was reaching for the doorknob when my hand in his squeezed and I said, "Wait."

He turned into me and looked down at me, brow raised.

Pol couldn't raise one brow and I liked it that Apollo could. It was sexy.

Okay, so pretty much everything about him was sexy.

That was not what I intended to share with him.

I looked to his throat, then his shoulder, trying to find the words.

No, trying to find the courage.

Crap.

"Poppy?"

I looked to his eyes, thought, *Fuck it*, and went for it.

"In my world, after a date," I began and his hand in mine tightened. "The guy...well, he..." I pulled in a deep breath and finished on a whisper, "At her door, he kisses her."

His eyes went lazy and his hand holding mine slid up his chest toward his shoulder as his other hand came out to cup my jaw and he murmured, "I see there may be things in your world that I would like."

A tingle slid up my spine as I watched his head descend. I then decided he shouldn't have to do all the work, so I rolled up to my toes.

His mouth hit mine and his fingers slid back into my hair as he molded our lips, taking his time. Finally, the tip of his tongue touched my lips.

I opened my mouth.

His tongue glided inside.

At the taste of him, a taste I really liked, I melted into him.

When I did, his hand let mine go and his arm wrapped around me tight. I curved my arm around his shoulders, going farther up on my toes as he slanted his head, I tilted mine and the kiss went from sweet and wet to sweet, wet and *wild*.

So, if that kiss was any indication, I was right about him not needing the adela tea to be good at this.

He was good at this.

Very good at it.

Way too soon, he broke the kiss but not the connection of our lips and his voice was rough when he said, "Oh yes, there are things from your world I like."

I knew what he meant, and it was sweet, so I smiled.

He moved away, grabbed my hand, threw open the door and pulled me inside.

He slammed it shut behind us, turned the lock, all of this with his hand still in mine which was good. It was good because, the minute the door was locked, he gave my arm a firm tug. I fell toward him, colliding with his body seeing as it was moving my way, and both my arms went around his shoulders as both his arms came around me. He started walking me backward and his head began to dip toward mine again.

My eyes were closing, my head tipping back, ready for it, wanting it, *all* of it, when suddenly he stopped us, and his head jerked up.

I was about to ask him why he'd stopped when I was unexpectedly flung to the side. I gave a small, surprised cry, my thigh hit a chair, I tumbled into a table, and as I reeled, I saw Apollo bend to his boot.

"Run, Maddie, *now*!" he roared.

I didn't run.

This was because my blood had turned to ice seeing as not one, not two, but *three* men all wielding freaking *swords* were flooding into the small sitting room of our suite.

As I noted, they had swords and there were three of them. But although Apollo had produced a knife, he had no sword and there was just one of him.

And they weren't delaying in attacking.

Shit!

What the fuck?

I watched as, with some fancy footwork, a lot of ducking and lunging, and his small blade crashing against their long ones, Apollo was holding his own. But even as he executed a ducking lunge and pulled another knife out of his other boot, I knew he couldn't hold his own for long.

No one could.

There were three of them!

With swords!

It hit my brain I couldn't run, because if I did, I'd be leaving him and there was no doubt in my mind that if I left him, I'd never see him again. Or I wouldn't see him when he was breathing.

I liked him breathing.

I just liked *him*.

And we'd just had a great first date. Sure, it started out rocky, but it ended up with that kiss, and I'd be damned if he was going to die as a finale.

Thus, I instantly prioritized and ran past the fray to the bedroom. I got to his saber that was resting against his trunk, grabbed it and extracted it from its scabbard on the dash back as I heard the battle clash on.

I will note this was hard because that mother was freaking *heavy*, but I still managed it.

I was thinking, in the movies, if you tossed a sword to someone who knew how to use it, they could catch it by the handle and carry on fighting without delay.

When Apollo had taken on Pol, he demonstrated he could use a sword.

I just hoped he was really good at it.

I hit the outer room and was thrilled beyond anything he was still holding his own.

But his attention was kind of taken.

Crap.

There was nothing for it.

I had to create an opening.

I grabbed the handle of the saber in both hands, shifted it so the flat was what sang through the air and did what Apollo did with Pol.

I smacked one of the bad guys upside the head with it.

Hard.

He staggered to the side.

Me entering the fray caused a diversion that Apollo took advantage of because it surprised the men, but not him.

He didn't miss a beat, shoved one of his knives in his belt, held a hand toward me and shouted, "Saber!"

God, I hoped he was as good as those guys in the movies.

I tossed it to him point up.

He caught it by the handle in one hand, whirled, and with a mid-body slice, gutted one of the bad dudes.

Holy crap!

When the guy's innards became outtards, bile shot up my throat and I staggered back.

But Apollo barked, "Maddie, *bloody go*!"

The one Apollo sliced was down on his back and I was thinking it was a good guess he was continuing the swordfight on some celestial plain. However, the one I'd conked was reentering the action and Apollo again had his hands full.

Two against one. Still no fair.

I focused and not on my wave of nausea. Instead, on a lamp on a table close by. I grabbed it and lifted it over my head. Shuffling this way and that around the battle, I tried to get my opening to smash it on one of the bad dudes' heads.

"*Maddie, what did I say?*" Apollo thundered, still clashing steel.

I ignored him because there it was.

My shot.

Crash!

I landed the glass lantern hard on the guy's head and he went down instantly, out like a light.

I turned to Apollo just in time to watch him make light work of the last one. That was, he disarmed him of his sword with a whirling flourish that actually pulled the sword from the guy's hand but kept control of it with the tip of his saber whereupon Apollo could twirl it aside, far out of reach.

Oh yeah. He was good at this sword shit.

Alas, as this was happening, Apollo was momentarily engaged in doing it, so the guy went for the knife on his belt.

Before I could cry out a warning, Apollo came back and carved his saber through the side of the guy's neck.

A sickening spray of blood spurted.

I gasped and took a step back.

The guy lifted a hand to his neck and then he fell down on his knees right before he crashed to his front.

Okay, well.

I was thinking he, too, was a goner.

Holy cow.

I stared at the bodies and blood littering our little sitting room and I did this for a millisecond before Apollo thundered, "When I tell you to run, you bloody *do what I say*!"

I looked to him to see his eyes were burning and not in a good way. Not that there was anyone left to talk to that wasn't dead or unconscious, but still, those burning eyes were locked on me.

"I—" I started.

He began to move my way and cut me off.

"Did it occur to you that if you'd run, you could have called for assistance?"

He stopped in front of me so close my head was tipped all the way back to keep hold of his gaze.

And seriously, our date—which included its shaky start, sure, but it also included great champagne, delicious food, and Apollo and I eventually chatting and laughing, another fab horse ride back with Apollo, a brilliant kiss and the promise of an orgasm (or more than one since he'd said we'd be doing it *repeatedly*)—but it ended in death and destruction and him shouting at me and being sarcastic, I don't think anyone would blame me that his words pissed me off.

"Did it occur to you that, seeing as I didn't run, *I* was your assistance?" I shot back.

His mouth clamped shut and a muscle ticked up his jaw and into his cheek.

I took that as "no." I also decided to take it as, "thank you for helping me defeat the bad guys," when he jerked away from me and stormed into the bedroom.

I decided the bedroom was a much better place to be than amongst the grisly mess in the sitting room, so I followed him.

When I did, I saw he was tugging on a velvet cord with a thick tassel at the end and he didn't do it once. I counted eleven times before he scowled at me and stormed back into the sitting room.

I really didn't want to go back there, but after what happened, I also really didn't want to be far away from Apollo and his sword. Therefore, I followed him back to see him bent over one of the guys, the unconscious one, his fist in the guy's hair holding his head up.

"Unconscious," he clipped. "Useless," he ground out as he threw the guy's head back and it thumped against the floor.

I put a hand to my belly, the gruesome tableau hitting me full on as Apollo stormed to one of the two dead bodies. He bent and started to go through the man's pockets.

"What are you doing?" I asked, deciding on focusing on him so I didn't focus on anything that might make me hurl.

His gaze cut to me and he didn't answer my question.

No.

Instead, he declared, "Four men in this room. Four weapons. And you."

"Apollo—"

"You could have been hurt."

Okay, I had to admit, it was sweet he was worried about me.

So I decided against throwing more attitude and whispered, "I wasn't."

"You could have been killed," he bit out, his handsome face still suffused with rage.

I swallowed because, after sitting room swordfights, it hit ridiculously late that that was what was causing his reaction.

"I wasn't, baby," I said gently.

He pierced me with a glower then went back to searching the man's pockets, muttering grouchily to himself, "She seduces me with this word. She also thinks she can use it to get away with madness."

It was then I decided quiet was in order, so I gave him that.

He stopped searching the one dead body and was moving to the other when a knock came at the door.

He went there, unlocked it, yanked it open, and I got one look at the maid outside, who got one look into the room and her face paled in a way I feared she'd pass out.

Luckily, Apollo started issuing orders so her attention shot to him.

"Send someone for the constable immediately. And send a man to the room with ropes. One of them is still alive and I want him bound. And find these men's horses. If they have possessions, I want them in this room without delay."

She visibly gulped, nodded and ran away.

I didn't blame her.

Apollo slammed the door and moved to the other body. I kept my silence as he searched his pockets then ran his hands along the inside of his cloak.

I watched his body suddenly still and then he straightened to his feet, his head bent, his fingers engaged with unfolding a piece of paper.

"What is it?" I asked.

"Bloody code," he bit out, sounding frustrated.

"Can I see it?" I queried.

His gaze sliced to me. "You can battle foes *and* decipher code?" he asked wryly.

I decided to let that slide and made a mental note that Apollo got grumpy after a swordfight.

"Can I just see it, honey?" I requested softly.

He gave me an annoyed look, but he finally stormed to me, his cape wafting out behind him, and we'll just say, grumpy Apollo after a swordfight was still hot.

When he got to me, he didn't hand me the note. He moved to my side and held it up so we could both look.

I stared down at the paper. It said:

C, E AT K – TR, BR, L, LE, C, DA, Z, FE, FAH, TE
U, I AT TL, V – BE, GR, ST

YEP. Code.

Crap.

I was handy with word puzzles, what with having a drug dealer husband, zero friends or family because my husband was a drug dealer and no one liked to hang with drug dealers (or their wives), no job because my drug dealer husband thought it reflected poorly on his ability to give me a good life through dealing drugs, so I had to find some way to spend my time, and I wasn't a fan of soap operas.

But this wasn't like a crossword, hangman, find-a-word or any of the puzzles I was used to solving.

Still, I kept staring at it, screwing up my eyes and trying to make the letters speak to me.

I continued to do so when a knock came at the door, Apollo grunted, "Come!" and I heard the door open. Apollo then commanded, "This one. Tie him up. Has the constable been called?"

"Yes, sir, and we're searching for the horses," a man's voice replied.

"Good," Apollo muttered, but he sounded distracted, and I knew the note had his attention again.

But as all this went on, somehow, some of the letters seemed to make sense to me, but mostly because they couldn't be a coincidence.

"I think..." I began but trailed off.

"What?" Apollo asked.

"I think..." I repeated but said no more.

"Madeleine, *what*?" Apollo clipped, impatient.

"I, well, could this mean...?" I lifted a hand to point at the note, the tip of my finger sliding under the bottom line. "Ulfr, Ilsa at Treeburn Lodge, Vasterhague. And then the three other groups of letters. I don't know..." I looked at the men on the floor then up at Apollo. "Maybe initials of first or last names of our attackers?"

He held my gaze, his jaw hard, then his focus went back to the note.

Mine did too and it did this with me muttering, "But the top line. I don't—"

I stopped talking abruptly and it felt like a cold hand squeezed my heart when it jumped out at me.

I knew Apollo got it at the same time because he barked, "Leave him! Saddle our horses, *now*!"

"Sir?" the employee who was tying up the now groaning man on the floor asked.

"Horses. Immediately," Apollo commanded, and when the man didn't move, he bellowed, "*Now!*"

The man jumped up and ran from the room.

My heart was tripping over itself as Apollo grabbed my hand and yanked me into the bedroom.

"But...I don't have a saddle," I stupidly told his back.

He bent to pick up his scabbard from where I dropped it on the floor and let me go to buckle it on, stating, "It's in the back of the sleigh."

Oh.

Well then.

Still.

I felt frustration build, all of it concentrating in my neck, making it tight because, seriously, this world was awesome, but there were times when cellphones would come in handy.

Like, big time, *now*.

"You need to go without me," I whispered.

"I'll not leave you unprotected," he said, moving to his trunk and throwing it open.

That was very sweet. But it also wasn't very smart.

"Honey, you'll make better time if—"

He turned to me and the expression on his face made me shut up.

"Fast, Madeleine, dress warm. *Very* warm."

I stared into his eyes a brief moment before I nodded and dashed to my trunks.

And this was because, if I was right about the bottom line, then the top one meant *Christophe, Élan at Karsvall.*

And ten men were going.

I got my hat, my gloves and wasted precious time I didn't know I'd be glad for later toeing off my boots in order to exchange my thin, eveningwear wool tights for thicker, warmer wool tights. I pulled my boots back on and barely straightened when Apollo had my hand, and he was dragging me to the door.

But he halted at the man on the floor who had his back resting against a heavy chest, his hands tied to the foot of it. He was also now groggy but conscious.

Apollo let me go to kneel beside him.

"Did they send ten men for my children?" he demanded to know.

The bad guy blinked at him.

Then he smiled.

It wasn't verbal. But it was an answer.

My heart thumped hard, and it hurt.

I held my breath as Apollo straightened, unsheathed his sword, flipped it so the blade was held in his gloved hand, and he whacked the guy across his cheek with the handle.

Blood flew from his mouth as his head lolled on his neck.

Out again.

I didn't get a chance to take in this latest ghastliness.

Apollo had my hand.

And we were away.

~

We rode hard the rest of the night and all the next day.

Five times, we stopped to exchange horses. With Apollo's commanding presence and heavy bag of coins, this took us less than five minutes each time. He only spent another thirty seconds the first change of horses to order Torment and Anguish sent to Karsvall.

And he asked only twice when we stopped if I needed food.

Both times, I shook my head. Both times he got that answer, Apollo's eyes held relief. And both times, without further delay, we were again off. He didn't waste time asking after that. He knew my answer.

I was not hungry.

I was also not tired.

I was terrified.

So terrified, my mind was gripped with it, so the long ride, the cold, the landscape, the villages flashing by, the horse straining under me, the pounding of my bones, none of it penetrated.

None of it.

Apollo had his guys at his house, and I'd seen Laures in action in the games, so I knew they knew what they were doing.

But those three men laid in wait for us. If the ones that were sent for Christophe and Élan were good at being sneaky...

I didn't let my mind go there. It kept *trying* to go there but I kept shutting it down. We would deal with what we found when we found it.

We just needed to get there to find whatever there was to find.

Thus, I bent over my horse and did my best to keep her at Apollo's heels, thanking God Hans was really good at teaching me how to ride and I'd had four months' practice.

I knew Apollo was terrified too. But hot-guy-badass-from-another-world terror manifested itself through fury. The kind of fury that wafted off him in a way that it seemed even the breeze was too scared of him to show up.

I kept on his heels as dusk of the next day moved into a dark evening and we finally galloped through the village where I'd spent the night at The Swan.

The village outside Karsvall.

Ten minutes later, we galloped up a pine-edged lane and I saw it.

Illumination, and it wasn't the moon.

We came out into a clearing and Apollo didn't slow so I didn't either. But I did see that torches and barrels of fire were all around, lighting the space. There were lots of horses. Lots of sleighs. Lots of men. Also a big house I didn't take in but I did take in the fact that a light was burning in every window.

This was not a good sign.

Apollo reined in and I did the same beside him at the front door.

And I saw that there were bodies lined up in the blood-spattered snow.

My eyes frantically slid over them, and although a couple of them were face down, none of them were faces I knew.

I had no time to feel this relief. Suddenly I was yanked from my saddle.

Apollo had his hands on my waist and he was tugging me down. When he had me on my feet, he grabbed my hand and dragged me to the house, barking, "My children?"

"They're fine, Lo." I heard Achilles say. "They're in Élan's room—"

He said no more as Apollo pushed through him and kept dragging me behind him. I had half a mind to at least aim a relieved smile at Achilles as Apollo pulled us by, but I had to keep up and watch my footing, so I had no shot.

It was a good plan because, in no time at all, I was going up stairs.

Then down a hall.

Then I was being hauled into a bright room, and with his hand firm in mine jerking me into his side, I came to a halt, lifted my eyes and caught sight of the children in the bed.

My systems shut down instantly.

All I could do was see.

A boy, I knew he was eight, almost nine. A girl I knew who was six.

They were all Apollo, the girl a female version, a very cute, very pretty female version, but they both were all him. No red hair. No brown eyes. No freckles.

Dark thick hair. Olive-toned skin.

Jade eyes.

They were beautiful.

Beautiful.

My heart started bleeding.

The boy was in bed with the girl, holding her close, and she was trembling so badly, she shook her brother, *and* I could see the tassels on the canopy on her bed shaking as well.

She was petrified, her face saturated with it.

There was no blood. No visible injuries.

But one of them had gotten to her.

I felt this realization hit Apollo as his rage permeated the room.

The girl whispered a trembling, "Papa."

At the sound of her little scared voice, it happened.

I was suddenly on fire. Every inch of my skin blistering. My eyes burning. My brain boiling.

Without a thought, not even knowing what I intended to do, I tore my hand from Apollo's and raced out of the room, down the hall, the stairs and out the opened front door, my heavy cloak billowing behind me.

I stopped in the snow, my cloak flying forward to wrap around me, and I counted.

Eight bodies.

I turned instantly to the man standing closest to me.

Gaston.

I stomped to him, wrapped my fist in his sweater and snapped, "Where are the other two?"

"Maddie—"

I beat his sweater into his chest, got up on my toes and screeched, "*Where are the other two?*"

His fingers began to curl on my biceps, and he started, "Maybe we should—"

I pulled from him, moved blindly away and saw it.

Tracks and drag marks in the snow leading along the front of the house and around the corner.

I sprinted that way, following the tracks. I raced down the side of the house, into the back garden, past a pretty gazebo, a large greenhouse and into the forest beyond where I saw two torches lighting the outside of a small outbuilding.

Without hesitation, I ran to it and stormed in.

There was a man hanging by his hands from a hook. He was shirtless and bleeding profusely from a variety of wounds as well as a serious pummeling he took to his face.

Hans and Remi were standing close to him.

There was another man, also shirtless and bleeding, tied to a chair in the center of the space.

Derrik was standing behind him.

Laures was working him.

When I arrived, all the men looked to me in surprise and they kept their focus on me when I stomped straight to the man in the chair, shoving past Laures and I bent, getting right in his face.

"*What did you do to her?*" I shrieked.

A hand came to rest on my shoulder, and I heard Remi whisper, "Maddie."

I shrugged it off and wrapped my gloved hand under the man's jaw and shoved it back.

He grunted but I dropped my face back to his and screamed, "*She's just a little girl!*" I got closer, my fingers curling deep into his flesh. "You monster! What did you do to her?"

"Mad—" Remi tried again but I whirled and shot past him.

My hand darting out, I nabbed the knife on Laures's belt.

"Bloody hell." I heard Hans mutter but I didn't hesitate.

No, I didn't.

I didn't hesitate *or* think.

I was fucking *focused.*

I turned back to the man in the chair, held the point of the knife to the hinge of his jaw and demanded, "Who sent you?"

The man's eyes held mine and he said nothing.

I pressed the tip into his flesh, he pushed back against the chair, and I screeched, "*Who sent you?*"

He again said nothing.

Controlled by emotion, still burning inside and out, I took the knife from his jaw and sunk it violently into the flesh of his shoulder.

He let out a pained grunt that didn't register on me.

I just pulled the knife out to three simultaneous masculine "*bloody hells*" and one "*by the gods*" and returned it to his jaw.

"*Who sent you?*"

Suddenly I wasn't in his face anymore, neither did I have the knife.

I was, instead, pressed back deep into Apollo's body with his arm around my belly.

And then, with Apollo, we leaned forward as he flashed the knife out.

And that was when I watched the gaping, red gash across the man's throat slither open, blood pouring down his chest. He sucked in a breath, got zero air, and an instant later, found his death with surprise in his eyes.

I had no reaction to this. I also had no time to have a reaction.

Without hesitation, Apollo turned both of us and we were across the room like a shot. He held me to his front as he held the knife to the man hanging on the hook's throat.

"Now you know I will not waver," he growled. "Who sent you?"

The man was staring with big eyes at the freshly dead man in the chair, but when Apollo pressed the knife to his throat, his attention shot to him.

And I watched him grow cold.

"The queen is just," he announced bizarrely.

"The queen is not here," Apollo returned.

"She'll not be best pleased, you dispense justice in your gardener's shack," he stated, and I finally looked around.

Yep. We were in a gardener's shack.

I turned my head, tipped it back and aimed my eyes at Apollo's stony face. "Honey, I bet I can make him to talk with those hedge clippers." I threw a hand toward the man's crotch. "He won't be needing *that* in prison."

Apollo spared me a glance as I heard Laures chuckle but just as quickly as he looked at me, he looked back to the man.

"Information or I get my lady some hedge clippers," he shared.

The man's eyes grew round for a half a second, before he covered it and declared, "I demand a trial."

"You'll not sit in prison, doling out information for leniency," Apollo shot back. "You talk here, or you die here."

Nice. That was a good line.

"You're already to answer to Queen Aurora for coldblooded murder," the man retorted, tipping his head toward the man in the chair.

"The queen is just," Apollo whispered. "But she also lost her husband to the schemes of traitors."

The man blanched.

Goodie.

Now we were getting somewhere.

Apollo moved back to target. "Who sent you?"

The man said nothing.

"Again, who sent you?" Apollo repeated.

The man remained silent.

I watched the staring contest from close up.

It was scary. It was also frustrating.

"For God's sake, would someone just get me the hedge clippers?" I snapped.

Apollo again looked down at me. A second later, he pulled me away from the man but pushed me gently to the side and I found myself not held by him, but I looked up, by Achilles.

"Take her to the dower house," he ordered. "Stay with her."

"But—" I started as Achilles rounded my waist with an arm and started pulling me away.

Apollo's eyes sliced to me.

"Dove," he said softly. "Go."

I glared at him. Then I glared at the man on the hook.

I transferred my glare back to Apollo and blew out on a sigh, "Oh, all right."

Apollo's eyes moved over my face, but I lost sight of him when Achilles turned me to the door.

I was out the door, but it wasn't yet closed behind me when I heard him say, "Hans, hand me those clippers."

The door banged shut.

I smiled.

13
LIONESS

In my crazy dream that was tinted blood red, I heard Apollo order from far away a growling, “Leave us. Now.”

My dream drifted to some ruins around a pool filled with blood when I felt my cloak that I’d wrapped around me to keep warm after Achilles finally got me to lay down thrown off.

I blinked.

My skirts were tossed up.

I blinked again, twice, fast.

And I came awake when my tights were torn down my legs.

My heart instantly racing, I shifted up hurriedly, pushing up the bed but got only so far when two strong hands wrapped around my ankles, dragged me back down and tugged them apart.

I gasped when a man covered me.

Through the firelight casting a weak glow through the room, I saw Apollo’s face.

I should have relaxed seeing as it was him, but the look on his face made my entire body go wired.

His hand drove into my hair, fisting as he rumbled, “You are a lioness.”

Hunh?

“What? What’s going on? Are you—?”

He cut me off. “Not even of your blood, not even a word exchanged, barely a glance, for them, you sank a blade into a man’s flesh.”

I thought I knew what he was talking about, so I said, “Well, yeah. I did. But why are you—?”

His mouth came to mine and I shut up because I could see his eyes were afire. They were searing into me and they were doing it in a particular way.

I knew that way. It was slightly different, not charged by adela tea.

But it was also the same.

His next words proved me right.

"You're going to take me now, Maddie, and warning, my dove, I'll not be gentle."

Yes, his eyes were burning in a particular way.

My stomach dropped.

"Apollo," I breathed, then he was gone.

But he didn't go far.

My skirts were thrown back up, my panties torn down my legs and his mouth was there.

Holy cow.

At his touch, more precisely how really good it was, my back arched off the bed and my heels dug into the mattress, but not for long. He grasped me behind the knees and threw my legs over his shoulders. After he accomplished that, he scooped my ass in both of his hands, brought it up, pressing me deeper into his mouth and he fed.

And boy, *how* he fed.

My hands went to his head, fingers sliding into his thick hair. My heels dug into his back. My neck arched and my lips parted, pants whispering out as Apollo wasted absolutely no time taking me there.

And then I was there, teetering over the edge, my orgasm within reach, it was going to be good, and I whispered, "Baby."

Then his mouth was gone.

Before I could even whimper, I was rolled to my stomach, my hips yanked up roughly and he pounded inside, filling me.

"Fuck yes," I breathed, my fingers curling into the covers.

"Ride my cock, Maddie, take it yourself," he ordered, and then I felt the slap of his hand sharp on my outer thigh.

I jumped even as heat radiated from the sting to right between my legs and I did what he ordered, rearing back, fucking myself on his cock.

Another smack to the thigh, another jump, more sting, more fire burning to the heart of me and, "Harder, poppy."

Oh God.

This was good.

I'd never been spanked and I wanted more.

I moved faster, took him harder, gasping and straining against him.

"Am I in there?" he growled.

Oh yes. Fuck yes. He was in there.

"Yes," I whispered.

His hands spanned my hips. His fingers digging in, he stopped my motion and slammed in himself, staying deep and grinding.

"Am I in there, Madeleine?"

"Yes," I gasped.

He started driving fast and deep and I got another smack on my thigh with, "Remove your gown. I want to see your skin."

As he fucked me from behind, I did my best to make short work of sliding out of the dress I'd worn on our first date, and an entire twenty-four hours (and more) besides. This left me in nothing but my black bustier, my breasts spilling out the cups with his violent movements, my nipples skimming the covers, and it started to move over me again.

"This arse, *gods*, your beautiful arse," Apollo groaned, running his hand over the cheek of my ass even as he continued to thrust inside me.

And I felt it. My climax was right there.

I reached for it.

He pulled out.

God!

"No!" I cried.

His hands came to my ribs. He yanked me up to kneeling in front of him and one hand went directly to my breast, cupping it, as the other one went between my legs.

"Not without me, dove," he growled in my ear.

"Hurry," I begged.

His finger hit the target as he rubbed his cock against my ass.

My head fell back into his shoulder.

Nice.

"You're magnificent," he groaned.

"Tha-thank you," I whimpered, pressing into his hand between my legs at the same time tipping my ass to push against his cock.

His finger and thumb found my nipple, rolled then pulled.

My entire body jerked, and I moaned, "Baby."

I got another roll of my nipple and a demanded, "Again."

"*Baby*," I breathed.

He buried his face in my neck. "*Gods*," he groaned before his teeth sank into my flesh.

God. *God.*

Amazing.

Then his teeth were gone. I was turned, pushed back to the bed and his hands were behind my knees. He pressed them high at the same time pulling them wide. His hands left my knees and went to my hips. He was sitting back on his calves and he yanked me up his thighs, the sensitive skin of my ass gliding against the rough hairs on his thighs, making me do a full-body quiver.

One of his hands left my hip and went to his cock. He guided the tip inside, his hand returned to my hip, and he hauled me up, filling me.

There it was.

"Yes, baby," I moaned.

His eyes locked to mine, he used me to fuck himself then stayed buried as he fell forward, his thighs going out from under me, his hands going to the bed beside me, arms straight, and he held himself over me as he drilled inside.

I lifted my hands to his chest, feverishly gliding them across the warm, hard wall and told him, "You're magnificent too."

"Keep your knees high for me, legs wide, poppy," he grunted, powering in, and I realized I was closing them in on him.

I stopped doing that, spread for him, exposed to him. It was wild, it was beautiful, it was hot, and I fucking *loved* it.

So much, I was nearly there.

"I'm close," I gasped. "Are you with me?"

He stopped thrusting, starting grinding and demanded, "Look at me."

I did, begging, "Apollo."

He dropped his body to mine, his eyes boring into mine, his hand going between us, his thumb hitting the target, and he pulled out, driving back in, groaning, "I'm bloody with you."

Then we both came.

His sounded really freaking good.

Mine was a whole lot better.

I knew this because I felt his hips pound into mine through his. But I was still gloriously riding my climax when he drove in and stayed planted and his nose was nuzzling the skin behind my ear by the time I started coming down.

He felt it and I knew that when he stopped nuzzling and his teeth nipped my earlobe before he said in my ear, "Next time I'll go slow and gentle."

I almost smiled.

I didn't.

When he'd lowered himself to me, he'd trapped my hands between us. I pushed them up his chest, his neck, and framed his face, lifting it and guiding it so I could catch his eyes.

"Are the children okay?"

His features softened to tender, and if that look was good normally (and it wasn't good, it was *good*), with him inside me, his face close, and after a fabulous orgasm, it was off-the-charts good.

He lifted a hand to cup my cheek, his thumb moving out to touch between my brows, gliding down over my nose to my lips, his gaze watching the trail of his thumb, that tender look not moving from his face.

That was sweet, *very* sweet. And I liked it. A whole lot.

But he didn't answer my question.

"Apollo," I called.

His eyes came to mine. "Élan has much exuberance for life, but she also has a sensitive soul," he whispered. "She merely heard the men battling and took fright. She saw none of it and was never in any danger. Neither of them were."

"Oh," I mumbled, suddenly feeling stupid. I was also thinking maybe he thought it less stupid and maybe a little scary-crazy seeing as I stabbed a man and threatened another's manhood with hedge clippers, all for nothing. "Well, then. Perhaps I overreacted."

His body started to shake with laughter, but abruptly it stopped and he closed his eyes, dropped his forehead to mine and slid his nose alongside mine.

Right. Maybe he didn't think I was scary-crazy.

I slid my hands down to his neck and he lifted his head half an inch.

"Tell me about the children you lost, poppy," he whispered.

That was a bolt out of the blue, a sneak attack, and my fingers flexed spasmodically in his flesh.

"Apollo—"

He pressed his body into mine and urged gently, "Tell me, dove."

I licked my lips.

He waited.

My teeth worried my lower lip.

He didn't move.

Shit.

Okay.

I looked deep into his eyes and saw he was not going anywhere until he had his answers.

Shit.

Okay.

Not that I wanted him to go anywhere, but we couldn't have our staring contest forever so, haltingly, I shared, "Uh...I lost my son when I was still pregnant. Pol got pissed for some reason and started to—"

"Speak no more," he growled, and I shut up as his anger saturated the room.

I started worrying my lip again.

He got a lock on it, but his voice was rough when he prompted, "And your daughter?"

"Miscarriage at six months," I whispered.

He closed his eyes and dropped his forehead to mine again.

It was my turn to wait.

He didn't make me wait long.

He lifted his head, gently slid out and rolled off me. I rolled to the side and curled up as he yanked the covers out from under me and tossed them over.

After that, naked, he walked to the fire, threw some logs on and came back to me.

He got under the covers and gathered me in his arms, holding me close, face to face with us on our sides, his hand moving up my spine to start sifting through my hair.

I drew in a deep breath and let it out, forcing myself to relax.

He spoke and he did it quietly.

"You're in the dower house. It's lovely, welcoming and warm. You'll like it. It's also, as you know, close to the main house. You're here so that you can control when you see the children rather than running into them in hallways or hiding away in an effort to avoid them."

Okay, I had to admit, I really liked that in the throes of all that was happening, he'd not only thought to give me that, he'd also given it to me.

He went on, "I've sent missives to Vasterhague for the return of our sleigh and belongings as well as Bellebryn to explain my delay and the information we gleaned from the perpetrator."

I tipped my head back to look at him. "You got something from him?"

He dipped his chin down to look at me. "Yes."

He said no more.

"Are you going to share what that was?" I asked.

"On the morrow," he answered.

I opened my mouth and he moved his hand from my hair to press his fingers against my lips.

"On the morrow, dove."

I stared into his eyes, and this time saw I would not get anything until "the morrow."

So I shut my mouth.

He removed his fingers from my lips and resumed gliding them through my hair as he kept talking.

"As my children have become acutely aware of the dangers lurking, I will obviously wish to spend time with them in order to assuage their fears as well as assess when this is accomplished."

"Of course."

"I also wish for you to meet them so you can spend time with them as well."

I didn't reply to that, but my body did. It got tight.

His hand in my hair moved to become a thumb and side of his finger at my chin and he dipped his face close.

"You will love them. They will love you," he whispered, and my breath caught at these words. "I know this because you did not even know them, only knew they'd been frightened, and you moved immediately to avenge them. It may be awkward and even difficult for you at first, but if you would do what you did this night without even knowing them, what could build if you did?"

He didn't give me the chance to answer, he answered himself.

"Something of great beauty. I am eager for you to give my children that, but, my poppy," he got closer, "I'm just as eager for you to have it."

God, that was beautiful.

I stared into his eyes, then, in order to hold it together as I felt it slipping apart, I slapped his arm.

"Don't make me cry," I snapped. "I've had a couple of really bad days."

He grinned, dipped even closer and touched his mouth to mine.

After he pulled back, he declared, "I will, of course, be spending my nights here. In this bed. With you."

I rolled my eyes.

His danced with humor and he carried on.

"And as I sense you'll require time before you spend some with Christophe and Élan, and I also want to spend time with you, and because I don't want the children around when it's done, the plans that need to be made after the information we learned this night will be done here. So you will be hosting my men."

That didn't sound bad. In fact, I missed the guys, so it sounded awesome.

"Okeydokey," I agreed and that got me a smile.

His arms went around me, he pulled me closer, and I snuggled into his heat.

After a long ride, me going temporarily insane and Apollo doing...whatever it was he did that night, the hard part was done. The good part was coming. That being sleep, of which, since it was still dark outside, it took a while for Achilles to calm me down (he used booze—it was a good choice) and talk me into lying down, I was guessing I didn't have much of it. Therefore, I was looking forward to it.

My eyes were especially, and I knew this because they were drooping.

"You rode hard at my heels, not eating, not sleeping, not speaking, at my side the whole way to get me back to my children," he whispered.

I didn't say anything.

He did.

He cuddled me even closer, kissed the top of my head and kept whispering when he said, "Thank you, my dove."

My answer was to press my cheek into his chest.

He fell silent.

I was warm and cozy under the covers, wrapped up in him, having had a really great orgasm, so my eyelids started drooping again.

"You liked our play."

This was Apollo, and my eyes stopped drooping mostly because I didn't know what he was talking about.

This time, I spoke.

"Sorry?"

His arms tightened. "Our play, Maddie, was rough. Very much so. And you liked it. Also very much so."

He could say that again.

But how embarrassing was this?

"Well...uh...the adela tea—"

"Yes, I sense this opened even more doors for us than I earlier imagined."

I tipped my head back to look at him again.

"Sorry?"

"You took my cock yourself. And I could feel your excitement grow when you were spanked. Further, you kept yourself spread for me at my command," he stopped. I was certain I blushed. His eyes narrowed slightly, and he went on almost musingly, "In fact, you did everything I commanded."

Oh boy.

"Apollo—"

"And your climax was very long."

Yes. I was blushing.

"Ap—"

He continued while his hand drifted up my back to cup my head and press my face in his throat. "We will explore this."

Oh boy!

"Deeply," he decreed.

Oh my.

He pulled me even closer and tangled his heavy legs with mine, murmuring, "I will enjoy taking you on your knees, seeing your arse red from my hand."

God.

I was no longer blushing, but I *was* exhausted, mortified, and still he was totally turning me on.

"Now we sleep," he announced.

Thank God.

I burrowed in closer and set about faking falling asleep fast so he couldn't do or say anything more to freak me out.

This mission failed.

And it did when he whispered, his voice gruff, on another squeeze of his arms, this one fierce, "You are a lioness."

I closed my eyes tight and said nothing.

He did.

"This pleases me."

I pressed closer and sighed.

Oh boy.

14

HEART TOO SOFT FOR A SOLDIER

Apollo sat on the side of the bed, shifted the weight of Maddie's auburn mane from her neck and curled his hand there.

He bent close and urged gently, "Wake, Madeleine."

She didn't, until he carefully pressed his fingers into her neck. Then her eyes slowly fluttered open and she turned her head on the pillow, focusing sleepily on him.

"Hey," she murmured.

He felt his gut tighten.

How could a single syllable be so sweet?

"You do not need to rouse," he whispered. "I just wished to inform you that I'm away to breakfast with my children."

"Okay, honey," she replied.

He'd heard this endearment used by the other women of her world with their men. It never occurred to him he would one day have it.

And if it did, he could not have known how much he would like it.

"I'll likely be busy throughout the day, but I'll take dinner with you," he told her.

"All right," she agreed drowsily.

"Go back to sleep, dove," he finished.

"Right, baby," she murmured.

And this endearment, he had no idea why, he felt in his cock. Every time. Even when she gave it to him while he was searching a dead man's pockets.

On this thought, his whole body stilled when she turned her head and touched her lips to the inside of his wrist, sweet, light, loving.

He had not recovered from her brief touch before she turned her face away and nuzzled into the pillows, mumbling, "Later."

He didn't move even as he sensed her slipping back to sleep. Instead, he sat there, staring at her, wondering what could move a man to strike her.

Cow her.

Make her live in fear.

Make her endure a life running.

Hurt her in any way.

Ever.

He could not allow himself to think of the other him raising his hand and killing the Christophe of that world while he grew inside his Madeleine.

He would think about that later when he next saw Valentine. And then he would give her another Sjofn diamond, or a chest of them, to see to doing what needed to be done to the Apollo of the other world.

That was not for now.

For now, there was much to be done.

With reluctance, for he would much prefer to remove his clothes and return to her warm softness in the bed, he instead left her and the house. He went to the dower house's small four-stall stable and saddled the horse he'd ridden there. He mounted the gelding and headed home.

The short ride to the main house of Karsvall should have been taken up with his thoughts of the many things he needed to do. And if not those, then of his children.

But they were not.

They were taken with Madeleine.

His Madeleine who rushed to avenge his children. His Madeleine whose shrieks of fury he heard as he ran to the gardener's shed the night before. His Madeleine who he saw sink a blade in a man and heard threaten another, all in defense of his children.

His Madeleine who reared into his cock, whimpered and moaned as she did as he bid, climaxing so strongly, her sex convulsed around his shaft, milking him and prolonging his climax in a way he'd never experienced.

A way he liked very much.

Keeping the horse at a sedate walk, his thoughts turned troubled as they moved to Ilsa.

His wife had not been adventurous during play. He did not mind, her appetites were strong and healthy, regardless that they were conservative. She had aroused him greatly and sated him almost nightly throughout their marriage.

However, it was not lost on him that there was often more that he wanted, desires he introduced to his marriage bed that were not spurned, but they were gently denied.

He had more than once considered suggesting adela tea to Ilsa when she was alive. In the end it was only time, and the fact that he'd run out of it that disallowed the discussion.

With only two sessions, Madeleine had gone further with him than the years he'd had with Ilsa.

The first time—when she'd taken his shaft so deep, he could feel the tip graze the back of her throat and when she'd taken his thumb in her arse, moaning and bucking into it powerfully —he could attribute to the adela tea.

Last night, no.

Last night, with no tea, she'd given herself with equal abandon. He had gone to her wrought with emotion for all she'd done, burning with need and taken her in the throes of it.

But she was not frightened or repulsed. She met his passion and even bested it.

And during their play, he did not need to be cautious, to curb his desires, to do or be anything but himself and take what he wished with Maddie giving it to him.

Gladly.

He was very aware that, as they became attuned to each other, learned about each other, got used to each other, he would make comparisons between what he was building with Madeleine and what he had had with Ilsa. This would happen even if she did not look like Ilsa.

What he would not have imagined, after the loss he suffered when he lost Ilsa, was that Madeleine, it would seem, in a very short time was beginning to surpass all the beauty, intelligence and strength that had been his wife.

Fifteen years ago, his eyes fell on Ilsa, he quickly became smitten and not long after fell deeply in love.

With Madeleine, it was something else.

He could not turn his mind from her. Her smiles felt like gifts. Her laughter, a triumph. Every "honey" a treasure. Every "baby" sent a pulse through his cock.

He was not smitten.

He was growing consumed.

And he was troubled by it.

Not that it was happening. Not that some part of him felt this swift response to Madeleine was a betrayal of Ilsa.

No, because if his world could turn dark at the loss of Ilsa and these feelings he had for Madeleine grew, what would become of him if he lost her?

The horse reached the clearing of the trees and Apollo's attention was taken from Maddie when he saw Achilles and Draven on the front steps of Karsvall, a horse at the foot, Derrik packing it.

All that needed to be done last night was done with the swiftness it required.

Therefore, he had little time to speak to any of his men as he did it, other than to give orders. And he'd gone directly to Maddie, so there was no time after it was done.

Regardless, he would not have been able to talk to Derrik, for after they extracted the information from the assassin, Derrik had absented himself completely.

At the juncture, Apollo had neither the time nor the desire to search him out and share gratitude for his efforts at keeping Christophe, Élan and Karsvall safe.

Now, he would take that time and hope what had elapsed since he'd last seen his friend had helped to cool his ire.

He kicked his horse to a trot and reined in when he was close to Derrik's mount, seeing it packed for a journey.

Apollo home, clearly Derrik was returning to the Lazarus seat.

Perhaps his ire had not cooled.

His eyes slid through Achilles and Draven.

Draven looked annoyed. Achilles looked thoughtful. This told him nothing.

Although Draven was not often annoyed, it was known he could get that way on occasion.

Achilles was much like any Ulfr. In most cases, he kept his emotions to himself. Achilles, however, was a master of this.

Apollo dismounted and approached the men. They all watched, but only Derrik did so with cold eyes.

"Morning, Lo," Achilles called.

Apollo raised a hand to Achilles and Draven and turned his attention to Derrik when he stopped three feet from him.

"You journey to Lazarus?" he asked quietly.

"I journey to Specter Isle," Derrik announced, voice not quiet but still cold, his words sparking *Apollo's* ire.

He narrowed his eyes on Derrik, his voice no longer quiet but impatient when he returned, "Don't be foolish."

Specter Isle, they'd learned last night, if the conspirator was to be believed, was where Minerva, Baldur, and the two Valearian witches they were conspiring with, Edith and Helda, were hiding.

Seeing Derrik's jaw set, Apollo kept speaking.

"Last night, I spent half the night writing missives to—"

"And the second half you spent fucking Maddie," Derrik interrupted him to bite out.

Apollo clenched his teeth.

He didn't fully understand every word, but he didn't need to in order to understand his meaning.

This was proved when Draven growled, "Careful, Rik."

Derrik didn't tear his eyes from Apollo, and he knew him well, so he read him.

This made him tip his head to the side in mock curiosity. "Has she not shared that with you? Her world's word of fuck? It has many uses, brother. When she has a few ales, a few glasses of wine, her tongue loosens." He threw out an arm to indicate Achilles and Draven. "She shared with all of us the curse words of the other world. That was my particular favorite."

"Fascinating," Apollo returned, his word dry.

"Though, I would guess, if *you* got a few ales in her, with her tongue loose, you'd find other uses for it."

At that, Apollo growled, Draven did it again, and both of them moved.

Achilles moved as well, but he could only stop Draven.

He didn't stop Apollo and thus Apollo's fist connected powerfully with Derrik's jaw. With satisfaction, he saw his friend's head flash to the side, blood spraying from his mouth into the snow. After this, Derrik instantly took a step back but lifted his fists, body loose.

Ready.

Apollo didn't lift his fists. Focus locked to Derrik, he didn't give him even that. His friend knew from years of sparring for sport who would be bested in the end. And it would not be Apollo.

Achilles moved between them, arms lifted, and he clipped, "Think, brothers."

He would not think.

He would warn.

"One more word from your mouth like that about Madeleine, you'll be picking your teeth from the snow."

"By the gods, you speak of Maddie," Draven put in angrily. "One more word like that and half the men will be sending your teeth into the snow."

Derrik dropped his fists and crossed his arms on his chest but said nothing. Through these exchanges, he didn't take his eyes from Apollo.

Achilles took a tentative step from between the men, but he stayed close and suggested, "Let's move on from this. We should be discussing your journey, Rik. Obviously, Lo agrees with what Draven and I have been trying to impress on you all morning. It's more than foolhardy."

Derrik tore his attention from Apollo to look at Achilles. "I simply go to scout."

Achilles eyebrows went up. "Alone, without a single man at your back or a witch for protection?" He shook his head. "You know this is reckless. It hardly helps the cause losing a good man and it definitely wouldn't help, losing a brother."

"Nothing will be lost. I'm skilled at it," Derrik returned.

Apollo knew he was not wrong. If they needed a scout, Derrik always led the party. He wasn't skilled at it. He excelled at it.

But they were talking about a she-god and two witches that were known to wield nearly as much power as Minerva. He'd not even turn his eyes to Specter Isle without being detected.

And dispatched.

"The birds were sent to Houllebec last night," Apollo told him. "Frey may have some men in the village and it's only a three days' ride—"

"Hard ride," Derrik cut in. "And do you think, *brother*, that we have three days before we face something further after what happened last night?"

"It was a play, Rik," Achilles stated, and Derrik looked to him. "You heard the man. They were sent to assassinate Lo, Maddie, and the children as a warning to the others to concede without a fight. They didn't even use magic."

"It was a first strike," Derrik contradicted. "We're at war."

Unfortunately, he was not wrong.

"A first strike where we prevailed," Achilles reminded him.

"And what? We sit and wait for the second?" Derrik asked derisively.

"A war fought on many fronts weakens the enemy," Apollo said low. "You know that. If Frey, Lahn, Tor and I were to amass in one place, Minerva would have to conjure and send one set of creatures. With us separate, she has to create at least two armies and send them to two locations, depending on where the other men are now. Her magic has already been weakened after what she sent at Tor in the other world, and you know magic does not renew quickly. If she were to need to do this, it would cost her."

"And clearly this strategy was decided by you and you alone last night," Derrik returned. "For just days ago, you were off to Bellebryn to meet the others."

"And was I not brought on by Frey and Queen Aurora to do just that?" Apollo shot back. "Provide strategy?"

Derrik clamped his mouth shut for he knew he was.

"With this foe, it has always been the plan to seek information, strategize, prepare and not attack until they do and thus, they're weakened," Apollo decreed.

"Then we withstand whatever they throw at us in the meantime?" Derrik pushed. "Alone. And the others withstand whatever may be happening to them, and they be damned?"

"We are constrained by slow communication, brother. And it takes a bird in flight or a man and horse much less time to travel the distance than it does a man escorting a woman in a sleigh. If the others disagree and feel there is safety in numbers, this will be discussed. But I took on three men with swords, armed only with my knives. They were quite skilled and I do not like to think how that would have gone if Maddie wasn't there to assist me." His eyes grew sharp on Derrik. "Nor do I wish to think what would have become of her had I fallen and they turned to her."

Derrik's jaw again went hard and Apollo knew his point was made.

Therefore, he continued.

"And my children were threatened," he said with deadly quiet. "I will not leave them. I will stay and protect my family and my home. This is my decision, and it is strategic, but it is also the decision of a man, a husband and a father. It is not 'the others be damned' for I know with no doubts that Frey, Lahn and Tor would do precisely the same thing."

"So, you wed her along the way," Derrik replied.

Apollo took in an irritated breath at being back on the subject of Maddie. "No."

"Then you are not her husband."

"Not yet."

"But it's your intention to take her to wife," Derrik went on.

Apollo held his eyes for long moments before he said, "Yes."

Something shifted in Derrik's gaze that Apollo, in all their years of knowing each other, and there had been many, had never seen.

Then he said softly, "So she is Maddie to you, but who are you to her, brother?"

"Is this drivel necessary?" Draven cut in to ask.

But Derrik didn't look away from Apollo and he kept speaking.

"Has it occurred to you that when she gazes up at you while you take her, she sees the husband of the other world that she felt wrong in loving, the husband of the other world she wished she had, not you?"

Apollo stayed perfectly still, because if he didn't, he would not be responsible for what he did do.

Also because that had not occurred to him.

Not once.

She called the other him "Pol." She'd never slipped and even started to call him that name.

So this couldn't be.

Could it?

"I've had four months with her and she told me much about this man," Derrik stated.

At that, uncharacteristically, Achilles lost his temper, and he did it clipping out, "She told you much and she did it because she trusted you. Do not betray that now, Rik."

Derrik's mask slipped, remorse shining through as he glanced at Achilles then he looked back at Apollo, opening his mouth to speak.

"And right now you taste the blood Lo put in your mouth, Rik," Draven stated before Derrik could say a word. He moved to stand close to Apollo and finished, "But if more comes out of that mouth about Maddie, you won't be picking your teeth out of the snow. You'll be coughing them up from your gut."

Through this, Apollo remained still and silent.

And through it, Derrik glared at Apollo. When he got nothing, he transferred his glare to Draven, then Achilles, and finally he moved to his horse, muttering, "I'm away to Specter Isle."

"Do you wish to be buried on Lazarus land, or Ulfr?" Draven asked after him as he mounted.

Derrik looked down at them all.

"If that decision needs to be made, I'll be dead, so do I care?"

After that, he clicked his teeth, sent his heels into his steed and burst through the snow.

When Apollo lost sight of him, he turned to the other men and asked, "Was it Derrik's decision not to stay at my castle in The Vale?"

"He did decide our route, Lo," Achilles answered quietly.

"Did he share the reason he steered you from such luxurious accommodation when it was along the straightest route to the port? Not to mention, he seemed quite keen on showing Maddie much of this world. I've asked and she's seen not a single castle except from afar when she spied Bellebryn from the ship."

"No," Draven replied shortly.

Apollo looked back to the lane, murmuring, "He is not right."

"Lo, you should know, he seemed quite taken with her from almost the beginning," Achilles shared.

Apollo turned again to his cousin, repeating, "He is not right."

"He's a man in love," Achilles returned carefully, his astute eyes on Apollo. "They do many things that are not right."

"You, alongside me, grew up with that man, cousin. That man who just rode away is not the man we grew up with. Again, he...is...not...*right*."

"I agree with Lo," Draven stated. "He's not right."

"And what do you think this is?" Achilles asked.

"I think that after what Minerva forced Tor and Cora to endure, the blackness of soul that Baldur has always had, the magic at their command, we should be very aware of anything that is not right," Apollo replied. He looked at Draven. "Set a man to following him."

Draven nodded and turned instantly to the house.

Apollo shifted his attention to Achilles.

Achilles spoke and he did it quietly.

"He may not be acting as Derrik, but he was not wrong earlier. You spent the night with Maddie."

"And this is your concern?" Apollo asked.

"It's been just days. Has it come so far so fast, cousin?" Achilles asked back.

"I'll repeat, this is your concern?"

"You just noted we should be aware of anything that is not right," Achilles pointed out.

He did indeed.

Apollo sighed and shared, "The witch with the green magic introduced her to adela tea." He paused and held his cousin's eyes before concluding, "And I was close."

Achilles brows shot up. "You took advantage?"

Apollo straightened his spine, and his tone was low when he stated, "Maddie and I have worked through that."

"You took advantage," Achilles murmured, studying him.

Apollo felt his skin prickling. "I'll answer my earlier question for you. This isn't your concern."

"She's vulnerable," Achilles warned.

"Agreed. This is why she needs me."

His gaze never leaving Apollo, Achilles tipped his head to the side, and he noted, "You care for her."

Apollo didn't hesitate and his voice was firm when he replied, "Greatly."

His cousin's lips twitched. "It's not a surprise *that* didn't take long."

Apollo had no reply for he spoke truth.

Achilles remarked quietly, "She also shared with me, cousin, and she would not take him."

Apollo felt his brows draw together. "Pardon?"

"It is hers to share with you, the knowledge she trusted to me. But you need to know so the seed Derrik planted does not grow. She would not take him to her bed. Not of her will. Never again. Whatever they had, he killed a long time ago. If she's taking you, it's *you* she's taking."

Apollo felt the tension ebb from his body at these words.

Then he jerked up his chin and moved to the steps, murmuring, "I'm off to have breakfast with my children."

He was nearly to the doors when Achilles called his name.

He stopped, turned and looked down at his cousin.

"Years, I have watched you mourn," Achilles started. "It saddened me. Now, it pleases me to see you again reaching to happiness." He paused and finished, "I wish you speed in grasping it."

His throat prickled but his lips said, "Your heart is too soft for a soldier."

"Says the man who grieved for his wife for four and a half years," Achilles swiftly returned.

Unfortunately, to that, Apollo had no retort.

Achilles knew it and this was why he smiled before he turned and sauntered away.

Apollo sighed again and headed to his children.

~

"When is the fire-haired lady going to come and see us, Papa?"

Élan was on her knees beside him on the sofa, leaning in, resting her little body on his side. She was also, for some little girl reason, curling the ends of his hair around her fingers.

But as she asked her question, Apollo's focus stayed locked on his son.

Christophe was on his belly on the floor, knees bent, ankles crossed, feet in the air. He had a board in front of him, chalk in his hand. He was drawing, but at his sister's question, the chalk arrested on the board.

This did not bode well.

He turned his head to look at his daughter, and watching her closely, being cautious with his words so as not to rekindle her fears of the night before, he said, "She rode with me through the night as well as the day to get to you, precious girl. Because of this, she was tired and today she's resting."

Not showing any signs this reminder distressed her, Élan nodded but asked, "Will she come tomorrow?"

"Perhaps," Apollo answered.

Élan tipped her head to the side and noted, "She's very pretty."

"She is," Apollo agreed.

Élan screwed up her mouth before she stated, "She looked very angry."

Apollo felt something coming from his son, but he kept his eyes on his daughter. "She was upset you were frightened."

"I was upset I was frightened too," she declared.

He smiled, turned to her and pulled her in his arms. She screeched in mock protest, as she always did. But when he blew a wet kiss on her neck, she giggled.

When he lifted his head, she put her hand on his face and told him, "I'm glad we're not at school anymore, Papa."

Apollo was glad as well. Even when times weren't troubled, he disliked them being so far away. It might be wrong, but he felt this especially this year, Élan's first. But he was a father, and she was his daughter, and he couldn't imagine any father happily sending his little girl two countries away to school.

His son was not only a boy but the oldest child. He was also much like his mother, extremely intelligent and self-assured. Christophe uncannily had displayed signs of both from a very young age. Although Apollo had not liked sending him either, it had caused less unease.

However, Ilsa had gone to that school, as her father had before her and his before him. It was, in truth, the finest school in the Northlands. And it had always been her wish that her children would attend it.

So he gave into that wish, even after her death.

Maybe especially after her death.

When she was alive, they had had plans, of course, to spend much of their time in Benies while the children were at school. And when it was safe for them to go back, Apollo decided that he and Madeleine would do just that.

"I'm glad you're home too, darling girl," he replied then arranged his face into mock severity. "But don't think with your papa home today and me allowing you to be away from your studies that you can be lazy every day. It's back to your tutor on the morrow."

She made a face, clearly not looking forward to this, and he again smiled.

"Élan, my love, bath time," Bella, the children's maid called from the door.

"Oh no!" Élan cried, twisting and sitting in her father's lap to look to her maid. "I don't want to take a bath now."

Bella put her hands on her hips. "Then can you tell me when you'd desire your bath, little miss?"

"In an hour," Élan tried.

"In an hour, you're to bed, eyes closed, dreaming good dreams," Bella returned.

Élan gave it a moment and came up with a different plan.

"How about I skip it tonight and take one tomorrow?" she pushed.

"I don't mind if you don't bathe," Apollo put in and his daughter's happy eyes came to him. "In fact, you are more than welcome never to bathe again. However, this would make you stinky and I wouldn't hold my girl in my lap if she was smelly."

Élan made another face, this time scrunching her nose. But his words also served to get her moving. She jumped from his lap only to dash two steps toward Bella, stop and dash back.

She jumped back on the sofa, threw her arms around Apollo and whispered in his ear, "I'm happy you're back, Papa."

Apollo wrapped his arms around her, pulled her close and took in her scent, which was far from unpleasant.

Then he returned her whisper in her ear and said, "Give your father a good-night kiss and go to Bella."

She pulled back, grabbed his face in both hands and gave him a loud kiss on the cheek before she again jumped off the couch and ran to Bella.

Taking her outstretched hand, she followed the maid out as Bella called, "Chris, you're next."

"All right, Bella," Christophe called back.

Apollo's eyes went to him. "Son?"

Christophe looked up at his father.

"Sit with me," he ordered.

Rolling side-to-side as only a child would do, he got his feet under him and came to the sofa.

Apollo studied him as he did so.

Christophe had, some time ago, eschewed what he called "little boys' clothes" and demanded to wear breeches, or trousers and high boots, not just breeches and ankle boots. He'd also taken to wearing full cloaks that fell to his calves, not short ones that fell to his backside.

Apollo had allowed this. If his son wanted to be a little man, there was no reason why he couldn't be. He was excellent at his studies and talented on a horse, not to mention showed great promise with a bow and his wooden sword.

And anyway, Apollo had hated ankle boots when he was Christophe's age, so he saw no reason to force his son to wear them until he was thirteen.

Apollo watched as Christophe sat on the sofa at the opposite end to him, arranging his boy's body in his father's exact pose as best he could with his much shorter frame. That was to say, leaned back with one leg crossed, ankle resting on the other knee. However, he didn't have his arms spread wide along the back and the arm of the couch as his arms didn't reach.

Apollo quelled his smile and caught his son's eyes.

"With your sister gone, I thought we'd talk, man to man," he began.

Christophe's chest swelled and Apollo was forced to quell another smile.

"You're well?" he asked quietly.

Christophe nodded. "Yes, Papa. I'm all right. And Élan is too. I knew Achilles and Derrik wouldn't let them get to us."

"That's not what I'm talking about, son," Apollo noted carefully.

Christophe looked to the carpets. He knew what he was talking about.

"Look at me, Chris," Apollo urged, and Christophe looked back to his father. "Madeleine, which is what she wishes to be referred as in this world, is very anxious about meeting you, knowing how she will appear to you."

Christophe said nothing for long moments, but he didn't look away from his father.

Then, he blurted, "Nathaniel told me."

Apollo blinked.

Perplexed at this change in subject, he asked, "Nathaniel told you what?"

"He was watching through a crack," Christophe went on, still not making sense.

"Son," Apollo started. "Explain."

"A crack," he hesitated, "in the gardener's shed."

Apollo drew in a sharp breath.

Christophe took his ankle from his knee and leaned into his hand in the sofa, asking excitedly, "Did she really stick a man with a knife, Papa?"

Apollo stared into his son's bright eyes and did not answer. Instead, he stated, "Nathaniel should not have been doing that nor should he have shared what he saw with you."

Christophe held his gaze.

Then he whispered, "She did."

Bloody hell.

"She was tired and cross," Apollo told him.

He watched his son's mouth quirk before he remarked, "She'd have to be very tired and very cross to stick a man."

In other circumstances, not these, he would agree with his son that this was amusing.

This time, he didn't.

He had other concerns.

"What else did Nathaniel tell you he saw?"

Christophe sat back, his shoulders slumping. "Nothing. Lees saw him when he was taking the lady...I mean, Madeleine out and he pointed at him, so he thought it best to run away."

Apollo relaxed.

"He said she was meaner even than Laures," Christophe went on.

"Again, she was not in a good state," Apollo replied.

One side of his son's mouth hitched up as he commented, "Nathaniel said it was grand. She grabbed his face and took Laures's knife and—"

He stopped talking when Apollo took his arms from the sofa, leaned into him and quietly shared, "Do you remember what I told you on the ship on the way home about the two worlds?"

"Yes, Papa," Christophe answered.

"In her world, she lost you and Élan."

Christophe snapped his mouth shut.

"In that world, your twins were never born. But she carried both and your twins in that world were taken from her before they took their first breaths."

Christophe held his father's eyes, his now stricken.

Nevertheless, Apollo kept speaking.

"She grieves this still. And when she saw the children she never had, and saw them frightened, she reacted. She did what she would have done if you were her own. It is not grand what she did, Chris. It is beautiful. Don't you think?"

Christophe nodded slowly.

"Your sister doesn't understand this because she doesn't remember losing her mother. But I think you do. She lost her Christophe and Élan. You lost your mother. Of anyone, you and I, we understand. Do you agree?"

His son again nodded slowly.

"She will need some time to gather the courage to meet you and your sister. Can you help me contain your sister's excitement in order to give her this time?"

"Yes, Papa," Christophe whispered.

"Thank you, son," Apollo murmured, lifting a hand and cupping it on the side of his son's neck. "Now, go to your bath. I'll see you at breakfast tomorrow."

"Al'right, Papa."

Apollo watched him jump from the sofa and he got no hugs from his son. Even at eight (nearly nine), Christophe was far too old for that.

But he still turned at the door and called, "When you see her, will you tell her Élan's excited to meet her?"

This meant something else entirely.

Apollo felt the tightness in his gut loosen and he answered, "I will."

Christophe nodded and dashed out of the room.

Apollo took in a deep breath and let it out. He then straightened out of the sofa and moved from the room. He found a servant and ordered a horse to be brought around. He then found Laures and told him of Nathaniel. He also ordered him to find Nathaniel, discover all he'd seen, extract a promise he would cease talking about it as well as another he wouldn't do anything as foolish again.

Finally, Apollo went to his cloak and swung it on, left the house and moved to the horse saddled and waiting for him at the front of the house.

It was not a sedate walk at which he rode to the dower house.

But when he came into the small clearing, he pulled back the reins at what he saw.

Two torches outside lighting the front door and casting a glow on the glade.

And in that glade were not one, not two, but three snowmen.

He peered closer and saw he stood corrected.

Two snowmen and a snow*woman*.

Maddie clearly had found a way to keep herself occupied that day.

His lips twitched before he clicked his tongue against his teeth and led the horse to the stables. But when he went to stall his horse for the night, he saw three stalls were taken.

This meant when he walked into the front room, he saw Remi, Alek and Draven lounging on his dead mother's furniture. Maddie was sitting on the floor. And a game of tuble was in progress on the low table they were all seated around.

All the men had mugs of ale. Maddie had a glass of wine.

He also walked in on them all laughing.

Remi saw him first and immediately shared, "Maddie has mastered the art of the cheat."

Apollo crossed his arms on his chest and asked, "Indeed?"

"She's taken every hand!" Alek exclaimed and went on, "She has very nimble fingers."

His eyes went to Madeleine to see her head tipped back and hers on him and his voice was much changed when he repeated, "Indeed?"

Pink crept in her cheeks as she looked away.

"Sit for a hand?" Draven asked, gathering the cards to shuffle them.

"I would like nothing more, but, you see, my lady and I were set upon only two nights' past and my children last night, so I'm afraid I won't have my mind on the cards."

The men looked at each other, grinning, and Maddie quickly got to her feet.

"I'll get you an ale. Or do you want wine?" she asked.

She asked this to him, he knew, however, strangely she didn't ask his face.

She asked his chest.

"Wine, dove," he told her.

"There's a lady, um...in the kitchens. She says she's to cook and serve. I've told her the men are staying for dinner," she shared, this time to his shoulder.

This did not please him. He'd wished to dine alone with her. However, he did not share this with her in a room full of his men.

What also didn't please him was that, for some reason, she seemed unable to meet his eyes.

"I hope she told you her name is Cristiana and she's to keep this house for you, Maddie," he murmured.

She nodded, and she did this to his ear.

What in bloody hell?

When she didn't move, he prompted, "Wine would be warming, poppy."

Her eyes flitted through his before she skirted him and moved quickly down the hall.

He watched her until his attention was taken with the outer door opening. He looked over his shoulder to see Achilles and Gaston joining them.

"The children," he said to them.

"Laures and Hans are patrolling the grounds," Achilles stated, walking in and stopping close to Apollo. "You've spent the day with your children and there's much to be discussed."

Apollo nodded and moved into the room. This commenced their discussion, which took them through dinner.

And through this, when his mind wasn't on the matters at hand, it was on the fact that Maddie was there, but she wasn't.

That was to say, she was there, smiling, answering a question if one was aimed at her from one from the men, talking to them softly, even laughing twice at something Remi had to say.

What she wasn't was giving any indication she knew Apollo existed.

The only time he forced his existence on her was when Cristiana cleared the dishes. This was because Maddie rose to help her, but when she neared him,

Apollo caught her hand and forced her into the chair beside him, a chair vacated by Gaston, who had gone to the main house.

He leaned into her and shared, "Lady Ulfr does not clear."

She turned wide eyes to him then moved them through him and nodded.

It was at that point that his bemusement at her behavior turned to annoyance.

And this annoyance escalated when they moved from the dining table to the sitting room with their whiskeys (though Maddie was still drinking wine) and she continued to be jovial and animated with his men but distant with him to the point of ignoring him.

Thus, he was glad when the business was concluded, the plans made, the men had their orders and they took their leave.

Apollo and Maddie saw them to the door.

And the minute the last farewell was thrown she ducked by him and moved into the house.

Much more slowly, he followed her.

Further irritating him, he found her tidying the glasses in the sitting room.

Her eyes slid through him once again as she passed him and he watched her walk to the kitchen.

He walked into the room, sat and took a deep calming breath.

She returned, her gaze avoiding his, but she bent not close, but not far, to grab a glass.

He bent deep, to grab her hips.

He then sat back, taking her with him, and planted her arse in his lap.

She stiffened completely except to look at his face then drop her gaze to his throat.

"What did I say about clearing?" he asked softly.

Her teeth appeared to worry her lip a brief moment before they disappeared and she mumbled, "Sorry."

He kept his voice soft when he queried, "Is there something amiss?"

"Amiss?" she queried back, but she asked his ear.

He gave her a gentle shake. "Maddie. Look at me."

Her eyes, with difficulty and too damned much time, finally found his.

There was fear in them.

Bloody hell, did he frighten her last night with his lovemaking?

On this thought, he gentled his tone further and slid his hand up her spine to her neck, pulling her down to him as his other arm rounded her waist and he remarked, "You're behaving strangely tonight."

"Um..." she mumbled but said no more.

"Maddie," he prompted.

Her eyes started to drift away but his hand tightened on her neck, and they shot back.

But she said not a word.

"Madeleine," he growled, his gentle tone slipping as did his patience.

"I'm not crazy," she whispered.

He blinked at this bizarre declaration. "Pardon?"

She shook her head sharply then announced, "You're being very cool."

Another bizarre declaration.

When she did not explain, cautiously he asked, "How am I being very...cool?"

"Not bringing it up or flipping out about it. I mean, sure, right after, you slit his throat but you're a dude in a parallel universe. You cut off Pol's hand. Gutted that other dude. Then there was the neck slice you delivered to that other *other* dude. I'm getting that here, things are a little bit more vio—"

She was rambling, and making little sense doing it, so he gave her another gentle shake and interrupted her with, "Maddie, I don't know what the bloody hell you're on about."

"I stabbed a man," she whispered, her voice horrified. "And I would guess, I think...well, I don't know about this world, but in my world, we're not hot on that. So I'm thinking that's not all that, um...*attractive* and that you might think me going half-cocked like that is actually, well...*crazy*."

He felt the tension release in his shoulders.

She was worried what he thought of her behavior the night before.

"You were overwrought," he reminded her quietly.

"You can say that again," she mumbled.

He dropped his voice low. "And you will remember how I reacted to your behavior when I joined you in bed last night."

She closed her mouth and pink again tinged her cheeks.

She remembered.

"After that, Maddie, how can you misconstrue my response to your actions?"

"He was tied to a chair." She was still whispering, her voice troubled. "Defenseless."

"That man was not defenseless," Apollo declared.

Surprising him at her swift change in tone, she cried, "He was, Apollo! He was tied to a chair!"

"Poppy, he came to my home with the intent to murder my children. He might have been defenseless in that moment, but do not mistake, my dove, even for a moment that if he was not tied to that chair and given opportunity and a weapon, he would not have brought you low. Me low. Any of my men low. Or Christophe and Élan low."

She was wide-eyed and it was no less adorable, but it had less of an effect on him due to why.

She was also breathing heavily.

And through her breathing, she stated, "Maybe I need to understand what the fuck is going on."

"You're aware that I was worried we were in danger, Maddie, and the past few days proved we are."

"But...children?" she asked quietly.

"Unfortunately, this thoroughly defines the wickedness of our foes. Although unfortunate they are this wicked, it is a twisted boon for we now know what to expect."

Suddenly, she turned toward him and lifted a hand to curl it around his neck, dipping her face closer to his.

"Right. Here goes. I'm laying it out there," she began, then announced, "I'm scared, Apollo. Freaking *terrified*. This shit is whacked. Totally *whacked*. I've had a day to think on all this crap and it *freaks me out*! I stabbed a man. You killed *three*. Right in front of me. Your kids in danger. And your guys are drinking ale, playing tuble like nothing's the matter when *it is*! Last night you tortured information from an assassin! Tonight, you're sitting around the dinner table talking about witches and missives and scouting parties and inventorying the armory like you're discussing the scores of the Lakers versus Celtics game. That shit is not right!"

"My dove—" he began, but she shook her head vehemently and dug her fingers into his neck.

"Unh-unh, you can't give me one of your sweet, sexy, tender, kickass 'my doves' and calm this storm, baby. I'm...*freaked...out*!"

He fought back his humor at her words and remarked, "I can assume that means frightened."

"Fuck yes!" she cried.

He started to stroke her back and whispered, "Calm."

Her eyes got huge again, it was still adorable, and this time the effect was what it usually was even when she went on.

"Calm? *You* calm!" she returned. "I stabbed a man!"

"Madeleine—"

Abruptly, her forehead dropped to his and she whispered, "I stabbed a man. And honestly? If you gave me those hedge clippers? In that moment, I don't know what I would have done. I was totally out of control. And you didn't even blink before you cut his throat."

He was belatedly seeing his mistake. One he would from then on rectify.

"I should have sheltered you from that. Alas, I was not thinking clearly at the time," he told her, and she lifted her head.

"I think it's safe to say neither of us was."

"That happens when you love your children," he told her, and she pulled in an audible breath.

He wrapped his arms around her and gathered her closer.

"Listen to me," he said gently. "A great deal has happened in the last two days, and unfortunately some of it you weren't shielded from due to necessity. And I will remind you of the fact that in the beginning, when we were set upon in Vasterhague, I told you to run and you did not run so I *couldn't* shield you from seeing me do what had to be done."

Her eyes grew sharp and he nearly smiled.

He didn't. He carried on.

"And the men spoke freely tonight around you. You'll be shielded from that in the future as well."

"I prefer to know what's going on."

"And I prefer you don't if it frightens you."

She drew in a very deep breath and sat back, pulling at his arms. He didn't gather her closer again because, for some strange reason, she drew a cross over her heart and lifted up two fingers.

Then she declared, "I'll put my big-girl panties on and suck it up from now on, cross my heart, scouts honor, swear." She dropped her hand. "But I'd really rather not stab anyone in the future, especially not if they're tied to a chair."

"I'll see what I can do," he murmured.

Her head tipped to the side and her eyes narrowed right before she asked. "Do you think this is funny?"

"The situation? No. Your reaction to it? Absolutely."

She glared at him.

He'd allowed her distance and now he was done allowing it.

So he again gathered her closer.

And his tone was very gentle when he explained, "Maddie, for many, *many* months we have lived under the threat of knowing very powerful conspirators with evil motives may unleash mayhem across the land. Today, you breathe, my children breathe, I breathe. So I feel relief and now we can take this as an opportunity to read their first strike, glean what we can from it and prepare. All this is foreign to you, thus frightening. But in the end, it's good."

"I'm uncertain I can see the good, Apollo," she admitted.

"Then I'll share that they didn't use magic. This could mean Minerva is weakened more than we knew, the witches she's aligned with not as powerful as we've assumed, or they fear the combined magic of Lavinia and Valentine, not to mention Frey, who commands both dragons and elves."

"None of that seems definite," she noted.

"It's not, but I've never known a battle where a warning shot was fired with a dart."

She blinked and asked, "What?"

"If you have a cannon or a flaming arrow, you would use that."

"Oh," she whispered, and he felt his lips curl up.

He wrapped the tail of her hair around his hand and brought her face closer.

"It has begun. We don't live under the threat of it, it's happening. This may not seem an advantage, my dove, but it is. It is much better to be *doing* something than awaiting the unknown. Now, I fortify the men at my home to keep my children and you safe for I *know* you are not, rather than guessing it or how I might protect you from it. Now, Queen Aurora can gather her troops. Now, Lavinia and Valentine may be able to focus their attention, for we may have knowledge of where the conspirators hide. But to end, poppy, now we can do *something*."

"I'm seeing the benefits of this for an action man," she noted.

He grinned.

"But for a chick from another world, this shit is still whacked," she concluded.

"Then let's agree that I shield my *chick* from another world from all of this so she enjoys her days making snowmen, playing tuble with her friends, her evenings with the company in her bed, all of this as she raises the courage to meet my children and tries to figure out what she intends to do with her life in her new world, shall we?"

"I really don't like things kept from me, Apollo," she whispered.

"I have received that message clearly, Madeleine," he whispered back. "So part of our bargain will be that you trust me to share with you what you need to know and the rest of it, I will keep to myself so you can be free to find your footing in your new life? Are we agreed?"

She held his eyes and she did this for some time.

He fought against holding his breath.

Finally, she nodded.

Thank the gods.

"Excellent," he muttered, rising and lifting her with him. "Let's go to bed."

As he moved from the room, he heard her mumble, "Oh boy."

And again, he smiled.

~

"*Baby*," she breathed.

Apollo slowly slid out, but he didn't slide back in.

He gave her just the tip of his cock and whispered against the skin of her neck, "Again."

To which, instantly she whispered back, "Baby."

He slowly slid inside, then glided out, and repeat, and again, his hands moving on her skin, his lips skating across her neck, down her jaw and up. His eyes open, holding hers captive, he took her mouth, sliding his tongue in and coaxing hers to dance with his.

Gratifyingly, with but a moment's coaxing, she gave him what he wanted.

When he broke the kiss but not the connection of his lips, she whispered, "You need to go faster, sweetheart."

Instantly, he gave her what she wanted.

He felt her tighten her legs that were curved around his thighs, and she slid her cheek along his, lifting her head to bury her face in his neck.

So bloody sweet.

"Maddie," he groaned into hers.

"Harder, baby," she begged, and his hand at her side drifted down to her waist, in over the small of her back and down to cup her arse.

He lifted her and gave her harder.

And deeper.

He heard her breath hitch and she ran the edge of her teeth along his shoulder.

When she did, a shudder tore through him. He shifted all his power to his hips and his thrusts turned to pounds.

"*Apollo*," she breathed, and he felt her sex clutching him tight.

Gods.

Magnificent.

"You grow close," he grunted. "Look at me, poppy. I wish to see your face as it takes you."

She dropped her head to the pillows, and at the sight of him, her eyes heated, she gasped, he thrust, and it took her.

She pushed her head into the pillows as her hand shot up and fisted in his hair.

"*Magnificent*," he growled.

Her orgasm shook her then started drifting away and he saw her eyes open just before his head jerked back, he felt the muscles in his neck straining, his hips bucking, before his head fell forward and he buried his face in her neck, driving deep, staying planted, and he groaned.

Yes.

Magnificent.

She held him to her as it shuddered through his frame, and he felt her press her lips to his neck.

So damned sweet.

Finally, he drew in a deep breath before he slid his tongue up her neck.

At that, he absorbed her shiver.

He lifted his head and caught her eyes.

"How's this for *in there*, dove?"

She lifted her head, shoved her face in his throat and let out a giggle.

That giggle, another triumph.

He twisted his neck and skimmed her temple with his lips. She dropped her head to the pillow and he smiled at her.

Her hand moved from his hair to his cheek, and she whispered, "God, you're beautiful."

Those words cutting through him, he closed his eyes, turned his head and kissed her palm.

Then he moved his lips to her nose where he kissed her before he pulled back an inch and looked into her eyes.

"I don't know what you prefer, Maddie, but I'll tell you, I prefer you sleep in nothing. I want to feel your skin against mine tonight."

"Okay," she agreed quietly.

He dipped his head to brush his mouth against hers.

"I'll deal with the sheath and return."

"Okeydokey."

At that, he gave her another brush of his lips, and, with great satisfaction, he watched her lips part as he slid slowly out. Once he lost her, he bent his head deeper and glided his lips across her throat before he rolled off the bed.

He tossed the covers over her and watched her turn to the side, curling into herself. Only when she settled did he move away from the bed and into the shadows.

He made short work of dealing with the sheath and emerged from the darkness. He felt her eyes on him as, naked, he moved to the fire, threw on some logs, stirred it then went back to her.

He joined her in bed, yanked the covers up to his waist and pulled her into his arms, tangling their limbs and doing it tight.

She pressed her cheek into his chest.

"I'm assuming from what just occurred, you also enjoy gentle and slow," he noted, sliding his fingers through her hair.

She emitted a short, sweet giggle and replied, "Yeah, that worked for me."

He stopped moving his fingers through her hair and pulled her closer.

She snuggled even deeper.

Then he felt her draw in a deep breath before she murmured, "Just so you know, honey, if your intention in bringing me to this world was to give me better, swordfights and bloodshed notwithstanding, you're succeeding."

His chest warmed, his heart squeezed, his arm around her got tight and he felt a rumble roll up his chest.

But instead of howling his elation, Apollo put his other hand to her jaw, tipping it so his mouth could crush down on hers.

He took her open-mouthed and wet. He did it deeply. He did it thoroughly. He drank from her, taking as much as he wanted for as long as he wanted. And as long as he wanted meant he did it a bloody long time.

When he finally released her mouth, she gasped, "And it keeps getting better."

"Cease talking, Madeleine. The children are expecting me for breakfast, and if you don't, we'll both get no sleep tonight, I'll eventually sleep late, and they'll eat alone."

He watched her press her lips together.

He shook his head, but he did it quelling a smile, before he rolled to his back, taking her with him so she rolled over him.

He turned out the lamp by the bed.

He rolled them back and arranged them in the exact position they were in.

She cuddled deeper and mumbled, "'Night, baby."

His arms got tighter, and he whispered, "Goodnight, my dove."

He felt her face move against his chest and he knew it was with a smile.

Apollo held her close and within minutes, he felt her sleep.

Just so you know, honey, if your intention is to give me better...you're succeeding.

And there it was.

It was indeed *he* she saw when she looked into his eyes while he was taking her, or any other time she did it.

And *he* was giving her better.

He didn't quell that smile. He let himself have it before he rolled into her and joined her in sleep.

THREE HOURS LATER, Apollo opened his eyes to a mostly dark room, the firelight only casting a dim glow.

Maddie's soft naked body was pressed to him, her cheek on his shoulder, her arm heavy across his stomach. He felt her warm weight. Her closeness. Her soft breaths against his skin.

But in that moment, having her as he wanted, his mind could finally move to other things.

And when it did, his lips whispered into the dark, "Why did they not use magic?"

15
HAPPIER

I pulled the nightgown over my head and let it slide down my body, the hem of sapphire satin swirling around my ankles.

Apollo was in the bedroom undressing for bed. I was in the dressing room off the bedroom, doing the opposite.

It had been three days since our mad dash back to Karsvall.

The good news was, in that time, Apollo hadn't killed anybody, and I hadn't threatened anyone with hedge clippers.

There was no bad news.

This didn't mean that things hadn't been eventful. They had.

At first, I was worried that it would be boring.

Sure, when I lived with Pol, we had a cleaning lady and most of his clothes were of the dry cleaning variety, and seeing as I had no job, there wasn't much to do. But I still did our laundry, the dishes, cooked. It wasn't like we had a house full of kids where I spent my time tidying toys or bandaging knees, but I had things to do.

The second full day I was there, Cristiana did everything, like putting away the contents of my trunks that had arrived from Vasterhague and even making the bed.

This left me with nothing. I'd already made snowmen and the guys had preparations for war to carry out, so I was at a loss seeing as I couldn't hang out with them.

And then, in the afternoon, Loretta and Meeta arrived.

They were my lady's maids.

This made Cristiana's job even easier as Apollo had brought them to the house, introduced them to me and explained their duties were to look after my "bedchamber" and my "person," so even Cristiana didn't have to tidy my clothes or make the bed anymore.

And seeing as I didn't even have to look after my "person," the presence of Loretta and Meeta meant I'd have *nothing* to do.

Further, Loretta either knew or had seen the other me around because she freaked way the heck out the minute she saw me (in a quiet way—that would be, her mouth dropping open and her eyes bugging out). This wasn't unusual but it was getting tired.

Fortunately, Meeta didn't.

And Meeta surprised me because she was Black, and I hadn't seen a Black person the entire time I was in that world. She was also pretty, with her hair clipped short to her head, very dark, smooth skin and a beautiful long, elegant neck that was to die for. Oh, and she had very intelligent, very assessing eyes.

And last, she had an easy, white smile that made me like her instantly.

But the introduction of Loretta and Meeta became a boon because, with none of the women having much to do, this meant we could spend our afternoons gabbing, something we did.

Fortunately, like everyone who knew the Ilsa before me, Loretta got over the resemblance quickly.

Unfortunately, the gabbing included Meeta matter-of-factly sharing that she was from the Southlands, a country called Maroo, and she had been a slave.

Yes.

A slave.

She then shared she was captured as a young woman and taken to another country called Keenhak where she was put into service against her will.

She also shared she wasn't really fond of that slave business (understatement). So she conked her "master" on the head, stole some of his valuables, spirited herself into the night and traded the stuff for passage on a pirate ship that took her to the Northlands.

Yes.

A pirate ship.

No kidding, this was her story.

She got as far away as she could, that being Lunwyn.

"I will take the cold and all these clothes," she said in her smooth but accented voice, her graceful hand indicating her clothing. "And do it happily to earn a wage and lay my head down free every night."

I was totally with her.

I'd also learned that Loretta had been laid by Hans. This I found because the guys still came around even if their strategy sessions were no longer held at the house. And I found it when he walked in, totally ignored her and greeted me like I was his long-lost sister, even though he'd seen me two days before.

Loretta watched this, got teary-eyed, mumbled an excuse and exited the room. Cristiana later shared why, this being that Loretta had slept with Hans, he hadn't come back for seconds, and she still had a big old crush on him.

Cristiana also took this opportunity to share that Apollo's men were quite active in the village and amongst the servants so, "Every other maid you'll pass, dearie, will have known the stroke of an Ulfr soldier's cock."

By the way, during my gabs with the girls, I learned that sexual mores here were a lot more lax. This being demonstrated by Cristiana's words.

And also, by the way, knowing this about the boys, I was glad Cristiana was over fifty years old and married, "To the love of my life, the stubborn, useless cuss," (her words). Therefore, she wasn't in danger of getting laid by one of the guys (I hoped).

I liked these ladies a lot and it was fun making friends again. There was a time when I had friends, but Pol, just being Pol but also doing what he did, scared them all away.

It felt good to gab with the girls, get to know them, and in doing it feel more settled in this world.

The other thing that was good was the dower house.

Outside, it was made of lacy, carved wood that had been weathered to a dark finish that made me think of chalets in the Alps.

Inside, it was what Apollo said it was, warm and welcoming.

But there was nothing rustic about the dower house of Karsvall. Its décor was sumptuous (though not as refined as the house in Fleuridia), yet tasteful.

That said, it seemed lived-in and loved. There were beautiful pictures of flowers on the walls and graceful vases or figurines here and there. And there were warm throws and fluffy toss pillows that made cuddling up with a book or having a gab with the girls feel homey and cozy.

It had a formal sitting room and dining room as well as a big kitchen downstairs. There was also a study that doubled as a library (thank God, more books!) and a small sewing room. But the best part of the downstairs was the conservatory at the back, made of glass and filled with plants—on tables, hanging from baskets, the windows dripping with damp.

The upstairs had three bedrooms with the "master bedchamber" having a dressing room, a bathing room and an additional small room (yes, for the chamber pot). It also had a massive fireplace with a cream marble mantel that provided a beautiful contrast against the dark wood paneling of the walls. It was decorated in creams and soft yellows with hints of peach and was quite feminine, the down comforter even tipped with dripping scallops of eyelet.

I'd learned that Apollo's mother lived there but not much more as Loretta and Cristiana gave each other big eyes and changed the subject practically before it was brought up.

I didn't push it. I didn't want to make them feel weird or force them to share anything that might annoy Apollo.

And anyway, I wanted him to tell me himself, in his time.

As for Apollo and me, our days had found a rhythm. This being him getting up way early in the morning, waking me to tell me he was going to eat breakfast with his kids, then he'd touch his mouth to mine and leave.

During the day, he'd mostly be away unless he had some free time. If he did, he'd come visit, but it was never for long.

Still, it was nice he did that.

And in the evening, he arrived just in time for a late dinner, which was after his kids had gone to have a bath then to bed.

Up next was the best part of any day, when *we* would go to bed and he'd make love to me. We'd spend some time whispering after we made love, these mostly sweet nothings while we cuddled (the second-best part of any day). Then he'd either make love to me again or we'd go to sleep.

Tonight, though, he'd sent Alek with the message he'd be late and that I should eat, and if he was very late, go to bed without him.

I'd been preparing to do this when I'd heard him hit the room five minutes ago and call, "Maddie!"

To which I called back, "I'm changing."

To which I heard nothing but his boots and belt hitting the floor, which meant he was getting ready for bed.

We'd also had one other change of circumstance since things settled in. This was Apollo getting me pennyrium, which he'd brought along with Loretta and Meeta.

So all was good on that front and sheaths were no longer necessary.

But it wasn't lost on me that we hadn't "explored" the "play" we'd engaged in that night we arrived in Karsvall, deeply or otherwise.

When he made love to me, it was sweet. It was slow. It was taking our time, building it then letting it explode.

It was also awesome.

But I had to admit, that night was hot. As in h-o-t, *hot.* I also had to admit I wouldn't mind exploring it (at all). Deep or otherwise.

That said, even slow and gentle, every time was good and there was no denying that the adela tea led us to understand each other better, what we liked, deepening the experience, making it richer than any I'd ever had or could even imagine having. There was a freedom to it, no being worried about what he'd think of my body or if I was doing something right. We had a kind of harmony in bed. It was about each other, togetherness, the experience and climax, all of this making the togetherness more meaningful. Even out of bed.

It was amazing.

Actually, Apollo was amazing. Tender, sweet, forthcoming, funny, and tender was worth another mention, especially the way Apollo did it.

And that was to say, the way he did it was just the way he was.

Sure, there was an arrogance about him that most likely came with his position in society and his family. But also, it just came naturally. A man of his looks, wealth, status and intelligence, this could happen. And with Apollo, it did.

That said, this was simply one small nuance of his personality. The rest, or the Apollo he gave me, was so much more.

An example being it had been three days and he'd made his point about wanting me to meet his kids and he didn't mention it again. No pressure. I was a ten-minute horse ride away, but he was a busy guy and he still split his time between me and them and didn't utter a word.

Nothing.

He just did it. He didn't bitch. He didn't push.

I had to admit, I loved that.

Actually, I was realizing there were a lot of things I loved about Apollo, and as I smoothed my hands over my nightgown at my hips, I knew I was excited to walk into the room and be with him. I didn't care if we made love, if we just talked, if we didn't talk and just cuddled.

I just wanted to be with him.

I never thought I'd feel that way about a man. Not again. I was done with all men after Pol.

So to feel that way about Pol's twin was crazy.

But as the days slid by, Apollo was making it crazy-beautiful.

On that thought, I wandered out of the dressing room into the bedroom and stopped.

He was in bed, smack in the middle, sitting up. He had the duvet to his waist, his wide chest on display, his dark hair was a mess from riding to the house, and he hadn't even bothered running his hands through it to give it some order.

He also had a sheaf of papers in his hands, his attention to them, and there was something about his big guy, muscled, powerful, commanding masculinity amongst all that cream, yellow, peach and eyelet that made my mouth water.

Then again, whenever I saw him, my mouth watered.

Also, there was the small fact that I knew he was naked under that duvet. Apollo never went to bed with clothes on unless he was doing it in the middle of taking them off.

His head came up, his gaze instantly slid down my body then it moved up, and when it made it to mine, I said softly, "Hey."

His face shifted to that tender look I felt in my belly and around my heart.

"Come here, dove," he said softly back.

I went there. While he tossed the papers to the nightstand, I lifted my nightgown to my hips and crawled into the bed on my knees. When I got to him, I threw a leg over and straddled his lap. His hands came to rest on my ass as my eyes found his.

"I've changed my mind about preferring you pressed to me, sleeping naked," he declared, his fingers accentuating his point by gliding over the satin at my ass.

"I have a lot of kickass nightgowns you've been missing out on, sweetheart," I replied.

"Mm," he murmured, this noise also hitting me in my belly but in a different way.

His eyes dropped to my chest and his hands started sliding up my sides.

I caught them at the wrists and he looked back to me.

"Baby, we've gotta talk."

That was when he did what Apollo always did.

He wrapped his arms around me, pulled me close and gave me what I asked for instantly.

"About what, poppy?"

God, I loved it that he could be this way.

I put my hands to his chest. "About three things. Then we can move on to the good stuff."

His lips twitched, his arms gave me a squeeze and he said, "Go on."

"Well," I started. "It's come to my attention that your boys are kind of..." I hesitated, "*active* at the main house and in the village."

His head cocked slightly to the side. "Active?"

"Very active."

"They are indeed active, Maddie. Though I'm thinking I don't understand what you're truly saying."

"Hans has slept with Loretta."

"And?"

"And...Loretta's my lady's maid."

"Yes?"

I stared at him, then said, "Well, Hans is one of your men and a friend of mine. And he's around the house, not often but he's around."

"This is true," he stated, patient but bemused.

Okay, surprisingly it seemed I had to explain this to him.

I moved a bit closer, sliding my hands up his chest to curl my fingers on his shoulders and I shared, "He's been here twice since Loretta came on board and he hasn't even looked at her. She's crushing on him big time—"

"Crushing?" he queried, his brows drawing together.

"She likes him."

"Ah," he murmured, his brow clearing.

"It's awkward," I told him.

"She shouldn't have taken him to her bed."

I blinked.

Then I said, "Actually, I was thinking you might have a word with the boys so *they* would be more discreet, and by that, I mean appropriate, and by that, I mean they might wish to go further afield when they're selecting their, um... play partners."

This time, Apollo stared at me.

Then his arms convulsed around me and he burst out laughing.

When he was down to chuckling, his arms came from around me so he could frame my face in his hands. He pulled my mouth down to his and gave me a brief, hard kiss with his still-chuckling lips before he wrapped his arms around me again and stated, "You amuse me, poppy."

"I was being serious."

He was *still* chuckling, but he blinked while doing it. "Pardon?"

"I was being serious," I repeated. "See, it's kind of..." I searched for a word and found it. "Uncouth for the hot guys of the manor to go around having their fun, leaving a trail of broken hearts in their wake. There has to be somewhere else they can go to get their..." I struggled again to find the right word. "Fun."

"And waste time astride a horse when they could be riding something else close to home?" he asked with mild disbelief.

My eyes got big, his lips curved into a smile, and I opened my mouth to speak, but he beat me to it.

"This is the way it is here, Maddie."

"I—"

He put his fingers to my lips and whispered, "Quiet. Please?"

I was quiet but only because he said "please." I really liked that he said it and I also liked his deep voice wrapping around that word.

He made sure I was quiet, removed his hand so he could wrap his arm around me again and went on.

"The people of this world are very free..." he paused, "sexually. The Vale, there are more strictures than Lunwyn. Fleuridia, less. But here, men *and* women enjoy each other openly and frequently. If Loretta has feelings for Hans that are not returned, that's unfortunate. But it happens. Does this not happen in your world?"

Actually, it did.

I bit my lip.

He nodded, correctly reading my non-verbalized answer.

"I'm sorry things are awkward, dove," he said gently. "But she is not under any misconceptions, I'm certain. She knows the ways of this culture. And it is highly probable she will find someone else to turn her attentions to. But this may happen again until she finds the man who...*crushes* on her as she does him."

This was how it happened in my culture too.

Drat.

"Are we done with that topic?" he asked, knowing the answer from reading my face.

I gave him a different one, however. "Kind of."

"What more is there?" he queried.

I thought about the Fleuridian prostitute and the fact that Apollo was most definitely a man and a man who liked to get him some.

"Have you, um...?" I trailed off.

"Never," he stated.

It was my turn to blink. "Never?"

"Never...recently," he amended.

There it was.

"Mm-hmm," I mumbled.

He drew me nearer, gentled his voice and explained.

"There are Heads of Houses who do these things. I am not one of them. I was married, my wife my one and only. After that, but I learned it before I was married, my dove, I found it uncomfortable to be around maids who knew me in this manner."

"In other words, they all fell for you," I deduced.

He nodded. "It's difficult to sit at dinner when the woman serving it is giving you longing eyes and you have had your fill and don't intend to drink more from that cup."

I looked away, murmuring, "I bet."

When I didn't turn back, Apollo's hand at my jaw brought me back. "Is there something else on your mind?"

I peered into his eyes, trying to decide whether or not to bring it up.

Then I brought it up.

"There was this woman who visited the house the night after you left me in Fleuridia."

His brows shot together and not in a confused way but in an annoyed one.

"Celise came to the house while you were there?"

"Well...yeah."

"She was not invited," he stated.

"She seemed to..." I hesitated, "well, it appeared she..."

"I have had her," he shared straight up. "Repeatedly. She visits me when I'm in Fleuridia."

Oh boy.

He kept going. "She has great beauty and she's very expensive because of it, that as well as her talent with her mouth."

Okay. There was my answer. Too late.

I shouldn't have brought it up.

"Uh, maybe we should stop talking about this," I suggested.

"You do not have whores in your world?" he asked.

"Well, yeah, but it isn't exactly bragged about, going to one."

"Why not?"

I stared at him.

"It's an honorable profession," he declared.

I kept staring at him.

"And only the best practice it. There are those who offer their services for a tumble, of course, but they cost little coin. However, they make much more than," he paused for emphasis, "a barmaid."

Eek!

He kept talking. "But there are those who cater to those of us who can afford the more skilled of their set, and they are quite talented. Some are even famous. Celise is one of them."

"That's crazy," I whispered.

"How so?" he asked.

"How not?" I asked back.

"This is not an answer to my question, poppy. Are whores not celebrated in your world?" he asked.

I shook my head. "No."

"Strange," he muttered then focused on me. "There are men, and women, who holiday in Fleuridia just to visit Fleuridian whores. They are the best in the Northlands."

"That's...well, I guess I find that kind of shocking," I told him.

"As I find it equally shocking providing such a service and being celebrated for your talent in doing it would be looked down upon in your world, as your reaction clearly states they are."

He looked like he was disappointed in me.

"We're not as free sexually as you are here, I'm getting," I explained.

His eyes grew dark, and I would know why when he inquired, "Do you feel guilt for what you do with me?"

"No," I told him quickly.

"If our coupling would be looked down upon in your world, why not?"

"Because I enjoy it and I like you and I like spending time with you and being close to you. So much, if we were in my world, I wouldn't care what people think."

His eyes shot straight to tender, and he said softly, "This is a good answer, my poppy."

I felt the tenderness in his eyes sliding through my insides, however, I did feel it necessary to point out, "Just to say, the men who pay for it in my world, and the women who get paid, are what's looked down on, Apollo. There's more sexual freedom for those who are free to be...uh, sexually free."

"Very odd," he murmured and again focused more closely on me to say, "If Celise made you uncomfortable, my poppy, I apologize. She was not scheduled to meet me that night. However, she has favorite clients, and I am one, so I'm not surprised."

And I wasn't surprised he was a favorite of the famous Celise whoever-she-was.

But I did wonder if he'd ever spanked her, drank adela tea with her or "explored" other things with her, and I knew, for some reason, if he had, that would upset me.

A lot.

"Now, are we done with this topic?" he asked.

"Yes," I answered, not about to get into how much he explored the beautiful Celise.

His hands moved over my nightgown, and he urged, "Then let's move on to the other ones so I can get this charming but entirely in the way nightgown off you."

I was suddenly not all that fired up about the other ones since they were harder but also because I wanted him to get my nightgown off of me.

Nevertheless, I persevered by stating, "What happened to bring us back to Karsvall, you've not mentioned it again."

"No," he confirmed readily. "This is because naught is happening. We're waiting for men and missives to arrive, but I don't expect any of either until tomorrow."

I loved it that he explained that to me, but that wasn't where I was going.

"Thank you for sharing that with me, baby," I whispered, and his hands stopped roaming so his arms could wrap around me again. "But that wasn't why I mentioned it. I had a question."

"And that question would be?"

"Well, the boys said frequently during dinner that night that we're kind of at war."

"Yes," he stated.

"I've been thinking on it and that seems weird."

"All of it is strange," he agreed.

"No, I mean the part about being at war and that happening because someone attacked you and your family. I mean, a king somewhere, I would get. But why were you a target?"

His body went still.

Uh-oh.

"Apollo?" I called, even though he was right there. But his eyes had grown distant, and I didn't like that all that much.

He focused on me and I held my breath as he did this for a good long time without speaking.

I let out my breath when he broke his silence.

"There are two possible reasons for this," he said.

"Okay," I replied when he said no more.

"One is that I'm Queen Aurora's strategist. I also served under King Atticus in this same position. This mostly included negotiations but there were skirmishes. Baldur was always conniving, he'd made some plays to wrest land from Lunwyn when he was the ruler of the now-gone Middleland. Most in Lunwyn don't know about them because my men and I stopped them before they took hold."

"Oh," I whispered, unsure about where this was going, though still thinking it was pretty cool badass Apollo and his badass boys nipped that shit in the bud.

"Frey is a raider," Apollo continued. "He is not a soldier. Lahn is a warrior, but his country in the Southlands is much different than those in the Northlands. His army is highly trained, highly skilled, large in number and thus unbeatable."

"Right," I mumbled, thinking this was good news.

"What I'm saying is, although Lahn is very intelligent, and strategy would factor into what he does, his warriors are so trained they need little direction, and so mighty they always best a challenge. They're known for it. This leaves Tor, who is also a warrior *and* a strategist. However, against our foes, we must put all our best minds together and Queen Aurora called upon me to be involved from the beginning. This could have made me a target, as any ruler or high-ranking general would be."

This made sense. It sucked, but it made sense.

"And the other possible reason?" I prompted.

He held my eyes, hesitated, but still he gave it to me. "It could be that you were the target."

What?

And *why*?

I picked one question and breathed it out.

"*What?*"

"Baldur has reason to be angry with all the couples who were brought together over the worlds. And Minerva herself connived to keep Tor and Cora apart by splitting Tor's soul and putting the other half in a woman from your world. This, we feel, is not a coincidence."

Oh boy.

"And you and I are now a couple brought together over the worlds," he concluded.

It felt good him saying we were a couple. We hadn't been together long but the time we had been together was intense. So yes, definitely good.

It didn't feel good me being a possible target of angry ex-rulers and she-gods, though.

"This doesn't make me feel warm and fuzzy, Apollo," I told him.

"It doesn't me either, poppy. But we can't know why they do what they do. We can only guess. And the coincidence is not something we can ignore."

"Does Baldur have reason to be angry with you?"

"Except for fighting in the war against the traitors who killed Atticus and imprisoned Aurora and Finnie, a war where his son was slain, not especially."

Well at least that was good.

"And...um, does he have a reason to be angry with the other me?" I asked hesitantly.

"No. Although I have met him at a variety of state affairs, and at some of them Ilsa was on my arm. But their meetings would be brief and insignificant to a man like Baldur."

I nodded.

That was good too.

Except for one thing.

"So, with the attack, it was probably directed at you," I guessed.

It was his turn to nod. "I have been thinking on this, Maddie, as it doesn't make sense. The only thing I can consider that does is that they fired their dart to make a statement. That being, they didn't have to use the mightiest weapons in their arsenal to make their first strike. The men who attacked us in Vasterhague were skilled. I do not like to think, if you hadn't intervened, how that would have ended."

I knew my face said "I told you so" when his lips curled up and his eyes lit with humor, so I decided not to say it out loud.

He kept going.

"Lees reports that the men here were equally skilled. Although, thankfully, no one was wounded, this was because my men are more skilled and also knew the lay of the land." He paused before, his voice deeper and rougher, he stated, "And I do not like to think of what might have happened if that wasn't the case."

I shifted a hand to his neck. "Then don't think about it, sweetheart."

He held my gaze and again nodded.

"What I'm saying is, they took those attacks seriously. They did not send easily bested adversaries. They planned to succeed. And this would make quite the statement, that they could get to me, to you, to my children, invading my home and taking all of our lives without even using all the power at their command. It would be such a statement that it might strike fear. Frey, Lahn and Tor are not men who are easily cowed by fear or maybe *ever* cowed by it.

But I think it's safe to say, if their wives or families were in greater jeopardy than we originally thought, that would do it."

The more he talked about these men, Frey, Lahn and Tor, the more I knew I would like them.

"Are we done with that topic?" he asked.

"Just one more thing," I answered.

"Speak it," he ordered, and I grinned.

Then I queried, "Where's Derrik? I've seen all the guys and not him since that night in the gardener's shed."

A shadow passed over his features before he replied, "He is away on assignment. A self-imposed assignment, but he is away on it."

I didn't get the feeling Apollo was happy about this.

"Self-imposed?" I asked.

"He was not commanded by me to take this assignment. I do not wish him on this assignment. He is under my command, but he is still his own man. I had no choice but to let him go."

I studied him closely.

"You're worried," I guessed softly.

"Indeed," he agreed.

That meant I was now worried and I wanted to know more.

But I didn't want to make Apollo tell me more when it was clear he didn't like talking about it.

"Okay, then, let's stop talking about that," I offered.

"I would be obliged," he accepted, his voice soft. "Now are we done with that topic?"

I nodded.

His hands started roaming.

"I have one more topic," I reminded him.

"Speak of it quickly, I grow impatient," he replied, his voice again low and rough but in a different way and this way I felt between my legs.

"Okay. Then, here it is. I made chocolate chip cookies," I announced.

His hands stopped roaming and he blinked. "Pardon?"

"Well, they're more like chocolate chunk since you don't have chocolate chips here and I had to bash some chocolate to make chunks and some of the shards got in the dough so they're kind of chocolate, chocolate chip coo—"

I was babbling.

Apollo heard it and interrupted me with, "Cease. Explain. *Clearly*."

See?

Arrogant.

Also dictatorial.

Unfortunately, still hot.

Whatever.

I sat up away from him and he let me. "Okay. Do you know what cookies are?"

He shook his head.

"Cookies are like little cakes. Except moister, richer, yummier. And the ones I made are the most favorite of most anyone in my world."

"And you made these today?" he asked.

"Yes," I answered.

His face changed, his hands slid back up my sides but did that pulling me to him again and his voice was *very* low and rough when he queried, "For me?"

I held his gaze and whispered. "Yes. For you. Also for you to take to Christophe and Élan."

His entire frame stilled.

Oh boy.

Okay, see, I had a plan.

Earn their hearts through their stomachs.

They were kids. That would work. Right?

When he said nothing, I said haltingly, "I, well...thought I would give them, um...a bit of my world. The kind of bit kids in my world like. And they might, uh...enjoy that."

"You're coming to meet them." It was a question said in a statement.

"Yes, maybe..." I pulled in a huge breath and finished on a question, "The day after tomorrow?"

"We will dine together," he decided.

Shit.

Crap.

Shit.

"Okay," I mumbled.

Apollo wrapped his arms around me. "They will like your cookies, poppy. They both have a weakness for sweets."

I nodded.

He pulled me closer. "And they will like you."

I swallowed.

"They will," he pushed.

"Okay," I muttered.

"This makes me happy, my dove," he whispered.

Okay. Well.

Him being happy made me happy.

"Good," I whispered back.

"Now have we covered everything you wished to discuss?" he asked, his hands beginning to roam again, his eyes warming, his lids lowering and all that was hot.

And him and all his masculine beauty in that bed with its cream eyelet duvet cover and pale-yellow sheets with peach embroidery, his broad shoulders against the headboard, his chest right there, I suddenly had something else to discuss.

"I have one more topic," I shared.

"Speak," he ordered, and I smiled a small smile that for some reason made the warmth in his eyes fire.

I didn't speak.

I reached for his wrists and wrapped my fingers around. I then pulled his hands from my body and stretched one of his arms along the top of the headboard, curling his fingers around the edge.

When my eyes went from his arm to his, I saw now they'd *really* fired. At seeing it, I fought squirming in his lap, took heart that he liked what I was doing, stretched his other arm out and did the same thing.

When I looked back at him, his eyes were ablaze, and I couldn't fight the squirm.

"You said we'd explore," I whispered, and his eyes scorched into me. "I want to explore." I kept whispering.

He said nothing, just held my gaze, his burning into mine causing a burn in *me*.

"Will you hold on to the headboard while I explore, baby?"

At that, his eyes flared, and his voice was a growl when he said, "For you, poppy, I'll try."

I felt my sex convulse at his answer.

"Thank you, honey."

His look was so hot, making me so hot, I didn't delay.

I put my lips to him and explored.

Running them and my tongue up his neck, across his throat, along his collarbone, I moved down and added my hands. I traced the bulges of his pectorals with my lips then moved to his nipples. With my thumb rubbing one, my tongue lashed the other.

His hips bucked and a stifled groan rumbled in his chest.

He liked it.

Thank God, he liked it.

So I gave him more, taking my time, sometimes lifting my eyes to see his face darkened, his eyes heated, watching me.

And I liked that.

Thus, I gave him more. Scooting down, I pushed the covers down with me.

And there he was. Hard, long and thick, standing proud, an invitation for my attention.

God, *gorgeous*.

I adjusted in a way he knew what I wanted and he spread his legs. I fell through and he lifted his knees, legs now wide.

I took him in, spread. For me. His gorgeous cock rock-hard. For me. All the power of him contained and waiting. For me.

All his beauty...for me.

Oh yes.

My nipples throbbed, my breasts felt heavy, the satin against them glorious torture, the area between my legs wet, I curled up between his legs, dipped close and ran the tip of my tongue up the underside of his hard cock, from base to the ridge of the tip.

Another groan, this one not stifled, and another buck of his hips.

I looked up at him to see the muscles in his arms and chest straining and the veins of his arms had popped out. His hands were gripping the headboard hard and I swallowed a whimper at seeing his power leashed, his passion controlled.

For me.

I gave him a small smile.

"Take my cock," he ordered, his voice thick.

I dropped my head and kissed the tip but gave him no more.

"Maddie—"

I moved and ran my tongue along the juncture of his hip and thigh. He shifted with agitation. I did too, then I moved to run my tongue along the other juncture.

"Take my cock, Maddie," he rumbled.

I looked up at him, holding his eyes as I again ran my tongue along the underside of his shaft.

"*Gods,*" he groaned, his head going back, his corded throat and the bottom of his strong, square jaw exposed. Taking all that in, I felt my clit start to pulse.

"You're so freaking beautiful," I whispered, and his chin tipped down.

"Take my cock," he clipped.

"So unbelievably beautiful."

"Take me, Madeleine."

I slid my tongue out slowly, touching its tip to the tip of his cock.

A rumble tore from his chest, and I saw now the muscles of his arms straining and his fingers were gripping the headboard so hard I feared he'd tear it apart.

At that, I decided it was time to give him more.

I wrapped my hand around his cock, brought it to me and took it deep.

"*Thank the gods,*" he rasped out, his neck again arching.

Then I gave it to him, mouth, tongue and hand. I sucked deep. I wrapped my hand tight and stroked hard. I vaguely noticed that now, his whole body was straining, even his legs, and I knew he was fighting back surging up and fucking my mouth.

And that turned me on more.

His rumbles became groans, spurring me on, and when they deepened and I felt his body tightening, I slid him out and sat up.

His head came up and his eyes seared into me.

"I want you to take my seed down your throat," he commanded, and at his words, another rush of wetness saturated my sex.

But I fell to my hip, yanked up my nightgown and tugged down my panties.

Swiftly, I shifted to straddling him, grabbed my nightgown and pulled it over my head, tossing it away.

"Another time, baby," I offered, reached between us and curled my fingers around his cock.

"Take me deep and ride hard, poppy."

He wasn't getting this. He didn't get to give orders.

But, damn, I liked how he did.

Still, I slid his tip through my wetness and whispered, "In a minute."

"Now."

I moved him to my clit, used him to rub hard against it and that felt fucking *awesome*.

"In a minute," I gasped.

"Now, Madeleine."

I rubbed him harder against me and made a mistake.

My head had fallen back, what he was giving me and *I* was giving me consuming me, I repeated myself.

But added the word "baby."

Suddenly I found my hand pulled from his cock. I righted my head just as he positioned himself to my entrance and both his hands grasped my waist. Fingers digging in, he drove me down.

My head fell back again as I breathed, "*Fuck yes.*"

And before I could start to move on him, his arms clamped around me.

My head came back up in surprise and I saw his face.

He was gone. It was like the night we arrived in Karsvall.

There was no control.

There was nothing but want. Hunger. Heat.

He shifted to his knees, taking me with him. As he did this, he lifted me up and my weight and the power of his arms slammed me brutally back down on his cock.

I loved it. It tore through me, pushing me straight to the edge. I was teetering as he fell forward, dropping me to my back in the bed.

But he lifted right back up. His fingers finding my ankles, he yanked my legs high, pressing them to his torso, pushing my heels into his shoulders as his hips pounded into mine, our eyes locked.

"Baby," I whispered.

"Touch yourself," he ordered, thrusting violent and deep, his fingers tight around my ankles.

"I'm close," I gasped. "If I do that, I'll come apart."

"Touch yourself, Maddie," he growled.

My head shook on the bed. "Baby, I—"

He pulled out, swung my legs around so he could roll me to my belly then he yanked up my hips so I was face down but ass up in the bed.

Then his hand cracked against my ass.

Oh God. God, God, *God.*

Yes.

My hips jerked, my ass stung, my body fucking *burned.*

"Touch yourself," he demanded.

Instantly, I lifted a hand between my legs and touched myself. Within a second, I was whimpering uncontrollably.

His hand cracked against my ass again.

"Yes," I breathed, pressing my fingers deeper, circling hard, lifting my ass to communicate I wanted more.

He gave it to me.

"Oh my God, Lo," I moaned.

Another smack.

My head flew back. "*Yes.*"

Another one.

"God, Lo, *yes,*" I exclaimed and came, *hard,* my cries sharp and piercing the dark.

I kept coming even as I felt him slam into me from behind and keep doing it.

And I kept coming with his fingers wrapped tight around my hips, yanking me back hard even as he thrust in harder. I was only just coming down when he drove in, ground in, and I heard his grunt of release that was so deep, I felt it vibrate through his cock right to the heart of me.

An aftermath quiver shuddered through me just listening, not to mention *feeling.*

He couldn't have come down before he pulled out, yanked me up and pressed his cock so that he'd buried it along the crevice of my ass.

But his arms wrapped around me tight, one at my ribs, one at my chest, and he shoved his face in my neck.

"You called me Lo," he said there, his breaths labored, his voice gruff.

Suddenly uncertain, I whispered, "Yes. I've heard the guys call you—"

He shoved his face deeper into my skin and squeezed so powerfully with his arms, my breath left me in a gush.

"This pleases me," he whispered back.

Thank God.

I relaxed into him.

He kept whispering, his words soothing into my skin. "*You* please me."

I closed my eyes but lifted my hands to his forearms, curling my fingers around tight.

He gave me another squeeze even as his hips pushed in, pressing his cock deeper between the cheeks of my ass. "Are you tender, dove?"

"Yes."

"But all right?"

"Oh yes," I breathed.

That got me another squeeze.

Then his arms relaxed (slightly) and his lips glided up my neck to my ear. "Some other time, I will take this arse," and his hips pushed in again, so I knew what he was saying.

A tremor shook my body.

I'd never done that.

But I wanted Apollo to do it to me. I wanted him to take me any way he could. I wanted to take him any way I could. I wanted to own him and I wanted him to own me.

And this knowledge shook me.

He wasn't done.

"Your arse again red, your fingers working between your legs, you'll climax with me buried inside it."

Okay, now I was thinking I wanted that immediately.

"We'll need oil," I said softly, and his teeth sank into my earlobe, which got another tremor before he shifted his lips to the skin at the back of my ear.

"I'll get some," he murmured there.

Goodie.

His arms moved. The one at my chest slanting to cup my breast. The one at my ribs doing the same to cup my sex.

"You give me this," he said gently.

"Yes."

"Freely," he added.

"Yes."

"With abandon," he finished, and he didn't hide this pleased him as well.

I said nothing but I felt a lot. God, so much. It was almost impossible to contain.

He pulled me deeper into his body and again shoved his face into my neck. "This makes me happy."

Oh *God*.

"I'm glad, Lo."

His mouth went back to my ear. "Is my dove happy?" he asked tenderly, and I bit my lip and felt even *more*.

So much more, it was devouring me.

And I didn't mind fading into it.

That shook me too.

My fingers tightened into his forearms, and I answered, "Yes, I'm happy, Apollo."

He said nothing for long moments. He just held me intimately, pressed close, both of us on our knees.

Finally, he broke the silence. "You're seeping. I will wash you and we will sleep."

"Okay," I agreed.

That got me another squeeze and a kiss on the neck.

Then he moved away to settle me gently in the bed and he bent to brush his lips on my jaw before he left me.

Then he set about undoing me.

And he did this by washing me, sliding my nightgown on me, smoothing his hands over the material then joining me in the bed, pulling the covers up to my shoulders and gathering me close, tangling me up in him. He did all this tenderly, with that look I felt in my belly and around my heart on his face.

He also did it like I was breakable, but precious.

Cherished.

No one had touched me that way.

Not in my life.

He held me tight to him as he rolled side to side to turn out the gas lamps beside the bed, leaving us with nothing but the firelight.

When he settled us on our sides, he drew me even nearer and I felt his lips at the top of my hair.

"I tell you now, my poppy, for years, I never thought I would again be happy. Never again." He tucked me closer and finished on a rough whisper. "So I never imagined I could be *happier*."

At his words and all they meant, my heart slammed in my chest, but I burrowed deeper, shoving my face in his throat, unable to say anything. Only able to feel.

"Sleep, Maddie," he murmured.

"Okay, honey," I forced out.

I felt his lips leave my hair and he kept one arm around my shoulders, holding tight while the other one moved down my back to smooth over my bottom, cupping me there lightly as if he wished to sooth the warmth that his hand left there. Warmth I didn't mind in the slightest.

I should have slept. Everything I knew, everything I'd learned, everything that was me told me to keep my mouth shut.

But in his arms, all he'd said, all he'd done, all we gave each other, I didn't.

My voice so quiet, it was even difficult for me to hear, I told him, "All my life, I've never been happy. So I never imagined even being that way. Until now."

He heard me.

I knew because that got me another powerful squeeze that took my breath away and I felt his lips back at my hair.

"I wish you to share why this was with me, Madeleine."

"I will, honey," I wheezed.

He heard the wheeze and loosened his arms.

"Not now. Now we sleep," he commanded, and at his arrogant, bossy command, I smiled against his skin.

"Right," I muttered.

"But I want you to sleep knowing how much it means to me that I've made you happy."

I took in a trembling breath, and to let him know I knew how much it meant and hopefully let him know how much what he said meant to me, I pressed my lips to the skin of his throat for a kiss. Then I turned my head and pressed my cheek at its base.

He continued to hold me close.

I burrowed closer, tightening my arms around him.

And I slept.

16

SKULKING

"I cannot believe we're doing this."

That was Meeta.

"Shh!"

That was Loretta.

We were skulking through the forest toward the main house.

We were doing this because Apollo told me two things the night before.

One, the men he was waiting for had arrived, they'd been set to patrolling and thus all of Ulfr land was now protected. This meant it was safe for us to leave the house and wander around without an escort. Apparently, his soldiers had been out on leave (kind of, I had a feeling "leave" meant "leave on missions Apollo didn't think it necessary for me to know," and I didn't really want to know so I was okay with that), but now they were back.

Two, he'd given the children my cookies and they'd loved them.

"It's lucky I had one before I gave them to Christophe and Élan," he'd told me, grinning. "For when I went back for more, they were gone."

This made me happy. Not only that the kids had liked them but also that he'd gone back for more which meant *he* liked them.

That night, I was to have dinner with them.

Suffice it to say, I was freaking out.

I wanted to ask Apollo for one more day (or seven of them) in which I could make them a variety of things. Snickerdoodles. Chocolate fudge. Lemon meringue pie. And I wanted to do this because I wanted them good and primed to meet me.

But I'd told Apollo I'd have dinner with them that night and I couldn't go back on that now. He was excited (in his badass-otherworld soldier type of way) for me to do it, so I had to do it.

For him.

But in thinking about it (okay, fretting about it), I decided that I couldn't walk into a room with them and keep my cool.

Unless I saw them again.

Therefore, during dinner one night when Apollo offhandedly told me their schedule—breakfast with him, studies, lunch, outdoor activities then back to studies before he spent time with them in the evenings—I was skulking through the forest with Meeta and Loretta in order to spy on them during their "outdoor activities" (whatever those were).

For moral support, I'd brought Meeta and Loretta along.

For obvious reasons, I had not shared with either woman, or Cristiana, that I was from another world. But knowing I looked so much like the other Ilsa, in other words, their dead mother, Loretta got me and understood my concerns about how the kids would react to me (if not all my concerns about why I was the way I was about them).

Meeta, however, watched me shrewdly in a way that felt weirdly like she'd figured things out, something she couldn't possibly do as, according to Apollo, only those who needed to know about the two worlds knew (with the warning I was to keep it that way, no matter how close I grew to the women).

That said, Meeta had agreed to go, if reluctantly. Though, mostly this was because, having been born and raised in the sun, heat and sand of the Southlands (this I knew because she'd described it), being out in the cold was not one of her favorite things.

So now we were skulking.

I'd been reduced to skulking.

I felt I should be slightly embarrassed about this, but mostly I was anxious about dinner that night and I didn't have it in me to be both embarrassed *and* anxious. Therefore, anxious won out.

"They can hardly hear us from this distance," Meeta pointed out to Loretta as I kept moving ever closer, using the horse tracks in the snow as my guide to the house.

"You never know," Loretta returned.

"Do they have unnatural hearing?" Meeta shot back.

"Not that I know of," Loretta replied.

"Then they will not hear," Meeta stated with clearly strained patience.

I was no longer listening to their somewhat ridiculous conversation, a conversation that would usually make me laugh, or at least smile.

In the last few days, they'd had these a lot. This was mostly because Meeta was highly intelligent, highly logical and not overly emotional (or, at least, she didn't show it). She was like a Maroovian Spock. Loretta, on the other hand, was not stupid but she was excitable and emotional, so she wasn't exactly Uhura or even Dr. McCoy. More like an honor roll cheerleader who'd been beamed aboard the *Enterprise*.

This made me Captain Kirk, for I was leading them on a misguided venture, and I hoped, like Kirk seemed able to do, I could get us through it unscathed.

On this thought, I saw it through the trees.

The main house.

Karsvall.

And *what* a house.

I had taken not one thing in when we'd arrived there days before.

Now, as I cleared the trees but stood behind one, peered around it and stared, I had no choice but to take it in.

This was because it was massive, long and four stories tall.

It was also made of the same lacy-carved, dark woodwork as the dower house but there was a lot more of it. *Tons* more.

The windows on the bottom floor were all arched and each as tall as a man. Along the front of the house there were decorative iron torches planted every three or four feet at a diagonal pointed away from the house. And on the second floor, every few windows, there were French doors that led to balconies with a carved wood balustrade surrounding them.

I noticed, taking it all in as I moved behind a border of trees, that the whole thing cut stark in the white snow. All around it was cleared so the dark pines and leafless trees framed it from a distance, making it look like something from a postcard.

I also noticed, as I got to the back, it was about symmetry.

The front had nothing leading up to it but a lane through a proud stand of pines that had clearly been planted in a way they looked like tall green soldiers at attention.

The back had matching gazebos, one on each side. Beyond the gazebos, there were large matching greenhouses with peaked roofs and ironwork shooting into the sky. And there was a line of short evergreen shrubs trimmed in perfect cones between the gazebos and the greenhouses, the shrubs delineating what my guess was the backyard, which was family-related, from what was probably more servant-related, the greenhouses.

And somehow, I had no idea how (they must have been dug by hand), twin rushing streams flowed in straight lines from the forest into a fountain that sat between the gazebos. Its waters brimmed forth from the tip of what looked like a carved marble saber. This water ran over frozen ice, the water and ice setting diamond twinkles into the sun. The streams also flooded out from the base of the fountain going toward the house and disappearing under it.

I took it all in and found it breathtaking in its frozen serene simplicity.

But what stole my breath completely was seeing Christophe wearing a mini-me Apollo outfit including a long cape. He had a bow and arrow and was aiming at a target some distance away.

Not too far from him, Élan was on her knees in the snow, not building a snowman but building what looked like a snow castle.

I noticed two things immediately.

One, they were even more beautiful out in the sun, doing things they enjoyed, not cowering in a bed, terrified out of their minds.

The other was that they both needed to put on hats.

"They should have hats," I murmured, staring at them, my heart pounding, my eyes beginning to hurt from just looking at all the beauty that was them.

"Try getting a hat on young master Christophe," Loretta mumbled. "I've heard he's stubborn, that one. His father doesn't wear a hat, he won't either."

At her words, I felt my lips curve even as my eyes kept burning.

"They're beautiful," I whispered.

"They are, indeed, Maddie," Meeta agreed from up close, her hand coming out to hold mine.

Christophe let his arrow fly. It hit just outside the bullseye, and I fought against cheering at the same time I fought against crying.

"They need a mother," Meeta went on and my heart squeezed just as her hand squeezed mine. "A mother would put hats on them."

She would. A mother would put hats on them. And tell them to eat their vegetables. And cheer when they made an almost bullseye. And help them make snow castles.

My throat started burning at the same time my scalp prickled in a weird warning and it was the latter that caught my attention.

I tore my eyes away from the children to do a scan of the area and I saw two men I'd never seen before in the forest by the furthest gazebo.

And they too were skulking, their eyes, I was sure even though I was far away, aimed at the kids.

Shit!

Apollo's men wouldn't skulk. They would have no need to skulk. It surprised me to know it, but with the presence of two skulking men, men who obviously weren't supposed to be there, it was apparent Apollo's men were falling down on the job at keeping Ulfr land safe.

But I couldn't think of that.

All I could think was that two rough-looking men were skulking towards the kids. And (except the way Loretta, Meeta and I were doing it), I knew skulking led to no good.

Therefore, quickly, I let Meeta's hand go and moved away from the tree I was hiding behind, looking this way and that, ordering in a quiet but urgent voice, "Go! Around the front. Head to the house. Find someone and tell them there's a threat to the children in the back garden."

"Maddie—" Loretta started as I found what I was looking for, dashed forward and pulled a stout, fallen branch out of the snow.

I whipped around to the girls. "Go!" I snapped and didn't wait to see if they did as I told them to do.

I moved.

Darting through the trees on the edge of the clearing, I kept my eyes to the men who were rounding the kids the other way. They weren't rushing (one couldn't rush while skulking) and I was, so I got close fast as they moved into the clearing, their focus on the kids, their bodies bent low in a threatening way, their clothing warm but rough, heavy beards on their faces.

I moved in from behind.

The one coming up the rear heard my boots in the snow, turned, and I saw his eyes widen in surprise because I was ready to strike. I had the branch back, I closed in on him quickly and swung at him with everything I had.

Unfortunately, he had time to lift up a forearm, so he caught the force of my blow there when I was aiming at his head.

Fortunately, I had another weapon at my disposal, my big mouth.

"*Kids! Run!*" I shouted just as the big guy with his scruffy beard caught the branch and wrested it from my hands. "*Run!*" I shrieked, launching myself at him, uncertain what I intended to do, just that I intended to do something.

I didn't make it.

Not because he fended me off.

No, because an iron arm clamped around my waist from behind and I was hauled back into a strong body.

I knew that body *and* that hold.

"Maddie, what on earth are you doing?" Apollo said in my ear at the same time Élan screeched, "*Uncle Quincy!*" And after that I heard Christophe shout, "Uncle Balthazar!"

Then I watched the kids run through the snow and throw themselves at the two rough men. The one I hit picked up Élan and gave her a cuddle. The one in front allowed Christophe to give him a brief hug around his middle before Christophe stepped back and the man put his big hand on Christophe's shoulder to give it a squeeze while he grinned down at him.

Oh shit.

It seemed I'd overreacted again.

I twisted my neck to look up at Apollo, saw his attention on me and explained in a whisper, "They were skulking."

His brows shot up (both of them this time) as his eyes lit with humor and he replied, "Skulking? Well, thank the gods you put a stop to that."

Crap.

I set my teeth to worrying my lip.

Apollo's arm gave me a fierce squeeze when he burst out laughing.

Crap!

Avoiding the children's gazes, I looked back to the man I hit, and when Apollo's laughter waned, I muttered, "Sorry I hit you with a branch. I thought you were a threat."

"I gathered that," he replied, his teeth very white against his russet beard, and I saw this because he was smiling huge. "Or, at least, I hoped that wasn't your form of welcome because I can't say much for it."

I heard Apollo's continued soft laughter (though I didn't laugh, even if the guy was being funny, not to mention nice about me hitting him with a branch) as he let me go but took my hand.

Placing it in the curve of his arm, he tucked it close to his side, bringing me with it, and moved us forward. "Quincy, Balthazar, meet Lady Madeleine."

I got two chin lifts and two big smiles from the men.

"Maddie," Apollo's voice was lower when he went on, "meet my children, Christophe and Élan."

"Hullo!" Élan chirped on an adorable, wide wave and my heart skipped a beat.

"Lady Madeleine," Christophe said.

I looked to him to see he was very like his father, and at that moment that included his green eyes dancing with amusement, and he was fighting back a smile.

I'd totally made a fool of myself. Captain Kirk never made a fool of himself.

I swallowed nervously.

Apollo spoke and I looked up at him.

"Now that you've explained your brave but erroneous attack on one of Frey's men..." Great. They were Frey's men. "Maybe you can explain why you're here. Dinner isn't until later."

"Loretta, Meeta and I were having a wander," I shared slightly dishonestly (okay, mostly dishonestly).

"Indeed," Apollo replied, his voice rumbling with humor, "I saw you three in the forest." He leaned into me and finished on a whisper that hopefully only I could hear, "*Skulking*."

God!

Someone kill me.

His beautiful full lips spread in a smile.

I decided to be pissed off as that was better than mortified so I narrowed my eyes at him.

He chuckled, pulled me closer and aimed his eyes at our onlookers.

"Christophe, Élan, it's time to get back to your studies. You'll be able to visit with Madeleine at dinner."

That got a nod from Christophe, but Élan opened her mouth to speak.

Apollo cut her off.

"Studies, precious girl," he said firmly but gently.

He called her "precious girl."

That was so freaking sweet it made my jaw hurt.

I closed my eyes.

"See you at dinner, Lady Madeleine," Christophe said, and I opened my eyes.

I nodded and forced out, "Looking forward to it, honey."

He grinned at his dad, went to his sister and grabbed her hand, pulling her as he moved to the house.

"I liked your cookies!" she told me excitedly as she was dragged behind her brother.

"I'm glad, sweetheart," I replied.

"You need to make more," she shared.

"Élan," Apollo said in a warning father's voice.

"I will," I told her quickly. "Sugar cookies next time."

"Hurrah!" she cried even though I knew she had no clue what sugar cookies were just as her brother tugged her nearer the house, murmuring, "Come *on*, Élan."

She waved at me.

I waved back.

They disappeared into the house.

Okay, well, one could say Captain Kirk was a whole lot better getting the crew of the *Enterprise* in and *out* of trouble than I was.

But I had the in part down.

"Quincy, Zar, we're to meet," Apollo stated.

I stopped kicking myself and looked to him then to the men.

"This may be delayed as I'll need a medic to look at my arm. I think it's fractured," Quincy, the tall, strapping, fair-haired, russet-bearded one declared.

Oh shit.

"If it is, I'm sending a bird straight to Kell so he can share with the boys that you got your arm broken by a woman," Balthazar, the tall, strapping, dark-haired, dark-bearded one said as he walked to Quincy and stopped.

A bird?

Before I could ask about the bird, Quincy told Balthazar, "She got the drop on me and clobbered me with a branch, Zar."

"She got the drop on you and clobbered you with a branch, Quince, and the operative word in that is *she*," Balthazar returned, grinning big.

"*She* is also handy with a blade," Apollo put in. "And swords. As well as lamps."

"Sounds like there's a story there," Quincy noted.

"Two," Apollo agreed and then he must have communicated something in man-waves because all three of them exploded in laughter.

Well!

"If you're done making fun of me," I cut into their amusement. "I'll *skulk* back to my house and return later for dinner."

Apollo turned smiling eyes to me and assured quietly, "We're not making fun of you, poppy."

"Really? I'm just a *woman* but I can speak Eng...I mean, the language of the Vale so I'm pretty certain I'm not mistaken that *you are*."

He looked to the men and explained, "She's very spirited as well."

"*She's* standing right here," I snapped.

He looked back to me and that tender look seeped into his eyes.

"Calm, dove," he said softly. "Do you think I or these men who are friends to my family think anything is unseemly about you being spirited or moving...*again*...to protect my children?"

Hmm.

Probably not.

I decided not to respond.

Apollo knew what my non-response meant and turned into me so we were standing front to front.

"Now, you're here and there's no reason for you to go back. Take your time, tour my home. The children are at their studies so you won't see them. I'll meet you before and take you to them. We'll sit and talk in order that you can get to know them a little better before we dine."

I was seeing the error of my ways (or errors, plural) in engaging on my skulking mission with Loretta and Meeta, but it was too late. We had an audience, an audience that was watching and not moving, and I couldn't have the conversation I needed to have with Apollo right then. And I could tell by the look in his eyes that Apollo very much wanted me to stay, tour his home and meet him before he took me to dine with his kids.

And I very much wanted Apollo to have whatever he wanted.

Shit.

"Okay," I told him. "I'll tour your house. From the size of it, that should take me about seven hours, though. If I get lost, send a search party."

His lips twitched before he leaned into me and used them to kiss my nose.

He moved back, caught my eyes and murmured, "Thank you, poppy."

I nodded, pulled in a deep breath and turned to the men. "It was lovely meeting you, after, of course," I looked to Quincy, "I attacked you."

"And you," Quincy replied, "after, of course, you attacked me."

He really was funny, and under all that rough, kind of cute.

Unfortunately, I wasn't in the mood to laugh or appreciate his cuteness.

But I did give him a smile.

Apollo let me go but put a hand to the small of my back and gave me a gentle shove toward the house, murmuring, "Go, Maddie."

I went, trying to be game and turning as I did to give them a small wave.

I got no waves back. Instead, I got a chin lift from Balthazar (who was also cute under all that rough), a grin from Quincy and a wink from Apollo who added a grin.

The wink was sweet.

And hot.

On that thought, I moved quickly to the house and disappeared inside feeling like a dork but thinking something good had come of that fiasco.

I had met the kids. I'd even spoken to them. Okay, so I'd also acted like an idiot around them.

But the hard part was done.

And now I could move on.

So maybe I wasn't so bad at this Captain Kirk stuff.

Though, I figured that still remained to be seen.

I STOOD at the massive picture window that rose two stories. A window that was one of twin windows on either side of a tall grand fireplace, its mantel of chocolate marble veined in cream, silver, gold and jade sweeping into the high ceiling.

I was looking out into the back garden, thinking.

Not surprisingly, Apollo's home was amazing. Far grander but no less warm and welcoming than the dower house, though also far more masculine.

It took ages for me to tour it, what with it having a formal sitting room, a formal drawing room, a massive library, a formal dining room (with a long table that seated twenty-six, yes, *twenty-six*), a morning room, an informal sitting room *and* dining room, as well as an octagon shaped conservatory off the informal sitting room.

There were kitchens, too, but I didn't go there because I was avoiding people (for obvious reasons).

Further, there was a room that looked kind of like it was a billiards room, but the table was much bigger and some of the holes led to shoots that expelled the ball back onto the table.

There was also a closed door which I took to be Apollo's study.

And last, there was the sunken great room that was the showstopper of the house. It was huge, its beamed ceilings vaulted, you walked in the front door over polished dark wood floors with fabulous rugs and that was what you saw before you. That fireplace. Those tall arched windows. That ceiling. And that room sunken into the floor, holding a vast array of comfy, deep-seated, supple leather couches arranged in a way that invited sinking into them with good company and a bottle of wine and wiling away hours.

The great room was the bomb. I'd never seen its like and probably never would again. Not even in this fantastical world. That was just how awesome it was.

During my tour, I also discovered the second floor (which had a cut out in the middle to afford the great room it's tall ceilings) was bedrooms, the third floor a ballroom (a ballroom that ran the length of the massive house!), but the floor above I didn't spend much time in because it looked like storage and servants' quarters. Not to mention, I could hear the kids down the hall, likely conversing with their tutor.

It took me two hours to explore it all, and not just because there was a lot of it but there was a lot to it. Portraits, objects d'art, rugs, tapestries, even the way the furniture was made and upholstered took my attention.

It was not a surprise with all his money that Apollo had a beautiful home. It also wasn't a surprise that it was comfortable and inviting.

What was a surprise was that it was *so much* of the latter. He was the only member of aristocracy I knew in that world (or my own). But even as huge as his house was, it was not imposing.

It was a home.

And I loved that.

This was what I was thinking when I heard boots on floor.

I turned from the window to see Apollo moving my way.

Burgundy turtleneck, brown breeches, his shined yet scuffed boots, and hair that was unusually swept neatly back from his face making me wonder if I liked it disheveled more than I liked it groomed.

"Hey," I called to get my mind off his fantastic hair (and to be honest, his breeches).

He smiled but didn't speak until he made it to me, curled his arms loosely around me and I'd put my hands to his chest.

Then his deep voice rumbled, "Hey."

That wasn't a word he'd ever used. It was a my-world word. And something about him using it made my heart sigh.

To get my mind off that, I shared, "I like your house."

His warm eyes got warmer, and he gathered me closer, but he kind of freaked me out when he did this at the same time he asked, "I would assume with the other me's nefarious dealings, he could provide you with a grand home."

"You would, uh...assume correctly," I confirmed hesitantly.

"Is mine grander?" he queried.

At that, I got it.

It was Apollo wanting to give me better.

I smiled and leaned into him. "Yeah, by, like, *a lot*."

He smiled back, pulled me closer and murmured, "This pleases me."

I felt all gushy because Apollo was pleased and I liked it when he was pleased.

Damn, I was fading fast. Fading into this world. Fading into him. And I didn't mind. Not even a little bit.

It was the fact I didn't mind that freaked me.

That was, I didn't mind until he announced, "As my home is agreeable to you, I'll charge Loretta and Meeta with packing your things and we'll move you here tomorrow morning."

I forgot all about fading and blinked.

"What?"

"Tomorrow, we shall move you here. It's not far to get to you, my dove, but it'll be far better to take dinner with you here and go to bed with you, also here, which means I'll wake here as well."

Um...

Move in with him.

Tomorrow?

Was he nuts?

"Uh, Apollo, by tomorrow I will twice have done something crazy in front of your kids and once, hopefully, acted like a sane person through a dinner with them. That's hardly time to move me in."

"You will have met them. You will be getting to know them. Thus, there will no longer be reasons for you to avoid them. You like my home. I see no purpose in us continuing our current arrangement."

"It's too soon," I told him, by a miracle succeeding in not letting my voice rise in panic.

"Too soon?" he asked, clearly perplexed.

"Yes. Too soon for them. Too soon for you and me."

"Maddie, how is it too soon?"

Yep. He was perplexed. And I was perplexed at how he could be.

I leaned back in his arms. "I've only," I lifted my hands and did air quotation marks, "*known you* for a week. A week is way too soon to live together."

"And how are we not living together now?" he asked. "We dine together. We go to bed together. We wake together."

Alas, this was a good point.

Luckily, I also had a good point.

"What about the kids?"

"What about them?" he asked, and I blinked again.

"Apollo, you can't seriously be suggesting I move in with two kids who I've said half a dozen words to."

"No, I'm suggesting you move in tomorrow morning when hopefully through dinner you've said much more."

I could tell he was getting impatient because his tone was sliding along the edge of sarcastic.

I lowered my voice to one I thought would calm him when I explained, "It's way too soon for the children. Honey," I hesitated then reminded him of something I knew I didn't have to remind him of, "I look like their mother."

"Élan doesn't remember her mother," he replied instantly. "And Christophe is an Ulfr male. This means that he may not show it, but he feels deeply. His friend shared with him what you did to avenge him and he admires this. I have shared with him the loss you suffered and he sympathizes as he has suffered his own. Therefore, he's keen to get to know you."

Apollo kept talking even though halfway through what he said I knew my mouth had dropped open and my eyes got big.

When he was done speaking, I asked, "He knows I stabbed a man?"

"Maddie, as you yourself have discovered, our world is quite different than yours and he's a boy who wishes to grow up and be a soldier like his father. These things don't upset him like they do you. He does indeed know you stabbed a man. He also admires it."

That I could let slide. Boys in my world would probably think the same thing.

Apollo wasn't done.

"But in knowing about the children you lost, dove, he respects it."

That I *couldn't* let slide.

"How could you tell him that?" I whispered.

Apollo's brows shot together. "And why would I not?"

"Because it's mine."

His brow cleared and he tried to gather me closer, but when I tightened my body and leaned away, he gave up and just brought his face closer.

"Do you not think," he began, his tone gentle, "that one day not one but both of them would put together the way it is with our worlds and wonder? Wonder why there isn't a them in your world or if you left their twins behind? You do not know him yet, poppy, but Christophe is very bright, as is Élan. They would eventually think on these things."

"Okay, I'll give you that," I replied. "But did this have to happen now?"

"I wish for my children to know the woman I intend to marry and I wish the same for the woman who is to be my wife. So yes, it had to happen now. There's no reason to delay."

"Did you think about maybe discussing with me what *about* me you could or could not share with your kids or, say, *anyone* at this juncture or any other juncture for that matter?" I inquired.

"What I wish to know," he replied, but did it carefully, "is why this is a secret? Maddie, you did nothing wrong."

He wasn't right about that.

I didn't share the ways he wasn't right.

I said instead, "That's not the point."

"Could you please explain the point?" he asked gently.

He was being gentle and he'd said please.

But he wanted me to move in with him *and* his kids.

Tomorrow!

"The point is this is moving too fast."

His tone was less gentle when he noted, "You say this often."

"Because you move too fast often."

"We clearly disagree on this," he returned.

"Apollo, it's been *a week*."

"And again, I will state we share the same table every evening and the same bed every night. I don't understand why it has to be in separate homes."

"Because there are children involved," I hissed.

"And this factors how?" he shot back, definitely less gentle and getting impatient again.

But I felt my own brows rise.

"How?"

"That's what I asked," he returned. "You see, my dove, it isn't you saying good-bye to your children and riding through the snow every night."

All right. Fine.

I could see that.

"Okay then, if that's a pain in your ass, and I could see that it would be night after night, then I'll sneak in the house after they go to bed."

He's brows knit. "Sneak?"

"Yes."

"Why would you sneak?"

He *was* crazy.

"Because, honey, I'd be arriving to crawl in your bed with you and do the nasty."

His jaw got hard, and his arms got tight. "What we do in bed is *not* nasty."

Uh-oh.

Obviously, he got the wrong idea about that.

I shook my head quickly and set about righting that wrong. "No. That's not what I meant. It's a turn of phrase in my world."

He dropped his arms and took a step back. "It doesn't surprise me that those of your world would use that word for lovemaking. However, they are wrong and *you* are wrong for using it to refer to what *we* do."

Now I could see he was getting angry, so I erased the space he put between us and placed my hand on his chest. "You're right. I'd never thought of it like that, but you're right and it absolutely does not define in any way what we do in bed or how I think of it."

"Yet you discuss sneaking into my home to avoid my children knowing you're here and in my bed, so you must hold some scorn or guilt for what we do," he returned.

"No," I shook my head again, leaning deeper into him. "Not at all. But they're *kids* Apollo. Young kids. And they don't need to know their father has a bed partner."

"I won't exactly be sharing our play second for second at the breakfast table, Madeleine," he stated, his voice turning cold. "But to share your bed with a woman you care about is not something to be ashamed of."

"No, of course not, but—"

"And I'll not communicate that by hiding who you are to me."

That was nice, so nice.

But that didn't mean he wasn't moving too fast.

"That's sweet, honey, but—"

"And I'll not have it communicated to my children...in *any* way...that the act of love between two agreeable adults is something to hide because it's shameful."

"Right, I get that, sweetheart. I totally do. But—"

"If you get it, then you move in tomorrow," he declared.

"Listen—"

"Tomorrow, Madeleine," he decreed.

Unfortunately, he was cutting me off and being arrogant and bossy all at the same time and this was serving to piss me off.

"Okay," I began, "you know your children better than me, obviously, so let's just say this is moving too fast *for me*."

"I do not understand how," he returned.

"Apollo," with effort, I controlled the snap in my voice, "I haven't had the chance to figure out what I'm going to do with my life, what with war breaking out and everything."

"And this requires you being in the dower house?"

"It requires time to think." When he opened his mouth, I hastened to add, "*Alone* time."

"Maddie, the children are with their tutors all day and I'm equally busy. You'll have plenty of *alone time*."

"You don't understand," I pointed out the obvious.

"No, I do not," he agreed to the obvious. "What I *do* understand is that whatever you're going to do with your life, you'll be doing it as my wife, living with *me* and my *children* in this bloody *house*. So you're very correct. I don't understand why you need to be in a home ten minutes away to *figure that out* delaying the inevitable, that being *moving in here*."

I tried to go gentle when I stated, "It isn't the inevitable. None of that has been decided, Apollo."

I didn't go gently enough.

I knew this when his eyes blanked, his face turned to stone and he asked, "And your choices are vast?"

Oh boy.

Now *I* was getting mad.

"Apollo—"

"So vast, it requires great blocks of *alone* time to consider all your options?"

"What I'm saying is—"

"And those options include options that are better than what I give to you and could give to you," he swept out an arm then leaned into me, "if you'd *bloody move in.*"

"You don't understand me—" I started but didn't finish.

"No, I don't," he clipped. "We've established that."

"What I mean is," I snapped. "You don't understand me and mostly, right now, you don't because you won't let me *bloody* finish."

He clamped his mouth shut, crossed his arms on his chest and scowled at me.

But when he did, I was so angry and all he'd said started crashing into my brain (because he was right, my choices *weren't* vast, in fact, they were practically non-existent), I couldn't get my head together enough to say a word.

"So." He threw out a hand and invited, "Speak."

"I need a second," I bit out.

"I don't have a second, Madeleine. I have a meeting with my secretary that should have started ten minutes ago."

Unfortunately, that led me straight into bitchy.

"Well, I apologize for being a drain on your time and taking you away from your schedule. If you're that busy, please don't let me keep you. I mean, we're just discussing our future."

"According to you, my dove, we don't have a future."

"That's not what I said," I hissed.

"Oh yes," he whispered. "It is."

Seriously?

"Apollo—"

He was not whispering when he said, "If you can manage it without attacking anyone, see yourself home. I'll give your apologies to the children that you couldn't make dinner tonight. I'll also not be joining you later this evening. However, this will serve to give you alone time to make important decisions about your future. And when you do, please share them with me so I can make some about mine as well."

With that, he turned on his boot and walked away, not realizing he left me gutted.

Or maybe he did, and he just didn't care, seeing as he was the one who'd gutted me.

17
HUZZAH!

I sat in the front room of the dower house, my crossed arms draped over the back of a couch, head down, cheek resting on them, staring at the light snow falling outside.

It really was pretty. Like a movie, so perfect it was unbelievable.

And that sucked.

For the first time since I'd been there, I wanted to go back to my world.

It had been four days since Apollo and I had fought. I had not seen him or heard from him in all that time. I hadn't even seen any of the guys.

Apparently, Apollo got the boys in our fight. Not surprising but it made things feel worse than they already did.

And I was getting the sense from not seeing him that things were pretty bad.

In other words, it had not been a good four days.

At first, I was pissed at Apollo and how he'd behaved like an arrogant ass who got what he wanted, and when he didn't, he threw a macho man hissy fit. I was also pissed at him because, although I'd been anxious at the time, I missed dinner with the kids and that hurt. Because he was right, they seemed to like meeting me (and I definitely liked meeting them, if you didn't count the part where I made a fool of myself). So, since the hard part was done, I wanted the second less-hard part to happen and I wanted that *bad*.

Then, of course, seeing as he was an arrogant ass, but he was also Apollo and I liked him, as one day wore into two, I started to miss him.

Now, on day four, I knew where I stood.

Therefore, I knew I needed to make a plan.

That was, figure out what to do with my life in this world.

A life without Apollo and his kids in it.

The problem was, I had no clue what to do with that life.

See, I really didn't want to be a prostitute. Even if they were revered in this world, I still thought that would suck.

And I couldn't be a lady's maid. I knew this because I couldn't do hair and had no clue how to iron clothes in this world.

A barmaid seemed kind of fun, but they didn't exactly wear nice clothes or hang with the best crowds, and Lord knew with my allure for trouble it would find me, and bars were where trouble often started seeing as alcohol was imbibed in them.

I could probably work in a kitchen since I knew how to cook, but we could just say that baking those cookies was a pain in the ass. It was worth it in the end, but they didn't have measuring cups in this world. Or ovens that had temperature controls. I could go on. Those cookies were touch and go from the start and I considered it a miracle they worked out okay.

I considered the option of starting my own business. They didn't have pizza in this world and everyone liked pizza. They liked it more when it was delivered to their house and the only thing they had to do was eat it and throw away the box. But, alas, I didn't figure pizza would stay warm being delivered in a sleigh. And starting my own business would require money, which I didn't have.

In other words, there really weren't a lot of opportunities that I'd seen for women in this world. In my world, I could get by. Sure, I would have to go back on the run. But before I took off, I stole a bucketload of Apollo's money that I'd stashed in safe places all over, so I didn't actually have to make a living.

Just run.

And hide.

But I couldn't get back to my world.

I had a medieval history degree and department store experience in a world that was kind of living its medieval history and had no department stores.

I was fucked.

Apollo was right, my options were not vast. I really only had one.

Marry him.

And honestly, when he wasn't being an arrogant ass, that was far from a bad choice. He came with a great house, cute kids and a pack of good friends, not to mention kickass clothes.

He also came with tender looks, interesting conversation, laughter, the ability to make me feel cherished and unbelievably great sex.

But now, I didn't have any of that because he was making it clear he didn't want me anymore.

Yes, I was fucked.

I sighed and it was a big one.

The one bit of good news in the last four days was that I started my period. So I wasn't pregnant.

Though, it must be said, having your cycle in that world was not fun and games, seeing as their sanitary products were as medieval as the rest of the world was. I'd learned this on the journey from Fleuridia (not fun to start your period around a bunch of guys you couldn't ask about tampons or pads and find a way to make do) and, like chamber pots, I still wasn't used to it.

I drew in a big breath and sighed again.

"Miss Maddie?"

I turned my head to see Cristiana standing in the doorway.

The one saving grace these last four days was that Apollo left me with my girls. At first, they'd acted the same, except a little cautious because of my mood. Now, they were watchful—in a caring way, of course, seeing as that was how they were.

But I hadn't shared what happened and twice I'd seen Loretta open her mouth only to have Meeta give her an elbow to the ribs. Thus, I knew they were worried.

I also knew I should open up to them. They were my friends. Or they were becoming my friends.

And even Captain Kirk had chats with Spock and Bones. Mostly, it was mild arguing or banter, but he shared his troubles with them. He was not the man, the island. Of course, the crew of the *Enterprise* was always in a life-or-death situation and that tended to promote sharing. Still.

It was just that it had been so long since I'd had friends, or *anyone* to open up to, I'd forgotten how.

And, in thinking about it (which I tried not to do, and failed), it occurred to me I really never had good friends I could open up to. When I was a kid, I didn't want to bring friends to my house because I didn't even like being in my house. This meant invitations to their houses dried up and I was often left out.

Thinking on this, I realized, as I grew older, my solitude kind of became habit. I had friends, just never really close ones.

Even though I hadn't opened up to the girls, it wasn't lost on them things weren't great. This was because I was moping and also because Apollo hadn't shown in four days.

"Hey," I called to Cristiana.

She smiled a small smile, her eyes on me assessing in a kindly way, and she moved into the room.

"Can I get you anything?" she asked. "Tea, perhaps?"

"I'm good, honey, thanks," I murmured.

She sat on the couch with me and looked out the window.

I looked back out it too.

"Ulfr doesn't come."

When she spoke, I looked back to her.

"Sorry?"

She gave me her regard, no less assessing, no less kind, but now astute. "Four nights he has not been here."

"No," I agreed.

"Will we see him tonight?"

I looked back to the falling snow and whispered, "I doubt it."

There was a long moment of silence before Cristiana broke it.

"May I ask, Miss Maddie, why you delay so long in healing this breach?"

I turned surprised eyes to her. "Sorry?"

"It's yours to heal and you delay. This isn't right."

"I..." I began and trailed off.

What was she talking about? How was it *my* breach to heal?

Had Apollo said something to her?

"Um...Cristiana, no offense," I pulled it together to say, "but you don't know what happened. I'm not sure it's my breach to heal."

"We women," she started, "it rarely is but it always *is*. Learn from me. I have thirty-five years with my husband. He is proud. He is stubborn. Therefore, when we have words and distance forms, it's up to me to close it."

There it was. One thing that was the same in both worlds.

"That isn't right," I told her the truth.

"It isn't but there are a lot of things that aren't right or fair in this world and this also pertains to relations between men and women."

She wasn't wrong about that.

"This, I know," she began, and I braced because her voice had gentled and she'd leaned into me when she spoke. I took these as warning signs and I was glad I did when she continued. "I have worked at Karsvall for twenty-three years. And thus, I was there when Ulfr brought home his bride."

I pulled in a sharp breath.

She kept going.

"Honestly, I knew no husband and wife who settled into marriage, and then parenthood, with the ease in which those two did. They had a steadiness that would have seemed unnatural if it wasn't so beautiful."

This, I did not need to hear.

Since I knew she was trying to be nice, I didn't tell her that and she kept talking.

"When she grew ill, he went to her several times a day, every day, and from their bedchamber, you would hear laughter. You would think nothing was amiss from the merriment coming from that room. But when he left and the door closed behind him, the cloud would descend. She was in her bed, she never felt it, but it followed him with every step he took. He is a good man, neither servant nor soldier bore the brunt of that illness eating away the woman he loved. But as it ate her away, it ate him too. And when she was lost, that cloud descended and stuck, immovable, shadowing him everywhere he went, except when he was with his children."

I pressed my lips together as I felt my eyes sting with tears.

That was so Apollo, to go to Ilsa when she was sick. Visit with her. Make her laugh.

But every time he did it, it had to kill him more and more.

I hated this for Apollo. *Hated* it.

"Then came you," she stated.

At that, my lips parted.

She kept going. "At first, when I laid eyes on you, your resemblance... extraordinary. I feared I understood his attraction to you and it was not healthy."

I held her gaze.

She went on.

"But what I saw was not him attempting to recreate what he had with Lady Ilsa. It was him building something new with you. Although she could make him laugh, the air did not ring with the richness of it near as often as it does with you. Although she was his wife and the mother of his children and he is a certain type of man, the type who would lay down his life to protect theirs, he did not look on her as if he needed to spring to her side at any given moment to shelter her from a storm."

Oh God.

Apollo looked at me like that?

My heart clutched.

She kept talking but did it softly.

"What you have is new. You may not know him well enough to understand, even if it is he who should ride to you to heal what has broken between you, his pride will not allow it. It may be that whatever happened between you is keeping him awake at night. He still won't do it. He is a man, but he is also an Ulfr. They have many qualities that are very good and these qualities make them the best House in Lunwyn. But with any good comes bad. I mentioned he is proud. But he's also stubborn. And last, he is a man used to getting his own way. And these three together will make things difficult at times for the people around him, most specifically the woman who warms his bed."

"I get you, Cristiana, boy do I get you," I told her. "But when he has something to say, he doesn't let me get a word in edgewise."

"Then, dearie," she leaned deeper into me, grabbed my hand and held it tight, "you must find a way to communicate, to *make* him listen, and that way may not be through words."

She was making all sorts of sense and it was an understatement to say that I liked—no, I had to admit I *loved* some of what she was saying.

But I didn't get that.

"I'm sorry, Cristiana, I don't understand what you're saying."

"Pay attention, Miss Maddie," she whispered. "For, if a woman is clever, and she pays heed, every man will give her clues as to how to make her will be known and even how to make her will be done and have *he* be the one who's doing it."

Holy crap.

"Are you talking about using sex?" I breathed.

She sat back and let my hand go so she could throw out hers. "If that works on a particular man, absolutely."

I pulled in a breath.

She had been doing great, but I didn't think that was good advice. Not with Apollo.

"However, Ulfr is not a man like that," she continued, and I let out my breath. "If you did not please him in the bedroom, he would not return to it night after night. That's certain. But he is not a man to be ruled by his body."

Okay, she was getting back on track.

"No, you, for him, it's something different," she declared.

"So," I started hesitantly, "you're saying I should play mind games."

"No," she replied. "I'm saying you should find your way to get his attention. This may be honesty. It may be emotion, as long as that, too, is honest. Ulfr is also not a man who would countenance games, as you call them. Manipulation is not the key to a man like Ulfr."

Definitely getting back on track.

And I knew it because Apollo had often made it clear he wanted more from me, and the more he wanted was me to share myself with him in more than time and sex.

So I whispered, "Right."

She nodded but carried on.

"He is also not a man who wastes time. He knows better than most how precious it is. And if given time because one is wasting it, he could make a decision that would be sad..." she paused, staring me direct in the eyes, "for him, for you *and* for his children."

"Giving up on me," I guessed, my voice quiet, my heart beating hard.

Then she got so on track, she was a freaking monorail.

"It's crucial, not only building something with someone but maintaining it, to show you care about the things they care about," she told me. "It is also crucial for you to demonstrate that you will handle their needs with care, just as they do the same for you. Apollo Ulfr would strike no one as a needy man. That does not mean he's not a man who has needs."

She was right. Because he was so strong, so imposing, it didn't hit me.

Apollo had needs.

He needed to protect his children and me against whatever was happening out there. And he was driven to do more, and that would be make us all happy, give us a good life, even when times were uncertain. And he needed to do what he had to do to keep his people—the people of his House, his soldiers, hell, all of the people of Lunwyn and the entirety of two freaking continents—safe.

And he didn't need to be fucking around with my issues because his were a whole lot more important than me figuring out I didn't want a career in prostitution and couldn't start a pizza delivery service.

In other words, I'd fucked up.

Shit, I'd fucked up!

And I had to sort it out.

Immediately.

I stood and announced, "I have to go to the main house."

Smiling, Cristiana stood with me. "You do, indeed."

I sucked in a huge breath and gave her a shaky smile.

When I did that but didn't move, she noted, "You're not making haste to Karsvall."

"Right," I said and jumped to it, moving swiftly to the door. But I stopped in it and turned. "Thanks, honey," I whispered.

"Go, Miss Maddie," she replied.

I nodded and ran to the hooks by the front door. I grabbed one of my cloaks and threw it on. I opened the trunk under the hooks, nabbed some gloves and pulled those on too.

Then I was out the door.

I had no horse of my own in the stables, so I had no choice but to walk to the main house. I did this as swiftly as I could, following the snowed over (as there hadn't been any of late) trail Apollo and the men's horses had made.

It still was a fifteen-minute walk, and even with my fur-lined cloak and gloves, I was frozen through by the time I hit the front door of Karsvall.

I stood there not knowing what to do.

Should I knock?

And what if the kids saw me?

Then it hit me it was early afternoon, after lunch and outdoor activities. They should be at their studies. So at least that was safe.

Talking to Apollo, that was another story.

I lifted my hand, not knowing whether to go for the doorknob or rap on it when it was opened.

Achilles was standing there.

"Hey," I greeted.

"Maddie," he replied, openly studying me, but he didn't hesitate to reach out, wrap his fingers around my elbow and pull me out of the cold. "It's been a long time since I've seen you," he noted, closing the door.

"Uh...yeah," I replied, looking nervously into the house and seeing nothing but Apollo's fabulous décor.

"You've been well?" Achilles inquired.

I turned back to him. "Yes...no. That is, yes-*ish*, but I would say no more," I replied and his head tipped to the side.

I could get he was confused at my answer, but I didn't have time for this. I had just spent fifteen minutes walking, time that ate away at my courage. I had to get down to this and pronto.

"Listen honey," I went on, moving closer to him. "I'd love to visit but I need to speak with Apollo."

"Is anything amiss?" he asked.

"No, but yes," I answered.

His lips curved up as he murmured, "She speaks in riddles."

"I need to talk to Apollo," I repeated on a whisper.

His eyes moved over my face and it was Achilles that got closer and his voice got lower when he said, "I'm sorry, Maddie, but he's away to the Drakkar seat."

My heart thumped so hard it hurt.

"Away? You mean, he's gone?"

"No. Not yet, but he's preparing to go and will be leaving soon and with haste. He has a long journey and must make it in time for the gale."

Shit!

"I really need to talk with him, Achilles."

He hesitated a moment, and I had to give it to him, his voice was kind when he lowered the boom.

"He would not welcome this talk, little bug."

Shit!

Apollo had spoken to Achilles, or he'd also been in a dark mood, and Achilles, not a dim bulb by a long shot, had read it.

"I still need to do it," I declared with more bravado than bravery.

He held my eyes an excruciatingly long moment before he nodded. "Then he's in his room. Do you know where that is?"

I had not officially been shown there, but during my tour I'd hit the master's bedchamber. I knew it was that because it was mammoth, richly appointed (and since everything else was seriously appointed, that room being *richly* appointed was saying something) and awesome.

It also smelled like his cologne and, well, *him*.

"I do," I told Achilles.

"Then go," he urged.

I smiled a shaky smile and took off toward the wide, carved wooden staircase.

I went as fast as I could go because with every step, I was losing the nerve to take the next one.

What if he was still pissed and was an asshole again?

What if in the last four days he'd figured out I wasn't worth it?

What if I got there and screwed everything up, said something stupid and damaged what was already broken to the point it couldn't be repaired?

These thoughts assailed me as I made it to his rooms and saw the door open.

Without knocking, I ran in.

His rooms were decorated in cream, jade and browns, mostly the latter two. He also had a small anteroom that I couldn't imagine he used much mostly because it contained nothing but a handsome round table with a carved support that had four clawed feet. This sat next to a coffee-brown leather chaise lounge overhung with a floor lamp.

I moved through, turned right to face where his massive bedroom was and stopped dead.

Apollo was prowling through the room, swinging his cloak over his shoulder, his head down so he could watch his hand catch the strap under his arm. His tall, powerful body in motion, that cloak flying out behind him, his thick chocolate-brown wool turtleneck and matching breeches, I forgot what a commanding presence he had, and my mouth went dry.

His head came up and he stopped too.

That was when my heart stopped.

Because without a flash, not even a flicker, he gave me nothing. His eyes settled on me, and they were blank, his beautiful face carved from stone.

There was no warmth. There was also no anger. Definitely no tenderness.

There was nothing.

I was too late.

"Now is not a good time, Madeleine," he stated, holding my gaze as he started walking again, buckling his cloak on his chest. "I'm away on an important errand and need to leave immediately."

He passed me and I turned with him at the same time I forced my lips to move.

"What I have to say is important," I told him.

He again stopped and turned to me. "Then say it. And quickly."

It was a lot less attractive, him being bossy and arrogant when he was looking at me with his beautiful eyes void of emotion.

No. Not attractive.

It was crushing.

"I...well, I thought you'd want to know, I'm, um...not pregnant."

Crap!

That wasn't what I wanted to say!

"Excellent," he returned, his voice cold, and he again moved as if he was going to leave.

"Wait!" I cried, taking a step toward him but I halted when he again turned to me.

When I got his attention, the words clogged in my throat and he finally gave me something.

Remote impatience.

"Madeleine, as I told you, I need to leave immediately." He swept me top to toe with a glance and finished, "If you have concerns about my absence, you've nothing to fear while I'm away. You'll be protected. Most of my men have returned and the property is heavily guarded. And Lavinia is en route. She will ensure that the witch I've engaged has made certain no enchantments can be cast on the house or the grounds."

"I...that's good," I stammered. "Thank you. But, Apollo," I took a tentative step toward him, "we have to talk."

"If you have something to discuss with me, you can do it when I return in three weeks."

Three weeks! He was going to be gone for three weeks?

"Now I must go," he finished.

He gave me his back and started to the door.

Without even a good-bye.

I closed my eyes and looked to the floor, my throat closing.

I was right, I was too late.

"Are you going to come with me or are you going to stand in my bedchamber staring at the floor?" he asked, and my head shot up. His first words were a ray of hope that he meant to take me with him. But when I caught his gaze, his next words smothered that ray. "I'll escort you to the front door and have a man take you to the dower house."

Yes.

Too late.

"You're in a hurry. You don't need to trouble yourself with me. I can get to the house, don't worry," I said quietly.

"Madeleine, it's snowing and now doing it heavily," he replied with clearly strained patience.

I looked to the windows and saw he was right. The snow was coming down a lot harder now.

I kept my eyes to the window and told him, "I'll be okay."

"You'll be more okay escorted by one of my men."

I looked to him, and he was wavy through the tears that had formed, but I swallowed and pushed out, "I'll be fine."

He didn't move so I did.

Dipping my chin to stare at my feet, I walked his way, and when I got close, I murmured, "Be safe on your journey, Apollo."

I didn't get by him. He caught my bicep in his hand and brought me up short.

I drew in a deep breath and tipped my head back to look at him.

"Are you distressed you aren't with child?" he asked.

I forced another swallow down a now swollen throat.

God.

Men.

In any world, they were totally clueless.

"No," I answered, my voice croaky.

"Then would you care to share why you walked through the snow to speak with me?"

"You're away on an important errand," I reminded him. "It can wait."

"I'm not fond of leaving women weeping in my bedchamber."

"I'm not weeping," I informed him, and it was the truth.

I *wanted* to weep. I was *going to* weep when the big gorgeous hot guy who didn't want me anymore finally was "away." And sure, there were tears in my eyes.

But I wasn't *weeping*.

"Madeleine, your eyes are swimming with tears."

Suddenly, I was done with this.

"Apollo, just let me go so *you* can go."

"Speak," he demanded.

I twisted my arm in his hold, repeating quietly, "Please, let me go."

"Madeleine." He dipped his face to mine, definitely impatient now and not remotely. "*Speak.*"

"I made a mistake," I whispered.

"In coming here?" he asked.

"In marrying Pol."

He went still. He was right, my eyes were swimming in tears so he was hazy, but he went so still, I could feel it.

"I have this...thing about me." My mouth kept going. "It's a weakness. A failing, really. And I...well, it led me to Pol. Actually, it led to a lot of bad things, but they all came through Pol. Because of this flaw, I didn't make the right decisions. I didn't listen to people who were telling me things I should hear. I saw what I wanted and went for it, consequences be damned."

He said nothing, didn't move, didn't take his hand off me.

So my mouth kept going.

"My father told me. He told me that I shouldn't marry Pol. And the first time it was bad, *really* bad in a way I knew it wasn't going to get better, it was only going to get worse, I should have driven myself to the hospital. Instead, I drove myself to my parents' house." I took a shuddering breath and slid my eyes to his shoulder. "He opened the door to me, one eye swelling shut, my nose bleeding, every breath shooting fire through me because my ribs were broken, he took one look at me and shut the door in my face."

Apollo did something then, his hand tightened around my arm.

But that was it.

"I don't know...I don't know how to be taken care of," I stammered my admission. "Because I've never had that. And looking back, my father was always that way. He was a bus driver and my mom worked too. But she made sure to rush home and have dinner on the table because that was what he expected. She worked as many hours as he did and still, she cooked dinner, did the dishes, the laundry, the shopping, cleaned the house. His job was driving buses, watching TV and complaining about everything under the sun *all the time*. The president and his policies. The Seahawks offensive coach. The number of Japanese cars on the road. I guess she did what she did, cowing to his every whim, just so she didn't have to listen to him bitch if she didn't."

I shook my head again, eyes still to Apollo's shoulder, and kept blathering.

"That negativity...constant," I kept on. "My mother, by the time I could cogitate, was buried under it. So buried she was barely even there. It consumed the air we breathed. She seemed to just drift through life with him, I swear, like she was doing her time, waiting for it to be over."

Apollo said nothing.

I looked to his throat.

"I was trying to do right," I said quietly. "When I got to this world. When I got a new start. I was trying to do right by finding a way to look after myself and do it not depending on someone to look after me. Finally, for once, being smart and learning to take care of myself. I depended on someone to look after me and he wasn't up to that job and worse, he was what I needed to protect myself from." My voice dropped lower. "I thought I had to learn from that. To be smart. To find a way to take care of myself."

Finally, he let me go and spoke.

"I am not your husband."

"I know," I whispered.

"If you do, then you speak of him now because..." he trailed off on a prompt.

"Because you're giving me everything he gave me except *more* and *better*. He gave me everything too and made it a curse."

His voice was still cold when he stated, "And you assume I'll do the same."

"I don't assume anything." I lifted my eyes to his still blank ones. "I don't think anything. I don't *know* anything. Not even who I am. And that's the point. I don't know who I am. I don't know how to be me. All I knew was living surrounded with negativity with two parents, one who was pissed at the world for what seemed no reason, one who was so gone, she was like a ghost. And my whole life both of them seemed like they didn't know I was around, and clearly, they didn't care much after I was gone. Then I was living in fear with Pol and breaking free only to live on the run, hiding from him, afraid for a different reason and that was that he'd find me."

"Maddie, your point," he pushed, and my heart sunk.

And it sunk because I was making my point, doing it honestly, sharing openly, and he still wasn't listening.

So, I got down to my final point so this could be done.

"Well, *I* need to find me. And I need time to do that."

His voice was arctic when he stated, "Alone time."

"No, Apollo." I shook my head again. "Just *time*." I threw out a hand. "Do you have any clue what it's like to live on the run, to live in fear, to know that if the man who seeks you finds you, you might have to take his life to save yours? Do you have any idea what it's like to live for over a fucking *decade* knowing you gave into your weakness and made a mistake that you paid for not only in pain and misery but the death of your *child*?"

I crossed both arms over my belly and looked to the windows.

"This has been lovely, amazing, all of it, everything you've given me. Even fighting with you because you showed me it was safe. I could say what I had to say without your fist connecting with my face." I said softly. "But it takes more than fairytale worlds to fix what's broken in me. And this is because I live every day knowing it was *me* who broke it."

Suddenly, I felt him move and looked his way to see he was sauntering to the jade brocade cord with its golden tassel that was by the bed. He stopped at it and gave it a tug.

I then watched him move toward the windows and he did this to round the heavy handsome dark wood desk that was sitting at a diagonal in the corner, facing the room. Confusion filtered through my sadness as he pulled open a drawer and unearthed a sheet of paper.

He was picking up a quill (yes, a quill, I'd learned months ago they didn't do ballpoints in this world) and opening a pot of ink when I got my shit together.

"I'm sorry," I whispered. "I'm being selfish. You need to go."

"Quiet, Madeleine," he muttered, scratching his quill on the paper.

I got quiet and watched. Back to the inkpot and to the paper. Ink. Paper. Another line. More ink. Another line.

I was so weirdly enthralled with this, caught up in my gloom, I jumped when a young boy came rushing into the room.

He looked at me, jerked his head down and up, then looked at Apollo.

"Sir?"

"A moment, Nathaniel," Apollo replied and kept scratching.

The boy and I watched.

Finally, Apollo tossed the quill down, put the lid on the inkpot and grabbed the paper. Straightening away from the desk, he moved around it, focus on the boy.

"Send someone to the dower house. Have them tell Loretta and Meeta that they need to prepare Lady Ulfr for the journey to the Drakkar seat," he ordered, and I sucked in breath, feeling my eyes getting huge. "Make certain it's explained to them that Lady Ulfr needs to be equipped to attend a gale. They will also be accompanying her."

He was folding the paper as he stopped by the boy. Once folded, he handed it to him and kept talking.

"They must make haste. We leave in an hour."

"Right, sir," the boy murmured.

"And take that to Achilles," Apollo went on, dipping his head to the paper.

The boy nodded.

"Go, Nat," Apollo commanded quietly.

The boy dashed out.

Apollo turned to me just as I forced myself to start breathing again.

And when he did, he said softly, "Come here, Maddie."

Without delay, walking woodenly, my eyes glued to his, I walked to him. And I was staring in his eyes because they were not blank. His face was not cold. Instead, his gaze was warm on me, his face soft.

I didn't want to hope.

But with what he said, his expression, I was hoping.

When I made it close to him, he reached and curled his fingers around my waist, pulling me closer then curving me into his arms.

"When we return," he continued in his soft voice, "you will remain at the dower house for as long as you need in order to..." he hesitated and finished, "find yourself."

Oh my God!

Was this happening?

"However, I would ask that you do this while spending some of your time with me and my children."

Holy cow.

It was happening.

I nodded and did it quickly.

His arms grew tighter. "Alas, for the next three weeks, I cannot guarantee you will have alone time."

"I, uh...well, that's, um...okay," I stammered, and I did that quickly as well.

"We will be traveling with a guard," he continued, and his hold tightened further. "And the children."

Oh boy.

I was freaking about a variety of things, including that new addition, but I said nothing.

"After what happened, I will not leave them," he carried on. "I would not have left you, but the way things were between us..."

He trailed off and I nodded again, this time that I understood.

One of his hands came up to cup my jaw just as his face dipped very close to mine.

"You must share with me more, poppy," he urged gently. "And you must do this in order that I can know how your mind works and won't come to mistaken conclusions just having your words that often cover much and say nothing."

He was right. So right.

I nodded yet again and whispered, "I'll try."

His thumb swept my cheek, and his voice was lower, deeper when he went on, still gentle. "I do now understand that it's difficult for you to speak of these things. So in return, I will try to be more patient."

God.

God.

He was beautiful, so, *so* beautiful.

In more ways than one.

I felt tears again sting my eyes.

"I'm sorry I screwed things up." I was still whispering. "I was just...I'm just—"

"Cease, dove, I know what you were."

I pulled in a breath and forged on.

"Well, since I'm explaining things, you should also know that in my world, when something happens and there are children involved, like, you know, one of the parents," I swallowed, "died or there's a divorce or something, we go a lot more slowly when introducing a new, well...partner to the kids. I understand," I continued quickly, "that you think differently and they're your kids so it's your decision to make. But it was strange to me. Very strange. When we argued, I was thinking of my need for time, but I was also thinking that they should have time to get used to me, get to know me, before they had to see me at the dinner table every night. It was...well, I thought it would be kinder to them to allow them an adjustment period. I mean, I'm not a bitch or anything, but you know, for kids who for a long time have had their father all to themselves, introducing them to the woman in his life is a lot for them to take."

"I have not introduced my children to another..." he paused, his mouth quirking, "*partner*, so in retrospect, I see this as wise."

He saw this as wise.

Thank God.

I relaxed in his arms.

He slid his hand down to my neck and gave me a squeeze, saying, "We must learn to talk like this, Maddie."

Again, he was *so* right.

And again, I nodded.

That tender look slid into his eyes before he bent his neck to touch his mouth to mine, and I swear it was crazy, I knew it, but I had to fight back bursting into tears because I missed that look and his touch so...*damned...much.*

"I do not like to think of your father leaving you to that man when you approached him for aid," he whispered, and I pressed my lips together and inhaled through my nose in a continued effort to fight back the tears. "You will not find such disregard here, my dove. So I urge you, along with discovering yourself, to find a way to get used to that."

I lifted my hands to the sides of his sweater, curling my fingers in to hold on and forced myself to nod while blinking away the tears that threatened to flood my eyes.

Yes. He was beautiful. In *way* more ways than one.

He slid his hand back up to my jaw so he could again sweep his thumb across my cheek and moved in to kiss my forehead.

Then he moved back, the pads of his fingers digging in gently and announced, "Now, we go tell Christophe and Élan you journey with us to Brunskar."

My stomach lurched but I said nothing.

Crisis averted, a new trauma right on its heels.

Such was my life.

Oh boy.

TEN MINUTES LATER, I stood in the great room trying not to fidget with my hands. Apollo was standing up in the entryway listening to something Laures had to say but his eyes were on me.

The minute we got downstairs, we'd run into a maid, and he'd called for the kids.

I was trying to keep it together, but I feared if I had to wait one more second, I'd fail.

At that thought, luckily (kind of) I heard a commotion and saw Élan round the corner at a run, Christophe coming slower at her heels.

She stopped dead when she saw me.

I clenched my hands together and tried not to hyperventilate.

Her gaze shot to her dad.

"Is Miss Madeleine coming with us?" she called across the expanse to her father.

"Indeed, precious girl," Apollo called back.

She instantly threw both her hands up in the air and cried, "Huzzah!" sticking out her booty and shaking it side to side.

Abruptly she stopped doing this and turned to her brother pointing at him, a triumphant look on her face.

She then announced, "Ha, Chris! Another girl is coming with us. That means when we stop to take lunch, we don't have to shoot at things with arrows and have snowball fights. That means we can make snow castles and talk to the bunnies!" She stuck her booty back out and swung it around again, pumping her arms at her sides and crying, "Huzzah! Huzzah-huzzah-*huzzah*!"

I looked to Christophe.

He was watching his sister with a disgusted look on his face.

Shit.

He turned his eyes to me, that look dissolved, and he grinned.

My heart thumped.

I grinned back then looked to Apollo.

He was smiling at his children.

Then he said, "Let us go."

Élan dashed to me, grabbed my hand and started tugging me toward the stairs.

Feeling her little hand in mine made me catch my breath so hard, it hurt, but I didn't mind the pain.

I let her lead me up the steps, Christophe joined his father, and they walked out first, Élan now skipping beside me as we followed and I tried to hold her hand in a casual way when I wanted to hold her so tight I'd never be able to let go.

Apollo looked over his shoulder as he descended the front steps, his eyes dropping to his daughter then coming to mine.

And on his face, that tender look was way, way, *way* off the fucking charts.

Thus, every inch of me warmed in a way I knew I could put on a bikini and the chill of Lunwyn wouldn't touch me.

Élan was right.

Huzzah!

One hour and fifteen minutes later, my trunks packed into one of two sleighs, the guys on horses all around (including Quincy and Balthazar, Apollo, of course, and Christophe on his own mount, like his dad), I got into the sleigh I'd be driving, my eyes on Élan who was bouncing on her bottom in the seat, the fur throw in her hands, crying, "Sit, Miss Madeleine. Sit. *Sit!* Let's be away!"

I looked to the sleigh behind mine that held Loretta, Meeta and Bella, the children's maid.

I then looked to Apollo who was talking to Remi.

Finally, I sat, Élan threw the throw over me and I took the reins.

"Miss Madeleine is in, Papa!" Christophe called.

"Excellent," Apollo replied then ordered to the group of ten riders and two sleighs, "Proceed!"

I flicked the reins, the horses moved, the sleigh started gliding over the snow as fat, fluffy flakes of more drifted down, and the horses around us closed ranks.

But I looked back to the house to see Cristiana standing in the opened front door.

When I caught her eye, she waved. Then she winked.

I smiled and blew her a kiss.

Then I turned to facing front just as Élan asked, "Do you know how to make snow castles, Miss Madeleine?"

"No, honey," I answered quietly.

"I'll teach you," she declared.

My lips curved up.

Hu...

Fucking...

Zah!

18
BRUNSKAR

"Wake her, Maddie."

I heard Apollo's soft words and looked up at him standing beside the sleigh.

Élan was tucked to my side, sleeping.

From my experience, the days were always short in Lunwyn, so it was dark. That said, it was also late.

And we'd made it to Brunskar, the Drakkar seat.

We'd been traveling for ten days through Lunwyn, and I knew the distance was long and the errand important because our hours on the go were longer than when Apollo and I were away on our aborted journey to Bellebryn.

This meant we usually took lunch *and* dinner by stopping along the way. It also meant Christophe was near-on dropping from his horse (but he'd never do that, as his father would never do that, and Chris, I'd learned, was keen to do *everything* like his dad).

And usually, at the end of the day, Élan was asleep at my side.

So when we stopped, it was to get a sleepy Élan and an exhausted Christophe to their baths (Bella oversaw this), take our own (Meeta and Loretta took care of mine) and hit the sack.

During our long journey I'd learned that Christophe liked studying math and also English (or the language of the Vale). He timidly shared that he liked to study the language of the Vale because he wrote stories (this timidity evaporated when Apollo straight up bragged about how great they were, which meant I was able to talk Chris into letting me read one when we got back to Karsvall). Adding to his artistic bent, he liked to draw.

But best of all, he liked to shoot his bow and arrow (and that bullseye was no fluke, he practiced any chance he got, even in the midst of eating a sandwich, and I saw close up that he was good at it).

This last was because he also shared what his father already shared with me. He wanted to be a soldier, *just* like his father.

Élan, I'd learned, did not like *any* studies. However, she did like "serving tea" (when this was described I knew she was talking about tea parties since Bella, various maids at Karsvall and her dolls were the usual attendees). She also liked to make snow castles and snow witches (what were referred to as snow angels in my world, except you punched a hat into the snow when you were done). And she liked pretty much everything else under the sun.

When she grew up, on the other hand, she was determined to marry Frey Drakkar, "The handsomest man in Lunwyn," she'd breathed. This was her heart's desire and she didn't care that he was too old for her. She also didn't care that he was married to Sjofn, or Finnie, the Ice Princess of Lunwyn. How she intended to overcome these rather large obstacles, I had no clue and didn't ask. She didn't need to know how huge they were, so I didn't share. She would grow out of it and find her own (age-appropriate, single, I hoped) hot guy.

I'd learned all this because Christophe often rode by our sleigh and chatted. He also would take his lunch and dinner with his sister and me. Part of this, I thought, was that he was intrigued with me and not because I looked like his mom. Instead, because I stabbed a man and hit another one with a branch and a woman doing those things in this world was intriguing, especially to a boy. But most of it was because his father took his meals with us and nearly always rode by our sleigh, and Chris did what Apollo did.

I'd learned all I'd learned about Élan because she rode with me in my sleigh, was extremely talkative and got excited at every snowflake, stand of trees or bunny who hopped across our path, and she felt I needed to share in her excitement.

I didn't care if she talked my ear off.

I would listen even if doing it lasted an eternity.

Needless to say, our days in the sleigh were little snatches of heaven for me. I loved getting to know the kids, especially since they were bright, funny, open and interesting.

The nights were the same.

Little snatches of heaven.

This was because, without me asking him to do so, the first inn we stopped in for the night, Apollo ordered a room for each of us and kept doing this throughout the journey. This meant, if the opportunity arose, the children saw him going to his room and me to mine.

But once they were tucked away, he came and slept with me in mine.

Before he slept though, he made sure *I* came, repeatedly.

Suffice it to say, Apollo missed me too. The first night we were back together, he'd communicated this by holding me in his arms all night (seeing as I was still on my period). He communicated this the first night my cycle was done by not delaying in giving it to me fast and heated (though the second time that night had been slow, gentle and sweet, as had the third).

Since that night, he just gave me the slow, gentle and sweet.

And every night, in his arms, I gave him not-so-fun bedtime stories (though, he'd asked for them) of my life growing up, my mom, my dad, my (kind of) friends and school. Anything and everything he asked, I'd whisper to him as he held me, stroked me, and I talked myself to sleep.

He had not yet coaxed me to talk about Pol.

But I knew that was coming.

He had also not shared much about himself.

But I'd see to that once I knew I'd given him what he needed from me.

In other words, although that long cold journey should have been tedious, it was anything but. I loved every second and I'd do it again in a heartbeat.

So I was disappointed we were there.

Brunskar, Frey Drakkar's family seat.

Their annual gale was tomorrow evening.

We'd made it in time.

I looked from Apollo to Élan and gave her a gentle squeeze.

"Wake up, honey bunch, it's time for bath and bed."

She snuggled closer and my heart turned over. I wanted to let her snooze the night away, holding her close, keeping her warm. But I knew I couldn't do that (as much as I wanted it) so I gave her another squeeze.

"Come on, Élan, time to get clean and then get warm."

"I'm warm," she mumbled into my cloak.

"You'll be warmer in bed," her father butted in, entering the sleigh.

He pulled the furs from her and put his hands under her arms, lifting her up.

When he had her close, she tucked her face in his neck, wrapped her arms around his shoulders and her legs around his waist.

He looked down to me, but I was already staring up at him.

Every time I saw him with his kids, holding sleepy Élan close, smiling as Chris chattered at him, I thought he'd never looked more beautiful.

Including now.

"I'll take her in. Stay close to Draven, poppy, until you get in your room," he ordered quietly.

I nodded.

He walked his daughter to the front door of the inn, and I saw Christophe and Hans standing there, Chris holding the door open for Bella to precede him and keeping hold on the door so his father could do the same.

I looked away and aimed my eyes forward and up.

I'd seen it from a distance, and when I did, I was glad that Élan had already fallen asleep.

This was because Brunskar was not like Apollo's home or any of the finer homes we'd slid by on our way.

Brunskar was creepy as all get out and scary as hell.

Of course, it was dark but the front of it was lit up by what seemed like hundreds of torches, even some on its face up four stories and more on the roof.

Its stone looked black against the gloomy firelight and its white backdrop of snow. Its lines were straight and aggressive with five towers spiking into the air. Many of the windows were lit, likely because they had guests for the gale, and those windows, too, seemed aggressive. Whereas the windows at Apollo's house were rounded in attractive trefoil arches, the windows of Brunskar were cut into spiked ogee ones.

And the castle (it had to be a castle, no other building had that shape) was set high into what appeared from the dark peaks that stood black against the starry midnight blue of the sky, to be a rather impressive mountain range. And in this world that didn't have motorized cranes or excavators, it was set surprisingly *high* into the face of those mountains in a way that it seemed to watch over the village below (also named Brunskar), and that way was not a good one.

It must be said I did *not* get a happy feel from the place. This was weird since I wasn't superstitious and I'd never felt that way about anywhere I'd been before except, say, when I was walking into a room Pol was in. But that was learned behavior. This wasn't the same.

I just didn't like it there.

And worse, I didn't have a good feeling about how things were going to go down there.

One thing Apollo did share during pillow talk was the fact that Frey was not Head of the Drakkar House, although he should have been, even if his father still lived. He just didn't want to be and I could understand that.

He had his hands full. He commanded elves and dragons, was a raider on the high seas (in other words, kind of like a pirate...well, actually a lot like a pirate, it was just that Apollo told me Frey's kind was the "good" kind, however that would go) and was married to a princess.

Alas, Apollo also shared that after the war that reunited Lunwyn and Middleland, Eirik, Frey's father, had been relieved by Frey of his responsibilities as Head of the House. Frey had then given these to his brother, Calder.

This had not made Eirik or Frey's mother, Valeria happy.

And intelligence had come to Apollo that one, the other, both or another member of the Drakkar family were in cahoots with the evil Minerva, her malevolent witch sidekicks, Edith and Helda, and the dastardly Baldur.

Therefore, Apollo reversed his decision not to attend their gale as he had been doing, but only since Calder and his wife Melba took over the House. He packed us all up and here we were.

And I didn't have a good feeling about it.

Any of it.

Especially that castle.

What I did have was Apollo as well as Draven, Hans, Alek, Remi, Gaston and Laures, not to mention Quincy and Balthazar, and they were armed to the teeth. I'd seen what lay under the green tarps in the back of the sleigh Loretta, Meeta and Bella were in, so I knew they understood the dangers and were not messing around.

Luckily, the kids didn't notice this, but I was thinking even if they did, they wouldn't care. This was because Apollo had clearly created a close relationship between his men and his children, and it was obvious the trust the kids shared with Apollo's boys was absolute.

They were a family—a familiar, caring, teasing, loving family.

This was another thing that made the journey good. I'd never had anything like it, never experienced anything so beautiful, not even on the long trip up from Fleuridia, though that was close. But the addition of the kids and my friends made it even better.

And I loved every second of it.

"Maddie." I heard Draven call, and I looked his way.

He was standing by my sleigh, offering his hand.

I threw the furs off, got up, reached out and took it.

Draven helped me out of the sleigh and tucked me close with my hand curved around his elbow as he walked me to the door of the inn.

"Are you all right?" he asked as we moved through the packed snow. "You seem preoccupied."

"That castle is freaking me out," I admitted.

"Good instincts," he murmured, reaching out to open the door for us.

But I stopped and looked up at him.

"What do you mean?" I asked.

He looked down at me. "The Drakkars," he shook his head, "except for Frey, Calder and their other brother Garik, den of vipers. Every last one."

Fabulous.

He drew me inside, saying, "You have no worries, my sweet. They're vipers, but they're far from stupid."

Well, that was good, I guess.

But with the feel of that place, I had to know for sure.

So I asked, "Okay, what does that mean?"

He stopped at the foot of the wooden stairs and looked down at me.

"That means tomorrow you walk into their gale on the arm of Apollo Ulfr and nothing but that matters. Lo is not a man to cross and they know it. And if anything is done or said to upset you, he would not hesitate to let his displeasure be known in ways they would not like."

Oh boy.

"Okay, now what does *that* mean?" I mostly repeated.

"It means, Maddie," he started quietly and bent close, "you look like Ilsa."

Oh shit.

I forgot.

How could I forget?

"Right," I whispered.

"This will be your first event amongst the Houses, love. It has been spread far that the resemblance between you and her is uncanny. I still don't think that will prepare many for what they'll see. Most will be well-mannered. The Drakkars, however, don't often concern themselves with manners."

Great. Just great.

"It isn't like you haven't been confronted with this very thing, repeatedly," he reminded me gently.

I turned us back to the stairs. "You're right. I have."

He stopped us again and I looked up at him.

"There are people who it matters what they think. And then there are those who it does not. I can tell you now, in the case of the Drakkars and anyone who might say or do something that would upset you, they do not matter."

"I see you feel in the mood to be a soldier philosopher," I remarked, and he grinned.

"I'm always at your service to impart wisdom," he offered.

"I know and sometimes it's annoying," I teasingly returned. "But this time, it's just plain scary."

He burst out laughing and moved us up the stairs.

I smiled and leaned into him as we made our ascent.

But inside I was thinking about that creepy castle, the not-so-nice family who claimed it, and the fact that my first gale was probably going to suck.

No, I didn't like it in Brunskar.

Not at all.

"I DO NOT THINK good thoughts about this place," Loretta declared.

I'd had my bath, and even though I could do it, she was brushing my hair. Meeta was across the room, arranging my clothes for the next day.

"I do not either," Meeta agreed. I looked to her in surprise at her words. She was supposed to be my Spock—level-headed, not irrational. "There's a chill coming down from that mountain," she went on, and I felt a chill slide across my skin when she did. Her eyes came to mine. "And it is not the normal chill of this icy place."

"It's all going to be fine," I lied, and I did this because I was Captain Kirk. I was supposed to be confident and reassuring, even if I was totally full of shit.

"It will be for you in about ten minutes when Ulfr strides through that door," Loretta noted, putting down the brush and arranging my hair on my shoulders.

I watched Meeta's foreboding expression change to a knowing one. A small smile lit her face as she threw the dress I was to wear tomorrow over a chair and did this still smiling.

I had no response because this was true, when Apollo walked through my door, everything would be fine. At least for me.

Loretta scooted her chair around to face the one I was in and remarked, "He has not had maid or cook or wench from the village."

This confirmation of what Apollo told me was good to know. Even so, I had no clue where she was going with it.

Then she gave me a clue where she was going with it.

"So what's he like?" she asked.

"Do not answer that," Meeta demanded. "I have not had a lover in months, my hand is getting tired, and I share a bed with you." She pinpointed her gaze on Loretta. "Therefore, that won't even be of use until we're home."

This was not good news. Not that Meeta couldn't engage in certain activities. No, that coupled with the fact she hadn't gotten herself any in months and a bevy of Apollo's boys was around, she was gorgeous, and they were active.

"I won't answer," I stated and aimed a smile at Loretta. "I'm sorry, honey, but that's private."

Her head tipped to the side. "Private?"

"As in, none of your business," Meeta clarified.

"I know what it means," Loretta retorted. "I just don't know why she thinks it is."

"Because she thinks it is," Meeta returned.

"But that's mad," Loretta shot back. "Everyone talks about what they get up to under the duvet."

"I think you may have noticed, doe, Miss Maddie is not everyone," Meeta replied.

Well, that was nice.

Loretta looked at me, now grinning. "That's the gods' truth. If you were, Ulfr would not be striding in here at any moment."

"He has good taste," Meeta murmured, and I started feeling squishy because that was *really* nice.

"Thanks, honey." I said softly and she looked at me.

"You're gentle. You're kind. And you're amusing. A woman who looks like you is rarely any of these things, much less all of them."

"And that's the gods' truth too," Loretta agreed. "They're usually vain and smug."

"And demanding," Meeta added.

"And attention-seeking," Loretta put in.

"But you're none of that," Meeta concluded.

"Which makes you grand," Loretta finished on a big smile directed at me.

Now they were both being nice.

"Uh...not sure you two have looked in the mirror lately, but you're both all those and neither of you are hard to look at," I pointed out.

"Hans seems not to think so. It seems he finds me very hard to look at," Loretta murmured.

I could see that still stung, worse now since we were traveling with him and she had to deal with him ignoring her for hours on end day after day.

And truth be told, I didn't get why Hans didn't think Loretta was the bomb and go back for more. Or simply just go back to stay.

She was very curvy, quite petite, had lovely light-brown hair and beautiful bright, blue eyes. She was funny. She was sweet. She held an excitement for life that was almost akin to Élan's. And, last, she was loyal to the core. I knew this because I knew she felt this for me, even if we hadn't known each other for very long.

Hans could do worse, but I didn't know how he could do better.

On these thoughts, I reached out and grabbed her hand. "Then why don't *you* look elsewhere, maybe to someone who'll see all that's you. But not one of Apollo's men," I hastened to add. "None of them seem quite ready to settle down...yet. And I think you are."

"She has great beauty, is gentle, kind, amusing *and* wise," Meeta decreed, coming our way and grabbing Loretta's other hand to pull her out of the chair, her meaning clear.

I let Loretta go as she stood.

"You guys get some rest," I called as they moved to the door.

Meeta arched her long elegant neck toward me.

Loretta waved.

"And, as usual, thanks for everything," I finished as they disappeared out the door.

All except Meeta's head, which she dipped my way before she closed the door.

I got out of my chair and pulled my soft wool robe tighter around me as I walked to the window.

We were at an inn on the nicer spectrum. It was clean, well-decorated and had its own restaurant downstairs. And the rooms had thick rugs on the floors so the cold couldn't seep through and heavy draperies so the chill couldn't come through the windows.

Still, I braved it to pull a curtain back and look out at Brunskar.

Yep.

Still creepy.

Totally.

"Maddie, dove, drop the draperies. You're letting in a draught."

I dropped the draperies at Apollo's voice and turned away from the window to see him in my room. No cloak, hair a mess (but in a good way) and hot.

My belly fluttered.

"Hey," I greeted.

"Come here and say that in my arms," he returned.

I smiled a small smile and did as he bid, walking to him and putting my arms around him as he did the same to me.

"Hey," I repeated a lot softer this time.

"Hey," he replied, also soft, and sweet, and that got a belly flutter too.

He bent his head to touch his mouth to mine.

Usually, this led direct to other things, including me taking his clothes off, him divesting me of my robe, nightgown and panties, and the fun didn't stop there.

But after he brushed his lips against mine, he lifted them to kiss my nose, let me go and moved to the bed.

I stood where he left me and watched him sit on it. Then I watched him take off his boots.

"Is everything okay?" I asked when he reached both hands back between his shoulders in preparation to take off his sweater.

His eyes came to mine. "We're in Brunskar," he told me something I knew and pulled off his turtleneck.

I ignored him unveiling the wall of his magnificent chest, not to mention the span of his wide shoulders (okay, I didn't ignore it, but I tried to) and said, "Uh...yeah. We're in Brunskar."

"No good can come of a visit to Brunskar," he muttered, standing and putting his hands to his breeches.

Great.

Now even Apollo was freaking me out about this place.

"Do you want to explain that?" I asked.

His belt undone, his fingers at the buttons of his fly, he looked to me again.

"No, I want your mouth between my legs. Then I want to watch you ride my cock. When we've both climaxed and my seed is dripping from inside you, I'll explain about Brunskar."

Suddenly, I didn't give a damn about Brunskar.

I gave less of one when he pulled down his breeches and I saw he was *very* ready for my mouth to be between his legs.

And I didn't even remember there was a Brunskar when he got in bed, put his back to the headboard, spread his legs, cocked his knees, and leveled his eyes to me even as he wrapped his big hand around his hard, thick cock and began stroking.

Every inch of me started tingling, most specifically my nipples and the area between my legs.

I had a feeling we weren't going slow and sweet tonight.

And I was looking forward to it.

"Remove your robe and gown before you join me, poppy," he murmured.

I couldn't be sure, I didn't think they recorded those types of things for the books, but I was relatively certain I had my robe and nightgown off in record time.

He liked what he saw, and I knew this because his voice was gruff when he ordered, "Crawl up the bed from the bottom."

Oh God.

Hot.

I didn't delay and moved to the foot of the bed.

"Slow," he commanded, and I swallowed.

I put my hands to the bed, then my knees and did as ordered, the whole way my eyes to his hand working his cock.

I got to my destination and felt his other hand cup the side of my face. I guessed what that meant and stilled so he could feed himself to me. I guessed right. Shifting the tip to my lips, his hand at my face slid up into my hair and put gentle pressure on until I took him inside.

His voice was thick when he whispered, "That's it, dove."

He was right.

That was it.

Or it was for right then.

I would get a whole lot more later.

Later, I remembered Brunskar because I'd climaxed, so had Apollo, his "seed" was seeping out of me and his hand was smoothing over my hip when he murmured, "Brunskar."

"Yes?" I prompted when he said no more.

His arms closed around me, and he gathered me closer so we were pressed front to front on our sides.

"The Drakkars, save Frey and his two brothers, are a vicious lot, greedy, lascivious and spiteful. Some are even cruel. They like to play and their favorite toys are people."

Wonderful. More good news about the Drakkars.

Ugh.

"Draven kind of warned me about them," I shared.

"Good," he muttered. "I would have done the same, but I've been struggling with whether or not to take you to the gale. Being here, the feel of the place, which I forgot just how unpleasant it could be, I think not."

That surprised me and I tipped my head back to look at the firelight playing on the angles of his face.

"Seriously?"

He looked down at me. "I do not like the idea of my dove being toyed with."

God, that was sweet.

"Ilsa," I whispered, telling him I knew what he was talking about.

He nodded. "That will be fodder, I'm certain. But they don't need it."

"I'll be okay," I assured him, though I wasn't exactly assured myself. That said, I knew I would be okay in the end because he'd make me that way.

This realization pretty much rocked my world, but I couldn't give into that feeling when Apollo kept talking.

"I don't want you just to be okay. I want you to feel safe and that will not be safe."

"Honey," I slid my hand up his chest to curl it around his neck, "I've endured far worse than mean people."

"Yes, you have," he agreed. "But that does not mean you need to continue to do it."

"What I'm saying is, that kind of thing doesn't faze me. And the Ilsa thing, it's not like I haven't had practice dealing with that too."

He made no reply.

I pressed closer. "Does it occur to you that I don't want you to go into what Draven called a den of vipers alone either?"

He sounded surprised when he asked, "You seek to protect me?"

"Well, you're a big guy who can look out for himself. But still. Unpleasant situations are a lot easier to deal with for anyone when they have someone at their back. Or in this case, on their arm."

At that, his hand slid up to my neck, then into my hair and he pressed my face in his throat while his other arm gave me a squeeze and I felt his lips at the top of my hair.

"I take it that means I'm going," I guessed.

"I have still to decide."

I sighed.

Then I pulled out the big guns.

"If you don't let me go, I can't wear one of my kickass gowns. I've been looking forward to wearing one of those gowns since I saw them in Vasterhague. And with us at war, if we're not at some gale where intrigues are happening and conspirators are conniving, where am I going to wear my gowns?"

He chuckled, taking the pressure off my head so I could tip it back. The instant I did, he moved in and gave me a sweet deep kiss with tongues.

When he was done, slightly breathless and tucked very close, I asked, "So, am I going?"

"I wouldn't wish to deprive you of your chance to wear your," he paused, "kickass gown."

"Awesome," I whispered, and he wrapped both arms around me even as I felt his body move with his silent laughter.

When he was done, he whispered, "Sleep, dove."

"Okay, baby."

At that, I got another squeeze and closed my eyes.

Minutes later, I slept.

I FELT the bed move and my eyes fluttered open.

This was because Apollo was joining me which made me groggily wonder why he hadn't been with me. He never left me, except to feed fuel on the fire.

I had no idea what time it was. I just knew I'd been dead asleep. I also knew his body seemed strangely cold when it moved into mine, colder than it would be just leaving the covers. And last, I knew he had something on his mind, and I knew what that was with the way he moved into me. That was to say, shifting me to my back, covering me and rocking his hips until my legs opened and they fell through.

"Baby?" I called, sounding sleepy and confused because I was both.

His hand found mine and guided it between us, straight to his hard cock.

Yep. I knew what was on his mind.

"Baby," I whispered.

"Guide me inside, poppy," he whispered back.

I did what he asked.

Once I'd positioned the tip, he took over, sliding slowly in the rest of the way.

My neck arched as he filled me and I wrapped myself around him.

His lips went to the skin under my ear. He moved his hips and started stroking.

My lips went to his ear, and I asked, "Is everything okay?"

"It is now," he answered.

I didn't think he meant it was because he was making love to me.

But I didn't get to ask him to clarify.

His hand came to my face, tilted it his way and he kissed me, slow, sweet, wet and deep.

I kissed him back the same way.

And the same way, he made love to me, building the burn, taking his time, then taking us both there.

I gasped my climax into his mouth.

He groaned his into mine.

When we both came down, he rolled us to our sides but kept one of my legs hitched over his hip so he had an easier reach to stroke my ass.

"Sleep, Maddie," he urged.

I'd just come. It was sweet but it was hard. And I was wrapped around Apollo and he was stroking my ass.

So he didn't have to urge me to sleep because, seconds after he did, I was there.

19

Intrigue Always Has Consequences

"You look like a princess!" Élan cried.

I turned from the mirror to Élan, who had come into my room and was gazing up at me like I'd gazed up at Cinderella at Disney World when I was seven, the one and only time my father took us on a family vacation. A vacation that didn't go well because Dad was the only person in the world who could find the most magical place on earth annoying and didn't mind sharing it, *all day*. This made me meeting Cinderella pretty much the only good part of it (save the Matterhorn and Space Mountain, both of which I'd *loved*).

Shoving that memory aside, I decided instead to let flow over me how freaking *great* it felt to have Élan staring at me like I walked right of a movie.

But it must be said, she was right. I totally looked like a fairy princess, or at least one who lived in a country covered in ice.

I gave her dazzled eyes a smile then looked beyond her to see Chris had come in with her.

He, on the other hand, didn't look dazzled. He looked startled and was hanging back. That was unusual behavior for him. If not as effervescent as his sister, he wasn't detached. And I'd never seen him startled by anything.

Before I could make anything of it, my attention went to Apollo, who had brought the children in. But when I looked at him, my heart stopped.

He didn't look dazzled either.

No.

Instead, he looked like he very much liked the dress. So much, he looked like he'd very much like to rip it off me. He had control and this control kept him across the room. But there wasn't much of it. I could see it in his face, something I'd seen before, that hunger, that heat. It was so strong, it communicated itself to me. I felt it sear through me and everything melted but him and that heat.

That need.

This was heightened significantly by the way *he* looked. Thick hair swept back. Dark-brown trousers tucked into shined boots, and his dark-brown cloak lined in almost-black-brown fur.

But his forest-green shirt had a high collar, and this time he was wearing a neck cloth.

If you'd asked me five months ago if I thought that look was hot, I would have said, *hell no.*

But believe me, it wasn't hot. It was freaking *hot.*

Bella broke into our scorching staring contest by ordering, "Say good-bye to your father and Miss Maddie. They're away to the gale."

"I can't *wait* until Frey Drakkar takes me to my first gale," Élan breathed, and I tore my gaze from Apollo and looked down at her. "I'm going to wear that *exact* dress."

"I'll save it for you, honey bunch," I promised.

"Hurrah!" she cried.

Thus commenced Élan dashing forward to give me a quick hug, Chris approaching his father, getting a squeeze on the side of the neck and then Chris turned to me to dip his chin.

But he didn't approach.

Again, odd. We rarely got physical, but he did get close to give my hand a squeeze when we had the occasion to say goodnight.

Bella, Loretta and Meeta, however, did approach.

Meeta did it to me, bringing with her my bronze velvet cloak.

Loretta also did it to me, carrying my satin evening bag.

Bella did it to the kids, huddling them and herding them out as Élan waved and cried, "Don't forget to dance!"

Oh shit.

There was going to be dancing?

Oh shit!

Of course there was going to be dancing. It was a ball.

The problem was, I didn't know how to dance.

Crap.

I couldn't think on that, the kids were leaving so I called, "Sleep tight!"

"We will," Élan called back before she disappeared.

Chris said nothing.

Again, *odd.*

My mind was turned from Chris this time as Meeta arranged the cloak on my shoulders then Loretta moved in and gave me my bag.

I bent in to kiss Loretta's cheek and turned to Meeta.

When I did, smiling, I looked into her eyes. At what I saw there, the smile froze on my face, and I stilled.

"Enjoy your evening, Miss Maddie," she murmured.

But she didn't mean that.

She meant, *Be careful and stay safe.*

How I knew this, I didn't know. I just knew her eyes were troubled, even alarmed, and that freaked me way the hell out.

"Madeleine, our sleigh is waiting," Apollo cut into these thoughts, and I looked to him to see he had his hand extended to me.

"Remember everything...eh...vree...*thing*. We want to hear it all on your return," Loretta ordered, coming forward to fuss with the folds of my cloak as I moved to Apollo.

I had a feeling from Apollo's earlier look that I wasn't going to be having girlie time "on my return."

I was coming to love my girls. But from that look, I was good to wait until the morning.

I didn't share this with Loretta.

I told her, "I'll remember, honey, promise."

I got close to Apollo, and he took my hand, lifted it and curved it around the inside of his elbow. Without delay, he moved us to the door.

Right before we went through it, I looked over my shoulder at Meeta.

She was watching me with a weird intensity that was unsettling, her expression clouded. Then, she strangely lifted up a hand, only a slim forefinger extended, and touched the tip of it between her eyes.

I didn't know what that meant. I just knew it meant something.

I obviously couldn't ask and I couldn't think on it either. Apollo was moving swiftly, and I had to think about keeping up with him and not tripping.

Before I knew it, we were in one of his sleighs with the furs over our laps and he'd snapped the reins. The chill air bit at my cheeks and through the heavy (but not as heavy as fur) velvet cloak. I shivered for more than one reason as my eyes lifted to the torchlit castle.

Apollo must have felt it, for he curved an arm around me and tucked me close to his side.

That felt better.

He then dipped his head and murmured into the top of my hair, "Your beauty tonight is unsurpassed."

That warmed me all the way through to the point where my toes curled in my beaded velvet slippers.

Because I knew what he meant and it meant the world.

I looked exactly like his dead wife. But tonight, I knew I looked better.

It might be greedy and wrong to love that, but I had to admit, I did.

Then again, even I was stunned at how awesome I looked.

I had help and not just Loretta and Meeta's awesome skills with hair and makeup.

There was no other way to describe it, my gown was *sublime*. A dark-green velvet that skimmed my figure to the bottom of my hips and flared out into a full skirt. The velvet led up to a strapless bodice, but this was covered in a fabulous topaz lace that melted down my torso, disappearing at my hips.

The lace formed a Sabrina neckline and dipped a little at the back, which was kind of backless. The kind of part was that the velvet came only to the small of my back and up my sides, but that extraordinary lace covered my skin, providing an elegant, peekaboo back done up the middle with lace covered buttons.

The dress was sleeveless, so I wore long, bronze satin gloves that fit tight up to my mid-upper arm. My feet were covered in flat green velvet slippers with a thick suede sole and topaz beading at the pointed toe.

My makeup was heavy, smoky and *fabulous* (Loretta's doing).

And the neckline of the dress was so perfect I needed no jewelry at my throat. But Loretta gave me emerald and topaz chandelier earrings to put in my ears as Meeta linked chain after chain of emerald and topaz bracelets around my right wrist.

And last, my hair was swept loosely back to a smooth, but large, lovely chignon Meeta fastened at the nape of my neck then, on each side close to the bun, she slid in extravagant combs that had ends which were large sprays of emeralds and topaz that glittered against my hair.

I had not, for some reason, perused the entirety of the jewelry collection Apollo had given me. But once my girls had outfitted me, I decided to rectify this error at my earliest convenience.

That said, it gave me a niggle of unease, for it was very clear not only the dress and shoes, but especially the jewelry, were costly and it was yet another thing that Apollo gave me that made me feel strange. Like our relationship was lopsided—he the giver, me the taker.

But I didn't have time to think on that too much either, what with my transformation from just me to Glamor Girl Me.

And Apollo liked Glamor Girl Me.

And as ever, when Apollo liked something, I liked that.

I pressed closer, put my cheek to his shoulder and admitted, "Every time I look at you, I think your beauty is unsurpassed."

He clearly thought this was amusing and I knew this when his arm gave me a squeeze and he chuckled.

"I'm being serious," I told him, tipping my head back to look at his jaw. He looked down at me, still smiling, and I went on, "The best, though, is when you're with your kids. I don't know exactly what it is, but there's something seriously gorgeous about a hot guy being a loving dad."

He stopped smiling at my words, his arm tightened further so he could pull me up as his head came down and he did this so he could kiss me hard.

And also wet.

Totally ruining my lip gloss, I was sure (yes, they had lip gloss here, and all kinds of makeup, the containers and applicators were a bit rough, but it worked).

I didn't care even a little bit. Lip gloss could be fixed. It would be a crime if that kiss had been missed.

When he lifted his head, I blurted, "I've no clue how to dance."

That got me his smile back and he relaxed his arm so I could again relax into his side as he looked ahead. "Matters not. I detest dancing and don't do it. So if others invite you to the floor, I'll be there to ward them off."

Thank God.

One thing on my list of things to fret about that night that I could tick off.

"Maddie, please remember what I told you this morning."

I stifled a sigh.

Before we left bed to have breakfast with the kids (and after, for me to hang with them outside while they did their thing and Apollo went off to do Apollo things), he'd been very clear about how tonight was going to go. As in *very* clear, giving bossy orders and pressing me to promise (out loud) to heed them.

"I remember," I told him.

"The men are already there, except Laures, who follows this sleigh. You will not see any of them all night. But they'll always be close."

I put my cheek back to his shoulder and nodded, knowing, for whatever reason, he had to reiterate himself, so I was going to let him do it.

"I am not out of your sight the entire evening," he continued.

I made a mental note not to drink too much, thus necessitating the chamber pot, and snaked my arm across his belly in order to give him a squeeze to indicate I heard and understood.

"And this means you are never far so, if needs be, I'll be at your side within seconds."

"It's going to be okay, honey," I assured him quietly.

He said nothing.

I again tipped my head to look at his jaw. "You have a bad feeling," I guessed.

"We're in Brunskar," he told the horses, not giving me his eyes.

I cuddled into him again, aiming my eyes at the castle and this time I said nothing because, seriously, we were in Brunskar, and I was getting that that was enough said.

I watched the castle get closer and spent the time I did doing my best to hold back the foreboding that got greaterm when suddenly, Apollo spoke.

"Do you love wearing that gown as much as I love seeing you in it?"

There it was again.

He didn't like my gown. He didn't even seriously like my gown.

He loved it.

And I loved that.

So much, it made me feel squishy inside, but still, I answered hesitantly, "Uh...I think so."

"I hope so, my poppy. I hope you love wearing it very much. Enough to make wearing it worth whatever comes this night."

Oh boy.

"Just to say, you're freaking me out," I shared.

"Good," he replied immediately. "This means you'll remain aware and cautious."

"Now you're *really* freaking me out," I told him.

"Excellent," he stated. "This means you'll remain *really* aware and cautious."

I decided to shut up and continue my freakout in silence.

And I did this while I watched the castle get closer.

WITHIN HALF AN HOUR of being at the gale, I learned a number of things.

One was that Houses had colors. This was why Karsvall was decorated in a lot of greens, browns and golds, because those were Apollo's House's colors. And this was why anyone who was at the ball who belonged to a House was wearing matching colors to their mate, like I was with Apollo. And I learned this because Apollo whispered it to me when I asked him what the deal was with that.

I also learned that the inside of the castle of Brunskar was way creepier than the outside. In fact, it was so creepy, it was a miracle of creepiness.

This was because the colors of the House of Drakkar were blood red and black and they decorated liberally in both. It looked like the home of Dracula's way more evil brother. The one they couldn't write books about because he'd scare the beejeezus out of even the most hardcore horror fan.

I further learned that the Drakkar's didn't like light. At least not inside. The outside was lit like they were hoping to make it seen from space. Once I'd hit the gloomy inside, I figured this was because they wanted it seen...and feared.

But inside, although there were tons of people milling about, it still had only the minimum of lamps and candles lit to help guide your way.

And last, I learned that Apollo and Draven were right.

Quickly upon arrival, Apollo found Calder Drakkar and his wife Melba to give them his greetings and introduce them to me.

Incongruous to the surroundings that were her home, Melba was sweet with kind eyes, and when we met, she gave me a cheek touch. Calder was very handsome and only showed a moment of shock when he looked at me before he hid it and lifted my hand to touch his lips to my knuckles. We chatted with them briefly, it was warm and welcoming, then Apollo let them go so they could see to their other guests.

Shortly thereafter, he found Garik Drakkar who was also very handsome and who also only allowed a brief moment of his surprise to show before he hid it and lifted my hand to his lips.

He and Apollo spent much more time talking. Through this, I noted they might not have been best buds, but they clearly had respect and regard for each other. Both men smoothly included me in the conversation in a way that I knew, if given time, I would have respect and regard for Garik too.

But after Garik moved away, Apollo wasted no time leading me through the crowd and pointing out the other Drakkars, noting the ones I should be most wary of.

He didn't have to.

The minute I laid eyes on them, I knew it. I hadn't lived with Pol for years not to be able to read evil.

"Kristian," he'd muttered, having given me a glass of champagne he'd grabbed off a passing tray and drawn me toward a wall with a vantage point to most of the enormous ballroom.

He'd turned my attention to another somewhat good-looking man (though, not nearly as handsome as Calder and Garik).

Kristian Drakkar.

"Frey's cousin, brother to Franka," Apollo went on "He's not near as clever as the rest, and thus is often a target for all. But even the most simpleminded of animals, if they have claws, will strike when they've been played with enough."

Apollo turned me slightly and gave an almost imperceptible jerk of his head toward an older man who had Drakkar written all over him. A man I knew at a glance I would not like, mostly because my flesh started to crawl the instant I laid eyes on him.

"Eirik," Apollo stated. "Frey's father. He's vain and vulgar. At his side is Valeria, Frey's mother."

I turned my attention to her. She was older but still very beautiful.

And she knew it. Yes, it was that obvious that I could read it across the room.

Apollo kept talking.

"She, too, is vain. She's also greedy. And lastly, she's conniving." He moved closer to me and dipped his head so his lips were at my ear. "If they conspire, it will have been her idea."

I nodded and he lifted his head but shifted me slightly.

"If you look about the room, you'll see a woman in a dress not fitting society. Her eyes are on you," he stated.

I scanned the room and found her.

Her eyes were, indeed, on me.

And I knew, of all of them, she was the one to watch out for.

I looked quickly away, hiding it by taking a sip of champagne.

"Franka," Apollo said. "Vain. Debauched. Unscrupulous. Calculating. Heartless and tirelessly cruel. Avoid her at all costs, my dove."

He didn't have to tell me that. I knew it the instant I laid eyes on her.

"Right," I murmured.

He shifted to stand in front of me, so I lifted my eyes to his.

"I must approach Eirik and Valeria, but I do not want you at my side when I do."

"I'll be okay," I told him.

He studied me for a moment and his voice was soft when he replied, "I believe you will. I still don't want you at my side. Ravenscroft is here. He's an acquaintance I trust. I will leave you with him. Before I do that, I'll explain I need to have words with Frey's parents and that I'm loath for them to meet you but wish to remain close to you." He dipped his head to mine. "Your appearance, poppy, he'll understand and take care of you."

He needed to do what he needed to do and not have me argue about it with him, even though I didn't want him anywhere near those people without me. So I let it go and nodded.

He took me to Ravenscroft, a tall, slim, dashing older man with kindly eyes who we chatted with briefly before Apollo leaned in and spoke quietly in his ear.

Ravenscroft looked Eirik and Valeria's way, then back to Apollo. He nodded and turned to me.

"My dear, why don't we get you something to eat?" he asked.

I looked to the tables filled with food. They were between us and Eirik and Valeria, the perfect spot for us to be occupied doing something it would seem natural to do, but me not being out of eyesight of Apollo while doing it.

"I'd like that," I said, taking the arm he was offering. "I'm famished."

Apollo caught my eyes as we moved away, and I smiled at him.

His lips curved up, his face got soft and then he looked to the Drakkars, and the softness vanished.

I'd lied about being famished, of course. My stomach was in knots. But I did my best not to show it as Ravenscroft (his first name was Norfolk), guided me around the food tables, sharing with me his favorite nibbles, all of which I tried.

And when I did, I decided it sucked my stomach was in knots, because if I wasn't in a creepy castle with icky people all around, I knew I would find them all tasty.

I was thinking that when Norfolk put his hand to my elbow and squeezed.

"Come away," he whispered urgently, his mouth suddenly at my ear.

I turned to look up at him in surprise, infinitely aware and cautious, as Apollo's warnings and creepy castles made me be, and his sudden demand concerned me.

My eyes slid to Apollo, who was talking with Eirik (an Eirik who was staring beyond Apollo even though Apollo was speaking to him, and when I glanced, I saw it was at a woman's décolletage) and Valeria, whose attention was pinpointed on Apollo, her expression giving me a chill.

I looked back at Norfolk, who was putting pressure on my arm.

"If you don't mind, I'd like to remain here," I told him.

"Then remain close," he told me, fairly yanking me to his side, his eyes not on me but over my shoulder.

I looked there just as Franka Drakkar murmured a purring, "Norfolk."

But her focus was on me.

Oh boy.

Here we go.

I straightened my shoulders.

"Who do we have here?" She kept purring before Norfolk could return her greeting.

"Franka," Norfolk stated tersely. "This is Lady Madeleine. Madeleine," he looked down at me, "I present Franka Drakkar, cousin to Calder."

"Cousin to The Frey," she corrected, an edge to her voice, her meaning clear. She had that powerful connection; she was not to be trifled with.

Frey was known as The Frey and The Drakkar. The first meant he commanded the elves, the second, dragons.

In other words, a very powerful connection.

"And cousin to Frey Drakkar," Norfolk bit out, humanizing Frey and telling her, I guessed, to go fuck herself.

"Lovely to meet you," I murmured into the exchange, deciding to be rude and not offer my hand.

"Oh, agreed," she whispered in a way that I could swear sounded suggestive.

"We're to dance," Norfolk declared, and that was a good gambit to get us away from this obviously vile woman, but still, my heart lurched.

I wanted to get away from her, but I'd seen the dancing. They weren't swaying to rock ballads (which I could do, no sweat) or waltzing a basic box step (which I could *try* to do and might have a small chance of not making a fool of myself doing it). No, each dance had steps, some seemed complicated, but it wouldn't matter because I knew none of them.

Franka's eyes moved to Norfolk. "But I've just met this lovely specimen," she protested. Her gaze came back and at the wicked look in her dancing eyes, I felt my neck get tight. "Or have I? You seem *very* familiar."

Bitch.

"She is of Ilsa's blood," Norfolk put in curtly.

"*Of* her blood or *is* her blood?" Franka asked, not looking from me, her voice saccharine sweet.

"A distant cousin," Norfolk stated like he'd rather have acid poured on his skin than continue the conversation, but clearly, he was momentarily stuck by good(ish) manners as Franka was refusing to let us go.

"Not that distant," she replied, keeping her gaze glued to me. "Ulfr seems smitten, but I suppose I shouldn't be surprised at *that*."

Total bitch.

"What surprises *me*," Norfolk started firmly, "is that you've noted she has Ulfr's arm and yet you approach with claws bared. You're craftier than that, Franka, surely."

"Oh dear," she put her hand to her spilling cleavage, and I was a girl who figured if you had it, you should flaunt it. That said, you shouldn't *expose* it. "Have I been rude?"

It was safe to say I was done with this.

"No, you've been reckless," I told her.

But I didn't stop there.

It was maybe stupid, but seriously, my life hadn't been all that great (until recently) and I didn't need to put up with catty bullshit. In fact, no one *ever* needed to put up with catty bullshit.

"Yes, I am aware I very closely resemble Apollo's sadly deceased wife, unfortunately for you, as you clearly wish you could have drawn blood by imparting that wisdom. But as you've noted and Ravenscroft confirmed, I have Apollo's arm. So I must admit, I'm disappointed. I've heard a bit about you and thought you were far cleverer than instigating a thinly veiled frontal attack. One I can assure you Apollo won't need me to inform him of since he's quite protective of me and is no doubt watching this exchange. And I would suppose you also already know that this exchange is one which will displease him greatly."

Her expression showed excitement as she tipped her head and asked, "Is that an invitation to instigate a different kind of attack?"

"Do as you wish," I returned. "However, you should know, I find games tedious and tend not to play them."

"Now *that* I find unfortunate," she replied on a venomous grin, which stated plainly she didn't care if I was going to play or not.

She was.

"And *that* I find unsurprising," I retorted. "You're obvious. Which means, if I did intend to engage in such diversions, I would hardly choose to do it with you. If you're going to spend time in such pursuits, it should be worth it, not an easily bested challenge."

Norfolk's hand still on my arm squeezed and he let out a strangled noise that sounded like a smothered laugh.

Franka's eyes narrowed.

"I think you mistake me," she said.

"I think I don't and that's why you're a disappointment," I countered. "I had hoped, when you made the approach you so obviously couldn't wait to make, that this would be much more fun. Instead, it's been rather boring."

This time, Norfolk coughed to hide his chuckle and Franka's eyes turned cold.

"I'll clarify. It's a mistake to *underestimate* me," she stated flat out.

"And it's a mistake to *threaten* me," I shot back. "For I have the arm of Ulfr and I'm not averse to calling in reinforcements."

Franka opened her mouth to speak but Norfolk got there before her.

"I find it's always best, Franka, when blood has been drawn, to retreat at least long enough to assess the damage."

Her gaze snapped to him, but he wasn't finished and his voice lowered meaningfully when he did.

"And when you retreat, I urge you to grasp, however belatedly, the fact that you've discovered a worthy adversary at the same time realize the she-pup you thought to play with has an alpha who, when a member of his pack is threatened, will not hesitate to tear you apart *with his teeth*."

She glared at him for long moments before she sent a cold look to me and turned, gliding away.

"Well done, my dear," Norfolk said into my ear, moving me from the food tables and positioning us by a wall that was close to Apollo, but not too close.

"Thanks," I murmured, looking Apollo's way to see his face stone-cold, his eyes aimed where Franka's departing back had just been before they turned to me.

I gave him a grin, a wink and added a finger wave for good measure.

His chin jerked slightly back when I did, even as he blinked.

Then he smiled.

Slowly.

God, seriously, I'd essentially been looking at that face for over a decade and still, seeing it as Apollo, I wondered if I'd ever get used to his beauty.

He turned his attention back to the Drakkars.

I gave mine to Norfolk.

"Thank you for being so..." I tried to find a this-world word since I didn't think he'd get "cool" or "awesome" or at least not the ways I intended them. I settled on, "Lovely."

"It is my pleasure," he replied on a smile. "Ulfr is a friend, he is loyal to my cousins, the queen and our Winter Princess, and he is a good man."

"He is all that," I affirmed, and he chuckled.

But he sobered before he noted, "You seem very used to the reactions to your resemblance to Ilsa."

"Although I'd never met her, in the time I've been in Lunwyn, it's become very clear I look exactly like her so I've had no choice but to become used to them."

"I must say, Lady Madeleine, that it's not uncanny, the resemblance. It's uncanny the resemblance that includes the startling differences," he remarked.

I felt my head tip to the side in confusion. "Would you mind explaining?" I asked.

"Only if this discussion doesn't offend you," he answered.

I shook my head, so he continued.

"I could not know, I have not been around when Franka and Ilsa were conversing, but, like you, Ilsa would not countenance Franka's rot. However, she would do that by walking away."

I wondered briefly if that was the way I should have played it, and this was brief because he went on.

"It's more fun your way."

I grinned at him and he returned the gesture.

"Have you met my cousin, Lunwyn's Ice Princess, Sjofn?" he queried.

I shook my head. "No."

"She will like you," he told me, patting my hand in the curve of his arm. "Greatly."

"Awe..." I started, stopped and finished more appropriately, "Well, that's just grand."

"Am I to set a course where Kristian cuts off his sister's allowance?" I heard Apollo ask.

I turned when I felt his hand come to rest on the small of my back.

In a sweet changing of the guards, Norfolk uncurled my hand from his elbow but gave it a squeeze before he let it go as he replied, "You may wish to give Franka some time to dress her wounds. Our Lady Madeleine proved her knives are sharper and she has greater skill in using them."

Apollo looked down at me, his hand gliding along my back so he could curl it around my waist and pull me close. "Indeed?"

"Amateur," I murmured, and he threw back his head and burst out laughing.

Norfolk added his chuckles.

Apollo stopped laughing and leveled his eyes at Norfolk. "I owe you a debt."

Norfolk threw out a hand. "Not at all." He looked to me. "It's been a pleasure."

Aw, that was sweet.

"You're very kind," I murmured.

"And you are a delight," he replied, smiling. He turned to Apollo. "I will leave you to your charming company."

Apollo inclined his head.

Norfolk dipped his chin to me and moved away.

After he did, Apollo moved me from the wall and started us walking slowly through the crowded space.

I took a sip of my champagne and muttered, "What now?"

"Now, we socialize."

Ugh.

"That's it?" I inquired.

"Well, to quench your need for excitement, I could challenge someone to a duel, but outside of the Drakkars, there's no one here whose blood I'd relish drawing."

I stopped and looked up at him and he stopped with me.

"You duel in this world?" I asked quietly.

"Indeed," he replied. "But only when honor is at stake."

"I don't suppose women engage in duels," I remarked.

He raised a brow, his lips twitching. "Wanting another go at Franka?"

"She's not very nice," I said by way of answer.

"If given the opportunity, I'd prefer observing you besting her with her own weapons," he murmured.

"Then I hope she's stupid enough to make another approach."

He shook his head, grinned and started us moseying again.

"Did you get anything out of Eirik and Valeria?" I queried.

"Dove, they'll hardly admit to conspiring during a trivial conversation at a gale," he replied.

"Of course not," I returned. "But they don't have to admit it straight out for you to get something from them."

He stopped this time, exchanging my half-drunk champagne glass with a fresh one and getting one of his own.

"My role this evening is to be here and keep an eye on Franka, Kristian, Eirik and Valeria as Remi and Hans find maids, charm the information out of them that would lead to the rooms of those particular Drakkars and search them."

Interesting.

"Just those Drakkars?" I asked.

"Alas, our informant was quite cagey about who was doing the conspiring.

But only those Drakkars would be foolish or spiteful enough to court the wrath of a man who commands elves and dragons."

I nodded, putting my glass to my lips and searching the crowd until I found Kristian.

"Kristian?" I murmured into my champagne before taking a sip.

"He would be the foolish one," Apollo replied.

"Hmm..." I mumbled, looking from Kristian to Apollo. "I must say, Lo, that this world is a whole lot more intriguing than mine."

His eyes warmed when I used his nickname, but his lips warned, "Intrigue always has consequences, poppy. We just need to ensure that those who deserve them are the ones who get them."

"Well, I'll keep track of Franka and Kristian and you keep an eye on Eirik and Valeria. Does that sound like a plan?" I offered.

His look got warmer as he started us moving again, murmuring, "And she gives me more reason than just that gown not to regret introducing her to a den of vipers."

"I aim to please," I replied quietly, scanning for and locating Franka.

But as I did, I suddenly felt Apollo's lips at my ear.

"You do, Madeleine, always. And tonight, we'll be exploring new ways for you to accomplish that."

Something to look forward to after we left Creepy Castle with its (mostly) Foul Family.

And I so looked forward to it, when Apollo moved his lips away, I caught his eyes from under my lashes and gave him a small smile.

He one-upped the promise made by my smile by staring at my mouth while he ran his tongue along his lower lip.

My clit pulsed and my lips parted.

His gaze came to mine, and he whispered, "Come, dove, I'll introduce you to Sinclair, Draven's uncle."

A diversion.

I nodded and gave him a different kind of smile.

He tucked me close, moved me through the crowd and introduced me to Walter Sinclair, who, like Norfolk, was also kindly and older. And I found when I shared it openly with him, he was a man who very much appreciated the fact that I cared deeply for his nephew.

20
HEWCROWS

Creepy Castles and (mostly) Foul Families aside, as I moved down the front steps of Brunskar hours later, Apollo guiding me to our sleigh, I was pretty pleased the night went so well.

Actually, intrigue was kind of fun (though I wouldn't tell Apollo that since he obviously didn't enjoy it much).

And I noticed he had steered me clear of a variety of people just as he steered me to closer acquaintances who would not be unkind or inappropriate.

Always looking out for me.

It was a weird sensation.

But once I got over the weirdness, it was a sensation I liked.

We made it to the bottom of the steps, and I pulled my cloak closer around me, noting, "Tonight was fun."

He moved ahead of me, reaching out to open the door of the sleigh, but looked back at me, smiling a bemused smile.

"You have an interesting idea of fun, poppy."

I stopped at the bottom step and tipped my head to the side. "I do?" I asked and didn't wait for him to answer. "Champagne. Good food and lovely company. And you looking hot and me looking fabulous in a gorgeous dress. Isn't that everyone's idea of fun?"

"I may take this neck cloth off, guide the sleigh to a cliff and throw it over," he said by way of answer, and I giggled.

"Can I take it from that you don't like neck cloths?" I asked the obvious.

He lifted a hand my way, and chuckling, replied, "You can indeed."

But I wasn't paying attention to his words, his hand or his humor.

This was because I was trying to lift my foot, but it seemed frozen to the step.

I looked down. It was freaking cold there but to have your foot freeze to a step?

It didn't matter. The black stone steps were cleared of snow and ice so this couldn't be.

"Maddie, cease your play. It's cold and I'm keen to get to the inn and get warm, but mostly get *you* warm," Apollo urged, saying things I normally would like very much.

But this was lost on me because I tried lifting my other foot and that wouldn't budge either.

Something was not right and that not right was *really* not right.

Panic surged inside me and I lifted my head.

"Ap—" I started but didn't get it all out.

He was dissolving.

No.

Fear shot through me because he wasn't dissolving.

I was.

I heard him roar, "*Madeleine*!"

Then I heard nothing. I saw nothing. I felt nothing.

I was surrounded in black mist.

Oh fuck.

Suddenly I was falling.

Falling through *nothing*.

Oh *fuck*!

I hit snow, the abrupt impact jarring my entire body, shooting pain through my legs and knees. Both crumpled and I landed heavily on my side in the snow.

Quickly, I raised my head and peered around to assess the situation.

Moonlight.

Snow.

Trees.

Nothing else.

No light. No castle. No sleighs. No noise. No people.

I was alone in a forest somewhere and I had no clue where.

Well, I guessed Minerva and her minions had decided to use magic.

On me.

Shit.

I pushed up to my knees and brushed the snow off my thin gloves. Gloves meant to be worn to a ball. My cloak meant to be worn in a sleigh with a fur over me, curled into the side of a hot guy.

I was not prepared to be in the cold in the middle of nowhere.

This was not good.

And it got worse when I caught movement through the moonlit forest.

I shot to my feet, my eyes glued to where I caught the movement.

Then I saw something out of the corner of my eye, moving in another direction.

I turned to that and started backing up.

Another movement from yet another direction.

I put one hand behind me in order not to slam into a tree and kept backing up.

One of the things moving stepped out from behind the shadow of the trees.

And at the impossibleness of what I saw, I went completely still.

It was a man, a sword at a slant on his back.

But his head was the head of a bird with a sharp, pointed terrifying beak and creepy beady eyes.

"What the hell?" I breathed.

He lifted his hand and went for his sword.

I saw another movement as another one stepped out of the shadows.

He was going for his sword too as I heard the hiss of steel when the other one drew his from his scabbard.

Another one appeared in the moonlight, his sword already unsheathed.

Okay.

Well.

I was *so totally* right.

This was *not good.*

And in my fabulous gown in the middle of a forest, not knowing where the heck I was, I had one option open to me.

Run like hell.

I took that option, turned, grabbed my skirts and did that like the devil himself was on my heels.

And, seriously, he was.

All four of him.

I didn't glance back. I was not going to fall over a fallen branch like some stupid bitch in a horror movie.

No fucking way.

If they were going to get me, they were going to have to catch me.

I had no idea where I was running and I didn't care.

I just ran.

I heard them giving chase behind me and they seemed close.

Fuck.

Shit.

Fuck.

I kept going.

Then I heard something from in front of me. It sounded like someone (or something) crashing through the snow.

They were coming at me from another side.

Crap!

I shot to the side and kept going, my breathing labored, my slippers encased in snow, the tops of my feet covered in it. It was awkward dashing through tall snow, and thus not easy, but I kept right on going.

"*Miss Maddie!*" I heard shrieked.

I kept going but I knew that voice and I couldn't believe I heard that voice where I was.

That voice was Loretta's.

Then I saw her and Meeta racing through the snow ten feet to my left.

What the hell?

I couldn't ask what the hell. I could only do one thing.

So I did it.

I ran their way, shouting, "Keep going. Go, go, *go*!"

They kept running as I ran to them and felt and heard those things chasing me.

I made it to them and Meeta threw back her cloak. On the run, she handed me a dagger.

I took it and suffice it to say I wouldn't have a problem using it on whatever creatures were chasing us. If I got that chance (which I hoped I didn't), I wouldn't hesitate.

But as I took it, I saw she was heavily armed. She had a knife belt on with more weapons. I was still running so I didn't have it in me to count all the blades she brought, but what I saw made me feel hope, even as I felt shock, not only that they were there but that they'd come prepared.

"Where are we?" I asked, still running.

"We run toward Brunskar," Meeta gasped.

I wasn't sure I wanted to go back there.

"But—"

Meeta cut me off. "No talk! Run!"

I thought this was good advice, so I kept running.

Until I heard them close in. Loretta cried out and I looked over my shoulder to see one of the bird-headed men had her.

Fuck!

"*No!*" I shrieked, turned, but Meeta was already there.

She yanked a short sword out of her belt, and without delay and looking like it wasn't the first time she did it, she cut his head off.

Okay. Maybe she wasn't Spock.

Maybe she was a Maroovian Russell Crowe-ian type gladiator.

There was no time to cheer, however, the others closed in.

One was close to me and I ducked like I saw Apollo duck when he was in the swordfight back at the inn. His sword whiffed over my head, and I came up, already thrusting my dagger forward. I plunged it in his gut and he fell back.

"Bad magic," Meeta whispered.

I turned to her to see her beating back another one.

I also noted the one whose head she cut off didn't fall even as I noticed Loretta was down, back on her hand, her own short sword raised, fending off a third.

No, the one with his head cut off just stood there as another head was growing in its place.

And worse. Another creature was growing from his severed head!

I had no time to totally freak right the fuck out at this, another one was rushing to attack me.

"Aim to maim!" I shouted. "You cut something off, it grows a new one."

Alas, Loretta had managed to cut the arm off the one she was fighting and get back to her feet, and the severed arm instantly started forming another creature.

I got my dagger in one and he fell back from me only for another one to close in.

"Keep moving toward Brunskar!" Meeta shouted, leading the one she was fighting in the direction we'd been going.

It must be said, I liked her mettle, but we couldn't see any light through the trees. Even if we were heading that direction, the castle was far away. We couldn't fight and make it there.

The good news was, I was a total amateur and I could tell these—whatever-they-were—were not real good at this shit.

The bad news was, their arms were longer, as were their swords, and as I fought the one I had on my hands, I noticed two more form out nothing.

"She sends more," Meeta snapped, sounding peeved.

Just peeved.

Seriously?

I felt even more but I couldn't tell seeing as now I was battling three.

All with one dagger.

We'll just say I was doing a lot of lunging, ducking, swaying my torso back and rolling through the snow.

My dress was totally ruined.

As were my cloak and shoes.

And I was pretty certain I'd lost a comb along the way.

This all sucked.

What sucked *way* worse was that I knew we were all dead.

This was because we were surrounded. I couldn't miss it even as I battled on, breathing heavy, my heart thumping in my chest, my blood roaring in my ears. I heard Loretta's terrified pants and Meeta's grunts of effort.

We were surrounded.

They were pressing us in.

I felt Loretta's back hit mine. Then Meeta's.

If just one of them got a good swipe in, they could take all three of us out.

We were done for.

I was going to die with two fabulous women who somehow had come to my aid and who I wished I had a lot more time to get to know.

I wasn't ever going to see Élan dressed for her first gale.

I wasn't going to see Christophe become a soldier.

I was never going to feel Apollo's hands on me again. His mouth. See his smile. Take in all the beauty that was him.

I was going to die in the cold and snow of a parallel universe having tasted a beautiful life I knew I'd grown to love but had not allowed myself to trust. Tasted it for a brief snatch of time and then it was going to be whisked away.

"You guys are the freaking greatest!" I shouted, grunting as I lunged forward and got one in the gut.

He fell back.

Another took his place.

"I die with you in my heart, Miss Maddie and Meeta," Loretta yelled, Meeta's name ending in a pained yelp, and I knew one clipped her.

"*We do not die tonight!*" Meeta screeched, her voice so shrill, it was like she was trying to make that be by putting everything she was into her words.

I admired her grit.

But she was heartbreakingly wrong.

One of the things did an overhead slice and I caught it with my short blade sideways, but the strength of the slice took me down to my knee. My arms over my head, struggling to hold my attacker's blade, the rest of me was ripe for the pickin's.

But if I let go, he'd slice me in half.

I let out an ear-piercing scream of frustration, terror and heartache, and his sword disappeared.

He didn't. He stood before me, but he was looking over his shoulder.

I shot to standing and noted both Loretta and Meeta pressing to my back, but I heard no grunts of exertion, nor did I feel movement.

This was because all of the creatures were looking back.

I was about to start jabbing at random to create a hole in what looked like a six- or seven-creature-thick wall around us when all hell broke loose.

And by that, I mean I heard barking, growling, yapping, snarling and suddenly a line of sight cleared, and I couldn't believe my eyes.

Wolves.

All around.

Dozens of them.

No.

More.

Maybe *hundreds.*

All of them attacking the things.

"Oh my God," I whispered. "What's going—?"

I didn't finish.

This was because, behind the wolves more of the creatures formed out of nowhere just as a line of wolves ran, scampered or crawled on their bellies through the snow, and the now battling-with-wolves birdmen toward Meeta, Loretta and me.

We pressed back-to-back.

Great.

Birdmen and now wolves.

If certain death already wasn't bad enough.

I lifted my dagger but didn't use it.

This was because I was staring in shock as the wolves formed a circle around us, snarling, growling, snapping and biting at the birdmen who were pressing in.

Holy cow.

They were protecting us.

More wolves shot to the circle to keep the birdmen back.

Holy cow!

The wolves were totally protecting us!

How cool!

I reached out and grabbed Loretta's hand. "You okay?"

"Flesh wound, shoulder," Meeta answered for her. "It's deep and bleeding profusely, Miss Maddie. We must get her aid. She pales."

There was my Spock. Logical, for of course Loretta needed aid.

I just couldn't get it for her when we were surrounded by bedlam.

"Stick with us, honey," I said on a squeeze of Loretta's hand. "You with us?"

"Yes, Miss Maddie," she whispered, her voice trembling.

At the exhaustion, pain and fear in Loretta's voice, I decided that next time Spock and I went on an adventure, we were leaving the honor roll cheerleader behind.

Not that I had a choice this time.

"We'll get you taken care of as soon as this calms down," I assured her, hoping I wasn't lying.

"Right," she replied, holding my hand tight, her voice holding no hope.

But keeping an eye on the activity, although our ring of wolf protectors was prevailing, and although I could see in the distance the shadowy shape of more wolves heading our way, the birdmen were popping up everywhere.

And as if to prove that true, two popped into the circle close to the girls and me.

They didn't even get turned toward us before five wolves jumped them and viciously ripped them to shreds.

Blue sparks flew everywhere and the birdmen disappeared.

Wild.

Scary.

And totally fucked up.

The wolves didn't hesitate to close ranks and continue snarling and snapping at the pressing birdmen.

And blue sparks were flying everywhere.

Yelps of wounded wolves came fast and thick. I even saw some unmoving wolf bodies on the forest floor.

More birdmen formed.

Lots more.

I squeezed Loretta's hand.

The wolves around us backed in tighter, their tails brushing our skirts.

This was not good.

The wolves were losing.

Shit!

Then it happened.

Suddenly and with little warning, bedlam turned into Armageddon.

It started with wolves in the forest suddenly turning tail and running.

That did not give me a good feeling.

It continued with the wolf circle around us falling to their bellies and pushing snout first through the snow.

This definitely didn't give me a good feeling.

But it ended with Meeta shouting, "Down! Now!"

I hit the deck mostly because Meeta shoved me there, on top of Loretta, Meeta coming down on top of me.

Then a fiery blast of heat seared over us as the forest all around us burst into flame.

I just had the chance to peek up from under Meeta's arm that was wrapped around my head, and I kid you not, no joke, no fooling, flapping their webby wings terrifying overhead, breathing fire all around was not one...not two...but *three* gigantic dragons.

I stared in shock and awe, my mouth hanging open as they stopped breathing fire. Only one was in sight and I watched it flap down and settle his ass to the scorched earth, forked tongue out and snaking around, eyes intelligent and aimed in the distance.

Meeta got up and pulled me up. I pulled Loretta up.

And we stood there, staring around us.

This was because everything but a five-foot diameter of now melting snow around our feet was totally incinerated. Charred. Leveled. Still smoldering but there was nothing left.

Nothing but three big dragons with thin, lolling tongues and a circle of wolves who were now sitting around us, some cleaning themselves disinterestedly, some just panting, one was scratching behind his ear.

Meeta pressed close and Loretta made a noise of fear.

I looked into the smoldering shadows.

Through midnight and smoke, a man and woman appeared.

The man was tall, built and seriously hot.

The woman had fabulous white-blonde hair.

They came to a stop ten feet away and he opened his mouth to speak.

But I beat him to it.

"I take it you're Finnie and Frey."

He closed his mouth but used it to smile.

Yep, hot.

She grinned.

And she was cute.

Right. With dragons in the mix, I had a feeling everything was going to be okay.

So I smiled back.

21

THE PATH TO VENGEANCE

Apollo rode Anguish hard through the snow, the needles of the pines whipping unheeded against his face and body, his torso ducking and swaying to avoid branches.

His destination? Where he'd seen the dragons' blaze.

His lungs were burning fire throughout his frame.

His neck and shoulders were solid with tension.

His thoughts were tortured.

He hit the smoking wasteland and saw them.

Meeta and Loretta were there for some gods' forsaken reason.

Finnie and Frey were there, which was surprising but not, considering the dragons and their fire.

His wolves were there, which was as he'd arranged.

And then there was Maddie, looking wet, cold and disheveled.

But standing.

Breathing.

Alive.

Alive.

He rode straight to her, not slowing Anguish, and the huddle swayed out of his way as he threw his leg over the saddle and dismounted with Anguish still at a run.

His legs bore the impact of his dismount, but he didn't feel it.

He took two long strides to Madeleine, lifted his hands and framed her face. Unable to stop them, he moved them over her hair, down her neck, under her jaws and back to the sides of her head as his eyes scoured her face.

Standing.

Breathing.

Her eyes open and looking into his.

"I'm all right, Lo," she whispered, and he felt her hand light on his stomach as she leaned in. "I'm all right, baby."

At her words, he crushed his mouth down on hers, thrusting his tongue in, tasting her, drinking from her, devouring her.

Her arms curled around his middle and went tight as she tipped her head back to give him what he needed.

More.

Approaching horses and voices pierced his extreme relief and he tore his mouth from hers. When he did, he cupped the back of her head, shoved her face in his throat and curled an arm around her, hauling her deep so she was tight to his body and he could feel her everywhere. Smell her close. Absorb the fact she was still alive.

His eyes went to Frey.

"What was it?" he barked.

"Hewcrows," Frey answered. "Minerva," he went on, telling Apollo something he already knew.

Everyone knew the bird-headed hewcrows were Minerva's magic.

But the black mist that he'd seen envelope Maddie was something else.

He couldn't think of his Madeleine being attacked in the forest by hewcrows. Not then. His nerves were frayed, his fury at the surface. The thought of his broken dove battling hewcrows in the snow would cause him to lose control.

Instead, he glanced around at the destruction, taking in the three dragons at rest.

Hostilities had escalated.

"Lo," Maddie breathed.

He ignored her and looked back to Frey.

"You're here because?" Apollo asked.

"I'm here because my family gathers," Frey answered.

Enough said.

"I'm also here to seek Lavinia," Frey added.

"The others?" Apollo went on.

"We've had a message from the Circe of the other world. She wishes to help with our plight and she's discovered a way to recover her magic. It's a dangerous process and she would still consume all she recouped if she made the journey between worlds. We need Lavinia and Valentine to transport her here. Once here, she'll be a formidable addition. That said, she's explained this process and Circe, Cora, Tor, Lahn and their men journey to the font where Lahn's Circe can recoup her magic as well."

Apollo nodded.

"Lo," Madeline whispered.

He again ignored her and noted that Frey's men, Ruben and Thaddeus, had arrived and Annar, Lund, Oleg and Orion were riding to join their group. He turned his head and saw Laures, Remi, Hans and Alek had also made it. All of the men were still mounted, except Hans, who was close to Loretta, holding her while Meeta tied a strip of fabric she'd torn from her dress around a shoulder wound Loretta had sustained.

At the sight of the maid's blood, Apollo's mouth got tight and that burn in his chest came back.

"Get Loretta back to Brunskar," he ordered Hans.

Hans looked to him and nodded.

"Lo," Madeleine repeated.

"My mother?" Frey asked over her and Apollo looked to him, knowing the question.

That question being why Apollo was there.

And Frey knew the likely reason.

"She, or your father, Franka or Kristian. They're all here," Apollo answered.

This time, Frey's mouth got tight and his eyes slid to Ruben.

"I want them in the dungeons before night's end," he commanded.

Without delay, Ruben, Thad, Annar, Lund and the others whirled their horses, dug their heels in and shot through the smoke.

Apollo heard more horses and turned to see Draven and Gaston arrive.

They'd barely stopped their mounts before Apollo caught Laures's eyes. "One of you, assist Hans with Loretta and Meeta. The rest, aid Frey's men."

Gaston approached Hans and the women. The rest of his men dug their heels in their horses and galloped away.

"Lo!" Maddie wheezed into his throat.

He took the pressure off the back of her head and looked down at her. "Dove, *what?*"

She tipped her head back. "You're squeezing the breath out of me."

His arm around her back relaxed but he did not let her go.

She collapsed into him and pressed her face in his chest.

Seeing her do that, feeling it, he felt a muscle tick in his cheek right before he whistled sharply.

Maddie jumped in his arms and raised her head, but Apollo turned his eyes to the wolf who ran to him and stopped five feet away.

He heard Maddie catch her breath, but he spoke to the king of the wolves.

"How many did you lose?"

"Twenty-seven." He heard in his head as the wolf barked.

Twenty-seven.

Twenty-seven wolves.

Gods *damn it.*

"They will be avenged," Apollo promised.

The wolf yipped, bobbed his muzzle, turned and ran through the smolder.

"What was that?" Maddie asked, her voice breathy, now for a different reason.

Apollo looked down at her.

She was staring after the wolf.

He turned his head and gave a different kind of whistle.

Anguish trotted to him.

He heard Maddie gasp as he lifted her and planted her arse on his mount. He didn't delay in swinging behind her, jerking up his chin to Frey, dipping it to Finnie, clamping Maddie close to him and bending into her and his steed.

He dug his heels in Anguish's flanks.

His horse shot through the smoke.

Destination Brunskar.

And the path to vengeance.

His boots sounding sharp on the black stone floors of the Brunskar dungeons, Apollo was not surprised at what he saw at the end of the hall when he turned the corner.

Madeleine and Frey facing off.

She was wearing what he assumed was one of Melba's soft, peach gowns. He assumed this as he'd left her to Melba, a guard, one of Calder's witches, a physician called in from the village, as well as Meeta. They were all seeing to Loretta.

In other words, outside Melba, who'd essentially been elbowed aside by a rabidly protective Maddie and an equally rabidly protective Meeta, they were generally getting in the physician's way.

As he had things to do that didn't include watching a physician stitch flesh as his Maddie fanned Loretta and Meeta threatened the poor man if the stitches weren't tidy and straight, he'd left them to it.

Now she had found her way to the dungeons, the torches lit along the walls casting spare light into the gloom.

He was finding that was his Maddie. Assassins. Hewcrows. Dark magic. She was a fighter. She most definitely did not like to be kept in the dark and she didn't shy away from much.

Except emotion.

And she was learning to face that head on too.

And all of this, all of Maddie, pleased him very much.

Which meant the thirty minutes where he knew not whether she was still with him in this world, or she was not in any world, had been unadulterated anguish.

Apollo could not dwell on that however, for as he got close, he saw her face was set.

As was Frey's.

She heard his boots, looked his way and greeted, "Hey, honey."

Even as fury and fear still smoldered in his chest, at her greeting, Apollo nearly smiled.

However, he did not.

This was because she turned instantly back to Frey and opened her mouth.

But Frey got there first.

"You will not enter."

Apollo stopped close behind Maddie but had no chance to speak.

"Finnie's in there," she returned heatedly. "I saw her when you opened the door."

"My Finnie is an unusual woman and princess of this realm," Frey retorted.

"Well, *I'm* an unusual woman too. Seeing as she's of my people, we're the same kind of unusual and it was *me* and *my girls*," she jerked her thumb at herself with each stressed word then threw out an arm, "who were out there with those *things*."

Apollo felt his jaw grow tight at a reminder of the danger Madeleine had been in.

But Frey was not swayed.

"What you would see in there is not for women's eyes."

"Huh," Maddie huffed in disgust, and at that noise Apollo lost his disquiet and rage at the events of earlier that night and again almost smiled. "I've seen Lo slit a man's throat, gut another one, slice another one in the neck and cut off a man's hand." She twisted her neck and looked up at him. "What other carnage have you wrought in front of me, sweetheart?"

At that, there was no hope of stopping it, he smiled down at her.

"Lo, this is your decision," Frey stated, and Apollo looked to him.

"Let her enter."

He felt Maddie relax in front of him.

Frey nodded and turned instantly to the door he was blocking, opened it and moved inside.

He left it open, and Maddie began to move there, but he caught her arm and turned her to him.

"Apollo—" she started impatiently.

"One moment, my dove," he interrupted her gently. "Before you enter that room, you must be warned. You have seen Laures at work, but you were in no state to let it register and he had just gotten started. Oleg, Frey's man, is also skilled at extracting information. He does not relish using these skills, but he has them. What you may see in that room may be difficult to witness no matter the..." he paused, "carnage you've already beheld."

Boots were sounding down the hall, but he didn't look, nor did Madeleine.

Instead, she assured him, "I'll be fine, honey."

"If you wish to leave, you go. But you do not go alone. I or one of my men goes with you and takes you immediately to the witch."

"They have a witch in there," she told him. "I saw her too."

"Regardless, do as I say. Understood?"

She held his gaze as he felt others join them and he only looked to them when she nodded.

Alek and Hans had arrived.

"They have them?" Hans asked.

"All of them," Apollo answered. "Save Franka. She's staying at a cottage not far from here. They're collecting her."

Hans jerked up his chin.

"The children?" Apollo asked.

"Quincy and Balthazar play guard. Calder has sent a witch as well."

This time, Apollo jerked up his chin.

Hans looked to Maddie. "Word on Loretta?"

"She's fine, Hans," Maddie said quietly. "Stitched up and now resting."

With mild surprise, Apollo watched a cloud shadow Hans's face before he moved into the room. And this cloud formed even as the news he received about Loretta was good.

Alek had already gone in.

Apollo took Maddie's hand and led her in.

When they entered, he saw Eirik and Calder nose to nose. He also saw Valeria standing to the side, watching in a detached way, arms crossed on her chest. And last he saw Kristian squatting in a corner, head down between his knees, the fingers of both hands shoved in his hair.

Kristian. Clearly the weak link.

Apollo cast his eyes further through the room and saw Frey and his own men standing about, as well as Garik. Finnie was in the shadows resting one shoulder against the stone. Her booted feet were crossed at the ankle, her arms crossed on her chest, focus on Calder and Eirik.

When they entered, she looked over her shoulder, caught Apollo's eyes, then hers moved to Madeleine, down to their clasped hands and back to Apollo whereupon she winked.

He again felt his lips twitch.

Then his attention was taken by the action.

"Three witches I paid a fortune to watch over my wife, my unborn child and my home, and you connive to tear that protection away?" Calder clipped into his father's face.

Clearly, the interrogation had advanced during his absence. No one knew about the conspiracy.

Except the conspirators.

Apollo knew, however, that Frey had warned his brother and Calder had taken precautions. This was the reason why Apollo felt safe bringing the children and Maddie to Brunksar.

In his fury, Calder had obviously informed the occupants of this room who previously might not have known.

Unless they did.

Something they would soon find out.

"I've done no such thing," Eirik returned.

Calder's eyes sliced to the witch who was standing shoulders against the stone wall, eyes to the action.

"Indeed, as I reported, the enchantments we cast were broken," she stated.

Calder looked back at his father.

"Explain that," he demanded.

"I'd hardly connive to put my own son and unborn grandson in jeopardy," Eirik returned.

"Just to say, she carries a daughter," the witch put in.

"Your further input is hardly welcome," Eirik bit out.

Maddie leaned into him and whispered in his ear, "Cool that Melba and Calder are expecting a daughter."

Apollo shook his head while tipping his chin to look down at her and lifted a hand to press his finger to her lips.

She rolled her eyes.

He felt his mouth quirk as he returned to Eirik and Calder, dropped his finger from her lips but lifted the hand he was holding and folded it into his chest, drawing her nearer.

"You fail to grasp your position here, Father," Frey noted, and Eirik looked to him.

"I fail to do so because it's beyond unseemly to escort the Head of a House to his own dungeons," Eirik shot back.

Calder's back shot straight and his face went cold.

"I will repeat, you fail to grasp your position here, Father, and it would appear you do it in more ways than one for you have not been Head of this House for some time," Frey returned.

"Can I ask at this point," Valeria cut in in a bored voice, "if someone will bring me a chair? I've been dancing all night and my feet are killing me."

"Holy cow." Apollo heard Maddie breathe in disgusted shock and he squeezed her hand but did not take his eyes from the players on the stage.

"It would seem, Mother, that you too are uncomprehending of what is transpiring in this room," Frey noted.

"We have been informed of what occurred this night and really," she shook her head in mild rebuke, "my dear son, you know my husband, nor I, would conspire with malevolent forces to bring down the powers that be on two continents. Not with a son who is The Frey *and* The Drakkar. A son married to the Winter Princess and a grandson who inherits the crown to this realm, a realm that is vast in size now that it's rightfully reunified."

"Too true," Frey allowed, and his eyes dropped to his mother's throat. "Though I must take this moment to compliment you on the ice diamond you wear."

Apollo watched Valeria pale as her hand started to snake up to her throat, but she wisely thought better of bringing more attention to the stone, an extortionately costly one.

"But I must admit confusion," Frey continued. "Seeing as in his last message to me, Calder explained he had to curtail your allowance, along with father's, as your spending was unduly extravagant and it was threatening the livelihood of every member of the House of Drakkar. Can I take it that jewel is an indication of what my brother was referring to?"

Valeria lifted her chin, but her face briefly exposed a crack in her bravado that Apollo knew Frey would detect. "Your father purchased this stone for me before Calder assumed Head of the House."

"How odd, considering the condition of the Drakkar House's finances were in disarray prior to Calder assuming Head," Frey shot back instantly. "So, although Calder's revitalization of Drakkar family funds has been dramatic, my father would have had less resources when he was Head to provide you such a gift. Or perhaps gifts such as these were the reason the Drakkar assets were in such disarray."

Eirik had turned to his wife and Apollo saw his eyes narrowed on the diamond at her throat.

"That is not a gift from me," he told her. Then he looked to Frey and repeated, "That is not a gift from me. She got that elsewhere. She's addicted to her fripperies and finds her ways to get them. But it is most definitely not a gift from me."

Frey didn't take his attention from his mother. "Perhaps you'd like some time to formulate another lie. You've five seconds." Only then did he move his gaze to his father. "Even as she stands there, lying when treason is in question, it warms the heart how swiftly my sire so staunchly champions the woman who birthed me."

"As you say, treason is in question," Eirik returned, puffing out his chest.

"Yes, indeed," Frey replied. "And on behalf of my wife, this realm's princess, I thank you for your swift incrimination, no matter if only implied, of your own wife for our country of ice."

Eirik's face suffused red just as there was movement at the door and everyone turned to see Draven and Thad bringing Franka in.

Her eyes instantly scanned the room and stopped on Frey.

"We must stop meeting like this," she remarked cattily, a derisive smile on her face.

"Yes, Franka," Frey said low, his voice ominous. "We must."

It was almost imperceptible, but Apollo caught it.

She swallowed.

Missing this, Eirik demanded of his wife, "Who bought you that jewel?"

"It was you," she returned, her voice cold, her eyes level, but she couldn't completely mask her fear.

"I believe I would remember buying you an ice diamond of that size," Eirik returned.

"I've been dragged from my bed, and the company in it, to witness a domestic?" Franka asked, performing the remarkable feat of sounding both astonished and bored.

"I advise you keep quiet," Calder clipped at her.

"If I do, then how would you all know that Valeria has long since tired of her husband's wandering eye, and cock, and for years has been bedding Malcolm Turnish, a wealthy merchant who could afford dozens of those diamonds, and Korwahkian emeralds, sapphires, rubies." Franka threw out a hand. "I could go on. He would actually wed her if she would sever ties with Eirik and allow it. However, it's unlikely some of her acquaintances would invite her to their gales if she was on the arm of just a merchant. And we all know Valeria likes to dance."

She looked to Valeria and continued, what seemed genuinely.

"I'm sorry to tell tales of your wifely betrayal, darling, but I actually *like* Malcolm, regardless of his profession, and have desired for some time for you to be kept in the style to which you *should* be accustomed without needing to beg. Not to mention the not insignificant bonus of having a man known to be much endowed in a *variety* of ways."

Franka barely finished her words before Eirik roared, "*You betray me?*" and he made a move toward his wife.

He didn't get very far. Garik shifted in and detained him.

Eirik struggled infuriatedly, though futilely, against his son's hold while Valeria studied her husband like he was a specimen tacked to a board.

"I have not entertained you in my bed in fifteen years, husband. And I only took you before to get my sons, and after I had them, as duty to our marriage," she explained casually, as if she was informing him of the menu she'd chosen for the week.

Suddenly Eirik stood still and hissed, "You never had an interest in play."

"Oh no, darling," Valeria whispered. "I never had an interest in playing with a man who doesn't know how to use his cock. One who does is *very* different."

Franka emitted a purring chuckle.

Garik looked to his eldest brother. "Just to say, at this point, I don't know whether to vomit or cut off my ears."

Apollo was done as well.

And he communicated this by saying quietly, "Frey."

Frey looked to Apollo and nodded.

Then he moved his gaze from one brother to the next. "You might wish to leave."

"I'll be staying," Calder announced immediately.

"And I wouldn't miss this for the world," Garik murmured, pushing his father off and moving toward Finnie. He settled in, leaning his shoulders close to where she was still lounging.

Frey looked to Apollo. "Oleg or Laures?"

"Let's see what Laures can get," Apollo answered.

He felt Maddie's hand convulse in his and he reconsidered his decision to allow her to enter, especially as she was close to Laures and he did not like to think of her perception of him changing as he went about the unpleasant necessities of his work.

Before he could make his decision, Laures moved forward.

Valeria and Eirik came alert and started moving back as Franka watched Laures advance toward her brethren. She did this with a face showing only mild interest.

"Are you...do you mean to...to...*torture* us?" Eirik asked, his focus glued to Laures.

"No," Frey answered then finished, "If you don't make that necessary."

Eirik's eyes shot to his son. "I've told you, I know nothing of a conspiracy!"

"Can I go last?" Franka put in at this point. "I'd like to watch."

Frey looked to her, but Apollo had been finished with her games earlier that evening.

He was most assuredly done with her now.

To communicate this, he told her, "The last conspirator I faced who proved of no use got his throat slit."

Her gaze slid to him, and she raised her brows. "You'd take a blade to a woman?"

"Maybe not," Maddie butted in. "But I would."

Apollo stifled a sigh, looked down at her and murmured a warning, "Madeleine."

She turned her eyes up to him. "She's not very nice, Lo. The world would hardly be a poorer place without her in it."

"And you?" Franka's voice came at them, dripping with scorn. "The woman who uses a dead wife's charms to enchant her heartbroken husband so she can warm his bed in order to wear his jewels and earn her place on his arm? Is the world richer for your presence?"

Momentarily frozen with fury, Apollo went completely still even as he felt the air in the room turn thick, at the same he time he watched Maddie's face pale and she turned woodenly to Franka.

"Franka," Valeria surprisingly whispered, her voice cautious. "Take heed, dear."

Apollo forced himself to turn, drawing Maddie's stiff frame closer as he did so, and caught Franka looking to Valeria.

"I'll hardly be insulted in the seat of my own family by a whore who doesn't even have the courage to claim herself as such."

And that was when Apollo let Maddie go.

A second later, he had Franka pressed to the stone with his hand at her throat squeezing, his face dipped to hers.

"She battled hewcrows this evening," he growled.

Franka tore at his wrist with her nails, her mouth opening and closing, fighting for air.

"And," he got nose to nose with her, "*she has my arm*."

He felt her throat convulse under his hand as strangled noises escaped her mouth.

But Apollo had no patience for further delay.

So he finally got to the point.

"And last, a Keer parcel was found in your brother's rooms," Apollo went on and her wide eyes widened further. "You've had your play for the evening. You...are...*done*," he growled. "Now, we move to *my* games. Tell me, is it you ensnaring your brother in your schemes or are they his alone?"

"Honey, what's a Keer parcel?" Apollo heard Finnie ask her husband.

"Wee one, not now," Frey replied, and this reply came close to Apollo's back.

"There was no Keer parcel in my room."

That came from Kristian and Apollo looked to his left to see Kristian had come out of his crouch and was staring with wild eyes at Apollo and his sister.

The weak link bends.

"Why do you think you're here?" Frey asked his cousin.

"I had no Keer parcel," Kristian whispered, his eyes quickly moving from person to person through the room. "I don't even know a witch who could conjure a Keer parcel."

"Kristian, it was found in your rooms this eve when the floorboards were torn up after Madeleine was taken," Frey informed him.

Kristian frantically shook his head. "I have no knowledge of it."

"Intelligence came to me that a Drakkar was aligned with a conspiracy involving Minerva, her collaborators, and Baldur," Apollo informed him, and Kristian's panicked eyes grew wider.

"I have no involvement with Baldur!" he cried.

"Ah...pah...lo," Franka forced out and Apollo looked to her to see her beautiful face mottled, her eyes bugged out and her mouth still opening and closing as she tried to get air.

So he moved his face again close to hers and whispered, "This night for you is not over. But, if you leave this room intact and you ever again utter a word to or about my Madeleine, or even look her way should you again be in her presence, I will squeeze the life out of your throat, Franka. Do not mistake me. It will be done."

She nodded as best she could with his hand at her throat and he released her.

Instantly, she jerked to the side, folded double and lifted her hands to her neck, gasping in air.

Apollo dismissed her and looked to Frey.

"My Madeleine was under attack tonight, Frey. I grow weary of this banter. We remove the women and let Laures work."

"Apollo," Maddie called in protest at the same time Finnie said, "I don't think so, Frey."

Frey turned to his woman.

Apollo turned to his.

"You're a distraction, dove," he said quietly. She opened her mouth, but he saw her face was pale, her eyes haunted. He knew she would not spend one more minute in that room and he didn't care if he had to carry her out himself.

But first he tried, "Please."

She shut her mouth.

Thank the gods, that worked.

"Take the women to the witch," Frey ordered, and Thad moved toward Finnie.

Apollo looked to Draven, jerked his chin Madeleine's way and Draven moved toward her.

He watched them leave the room, noting Maddie left without glancing back. He then watched the door close behind them. Only when the door closed did he turn his eyes to Laures.

"Start with Franka," he ordered.

"What? No!" she cried, all her audacity lost, her eyes were huge and staring at Laures.

Laures looked to Apollo and Apollo knew why.

He drew a line at woman.

Apollo cut his gaze to Frey.

Frey nodded then looked to Oleg.

Oleg moved forward.

"I know nothing of conspiracy!" Franka exclaimed.

"Annar, get me a hook," Oleg said.

Franka's face lost all color.

Annar moved to the door and her attention followed him.

"I...you can't..." Her eyes shot to Frey. "Frey, you can't really believe I'd—"

Frey interrupted her. "Convince me you wouldn't, cousin, but do it fast."

Apollo saw her gaze flick in the direction of her brother before it moved back to Apollo. "The Drakkars are the most powerful family in Lunwyn. You know I value my ties to my family. You know why. We've been here before during the *last* conspiracy. What reason would any Drakkar have to—?"

But Frey had seen the glance too.

"Oleg, not Franka. Kristian," he ordered.

"*No!*" Franka shrieked as Kristian cowered into the wall.

"What has he done, Franka?" Apollo asked.

"He...he..." She shook her head. "Nothing."

Oleg started to move to Kristian and Kristian turned his side to the corner, pressing in like the stone could absorb him.

"What has he done, Franka?" Apollo asked.

Oleg made it to Kristian.

"Nothing!" Franka shouted and started toward Kristian, but Apollo caught her in the chest and shoved her back roughly. He watched without remorse as she lost her footing and went down on her arse.

He bent deep, leaning into her and roared, "*What has he done?*"

"*Nothing!*" she shrieked.

There was a thud of flesh hitting the wall and Franka's focus flew there. Apollo looked over his shoulder to see Kristian shoved face first in the wall, one of Oleg's hands at his neck keeping him there, the other wrapped around his wrist, twisting it behind his back.

Kristian was struggling and panting.

Oleg was looking at Frey.

"How ugly to start?" he asked.

"Mark him," Frey ordered.

Oleg turned back to Kristian.

"I have a lover!" Franka cried.

Apollo looked back to her.

"*Continue!*" he barked when she said no more.

She shook her head in short jerks, closed her eyes, opened them and whispered, "He's been taken to Specter Isle."

Gods *damn* it.

"And?" Apollo clipped.

"And they told me I have unique access to both Finnie and Ils...I mean," she corrected hurriedly at seeing the look that moved over Apollo's face, "Madeleine. They said if I could get them access, they would release him."

Bloody hell.

They were after the women.

"Why are Finnie and Madeleine targets?" Apollo asked curtly.

"They didn't share their strategy," she replied shakily.

As they wouldn't.

"They just told me, if I didn't, I'd receive his shaft back, the only part they said I liked, which isn't true," she spat. "And that was *all* I'd get back."

Shocked deeply she cared about anyone enough to risk her own neck, Apollo stared at her a moment before he went on. "And who approached you?"

"Helda," she answered.

"And is her magic black?" Apollo pressed.

She held his gaze but couldn't hold back her obvious shudder.

Helda's magic was black.

It was Helda's magic that spirited Maddie away.

So it would be Helda's head that rotted on a spike at Rimée Keep, the Queen's palace in Snowdon.

Apollo would take it there himself.

"They've hurt him," Apollo guessed quietly.

"She showed me a mirror. He was in it," she snapped. "And yes. Every day. On the hour. Every hour. They *hurt* him."

Apollo felt Frey draw close, but he didn't take his eyes off Franka.

"So you schemed to trap your brother, shift blame should this plan be discovered?" Frey asked.

"No," she replied. "The Keer parcel had to be laid somewhere in the house. A Keer parcel is easily detected as it glows when the magic outside is trying to pierce the enchantments protecting a location, so it had to be well-placed. Calder informed me there was no room for me."

She sent a bitter look to Calder, who Apollo already liked, but he grew in Apollo's estimation greatly, seeing it was clear he had no wish for Franka to be under his roof.

Her eyes came back to Frey. "So I shared what was happening with Kristian and begged for his help. He didn't want to do it," she hastened to add. "But, I... he..." She swallowed. "My brother has a soft heart."

Her attention went to her brother and she swallowed again.

Then she whispered to the floor, "He's always had a soft heart. It doesn't fit a Drakkar."

"Congratulations, cousin, with that you've spoken more truth tonight than you have since you emerged bawling from your mother's womb," Frey drawled, and she turned resentful eyes to him.

"They have my Antoine," she hissed.

"And did it occur to you that if you came direct to me with this problem, we could see about getting him back?" Frey returned.

"And why would you do me any favors?" she spat.

"Because I understand what it means to be in love, but, cousin, you surprisingly forget. I owe you a debt," Frey replied.

Her face grew cold as she slipped her mask in place.

"I'm not in love," she snapped.

"Tell yourself that, Franka," Frey said quietly. "But you do not commit treason for a heady climax and we both know it. It's just that you only know it deep inside, where you've buried any emotion that might make you resemble a human being."

She glared at her cousin but there was more that they needed to know.

"You sent the informant," Apollo remarked.

Her attention came to him, but she said nothing.

"You knew I'd sent my apologies for the Drakkar gale, and to lure me there, hoping I would bring Madeleine, you sent the informant."

She lifted her chin and confessed by saying, "Hope prevailed. It worked."

Apollo drew in a sharp breath and made note to send his men on a hunt.

The informant would not earn a spike, but he *would* earn a noose.

Franka tired of their discourse and demanded, "What do you do with Kristian and I now?"

"What I do is send my dragons to Specter Isle to annihilate it," Frey answered, and her expression filled with alarm.

"If you do that, they'll incinerate Antoine," she whispered.

"Franka," Frey started, his voice gentling. "It would end his pain *and...*" he stressed his last word when she opened her mouth to speak. "Ask yourself if one sacrifice is worth saving the lives of many. We know not what they plan, we just know it is ill and every soul on two continents is at risk."

Her eyes narrowed with hostility. "What I'll ask is for you to consider the same should it be Finnie who was obliterated and it was *you* facing an empty bed until the end of your days. Ask your bride. Your Winter Bride knows." She turned furious eyes to Apollo. "*You* know." She leaned toward him and hissed, "*You know*."

"You compare this loss to mine?" Apollo asked, his tone dripping with disgust.

"Is there ever a compare?" she shot back. "I couldn't begin to imagine what you lost for I never knew your wife in that manner. All I know is Antoine has a kind heart, a soft touch, and he is the one and only person on this earth who has ever made me feel like I was *me*. *Not* a Drakkar. You may not think that's worth saving. Worth treason. Worth dying for. But *I* do."

Apollo took a step away from her but kept his gaze on her.

She also did not move hers from him.

"Remember, Franka, what you did this night," he finally said quietly. "You nearly cost me something I've grown to cherish."

"I would apologize if the stakes were not so high," she returned, tossing her head, and when she was done speaking, pushing to her feet.

"You have no remorse," Apollo noted.

She straightened her shoulders. "I think I've made it known I have little regard for your Madeleine. And I know who she is." She looked to Frey. "I know where Finnie comes from, too. Helda told me." Her attention moved back to Apollo. "Regardless, I have little time for remorse knowing Antoine endures agony every hour. So pardon me for not admiring her spirit. But in the end, I've never been good at making friends."

Apollo drew in a deep breath and looked to Frey when he let it out.

Frey was studying Franka.

"Frey?" he called.

"Tonight, I send the dragons," Frey decided.

Apollo nodded. Franka uttered not a noise but that didn't mean the depth of emotion emanating from her didn't beat into both men.

It was just that, in times like these, soldiers had no choice but to be immune to it.

Frey turned to Ruben. "Sequester Kristian and Franka down here. Arrange for them to be made comfortable." He looked to his mother and father. "Will what you've seen and heard here be shared with anyone? Or do we have to arrange for your accommodation in Brunskar's dungeons as well?"

"*I* will not say a word," Valeria declared quickly.

"And I will be too busy dissolving my union with my wife to be bothered with this...*mess*," Eirik stated.

"My wife and son," Kristian said quietly.

Frey looked to his cousin. "They'll be sequestered with you."

Kristian opened his mouth to speak but Frey lifted a hand.

"Until the dragons return, it's necessary anyone who could be connected even remotely to the plot that evolved this evening needs to be isolated," Frey explained, turned his head and jerked his chin to Lund who immediately left the room.

Kristian took a step forward and regained Apollo's attention.

"They know nothing of this," he stated.

"They will be made comfortable."

"But—"

"Kristian," Frey interrupted him, his voice low with warning. "Your loyalty to your sister is admirable but it is also beyond foolhardy. You committed treason."

"But the...the..." his eyes darted to Apollo and back to Frey, "lady in question isn't even of this world."

"She is now and she's betrothed to the general who commands your queen's soldiers," Apollo returned and watched Kristian swallow.

"We'll discuss your situation after the dragons return," Frey decreed.

Kristian held his cousin's gaze before he looked to his sister almost beseechingly.

He clearly got nothing there because he then looked to his boots.

Frey turned to his parents. "A word is breathed, I'll know."

That was all he needed to say. Neither spoke but both of their faces did it for them.

They would speak not a word.

He gave his attention to Apollo.

Apollo jerked up his chin, moved from the room and felt Frey follow him out.

They'd turned the corner before he stopped and looked to his friend.

"They seek to assassinate the women," Apollo stated.

"I'm sending the dragons."

This, he predicted, would not work and he shared his concerns with Frey. "They'll have enchantments protecting Specter Isle."

Frey nodded. "It's likely the beasts won't succeed."

"It would take mighty magic to protect an entire island from dragon fire," Apollo noted.

Frey's lips moved up into a small smile. "They weaken."

They did. And this could be why they didn't waste magic on their first strike.

But their side needed an alternate plan. "Should the dragons return unsuccessful, we can use Franka and Kristian."

Frey nodded again. "Agreed."

"We need Lavinia."

"And Valentine."

This time, Apollo nodded. "The Circe of the other world, who used to be Baldur's sorceress, she's powerful?"

"It's said she is. As is Lahn's Circe. But he's had words with me and Tor. They seek to recoup her powers, and although Circe doesn't know this, Lahn is allowing it for her to use should she need to protect herself. He's forbidden us to use her in any way. She will volunteer, he's made that clear. But he will not allow it. He does not want her made vulnerable."

"Understandable," Apollo murmured.

Frey studied him closely and Apollo would know why when he asked quietly, "She pleases you?"

He was talking about Madeleine.

"She is nothing like her twin," Apollo said by way of reply.

"They never are," Frey murmured.

Apollo drew in a deep breath and admitted, "The loss was a long time ago, however the feelings felt fresh. Until her. But time may have dulled the memories. It feels a betrayal to Ilsa to speak these words, but I am enjoying my time with Madeleine..." he paused and finished, "maybe more."

At that, Frey smiled and responded, "They never are the same, but they are always better. And for you, my friend, she would need to be considering the other her was as she was, and you felt for her as you did."

Apollo felt his lips curving and concluded, "Yes. So, in other words, indeed. She pleases me. She vexes me often. But she pleases me more."

Frey's brows rose. "Ilsa did not vex you?"

"What we had was very steady."

Frey grinned. "You may have discovered that the vexing leads to many things and most of them are interesting. And most of those interesting things are *very* interesting."

Apollo started walking again, Frey falling in step beside him, and Apollo murmured, "I may be mad, but I simply find the vexing part interesting."

Frey chuckled and clapped Apollo on the back. "Do not share this with my wee Finnie, but I would agree."

They ascended the stairs and stopped again to go their separate ways.

"We leave on the morrow for Karsvall," Apollo told him. "Lavinia is there and it's safe. My children and Maddie are here where I feel it is not. You and Finnie are welcome."

"I'll report to you immediately about the dragons. And if they are not successful, we will discuss Franka and Kristian and how to use them," Frey replied. "I'll leave a man to deal with that and Finnie, my son and I will follow you to Karsvall."

Apollo lifted his chin.

Frey murmured, "I go to my dragons," as he turned to move away.

"Frey," Apollo called, and Frey stopped. "I have a man who makes his way to Specter Isle. A self-appointed mission to scout. I have another man who follows him. I would think they should be there by now, though I've heard no word."

"This is a foolhardy mission," Frey remarked.

"He was warned," Apollo shared.

"The dragons' missiles cannot be precise if we don't know where they are," Frey said quietly. "Upon approach to Brunskar, we saw the black magic in the forest and the blue of Minerva's sparks, as well as the sea of wolves, so we knew one of ours was under attack and I could instruct the beasts." He shook his head, watching Apollo closely. "Specter Isle is not vast, but it's far from small. Not knowing where they are, I cannot do the same for your men or Franka's lover."

Apollo drew in breath and looked away, wishing like all soldiers—futilely he knew—that there was a world with no war.

If Derrik reached Scepter Isle, and the dragons succeeded, he would be lost.

Apollo felt that score through his soul before he let out his breath slowly and looked back to Frey. "I will hope they have not yet made their destination."

"I will hope that as well," Frey replied.

Apollo drew in another breath, and on the exhale, whispered, "Thank you. For tonight what you did with your dragons in the forest, I owe you a debt."

"You owe me nothing," Frey replied quietly. "My wife was in a war zone, a princess surrounded by snakes. You were her one true ally who held power. You saw she took no venom. Tonight, I repaid *my* debt."

That he would allow so again Apollo lifted his chin.

Frey dipped his.

Then Apollo moved to find his Madeleine as Frey moved toward the front doors to command his dragons.

22

HOLD TIGHT TO HAPPINESS

Apollo's boots made no sound on the blood-red runner that ran the hall to the room in which the maid had told him he would find Maddie.

He was not surprised when, seven feet from the door, Madeleine's Maroovian maid stepped out, her eyes aimed to him.

He stopped three feet away and held her gaze as she closed the door with a soft click behind her.

Only then did he quietly state, "You are witch."

She shook her head.

He felt his eyes narrow at her lie. "You knew the danger, where she'd be. And you went there armed."

"I did," she agreed, steadily holding his gaze. She went on to explain, "My grandmother held magic. This was passed down to me through my mother, who did not. I am not witch, but I have the sight."

She had the sight.

And she was loyal to Madeleine. Loyal enough to put her own life on the line to protect her.

Bloody brilliant news.

"I warn you, wolf, it is not under my control," she continued. "I cannot call it up as my grandmother could. If I sense something, however, I can pinpoint it, keep it in focus, and it is never wrong."

Although brilliant, this was annoying.

"If you sense something in future, woman, I bid you to tell me," he commanded. "For tonight could have had a different ending."

She shook her head again.

"I saw the dragons," she whispered, and Apollo tipped his head to the side. "I knew Miss Maddie did not die tonight."

"If you saw all you saw, explain why you didn't share it with me."

"Dragons?" she asked, shaking her head yet again. "Impossible."

"Not in Lunwyn," he returned.

"I have heard much of this. However, I thought it lore. It was too fantastical." She drew in breath and finished, "It must be seen to be believed."

"Now you've seen it, believe it and share any future visions with me no matter how impossible you feel them to be," he ordered.

She held his gaze for a moment before nodding. However, she did not step away from the door.

He grew impatient with her delay as well as what he read behind it.

He disliked both, but more the latter.

"You will be recompensed for your actions and your loyalty displayed tonight," he said low.

"I wish nothing but to remain in service to Miss Maddie," she replied, and he felt his head twitch in surprise.

"That is not a difficult wish to grant. You excel at your job and she cares for you," Apollo told her. "That said, with what you did this night I will still reward you in coins or baubles, your choice. Simply tell Cristiana when we've returned and they will be provided for you."

"I will accept either to save for when I am no longer able to work. You choose which you will bestow. In the meantime, I simply wish to remain at Miss Madeleine's side."

Apollo felt his skin prickle at her reiteration of something he'd already assured her she'd have. Before he could ask after it, she told him.

"She is not of this world," she said softly.

He said nothing.

"She is special," she carried on.

He said something to that.

"She is," he agreed.

She drew in a breath through her nose, the long line of her neck lengthening, her eyes never leaving his.

Then, hesitantly, for her words were not those acceptable from one such as she to one such as him—not ever—she spoke.

"You should feel no guilt for this love you hold for her, this love that builds beyond imagining. It does not reflect on the love you had before."

With respect to her actions that night, instead of remonstrating her for her insolence, he simply replied, "This is not your concern."

She ignored him.

"Love like you build with Miss Madeleine is as she is. It is not of this world. Not of her world. It is beyond the worlds. It is beyond anything."

He was feeling that, he didn't need a lady's maid, no matter her intelligence or power, to tell him so.

Apollo looked beyond her to the door, starting to say, "We will not dis—"

"She is in grave danger."

He turned back to her.

"This I know," he growled.

"I do not know why these powers wish to extinguish this love beyond worlds. But this is their wish. I sense it. They wish to extinguish it, but they will wrest something from it." Her head cocked to the side. "There are others." It was a question and a statement.

"Three others," he confirmed.

"They are in grave danger as well," she informed him of something he knew.

"Woman, this is not something we don't know," he shared.

She didn't move.

He grew more impatient, but still, to learn what she might know, he waited.

Finally, she said, "The one with white hair we met tonight and Miss Maddie I see often surrounded in green. This green does not cause me dread. It means them no harm, in fact, the opposite. There is also one who is surrounded by gold. She, too, does not trouble me. You say there's another?"

He drew in breath and told her, "Cora, the Gracious. Princess of the Vale."

She nodded. "I will tell you if I see her."

Brilliant.

Now she needed to bloody move.

He didn't order this. He waited again, his patience waning.

"It is their love," she said softly, her eyes going unfocused.

"Pardon?" he asked.

She lifted a finger. Closing her eyes, she rubbed it between.

Finally, she dropped her hand and looked to him.

"The men of these women, they are hard to love," she declared, and Apollo clenched his teeth. "All for different reasons. All, if they had not found these women, would have lived lonely, untouched by that emotion, the companionship they enjoy, the contentment their lover brings them."

"I was touched by it," he reminded her, his voice cold.

"You were, and yet it was lost. Worse for you, as you know how that feels."

He wished she'd cease telling him things he knew and get out of his gods' damned way.

"And because you lost it," she continued, "*this* is why your love is not easy to win, and you not an easy man to love."

He said nothing for she was again telling him something he knew.

"I will share if I see more," she declared, finally moving out of the way.

"My gratitude," he muttered, shifting toward the door. Hand on the doorknob, he turned back to her. "I wish you to stay with Loretta tonight. Lady Madeleine and I will be going back to my children. We travel with a guard and a witch."

She nodded.

"You will be escorted back to her in the morning."

She again nodded.

He jerked up his chin. "Sleep well, Meeta," he muttered, turning from her, but before he could enter the room, she called, "Wolf."

He glanced back.

"You will not know," she started quietly. "You will never know. I have lived a life in service. That forced on me or that necessary to put food in my belly, clothes on my back. In this world, all have their place. In her world," she inclined her head to the door, "I sense, they do not. In her world, I am her equal. Thus, in this world, that is how she treats me. Even if I am in service to her, she never makes me feel this is the case. In this world, in my place, such as this is a gift more valuable than a hundred chests of gold. You can never understand this, but I do. And it is a treasure I wish to keep...for always."

"Then you shall keep it," he replied softly.

She dipped her chin.

When he regained her eyes, he said, "Thank you for what you did tonight, Meeta, and for all you do for my Madeleine."

Her mouth grew soft.

He nodded to her, finally turned to the door and entered the room.

Madeleine was curled up in a chair pulled to the windows. The curtains were open, and she had her chin to her raised knees, gazing at the village of Brunskar.

"My dove," he called gently and watched her body jerk, her head turning to him. "We must be away."

"Away?" she asked.

"To the children," he explained, walking toward her. When he got close to her chair, he crouched down at her side. "We will have a guard and a witch with us. The Keer parcel has been destroyed, the enchantments recast. We are safe to journey, poppy. But with what happened tonight, I do not wish to be far from you or my children."

She drew in a deep breath but nodded while doing it and unfolded from the chair.

He looked around the room. "Has Melba offered you a cloak?" he asked.

"No," she answered, and when he looked back to her, she was again gazing out the window.

"Maddie," he called, and her eyes came to his. "We will be safe, dove," he whispered.

Her teeth worried her lip, but she nodded.

"Loretta is to stay here and rest, Meeta is with her. They will return tomorrow and we'll be away to Karsvall."

She nodded again.

He held his hand to her. "Let us find you a cloak and be on our way."

She took his hand without a word and followed him out. Most of the servants were awake, seeing to the rush of activity that ended the night. Thus, they acquired a cloak easily.

However, Maddie swayed to a halt at his side when they hit the top of the steps outside the front door.

He looked into her pale face, understood her terror and bent instantly. He swung her into his arms and walked her down the steps as she held tightly to his shoulders, her cheek pressed against his.

She only let him go when he put her atop Anguish. He mounted behind her, leaned them both into the steed and kicked in his heels.

His men, Remi with the witch on the back of his horse, fell in around them.

The ride to the village was less than half the time it took when they rode to the castle in their sleigh. Once they reached the inn, Apollo escorted Maddie to her room, Gaston moving to stand sentry beside her door as he pulled her loosely in his arms just inside it.

"I will be back very shortly, poppy. I wish to check on the children."

She looked up at him, her face still pale, her eyes strange, but she nodded.

He would deal with her fears very soon.

For now, he bent to touch his lips to hers, and as he lifted his head, he shuffled her backwards deeper into the room and lowered his voice to say, "I wish to be present when you disrobe, dove. Do not change. Tonight, you sleep naked pressed beside me."

He watched with surprise and some confused disquiet as he thought he almost caught a wince before her expression cleared, she pressed into him and she whispered, "Okay, honey."

He drew in breath, let it go, gave her a squeeze and released her to see his children.

They were asleep in their beds, Balthazar in Élan's room, Quincy in Christophe's.

He got nods from the men, returned them and made his way back to Maddie.

When he closed and locked her door, he found her again staring out the window. Her borrowed cloak was thrown over a chair. Her borrowed dress still on.

She'd fed the fire and lit a lamp by the bed.

But now, she stood unmoving.

"Close the drapes, dove," he ordered gently and again watched her start and turn to him.

She nodded and did as ordered as he walked to the side of the bed closest to her and sat down.

"Come to me, Madeleine," he said, his voice still gentle.

As he wished, she came to him and she did it close, stopping between his spread legs.

He lifted his hands and put them to her hips, his head tipped back to keep hold of her eyes.

"Are you sore from your endeavors tonight, my poppy?" he asked.

"I don't feel anything," she answered.

He didn't relish the way she said that, her voice strangely without emotion. However, he suspected after all that had befallen her that eve, it would take much to process it, including time.

But he would be there to help her do it.

"You'll feel it on the morrow," he murmured.

"Probably," she murmured back.

"You're safe, Maddie," he assured her.

She drew in a breath and nodded to the headboard.

"Madeleine," he called, and she looked back to him. "I wish to ask something of you."

Her eyes held his in a way he found strange, moving, yet troubling, even as she lifted her hand and cupped his jaw.

Once she'd touched him, she whispered, "I'd do anything for you, Apollo."

Her words, the way she said them, now full of emotion, the way she touched him, gentle and light, he felt his gut tighten.

Perhaps she wasn't processing what happened that evening.

Perhaps she was processing something else entirely.

His gut tightened further.

"Give me your foot," he directed, his voice suddenly gruff.

She tipped her head to the side but dropped her hand and lifted her foot.

He slid her borrowed slipper off.

"The other," he said once he'd dropped it to the floor.

She did as bid.

He slid that one off as well.

"Now remove your dress, poppy."

She pressed her lips together, but her hands did not delay in moving to the fabric, bunching it in her fingers and pulling it up and off.

She let the dress glide from her fingers to the floor and stood before him wearing nothing but an emerald-green satin bustier that dipped low at the back, her breasts barely contained in the cups at the front, and it had bronze ribbons adorning its boning. She also wore a pair of matching satin panties.

He felt his cock pulse as his gaze moved over her. Her soft skin. Her curves. Her abundant hair glimmering in the firelight. Her beautiful eyes directed at him.

There she was.

His Maddie.

Alive.

Breathing.

Beautiful.

His.

His voice was now gruff for more than one reason when he instructed, "Discard your panties, Madeleine, then free me and climb in my lap."

He watched her lids lower, her lips part, and he felt both in his throat, his gut and his shaft. Then she slid her thumbs into her panties and tugged them down.

His cock started aching.

She bent to him and he felt her fingers working at the buttons of his trousers.

At that, his shaft throbbed.

She pulled him free and caught his eyes as she positioned, first one knee in the bed, then the other, climbing on.

"Guide me inside," he whispered.

She licked her lips, and he felt her reach between them, her hand wrapping around him. He stifled the rumble rolling up his chest as she slid the tip of him through her wet silkiness until he caught at her opening.

Gazing at him, slowly she glided down until he filled her.

Apollo wrapped his arms around her, head tipped back to keep her gaze, his voice nearly hoarse when he kept whispering. "This is us, my dove."

"It is, Lo," she whispered back, her sex pulsating around his shaft.

"You're safe," he repeated.

"Yes." She was still whispering.

"You're mine," he declared, his voice now almost guttural.

She closed her eyes, dropped her head so her forehead was resting on his and lifted both hands to wrap them around either side of his neck.

"Yes," she said quietly.

"Look at me, poppy."

Her eyes opened but she didn't lift her head.

"I wish to lie back and watch you take me."

Her forehead rolled on his as she nodded. "Anything, Apollo."

Gently disengaging from her hold, he lay back.

She kept his gaze as he did, and once he was settled, his hands at her hips, she started moving.

Apollo watched.

And felt.

And listened.

And as he did, he memorized it all. Every wet, sleek inch of her he could feel gliding on his cock, her thighs pressed to his hips, her hair tumbling over her shoulders, her breasts moving against the satin, her gaze on him heating with each stroke, her soft gasps each time she filled herself with him.

"Faster, dove," he encouraged.

"Yes," she breathed, moving faster on him as he watched.

And he watched as she raised her arms, her hands moving behind her neck, lifting up her hair as if its touch, the sway of it against her skin was too much.

His Madeleine.

Sheer beauty.

"Keep your hair up, Maddie," he groaned.

"Yes, baby," she whimpered, moving faster, her soft gasps coming quicker, deeper. "Lo, I need your thumb," she begged, and he immediately gave it to her.

When he pressed in and rolled, he watched her back arch.

"God," she moaned.

"Take me, Maddie," he ordered, now bucking his hips, watching her take him, her breasts nearly spilling out of the satin.

She dropped her arms to arch back further, riding him now as *he* took *her*, her fingers curling around his thighs.

"That's it, poppy," he rumbled, his one hand holding her steady, his other thumb circling deeper. "Take me."

"Lo."

He bucked harder.

"God! Lo!" she exclaimed, her sex convulsing around his shaft with her climax, her cries short and low, but sharp.

"Keep taking me," he grunted, driving his hips up into her beautiful bucking body.

"Yes, Lo, yes. Forever, baby. I'll take you forever," she gasped, still climaxing, and he exploded.

He pressed his head into the mattress. The muscles of his neck straining, he moved his thumb so that he could clamp both his hands on her hips to hold her tight to his cock. Thus, he shot his seed inside her on a grunt followed by a low rumbling groan that shook through him. And, at her whimper, he knew it shook through her.

He was barely recovered before he ordered brusquely. "Come here."

Instantly, she dropped forward, her weight landing on him, her hot, wet sex still enveloping him. When she got close, she shoved her face in his neck.

Apollo wrapped his arms around her and turned his head so he had her ear.

"This is us. That was us. We're here, my poppy. We're alive. We're together, my dove."

He felt her body still on his for a brief moment before she pressed it into his, pushing her face deeper into his neck.

"They will not take you from me," he vowed, and she slid her hand up his chest to curl her fingers around his neck and held on tight.

He memorized that too, everything, burning all that was Madeleine at that moment into his brain before he slowly sat up, taking her with him, reveling in the noise that was part surprise, part pleasure that glided up her throat.

He found his feet, holding her to him. She wrapped her legs around him and he moved through the room. He stopped by the pitcher of water left for them. He lifted her gently, sliding her off his cock and setting her on her feet. Holding her in his arm, carefully, he cleaned her as she leaned against him.

"Stay close, dove," he murmured as he let her go.

She did as ask and he disrobed, dropping his boots and clothes to the floor where they stood. He then moved his attention to her, unhooking the stays at her back and dropping her bustier to the floor.

Apollo then lifted her and carried her to the bed. Bending low, he threw back the covers, still holding her close. He placed her in the bed, joining her there the minute her back hit the mattress, covering her. He pulled the bedclothes over them and shifted his weight into a forearm.

He then looked down at her to see her gazing up at him. Her eyes warm and sleepy.

And trusting.

His chest warmed as he brushed a lock of hair from her face.

"I will ask one thing more of you before I let you sleep," he whispered.

She slid her arms around him as she replied, "Anything, Lo."

"I wish you to listen to me."

She nodded, her head moving on the pillow, her eyes never leaving his. "Of course, honey."

He cupped her cheek and dipped his face close before he began, "At first, we missed it."

He watched her blink in confusion, but he went on.

"The time she carried Élan, like with Christophe, was uneventful."

When understanding dawned, Apollo felt Maddie's body tighten under his, but he continued.

"The birth, however, was complicated. Christophe slid easily into this world. Élan gave Ilsa more difficulty."

"Apollo—" she whispered, and he pressed the pads of his finger in.

"Listen," he whispered back.

She closed her mouth and nodded again.

"Looking back, due to the birth, we both missed it. Even she, a physician. We thought her body was taking its time recovering from bringing Élan into this world. The extreme fatigue. The constant lethargy. Though, even if we caught it, there was nothing to be done."

"All right," Maddie whispered when he didn't go on.

"And then it happened fast," he told her softly. "She just started wasting away."

She closed her eyes.

Apollo slid his hand to her neck and she opened them again.

"We disagreed about Christophe, Ilsa and I," he shared. "She thought like a physician, sometimes clinically. Thus, she felt that life was life, and even for children, it was not wise to shelter them from it too much. He was only four. So very young. I did not want him to see his mother that way. To remember her that way. She was energetic. Lively, in her way. Not like Élan, the way she had was all Ilsa's. I didn't want him to see her thin, gaunt, in pain. I didn't want him to remember her that way. She wished to see her son, but I denied her. I did this for Christophe. I struggle still if I made the right decision."

"You did," she said gently, her arms around him tightening.

His Maddie, so loyal, telling him what he wanted to hear.

"I will never know if you speak true, my Maddie," he murmured. "They had a bond, much like what he has with me. And if it were me abed, my power stripped, sickness eating away at me, pain crippling me, I would wish him not to see me like that. I would wish him to remember his father as vital. Jovial. Whole."

"So you did the right thing," she replied.

"He did not see her at all the three months before she passed. I robbed them both of each other to protect my son."

Maddie swallowed but said nothing.

"It was torture," he whispered.

She pulled her arms from around him so she could slide them up his chest, his neck, to frame his face as she murmured an aching, "*Honey.*"

"All of it was, Madeleine, watching her waste away, watching the pain consume her, keeping our son from her. Torture. Every moment."

Her hands on him lightly squeezed.

"Tonight, the black mist took you, and I felt all that torture, months of it, condensed in an instant," he declared, and her gaze widened. "It was the most excruciating moment of my life."

At that, he watched her eyes fill with tears.

"Baby," she breathed.

Suddenly, he found his fingers shoving up into her hair, the pads digging into her scalp, and he brought his face to a breath from hers. "Tonight we learned we must hold tight to happiness, my dove. Every day...every *moment*...is a gift. We must hold tight to that, Madeleine, and never let go."

"Yes," she whispered.

He slid his nose along hers until their eyes were so close, if either of them blinked, their lashes would sweep the other's.

"I will not lose you," he growled.

"I'm right here, sweetheart," she soothed.

Apollo drew in a deep breath, released it then slanted his head so he could brush his mouth lightly against hers.

Only when he pulled back an inch did he reply, "You are, indeed."

She gave him a shaky smile.

"Thank you, my dove, for fighting so hard this night to save a life I cherish."

Her shaky smile wobbled as her face began to crumble but he saw no more when she lifted her head and shoved it in his neck.

"You-you-you're welcome," she stammered into his skin.

He gave her his weight for a brief moment in order to wrap his arms around her before he rolled them to their sides.

Putting his lips to her hair, he whispered, "Now you can sleep."

She took a shuddering breath that was half sniveling, half chortling and nodded, her face now pressed to his throat.

He held her close and stroked her back as she gained control of her emotions. When she did, she slid a hand from where it was pressed to his chest, rounding him with her arm, and she pressed closer.

Many minutes later, when her body had loosened, her breath had evened and he thought her close to sleep, she called a drowsy, "Lo?"

And, gods, but he treasured it when she called him "Lo."

"Yes, poppy," he replied, giving her a squeeze.

He felt her frame tense slightly when she began, "You know that I, uh...well, I um...pretty much cherish you too, right?"

Again that night, a night he would not think he would find anything amusing, he couldn't stop his body from shaking with laughter.

"Yes, Madeleine, I *pretty much* know you cherish me too."

She relaxed and murmured, "Cool."

He grinned at her hair and gave her another squeeze.

"Sleep, Maddie."

"Right away, boss," she muttered and again he grinned.

She settled in.

Apollo closed his eyes and saw the black mist shrouding her, so he opened them again and gathered her even closer.

He took a deep breath as she snuggled into his embrace.

He took another one when, moments later, he felt sleep claim her.

Love like you build with Miss Madeleine is as she is. It is not of this world. Not of her world. It is beyond the worlds. It is beyond anything.

Meeta's words filled his head and he was forced to take another deep breath.

Tonight, he almost lost her.

Tomorrow, he would set about making certain that did not happen.

He had no earthly clue how he would do it.

He just knew he bloody would.

Nothing could save Ilsa.

But nothing would ever again harm Maddie.

Not ever again.

Not ever.

~

His thoughts in turmoil, Apollo had no sleep. So he was awake when the soft knock came at the door.

He carefully disengaged from Maddie, strode swiftly to his trousers and yanked them on.

He then headed to the door.

He unlocked and opened it an inch.

Frey's man Ruben stood outside.

His deep voice was low and concerned when he stated, "The dragons failed."

Apollo felt his mouth get tight.

Very bad news.

But at least this meant his men lived.

And that their foe's magic had to be weakened.

"Frey will meet you here in an hour's time to discuss what we do next," Ruben went on.

Apollo nodded.

Ruben moved away from the door.

Apollo closed it, leaned against it and aimed his eyes at Maddie's sleeping form in the bed, his mind slotting the priorities in his head.

First, he would send men to find the false informant and put him in prison, awaiting trial.

Second, they would interrogate Franka, find the witch who created the Keer parcel and put her in prison to await trial.

Next, use Franka and Kristian to draw out the enemy.

Strike that.

Kristian could barely hold his water during the tame interrogation he'd endured.

Kristian and his family would "disappear."

Franka would be their tool.

And last, find bloody Valentine and put the woman to work.

She'd been paid a handsome fee.

It was her time to earn it.

On that thought, he moved to the bed and commenced in waking Maddie with his mouth.

Then he made her climax with it.

After, he made her climax on his cock.

And after he joined her, content he'd started her day with happiness, he kissed her so hard he bruised her lips and made her gasp with pleasured pain when he finally released her mouth.

He left her in order to continue down his path of vengeance.

The path that would end with her safety.

23
IT WAS ALL I HAD

"We cannot trust her."

Apollo tore his gaze away from the window where he was studying Maddie outside with his daughter.

He was also studying his son.

Maddie and Élan were smiling, and he often heard their laughter as they did whatever-they-were-doing in the snow outside the inn, waiting for Apollo and Frey to finish speaking so they could leave Brunskar and be away to Karsvall.

Seeing the vision outside the window, he was relieved that it seemed he had led Maddie beyond her concerns of last night, for she was no different than she normally was around his Élan.

Therefore, his thoughts were with Chris, who was not often far from his sister, and thus, of late, Maddie. But now, for some reason, he was well away from them both and not in a manner where he was simply interested in his own pursuits.

No, he appeared to be avoiding the two females.

This did not sit right with Apollo.

However, he had no time to dwell on it. He would keep his eye on the situation and approach his son later if need be.

Now, he was discussing their next steps with Frey.

"Indeed, Franka is not trustworthy," he told his friend as he turned his eyes to Frey. "And matters will be worse than before, for even if there is now hope she will get her lover back alive, she will not forget your willingness to sacrifice him."

Frey nodded. "This is true. And it seems Franka is unaware that if this Antoine has been tortured every hour for some time, if she gets him back, she may not find the man she knows returned."

"Undoubtedly," Apollo agreed.

Frey's expression turned pensive. "Or she is aware and doesn't care. She will simply take him as he comes."

"This may be the case as it would appear she's in love," Apollo pointed out.

Frey focused on Apollo and shook his head. "I do not wish to think that as it would be indication that the world is coming to an end."

Apollo chuckled and Frey gave him a smile.

"And you send the dragons again," Apollo stated.

This was another part of their new strategy. Bombard the isle with dragon fire in hopes to either weaken the shield or weaken their magic.

"Daily, randomly," Frey confirmed. "They will need to expend much magic to keep it strong against my dragons' blaze and do it constantly for they will not know when the next attack will occur."

"The elves?" Apollo asked.

"I always keep the branch close. I will visit them after I talk to Franka and before I join your party en route to Karsvall."

Apollo nodded.

During the last war, in his play to depose Finnie's father and unite Lunwyn and Middleland, Baldur's son Broderick's agents had burned all the adela trees to the ground. As these were the conduits used for the elves to ascend from their world under the ice, this was done to trap them and their formidable magic so they could not be of aid.

Since, Lavinia had made it her mission to plant new adelas all through Lunwyn. They were taking root, but it would be decades before they'd grow strong.

Which made it fortunate that Frey and his Raiders had purloined an ancient relic, a branch of adela that Frey could touch to the earth anywhere and summon the elves to the ice.

"I'm rethinking staying separated from Tor and Lahn," Apollo told him. "The magic you have at your command, Lavinia, and if we can find Valentine, Lunwyn is far safer for us all."

Frey shook his head. "That reasoning holds merit, cousin, but your suggestion to divide their energies is sound. There are far more witches in the Vale than Lunwyn. They don't hold the power of Lavinia and Valentine singly, and no one holds the power of the elves, save Minerva, but amassed these witches are formidable. Tor has amassed them. Though, we'll send birds and discuss how they feel about this course of action."

Apollo nodded his agreement.

Frey's eyes moved to the door and back to Apollo before he said, "We mustn't delay."

Apollo again looked toward the window, taking in Maddie, Élan and Christophe, who had not come any nearer to his sister, and thus Madeleine.

He turned his gaze back to Frey and said, "The sleighs should be ready. Finnie and Viktor will ride with Maddie and Élan. I ride at their side. We'll expect you tomorrow evening in Skógarholt."

Frey looked to the ceiling where Apollo knew Finnie was with their young son, Viktor, before his gaze came again to Apollo.

"Tomorrow evening in Skógarholt," he agreed.

"Until then," Apollo replied.

"Until then," Frey returned on a low wave as he walked out the door.

Apollo watched the door close before he returned his attention to the window.

He felt his lips curving up when he saw Élan lean heavily into Maddie, head tipped back, face alight. Maddie had her hand curved over the pink knit cap on his daughter's head, something she insisted Élan wear (she also insisted that Christophe wear a hat, but he had balked when Apollo approached him and Maddie didn't press).

She was looking down at Élan and her expression, too, was beaming.

His focus went to Chris to see he was making his way toward the door of the inn, and as he did this, he didn't even look Maddie and his sister's way.

Very strange.

Apollo decided to have a word.

But not now.

Now they needed to be away to get to Karsvall so that he could get his family to safety.

THAT NIGHT, Apollo turned the key to Maddie's room and entered to see her sitting in bed, a loosely-knit shawl around her shoulders to keep the chill at bay, the fire and all the lights blazing in the room. She had a book in her hands, but her attention was on him.

"How did the talk go?" she asked before he even got the door closed behind him.

He felt his lips curve up as he closed and locked the door.

She, too, had noticed that something was amiss with Christophe. She'd shared this when he'd told her he intended to have a word.

However, Christophe did not confide in his father during the talk.

Apollo was concerned, but not overly. He knew his son, and if he asked, and it was his time to share, Chris would explain. If it wasn't time, Christophe would explain when it was.

Maddie didn't know Christophe as well. She did, however, care.

A great deal.

Therefore, she was anxious.

He didn't like her to feel anxiety, but he liked why she did.

He didn't answer until he'd moved to her and sat beside her hip on the bed. Then he went about setting her mind at ease.

He leaned toward her and rested his weight into his fist in the bed. "He says all is well."

She pressed her lips together, indication she didn't believe this, and the corners of his mouth again turned up.

"We both know all is not well, my dove," he told her, and this had remained true through the ride as Chris did not stay close to Maddie's sleigh as usual. Instead, he'd ridden with Remi and Gaston. "However, I trust my son that, whatever is on his mind, he will share it with me when he's ready. Now, he's working through it and I need to give him time to do this."

"It started last night when he saw me before the gale," she told him.

Apollo tipped his head to the side. "You noticed it then?" he asked.

"Yes," she answered. "All day yesterday he was his usual Chris. When he came into my room with you and Élan, he seemed weird. Distant. He isn't as friendly with me as Élan but he's friendly. He's never behaved like that and his behavior hasn't changed all day."

At her words, thinking of her last night in her gown, the children coming with him to say goodnight, understanding dawned and Apollo felt a burn hit his chest.

"Lo?" she called, and he turned his attention back to her.

"Ilsa and I were social," he explained quietly. "My place in my House as well as my many enterprises dictate I need to be. Ilsa was because she enjoyed socializing. We traveled a great deal, and after we had Christophe, he came with us. Even as a babe. Ilsa didn't like to be without him and neither did I."

"Okay," she prompted softly when he ceased speaking.

"If we had an event we were going to, it was our habit that I would collect Chris as Ilsa finished preparing for the evening and I would bring him to her in order that she could say goodnight to her son."

He watched understanding light for her before she whispered, "Oh God."

But Apollo's attention again drifted, his thoughts turning to his son and what he must have felt the evening before, walking into Madeleine's room, seeing her dressed for the gale wearing the colors of Ulfr house, appearing much like his mother about to do something he saw his mother so often do.

He gave a start when he felt Maddie's hand light on his jaw, and he returned his gaze to her to see she'd risen from the bed and gotten close.

"I can imagine that, although I look like her, I didn't seem much like her, until last night," she noted.

"Yes," he agreed.

"And I can imagine that what I am to you could seem innocuous to him, until he understood what we were doing last night and what I am to you became clearer."

"Indeed," Apollo again agreed, although he felt some disquiet at her use of the words "what I am to you" rather than how she should refer to herself as "*who* I am to you."

"Crap," she murmured before he could remark on this, and he noticed her gaze had gone unfocused as her hand fell away from his jaw.

He caught her hand and gave it a squeeze to regain her attention. This succeeded and her eyes came back to his.

"We will give him his time, poppy," he told her. "Clearly, he wishes to try to sort through his emotions on his own. We must allow him to do that. We will, however, keep an eye on him, and if that time is too lengthy, I will have another word. Yes?"

Her brows drew together, and she queried, "Are you asking me or telling me?"

He moved a bit away from her, confused as to her question, but answering, "I'm asking."

Something shifted through her features, but she merely mumbled, "All right."

"Maddie," he started. "Why do you ask such a question?"

"Hmm?" she inquired in return, clearly evading his query with a vague one of her own.

"Is 'hmm' the answer to my question, dove?"

"Well..." she said but trailed off and said no more.

"Madeleine," he said her name as a warning, and he watched her draw in breath through her nose before she straightened her shoulders.

"I'm not his mother," she stated, her voice strange, quiet, and something else he'd never heard from her.

Something that sounded like pain.

"No, my poppy, you aren't," he replied gently. "But even so, I don't understand why you've mentioned it."

"Well, you asked what we should do with Chris, who has an issue he needs to sort out. And that's, well...it's not really any of my business how you deal with Chris. You're his father. I'm nothing to him."

At this, Apollo blinked and again felt fire in his chest. This time, it wasn't the fire of feeling the remembrance of the grief he'd not too long ago shirked, grief his son re-experienced just the night before.

This time, it was the fire of anger. Anger he controlled due to the subject and Maddie's sensitivity to it, but anger he felt nonetheless.

"You're nothing to him?" he asked, his tone soft with disbelief but tense with ire.

"I mean, not *nothing* nothing," she said quickly, reading his tone and undoubtedly the look in his eyes. "But I've no say in how—"

"Cease speaking," Apollo ordered, and she clamped her mouth shut. "It's my understanding that we're building a life together," he noted. "Am I mistaken in that?"

"No," she whispered.

He was pleased with her answer.

That said, he was still not pleased.

"And as you are in my life, my children are in my life, you are an adult who is close to them and will grow closer, do you not think we should confer as to how we deal with the varying matters that will arise as they mature?"

"I didn't think I—"

"Think it," he interrupted her. "It's preposterous to consider that you would be in my life, *will* be my wife, we'll live out our days together, days we will share with my children for years to come, and you will not help me to raise them."

She held his gaze, something working in hers. He again had not seen it before but this time it was not pain.

Far from it.

He felt the burn release his chest when he saw that this time, it was hope.

He watched her eyes get bright before he saw her swallow and then she whispered, "Okay, then I think it's a good idea to give Chris some time and then approach him if it doesn't seem like he's working it out on his own."

His voice was again gentle when he said, "Then we're agreed."

She nodded.

Apollo lifted her hand to his mouth and brushed his lips against her knuckles. She watched him do this and he watched her eyes get soft when she did.

"You keep giving me things," she remarked.

He liked very much that she thought of him wishing her to be a part in his children's lives in that way as him "giving her things."

It was arguable, but he could have liked it more, the look of contentment and gratitude on her face at receiving it.

"I would endeavor to become accustomed to that, Madeleine, for I intend to continue doing it."

Her eyes already warm, the skin around her mouth softened and she moved. Leaning in, she touched her lips to his and asked, "And what can I give you that you'd like to become accustomed to?"

He knew he had all of her that he could have. What he didn't have, night by night, day by day, she was giving to him. He asked questions, she answered, giving him her life, the vile people in it and the knowledge of the fractures they'd made to her soul. And he hoped this knowledge would provide him with the information he needed to heal what was broken inside her.

But what he wanted most was her heart.

He knew she "pretty much" cherished him.

He wanted more.

With Maddie, he always wanted more.

But he had to win that before she gifted it to him.

And he would.

He released her hand, moved his to her neck and slid his fingers back and up into her hair before he bared his teeth and nipped her lower lip.

He felt her breath rush against his mouth with her excited sigh before he murmured, "What I'd like to become accustomed to is you giving me whatever you wish...just as long as you keep finding things to give, for I never will lose interest in what you have to offer."

She placed her hands light on his chest before she slid them down in order to curl her fingers into his sweater.

"This would mean I'll have to get creative so I don't run out of things to give," she replied.

"Are you capable of that?" he teased.

She slid her nose along his and answered, "We'll see."

After she said her words, she pulled up his sweater.

He lifted his arms in order that she could yank it free.

She did, tossing it to the side and putting her hands to his chest to push him back to the bed.

He allowed this.

Then he allowed her to do other things.

And much later, he had proof that she was very capable.

Or additional proof as she'd proved it before.

Repeatedly.

"I LIKE FINNIE," she whispered into his neck much later, after she'd cleaned herself of him, pulled on her nightgown and slid back into bed to curl into his side.

"I'm glad."

"It's nice having someone from home here."

He squeezed her with the arm he had around her. "You are home, poppy."

"You know what I mean," she said sleepily, snuggling closer.

He did.

He still did not like her referring to the other world as home.

Home was a warm, safe place where you were always welcome. Where there was love and memories of laughter and happy times.

Home had never been that to her.

And her next words would strengthen this conclusion.

"I didn't have any friends at home," she told him, still drowsy, her body getting heavier against his side. "It feels good, finally having friends again."

Apollo closed his eyes.

As much as he wished her secrets, as determined as he was to mine the depth in her eyes, to lighten the darkness she held there, the years of mistreatment at the hands of everyone close to her tore at his heart.

"She's a bit crazy, though," she murmured, now sounding half-asleep.

This made Apollo open his eyes and smile into the dark.

"That she is."

"Crazy in a good way," she explained, but he could barely hear her, her voice was so sleepy.

This earned her another squeeze. "Go to sleep, my dove."

"Okay," she mumbled and seconds later, he had all of her weighing into his side.

He tightened his arm, gathering her closer while he pulled the covers higher up her shoulder.

Apollo stared at the ceiling not thinking of dragons and conspirators, witches and prisoners, Derrik and what he might be up to, or what may be assailing his son's thoughts.

No, he thought nothing of that and all about Maddie now having friends. Now understanding she had a say in the way he raised his children and how she clearly treasured that. Now having protection and kindness and care.

Now having a home.

And Apollo giving all of that to her.

Thus, it did not take long before Apollo followed her into a deep, restful, dreamless sleep as if all was right with the world.

Even when it was not.

~

Maddie

THREE DAYS LATER, I sat in the warm dining room at the inn where we'd stopped for the night. I had Viktor curled in my arms. His eyelids were drooping, a long day out in the snow having taken its toll.

My thoughts were on the precious bundle of toddler in my arms, but my eyes were on Chris all the way across the room.

I was thinking thoughts of Viktor in an effort not to think thoughts of Chris.

It had been days and he was still avoiding me.

In doing so, he was avoiding his sister which she didn't understand. This proved true what I'd guessed and that was they weren't just siblings, they were companions. Apollo had a young servant in his house. But Chris and Élan spent a great deal of time together out of necessity, necessity that was familial, warm, and if not overtly loving, the love was there all the same.

So, regardless of their different ages and genders, they were close.

Élan wishing to be near me meant her brother was not around her.

This, of course, made the little girl cross because any time she tried to get his attention, he continued to evade it. She didn't understand why and further didn't know how to communicate that.

I'd noticed Apollo was giving this situation a wide berth. I could see he was watchful, but he wasn't intervening.

I had agreed with him Christophe should be given some time. He was a boy, but he was keen to learn how to be a good man, and I figured this was one of Apollo's ways of teaching him how.

But four days seemed long enough to me.

Apollo said I had a say in raising his kids and that was perhaps the most beautiful gift anyone had ever given me. And considering Apollo had given me a vast amount of beauty that was saying something.

But his assessing if I agreed with his course of action and me bringing it up that I no longer agreed were two different things.

"He remembers his mother."

This came from Finnie who was sitting at my side.

I looked her way.

She really was very pretty, all that white-blonde hair, those fascinating ice-blue eyes.

Though she didn't look much like a princess and this mostly had to do with the fact she dressed like men from this world, in breeches, boots, sweaters and cloaks.

It also had to do with the fact that, if she was not in the sleigh with me or with her husband and/or son, she was practicing knife fighting with one of Frey's men or bows and arrows with Chris (and Frey *and* Apollo's men).

Frey had joined our party a couple of days before and I enjoyed watching them together even as it kind of broke my heart (I didn't think on this too much, if I did, the "kind of" part of that would be gone).

I loved how he called her "my wee Finnie." I loved how she addressed him as "husband" and he returned that by calling her "wife." I loved how they bantered and teased. I loved how his men were with her. I loved how they looked at each other. How they both clearly adored their son and equally clearly adored that the other adored their son.

It was so cool watching a man like Frey—in other words, a man just like Apollo in the macho department—who was entirely unconcerned with communicating to anybody who paid attention that his heart rested in the hands of his wife and the child she gave him.

No, it wasn't cool.

It was beautiful.

Finnie wasn't secretive about doting on her husband and son either. And I knew it wasn't hard to do, considering Frey was as he was, and Viktor was an immensely active child (in other words, the sleigh ride was akin to toddler torture), but a sweet one.

In another way Frey was like Apollo, Viktor looked nothing like Finnie. He had inherited his father's dark hair and green/brown eyes (or, they could also be brown/green, I hadn't yet decided).

I wondered, if given another shot and they had a girl, if she'd get Finnie's hair and eyes.

And I wondered, if given a shot with Apollo, if we'd make a girl (or a boy) who had my red hair and freckles.

"Maddie?" Finnie called.

I focused on her.

"Sorry, I was on another planet."

She grinned. "That happens."

At her response to my unintentional pun, I grinned back.

Her grin faded and her eyes grew assessing. "Would you like to share?"

I would.

In fact, I needed to share.

This, I found, happened when you actually had someone you could trust to share with. Then again, it happened when you didn't have someone too. It was just good that these days I had people to talk to.

Yet something more Apollo had given me.

"Yes, he remembers his mother," I responded to her earlier comment. "We were doing okay. I've been on this world for months now, but I've only known the kids a few weeks. He was fine until recently when Apollo and I went to the gale, something he saw his parents do often. I don't think before that he put the two of me being around and the two of me being *around* together. That night, seeing me with his father the way I was, he put it together."

"I'll bet," she replied.

"He's been detached since then," I shared. "He's told his father things are fine. And even though Apollo knows they aren't, he's letting him work through it on his own."

"That's a big thing to work through," she noted.

She was so totally right about that.

But I said nothing.

"Have you approached?" Finnie asked.

"I think I should follow his dad's lead," I answered. "And seeing as it's me he has a problem with, I'm not certain that's the way to go."

She screwed up her mouth as her gaze slid to Chris and she murmured, "I suppose you're right."

I supposed I was right too.

But only supposed.

"I'm happy for him," she said, her eyes still aimed in Christophe's direction, so I was confused.

"Chris?" I asked.

She turned and my breath caught at the look in her eyes.

"Apollo," she whispered.

"Oh," I whispered back.

"I...he is..." She shook her head. "He went through a dark time with me. In his way, he helped me through it, actually." Cautiously, eyeing me closely, she finished, "He understood."

I nodded.

"You know?" she asked.

"That you thought you lost Frey and that he lost Ilsa?"

It was her turn to nod.

"Yes. I know about Ilsa, and Apollo's told me the stories of all the other women of our world and their men. Or, what he knows to tell."

"Then you would understand how Apollo means a great deal to me."

"I do," I said quietly.

"So I'm happy. Watching you two. Seeing how he looks at you. Watching him smile and laugh. Honestly, Maddie, I've known him for over two years, and although I'd seen him smile, I don't know if I've ever heard him laugh. It makes me happy he has that. It makes me happy to see he's happy you give it to him."

I loved that.

I absolutely loved it.

I just wished I could give him more.

Not just smiles and laughter.

Things like what he gave me. Big things. Important things. Precious things.

Everything.

"It's not my place to thank you." She grinned. "But I'm going to do it anyway."

I grinned back, it was a tad forced, but it was mostly genuine. "Pleased to be of service, especially that kind."

"I appreciate you giving my wee wife a rest, Maddie, but I'll take him now."

I jumped slightly when Frey's rich, deep voice sounded at my other side. I had just enough time to turn my head and look up to see him already bending to me. Without delay, he whisked his son out of my arms.

He curled the tot to his broad chest, Viktor's legs dangling over his dad's forearm, his head resting on his shoulder, bringing to life the vision of one of those pictures with a hot guy and a kid that I used to see on calendars and such. Taking it in, I wondered if it would be hotter if Frey held a kitten instead of a kid.

Probably not.

Though, seeing him cradle his son, I'd like to see him cuddle a kitty.

Frey's gaze went to his wife.

"I'll put him down, my love."

"All right, honey," Finnie replied.

I felt something hollow out in my insides as I watched this exchange, but I made certain my lips were smiling when Frey's eyes came to my face before he dipped his chin and took off with Viktor.

I watched him go, and when I turned back to Finnie, I saw she was also watching her husband go with a expression on her face that I understood.

I felt that look. I felt it for Apollo. Maybe not that strong. Maybe without years and adventures and a baby making it stronger.

But I felt it.

Finnie gave her husband smiles and laughter. She also shared his adventures since they were both just that. Adventurers. She challenged his mind with her wit. She'd done brave things for a country that wasn't even hers (though, now it was), going so far as killing a man.

She had much to give.

That empty feeling inside me grew.

When Finnie finally caught my eyes, she blinked, and I knew by her expression she'd read my thoughts.

Quickly, so she wouldn't ask about it, I declared, "Frey and Apollo are a lot alike."

"Cousins," Finnie said.

"They are?" I asked, and she nodded.

"Yep. Frey's grandmother Eugenie was an Ulfr." Her lips were quirking when she remarked, "You've met the Drakkars."

I fought back my shudder before I confirmed, "Yes."

"Well then you know there had to be some good blood coming from somewhere to make Frey and his brothers." She leaned into me and her lips were no longer quirking. She caught me fighting back the shudder so she was now smiling. "That was Eugenie."

Well, that explained that.

"Ah," I murmured.

"Mm-hmm," she murmured back and after she did, she giggled.

And since she giggled, I giggled too.

We then giggled more.

We only stopped giggling when another rich, deep voice came from my side.

This one I liked a whole lot better.

It was Apollo's as he said, "I'm loathe to disturb your merriment, but the children will soon be heading up for their baths."

I looked up at Apollo, knowing what this meant.

We were riding back much as we'd ridden to Brunskar. This was with brief pit stops to stretch our legs, eat lunch, feed and water the horses, and then pressing forward.

But due to Loretta having an injury and Finnie having a toddler, we ended our rides early enough to settle in our rooms and get a good hot meal.

Therefore, the last few days, Apollo had set about making it so he and I spent time with Chris and Élan alone before they had their baths and went to bed.

This was, I knew, his way of dealing with the Chris situation as well as simply offering the children more opportunities to get to know "us" as an "us" and that meant more than just the Apollo and me "us" but the family "us."

Normally, I would love this.

The way Chris was remote during these times, which Apollo kept brief likely in deference to his son's feelings, I didn't like it all that much.

Nevertheless, I pinned a bright smile on my face and said, "Okeydokey."

The instant he heard me say that word, Apollo smiled a warm, intimate smile that should have warmed me through and through.

It didn't.

It simply made me feel emptier.

I didn't let him see this.

I said my goodnight to Finnie and took Apollo's hand.

He pulled me out of my seat and led us to his children.

THAT NIGHT after Apollo made love to me, we were lying face to face in each other's arms.

I was thinking of what Apollo would look like holding a kitten. Envisioning it in my head, I felt all warm and squishy inside (or warmer and squishier, I always felt pretty warm and squishy after Apollo made love to me).

I didn't know what Apollo was thinking.

Until he told me.

"You are very natural with Viktor," he murmured, his voice sexy-sleepy.

I had to admit, I appreciated his sexy-sleepy voice, and I wished I could focus on that.

But instead, I closed my eyes tight and pressed closer to his warmth, visions of Apollo cuddling a kitty disintegrating and visions of Apollo cradling our redheaded daughter (or son) crowding in.

They were beautiful.

And they hurt.

I opened my eyes and shared, "It's easy to be natural with him when he's tuckered out. I lost count of how many times he made a play toward the front of the sleigh so he could launch himself on Anguish's back."

"His father's son," Apollo murmured.

That was the truth.

He gathered me even closer, and his voice was still drowsy (and hot) when he said, "Watching you with Viktor, I now understand how you find me beautiful when you see me with my children."

Oh God.

He was killing me.

Since he was, and I was fighting that feeling (and that feeling took a lot of fighting), I said nothing.

Apollo, as was his way, read that I needed him to leave it at that. I knew it when he changed the subject to ask, "I must request a favor."

"Anything," I whispered, the feeling in that not hidden because I meant it.

I'd give him anything. Anything I had to give.

I just didn't have very much to give.

But what I had was his.

"Keep an eye on Loretta and Hans. Something is brewing."

This, too, was the truth.

It seemed a turnabout had happened.

Understandably, Loretta was a little freaked she'd fought a battle against magical creatures and sustained a war wound. The wound wasn't terrible, it wasn't great. There were some herbal remedies Draven was giving her that took the edge off the pain during the day, different ones that helped her sleep at night.

However, something had switched on for Hans, knowing the depths of Loretta's loyalty to me.

At the same time, something had switched off for Loretta, knowing he didn't want her before, the implication being perhaps he thought her frivolous and not worth his time, now something he knew not to be true (when, of course, it wasn't true before either).

The problem was, when a lady's maid was crushing on a handsome soldier with aristocratic blood, and he didn't return her feelings, she was screwed and not in the way she'd want to be.

But when a handsome soldier with aristocratic blood had his sights set on a pretty, spirited, loyal lady's maid, and she gave him the cold shoulder, shit could happen.

Hans was getting impatient.

Visibly.

Finnie, Meeta, Bella and I had been watching as this situation was unfolding and had conferred on it repeatedly over the last few days.

We thought it was *awesome.*

"I'm already keeping my eye on it," I told Apollo.

"Good," he murmured, his voice lower, quieter, even more drowsy, and thus very sweet.

Therefore, I whispered, "Goodnight, baby."

He gave me a light squeeze and whispered back, "Goodnight, dove."

I felt his big body relax, shifting slightly forward, some of his weight settling into mine.

And when it did, I tipped my head back.

Apollo had extinguished the lights but the fire in the grate was still blazing. Still, the weak light of the flames barely illuminated the shadows dancing across his features.

He was beautiful at rest.

He was beautiful all the time.

His beauty shined outwardly and reached deep into his soul.

He had it all to give and he wanted me to have it.

And I was taking it.

I lay in that bed in the warm safety of Apollo's arms, having it all.

Yet, I still felt empty.

Two nights later, the lamps out, the firelight dancing, Apollo having decided he wanted to feel the silk of my nightgown against him as he slept so he'd dressed me again after he'd made love to me, I lay on top of his body, running my lips along his collarbone.

"Can I ask you something?" I whispered against his skin.

His hands spanning my hips tensed, giving me a squeeze when he answered, "You can ask anything, poppy."

I lifted my head, slid up him and raised my hand. I watched my fingers drift through the dark hair that had fallen on his brow, smoothing it away, and I left my fingers in it as I turned my eyes to his.

"What gives with the wolves?" I asked.

His brows drew together as his hands at my hips glided around so he could hold me. "What...gives?"

It was cute and sweet, how he reacted to the way I said things in the terms of my world.

I didn't tell him that.

I explained, "That night, after those things attacked us and you showed, you talked to a wolf, and I mean, I know men can talk to wolves and such, but it seemed like something more."

"Ah," he murmured but said no more.

"Ah?" I pushed.

"You do not know."

"No, I do not know," I confirmed the obvious, since I was asking.

"I am an Ulfr," he stated, and I stared.

When he said no more, I informed him, "Uh, I know that, sweetheart."

"The Head of my House," he went on.

"I know that too."

"Ulfr Heads command the wolves."

At that, I blinked.

Apollo kept talking.

"The House of Ulfr has always commanded the wolves. It's more than talking to them. They do our bidding, specifically, if needed, during war."

Wow.

The book on the Houses that I read in Fleuridia hadn't mentioned that!

And that was cool!

"Seriously?" I asked.

He grinned and his arms tightened around me. "Seriously, dove."

"So, you bid them to help me when I was in danger?"

"For the most part, yes. The night before the gale I felt you were protected but I had concerns and wanted to be certain. So I called to the pack leaders and bid them to stay alert, patrol, and come to your aid if it was needed."

"That was what you were doing before you came back to bed," I noted.

"It was."

That explained that.

Apollo kept the information flowing. "The alliance between the Head of the House of Ulfr and the wolves is strong. This is because during war they can sustain many casualties. Thus, we do not call on them often, only if the situation is important or dire. And if they do sustain casualties, we avenge them. Therefore, someone involved in this plot, if found, tried and deemed guilty, as treason carries the death sentence without question, they will be turned over to the wolves. The wolves will then tear the perpetrator to shreds as vengeance."

Uh.

Gross!

"Holy cow," I breathed.

"It's unpleasant and has not happened in decades. But it is their due."

"Yuck," I mumbled.

Apollo again smiled, sliding a hand up my spine so his fingers could play with the ends of my hair.

"You will obviously not witness this," he declared.

Thank God.

"I'm down with that."

His smile turned into a grin.

"Now that I get the wolf business, what's with the birds?" I asked.

Again, his brows drew together. "What birds?"

"I've heard mention of sending 'a bird' more than once. What's the deal with that?"

His brow cleared, his fingers tangled deeper into my hair but the expression on his face changed in a way I felt deep in my belly. In a way that made my beautiful Apollo even more beautiful.

I would know why when he murmured, "I forget that you have been here such a short time. It feels I've had you in my arms for decades. Strangely, at the same time it feels like fleeting moments. Those kinds of moments that are precious. I forget you still have much to learn of my world. But when I remember, I also remember how I enjoy my opportunities to share with you about your new world."

I melted into him and whispered, "I enjoy it when you do too."

He gave me a squeeze, dipped his face close to touch the tip of his nose to mine before he drew away and stopped being impossibly wonderful and went back to just being normally wonderful.

"Communication in this world, as you know, is slow. You've explained your world with its phones and computers. As you also know, we have none of that. Messengers on fast horses are used. But if a message is urgent, we send it with a bird. A bird can fly faster and straighter than any horse."

"Carrier pigeons," I said, and his brows went up.

"They have these in the other world?" he asked.

"Yes, though they're not used anymore. Not like they used to be," I answered.

"Interesting," he murmured.

"So, do you use these birds a lot?" I queried.

Apollo nodded. "Yes, quite often. But not all the time. There are issues with this as the message is tied to the bird's leg so it cannot be very long. Thus, it has to be concise and cleverly written. Many a time a message was misinterpreted when the few words that can be written are not properly understood. And although birds are trained, if the distance is lengthy, they can come to harm or go astray and never deliver the message at all. Still, they are used regularly, and if a message is important, two, three, or even more birds are sent with the same message in hopes one of them gets through."

I studied his handsome face as thoughts leaked into my brain, thoughts that then leaked out of my mouth.

"Are there others with powers such as yours, bidding the wolves?" I asked.

"Outside Frey and some men who practice sorcery, thus are trained to wield power, no."

That said a lot. At least to me.

"So, has it occurred to you," I began quietly, "that it would seem that all the men in this scenario, the husbands of the women from my world, have special things about them? Frey with his dragons and elves. Lahn with his might. Tor, chosen for whatever reason to have his soul connected to Cora. You and your wolves?"

He held my eyes and his fingers stopped moving and tangled in my hair.

"Yes," he answered.

"Lo—"

"We are all special, Maddie."

He was right about that.

Save one.

Me.

On this thought, I dropped my head so I could press my face in his neck and his arms wrapped around me tight.

"You are safe," he stated firmly.

I was.

Because he made me be with him, his men, his *wolves*.

"You are safe, my dove," he repeated, quieter but just as firmly.

"I know, baby," I whispered and fell silent.

After some time, he rolled us to our sides and snuggled me closer.

"Enough talk. We have another long ride tomorrow. Now you must sleep, poppy."

"Okay, Lo."

He gave me a squeeze.

I nestled in and closed my eyes.

Apollo fell asleep before me.

And when I slept, I dreamed of wolves, black mist and disembodied beaks pecking at me.

Thus, I woke up fatigued and restless. And even waking with Apollo's hands moving on me, knowing all around me were special, adventurers and Raiders, warriors and warrior queens, lovers with interconnected souls, soldiers who commanded wolves...and then there was me, I woke still feeling empty.

~

Five evenings later, I had one hand to the headboard, one hand between my legs and both of Apollo's hands at my breasts, rolling and tugging my nipples.

Apollo was fucking my ass.

And, believe it or not, I loved it.

Every *freaking* stroke.

"Baby," I breathed.

He kept fucking me. "Do not climax, Madeleine."

"Honey, I'm about—"

He stroked in, filling me, a strange and brilliant feeling, especially since it came after he made me lie still while he touched me, then spanked me while he fucked me normally, then he oiled me, and finally, when I was primed, slowly took me.

He tugged on my nipples. "You climax at my command."

Oh God. That was *hot.*

"I'll try," I gasped.

He started stroking again. "This is all I ask, poppy."

He kept going and I kept moaning, touching myself, struggling to hold back my orgasm. The fight was making my muscles quiver and my fingers that were wrapped around the headboard dug in so hard I thought I'd break it with my hand.

"So beautiful," he grunted, plunging in.

God.

"So beautiful, Maddie," he rumbled. "Gods, I wish you could watch you taking me."

God!

He stroked in and pulled out, declaring in a thick voice, "We'll get a mirror."

"*Baby,*" I whimpered, his words driving me to the edge, and I wasn't going to be able to hold it.

He knew it and ordered gruffly, "Take me yourself, poppy, then take yourself there."

He'd slid out. I only had the tip, so I pushed back, taking him at the same time coming apart as my orgasm shook through me.

When it did, Apollo hauled us down the bed and pressed in so I was on my belly, all of this with me still taking him. As my orgasm continued to shudder through me, he kept fucking me before he pulled out and I heard his deep groans. I knew he'd slid off the sheath he'd put on when I felt him come on my ass.

So.

Totally.

Hot.

"Arse up for me, dove," he murmured after he'd lifted his weight from me, and I shivered as I slid my knees up under me.

He rubbed his "seed" into my delightfully sore ass, and I closed my eyes, my thighs quivering as the intimacy of that, the sexiness poured over me making me warm and hot again, all at once.

His thumb slid between my cheeks, coming to rest lightly on my anus, and he whispered, "Okay?"

"Totally," I whispered back.

I felt his hand curl around my hip, fingers digging in in an affectionate squeeze, as his thumb did some soothing circling. Then his hands left me, only for him to come back with a cloth. He wiped himself from me, the cloth was gone, and his hands were back, gently moving me so I was on my back and he was between my legs.

Then he surprised me by bending and kissing my belly, and as he was sliding down the bed, his eyes came to mine and he murmured, "Rest, my dove. You giving me that deserves a reward."

The minute he was done saying that, he draped my legs over his shoulders, dipped his head and gently, slowly, amazingly, *beautifully* ate me until I came again, my legs pressing into his shoulders, my heels in his back, my cries quiet but forceful.

By the time I came down from that one, I found myself on top of him, one of his arms wrapped tight around my back, the other hand cupped on my bottom, the tips of his fingers pressed into the inside curve of my cheek, soothing, claiming, possessive.

I closed my eyes.

"Did you like that, honey?" I murmured.

"You're very tight," he replied, his fingers giving me a squeeze.

I decided to take that as a yes.

He wasn't done.

"I want you facing a mirror, arse up, shoulders down, climaxing for me while you watch me move in your arse," he went on.

I swallowed an excited noise at his words.

He still wasn't done.

"But I prefer what's between your legs. It's wetter, sweeter, I can look into your eyes when I'm taking it and I can take it hard. And when you climax, it spasms, milking me of my seed in a way I like very much." His arm and hand at my ass gave me a squeeze. "*Very* much."

That was hot, what we just did, and I loved it.

But I had to admit, I was glad he preferred "taking" my normal girl parts mostly because he liked looking into my eyes when he was doing it.

His hold again tightened. "Now all of you knows the stroke of my cock." His voice lowered. "This is a gift, Maddie. One I cherish. Thank you for giving it to me."

He thought it was a gift.

Suddenly, as they had time and again since she'd said them, that detestable woman's words slid through my head, and I squeezed my closed eyes tighter.

And you? The woman who uses a dead wife's charms to enchant her heartbroken husband so she can warm his bed in order to wear his jewels and earn her place on his arm? Is the world richer for your presence?

The answer to her question was...no. It was not.

This world or my old one, neither of them was richer for my presence. I'd done nothing kind. Nothing thoughtful. Nothing witty or smart. Nothing brave.

Nothing at all.

This is us, my dove.

Apollo had said that to me when I'd taken his cock that same night.

He was right too.

This was us.

This was what I could give him. All I could give him.

He could give me clothes. Jewels. Beautiful houses. Fancy sleighs. Trips to balls where intrigue was happening. A home. Laughter. Safety. Kindness. Good friends.

Children.

I could give him my ass. My body. My cunt.

I could not be Ilsa. I could not do anything, have another purpose, give him more in any other way. I could not replace what he lost with her, something he'd gone out of his way to find again when he brought me to this world.

And this was good. Apollo didn't want me to be Ilsa.

But he did want this.

And I had this to give.

So I was going to give it to him.

I was giving it to him because he wanted it. I was giving it to him because I wanted him to have everything he wanted.

And I was giving it to him because it was all I had.

24

BECOME FOUND

"You rang?"

Apollo turned in his chair at his desk in his office at Karsvall.

He'd been looking out the window at the woods that led to the dower house. His thoughts so engrossed with Madeleine, as well as Christophe, he not only was not seeing the woods, he had not sensed her arrival.

But there she was, the witch Valentine, wearing a green dress, sitting in a chair opposite his desk, studying him like he was mildly interesting, but she had better things to do.

Instead of greeting her, he stated, "May I remind you that you've been paid handsomely to assist our efforts at quelling whatever evil threatens our land. Yet you've disappeared for weeks. Repeated messages sent from witches of this world have gone unanswered. Things have happened that have put Madeleine and my children in danger. You finally arrive and you're flippant?" He shook his head. "I'll warn you my patience is spent, witch, so there is none to test."

"You must know I've been keeping an eye and noted you've had matters in hand, *mon loup*." She smiled a sly smile. "*Well* in hand."

He knew precisely to what she was referring. It was annoying but he couldn't think on it, or it would spur him to action. They needed to speak, not argue.

Therefore, he informed her, "You have not been called here to discuss how things progress with Maddie."

Her smile stayed firmly in place when she told him, "We don't need to discuss how things are progressing with Madeleine." Her smile grew slier. "You have done well in the time I've been away, *chéri*."

He had.

Absolutely.

Perhaps *too* well.

Something was amiss with his Madeleine. Something troubling. Something Apollo could not put his finger on.

But not something he'd discuss with the witch.

Consequently, he moved their dialogue to what he would discuss.

"You've received the message from Lavinia," he said, but it was a question.

They had arrived back at Karsvall two days earlier. Lavinia was there, as planned. And upon their arrival, Frey and Apollo had asked her to contact her fellow witch as a matter of urgency.

Since the two were friends, he deduced that Lavinia's call was the one that was finally answered.

"I have indeed," she confirmed. "Although I will admit that I received other missives from your witches, another matter has been taking my time."

Apollo raised one brow. "And this other matter has priority over what's happening in this world? And by that, witch, I'm asking if your fee was higher considering we've paid you extortionately for your aid, something which we are not getting much of, but we've paid enough we should be your priority."

Her gaze was steady on his when she replied, "Perhaps the fee wasn't higher, although the Sjofn diamonds I received for the job I'm completing made an extraordinary necklace that I quite cherish."

He felt his shredded patience fray further, for he again knew to what she was referring.

He had given her a bag of Sjofn ice diamonds to find Maddie and bring her to him. He also knew the only other job she had on this world was his, something they assessed before paying her in order to be certain that they would have her undivided attention on this world.

Something they were not getting.

"I'll remind you, that job is complete. Maddie is here. She is safe. She is with me. We're building our life together and we're content."

Or...he was.

Maddie also was, on the outside.

But there was new darkness in her eyes. Something she wasn't sharing with him during their whispered conversations after lovemaking. Something that was eating deeper into her soul.

Christophe had remained distant. He took his meals and had his times with Madeleine, Apollo, his sister, but he made it clear in quiet, rebellious ways that were not his nature that he didn't like it.

This could be what was concerning Madeleine.

But Apollo sensed it was more.

These thoughts were troubling, but he came alert as he watched the normally unperturbed witch shift with what appeared to be agitation in her seat.

Seeing her do it, he did not get a good feeling and therefore commanded, "Speak."

She drew in a delicate breath before she stated, "I have some concerns."

"About?"

Again, she steadily held his gaze when she told him, "I cannot see the you of my world."

Apollo knew by her behavior this was not good news.

"This means?" he prompted when she spoke no further.

"He cannot hide himself from me," she explained. "In finding Madeleine for you, I found him first. As he was seeking her, I cast on him so I could watch him should he find her and lead me to her. For obvious reasons, I continued to watch him even after I found her. Since I discovered him, I have never had any trouble seeing him."

"And now you can't see him?"

She shook her head but continued to hold his eyes. "No. And to explain why this is a concern, he cannot hide himself from me. Even if he were to somehow understand that there are magical forces at work in our world, he could not do it himself. He'd need a witch." She paused. "A powerful one." Another pause on a deep intake of breath. "A *very* powerful one."

Apollo did not like where this was leading.

"He's here," he guessed quietly, his gut tightening, his skin prickling.

"I've no idea," she replied. "But I've spent some time searching for him. There has never been a spell cast to hide someone that I could not break. It is a certainty this cannot be done by any witch in my world. This would lead me to believe that there is a possibility that our foes have discovered his existence and recruited him."

"For what purpose?" Apollo asked, his words curt.

"What purpose do they have for anything they do, *chéri*?"

A valid question.

One with no answer.

The witch knew it for she continued speaking.

"However, he is vile. He is evil. He wishes Madeleine harm, and I daresay since you took his hand, he wishes you the same. He may not have magic. He may not be of this world. But he has motivation to do ill, he is skilled at it, and they can promise him great riches for this talent."

Apollo looked beyond her, muttering, "We do not need this."

"We do not, indeed," she agreed. "In my absence, I can assure you that I have not been dawdling, *mon loup*. I've been spending a good deal of time searching for the you of my world. I have also been in constant touch with Lavinia. I know what became of Madeleine in Brunskar. I know that it's the women they're targeting. I also know that they have not cast an enchantment on your comrade. The handsome Derrik acts out of his fondness for Madeleine and his absurd, but definitely masculine need to compete against another male, in this instance you, in the contest for her heart. His pride was injured when he was so swiftly replaced and the way that came about, and he set about doing something to heal it. I further know that he has breached Specter Isle. I have since lost sight of him. However, your other man wisely decided not to follow him to that Isle and is on his return."

Mixed news.

It was good to know Derrik was not enchanted but if he breached the Isle, they could have him. If they were torturing Franka's lover, Apollo did not like to think of what they would do to a soldier.

So he didn't think of it.

He thought on something he had some power to control.

"We must see that all the women are safe," he ordered.

Valentine nodded. "I am speaking with Lavinia after our discussion, *chéri*. The others have reached the font. Circe is currently performing the ritual to recoup her powers. This should be complete within a day or so. After that is done, my suggestion would be to bring all the women together so that Lavinia and I can keep them from harm."

Apollo shook his head.

"I don't think Tor and Lahn will allow their women to be away from them. Minerva and her allies are expending great amounts of magic enchanting Specter Isle to protect it from even dragon fire. Frey bombards them with his dragons every day so they must keep this shield strong, and dragon fire is potent, this cannot be easy for them. They've sent creatures to your world, utilized them here, and perhaps brought the other me back. They're wasting vast amounts of magic. Our separation from Lahn, Circe, Tor and Cora force them to concentrate on two fronts."

She threw out a hand before stating, "I see you wish to divide their energies and use this to conquer. But the women scattered also divides Lavinia and my energies. If the men come with them, so it will have to be, and you'll have to devise a new strategy."

He could not argue that, since he'd had the same thought, so he didn't.

Instead, he stated, "Frey has met with the elves. It was not in question they would provide us assistance, it's how they'll do this we must decide. They're conferring. Frey will meet them again soon to discuss how they'll be involved."

She nodded. "In the meantime, I will be bringing the Circe who lives in my world here. As for the others, it would take too long for them to journey here for they are in the heart of the Vale and the longer they remain separated from you, and thus Lavinia and I, even with Circe back to full power, I fear the more danger they're in. She has great power, but she does not have it at her command. It leaks out through her emotions. That could be a hindrance instead of a boon."

This time, Apollo nodded.

Then he leaned slightly forward in his chair, holding her eyes.

"The witch, Helda, if the dragons do not beat the shield and incinerate her, you must know, I want her captured, incapacitated and brought to me. She dies by no other hand. She's mine."

"Brunskar," Valentine whispered.

"Absolutely," Apollo replied.

Her lips curved up in a leisurely predatory way that Apollo suspected many men might find alluring. Men, unlike him, who preferred in such matters to be the predator.

"I will speak to Lavinia," she stated. "Then I will make my journeys and move our people into position."

"And then you will stay," he commanded, this getting him another sly grin.

"Of course, *chéri*."

Apollo remained silent and Valentine said no more, just sat there grinning at him.

As this lasted some time, Apollo was forced to suggest drily, "It would be beneficial if you saw to all this without delay."

Wisely, her eyes went hooded in order to shield her further amusement from him as she stood and lifted her hands.

The green mist immediately emanated from them, but as it did, she turned her attention back to Apollo and there was no more humor in it.

"Thank you."

Her words startled him, being those two words coming from her.

They did this just as they perplexed him.

"And what have I done for you, witch?" he asked as the green mist grew around her.

"Not one thing, *mon loup*," she replied, her body fading, her lips curving up. "I do not express my gratitude for me, but for my sister."

This perplexed him more.

"I do not know your sister," he told her something she knew.

"We women are all sisters," she told him something he did not.

Then she faded away.

However, he understood, and he wanted to feel satisfaction in knowing that she felt he gave something to one of her "sisters" that deserved gratitude.

He just didn't feel that way considering, with her manner of late, there was more work to do to mend his broken dove.

He needed to talk to Madeleine. It was just that he was forced to do it later and he was becoming more and more impatient with all the "laters" that were forced upon him. Laters that meant he didn't see to his dove. Laters that meant he didn't see to his son.

But now, he had to find Frey and report what just occurred. Then it would seem he'd need to give the order to prepare to have more people in his house and likely more soldiers on his grounds. Further, there was the matter of Franka and their next move, which needed to be intricately planned, which would mean they would need to be away to the Winter Palace for the Bitter Gales soon.

But presently, after talking with Frey, he needed to have lunch with his children.

He would send for Maddie to join them and speak with her after.

And after that, perhaps both of them would sit down with Christophe, whose distance Apollo felt had gone on long enough.

It was unfortunate he had to press this issue with his son.

But he wanted Madeleine bound tight to him *and* his children. He wanted them all to build their relationship as a family together. And he wanted his children settled with that, working toward that same goal, and not battling demons alone.

On this thought, he got up from his desk and was making his way around it when a knock came at the door. Before he could call out his command to enter, the door opened, and Achilles moved through.

He closed it behind him and stopped, as did Apollo.

But before Achilles could speak, Apollo did.

"The green witch was just here, cousin. I apologize, but I must find Frey."

"I was just with him and Lavinia. Lavinia sensed her and I came to see if she was visiting with you."

"She goes to Lavinia now," Apollo told him.

"Frey went to his wife on the same errand as mine."

"Then I must go to him and explain what we discussed. You should accompany me as you'll need to know as well."

"If it isn't urgent, while I have you alone, I'd like a moment before we go."

Apollo studied his cousin and asked, "Is what you need to speak with me about pressing?"

"It's about Maddie."

Anything about Maddie was pressing.

Therefore, Apollo crossed his arms on his chest, indication his cousin should proceed.

He did.

"I will preface this by saying that I understand it's not my place to pry, but Draven told me you, Maddie and the children were getting on well in getting to know each other while you were away. He's noted now that's changed, and since your return, I've seen Maddie often with Élan, never with Chris. He's your son, Lo, and you have your way with him, but I'm surprised you have not yet intervened." He tipped is head to the side and suddenly asked, "May I ask why Maddie's still at the dower house?"

Maddie continuing to dwell in the dower house was something Apollo had hoped would change when they returned. Weeks spent in the presence of the children, she had to feel that it was fitting that she move to the main house.

Further, Apollo felt that the more his son saw him with Madeleine, the more accustomed he would become to her, the more he would settle into the knowledge that Maddie was Maddie, not his mother. Also he would see she was important to Apollo and Christophe's sister, and in the end, come to the conclusion he should shirk his current behavior and settle into his place in the family Apollo was trying to build.

However, upon their arrival, Madeleine had balked at this, saying it was clear from Christophe's behavior that he was not ready for it, and Apollo could not disagree with her.

He didn't like it.

But he didn't disagree.

Thus, it was most definitely time to talk with his son.

And there was more than one reason he wished her in his home and his bed, a reason he had not yet shared with Madeleine.

She had shared greatly about her past life. She had only prodded gently about his.

They would have time for him to share his life, which was nowhere near as complex and heartbreaking as hers. And that time would come after he had all of her.

"It's precisely that Chris has distanced himself from Maddie that is the reason she's still at the dower house," he explained. "She feels the children should be comfortable with her presence and know her well before the manner of our relationship is further defined for them."

Achilles took a step toward him and stopped, saying, "I think this is wise. However, I also believe the manner of your relationship at this point is relatively clear, or as clear as their ages will allow it to be. Élan thinks the world of her and would benefit greatly with having a lady in the house that is not a servant. But allowing Christophe to act out, even silently, against the relationship you're building with the woman you intend to wed might not be sensible."

"Agreed. Thus, Madeleine and I will be speaking to him this afternoon."

Achilles nodded but his gaze grew intense. "I bring this up, Lo, not only due to what Draven shared about Chris, but also because Alek brought gossip from the village."

"Bloody hell," Apollo muttered, knowing exactly what the villagers were saying without having that information imparted.

"It is now known wide that you intend to wed her. But you're installing her in the dower house has brought up speculation that I'm sure won't surprise you. It would not serve you well if Maddie were to hear it without it being in context."

Apollo grew impatient with their discussion and repeated, "As I said, I'll be dealing with these issues shortly, Lees."

Achilles gaze did not lighten. It did the opposite as he asked, "Is Maddie all right?"

Apollo threw him a look before he sighed, leaned into a hand on the back of a chair in front of his desk and noted, "You're far too observant."

Achilles smiled a small smile. "You usually find this a boon."

He did.

Since Achilles knew it, he didn't confirm it.

Rather, he returned, "I'm uncertain I'm comfortable with the attention you're paying to Maddie."

Achilles's smile died. "You can't mean to imply—"

Apollo interrupted him. "Of course not. But I can handle my romantic affairs, Lees."

"I'm aware of that," Achilles retorted instantly. "But you grow close quickly. *Very* quickly. And Maddie is in danger." His expression changed and Apollo braced at witnessing it. "You've lost a great deal, Lo."

"I may have moved past that, cousin, but I do remember it," Apollo told him.

"Is she sharing with you?" Achilles asked quietly.

"Yes," Apollo answered.

"Are you sharing with her?" Achilles pressed.

Apollo straightened from the chair and again crossed his arms on his chest. "This is where I'll put a stop to your prying."

Achilles ignored that and carried on.

"She seems strong, surprisingly so after all she's endured. Draven explained that she recovered from the attack very quickly. Yet, since her arrival home, I can't help but think that something has changed."

"Again, I'll repeat that I'll be dealing with these issues shortly, Lees. And that time would come a great deal sooner if we could end this conversation."

Achilles studied him and Apollo allowed it.

For three seconds.

Then he uncrossed his arms and moved toward his cousin, stating, "We're done with this. Let us find Frey."

He stopped when Achilles put a hand to his shoulder.

"We now live with many unknowns," his cousin said softly. "For you, Maddie, your children, one less unknown, an important one, the solidity of your family, would be beneficial. Especially for Maddie, as this is something she's never known. She's adapting to a land that's very strange and doing it well." His lips quirked. "She's adapting to you and doing that well also. But with all that has occurred from Vasterhague to Brunskar, she is quite aware of the dangers lurking. She has lived long with dangers lurking, cousin. A foundation such as this, I can only assume, would go a long way to making her feel safe during troubled times."

Apollo raised his brows. "But a month ago you felt this was moving too fast. Now you're advising I speed things up?"

"But a month ago you had essentially just met. Now, I've seen her smile at you. I've seen you make her laugh. I've seen her do the same for you. I've seen how she is with Élan. She does not hide in the slightest that she feels deeply for you, cousin. For your children. You have all lost a great deal. It's a beautiful thing, watching you become found."

At his words, words he liked, Apollo sighed.

Then he shared, "She knows I wish to wed her, Lees. It's she who wishes to understand herself better before she allows this to happen."

Achilles dropped his hand from Apollo's shoulder as his brows shot together.

"How can a person not understand oneself?"

"I've no bloody clue," Apollo replied, shaking his head. "She's explained it. It made sense at the time. Or more accurately, what made sense was the emotion she felt behind the words she said which didn't make sense. However, they did to her, and she meant them a great deal. What I took from that is that she needs time. I'm giving it to her."

"This is uncharacteristic of you, cousin," Achilles remarked.

Apollo held his gaze when he replied firmly, "I'm a man falling in love. We do many things that are uncharacteristic."

He watched surprise suffuse his cousin's features before warmth overtook them.

"This makes me happy," he said quietly.

Apollo smiled at him. "It does me as well."

Achilles smiled back. "Obviously."

Apollo did not reply so Achilles spoke on.

"Now, I will cease causing a delay so you can see to important matters."

"Why do I not think you're referring to me speaking to Frey?"

"Because nothing is more important than the pursuit of happiness."

Yet another thing Apollo could not argue.

However, they had one other matter to discuss, and it unfortunately took them out of discussions about the pursuit of happiness.

"An important thing of note that the witch shared is that she has not been able to find my twin from the other world."

The warmth fled Achilles face and his eyes turned sharp.

"That does not seem to be good tidings, Lo," he noted.

"I don't believe it is. Neither does Valentine, who is speculating that he's in this world, veiled by our enemy, but brought here in order to do ill."

"If we remain in Lunwyn, with Frey here, the dragons and elves at his command, Lavinia and the green witch both providing their skills, they could be seeking non-magical means to bring harm to Maddie and the other women."

"Precisely," Apollo agreed. "And this other me has proved irrevocably he has no issue with bringing harm to Maddie and thus any woman."

"I will increase the guard on the dower house and her," Achilles declared.

"Also on Loretta, Meeta and Cristiana. They mean much to Maddie. If our enemy could get to them, they could be used to cause Madeleine harm."

"Done," Achilles stated. "I'll see to this before I join you and Frey."

Apollo lifted his chin.

Achilles nodded, and finally they moved to the doors.

An hour later, Apollo walked into his study, where he'd been told Maddie had gone to await him to take her to lunch with his children.

He found she was indeed there, standing at the side of his window, for some reason peering around the opened curtains as if she was using them to hide.

Whatever she was watching had her full attention. He knew this because she did not sense his presence and thus turn to greet him.

As he approached, he took her in wearing her dress that was nearly the color of the deep green of Valentine's. But hers was knit, covering her from its rolled neck that went up to her jaw and down to the tips of her boots. Her extraordinary hair was mostly down, but the front and sides had been pulled away from her face and arranged in soft curls at the back of her head. The dress hugged her upper body magnificently, down to her waist where it flared into the skirt. But even the skirt clung to her figure, specifically her hips and arse, and it did this in alluring ways that brought to mind the fact that he needed to order a mirror to be installed in his bedroom.

On this thought, he got close to her back and felt her jump when he slid his hands along her ribs.

She twisted her neck to look up at him and he smiled down at her.

"Hello, my dove," he greeted.

Her hand cut to her face, her finger extended over her lips, and she hissed, "*Shh!*" before she turned to look back outside.

He felt his brows draw together as he moved his gaze to the window. Then he felt his lips curve up when he saw Hans speaking with Loretta out in the snow at the side of the house.

Hans was standing very close to the maid.

Loretta didn't like this and was pulling back.

Thus, Hans had an arm around her waist, plastering her to his side, just as he had his neck bent so he could bring his face close to hers.

"They can hardly hear us, poppy," Apollo pointed out, still looking out the window.

"I'm concentrating," she told him.

"On what?" he asked.

"Reading Hans's lips."

This surprised him so much he cast his gaze to the top of her hair.

"You can read lips?"

"No!" she snapped impatiently, not tearing her eyes from the window. "That's why you have to shush so I can concentrate."

His body shook with laughter as he turned her resisting frame in his arms.

"Lo! I'm missing it," she bit out irritably when he had her front to his.

"Perhaps we should let whatever that is play out without an audience," he suggested.

"If we do, how can I report back to Finnie, Meeta and Bella?"

"You'll just have to ask Loretta what occurred when you have that opportunity."

Her expression changed to frustration when she shared, "She's being closed-lipped about the whole thing."

He was again surprised.

"I thought you women nattered about these things freely," he remarked and watched her eyes narrow.

"We *women* are vast in number, Apollo. Some do. And some, like Loretta, *don't*."

He grinned down at her. "All right. Then perhaps you should allow her to share, or not, as she wishes."

"What's the fun in that?"

She had him there, so he didn't answer.

Instead, he changed the subject. "How's her injury?"

He felt as well as heard her deep sigh as she gave into his demand that she leave his man and her woman alone, something she had no choice but to do with the hold he had on her, and she knew it.

Then she answered, "Healing nicely."

"And has she recovered from the incident?"

Her eyes slid to his shoulder as she replied, "That maybe isn't healing so nicely."

"It frightened her," Apollo deduced, and her gaze came back to him.

"It would anyone, Lo," she noted. "Those things were *creepy* and there were *a lot of them*."

He did not need the reminder of Maddie and her women out in the snow with a lot of "creepy" things.

Alas, he had it and they were discussing it, as they should. Avoiding it was not healthy.

Therefore, he pointed out, "She went to that forest of her own accord, poppy."

"She did," she agreed. "But that shit was extreme."

This was terminology he'd never heard, not even from Maddie.

He still understood it.

"Then let's hope Hans can get through to her. If anyone understands *shit* that's *extreme*, it's Hans."

"Good point," she murmured, her gaze now moving over her shoulder as she twisted somewhat in his arms to look back out the window. "I'll have to mention that to her."

"I would allow Hans to try to break through, Madeleine," he advised.

She looked back to him, her eyes wide. "Are you nuts?"

"No," he pointed out the obvious.

"I have to meddle. It's my sisterly duty."

He was further surprised at another reference to the heretofore unknown sisterhood of women.

Then again, he'd seen it at work the night Loretta and Meeta forged into the cold, heavily armed, doing so on the dubious, but eventually proved correct knowledge that Maddie might need them.

And the knowledge of a sisterhood of women was far from unwelcome in times like these.

"Before going to lunch, we have things to discuss," he told her.

She studied his face before she settled into his embrace, giving him some of her weight and lifting her hands to place them light on his biceps.

"What do we need to discuss?" she asked.

"After lunch with the children, I'd like you to remain at the house so we can talk."

"We're talking now," she noted.

"We need time, my poppy, and privacy. I would delay until later when we go back to the dower house this evening after dinner, but it's important."

Her body stiffened slightly in his arms when she asked, "What are we going to talk about?"

"Amongst other things, the timing of your moving into this house," he told her.

Her body stiffened more. "Apollo—"

He spoke over her. "And after our talk, we'll speak to Christophe together about his continued distance."

At this, her body relaxed, and he knew what that meant.

"I take it you agree it's time we confront him about it," he remarked.

"Yes," she replied. "Though, I'm not sure I should be there."

He shook his head. "In future, if there are issues that need discussion, outside of those that need to be dealt with man to man, you will be there. He must learn to get used to that and it's best he do it now."

Her head tipped to the side, her gaze went unfocused, and her teeth came out to worry her lip.

He gave her a squeeze and she again focused on him.

"Do you disagree?"

Hesitantly, she said, "Not exactly. It's just that I think my presence at this particular discussion may not be a good thing."

"Explain," he demanded.

"I can't," she returned. "I'm not a young boy who lost his mother and faces another woman in his life who looks exactly like her but is not her. I don't know what he's feeling. I just know it's *me* who's making him feel it." She pressed closer and got up on her toes. "And although I agree wholeheartedly that this has to be discussed, I think you, particularly you, Lo, need to be sensitive to all that. It causes me pain to cause others pain, the others being people who knew and loved Ilsa. It causes me more doing it to Chris, and I'd rather not do it, and instead give him my company when he wants it, not when it's pressed on him."

Listening to her, allowing her words to penetrate, he studied her exquisite face, the adorable freckles that danced on her nose, freckles that became more pronounced if she spent time outside, and he hoped they created a daughter that she bestowed those freckles on.

As well as her hair.

And those remarkable eyes.

Not to mention her sense of humor. Her bravery. Her fighting spirit. Her quick wit. Her loyalty. And her drive never to give up even when the odds were against her.

To communicate all this, when she'd finished speaking, he pulled her deeper into his arms, dipped his face closer to hers and whispered, "You'll make a wonderful mother."

Distractedly, he felt her entire body stiffen as her face froze.

And it was distractedly he noted both because Bella ran into the room and said on a near shout, "Lord Apollo!"

He turned, still holding Maddie in his arms, but it was Apollo who grew still as a stone when he looked into Bella's face.

"He's gone!" she cried.

He dropped one arm but held Madeleine's tense body tight to his side as he turned fully to the children's maid.

"Explain, Bella," he barked, the words harsh and abrasive as they scored through his throat.

"Chris!" she exclaimed, and Apollo's chest got tight as he felt Maddie's hand come up and curl into his sweater at his stomach. "The tutor said he left to go answer the call of nature, and when I went up to get them for lunch, he'd not returned." She shook her head frantically from side to side and lifted her hands in a helpless gesture that made every inch of skin on Apollo's frame feel like toxin was burning into it. "It's been some time since he left the school room. We've looked everywhere and we can't find him."

"Oh my God," Maddie breathed.

But Apollo moved.

He broke away from her but turned to her, leaned in and lifted a finger to within an inch of her face.

"You do not leave this house," he commanded.

"Okay, honey," she agreed instantly.

"Not for any reason, Madeleine," he clipped.

"Okay," she repeated. "Go," she whispered, her heart in her throat making it croaky, her eyes bright with fear.

He moved to the door as he ordered Bella, "Send a man to the dower house. Get Cristiana and Meeta here at once. And get Hans to bring Loretta inside."

"Yes, sir," she replied, and he felt her dashing out of the study behind him.

But he didn't look to see where she'd gone. He didn't look back to Madeleine.

He moved with purpose to find his men, give orders and then find his son.

Apollo on Torment dashed through the forest at a full gallop, so fast he could feel his cloak flying out behind him.

He was guiding his horse, his eyes riveted to the tracks in the snow.

But he let his steed avoid the trees and low hanging branches.

There were two sets of small tracks.

Two sets of small tracks that stated, unless Christophe was abducted by a dwarf, he'd run away with Nathaniel.

And if he'd done this, once they found him, he would embrace his son.

Then he'd tan his arse.

As if sensing these were his thoughts, he heard Achilles call out from behind him, "Stay calm, Lo."

Easy advice to give, not having a son in these times...or *ever*.

Not advice he could, or would, take.

"Apollo!" He heard Frey shout, also from behind him. These two being the two Apollo had chosen to search with him as the men separated in order to cover more ground.

It was not luck but good tracking skills that they'd noted quite close to the house how the boys had swept the snow to hide their tracks. They'd followed the well-disguised (but not well enough) trail. Then they'd found where the boys had thought they were safely away and had stopped bothering to hide their tracks.

At Frey's shout, he looked up from the snow and caught sight of what was approaching them.

It was a horse, and on it was a man who did not look like he belonged on a horse in a frozen forest, but instead would look perfectly at home on the deck of a ship.

And this was because he was the man who taught Frey everything he knew about ships.

The man who was now first mate on Frey's ship.

And a man who'd mastered the art of curmudgeonry.

Kell.

Kell's horse was dragging a narrow pack sleigh and perched precariously on top of its load was Nathaniel.

In front of Kell on the horse was Christophe.

Bridling fear that had turned into anger, Apollo reined in Torment and felt Frey and Achilles rein in on either side of him.

Kell approached and stopped his horse and sleigh but feet from the men.

Without a greeting, Kell looked right at Apollo and called out, "Found these two settin' up a tent and tryin' to build a fire. Seein' as I didn't 'spect you'd want your boy, and whoever that lad is," he jerked his head to indicate Nathaniel behind him, "to be bear food, I convinced 'em to come with me."

From the mutinous look on his son's face, and the terrified one on Nathaniel's as he eyed the Head of the House where he was employed, Apollo wondered briefly how Kell had convinced them of anything.

He had no opportunity to ask for Frey spoke.

"Bears are hibernating, Kell."

"Aye." Kell nodded. "Too true. But I reckon they'd come out for a tender morsel of boy meat."

Apollo watched his son pale and knew how Kell convinced them to go with him.

He dug his heels into Torment and his horse led him to the side of Kell's.

"Put him down," he commanded.

Kell's eyes in his weathered face gave Apollo a once-over.

And Apollo knew what he saw when he said, "Will do after you tell me your feelin's about corporal punishment."

Apollo speared him with his scowl.

"Put. Him. *Down.*"

Kell held his angry gaze for a moment before his went to Frey, and finally, he slid Christophe to his boots in the snow.

The minute Apollo heard the crunch, the leather of his saddle creaked as he dismounted.

He put a hand to his boy's shoulder and led him away from the horses and into the trees.

He felt his son's tight muscles and saw his set face, but when Apollo stopped them, Christophe didn't hesitate to tip his head back and look right into his father's eyes.

Now he felt pride, as well as anger.

Bloody hell.

Apollo took a deep breath and let it out before he said quietly, "You are very aware there is danger."

Christophe's eyes flashed, but he said nothing.

Apollo did not do the same.

"Thus, you would be very aware that the news you were missing would cause panic and distress."

He saw his son swallow, but he remained silent.

"Bella was beside herself," Apollo told him, and at that, he lost his son's gaze. "Look at me, Chris." Christophe looked back to him. "The news of your disappearance was kept from your sister. But if it had not been, if she was the one to discover you were gone, how do you think she'd feel?"

Finally, he spoke.

"Bella told us she was lunching with us."

"She?"

He watched Christophe clench his teeth, but he said nothing.

"So, you're not saying Maddie's name now?" he asked.

Christophe looked to the side.

"Give me your eyes, son," Apollo ordered on a squeeze of his shoulder.

Christophe looked back.

"Why did you run away?" he queried.

"I didn't want to be around her."

"Why did this make you run away?" Apollo pushed.

"I just didn't want to be around her."

"And you ran away instead of discussing this with me?"

His lips twisted into a half-sneer when he stated, "*You* want to be around her."

"I do," Apollo agreed. "She makes me laugh. She makes me happy. She—"

"She does all that because she looks like Mum," he bit out.

Apollo took in another deep breath and let it out.

Only then did he speak.

"You know that's not true."

"Yes?" he asked, his boy's voice filled with sarcasm. "How?"

"You've spent time with Maddie. You're very aware she isn't your mother."

"Yes. I'm *very* aware of that, Father. Are you?"

His hand again tensed on Christophe's shoulder but this time it did it of its own accord.

By the gods.

That grief.

That anger.

Apollo had been mistaken.

He should not have left it this long.

"Yes, son," he whispered. "I'm very aware of that. I'm very aware that losing your mother felt like half my soul had been torn away. I'm very aware that the only moments since she passed that gave me joy were the moments I spent with your sister and you. I'm very aware that I had grown so accustomed to feeling joyless that I lost hope I'd ever feel that way again, the way only your mother could give to me. I'm also very aware that at first, I was much like you. I felt anger that Madeleine could look so like your mother and not be her. This anger came after I held hope, even though I knew it was wrong, perhaps even cruel to expect that of Maddie, that she would be your mother returned. And I treated Madeleine to that anger when I understood she was not."

He watched the flash of relief hit his son's expression, relief that his father understood, and in a perfect world Apollo could leave it at that.

But this wasn't a perfect world. It was a complicated one. And it was Apollo's duty to guide his son into learning how to navigate it.

Thus, he forged ahead.

"However, once I shared time with her without those expectations and it became abundantly clear that Madeleine was not your mother, she did many things to bring me joy. She did many things to make me angry. She did many things to make me think. She did many things to make me wish to keep her safe. She did many things to make me *feel*."

He saw his son's face getting red, either increased anger or another emotion, Apollo did not know.

But he didn't stop.

"Your sister never knew your mother. But if you've been paying attention, and Chris, I know you pay very good attention, you'd have seen that Maddie does many things to bring your sister joy."

"Mum was a better mum," he stated mutinously. "Élan will never know. Élan will never know how good a mum Mum was."

That grief.

Gods.

He had been sorely mistaken.

"No," Apollo whispered. "And you are correct. Your mother was a better mother because you were hers and she was yours and there is never a better mother to have than your own. And your sister will never understand that which is a tragedy we both know well. But would you not allow me to have what Maddie gives me, allow your sister to have what she could give her, allow yourself to have what she so wants to offer you, even if it isn't the same, even if it isn't as good, simply because you deserve it, and she deserves the privilege of giving it?"

"You act like it's better than what Mum could give."

He was still whispering when he returned, "I have never done any such thing."

Christophe again looked to the side and said nothing.

Apollo didn't force back his eyes.

Instead, he moved his hand to curve his fingers around the side of his son's neck and dropped to a knee in the snow.

"You are my little man," he told him quietly.

Christophe didn't look back to his father, but he did swallow.

"I forget," Apollo went on. "You are such my little man, so brave, strong, grown-up, I forget that you're still my little boy."

Apollo watched his lips tremble, the vision cut deep into his soul, but he kept speaking.

"I was mistaken. I knew there was something amiss. I understood you were struggling. I understood why, Chris, seeing Maddie dressed in our House's colors, ready to take my arm. Something you remembered was your mother's and mine."

At that, Christophe cut his eyes to his father. There was anger in them, defiance.

But mostly pain.

Apollo sustained that wound and gave him a squeeze.

"I was mistaken," he repeated. "Mistaken in thinking that my little man could work through that hurt and see things as they are, the happiness your sister and I have with Madeleine in our lives. The happiness you could glean having her in yours. I forgot that you're still my little boy, and being such, I should see to you."

"I'm not a little boy," Christophe snapped.

"No, you aren't, yet you are. And, my son," Apollo leaned into him just as he pulled Christophe close so they were nearly nose to nose, "until you're a father, you won't understand this. But I was mistaken in something else. That being I *want* you to be my boy for as long as I can have that. I will have decades of you being a man. Now, I must cherish the time when you're my boy and take care of you as a father should while you are. This I will do. I will rectify these mistakes and from now on, look after you."

"Does that mean you'll be sending her away?" Christophe asked, his tone very much not like anything Apollo had heard from him.

It was ugly.

"Is that what you want?" he inquired. "For me to be alone again? For your sister to lose a woman's touch?"

"Élan has Bella," Christophe retorted.

"Indeed," Apollo acceded. "And what will you leave me?"

Christophe clenched his teeth.

Apollo did not give up, for he couldn't.

He loved his son.

And he was in love with Madeleine.

"And what will that leave Maddie?" he pressed. "I have you. Élan. Achilles. Draven. As you know that list goes on. If I were to send Maddie away as you wish, what would she have?"

Christophe knew the answer to that, but instead of saying it aloud, he slid his eyes away.

"I know not how to heal your hurt, for even having Maddie, I still mourn your mother," Apollo said gently. "I mourn her for myself, and I mourn her for you and your sister. Thus, I know that hurt will never completely fade away. What I also know is your mother is lost to us, but we still live. And the only way to do that is to *live*, finding as much laughter and happiness along the way as we can."

Christophe kept his gaze averted, and as he did, Apollo knew he was feeling too much for this to be sorted now, in the cold and snow, while men were out looking for his son and many were worried.

"We'll talk more when we're home and those who are worried know you're safe."

Christophe finally looked back to him. "I'll ride with Lees."

Apollo endured yet another wound and shook his head.

"You'll ride with your father."

Christophe clenched his teeth, but he said nothing further.

Apollo straightened from the snow and moved to Torment, guiding Christophe with his hand to his shoulder. Achilles, Frey, Kell and Nathaniel watched silently as he mounted then bent and pulled his son up in front of him.

Christophe held himself stiffly, clearly trying to stay as far away from his father as he could.

Without a word, Apollo spurred Torment into a canter, pulling ahead of the men who were silently following them, wishing to be home to put minds at ease, especially Maddie's.

He did this with his own mind in turmoil.

The Queen's strategist, general to her soldiers, as his thoughts chased each other through his brain, he could not settle on a strategy of how to help his son deal with his pain and his grief.

He'd expected too much from him.

But this was not Christophe's burden.

It was Apollo's mistake.

Madeleine looked like his mother and Christophe had not even reached double digits. He would not process the differences between the two women as an adult would.

He would struggle.

Apollo knew the instant he explained Maddie's existence months ago that Chris was uncomfortable with it.

He should have kept watch and planned how to battle it should demons arise.

He should have seen to his son.

These thoughts assailing him, his attention focused on the forest opening up in front of them as they arrived at the house, Frey growled, "Bloody hell."

Apollo knew why Frey sounded annoyed.

Finnie was atop a steed and galloping toward him.

Frey put heels to his horse and shot forward, thundering, "Wife! I told you—"

"Maddie!" she cried, cutting off her husband, her focus not on him but on Apollo, her horse in full gallop as it brought her toward them. "Maddie's gone!"

Even as he felt his son do the same, Apollo went completely still and only at the last minute reined in as Finnie pulled back her own reins so swiftly, her horse wheeled under her.

She turned her head as it did to keep her eyes on Apollo as she continued with her dire news.

"We've turned the house upside down, men have gone to the dower house." She finally stopped her horse. "Ruben found two sets of tracks, both he says were female, leading away from the house. All the women at the house are accounted for so we don't know for certain who's with her. But the tracks abruptly stopped and there's no other sign."

She drew in a breath, her eyes wide and concerned, before she finished on a whisper, her words landing yet another blow straight to Apollo's soul.

"She's disappeared."

25
FUCKED UP. HUGE

Something was not right.

And that something not right was not the fact that, thirty minutes ago, Cora, the Gracious surprised the absolute crap out of me by showing up in Apollo's study telling me that she and Prince Noctorno were riding to Karsvall and found a young boy Noctorno knew to be Apollo's son. Said boy refused to budge from where he'd dashed from them and was holed up in the trunk of a tree.

That was, he refused to budge unless he saw me.

The house was in disarray, people were freaked, most of the men were out looking for Chris, and I was alone in the study, fretting and wishing I could do something.

And this was something I could do.

Not to mention, this was Cora, the Gracious. A woman of my people. One of the women of four couples united over worlds.

One of us.

And let us not forget, I was freaked too.

Chris was gone, and with the enemies we had, that could mean anything.

None of it good and most of it *really* not good.

So I'd followed her seeing as she said Prince Noctorno was with Chris and seeing as she was Cora, the Gracious.

And I knew it was her. I'd seen newspapers in Hawkvale, and even Lunwyn, that had pen and ink drawings of her that were printed beside articles that described what she wore to some ball or when she'd do a good deed, like visiting a children's hospital.

Why she was there with Tor, and we didn't know they were coming, I didn't know.

Then again, Finnie and Frey had shown without warning, so maybe the bird sent with the message they were coming got shot for someone's supper (or something).

As I followed her, and followed her, *and followed her*, deep into the forest around Karsvall, worried we were getting into a zone that was unprotected by Apollo's witches, I began to realize that things were not right.

First, if I thought about it (which I hadn't), the fact that she'd mentioned Prince Noctorno repeatedly and she'd done it just like that was weird.

She called him *Prince Noctorno.*

Now, I didn't know any aristocracy from the Vale, so maybe I was wrong, but the dude was her husband, and she was from my world. I couldn't imagine she'd address her husband as Prince Noctorno unless she was at some official function. And truly, I couldn't even imagine her doing it then. I hadn't been to an official function with Apollo, but I couldn't imagine addressing him as anything but Apollo, even to servants, as he called me Lady Ulfr or Lady Madeleine to them.

And that was another thing. She was from my world.

But she spoke like she was from this world.

Now, I'd heard that Americans who lived in England (or wherever) could take on the accent. But she hadn't been in this world for decades, for goodness sakes. I couldn't imagine her talking just like people from this world.

Not yet.

Further, I couldn't imagine Christophe wanting to see me.

For two weeks he'd been doing his best to avoid me.

Demanding to see his father, sure.

But me?

Having time to think on it, lots of it as we trekked through the forest, that wasn't right either.

Not to mention, she'd said that *Prince Noctorno* was not far.

But he was.

We kept going (and going) and she had to know we were unprotected by men or weapons and the further away from the house we were, the more danger we'd be in.

Apollo had told me that all the women knew what was going on. Their men let them in on it so they could be vigilant and cautious (he'd also added the word "obedient," but I decided to forget he said that, though, it was becoming scarily apparent that I'd forgotten the "cautious" part too).

If she was leading me to her husband who was with Chris not too far away from Karsvall, I could get it.

But she was leading me to what seemed like nothing except deeper into the forest and far away from Karsvall.

And last, she had no guard.

Her husband had let her go like that, unprotected. From what I'd heard about him, that was not something he'd do.

Ever.

No.

This was not right.

I was getting the distinct feeling that I'd been an idiot.

I knew that feeling. It had happened often in my life, this one worse than the rest (except, of course, when I'd picked Pol to pledge my troth to, then again that remained to be seen depending on whether I could get myself out of what I was currently getting myself into).

I decided it was time to stop being an idiot and called, "Hey!"

She forged ahead, not looking back when she replied, "Not too far now."

"Uh, I'm thinking that we should turn back, find a man to find Apollo and have you lead him back to Tor and Christophe."

"We're not too far," she mostly repeated. "It would be foolish to turn back now."

I stared at her plowing through the snow.

Then I stopped.

"Hey!" I called again to her still moving form. "I'm thinking this isn't smart."

She looked back, stopped, and I saw annoyance flash through her features before she rearranged them and said yet again, "Really, it's not too far."

Did Cora, the Gracious, who was beloved across an entire country and visited children's hospitals (and homeless pet shelters, not to mention read to the blind) get annoyed?

I stared at her pretty face with all that fabulous, lustrous brown hair.

And as I did, it hit me.

And what hit me was that I hadn't been only an idiot.

I'd fucked up.

And huge.

Cora, the Gracious probably found occasion to be annoyed (especially if her husband was an other-worldly macho man like Apollo).

But Cora's twin, the one from this world, the one who'd disappeared after being kidnapped by Minerva and her crew, would totally get annoyed. From what Apollo told me, she was a screaming bitch.

This had to be her.

It had to.

Cora wouldn't lead me to danger. She wouldn't even suggest it.

Okay, I didn't know that for certain.

But if it were me, I wouldn't lead Cora to danger. Nothing even near it. Not in times like these.

Not ever!

God!

I'd totally fucked up!

I started backing away.

"Uh, how about you go on to Prince Noctorno and I'll go back to the house? When I find someone, I'll tell them to tell Apollo to follow our tracks to you," I suggested.

More annoyance sliced through her expression before she looked side to side in a weird way I did not like then began following me, her hand raised cajolingly my way.

"It's much further back than forward."

"I'm cool with that," I told her, moving more quickly.

She moved more quickly too, saying, "I fear for your safety, walking alone back to Karsvall."

"It's okay," I replied. "There are enchantments that'll keep me safe."

Again, she eyed side to side.

I kept backing up and eyed side to side too.

I also hoped like hell Apollo (or someone) found Chris and that they were now searching for me.

I'd take the verbal lashing Apollo was going to give me after he discovered I'd been a complete idiot, and I'd take it since it was deserved.

I just wanted to get back.

I didn't notice anything side to side, but when I looked down to ascertain that I was following the same tracks as I'd made coming out, not only so I could get home but so that anyone possibly looking for me would actually find me, I stopped dead.

There were no tracks.

I whipped my head around and looked behind me.

There were no tracks there either.

Uh-oh.

I looked back to my feet and took another step.

The instant my foot hit the snow, the snow reassembled where my print had been so there was no print at all.

Uh-oh.

One could say we'd definitely come out of the enchanted safety zone because that couldn't happen.

Except by magic.

Crap!

My head snapped up and my blood turned to ice when I saw Cora standing with her arms crossed in front of her, gloved hands up high, resting under her shoulders.

And she was smiling a very bitchy smile.

Shit!

At this point, three things happened at once.

The first was that I turned to run.

The second was that two men came barreling out from behind the trees, and the sight of them scared the complete beejeezus out of me.

This was because they were not like any men I'd ever seen in my life.

They were huge.

And when I say huge, I mean *huge.*

They had long black hair (one in a plait down his back, the other's was only pulled back at the top).

They were also wearing hides. *All* hides. Hide boots. Hide pants. Hide shirts laced up to their throats with thick hide threads and hide jackets that had long lapels that looked to be made of some short fur, like a cow's.

Oh, and they were carrying massive swords.

Massive.

Their swords had to be at least a foot longer than Apollo's and they were way heftier. Even at a glance, I figured they had to weigh double what Apollo's weighed and his was freaking *heavy.*

They were also running.

Toward *me.*

And the last thing that happened was an enormous flock of birds suddenly appeared in the sky. They were not pretty birds. They were ugly birds. And they were freaking scary birds that had webbed wings that made a sickening sound when they flapped.

And there so many of them, they blotted out the sun.

Yes.

Blotted. Out. *The sun.*

They were swooping in, also toward me.

I didn't scream (though I wanted to).

I didn't freeze.

I didn't stumble.

No.

I *ran.*

I heard the men running after me, so I did my best to run faster, knowing, with their long legs, they'd totally catch up.

But I wasn't going to give up.

Sure, if I made it to Karsvall, Apollo was going to be pissed.

But I'd take that over whatever those birds (and men) could do to me any day.

Within seconds, I felt the men were almost on me, and the instant I did, I heard a grunt of effort.

The next instant, almighty shrieks filled the air and a shower of blue sparks—sparks I'd seen before in a not-so-happy time—rained over me.

Not that I needed verification those birds were bad magic, still, those sparks gave it anyway.

When they bounced off my skin and hair, I stumbled but did not fall. I kept running doubled over, my hands in front of me to break it, should I fall, as I desperately tried to keep standing and most of all, *moving*.

I didn't fall because I got control, but I also didn't because a strong arm wrapped around my stomach and hauled me up. It held me to a big body as that body kept running before, still running, he put me back in the snow, forcing me to run with him running close to my back.

And over my head, he grunted nonsensically, "*Veeyoo maya*." Then he said, "Go," and finished on a roar, "*Fast!*"

I went and fast, and I did it feeling slightly better (slightly) because I had a feeling, seeing as I was still running and not thrown to the snow or being carried away, that these were the good guys.

Guys from my side.

He kept at my back, and I had no clue how we both ran so close together, but we did.

The one at my back had my back, literally.

The other one I knew was fighting those birds. I heard his grunts of efforts. I saw the flashes of blue sparks.

But there were tons of those birds. The sinister sound of their webby wings flapping filled the air all around. I could hear the shrieks as each arc of the guy's sword took out not one, not two, but what sounded like dozens.

And my body was electrified with terror.

We kept running and the man at my back twice put a hand to me to shove me in a different direction.

He knew the way home.

Thank God, he knew the way home.

On this thought, again he put a hand to me to shove me a different way, and I went that way, head up, watching where I was going so I wouldn't run into a tree or something.

And that was when I saw him.

And when I saw him, I nearly quit running.

Yes, my life was on the line, but at first sight of that man, I nearly quit running.

Because he was just...

That...

Magnificent.

Bigger than the men with me, strikingly beautiful, sitting atop a massive steed in much the same clothing as the other two (but the fur inside his jacket was thicker and longer), his hair not tied back. I knew the man who raced toward us on his magnificent beast was Dax Lahn.

The mightiest warrior in this world.

Before it even seemed possible, the men disappeared because Lahn and his horse were there.

Bent to the side, he swept me up and deposited me in front of him with a grace and fluidity that had my breath leaving me.

He wheeled the horse around and leaned in, pressing me almost to the horse's neck, covering me with his enormous torso to shield me from the birds. The horse then burst forward through the snow with such speed, my hair flew straight back and the icy air bit deep into the skin of my face.

The birds followed, I could hear them, but we didn't slow. He also didn't take the sword from the scabbard on his back.

We just flew.

Mere moments later, peeking in front of me through his horse's ears, I saw her.

The Golden Warrior Queen.

Circe.

She was on her own steed wearing her own hide coat, hers long, and a billow of richly colored material shot with threads of gold waved around her legs and boots.

Her hair was freaking amazing.

Her eyes were on us.

Lahn tore straight toward her, and she didn't move her horse an inch as we shot past her.

The instant the tail of Lahn's horse cleared the nose of Circe's, an almighty shriek filled the air, the snow all around flared blue, then everything went silent except the horse's hooves turning us around in the snow.

Well, there you go.

Apparently, we'd reached the edge of the enchantments Apollo's witches had cast.

I breathed a sigh of relief as Lahn straightened us on the horse.

Once turned, I saw the air cleared of birds, the snowy forest beyond tranquil, and Lahn trotted us back to his wife and stopped.

I looked to her to see she was already looking at me.

"Hey," I said, and she smiled.

Wow.

She was really something.

"Hey," she said back.

I smiled a shaky smile at her and looked up at Lahn to see him eyeing his wife. He felt my gaze and looked down at me.

Okay.

Seriously.

Charging toward me on a horse?

Magnificent.

Right there an inch away?

Spec-freaking-*tacular*.

"Hey," I breathed.

His mouth curved up in a blinding white, unbelievably gorgeous smile.

I fought against fainting.

Circe burst into laughter.

We waited just long enough for the other two guys to show (unscathed, thankfully), collect their horses that were milling about a bit away from Circe, Lahn and me, and for Circe to introduce them as Zahnin and Bain before we were on our way, cantering toward Karsvall.

Zahnin, by the way, was the one with the top of his hair pulled back. Bain was the one with his hair in a plait. I knew this because they grunted unintelligibly in turn when their names were said by their queen.

And eyeing them, it was insane. I had an awesome hot guy (as in *seriously* awesome and seriously *hot*), but I kind of wished I'd been transported to wherever they came from.

We started our journey with me feeling relieved I was alive and not pecked to death by a flock of magical birds.

This relief quickly melted to trepidation.

Because first, I had no clue what was happening with Christophe.

Had he been led away and then attacked by birds too?

And if so, had someone found him and saved him?

And second, if they had found Christophe (and I hoped to God they had), when we returned to Karsvall and Apollo learned what I'd done, he was going to lose his mind.

Christophe being led away was one thing. He was a kid.

Me?

Stupid.

And the worst part about all of it was that when Apollo lost it with me, it would be justifiable seeing as I'd been an idiot.

My feelings of trepidation ran so deep they forced words out of my mouth.

And these words were a muttered, "Apollo is going to lose his mind."

"Yes," Lahn stated immediately, the rumble of his deep voice sounding not only over my head but beating into my back.

I bit my lip and looked to Circe.

"You're safe," she noted. "He'll be upset, but once it sinks in that you're safe, it'll all be fine."

She was being reassuring, and I'd already decided I liked her, what with her kickass skirt and awesome hair and kind eyes and quick smiles and ability to land a serious hot guy, but at that, I decided I really liked her.

Then I saw her gaze shift up to her husband and whatever look he gave her made her look back to me and roll her eyes.

She was trying to reassure me.

Her husband was thinking thoughts of how he'd feel if Circe stupidly wandered off when malevolence was afoot, she knew it, and followed a stranger into danger anyway.

In other words, his look was stating clearly, he too would lose his mind.

In a big way.

Just like Apollo was going to do.

Crap.

"Cora's twin showed," I told Circe.

She nodded. "We know. Lahn saw her."

"I thought she was the real Cora," I shared something she probably had guessed. "Christophe, Apollo's son, has gone missing and she said she and Tor had found him and he'd only budge if he saw me. I was worried about Chris." I took in a deep breath to attempt to calm my fears. It didn't work, so I finished quietly. "I still am, and I didn't think."

"It is the not thinking that will make your warrior lose his mind," Lahn rumbled informatively, but scarily, from behind me.

I gave wide eyes to Circe.

She took them in before she turned her head and grinned down at her horse.

To take my mind off my rapidly growing apprehension, I cast a glance from side to side, then back, that being from Zahnin to Bain and back to Lahn, and said, "Uh...thanks for saving me from Cora, the Nasty and the magical birds."

After I spoke, Lahn spoke, but he said a bunch of stuff I had no clue what he was saying.

After he was done, Circe spoke, and I looked back to her.

"Zahnin and Bain know some English, since they've been around me for a while, and been in Hawkvale for another while, but they don't know much. Lahn was interpreting."

"Ah," I mumbled.

Zahnin said something in their language, and I watched Circe grin then quickly beat it back.

"What did he say?" I asked.

She again looked to me. "You don't want to know."

Zahnin also thought I'd been stupid.

I couldn't get uppity because he was *so* right.

I decided to remain silent.

Everyone else did too.

This did nothing for my trepidation.

Trepidation that turned into out and out panic when I noted Frey's men, Ruben and Oleg, ahead of us on horses. They were galloping through the snow what looked determinedly.

The second they saw us, they reined in, took us in, gave Lahn chin lifts then wheeled around and galloped away.

They had not been looking for Chris.

They'd been looking for me.

I hoped this meant someone had found Chris.

Though, I had a feeling it also meant they were heading straight back to share that Lahn and his crew had found me.

This didn't make me feel better.

I felt even worse when five minutes later the forest opened up and Karsvall came into view.

A Karsvall that had a shitload of men standing in front of it, one of them Apollo, as well as Chris looking healthy and fit (thank God), Finnie, Frey, some old guy I'd never seen before who had a weathered face and a shock of white hair that was such a shock it kind of freaked me out (more than I was already, that was), and finally, the redheaded witch, Valentine.

I couldn't think on the guy with white hair, or Valentine being there after months of not seeing her.

No, heads turned our way, but after quickly assessing our audience, I only had eyes for Apollo.

He was holding himself very still, and even from far away, I saw his face was granite.

Yep.

He was going to lose his mind.

Circe spurred her horse to go faster, Lahn followed suit and Zahnin and Bain did the same.

But Circe arrived first.

Without greeting, she launched right in, and when she did, even though it was not in question, I *totally* knew I liked her.

"She was led away by the twin of Cora," she stated.

Apollo didn't tear his attention from me when he ordered Lahn, also without greeting, "Put her down."

Crap.

"Now," he finished when Lahn didn't move quickly enough.

However, Lahn had moved and so I had feet to the snow way before I was ready.

"She couldn't know she was her twin, Apollo," Circe went on. "The other Cora hasn't been seen or heard from in months. We weren't even sure she was still alive. And she explained your son was missing and she was concerned. The other Cora told her that they'd found him and he'd only talk to her."

She was doing a bang-up job explaining, but I had a feeling so much blood was rushing to Apollo's head, he couldn't hear her because his reply was to me.

And it was another order.

"Come here."

I held his eyes and said softly, "I'm sorry. I screwed up."

"Come here," he repeated.

"I know it was a big screw up, honey," I told him.

"I do not know what this term means. I also do not give a bloody damn." He came unstuck to lean slightly toward me. "Now, come...*here*."

I took in a deep breath.

Then, keeping my gaze to his, I went there.

The instant I was in reach, he crushed me to him just like he'd done after Frey and his dragons saved Meeta, Loretta and me.

"I'm sorry," I wheezed against his chest.

He gave me a powerful squeeze that I thought might break a few ribs before he abruptly let me go.

He took a step back, and at the look on his face, which was not the relief I felt in his hug, I braced.

"You are lucky you have the opportunity to feel sorry, Madeleine. Your other choices were dead or captured, tortured and used to push me into doing something foolhardy to rescue you, and then who knows. Perhaps my children would be without a father as well as a mother."

Okay.

Yes.

Totally fucked up.

Huge.

I heard a noise I knew was from Christophe, it was small, but I felt it pierce my skin like a dagger.

"It was stupid," I admitted, because it was, and I wanted him to know I knew it.

"It bloody was," Apollo agreed.

"I was worried about Chris," I whispered.

It was lame.

I knew it.

So did Apollo.

"Before I left, I instructed that you not leave this house," he reminded me.

He totally did.

I set my teeth to worrying my lip.

"For any reason," Apollo continued.

I quit worrying my lip and asked cautiously, "Can we continue this inside?"

"We aren't continuing this at all," he clipped, his words ringing with an ominous finality that made me think that he was not talking about our discussion but something else entirely.

A chill slid over my skin that had not one thing to do with the cold.

Apollo turned to Achilles.

"Take her to the dower house."

My heart stuttered painfully in my chest at his words.

It stopped altogether when he turned his back to me, moved sideways a step and commandeered his son by clamping him on the shoulder. Then he led Chris into the house, Chris looking back at me with an expression I couldn't decipher.

There was relief there.

There was also, strangely, guilt.

Then the dark caverns of its interior closed in behind them and they disappeared.

~

LATE THAT EVENING, I sat in the sitting room at the dower house, curled on the sofa with a shawl around my shoulders in an effort to beat back the chill that even the roaring fire was not keeping from the room.

My eyes were aimed out the windows.

As she always did, Cristiana lit torches in front of the house just in case we had visitors.

Something we often had.

At the very least, Apollo came every night.

Now, staring into the torch-lit night, watching the heavy snow fall, I had a feeling Apollo wasn't going to come.

His reaction upon my return was not bizarre. He was big on retreating into anger. I'd learned that lesson the hard way.

But there was something weird about this.

Something wrong.

Something I wasn't certain I could set right.

I'd already apologized, admitted I'd messed up.

Now I didn't know what to do except give him some time.

Time I figured he'd take, considering the last time he retreated into anger it had taken four days and me approaching and laying myself bare to sort things out.

I wasn't going to give it four days this time.

But I was going to give him space.

This meant a thrill of surprise shot through me when I heard the front door open and close.

I turned my head to the door to the sitting room, half expecting someone else to show there. Therefore, I was even more surprised when Apollo's big frame filled the doorway.

He hesitated in it before he took a step inside the room.

I pulled myself out of my stupor and made a move to get to my feet.

I stopped when he ordered curtly, "Halt."

I blinked.

Halt?

His weirdly formal order made my heart begin to race as I stared up at him standing across the room from me.

Far away.

The length of a room that for some reason felt like an ocean.

And it felt like an ocean because his face was impassive. The same as he'd given me when he was angry at me before.

I hated it when he was like this, it scared the crap out of me.

But it was definitely better than him hitting me (or kicking me).

He also got over it.

And this time, I deserved it.

So I settled in to take it.

"What you did today was beyond foolish," he stated.

I drew in a deep breath, nodded and said softly, "I know, honey."

"My son missing, I did not need to bring him back to find you were the same."

"No," I agreed. "You didn't."

"I instructed you not to leave the house," he reminded me (again).

I took in another breath, this one through my nose, before I nodded and said, "I know, Lo. What I did was stupid. *So* stupid. And I'm so, *so* sorry."

He showed no indication he heard my apology.

Instead, he declared, "I'm uncertain if you've been informed, but unlike you, Christophe did not get played by trickery. He ran away."

"Cristiana explained," I told him, and she had, when Achilles escorted me home after Apollo turned his back on me.

This was not a surprise either. Chris had not been in a good way since Brunskar.

It sucked that he'd been moved to that. He had to be feeling things deeply, bad things, things he couldn't work through on his own in order to be moved to do something like that, especially in times like these. I was worried about why he had been and his current state of mind.

But I didn't figure now was the time to broach that particular subject.

"My son has a variety of things preying on his mind. He needs his father's attention," Apollo announced.

I again nodded, this time slowly. I didn't do it slowly because I wasn't expecting that Apollo would want to look after his son. I did it slowly because he was saying those words, but I got the impression he not only meant them but also something else.

"And I have a variety of things to think on," he continued.

That didn't sound good.

"Like what?" I asked, my voice weak with fear because I didn't like the way this conversation was going at all.

"I'll discuss that with you after I've thought on them," he stated. "In the meantime, I shall need to attend my son so I shall not be attending you."

Shit.

There it was.

Oh God.

God.

God.

My chest had compressed, making it hard to breathe, but I fought it and slowly gained my feet at the side of the sofa.

"Apollo—" I whispered.

He allowed me to get no further.

"I've made some grave mistakes. I must see to rectifying them."

What did that mean?

My heart started hammering in my chest, so my voice sounded breathy when I asked, "What mistakes?"

"I'll explain when I've thought on them, come up with a plan, put it in action and rectified them," he declared.

"You're still angry with me," I deduced quietly.

"Livid," he bit off, his formal aloof demeanor slipping as he said that two-syllable word in a tone that proved it absolutely true.

Then, unbelievably unfortunately, he spoke on.

I'd felt the edge of his tongue when he spoke without controlling his emotion before doing it.

Each time he'd done this, it had gutted me.

But this time, it destroyed me.

"It would seem I am much like your father, Madeleine, for no matter how I wish to keep you from harm, you consistently find your way into it by making rash decisions that lead to dire consequences."

After he finished, I stared at him hoping he did not just say that.

Or, since he obviously did, that he would immediately take it back.

I'd told him all about my father.

He knew. He freaking *knew*.

He knew that wasn't right and he knew how his saying that would make me feel.

I stood there, staring at him, and gave it time.

Apollo didn't take it back.

"He didn't wish to keep me from harm," I whispered, and I wanted to kick myself because it sounded uncertain and it bloody wasn't. Then I pointed out, "When offered the chance, he didn't even try."

"Or he may have been smart enough to know when he should give up."

Now, he did just say *that*.

He'd said it.

Straight up.

I knew because I felt the blow, and when I did, I flinched and put a hand to my belly to soothe the pain that shot through me.

Apollo's face didn't change in the slightest as he witnessed this.

I had fucked up. I knew it. I knew it was huge. I admitted it. I apologized for it.

But even as big as it was, an attack this brutal was undeserved.

Completely underserved.

"Attempt to stay safe and not do anything unwise, if you can manage that," he went on, his tone ominously final, and a chill of pure frost slid over my skin, making me shiver. "We will speak further when there's something to say."

I had things to say.

I had *tons* of things to say.

I didn't get a single thing out.

This was because, for the second time that day, for the fourth time of our acquaintance (yes, I fucking counted), without another word, after having lowered the boom on me, Apollo turned and walked away.

26

WHERE DID YOU GO FROM THERE?

"I've seen some serious stuff on this world, and I mean *serious*. Serious cool. Serious crazy. Serious sick. But this was serious *beautiful*."

Circe, Finnie, Loretta, Meeta and I were in the sitting room of the dower house and Circe was explaining the procedure of getting her magic back.

Loretta was cuddling and cooing to Circe's drowsy, close-to-a-nap baby daughter, Isis.

Meeta was cuddling (but not cooing) to Finnie's snoozing Viktor.

I was trying to contain a very active Tunahn, Circe's baby boy, a child Circe shared was immune to naps (and sleep on the whole most of the time).

I was listening because it was interesting.

I was also not listening because my heart was bleeding.

It had been two days since I'd fucked up huge, Apollo came and took his anger out on me, and I had not seen or heard from him since.

This was not a surprise. It must be said, the man could hold a grudge.

But this time it was worse.

He had a right to be angry.

But the way he expressed that was not okay.

In thinking on it, it occurred to me that it had not been okay the first time he did it. Or the second. And definitely not the last.

I'd run away from Pol so I wasn't his literal whipping post.

I didn't need to be with a man who used me as his verbal one.

I mean, seriously.

Since Apollo was again keeping a distance, Cristiana, Meeta and Loretta were keeping an eye on me, Cristiana especially. But this time, I didn't feel it was up to me to go to Apollo and apologize.

No way.

It wasn't like I'd screwed up and tried to pretend it wasn't a big deal and told him to just get over it. I'd owned up to it straight away.

Then he'd *way* overreacted.

In fact, I wasn't sure there was any situation where his reaction would be appropriate.

Or, honestly, forgivable.

Since we left Brunskar I'd been feeling more and more like shit because Apollo had so much to offer, and I had so little.

I sure as hell didn't need him to point that crap out.

The good news was, Apollo allowed Élan to come have lunch with me yesterday, at her request. This was super sweet, and I loved spending time with her because *she* was super sweet. She was also so exuberant, witnessing her natural delight at pretty much everything was the only time I could forget my growing anger.

The other good news was, Finnie and Circe came and went as they pleased. And with the men holed up talking about dragons, elves, witches and war plans, they had time to come and go as they pleased. So I was getting to know Finnie more and Circe better, which was nice, since they both were great.

The bad news was not only was Apollo entirely absent, so was Chris.

Chris had run away because of me.

This was weighing on my mind. I was worried. I was hoping Apollo was giving him what he needed. And I felt powerless because I couldn't do anything to help.

In fact, it was me that was the reason he hurt.

Knowing I was causing pain to Christophe didn't suck.

It killed.

That was also weighing on my mind, and call me selfish, I knew he had things weighing on his mind too, but Apollo had to know it.

And still he attacked.

I'd thought on it (and thought on it), and there was no way to twist what Apollo had said into being understandable.

It just wasn't right.

During her visit the day before, I had learned that Circe and Lahn, with Zahnin and Bain as Circe's personal guard, had been transported here by Valentine.

I say Circe's guard because Lahn didn't need a guard. He was a one-man guard all on his own and only a fool would attack that man. I mean, those birds didn't even attempt to peck away at him, and they were brainless creatures formed from magic, but still, they knew better than to even try.

Circe told me that upon arrival in Lunwyn, Valentine had immediately sensed I was in danger and Lahn, Zahnin, Bain (with Lahn bringing Circe along because he refused to be far from her) sprang to my rescue without telling Apollo or anyone they were here.

Apparently, the ritual Circe was conducting to recoup her powers had gone a lot faster than expected. Since Valentine was already there to tell them she was moving them all to Lunwyn when it was finished, she'd just moved them all to Lunwyn.

The real Cora and Tor were with them but could not come because he had something pressing happening, seeing as he was not only a marked man with a marked wife but also a prince of two realms, so shit had to get done.

They were arriving as soon as whatever royal stuff he had to do was done.

The other five hundred (yes, *five hundred*) members of Circe's personal guard that Lahn insisted accompany her to the Northlands were riding their horses up from the Vale seeing as Valentine wasn't real hip on transporting an entire army.

Depending on how good of time they made, they'd be here in three weeks to a month.

So now we were in my sitting room visiting.

And I was trying to figure out how I could sort the latest mess I'd gotten myself into.

What I was trying not to do was think about the fact that maybe I didn't want to.

I hadn't had any sleep since it happened. Not a wink. I was mentally exhausted (for Lord knew it was a veritable impossibility to become physically exhausted because, with a housekeeper and two lady's maids, there was nothing for me to do).

All I could do was think on what Apollo said to me. How ugly it was. How uncalled for it was. How he had to know how it would wound me.

And last, that he'd let it sit for two days, maybe expecting me to go to him and smooth things over like Cristiana advised before.

And perhaps I should.

But I felt deep down inside I shouldn't.

I took a lot from Pol.

I had to draw a line with Apollo.

But the man he was, maybe he wouldn't come to me.

See?

All this crap in my head, it was no wonder I couldn't sleep.

Not to mention, worrying about Christophe and still feeling like an idiot because I'd done something so immensely stupid to start all this off.

I was *so* over it.

The problem was, I was over it, but it just wasn't *over*.

I was beginning to see the wisdom of Captain Kirk loving them and leaving them as he boldly went where no man had gone before (in the case of some of his alien partners, probably in two ways).

Because it hurt to love.

Especially when you fucked up.

Huge.

Then they fucked up.

Arguably even more huge.

Because where did you go from there?

And yes, I loved Apollo. I fell for him the instant he'd looked at me, his eyes filled with tenderness and pain. I knew this because, alone at night (and also when I was alone during the day), when I wasn't worrying or being pissed, I ran over every moment we'd shared.

In doing this, I knew that a man who could look like that was a man who could feel anything, everything, and do it deeply, completely, magnificently.

Pretty much everything he'd done since had proved this irrevocably. Including (it sucked to admit, but it was true) how he expressed anger (though, that part wasn't magnificent).

On this thought, my attention came back into the room when I saw Zahnin walk past the windows, his head turned to look out into the glade.

Lahn was at Karsvall, holed up with Apollo, Frey, Valentine and the other witch I'd only met in passing (but who, unlike Valentine, was really sweet). Her name was Lavinia.

Circe and Finnie had come with Zahnin and Bain since Circe didn't move a muscle unless Lahn was at her side.

Or her guard was.

That was super sweet too.

"The cave was like nothing I'd ever seen," she said, taking me out of my thoughts, and I looked from Zahnin to her. "I mean, it *glittered*. Not like the stone it was made of had anything in it that sparkled. I don't know how to describe it, except it was magic."

"I *so* have to go there when all this business is finally done," Finnie declared.

"You *so* do. It was freaking *amazing*," Circe agreed.

"So, you just walked into the fountain in the cave and, *poof*, magic restored?" Loretta asked, her wide excited eyes on Circe.

"You're supposed to go every day for five days and walk in naked the instant the sun sets on the horizon, which isn't easy to time since you're in a cave and can't actually *see* the sun setting on the horizon. Luckily, Lahn has a good internal clock. Also luckily, it only took me three days and on day three," she shrugged, "I just filled up."

"Could you feel it?" Loretta queried.

Circe's eyes got kind of dreamy in this sexy way that laid even more testimony as to why she caught a hot guy the likes of Dax Lahn.

Then she whispered, "Oh yeah. I could feel it."

Just the way she looked and spoke gave me a tingle in a private place, which sucked because it made me miss Apollo even more.

And thus, be even more pissed at him.

"It seems strange," Meeta put in, "that you could do something so vital, so important as filling up your magic simply by wandering into a pool."

Circe looked to her. "I guess so. Of course, we had to solve five riddles every day then face five trials and each day they were different riddles *and* trials. We had to do this to make it through the interconnecting caves that led to the pool and the route was different each day. Then we had to leave the caves and start all over again the next day. Luckily, we only had to do that for three days rather than the full five."

She looked through the room but kept speaking.

"The place had tons of skeletons of those who'd failed to solve the riddles or failed at the trials. And there were a couple of fresh kills that were unpleasant. Then, of course, Lahn almost got his head chopped off once, but," she grinned, "I knew my man would prevail."

My mouth had dropped open and I still hadn't closed it when Loretta breathed, "He almost got his head chopped off?"

"We failed at that riddle the first time and these skeletons with swords came to life. He battled them." Another grin. "He won."

"Holy cow," I whispered.

"I know, it was awesome," she replied. "You would think I'd get used to how awesome he is, but I haven't."

I had a feeling I wouldn't either.

It was at this point I caught something out of the corner of my eye and looked back to the windows to see both Bain and Zahnin were standing out in the snow, their eyes turned to my front door.

I was getting a lot of visitors these days, Finnie, Circe, Élan.

But it was early afternoon. Élan would be at her studies and Finnie and Circe were already there.

I tensed when I heard the front door open, thinking maybe it was Apollo finally coming to call and wondering what I'd do if it was.

I soon found it wasn't.

It also wasn't Valentine or Lavinia, who the men at the main house were hogging. I hadn't even said word one to Valentine while she'd been there.

No.

It was Hans.

A Hans who only had eyes for Loretta.

My gaze shot to Meeta.

She looked to me and shook her head as if the Hans and Loretta situation was working her last nerve, she wanted them to end the drama and just get it on.

It wasn't working mine. It was something to keep my mind off my own situation.

I wanted Loretta to be happy, but I was proud of her. She'd crushed huge on Hans for a good long while. Now she had him and she was making him work for it.

As she should.

As he should.

I just had no idea how it would play out because she *seriously* was making him work for it, and I knew Hans, but I had no clue if he'd give up or fight until he got what he wanted.

I hoped it was the latter because Loretta was worth it.

I looked back to Hans when he spoke.

"Our talk was interrupted yesterday," he stated, eyes still pinned to Loretta, and he was speaking like she was the only one in the room. "I wish to finish that discussion now."

I looked to Loretta when she replied with fake sweetness, "Oh, were we having a discussion?"

I returned to Hans when he returned, "Indeed, we were."

Back to Loretta when she retorted, "Funny, I thought a discussion was when two people were talking. There were two people there, but only one of us was speaking. And that was *you*."

I pressed my lips together and turned to Hans, who did not look happy when he shot back, "Right, then I still have things to say, and this time you can use your mouth, but only after I say them, and when I finish, you won't be using it to speak."

Yowza!

My eyebrows darted up even as I pressed my lips tighter together and I cut my eyes back to Loretta to see her cheeks pink with anger, or embarrassment, or both.

"This would be why we aren't talking now or *ever*," she flashed sharply in return.

Back again to Hans when he ignored this and ordered, "Hand the child to Queen Circe and come."

Again, my gaze went to Loretta when she snapped, "I think not!"

"Woman," Hans growled impatiently.

"Man," Loretta bit out irritably.

That was it for Hans. I knew it when he strode forward purposefully, carefully gathered Isis from Loretta's arms, twisted to deposit her in Circe's, then he caught Loretta's hand. He yanked her out of the couch and dragged her from the room.

I watched, turning my neck to look over my shoulder and catch it all before I turned back to the room.

All the women were looking at each other silently with knowing eyes.

Except Meeta.

She had knowing eyes, but she was not silent.

Cuddling Viktor closer, she noted blandly, "It's my feeling that you females who allow yourselves to be caught by these overbearing men are quite mad."

"And when was the last time you got yourself some?" I asked, and she looked to me.

"Got myself some?" she queried on her brows rising elegantly.

"Were bedded," I explained in this-world language.

"Last night," she declared. "Ruben. That was seven nights in a row. He's an exceptional lover. By far the best I've ever had. He's especially talented with his fingers. He does things with his fingers I didn't even know were possible and I'm not inexperienced."

"I didn't need to know that," Finnie muttered.

I looked to Circe to see her smiling at Finnie.

I didn't smile. Not because it wasn't funny, but because these days, I didn't feel like smiling.

My eyes drifted back to the windows, and I saw no Zahnin or Bain.

I saw nothing but forest and trees.

As simple as the view was, it still was beautiful.

Even with that beauty, looking at it, it hit me, with all that we had in my world, traffic and malls and TV, even with the way my life had been there, it was still simpler than my life here.

I had one goal, stay away from Pol.

I couldn't say I was happy doing it.

I *could* say I had a mission. I had a purpose. I had something to do.

I didn't have much of a life and I wasn't content.

But I had a reason for being. It wasn't a great reason, but it was something.

Now, with all I had, these last two days I was reminded that I was still at Apollo's mercy.

He gave me everything.

And when he felt like it, he took it all away.

I heard the front door open and again went tense.

And again, it wasn't Apollo.

It was Lahn.

The sitting room wasn't small, it also wasn't large and there were a number of women in it. Still, the instant he walked in, the room seemed overfull, not only from his big man body but also the sheer force of his presence.

Like Hans, he only had eyes for his woman.

Unlike Hans, once his eyes moved over his queen they dropped to his daughter. Without delay, he strode to Circe, divested her of her baby burden and curled his girl into his arms.

Okay, no way he'd look better with a kitten.

True, he'd look hot cradling a kitten.

But the way he held his girl and looked down on her with unconcealed devotion in his fierce features, no kitten could top that, no matter how cute it was.

Once he'd showered silent adoration on his now sleeping daughter with four women raptly watching him do it (yes, even matter of fact Meeta, and as a Maroovian who were sworn enemies of Korwahk, that laid testimony to just how awesome Lahn was), he looked to me.

"A young female at Karsvall approached me prior to my leaving. She requests your attendance at a party in her chambers. I told her I'd have Zahnin bring you to her. He's waiting outside to take you there."

Only Élan would walk up to a huge-ass warrior and tell him to ask someone to one of her tea parties.

On that thought, I did smile. It was genuine, but it was small.

"It seems I've been summoned," I murmured as I got to my feet. Once up, I looked around the assemblage. "I hope you don't mind."

"Go," Finnie said on a grin.

"Tell her I want an invitation next time," Circe added, reaching out her arms so I could hand Tunahn to her.

This I did, saying, "Will do."

I glanced through the group as I gave my farewells, seeing Meeta watching me closely as I did so.

She did this often.

On our trip back from Brunskar, she'd explained she had "the sight." That was why she was in the woods, heavily armed, dragging Loretta with her. Though, Loretta was in on relating this story to me and she said she'd volunteered, but I had a feeling her volunteering was a bit coerced. That said, she'd come and got herself injured because of it so it didn't matter either way.

But now, I couldn't tell if Meeta was watching me because she'd had a vision.

I also didn't ask.

If I was going to be walking into another trap, I wanted to know.

The way she was looking at me now, speculative and troubled, I had a feeling she wasn't worried about me battling scary-as-hell birds but instead dealing with an alpha who could make me feel marvelous, and it was rare, but he could also make me feel like dirt.

I tipped my head to the side and gave her a small smile (that was not genuine) and headed to the door.

I threw on my cloak, pulled on my gloves and headed out to see Lahn had not lied. Zahnin was waiting on a horse for me.

I looked around as I made my way to him and saw no Bain.

Undoubtedly patrolling.

My attention diverted, I gasped when I got within arms' reach and Zahnin's arms did just that. He pulled me up to sitting in front of him on his horse.

Clearly, he wanted to run his errand and get back to guard duty because he no sooner settled my behind in front of him when he put his heels to his mount and we sprang forward through the snow.

He said nothing but then again, he didn't know very much English.

I knew no Korwahkian.

Thus, the ride was silent.

That was until he reined in at the front door to Karsvall.

I had a mind full of Apollo and what I'd do if I ran into him.

My mind was also full of what he might do and then what I might do in response to what he'd do.

In other words, after the five-minute ride, I had the beginnings of a headache.

To my surprise, Zahnin didn't put me to the steps he'd stopped beside and promptly take off.

Instead, he threw a leg over and dismounted. He then put his hands to my waist and pulled me off the horse.

He set me on my feet but didn't take my elbow or curl my hand in the bend of his.

He curved his fingers around my bicep and semi-led, semi-dragged me (his legs were longer so I couldn't quite keep up) up the steps, stopping at the door.

When he let me go, I tipped my head back to say thank you (words he had to know, or at least I hoped he did).

I didn't get those words out.

His rumbling voice sounded.

"I have wife."

I blinked in surprise, not only at his strange announcement, but that he spoke at all.

"Okay," I replied, hoping he knew that word too.

"We meet. She no talk," he declared.

I drew in breath.

He kept going.

"No good. Bad. Talk good."

Hmm.

Seems I was getting another Cristiana-style lecture with a lot fewer words.

"Talk *is* good, Zahnin," I agreed.

"Warrior. You. Talk."

Again, few words, but there was no mistaking it was an order.

I wasn't sure I was ready. I wasn't sure what to say. I just knew what I needed Apollo to say, but I wasn't sure he had it in him to say it.

And I didn't know how I'd feel even if he did.

Even so, I said, "Okay, Zahnin."

"Warrior suffers."

Oh God.

I stared up at him. "Apollo suffers?" I whispered.

"Warriors' women no talk, warriors suffer."

Okay, this guy was a big guy, a hot guy, a scary guy, because even if we couldn't converse all that great, you didn't need words to know he was seriously edgy.

But he cared about his wife, a lot.

And he was trying to do something nice for Apollo and me.

Which meant I hoped his wife cared about him too.

A lot.

Hesitantly, I touched his hand briefly and said, "Thank you. I'll think about it."

His brows shot together over narrowed eyes, and I was right.

Definitely edgy.

"No think." He leaned into me. "*Talk.*"

I thought it best to agree at that juncture, and not simply because his limited vocabulary meant we couldn't have a full-blown discussion.

So I did.

"Okay, Zahnin."

He nodded sharply once then instantly turned and prowled down the steps to his horse.

He mounted the horse in a fluid motion that in and of itself would get him a contract with a Hollywood agent, which would then lead to a resurgence of the western.

Once astride the mighty beast, he looked at me and called curtly, "Inside."

I pressed my lips together, nodded, waved my farewell, then put my hand to the doorknob and went inside.

Once I'd closed the door behind me, I took six tentative steps in and looked right.

The door to Apollo's study was closed.

That likely meant he was in there which thankfully meant I wouldn't run into him.

I let out the breath I didn't realize I was holding and hurried to the stairs. Once up them, taking no chances, I hurried to Élan's room.

The instant I appeared in the doorway, she looked up from pointing at a doll in a little chair and saying something to it (and it was clear the doll had misbehaved and Élan was telling her off), her beautiful green eyes came to me and lit.

"You came!" she cried delightedly, like the queen of Lunwyn had shown at her door (and this could happen for her, the country's princess was only a short horse ride away).

Taking her in, she was one thing my old world could not offer me. Not ever.

And she was perhaps the only thing that could make me forget everything and just feel happy.

"Of course I came," I replied, walking in taking off my gloves and grinning at her. "I haven't had a more important invitation in years. No," I corrected. "Decades."

Her head tipped to the side, and she planted her hands on her little hips, watching me undo the catches of the cloak at my throat.

She looked to my face.

"You're not wearing a hat," she observed.

"No," I agreed, swinging the cloak off my shoulders.

"You always make me wear a hat," she noted.

I dropped the cloak and gloves to an overstuffed flower print chair and turned my full attention to her.

"I do." I lifted my hands in front of me in the "don't shoot" position. "And before you say it, you're right. I should. Just like you always should. It's important to keep warm in order not to catch a chill and it's just as important for me as it is for you." I dropped my hands and grinned at her again. "It's just that I was so excited to get my invitation from Dax Lahn to attend your party, I forgot."

"Chris doesn't wear a hat," she pointed out.

I approached her and stopped when I was near.

I bent slightly at my knees as well as at the waist to get closer and stated, "He should. He should stay warm and healthy just like you and me. But he's a boy and boys have reasons for not doing things like that. Reasons we girls will never understand, no matter how hard we try. But we just have to be smart and do such thing as wear hats when it's cold and be even smarter, and when boys do things that make no sense, just let them do it. It'll be their price to pay in the end if they have a stuffy nose. Am I right?"

"Chris gets grumpy when he gets a stuffy nose," she informed me.

"We all do, honey bunch," I returned.

"Not me." She smiled. "That means I don't have to go to the school room. I can lie in bed and Bella will bring me flavored ices for my throat if it hurts and Papa will come up and read me stories."

Only Élan would find the silver lining of having a cold.

"I bet you'd prefer being outside making snow castles," I told her, and she screwed up her face.

It cleared and she said, "Bella gives me flavored ices even when my throat doesn't hurt, and Papa reads me stories too. So having that *and* being able to make snow castles is better."

I was glad she had come to that conclusion even if I didn't like suddenly having the vision of Apollo reading stories to his daughter in my head. It reminded me of how wonderful he was which could make me forget when he was not.

That had happened in the early days with Pol too. He'd do something awful then revert to the Pol I fell in love with and I'd forget. In the end, before I gave up the effort, I *made* myself forget.

Then, eventually there was enough bad that no amount of good could erase it.

If you put up with it, they dished it out.

Apollo was not Pol. I knew this completely.

The fact still remained that if you put up with it, they were going to dish it out.

And it got worse.

I'd put up with it from Apollo.

He'd again dished it out.

And it got worse.

I stopped thinking these dire thoughts when I felt Élan grab my hand and tug.

"You sit here, next to Ariel," she instructed, sitting me next to a doll with a crown and a very pretty knit dress the likes of which I had several of in my wardrobe.

But as she moved me, I caught something out of the corner of my eye and spied Christophe peeking just his head around the door.

My body gave a start as my eyes caught his. He was watching us and I couldn't know how long he'd been there. I also couldn't ask, for before I could say a word or even smile, he disappeared.

I drew in a breath as I let Élan seat me next to Ariel (not an easy task seeing as the chairs were not even half as tall as normal chairs) and my eyes drifted back to the door as she chattered and fake poured tea from an exquisite china teapot (that also wasn't half the size of a normal teapot).

Chris did not show.

I took this as a sign that whatever Apollo was doing with Chris wasn't working.

Once I processed that and let the heavy weight of it settle around my heart, I set it aside and turned my full attention to Élan.

She wanted me here, she had me here. And not with me moping or stuck in my head, worried about my life, Apollo or Christophe.

I'd sit through hundreds of tea parties.

I'd do it smiling.

And for Élan, those smiles would be genuine.

Every time.

27

REMEMBER THIS KISS

Thirty minutes later, Bella bustled into the room, shooting a smile my way but ending our tea party with, "Your tutor says you have writing to practice, little miss. Time to put away the teapot. You can finish whatever you were discussing at dinner tonight."

Fat chance that would happen.

For two nights I'd dined with Meeta, Loretta and Cristiana in the kitchen at the dower house.

They were good company (the jury was out on whether or not I was). But this meant for the first time in weeks I'd dined without Apollo and the kids.

I missed that too.

And he didn't blink in taking it from me either.

Completely at his mercy.

Ignoring the pout Élan aimed her way, Bella went on, "And, Miss Maddie, Lord Apollo has sent word that he'd like you to attend him in his study when your party with Élan was done."

Or maybe it wasn't a fat chance dinner would happen.

Then again, it was at Apollo's whim whether it would or wouldn't.

Not to mention, I really had no choice of whether I would attend him in his study or not.

As all this settled in my head, I felt something strange bubble up inside me. It wasn't a bad strange. It wasn't a good strange. It was something I never felt before.

It was a *nothing* strange.

I didn't think on it as Élan gave me a hug, and when she let me go, I bent down to kiss her cheek.

I pulled away and whispered, "Ask me again. That was fun."

She gave me one of her sweet smiles, a smile for some reason that I committed to memory like I wanted to file it away so I could call it up whenever I wanted, right before she chirped, "I will. We'll do it tomorrow! And we'll ask Frey to come!"

I tried to force my mind to wrap around a vision of Frey Drakkar folding his long body into one of Élan's little chairs and one of his big hands holding a daintier than dainty teacup. My mind refused to do it, but my lips smiled at the thought.

"Even if it's just you and me, I'll be here," I told her.

"Huzzah!" she cried.

She'd be happy with just me. Hell, she'd be happy with just her dolls. She was just a happy kid.

Though, I figured she'd be happier if Frey showed.

I kept smiling at her as I straightened. Then I aimed my smile at Bella and moved to my cloak.

"I'll see you both later," I called as I made my way to the door.

"See you at dinner!" Élan called back.

I shot another smile toward her, wondering if she would.

I then waved and walked out the door, busying myself with arranging the cloak over my arm, folding the gloves more firmly in my hand, trying to think what I was feeling.

And still, all I could come up with was that I was feeling nothing.

It was the nothing part that worried me, and I was so lost in thought as I made my way down the corridor, I barely processed the women's voices I heard coming from not close, but not too far away.

"I'm shocked," one said. "It's unlike Ulfr. His father, absolutely. Him? No. But what he's doing is much the same thing."

"It is and not much the same. Exactly the same," another voice replied. "And you know, I overheard Jeremiah. Apparently, Ulfr has a house in Estranvegue all set up for this Madeleine for when it's safe to send her away."

At hearing my name, I stopped dead.

Or, perhaps, it was hearing the part about Apollo sending me away.

"In Estranvegue?" the first voice asked.

"Yes," the second voice confirmed.

"Goodness, that's all the way across Lunwyn," the first voice noted.

"Indeed," the second voice stated. "He's also set up an account for her. Obviously, he still intends to take on the responsibility of caring for her, but he won't be doing it here."

"But," the first voice started, "I've heard they're to wed."

"I've heard that too. And maybe he intended to do that if the children had accepted her. Now, that's obviously not going to happen. I know little Élan likes her, but she likes everybody. Young Christophe doesn't like her. It's not in his nature to cause alarm by doing something like running away, even when things aren't topsy-turvy as they are now. Her being here, he ran away. And who can blame him? I've seen her and she's the image of his mother. It's uncanny. It's also downright cruel to force your lover on your son if she looks exactly like your dead wife. Ulfr may be behaving like his father, as shocking as that is, but I figure in the end, he won't do anything to harm his son."

My breath suddenly coming in pants, I was teetering on my feet. I should have shifted to the side to put a hand on the wall to hold myself up, but I couldn't find it in me to will my body to do so.

I could do nothing but listen.

"Cristiana tells me she's lovely," the first voice said.

"I've heard that as well. But she can be very lovely and that won't make her look any less like Christophe's departed mum. It's no surprise Ulfr took up with her, considering how severe he grieved the passing of his wife. She wouldn't even have to be lovely for him to do that. But when enough is enough, it'll be enough. And I reckon young Christophe running off like that, Ulfr will decide enough is enough."

It was at that, I swallowed and finally shuffled to the side. Leaning heavily into my hand on the wall, my head dropped because the effort of holding it up was too much as their words burned into my brain. My skin.

My soul.

"At least she's on pennyrium," the first voice noted. "Sally from the village said Ulfr gets Loretta to acquire it from her. Though, it's still shocking, what with what his father did to his mother. From how he is, it's impossible to believe he's repeating history like this. But it seems he is, since his father also installed his mistress at the dower house just like Ulfr has done with this Madeleine.

"But the old Ulfr did it to get her with child," the second voice remarked, and I blinked at my feet in shock.

There was a clucking noise before the first voice said, "I know. Desperate for an heir, he put his wife through that. Can you imagine, living in this house knowing your husband journeys ten minutes away every single night to engage in such activities?"

"Can you imagine living in the dower house knowing your lover leaves you for his barren wife and you'll never have him that way?" the second voice returned.

The first one's voice stated clearly she couldn't imagine it when she said, "I felt for her. For both of them. Especially when old Ulfr got his heir. All of that still going on, having the best of both worlds, but her sitting in the dower house having to wait for visits from her own son, who the lady of the house was raising, and poorly, seeing as she didn't think it all that grand having to raise her husband's child with another woman. A woman who was just along the way. I was here when it happened, and it was actually a relief when he finally sent her away."

What on *earth* were they talking about?

"With all that happening to his mum, Ulfr should know better," the second one stated firmly, cutting into my thoughts. "Everyone in the village is talking about this Madeleine. About how young Christophe ran away because he can't bear to be around her. How Ulfr is repeating history. You know, no one believes he's going to marry her. What I don't understand is why he dragged his children into this at all."

The first woman's voice was fading when she replied, "It's unlike him. Truly. And disappointing. But he's an Ulfr. He's Head of a House. They do what they will. They always have."

They were clearly departing because I barely heard the second one concur, "That they do."

I knew they were gone when I heard nothing more.

But I didn't move.

I couldn't know for certain because Apollo sure as hell didn't tell me, but it seemed like his mother had lived in my house, and she didn't do it after moving there when her husband died. She was not his father's wife, she didn't raise her son except for whatever visits Apollo's father let her have, and then she was sent away.

This was big shit.

Shit Apollo should have shared with me, perhaps, I didn't know, one of the freaking *dozens* of times we lay in bed whispering to each other.

And he had some house set up for me somewhere.

Somewhere far away.

With an account for me.

As devastating as this news should have been, it wasn't.

Because it wasn't a surprise.

Christophe had run away because of me and Apollo was clearly concerned with that. He'd also made it clear he was fed up with dealing with me. But he wouldn't turn me out or allow me to go it alone.

Apparently, in the last two days he'd made arrangements to keep me.

He just wasn't going to *keep me*.

At that thought, I knew why I was feeling nothing.

I was feeling nothing because that was the smartest way to feel, for if I felt what I should be feeling, it wouldn't gut me. It wouldn't destroy me.

It would annihilate me.

On that thought, I remembered Apollo was waiting for me. That bitter chill crept over my skin as I pushed away from the wall, squared my shoulders and raised my head.

And again, stopped dead.

This was because I saw Chris in the door to a room just two feet ahead of me, his head turned to look down the hall toward where the voices had disappeared.

That was his room.

The door had been open.

He'd heard.

I knew it because I only had his profile, but his face was pale and he looked stricken.

I moved and watched his body jump before his head whipped my way.

"Please don't run," I whispered.

Fortunately, he didn't.

"Thank you," I said when I'd stopped close.

Then I didn't waste any time saying what I had to say. I did this because I wanted him to listen to me and I didn't want him to dash away in the middle of what I had to say.

I also did it because I didn't want to torture him with my presence for too long.

"I won't take a lot of your time, Christophe. I just wanted to say that I'm sorry." I pulled in a deep breath, pulling it together at the same time, and went on, "I never meant to hurt you. Before I met you, I was very worried I would. I'm not surprised that I did. But I am sorry." I dipped my voice lower and held his eyes when I finished, "Very sorry, honey."

He stared up at me and said nothing, his face expressionless.

Looking at his face, I again thought that he was so like his father in so many ways.

But it was time for this to be done. He didn't need any further pain.

Neither did I.

"Even if I did hurt you," I began honestly, "for me, it was still an honor to have the opportunity to get to know you. You're a good brother. You're a great kid. And your father is very proud of you. You'll make an excellent soldier one day, Chris. In fact, you'll make an excellent anything you want to be."

He continued to stare up at me without a word.

I decided to finish up.

"Thank you for putting up with me for a spell. I wish that time came without me hurting you. But I'm still grateful that I've had it."

He swallowed.

That needed to be that, so I gave him a smile that was not genuine in the slightest, wishing I could touch him. I wouldn't be greedy, go for a hug, a kiss on the cheek. I just wanted to stroke his hair or run my finger along his cheek.

But I couldn't.

Because he wouldn't want that.

Instead, I turned away and moved quickly down the hall.

I didn't look back.

Speaking with Chris took a lot out of me. Too much. I was beginning to feel more than nothing. A lot more than nothing. And I needed that nothing in order to get through speaking with Apollo.

Then I needed to find Valentine.

And once I'd spoken to her, when she'd done what I'd asked, only then would I let myself feel something.

Now, I needed that nothing.

I held on to it as I made it down the stairs and directly to Apollo's study.

I didn't hesitate to knock.

I also didn't hesitate to put my hand to the knob, turn it and move into the room when I heard him call, "Come."

The minute I entered I noted that he was alone. He was at his desk, his head bent to some paper he was scribbling on.

And in that second I entered, my feeling of nothingness took another hit, because at one glance, I knew I missed him. I missed everything about him including watching him do something ordinary, like scribble on paper, and marveling at how beautiful he could be doing it.

The second after I came through the door, his head came up, his expression changed, and he dropped his quill.

I blocked out his expression.

I needed to. If I didn't, I'd feel something.

And not a little something.

I couldn't allow myself to do that.

So I didn't.

"Close the door, dove," he called quietly as he straightened from the desk.

I did as bid, steeling myself against him calling me "dove."

I'd missed that too.

I closed the door and positioned to stand in front of it, holding my cloak over my arm, my gloves tight in my hand.

Apollo moved to the front of his desk, his eyes on me as he did, and there he stopped.

"Will you come here?" he asked.

So Apollo, wanting me to go to him.

As irritating as that could be, I'd missed that too.

"No, thank you," I answered.

I saw his jaw clench.

He did this holding my gaze and he gave it a moment before he stated, "I said some things."

"Yes, you did," I agreed matter-of-factly.

He registered my tone immediately. I knew it because I saw his almost imperceptible flinch before he recovered and went on.

"I regret them, poppy."

I made no reply.

"I was worried about you," he told me.

I remained silent.

"And when we found him, Christophe shared things that were troubling."

I said nothing.

"I had many weighty matters on my mind. Too many, all at once."

I held my silence.

Apollo started toward me, saying, "Alas, my dove, I took that out on you."

I finally broke my silence, and he stopped moving when I said, "I'd actually prefer it if you stayed over there."

"Maddie—" he started, his voice soft, sweet.

I couldn't allow myself to hear that either.

If I did, his voice would definitely make me feel more than nothing.

So I interrupted him by announcing, "I want to go home."

His body stilled. All of it, top to toe. I watched the power of it still completely, and it must be said, it was a remarkable sight.

Then I watched it come alert and that was even more remarkable.

But (I told myself) neither of these made me feel anything.

"You are home," he said quietly.

"I'm not," I returned. "I'm in Karsvall, your home. Karsvall is in Lunwyn, your country. In the Northlands, your continent. All of that is in your world. I want to go back to my world."

He again started moving toward me, his eyes locked to mine. "I spoke harshly to you. I said things I deeply regret. It was inexcusable, Madeleine, and I apologize."

He meant that. Every word. I knew it. I knew by the way he was looking at me and I knew by the way his words sounded.

He meant it a great deal.

But it didn't make me feel a thing.

Or...at least that's what I told myself.

Instead, I held my ground and held his gaze. "I appreciate that. Now, if you'd lead me to Valentine, I'll be requesting that she send me home."

He stopped two feet in front of me and studied me closely.

I could read the anger in his eyes. Controlled anger.

I could also see the worry.

That was uncontrolled.

"You can't think I'd simply allow you return to your world," he remarked.

"No, I can't think that," I agreed. "You'll only *allow* me do what you *want* me to do. You have a way with getting your way and I have a way of giving it to you. I must admit, I've been too in pain to think about this rationally over the last couple of days. But just moments ago, on my way to you, it all became very clear what I have to do and where I have to be. Now, I've just had a lovely time with Élan, a time we both enjoyed. I'm not happy to leave her but I'm hoping that will be a nice memory to leave her with."

And I hoped it was.

When I was gone, I knew she'd miss me. She liked me. It would be a blow.

But better I leave now than later when her father sent me away.

As for me, I couldn't think about how leaving Élan would feel.

So I didn't.

Without pause, I kept going.

"And I happened on Christophe. I hope the words I found to say to him have helped in some way, though that's doubtful. But I only have one choice and it's not a good one, but it's the right one. Since Valentine is here, regardless of what you'd let me do, Apollo, she's the one who has the power to send me back and I'll be asking her to do it."

I could feel the emotion emanating from him. It wasn't good emotion. It was frightening emotion. But I told myself I didn't feel that either.

"You are not safe in the other world," he reminded me.

"I'm not safe here," I reminded him.

He shook his head. "What I said to you was unwarranted, Madeleine, this is true. But you strike back by committing the same sin? Inflicting your own wounds in this way? After all we've shared, all we've become to one another, asking with not one ounce of emotion to leave me?"

"What you said was inexcusable, unwarranted *and* unforgivable," I replied, holding his eyes and squaring my shoulders. "I'll not accept Pol's physical abuse for a decade only to come here and allow his twin to verbally abuse me."

I heard his sharp intake of breath even as his torso straightened abruptly and the mood in the room, already not good, degenerated further.

I told myself I didn't feel that either.

"I've said this before, but I will remind you again. I am not him, Maddie," he said shortly.

"You aren't," I stated on a sharp nod. "You strike out in a different way that's just as undeserved and perhaps not as physically painful, but it still hurts."

"I apologized."

"He used to do that too."

His head jerked and I got another flinch, this one not almost imperceptible.

This one I couldn't miss.

He felt those words. I'd wounded him.

No, I'd wounded him with the understanding of how deeply he'd wounded me.

I told myself I didn't feel that either.

"In all the beauty that we've shared, in all the beauty you've given me, I forgot," I told him. "I forgot I was trying to find my way. Forgot it so deeply, I lost it again. Until that woman pointed it out. And then you did what you did, and it became even clearer."

"What woman?" he asked, his brows drawing together.

"Franka Drakkar," I answered.

He shook his head again, but this time did it and took a step closer.

I didn't move.

He spoke.

"Nothing that woman says is worth hearing."

"You're wrong," I returned. "It was. After she said it, I took it in. I just took it in the wrong way. You see, how I see it is that I was Pol's whore. A whore with a ring on my finger. I bought that, being me. Being who I am. Being a woman who likes nice things and wanted a good life. A life not like the one my mother lived with my father. Scraping and saving, existing day to day, paycheck to paycheck, but not doing that happily, knowing my home was a warm place where love thrived. Doing it putting up with shit. Living with negativity choking her every breath. I wanted so badly to make sure I had none of that, but all I wanted, I was blinded to what I bought when I took the easy way out and became a whore."

"Madeleine—" he started, but I ignored the new look on his face. The look that was not confused or angry or concerned. The tortured look that hurt so much to witness, it threatened to make me feel something, and I talked over him.

"In my world, a man treats a whore like Pol treated me. He doesn't treat his wife like that." I threw a hand his way. "Now I'm your whore, but without the ring, even though you've offered it. And I don't want to be a whore, Apollo. I'm sure I could sally forth in this world and maybe make a living at it, and that's the only thing I could do. I'm good at nothing else. But I don't want that. I've been doing it way too long. I'm done with being a whore. So, since I can't get on in this world without whoring myself to you or someone else, I'd rather go home and take my chances."

"You are not my whore," he whispered, and it was not one of his sweet whispers. Not by a long shot.

It, like the look in his eyes, was tortured.

I told myself that didn't affect me either.

"Then what am I?" I asked.

"I want you to be my wife," he stated.

"And your son?" I pushed.

"He'll come around in time."

"Or maybe not," I retorted. "Maybe, for the father he adores, he'll just get better at hiding the pain."

Another flinch before Apollo closed the distance between us and lifted a hand to cup my jaw, murmuring, "Another fatal error."

I had no clue what he was talking about, but I wasn't going to ask.

He was touching me.

And I knew if I didn't end that, and this conversation, and *soon*, I'd most assuredly feel something.

So I started, "Apollo—" but he talked over me.

"Franka's drivel. This is what brought the dark to your eyes," he declared.

Oh.

That was what he was talking about.

He was absolutely right.

"Yes," I confirmed. "If there's dark in my eyes, she put it there. But she wasn't wrong. It wasn't nice how she said it but what she said was absolutely right. You have a lot to give, Apollo. I have nothing but my body. And I've taken what you can give. Including when you treat me like shit."

His fingers tensed into my skin as his eyes flashed, but I kept going.

"And really, is the world richer for me being in it?" I shook my head. "No. It isn't. Not in any—"

His fingers again tensed in my skin, his eyes again flashed, but brighter, angrier, before he interrupted me.

"Cease speaking."

"Cease interrupting me," I shot back.

When I did, suddenly (and worryingly), he smiled.

And I *so* wished he hadn't done that because I could tell myself I didn't feel a lot of things, but I couldn't tell myself I didn't feel that smile.

Crap.

"You listened to Franka's drivel, I won't listen to yours," he declared.

"Apollo—"

I stopped speaking this time not because he interrupted me but because he bent close even as his hand slid under my ear, his fingers curling back into my hair, and he pulled me closer.

"I have had maid and whore, paid for the best of the latter, and not one of them have I even remotely felt anything for. Certainly, I haven't fallen in love with them."

Oh my God.

Did he say what I thought he just said?

All of a sudden, I wasn't breathing.

"And, poppy," he kept going before I could cope with the bomb he'd just dropped, "can you honestly stand there and tell me the world isn't richer for you being in it when you just sat down to play at drinking tea with my daughter? I would doubt, if she understood the concept, that she would agree you do not make this world richer."

My heart clenched but I forced myself to breathe so I wouldn't pass out.

"As you know," he kept at me, "Christophe is reacting badly to the reminder that he lost his mother. He is far from unintelligent but too young to recognize what he's feeling is the resurgence of grief."

His hold on me tightened before he continued.

"And yes, poppy, this was caused by you, but that doesn't negate the fact that it has nothing to do with you and furthermore is not your fault."

I opened my mouth to say something, but Apollo didn't give me the opportunity.

"It's the fault of fate and it's *my* fault. He lashed out and I deserved it. I wasn't seeing to him and his making that clear caused me great pain. I deserved that too. But not for one second do I believe that my son won't come to terms with the situation and see the richness you bring to my life, my daughter's life, any life you touch, including his, and in the end, he will cherish it. I simply have to remember to take heed to the fact that he lost his mother and honor her memory, keep her alive for him in ways that don't involve you. This, I will do. And he will respond to it. I'm sure of it."

"You can't know that," I said quietly.

"I most assuredly can," he returned firmly.

And he didn't stop there.

"We're both agreed that the way I behaved after finding Christophe, and then finding you again in danger, was inexcusable. But Poppy," he leaned even closer, "*you followed the wrong Cora into the forest.* You put *yourself* in danger. Even if it was the right Cora, it would have been the wrong thing to do. Although I understand you were worried about Chris, it was reckless."

"I already admitted that," I pointed out.

"You did. And I let all that was happening get the better of me. I spoke careless words that harmed you. I forgot, with my son wishing so badly to be a man and thus acting with a maturity that is beyond his years, that he's just a boy. I also forgot, with the strength of will and heartiness of character you consistently display, that you are broken, and I must handle you with care."

Strength of will?

Heartiness of character?

He thought that of me?

And even with that, he also thought I was broken?

"I'm not broken," I whispered.

His voice went soft. "Dove, you're shattered. I know this because you think you're my whore. I know it because you think you don't have anything to offer when just your kindness moved two women who have not known you for long to arm themselves and venture into a frozen forest on the chance that you might need aid."

This, I had to admit, was true.

I just hadn't thought about it like that.

Apollo still wasn't done.

And he returned to an earlier theme I hadn't processed the first time he broached it, it pretty much rocked my world then, so I sure wasn't prepared to hear it a second time.

"It is my responsibility as the man who loves you and wants you to be his wife to mend what's broken in you. With Chris, I'll not forget again that I must care for my son. With you, I'll not forget again that I must treat you with care."

I stared into his eyes.

He stared into mine.

I waited for the room to melt. For the earth to shake. For someone wearing a trendy t-shirt and jeans to run into the room, point at me and shout that I'd been punked.

None of this happened.

So I asked, "You love me?"

"Yes, Maddie, I do," he replied instantly, and my stomach dropped.

But he *still* wasn't done.

"This being precisely why two days have passed with me needing to worry about the not insignificant fact we're at war, but the only thing on my mind was the look on my son's face when he showed me his pain and the look on yours when you gave me the same. Thus, for the first time in so long I don't think there was a time before, I had no idea what to do. I had to see to my son, who, I'm sorry, my dove, needed time away from you. But even so, I did not need the same. And I felt acutely the longer I left you with the words I spoke to you, the harder it would be for me to mend what I myself had broken. And *still* I was unable to act, fearing just this type of response. I only did anything because I'd been told you were in this house attending Élan, and I knew I could not have you under my roof and allow you to leave without at least you knowing the depth of my regret and the sincerity of my apology."

"You didn't know what to do?" I asked, my voice sounding as shocked as it was.

"No idea," he answered firmly, and it was not an admission.

It was a declaration.

Oh dear.

I had already started to feel something. A lot of somethings. A lot of *big* somethings.

But now I was feeling more.

And part of that was confusion.

"You didn't spend the last two days preparing to send me to Estranvegue?"

Suddenly, he dropped his hand and leaned away.

"Where did you hear of Estranvegue?" he asked in an eerily calm voice that I had the distinct feeling was not calm at all.

Uh-oh.

"It doesn't matter," I answered quickly.

"Oh yes," he returned. "It does."

"Apollo—"

"Where did you hear of Estranvegue?" he pushed.

I stared him in the eyes and didn't answer.

I had a more important question. I'd already asked it, but I still couldn't believe it.

So I asked it again.

"You're in love with me?"

"Yes, Madeleine," he bit out. "Now, where did you hear of Estranvegue?"

He was in love with me.

Apollo Ulfr (the good one) *was in love with me.*

Oh my *God.*

Oh yes.

I was feeling something.

Something big.

"You're in love with me," I breathed.

"Yes," he clipped, and his hand came back to curl around the side of my neck and he again bent close. "I'll ask again, poppy, where—?"

I cut him off with, "Why?"

He clamped his mouth shut then opened it to ask, "Why?"

"Yes. Why?"

He shook his head in confusion. "Why what?"

"Why are you in love with me?"

He blinked before he lifted his other hand to the other side of my neck, his eyes locked with mine and asked in return, "Why aren't you answering my question?"

"Because it's obviously more important to know why you're in love with me and because I'll get someone in trouble if I answer your question," I finally answered.

"You ask a question that has no answer," he returned. "Now answer mine which actually does."

Really?

He thought my question had no answer?

Honestly, I could not believe that men in this world, just like in my own, thought they could get away with that "I love you because I love you so just believe it and let me get back to the ballgame" nonsense.

Well, this man couldn't.

I mean, there was no ballgame to get back to. It was a war, and, well, a bunch of other stuff.

But still.

"It has an answer, Apollo," I retorted.

"You are correct. It does," he declared. "It has an answer that would take a decade to speak out loud. But, as you seem determined to have it, in an attempt to put it succinctly, I fell in love with you because I brought you to this world, a world all new to you, and turned my back on you. You didn't grow morose and retreat into yourself. You didn't become frightened, get overwhelmed by your fears and lock yourself away. You challenged a chef to a cooking duel over seafood."

I stared at him thinking that I did do that.

I didn't know it was hot-guy-from-another-world-love-worthy, but I did it.

Apollo kept talking.

"I fell in love with you because I was in a battle to the death and you didn't run, even when I told you to. You retrieved my sword and smashed a man on the head with a lamp in an effort to aid me."

I continued to stare mostly because I'd been so engrossed in all that was happening, I actually kind of forgot I did that.

That was something Finnie would do.

And the warrior queen Circe.

And, well...*me*.

Apollo continued to talk.

"Further, the most beautiful, most intelligent women I know have been torn to shreds in Franka Drakkar's claws. She got hold of you and you didn't blink." He paused and scowled at me. "Until she struck deeper, and you let it sink in then fester without speaking to me about it. That last is not part of why I love you, but it's part of you so it also is. Even though, at this point, it's bloody frustrating."

I wanted it, I'd demanded it, but I could take no more.

So I whispered, "You can stop talking now."

"Certainly," he replied. "Though I will only do so noting that I have not scratched the surface. For instance, I've not mentioned how it feels to have you give your body to me so freely, this freeing me in a manner I never had before. A manner I treasure. A manner that builds our closeness in ways I've also never experienced before. Or how magnificent it feels to know that my daughter extends an invitation to a tea party, and although things are not right between us, you still come and give her what she desires even knowing it might include a confrontation with me."

"You didn't stop talking," I pointed out shakily.

"No, I didn't. But I shall. Now, it's your turn to talk. How did you hear of Estranvegue?"

"I, well..." I paused. He kept scowling. So I went on, "Overheard two maids talking."

He didn't let me go but he straightened and looked over my head at the door as if he wanted to burn holes in it with his eyes.

Even though I didn't want to, I thought it prudent to get it all out there, so I added, "They said a few things about your mother, your father and, um...his wife."

He looked back at me, and when he did, it was me who felt like I'd go up in flames at the heat of his glare.

Thus, I blurted, "I'd kind of like to talk about you being in love with me again."

"Do you still wish to go to the other world?" he asked abruptly.

"We have more to talk about," I answered.

"Do you still wish to go to the other world?" he pressed.

I stared into his eyes.

Eyes that looked annoyed.

But they were the eyes of the man who loved me.

Then I whispered, "No."

"Do I have your love in return?" he asked.

Oh God.

God!

I swallowed.

Still staring into his eyes, I whispered, "Yes."

He slid his fingers up into my hair and instantly stopped looking annoyed.

He looked something *a whole lot* better.

Something that made a beautiful man impossibly more beautiful.

God.

"You love me," he whispered back.

I didn't repeat my response.

I repeated something else.

"We have a lot to talk about, Apollo."

"Yes, for instance, why *you* love *me*."

I was back to staring but it turned to glaring when I saw his lips twitch.

I didn't find anything funny. In fact, suddenly all that was happening overwhelmed me, all I'd held back feeling slammed into me, and I closed my eyes so I could focus on not letting it consume me.

He was in love with me.

Apollo Ulfr, general of a queen's army, man of many enterprises, father to two great kids, was in love with me.

I opened my eyes again when I felt his forehead come to rest on mine.

And the instant it did, he stated, "You have my vow that I will not speak to you in that manner again, Maddie. No matter what is on my mind, what I'm feeling, how significant the things are that are troubling me. Like my son, I lashed out at someone I loved, hoping they'd take the pain I was inflicting so I could release some of the pain I was feeling. I should be old enough to know better. You know I regret it. What I must know is that you trust it won't happen again."

"I...you...I," I stammered, pulled it together and finished, "Trust is built."

He moved away half an inch and stated, "Yes. But in this case, it must be earned. This I'll do."

Okay.

Yes.

This man loved me.

And I loved this man.

He pissed me off. Shit was crazy and it was extreme.

But I still loved him.

I didn't know if this was awesome or scary as shit.

Apollo's next words didn't help.

"Our last conversation prior to you doing something foolish and me retaliating by being cruel," he paused and stated severely, "something neither of us will repeat," he paused again and waited until I agreed to this demand by nodding before he continued, "was the beginning of a discussion about you moving to Karsvall. Alas, with things as they are with my son, you cannot do this. He is still struggling. This would not be wise."

I nodded because he was right.

It wouldn't be wise.

"However, I would like you to come to dinner," he carried on. "For myself. For Élan. She misses your presence at our meals, as do I. We'll dine together, watch and assess Chris's reaction. After, we'll discuss how we move on from there."

I missed him too.

And Élan.

And Chris.

But I didn't think dinner was a good idea.

So I told him, "Uh...Chris heard what the maids said as well. It was clear it freaked him. And when I, um...had words with him, they were kind of..." I paused to draw in a deep breath and finished, "Final."

I watched Apollo's jaw clench again before he released it and replied, "Then you will not come to dinner. You'll return to the dower house. I'll speak with my son about what he heard. Going forward, I wish Christophe to have my attention and presence and I hope you understand he must have both without you for a time. That said, it would be imprudent to continue your complete absence, for he must get used to you. But from this time forward, for his sake, we will take it much more slowly."

At that, I nodded.

"Tonight, I'll come to you after he's asleep," Apollo declared.

He'd come to me when Christophe was asleep.

I swallowed.

Then I nodded yet again.

"When I do, you and I will discuss all the things you wish to talk about," he concluded.

I found my voice and used it to say, "Okay."

He held my gaze and repeated my, "Okay," but his was way better.

It was way better because his eyes were warm, his voice was soft, and he was using his hands to pull me closer.

When he was a breath away, his gaze boring into mine, he whispered, "You love me."

I did.

I didn't say that.

I said, "I'm scared."

One of his hands moved from my hair so he could stroke my jaw with his thumb as something passed through his eyes that I felt in my belly. And it wasn't in a good way.

I would know why when he said quietly, "I have vowed to keep you safe, to make it so you never feel fear again, to give you better, and here I stand, with you so close but still holding yourself away, because it was me who failed at giving you all those things."

That wounded him too and I *so* knew how bad it felt when you did something stupid or thoughtless, something that affected other people.

It totally sucked.

Feeling that for him, I softly said, "Lo," and the instant I did, he closed his eyes.

Before I could say more, he opened them and promised, "I won't fail again, my dove."

He meant that.

Each word.

I felt wet hit my eyes as I replied with a shaky, "Okay, baby."

His fingers tensed against my scalp as the hand he'd slid to my jaw glided down my spine and he murmured, "And she gives herself back."

As if I wanted to prove his words true, I let my cloak and gloves fall to the floor, lifted my hands and pressed them to his chest.

"I will take care of all you give me this time, my poppy," he told me.

"I'm not sure what I give you, honey," I admitted. "But I appreciate that."

"Then part of how I'll take care of all you give me is to make certain you understand precisely what all of that is."

I thought that was a good plan.

Apollo was thinking something else.

I knew this when his arm wrapped around my waist and he pulled my body to his. My head tipped back. His dipped down. And then his lips were on mine.

But he didn't take my mouth.

"Remember this kiss," he ordered on a whisper, his eyes staring into mine.

There weren't many kisses Apollo had given me that I didn't remember.

I didn't share that.

I asked, "Why?"

"Because it is special," he answered.

"They're all special, Lo," I pointed out and watched his eyes smile even as I felt his lips do the same.

"They are, dove," he agreed. "But this one, the first I will give you knowing you return yours with love, will be the one I most treasure for the rest of my life."

Okay.

It was safe to say I was no longer uncertain if loving Apollo was awesome or scary as shit.

It was awesome.

It got more awesome when he quit rocking my world with words and did something else with his mouth, that being taking mine in a kiss.

It was deep. It was wet. It was long.

And it was unbearably sweet.

I slid my arms around his neck and melted into his kiss and I did it knowing my man was very right.

Because all of his kisses were special. All of them were worth remembering.

But the first one he gave me knowing that he loved me was the one I'd treasure most.

For the rest of my life.

28

I HAD A FEELING

Apollo stood at the top of the steps of Karsvall and watched Maddie with Achilles on Achilles' horse as they cantered out of sight into the woods toward the dower house.

As he watched, he did not allow himself to think on what she'd said, including the fact she was prepared to return to the other world and the life she led there that was no life at all, doing this rather than stay with him because he'd wounded her so with his words.

He thought only about the fact that he had her love and he hoped in having it, together, they could surmount the rest of their troubles.

His thoughts turning to those troubles, Apollo sighed as he moved to enter the house in order to find his son.

But he stopped when something caught the corner of his eye.

He turned that way and what he saw made him clench his teeth in frustration for it seemed even as he had managed to solve one important problem, he would yet again be delayed in attempting to solve another.

One could argue that nothing was more important than the woman he loved and his son.

Except, perhaps, the fate of two continents.

He stood and watched the sleigh moving toward the house, two of his men on horses leading the way, two following. Clearly, they'd intercepted it and decided to accompany the rider in the sleigh.

This was the right decision. He knew this when the sleigh got closer and he saw Valeria Drakkar.

His men guided her to the foot of the steps where they stopped.

Apollo stood and watched as she sat in the sleigh peering up at him from under her attractive fur cap. This went on for some time until it struck him that she was awaiting his descent in order for him to open the door of her sleigh for her.

Apollo held her gaze, planted his feet and crossed his arms on his chest.

He saw her face tighten with annoyance before she rose from her seat, throwing off the furs in her lap, and made her way out of the sleigh herself.

Apollo stayed unmoving as he watched her make her way up the steps, the luxurious heavy pelts of her cloak weighing it down so that it barely moved as she did, giving her the appearance of gliding.

When she was two steps away, he asked, "To what do I owe the honor of this visit?"

She stopped and looked up at him, her eyes narrowing. "Greetings to you too, Ulfr."

He inclined his head but said no more.

"Are we to speak on the steps to your familial home, or will you allow me entry in order that I can get warm?" she asked.

He would prefer to speak with her on the steps of his familial home.

Even so, he sighed and turned to the door. He opened it and shifted to the side, allowing her entry. She passed him without glancing at him, and as she did, he unfortunately got a whiff of her strong perfume.

He followed her in and shut the door against the cold.

He moved around her and caught her eyes before he swung out an arm.

"My study," he invited.

"My son?" she returned.

"I'll find him," he told her.

She made no move for long seconds before she tipped her head to the side. "Are you going to take my cloak?"

"As you won't be staying longer than needs be to explain why you're here, it would be a waste of effort for you to be far from it."

Again, her face tightened, but Apollo ignored it and tipped his head toward his study.

"I trust you can find your way there. I'll find Frey and we'll attend you shortly," he said.

"Would it be too much to ask if you could send a servant with a warm beverage?" she requested.

"Indeed, it would," he stated vaguely and moved away from her in order to search for Frey.

He could be anywhere. At the dower house to collect Finnie. With his men.

Fortunately, on his way to Frey and Finnie's room, the first place he intended to look, he ran into his housekeeper who was bustling his way.

"Do we have company?" she asked as Apollo stopped.

"We do," he answered. "I'll need hot tea served in my study. Also, set the staff to finding Drakkar and asking him to join me there."

"Of course," she murmured, nodding and turning to leave.

Seeing her do it, Apollo decided, since fate was not on his side in allowing him time to see to the variety of things he had to see to, he'd take his chances when he had them.

"Lucretia," he called, and his housekeeper stopped and turned a questioning gaze his way. "It's come to my attention that two maids were gossiping about myself and my family in the halls of Karsvall."

Her face paled and her eyes widened. She understood the severity of this.

Apollo kept speaking.

"This will not be countenanced. It's my understanding my son overheard their chatter. Although this is not a minor infraction, in this instance I will trust you to find the two maids who participated in this behavior and deal with them. However, all the staff should know, if it should happen again, I will be dealing with them." He paused and held her eyes before he finished, "Personally."

"Of course, Lord Apollo," she replied shakily.

"Now, please find Drakkar."

She nodded and hurried away.

Apollo did not hurry to the study.

When he arrived, he found that Valeria had the wherewithal to divest herself of her own cloak, gloves and hat, for she had. She'd tossed them on one of the chairs in front of his desk and was sitting in the other one, drumming her fingers on the arm.

He closed the door behind him and her head turned his way.

"You do know, I journey from Brunskar on an errand of urgency *and* assistance," she snapped as he made his way into the room.

"Actually, madam, I did not know that. I did ask your purpose here. You just didn't answer," he replied, moving to the side of his desk farthest away from her and leaning a thigh against it.

"Well, I have," she retorted.

"And, pray, what is this urgent errand?" he queried.

"I fear I'll have trouble sharing it, since my throat is still frozen from my mad dash across the tundra," she said by way of answer.

Apollo studied the woman, a woman he'd never liked because she gave him no reason to, wondering how on earth she had birthed Frey.

Then he told her, "Tea has been ordered. As has the attendance of your son. Although there are those capable of great magic in this house, I'm afraid no one here is at my command to snap their fingers and provide either for you."

She glared at him.

Apollo withstood it and suggested, "Perhaps we can begin this discussion prior to Frey joining us."

"If we do, I'll need to say twice what I could say just once."

"You could also simply tell me what you have to say and I could go to the taxing effort of reporting it to your son."

"I'm his mother," she returned. "I would also like to see him, and my grandchild."

She did not ask after Finnie. Although Apollo noted it, he didn't ask about it for he didn't care in the slightest about the answer.

And neither would Finnie.

When he made no response, her gaze turned shrewd and she asked, "You're attending the Bitter Gales?"

He didn't answer verbally. He simply inclined his head.

"And you'll be bringing the other Ilsa with you?"

He responded to that, and even if the way she asked her question irritated him, he didn't allow her to see it.

"Her name is Madeleine, and she is my betrothed, so yes. She will attend the Gales on my arm."

The shrewdness left her face and spite replaced it, reminding him precisely why he'd never liked her, and she declared, "You must know what everyone is saying about you and this...*Madeleine*."

"Indeed, I don't know," he replied. "I also don't care."

"*She* will care, especially as you take her to the Gales."

"That's doubtful," Apollo replied, and he would have believed this statement to be truth but weeks ago.

However, Maddie was vulnerable now.

He would have to have a word with Frey and Finnie, Lahn and Circe. At the Gales, they would need to keep an eye on his Maddie and assist him in keeping her away from those who would cause harm, either intentionally or not.

"Men do what they will and what others think matters not," she returned. "Women are not made that way."

Apollo shook his head. "I have had the rare and exquisitely pleasurable experience, madam, of learning with great fullness how each woman is quite unique. I'm certain there are some who are not made that way. I'm also certain there are those who are."

She clamped her mouth shut, and at that moment, thankfully, the door to his study opened and Frey strode in.

He took one look at his mother, his face hardened, but his lips muttered, "Brilliant."

Valeria's back shot straight before she snapped to her son, "Is that how you greet your mother?"

"I would say it is, since it was how I did," Frey replied, and Apollo fought back his smile as he looked to his boots.

"With the welcome I've received from the two of you, I'm uncertain I wish to relay the crucial message that's been given to me," she announced.

Frey stopped five feet from her and crossed his arms on his chest.

"I suppose you could make that decision. However, word has been received that father has wasted no time in petitioning the queen for a dissolution of his union to you. Should that happen, unless Calder is feeling generous, you'll need to fall back on your own House to absorb your upkeep. As you've been rather unfriendly to them over the decades, it's doubtful they'll be keen to do that. And if I have a word with Calder, I fear he won't be feeling very generous. So, in the end, you must hope Malcolm Turnish will take you to wife. But I assume your sojourn at Brunskar means Turnish has not offered you welcome."

Apollo looked from his boots to Frey's mother to see her eyes were aimed at her son and they were slits.

"What, precisely, have I done to you that you feel it's appropriate to treat me in this manner?" she asked.

"Precisely, nothing," Frey answered immediately. "And a mother who does nothing is no mother at all. Thus, I have no qualms treating you in this manner."

She stared at her son a moment before she swallowed.

Frey spoke on.

"Now, why are you here with bird nor man bringing news you would be?"

"My message was too sensitive to trust to bird or man," she answered.

"And your message?" Frey prompted.

She drew in breath through her nose, looked to Apollo, then back to her son and declared, "Antoine has perished."

"Fuck," Frey muttered as her words made Apollo straighten from the desk.

Frey looked to him and Apollo shook his head.

Frey turned his attention back to his mother.

"Franka sent you with this message," he stated.

"She did," she confirmed.

"How did he die?" Apollo asked.

Valeria looked to him. "They have had him, and have been torturing him, for a great deal of time. There is only so much a body can take. He simply expired."

Apollo raised a brow. "And they shared this directly with Franka?"

She shook her head. "As she would, during her discussions with them, Franka demanded to see him again to ascertain his condition. It was a coincidence, and I daresay a grave error...theirs...that when they opened the mirror to show him to her, he took his final breath."

At that, Apollo felt something he thought he would never in his life feel.

Sorry for Franka Drakkar.

He then felt Frey's gaze and turned his eyes to his cousin.

"They no longer have anything to hold over her," he noted.

"And therefore, she'd have no reason to act for them," Apollo replied.

"True," Valeria put in and both men looked to her. "But Franka is a Drakkar. As you bid, she shared with them that you erroneously came to the conclusion that it was Kristian who was behind the plot against," her eyes slid to Apollo, "*Madeleine.* Also as you bid, she shared that you've imprisoned him and his family in the dungeons of Brunskar to await transport to Snowdon to stand trial for treason. A guilty verdict that carries a sentence from which any sister would wish to save her brother. Although her lover is dead and they have nothing to hold over her, her brother is incarcerated and what he would face if found guilty means she has something to bargain with. And this she's doing. The plan proceeds as hatched, with that alteration."

"Her bargain?" Apollo prompted.

"That once they have done what they wish to do, Kristian and his family will be freed and she, as well as her brother, will be allowed to continue their lives unhindered by whatever malice they intend," Valeria answered. "But, as you wished, she has pressed them to act and do it quickly, now doing so in order to save Kristian rather than to halt the torture of her lover."

"And we're to believe Franka continues to put herself in jeopardy for kin and country?" Frey asked, his voice dripping with disbelief.

Valeria cut sharp eyes to her son. "They killed her lover."

"Indeed," Frey replied. "But this is Franka. I'm certain she'll find something to amuse her that will assuage her grief."

She lifted her chin and held her son's gaze. "It is clear you do not know your cousin well, my son. They *tortured* then *killed* the only man she's ever loved. This is not for kin and country. This is for vengeance."

"That, I can believe," Frey murmured.

"Then I bid you to believe it," Valeria retorted. "She was not wailing her despair when she imparted her message on me. But she was determined. Exceptionally determined. And I do believe you know your cousin well enough to know what that means."

It was then Frey lifted his chin.

He knew.

At this juncture, a knock came on the door and Apollo called, "Come."

Lucretia appeared holding a large silver tray on which was tea, to which Valeria said irately, "Finally."

Apollo ignored her and moved, ordering Lucretia, "See to Lady Drakkar."

When she nodded, he looked to Frey, but Frey was already heading to the door.

Once outside it, Apollo closed it and followed Frey who'd continued walking.

They stopped some ten feet away from the study and turned to each other.

"Your thoughts?" Frey asked.

"I would like to look in Franka's face when those words were delivered," Apollo answered. "But I cannot think that she spoke false to your mother. Our protections are such that they cannot break them. If she's shared our plan, they'd know it was an ambush and she would not be suggesting we carry on with it as it stands. She'd be altering it."

"Agreed. There are no vulnerabilities to our plans and Franka knows this."

Apollo nodded.

"I'll send a return message through my mother," Frey stated.

"And I'll leave you to do that. I must have a word with my son," Apollo replied, and Frey's focus on him intensified.

"All is well?"

"Not close," Apollo confided. "But I'm working on it."

"I couldn't help but note that today, Madeleine spent some time in your study with you," Frey observed.

"At least with that, all is well."

"I'm glad of it, cousin," Frey murmured. "The rift was concerning Finnie. However, she feels she doesn't know Maddie well enough to broach it."

He tipped his head to Frey. "Feel free to share this news with your wife to ease her worries. Now, I must see to my son." He looked to the door of the study then back to Frey. "In order to rest before she again leaves, your mother is welcome to stay the night here."

Frey grinned before noting, "Well done, saying that without wincing."

Apollo shook his head feeling his lips quirking.

"However," Frey went on, "I believe she'll be perfectly comfortable at The Swan."

Frey wanted her under Karsvall's roof less than Apollo did.

"Your choice," Apollo murmured.

Frey nodded and turned toward the study doors.

Apollo moved to the stairs.

He found Christophe in the first place he looked, his room.

His son was sitting at his desk, head bent, quill in hand, scribbling on a piece of paper.

His was so engrossed in this endeavor, Apollo leaned a shoulder against the doorjamb and took the time to enjoy watching his son's concentration for long moments before he saw Christophe start and look his way.

"Papa," he said.

"If you're at your studies, Chris, I won't disturb you," Apollo replied.

Chris quickly turned the paper on his desk over as he shook his head and stated, "I'm not at my studies."

He was writing and what he was writing was not Apollo's to see. That was his son's prerogative, it always was, and it always would be. Apollo never read Christophe's writing unless asked to do so. Indeed, no one did, unless it was an assignment from his tutor. And Christophe was very particular about who he allowed to read it.

It had heartened him when Christophe had offered that gift to Maddie on the way to Brunskar. However, as things were as they were, he had since reneged.

Still, Apollo took this as an invitation and entered the room.

Christophe didn't move from his chair, so Apollo came to a stop several feet in front of his desk.

"I've been told," he started cautiously, not sharing who told him even knowing his son would know, "that you've overhead some servants gossiping."

Red crept into Christophe's cheeks as he looked down to the quill he was still holding, a quill he was twirling in his fingers.

Apollo waited the time it took Christophe to speak.

Finally, he did.

"They said some things about Grandpapa."

"I know," Apollo told him and gained his son's eyes. "This is unfortunate, Chris. Although unfortunate, I wish you to know that I had intended to share this with you when you were older."

A stubborn firmness started setting in Christophe's face, that same firmness Apollo had seen often whenever it was mentioned he was too young for anything, so Apollo continued.

"Alas, you know of it now. Likely not all of it and I will not take this opportunity to share the rest. You're still too young."

"But—" Christophe started.

"You're too young, my son," Apollo stated quietly. "What I will tell you now is that a long time ago, your grandfather made a decision. It is my opinion that it was the wrong decision. When it's your time to know the fullness of this story, you'll be old enough to form your own opinion. But regardless of either of our opinions, it has all long since happened and there is nothing we can do to change it now."

Christophe held his gaze and declared, "Auntie Lynne was your mother."

"She was, and in the ways she could be, she was a good one."

"You grew up without her."

"I did and I didn't." It was he who held his son's gaze when he shared, "There is much a mother will do to be with her children. My mother did all that."

Christophe looked back to his quill. "You...you had to..." he trailed off and said no more.

"Chris, son, please look at me," Apollo called, and Christophe lifted his eyes to his father. "I did not suffer. It was the life I knew and I had her love. I had my father's love. It was not a usual situation, but it was mine."

"Is this why Grandmother never comes to see us?" he asked. "Because we aren't hers?"

"It is," Apollo confirmed.

"Is she angry?" he asked.

"I can't know. What I do know is that she's feeling something that keeps her away and that might be what she's feeling. She also may be sad. But whatever it is, it's hers to feel and her decision to stay away."

"Was she mean to you?" he whispered.

"Never," Apollo replied. "When I was older, I would understand why she was as she was with her husband. But she never was that way with me."

"The maids said—"

"The maids know little and should have said nothing at all. And this, Chris, is the lesson you should take from what's happened. When you speak, you must be aware of what you say, how it can be taken and who may hear it. But mostly, if you speak at all, you should know what you're talking about."

He nodded to confirm he'd heard his father's message then rubbed his lips together before he asked, "Did...erm, well...Maddie...is she...?" He drew in a deep breath and let it out, saying quietly, "She seemed very sad."

"What they said wounded her deeply. We talked about this. She's feeling better now."

Apollo felt relief sweep through him when he saw the same on his son's face.

This was short-lived, however, before he returned to looking troubled.

Apollo would know why when he asked, "Are you sending her away?"

"No," Apollo replied, and when he did, unfortunately, his son hid his reaction so Apollo could not know his thoughts.

"They said you were sending her away," Christophe noted.

"They were in error," Apollo explained.

Christophe rubbed his lips together again.

Apollo let him for a while before he took a chance.

"As I explained, your sister and I enjoy her company. Maddie also enjoys ours. I've asked her to dinner tonight, but she has refused, worried about you and what you'd heard. She also is simply worried about you. I would like for her to join us again soon. I can find my times with her, as can Élan, times we don't share with you. Therefore, if you don't wish her company, I need you to tell me." He lowered his voice when he finished, "But I must be honest with you, my son. You must follow your heart and I hope you always share with me freely what's in it. I will do my best to listen with no recriminations. I will return that favor right now and share that for your sister, for me, and also for Maddie, I would hope you will dig deep and find times that we can all share together. If you can't, this will be understood. But that does not negate the fact that I hope that you can."

"I think..." Christophe shook his head but then kept talking. "I think she was so sad because she thought you were sending her away."

"You think correctly."

He rubbed his lips together some more before he noted, "She's nice to Élan."

"She cares for her deeply."

Christophe looked back at his quill and kept his attention there when he spoke on. "You were angry with her for looking for me."

"I was," Apollo confirmed.

"I got her into trouble," Chris whispered to his quill and Apollo's gut tightened with hope.

"She and I have spoken, Chris," he said gently. "And that is past. She will not do something so foolish again, even if moved to do it through her concern for you and Élan, and I will not lose my temper with her in the manner I did."

Christophe said nothing, simply contemplated his quill.

Apollo decided he'd had enough.

He changed the subject by asking softly, "Are you done with your studies, son?"

Christophe looked to him and nodded.

"I have not tested you with your sword in some time," Apollo remarked and watched his son's eyes light. He smiled at him and turned to the door, ordering, "Get our swords. I'll meet you outside."

"But...it's gone dark, Papa," Christophe called to his back.

At the door, Apollo turned back to his son.

"Then it's good we have torches. But not every swordfight is fought in the sun, Chris. To be prepared, you must be prepared for anything."

Christophe nodded enthusiastically.

"Swords," Apollo prompted.

Down went the quill and up went his son out of his seat.

He dashed to his wardrobe.

Apollo drew in a breath and let it out as he walked out of the room.

It was only when he was well down the hall that he allowed himself to smile.

~

"AND AT THAT, Princess Arianna stepped onto the cloud..."

Apollo stopped reading and looked down at his daughter.

She was asleep.

Then again, she always fell asleep at that part the third time he read it.

He closed the book softly and laid it on her nightstand. Carefully disengaging her from his arm around her, he rolled her to her side and exited her bed. He pulled the covers up high over her and tucked her in before he bent deep to brush a kiss on her temple. He then straightened, turned out the lamps and walked out of the room, keeping the door open an inch as she liked it.

He moved to Christophe's room and saw his door opened an inch.

As he liked it.

He pushed it open further and moved through the darkened room toward his son's bed. The light from the hall barely illuminated the space. Therefore, Apollo gave it time for his eyes to adjust before he bent over his boy, pulled the covers to his neck and carefully tucked him in.

Awake, he was too old for it.

Asleep, Apollo could do as he liked.

So he brushed his fingers across his son's brow, sweeping the hair away from his skin. Then he bent and touched his lips to that hair before he straightened and moved away.

He was halfway across the room when he heard a sleepy, "Papa."

He turned and softly replied, "I woke you."

"No."

Apollo said nothing.

Christophe didn't either.

When this lasted some time, Apollo asked, "Do you need something, Chris?"

There was a long hesitation before Christophe answered, "No...I just..." Another hesitation before, "I just wanted to say goodnight."

Apollo strode back to the bed, bent in and wrapped his hand around the side of his son's neck.

"Goodnight, my son," he whispered.

"'Night, Papa," Chris whispered back.

Apollo gave his neck a squeeze then moved back to the door. He pulled it to almost closed behind him but kept it open an inch.

He then strode to his room, grabbed the cloak that was lying across the foot of his bed and exited, swinging it on.

He found Torment as he requested, blanketed and saddled, waiting for him at the foot of the steps at the front of Karsvall.

He mounted his horse and kicked in his heels.

Torment burst into a gallop across the snow.

He made the dower house quickly and noted when he did that there were lights streaming around the curtains from more windows than normal. The front sitting room. Maddie's upstairs bedroom. From the side where the kitchen was. From the back where her maids stayed.

He rode Torment to the stables, made short work of settling him in for the night, and as he left, he made certain to secure the door against the chill.

Instead of moving to the front of the house as he would normally do, with the light coming from the kitchen, thinking perhaps Maddie sat with her friends there for an evening natter, he approached the side door.

He opened it and closed it swiftly to limit the draught he allowed in. Once he'd dropped the bar to lock it for the night, he turned to the kitchen to see only Cristiana sitting in a tufted chair by the fire, feet up on a small padded stool, shawl around her shoulders, knitting in her lap.

Her head was turned to him and her face was expressionless when she greeted him much less enthusiastically than normally.

"Lord Apollo."

"Cristiana," he returned. "Where's Maddie?"

She returned her attention to her knitting, saying, "Sitting room."

Apollo began to move that way before he stopped and looked back at the woman.

"Don't you have a husband to look after?"

Her lips quirked as her eyes came back to him. "I'd hope, by this time and with his age, he's able to look after himself." Sharpness entered her gaze when she finished, "I also have a girl to look after."

Her loyalty to Madeleine was welcome.

Her inference was not.

He said nothing.

He just dipped his chin and moved from the room.

He found Cristiana was correct. Maddie was in the sitting room, and he had a sense of foreboding when he saw her not reclining on the sofa reading, or chatting with Loretta and Meeta, but at the window. She'd pulled a curtain slightly back and was staring out into the night, her expression unreadable.

He'd seen her like that before, the night Franka Drakkar had said words that tore into her soul.

He had hoped their earlier discussion had given her much to think on that would prove Franka's words for what they were, intentionally malicious and utterly untrue.

It would appear it hadn't.

"I hope, my dove, that Hans and Loretta aren't out in this chill," he quipped as he entered the room and her head whipped his way. "And if they are, I would hope Hans is keeping her warm. But if he is, I would guess it's in a way that you should not be witnessing."

"They're not out there," she told him, and he stopped advancing to her, this placing him in the center of the room.

"Then what are you looking at, poppy?"

"I..." She looked to the window before she dropped the curtain and turned to him. "Nothing. I was thinking. I don't know why I do that standing at a draughty window, but I guess it's because it seems so serene out there. It helps me order my thoughts." She shrugged. "There aren't a lot of windows you can look out of in my world and witness complete stillness."

"The other world," he corrected.

"What?" she asked.

"This is your world, Maddie. It's the *other* world that has limited stillness."

Her teeth came out to worry her lip.

Apollo didn't like that either, but he continued to give her distance and asked quietly, "What were you thinking on, Maddie?"

"How's Chris?" she asked immediately in return.

If he was told to guess what filled her thoughts that would be it.

"We talked," he answered. "Considering the subject matter, there was not much I could share. This frustrates him for he's nearly nine, but he thinks he's thirty-nine. However, we ended our talk by battling with wooden swords in the snow. So I think, for now, he's fine."

"You battled?" she asked, eyes wide.

"It's play," he explained. "Élan enjoys tea parties. Chris enjoys swordplay."

"Oh," she whispered, but said no more.

Therefore, he pressed, "Was Chris the only thing on your mind?"

"Not exactly," she replied.

He felt his face go soft when he went on, "And what else was on your mind?"

"Well," she began and threw out a hand. "The subject matter."

"My father, my mother and Lady Ulfr," he stated.

She nodded and Apollo didn't delay in sharing what she clearly wished to know.

"As still happens today, my father's marriage was arranged. He could have opposed it, but he did not. This was because, although she came from a much lesser House, his intended held great beauty."

She nodded again as she leaned her weight into a hand on the back of the sofa, settling in for his story.

He didn't like this for it meant she settled in away from him.

But he sensed she needed it, so he gave it to her and carried on.

"She was also a kind woman, if a quiet one. Unfortunately, it became clear early in their marriage that she could not provide him an heir. When this happens, the Head of a House can accept it and the next in line will inherit his role. My father could not know this, for Achilles was born after me, but we know now that Achilles, who would have been the next in line, would have made a fine Head for the House of Ulfr. Though, he should have known it for my uncle was as fine a man as Achilles. But even if he could know it, the man he was, Father would still have made the decision he made. A decision that many Heads made then, before then and even now, should they find their wives unable to provide an heir. They find a surrogate so they can see to that task personally."

He knew this information shocked her by the expression on her face.

But all she said was, "Okay."

"My mother, however, was no surrogate," he went on. "She too, had great beauty and my father held some affection for her. Thus, he installed her in this house, and if lore is true, fully enjoyed her being here."

He witnessed her flinch, but even so, he continued.

"She had me. As she was no surrogate arranged to provide an heir, although I believe she knew her place, she still expected to enjoy raising the son she bore for her lover. This didn't happen. I was raised in Karsvall with my father and his wife. Although she lived quite close and I visited her regularly, it was not as regular as my mother would have liked. This caused her to protect against another pregnancy. Time passed and I was too young to know what occurred in that time or how those involved felt about it. I just know that many years after she had me, my father sent my mother away and I was raised fully here in Karsvall with him and his wife, seeing my mother only during short visits my father would allow."

"That's awful," she whispered, the tone she said those words stating clear she felt it was exactly that.

"It is, yet it isn't," he replied. "I know the gossip, but those who speak it don't know either how those involved felt about what was happening. I only know that Patience Ulfr was a good woman who may not have showered me with adoration, but that simply wasn't her nature. She was thoughtful. She was kind. But she was sad. Perhaps sad her marriage became what it became, for I cannot know how they were before I came into this world, but they were very distant in the time I spent with them. Perhaps she was sad because I was not hers and she wished her own child. Perhaps sadness was simply part of her disposition. I cannot know. I never asked, but even if I did, she was not the kind of woman to tell. Though, regardless of her consistent sadness, she never made me suffer for it."

"And your mother?"

"Once I became old enough to decide how I would spend my time, I saw her far more frequently. After my father passed and Lady Patience returned to her own House, I moved my mother back to this one. She left this world a year after Ilsa died."

When he stopped speaking, she studied him and said nothing.

He allowed this for some time before he stopped doing so.

"Now that I've shared that, my dove, may I ask why you're so far away?"

She didn't answer him.

She asked her own question.

"Is that why you seem to have an issue with me being in this house?"

"It is," he confirmed. "I have many good memories of the times I shared with my mother in this house, both before my father died and after she returned. But you are not her. I don't like you here not only because it reminds me of who she was to my father, but also it reminds those around us of the same. And I do not want them to think of you in that way for you are not that to me. You are far more."

He watched her features soften as she noted, "But now, with the way Chris is feeling, I can't move."

"Alas, you cannot. However, you were right those weeks ago. For him, you should remain here until he's comfortable with you being there."

She pressed her lips together, looking uncertain for a moment, before she asked quietly, "Why didn't you tell me any of this?"

"You must agree that we had more important things to discuss," he remarked, and her brows shot up.

"More important than that?" she queried.

"Absolutely," he returned.

"But...I mean..." She shook her head as if clearing it. "Apollo, your mother, your father, growing up like that, what you must have felt, there really isn't much that's more important than that."

"There is," he retorted. "You."

The instant his last word passed his lips, he watched her entire body sway back as her lips parted.

Then he watched her eyes get bright.

And at that, he was done.

So he inquired, "Now, will you come to me or will I be going to you?"

She again didn't answer him.

She whispered, "I should have shared."

"What?" he asked.

She held his eyes, hers still bright, and repeated, "I should have shared."

"Poppy—"

She interrupted him to explain. "I should have shared what that woman said bothered me so much."

"You should have," he agreed gently.

"I'm not what she said I was," she stated.

"No." His agreement to that was far less gentle. "You aren't."

He watched her draw in a deep breath before she admitted, "I still don't know what I am."

"To that, what I must ask, my dove, is why you need to be anything but you?"

She blinked as if supremely perplexed by his comment.

"Sorry?"

"You are amusing. You are spirited. You are intelligent, loyal and brave. And you've led a life where lesser women, women such as your own mother, would long since have admitted defeat. But you never did. Can you not be content with all that is you, knowing there is so much of it, and enjoy what those around can offer you in return? Most specifically me, who simply wants you to leave the life you led behind, as well as the demons it left you with, and have one where I can make you happy."

And again, she did not answer.

She looked to the seat of the sofa.

But he saw the tear slide from her eye and glide down her cheek.

He felt the sight of that lone tear pierce his heart.

"Madeleine, please come to me," he whispered, and she returned her attention to him.

"You give me a lot," she whispered back.

"I do. But that scale is not unbalanced."

"I—"

"Maddie, please cease listening and *hear* me. I shared earlier the gifts you've bestowed on me, these being the reasons why I love you. And even after sharing those, you gifted me with something I treasure above all, your love. I don't know how to guide you into seeing that there is nothing you must do or be or give for others to understand irrevocably having you in our lives is worthwhile. Again, specifically *me*, for I have you in ways others don't. I have your heart."

"Is that enough?" she asked, and at her question, Apollo fought back the searing sensation that burned through his chest.

And that sensation made his tone harsh when he declared, "Would that I had the time to find the other me, to locate your father, to take my time in ways they would most assuredly not enjoy to communicate *precisely* how I feel that they have given you what they gave you that you'd ever think to utter such a question."

She stared at him.

Then she said, "I take it that's enough."

"It bloody is," he bit out.

"Okay," she whispered.

"Now, you have one second to come to me. If you don't—"

He didn't finish.

She took a step to him.

Then she took another.

That was the last simple step she took.

The rest of the way, she ran.

His body rocked back when hers hit his. But when it did, he locked his arms around her, hers curved around his shoulders and she shoved her face in his neck.

"I was rather hoping once you ceased standing across the bloody room and came to where you belonged, you'd press your mouth somewhere else," he muttered irritably.

Her body shook in his arms for several seconds before her laughter became audible.

Still laughing, she pulled her face out of his neck, rolled up on her toes and pressed her closed lips hard against his.

That was better.

It didn't remain that way, for she almost instantly pulled away.

"Does that work?" she asked, her eyes still bright with unshed tears but those tears were going nowhere. He knew this because behind the wet was the light of amusement.

He missed that light.

And he was immensely pleased to have it back.

"Barely," he drawled in answer.

The amusement in her eyes flared then slowly died but only so the skin around her mouth could soften as her gaze roamed his face.

It found his and his breath stuck in his throat at what he saw as she whispered, "So this is what it feels like not to be broken."

Bloody hell.

His arms around her convulsed, but for the life of him, he couldn't get his mouth to move in answer.

She didn't need it.

She had something else to say.

And that was, "Love you, Lo."

Suddenly, Apollo was done talking.

So he stopped them doing it.

But how he did that, he used his mouth.

And in return, his Maddie used hers.

THE ROOM DARK, the weight of Maddie's soft warm naked body resting on him, her knees high at his sides, her forehead in his throat, her fingers trailing lazily along his shoulder, when he thought she was near sleep and was looking forward to the same with his dove held close, he felt her move.

No.

He felt her shake.

"Madeleine?"

She started shaking more.

His arms, already around her, tightened as he lifted his head in an attempt to peer at her through the dark. This attempt failed. All he could see were the poppy highlights in her auburn hair sparkling in the firelight.

"Maddie," he said more sharply.

She tilted her head and shoved her face in the side of his neck, her body shaking harder.

He thought she was weeping and could not imagine why, when a delicate snort filled the room, and she shook even harder.

That snort was not from weeping.

It was from laughing.

He rolled her to her back, mostly covering her, and lifted his head to look down at her just as her laughter became audible.

She clutched at him as it did, giggling uncontrollably.

"What is funny?" he demanded to know.

She kept laughing, and also shaking, and further snorting, but she didn't speak.

"Madeleine," he gave her a squeeze, "what is funny?"

She pulled her face out of his neck, and still laughing, stammered, "I...you...I was..."

Then she shoved her face back into his neck, clutched him tighter, and burst into renewed laughter.

He waited.

This took some time.

Finally, her laughter began to wane, and he said, "Now, would you please share your amusement?"

She dropped her head to the bed, but did this still holding on to him, and found his eyes in the dark.

"You know," she began, "since practically the minute this started between us, I felt shit because of all the things you were giving me."

He found this alarming but had no chance to remark on it.

She lifted her head slightly from the pillow and slid her hand to his jaw.

"I like nice things, Apollo."

She said this like it was an admission when he knew not one soul who didn't.

Thus, he replied, "I do as well, Madeleine. Everyone does."

He felt her body stiffen slightly under his and he knew that thought had not occurred to her.

When she said nothing, he prompted, "And this caused your hilarity?"

"No. I mean, yes...I mean, not entirely. Why I was laughing is that you were giving me so much. Nice clothes. A lovely home. Friends." She paused, sweeping his lower lip with her thumb, before she whispered, "Élan. *You.*"

He felt his gut warm, but she was not finished.

"And now I get that's how it is, if people care about each other. There are lots of ways to give."

His voice was gruff when he agreed, "There are."

She slid her hand back into his hair in order to pull his face closer to hers as she continued to explain. "Why I was laughing, sweetheart, is that today, you gave me something else."

"And what I gave you was funny?" he inquired.

"Yes," she replied.

"And what was that?"

He felt her body soften under his as she tensed her hand at his head and brought him ever nearer.

And her voice was teasing, yet husky, when she answered, "Oh, nothing big. Not like a really nice cloak or a kickass dress." Her voice dipped low. "Just your love and, well...*me*."

The warmth in his gut increased as he slid his hand up her side and queried, "You?"

She nodded. "You gave me me. All those things I felt guilty for, and your grand finale was falling in love with me and giving me back *me*."

His gut still warm, the area around his heart now warming, he continued to slide his hand up and in, over her chest to her throat until he had it at her jaw.

"I'll warn you, my dove, that was hardly my grand finale."

She turned her head so she could kiss the palm of his hand and the warmth inside intensified as she righted her head and whispered, "I had a feeling."

The moment she finished uttering the words, she lifted her head and pressed her mouth to his.

Apollo slanted his head and took what she offered.

Then he gave her more.

29

HAPPY?

I collapsed on the somewhat dingy, overstuffed couch by the fire and muttered, "This world needs at least trains."

I heard Circe and Finnie's quiet chuckles as I gratefully stretched my legs out in front of me.

"You'll get used to it," Finnie said, and I looked to her.

"Easy for you to say," I returned on a smile. "You spend most of your time on a galleon having adventures on the high seas. Who cares if a galleon goes fast? You're having adventures on the high seas."

"I've sat often enough in a sleigh to get you," she replied.

I figured she did, so I said nothing.

"Tomorrow, we'll make Fyngaard and the Winter Palace and we won't see a sleigh for, oh, I don't know, at least three days," Finnie went on.

"It isn't much," I mumbled. "But it's something."

"You also get to meet Cora and Tor," Circe added. "Lahn told me they're already there, Valentine with them, casting enchantments or...whatever."

At least there was meeting Cora (the real one) and Tor to look forward to.

"The dream team unites," I murmured.

Circe grinned at me before she grinned at Finnie.

At this point, Meeta collapsed on the couch beside me (but she did it far more elegantly than I did).

Watching her do it, it occurred to me that Meeta had been within spitting distance of me any time she could since we left Karsvall.

Then again, she was Spock to my Kirk. That was where she was supposed to be.

Not to mention, the last time we took a road trip, things got extreme.

Once settled, she muttered, "If I sit my arse in another one of those contraptions and glide through the frost that settles in the bones never again in my life, I will be content."

At her words, I burst out laughing.

Obviously, we were on our way to Fyngaard to attend the Bitter Gales. All of us. Apollo's men. Frey's men. And Lahn's men. The only ones who weren't there were Lavinia and Valentine. They were off on unexplained magical errands seeing to the safety of two continents.

The good news about this was that I got to wear another awesome gown and attend a ball where intrigue was afoot (and the gown I'd been fitted for for the Bitter Gales was not just awesome, it was *awesome*).

The bad news about this was that Fyngaard was a two weeks' ride away from Karsvall and I was d-o-n-e *done* with sleigh rides.

Sure, at first, they seemed great.

But after you'd spent a bazillion hours in a sleigh, not so much.

On this thought, Tunahn, who was cavorting on the floor, grabbed hold of my skirt and tugged hard (and cavorting for Tunahn included finding ways to get into trouble, thus earning a scolding from his mother, a scolding he would ignore, for the instant she set him down again he'd merrily go about his business finding another way to get into trouble).

Since he was freaking strong and his tug was misshaping the knit of my skirt, I bent forward, snatched him up and held his heavy, squirming, big boy baby body in front of me.

I looked into his eyes and shared, "It's rude to pull a woman's skirt."

His response was to curl his fingers into the low square neckline of my gown and yank it out.

I cuddled him to me, laughing, but effectively stopping him from exposing me to everyone in the lounge of the inn where we were staying.

I tipped my chin down to see his intelligent, but annoyed, dark eyes were tipped up to me, and I shared, "And that's even ruder."

He slapped my chest with his hand.

I laughed again, but as I did it, I felt something from across the room, so I turned my eyes that way.

My breath caught when I saw Apollo standing and talking with Laures, but his gaze was on me.

And the look on his face was hot, sweet, and like all things Apollo, beautiful.

I liked that look. I liked what I figured that look said. But as much as I liked all this, I felt something else, and my eyes moved again.

This time they caught on Chris and my heart stuttered in my chest as I saw he was watching his father.

Not looking at him.

Watching him.

Then my heart stuttered again when Chris's focus slid to me.

I swallowed before I sent a small smile his way.

He lifted his chin and looked away.

Progress.

Only a little, but I'd take what I could get.

We could just say things had not changed much with Chris in the three days we were at Karsvall before heading to Fyngaard. The last night we were there, though, he did find Apollo and tell him he was okay with me coming to dinner.

But that was it.

And dinner went fine. He wasn't withdrawn. He also wasn't his usual self.

What he was was watchful. Watchful of how Élan chattered with me. Watchful of how his father spoke and looked at me.

Watchful of everything.

I did my best at being my normal self, hoping, if his father could find things to love about me, Chris would at least find things to like about me.

By all indications, he had not (yet).

But on the ride, sometimes he maneuvered his horse close to Élan and my sleigh. He wasn't talkative as he'd been when we made our way to Brunskar, but Élan was, so he didn't need to be and all she needed was her brother near.

I decided to take that as more progress.

By the by, Apollo didn't push any of this.

I had my time with him. I had my time with Élan. And I had my time with both of them.

Chris chose his times to participate in the last part.

Although things were progressing slowly with Christophe, they were not with Élan. As with our last ride, and even before we left Karsvall, she wanted me around all the time.

She wanted me.

She had me.

I'd fallen in love with her father.

It took far less time to fall in love with her.

Things did not progress slowly with Apollo either. For Chris's sake, we had to go back to his nights at the dower house with me, up early to breakfast with his children, and he stayed even later to dine with them and didn't leave until they were in bed.

But Apollo found times to visit me, me to visit him, and we made it work.

No.

It was more than making it work.

It was making both of us happy.

Absolutely, Apollo worried about his son. This was true. We discussed it often.

But I found he told no lies when he said having my heart was enough.

He was just happy to be with me.

Me. As I was.

It was awesome.

After he told me he loved me, me returning that gesture, and getting all that crap out, with nothing eating at me, things changed.

No strings. No doubts. Nothing plaguing me.

Nothing broken.

All healthy, real.

Strong.

Living the life I'd led, it was hard as hell to get used to.

I had known happiness, Apollo gave it to me.

I'd known contentedness, Apollo gave me that too.

But both of them together with a settled feeling and Élan thrown in to sweeten the pot?

Bliss.

These were my thoughts, and I was lost in them, so I jumped when suddenly Tunahn was no longer in my arms.

He was in his father's, a father who was walking away, murmuring to his son in Korwahkian.

I had no clue what he was saying.

Circe did and I knew this when she snapped, "Lahn!"

He sent her a look that was so severe it made me give an "eek" face to Finnie.

Finnie witnessed the look too and thus returned my "eek" face.

Circe didn't see this. She was concentrating on her husband. And she did not have an "eek" face.

She was snapping something else to him, but in Korwahk.

His reply was, "*Rayloo, kah rahna fauna.*"

"Don't tell me *rayloo, kah Dax,*" she retorted.

Suddenly, he grinned at her, and at that, I made no "eek" face.

Neither did Finnie.

Neither did Circe. She turned away from her husband on a "humph."

He moved away with his son.

When he did, she groused, "It really sucks he's so hot. He gets away with a lot of shit being that hot. Add him calling me his *rahna fauna*, he can get away with practically anything. Even doing idiot dad things." Her eyes went to Finnie. "Do you get me?"

"I so totally do," Finnie replied, and Circe looked to me.

"Beware of that," she advised.

I nodded my head, unable to speak at the idea of having the opportunity to experience Apollo doing idiot dad things with a child we shared (even though I knew that was something he wouldn't do). At the same time, I was thinking my future held a lot of him getting away with a lot of things, being so beautiful and also utilizing that "my dove" business.

"What did he say to Tunahn?" Finnie asked, taking me out of my thoughts.

Circe leaned in. Finnie and I leaned in. Meeta did not lean in.

When we were in position, on a hissed whisper, Circe shared, "He told his son he was not to tear at a woman's clothes until he'd learned to use his cock."

I felt my eyes get huge.

"See what I'm saying?" Circe asked, taking in my wide eyes. "Idiot dad things and he walks away with me not verbally kicking his ass because he's hot."

I looked to Finnie. "Does Frey do idiot dad things?"

"I don't know," she replied. "When Viktor couldn't sleep, does Frey taking him to the wheel of his ship in the middle of the night and keeping him there for hours as he navigated the waters count as an idiot dad thing? And just to note, it was cold as hell outside, and Viktor was so excited to be with his dad out in the sea air, he didn't sleep a wink so he was grouchy all the next day and had a runny nose. Is that an idiot dad thing?"

"Yes," I answered.

"Right," Finnie began. "Then I'll tell you that after he did that, I had words with him. Frey accepted about four of them before he grabbed me, kissed me and said, 'He's healthy and strong, strong enough to survive a nip in the air, my wee one. Leave it alone.' Then he let me go and walked away. But he didn't have to call me his wee one or even speak. I was stuck back at the kiss."

I was thinking I should find some way to shore myself against Apollo's awesomeness should it happen that he gave me something I'd treasure just as much as his love—a baby—when Isis scampered across the rug between the two couches the women were sitting on.

She was being chased by Viktor, who had an unfair advantage. He was steady on his feet.

Therefore, he caught her by falling on her, rolling her, and giving her a sloppy wet kiss on her giggling rosy lips.

"Dear God," Finnie muttered and flopped back on the couch across from mine.

I couldn't help but grin but did it turning my eyes to Meeta when she spoke.

She was looking to Finnie.

"Your son *is* healthy and strong and can survive a nip in the air. I know this because he did." After delivering that, she then looked to Circe and pointed out logically, "And it is true. Your son shouldn't tear at a woman's clothes until he knows how to use his cock."

"He's barely a year old," Circe replied.

Meeta arched her brows and inquired, "Does this make your king's statement any less true?"

Circe shut her mouth.

At this juncture, Loretta threw herself on the couch on my other side me and asked, "You're all laughing. What'd I miss?"

Everyone looked at her, but no one said a word.

Then we looked to the ground for Isis was squealing and this was because Viktor was up and appeared to be attempting to lift her in his arms in order to do God knew what with her.

This meant Loretta still didn't get an answer because, before Circe or Finnie could make the move they were preparing to make to separate the young lovebirds, Lahn swooped in. He scooped up his daughter, and without a glance at anyone, sauntered away with both of his offspring held close to his massive chest.

Tunahn was squirming.

Isis immediately began snuggling into her daddy.

Loretta took this opportunity to change her question, this one uttered after tearing her eyes from Lahn and directing them to Circe.

"You say both Bain and Zahnin are taken?"

Again, she got no answer.

This time she didn't because we were all too busy again laughing.

"AND...AT that...Princess Arianna stepped onto...the...cloud..."

No.

At that, Élan, who was reading to me, fell dead asleep in the middle of doing it.

When she did (after grinning), I carefully tugged the book from her hands and set it on the nightstand. Then I leaned into her and kissed the top of her shining dark hair. Finally, I disengaged from her body leaning against my side.

I found my feet at the side of the bed and bent in to pull the covers high and tuck her in. After that, she snuggled deeper into them and turned to her side. Afforded a new opportunity, I slid the hair from her face and bent deeper to touch my lips to her cheek.

When I pulled away, I took the time to enjoy watching her little girl beauty in sleep. After long moments of doing this, I blew out the lamp by her bed, moved to the fire, pulled away the screen, threw a few logs on and moved to the other side of the bed. I blew out that lamp and left the room.

In the hall, I saw Gaston patrolling close to Élan's room.

He saw me as well, and on a smile, asked, "Is she down?"

"After reading her book to me three times, yes, she's finally down."

Gaston approached, still smiling, and noted, "Lo reads to her."

I tipped my head to the side. "Sorry?"

"Lo reads to her when he's around in the evenings. I know this because she likes it when he does so she mentions it after he does. Often. But it is she who reads to you." His smile got bigger. "Trying to impress you."

Warmth swept through me at his words, though I figured something else was at play.

"And she has her father wrapped around her finger," I returned.

His eyes lit and he murmured, "There is that."

That sent more warmth through me as I looked down the hall and saw Frey's man, Lund, standing sentry at the top of the stairs.

Weirdly, this didn't feel like protection that would then be a reminder of danger.

Weirdly, it just felt like family.

And not weirdly, more warmth moved through me.

"All's safe, Maddie, you can seek your bed," Gaston told me.

I looked beyond him to the other end of the hall then back to him.

"Do you know where Lo is?" I asked.

"Still in with Christophe," he answered.

"If he leaves Chris and heads to my room, can you tell him I'm in with Loretta?"

Gaston nodded.

I leaned in and rolled up on my toes to touch my cheek to his.

With it there, I said, "If I don't see you again, have a good night."

"You as well, love," he muttered.

I pulled back, gave him a grin then headed down the hall.

I was in my nightgown and robe, fur-lined slippers on my feet, ready for bed as Loretta and Meeta, as usual, assisted me in being. Then came the request from Élan that I listen to her read so I headed to her room as my girls headed to theirs.

Meeta, no doubt, would by now be with Ruben in his.

That situation was continuing quietly, without fanfare, as was Meeta's way. This didn't mean she was entirely matter of fact about it. I often saw her search for Ruben on his mount with her eyes as we traversed the snow.

She liked him.

Alas, she was not a woman who would respond (at all) to me teasing her about it, and since that would be a waste of effort (and good teasing), I didn't.

But I wished I could.

Loretta, however, would be sleeping in an empty bed tonight.

Surprisingly, Hans had made no headway.

Unsurprisingly, as a great deal of time had passed, he'd backed off.

Though he didn't do it happily and his near-constant glower often aimed Loretta's way told me so. It also pretty much told the same to anyone who witnessed it.

And everyone witnessed it.

For some reason, this didn't sit well with me. And although she did it jokingly, earlier that evening, her asking after Bain and Zahnin's relationship status also struck me wrong.

She'd been into Hans.

I thought she'd cave (eventually).

She didn't.

She also hadn't shared.

Friends were supposed to look after friends—I guessed, since I didn't have a lot of experience. But the friends I had now looked after me.

And I wasn't sure I was looking after her.

So there I was, heading to her door.

Once I'd made it, before I could chicken out, I lifted my hand to knock.

I didn't get it in because I heard the door behind me open.

I twisted that way and saw that Meeta stood in it.

"Hey, honey," I greeted.

"Miss Maddie," she replied.

A chill slid over my skin when I caught the look on her face.

Since she was studying me closely in a way that kind of freaked me out, I turned fully to her.

"Everything okay?" I asked.

She kept studying me and didn't answer.

"Meeta?" I prompted.

She tipped her head to the side.

Yes, freaking me out.

Suddenly, her face cleared, and she said, "Everything is fine."

The chill left.

If Meeta said everything was fine, she would not lie.

A brawny arm appeared, that arm wrapping itself around Meeta's chest.

Then the handsome face of Ruben appeared at the side of her head.

He dipped his chin to me and gave me a wolfish grin.

Half a second later, Meeta disappeared, and the door clicked shut.

I grinned at the door before I turned and knocked on Loretta's.

Within moments, I heard the lock turn, and the door opened a few inches.

When she spied me, she opened it further and frowned.

"Is everything all right, Miss Maddie?" she asked.

"Everything's fine, honey," I answered. "Can I come in for a sec and chat?"

She looked confused but opened the door further and invited me in, saying, "Of course."

I moved into her room and noted that the fire was blazing, the lamp by her bed was lit and a book was upside down on the bedclothes.

I turned to her. "I'm sorry, you were all settled in."

"I'm always happy for a visit from you, Miss Maddie," she replied, moving to the bed, sitting on its edge, grabbing her book and setting it on the nightstand, finishing, "It's nice anytime but definitely much better than this book."

I followed and sat beside her. "No good?"

"I'm not sure the hero is going to end up with the heroine." She grinned at me. "I prefer a happy ending."

I did too.

And I was there to ask about hers.

"Okay, honey," I started. "Just to say, this isn't any of my business and you don't have to talk about it, but it seems you've managed to put Hans off."

She looked to her knees, murmuring, "Finally."

That word should have held relief.

But I didn't hear relief.

I just didn't know what I heard.

"Can I..." I paused and she returned her eyes to me, "ask why?"

"Why?"

"Hans is a good man, Loretta, and you liked him a great deal before what happened in Brunskar."

She looked back to her knees and it seemed she was uncomfortable.

Okay, maybe I'd screwed up. Maybe friends weren't supposed to stick their noses in their friend's business.

Backtracking, I assured her quickly, "You don't have to talk about it with me. It's your business. Not mine."

Her gaze came again to me. "I'm...choosy," she declared.

"Choosy?" I asked.

She turned fully to me. "I enjoy bedplay. Most definitely. But I'm choosy with who I do it with. I haven't had a great number of partners because of that," she stated openly.

"Okay," I replied slowly when she didn't continue.

"He pursued me," she went on.

"Are we talking about the first time?" I asked.

She nodded. "I thought...well, the first time, he was like he was this last time, obviously not as much because I gave in, but he seemed," she shrugged, "interested in me. For more than bedplay."

"And you were disappointed when he wasn't," I guessed.

"Yes," she confirmed. "But it was more. It was clear he was very good at it, for I greatly enjoyed what we did. Much more than I'd ever enjoyed it before.

But when he wanted no more, I thought perhaps I...well...*wasn't*. Good at it that is."

Ouch.

That had to sting.

I didn't get to share that, she kept talking.

"In his pursuit, I also got to know him. And I liked what I knew. You're right. He is a good man and he treated me in ways I liked. Then, after he had me, all that just...went away."

I felt my mouth get tight.

Stupid Hans.

"I know that had to feel awful," I said, reaching out and grabbing her hand.

Her fingers curled around mine as she agreed, "It did. It hurt a whole lot. And it made me angry when he was suddenly interested in me again after what happened in Brunskar. It was like all that went before was play. He'd asked about me, as if he wished to get to know me, but it was a means to an end. He didn't wish to get to know me. I don't think he even listened. He just did it to get what he wanted. Then, when what occurred at Brunskar occurred, suddenly, it was like he decided I was worthwhile—"

"When you were that before," I finished for her.

"I hope so," she replied.

"You were," I assured her. "You are."

"I hope so, Miss Maddie," she whispered.

I squeezed her hand and leaned in. "You were. You *are*," I repeated firmly, and I leaned closer. "I've learned very recently that there are things inside us we have to offer that the way those around us behave, how they treat us, can make us not see that we have them to give. I would think, sweetheart, that it also goes the other way around. That those around us have things that make them blind to what we have to offer, until something happens where suddenly," I clenched her hand in mine, "*they see*."

She said nothing so I kept going.

"And we can just say that what happened at Brunskar, what you and Meeta did for me, was a very big thing. Truthfully, in normal times, you showing that kind of bravery would never have the chance to happen. And Hans is a man who very much values bravery, loyalty, things you displayed in abundance. So he may never have known all there is to you because he wasn't opening his eyes to see, but also because there wasn't the opportunity for him to see just all there is."

I took a breath before I laid out the hard part.

"But I have to admit, the way you explain it, I hate to say this, it does sound like Hans was out just to have some fun."

"Yes," she said softly.

"But then he *saw* you."

She studied me a moment before she declared, "You want me with him."

I shook my head. "I want you to have what you want. What you deserve. I just can't help but think that you wanted him before, very much so, and although I totally get why you wouldn't want him now, I can't forget how you felt before. But in the end," I gave her hand another squeeze, "I just want you to be happy."

"I...well..." she stammered then looked away and suddenly exclaimed, "Oh blast!"

"What?" I asked.

Her eyes came back to mine. "Now I'm angry he stopped."

I blinked before I repeated, "What?"

"I am...I have...well, Miss Maddie, I must admit, I wanted to know this time his interest was genuine, was *more*, so I was," she made an embarrassed scrunchy face, "*testing* him."

Oh boy.

"And he gave up," she continued.

Crap.

"Now I don't know what to do," she confided. "Because now he's only doing what I *told* him to do, which is leave me be, and not doing what I *want* him to do, which is work to win me."

"Do you want me to have a word with him?" I asked, hoping she didn't because Hans liked me, but I had a feeling he wouldn't like me getting involved.

Still, I'd do it.

For my Loretta.

To which she immediately (and thankfully) cried, "No!"

"Okay," I said hurriedly. "I won't."

"I've made a terrible mistake," she declared. "He's very handsome and he's of a House, and since Brunskar, when he wasn't being bossy and annoying, he was very sweet. I was lucky to catch his eye in the first place."

Oh no she didn't.

"That's where you're absolutely wrong," I told her. "He was lucky to earn your attention. You're lovely, honey, every part of you. Inside and out."

She smiled a small smile as her hand in mine squeezed, but then the smile faded, and she looked back to her knees.

"I don't know what to do."

"Well, I'm no relationship expert, not by a long shot," I started, and she looked back at me.

"A long shot?"

"A...well, let's just say I'm not very good at this kind of thing," I explained.

"But...Lord Apollo adores you."

He did indeed.

I couldn't bite back the grin that reminder caused, so I didn't.

Then I kept on target.

"What I'm saying is, although I landed my guy, and he's a good one, it was a bumpy road before that where I made some mistakes. So, take my advice knowing that. But I'm thinking you both need to quit playing games and get real."

Her brows drew together. "Get real?"

"Talk to him. Share your feelings. Tell him how he hurt you before, explain you admire him and you don't want a roll in the hay." When she looked confused again, I stated, "Just bedplay. If he's not interested, tell him you want to know that so you both can move on. But if this is more to him, then you'll know."

"He may be angry with me for playing these...games."

"He might," I agreed. "Then again, he might realize he bought that and suck it up."

She stared at me. "Sometimes you speak very strangely, Miss Maddie."

It sucked I had to keep the secret of who I really was from a friend, and this was the kind of time when it sucked more.

Still, she couldn't know so I couldn't tell her.

Instead, I said, "We have different ways of saying things where I come from in the Vale."

"I've noticed," she murmured.

It was time to leave her alone, so I bumped my shoulder against hers and lifted our hands, doing this while offering, "If you ever need to talk about this kind of thing, or anything, I'm here. And if you don't want to talk about it, that's okay too. I just want you to know you have both from me. Yes?"

She smiled and this time it wasn't small. "Yes, Miss Maddie."

I smiled back. "Now, you sleep tight, sweetheart."

"You too."

I let her hand go but twisted to her to give her a hug. She gave it back. And when her arms closed around me, I wondered how I'd existed for so long in a life untouched by good people.

Then again, it didn't matter.

Because I lived that life no longer.

I let her go, straightened from the bed and winked at her before I headed out the door.

When I got into the hall, I noticed Gaston was down at the other end and Lund was still at his position at the top of the stairs.

But as I moved toward my room, I also noticed one of the doors in the hall was cracked open.

It was Christophe's.

I thought Apollo had left it open for some reason and was wondering why when I got closer and saw Christophe's eye peering out the crack.

I looked quickly away, his position telling me he didn't want to be caught peeking out and made note to tell his father he was still awake and something was up as I walked by his door, pretending I didn't know he was there.

I got two steps past it when I heard him call, "Miss Maddie."

My heart jumped in my chest as I turned and saw he'd stuck his head out of the door.

His eyes were on me.

And he was addressing me.

Directly.

"Are you all right, Chris?" I asked.

His head turned to look toward the other end of the hall then he looked back to me.

"Did you talk Loretta into being with Hans?"

I stared at him, surprised at his question.

A question that laid testimony to the fact that Chris didn't only watch his father, sister and me.

It would seem Chris paid attention to everything.

Then I forced myself to speak. "Um...well, no. Not exactly."

He looked disappointed.

"She is..." I didn't know what to share and decided on, "She has some issues."

"Hans likes her," he stated.

"Well, yes," I replied.

"The handsome soldier is supposed to get the maiden he desires at the end of the story," he declared, and I felt my lips twitch as I fought back a smile.

"You're absolutely right," I told him.

"So what's wrong with Loretta? She's ruining the story," he told me.

I again beat back my smile, doing it thinking that I wanted to walk to him. To get close. To crouch in front of him and hold his eyes when I spoke my next words.

But this was not small progress.

This was huge progress.

So I didn't push it.

"Some stories have twists and turns, Chris. It could be that those twists and turns will lead to Hans winning Loretta. It could be he thinks she's the maiden he desires but yet another is on the horizon, and it will be her he seeks to win, and does. As with any good story, we just have to watch it play out and see."

"She's the maiden he desires," Chris informed me authoritatively. "I heard him tell Remi he thinks she's very pretty."

"I'm glad to know that," I replied softly.

"So she needs to stop being so stubborn," he asserted.

"Well, hopefully I gave her a few things to think about in regard to Hans," I shared.

"Hopefully you did," he agreed.

At that, I let myself smile and said quietly, "But we'll just watch it play out, shall we?"

He was looking at my smile. His eyes shifted up and he nodded.

"Now, do you want me to find your father and ask him to come and tuck you in, or are you good?" I queried.

His head (the only thing I could see around the jamb) lifted up two inches before he stated, "I can tuck myself in."

"Of course," I murmured. Then louder, I said, "Now you sleep tight, sweetheart."

Something moved over his face at the endearment. Something I couldn't quite catch before he called, "You sleep tight too."

And without further ado, his head disappeared, and he closed the door.

I turned swiftly, catching myself from twirling with glee.

I waved to Lund and Gaston as I rushed down the hall, catching myself from skipping.

I threw open the door and saw Apollo sitting in a chair in my room, tugging off his boot. His head came up, his face got soft when he saw me, I liked that a whole lot, and I closed the door behind me.

"Lock that, poppy," he ordered.

I didn't lock it.

I let myself skip across the room to him, watching him watch me as he dropped his boot and straightened in the chair.

When I arrived at him, I let myself twirl and I ended my twirl falling into his lap.

His arms instantly closed around me.

I instantly lifted my hands and slapped them against his chest.

"Guess what?" I asked.

He was grinning down at me as he asked back, "What?"

I pushed closer, and when we were nearly nose to nose, I shared, "Chris just caught me in the hall and *instigated a conversation with me*."

His eyes flared, his arms convulsed, and his lips curled deeper.

"Good," he murmured, and I shot backward, away from him.

"Good?" I asked before I slapped my hands on his chest and leaned in again. "*Great!*"

"Yes, dove, it is great," he agreed, his arms closing tighter around me, bringing me closer, his jade eyes dancing with amusement. The dancing stopped and warmth settled in before he whispered, "Happy?"

He wanted very badly for that answer to be yes.

He'd worked hard at making that answer yes.

So it was with deep gratification that I slid my hand up his chest to curl it around his neck and whispered back, "Very."

He dipped his head so his lips were a breath away from mine.

"Now, let us see if I can make you happier."

His words. His tone. The warmth that had heated in his eyes.

I squirmed.

"Okay," I breathed.

"Go lock the door, my dove. But when you join me in bed, I want just you and not your clothes joining me."

I could *so* do that.

So, without a second's hesitation, I did.

God, he was killing me.

"Lo," I breathed.

Apollo and I were under the covers, facing each other on the bed. We were naked. He had my leg draped over his hip, his thigh hitched between my legs, and his fingers were toying there as they had been for a long time.

A very long time.

"Look at me, Maddie."

I lifted my gaze from an unfocused study of his throat, pressed my hips into his hand, and caught his eyes even as his fingers whispered away.

"*Lo*," I breathed again, this time it was a plea.

His mouth came to mine, his eyes held mine, and his lips whispered, "Marry me."

All my breath left me.

Okay.

Now that...

That was a marriage proposal.

His fingers whispered back before they again slithered away.

"Marry me, Maddie," he repeated.

Oh God.

"Apollo," I said his name softly but said no more.

I couldn't. His fingers returned, gliding over my clit then shifting back, one catching at the entrance to the core of me.

"Say you'll marry me," he ordered gently.

I bit my lip.

His finger circled.

I whimpered.

"Say it, poppy."

"I'll marry you, baby."

His finger filled me.

I closed my eyes, pressed my hips down and arched my back.

Apollo moved his mouth to my neck as he slid his finger out.

On the inward glide, he asked, "You'll spend the rest of your life with me?"

"Yes."

His finger went out then in.

"Content at my side."

"Yes, Lo."

Out then in.

"On my arm."

"Yes, honey."

Out, in and then gently circling.

Yes.

God.

Killing me.

And I loved it.

"Always with me," he went on.

"Absolutely."

"Will you try and make a baby with me?"

My body bucked and my hands at his chest pressed deep.

But my answer to his question was, "*Please.*"

The second he got it, he lifted his head, caught my mouth in a deep, wet, searing kiss as his finger slid out and he pressed his big body into mine.

I fell to my back, Apollo covered me and his hips fell between my legs. He broke the kiss and braced on a forearm, his other hand going between us. I felt the head of his cock gliding where his fingers had been.

But not coming inside.

I lifted my head and shoved my face in his neck.

"Lo, please."

He traced my ear with his nose before he did the same with his tongue as he rubbed the tip of his cock against my clit.

I gasped.

"Do you love me?" he whispered in my ear.

"Yes," I whispered against his skin.

"Say it."

"I love you, baby."

He slid his cock back and it caught right where it needed to be.

But he didn't go inside.

"Say it again."

"I love you, Lo."

He gave me an inch.

I strained for more and wrapped my arms around him, lifting my knees high at the sides.

"Again, poppy."

"Love you, Lo," I breathed.

I got another inch.

I bit my lip and slid a hand up his back to clench my fingers in his hair.

His voice was rough when he ordered, "Again."

"Love you."

Another inch.

"Love you, honey," I repeated without his prompt this time.

And that was when I got it all.

Then again, I already had it all.

Apollo had given it to me.

He was just giving me more.

He moved and I moved with him, hearing his quickened breathing in my ear, feeling it tingle over my skin.

He moved faster, thrust harder, and I listened to his breathing as it turned labored, my body tingling everywhere, pressure building.

I clutched at him with my hands, pressing my thighs tight to his sides, and gasped, "Baby."

"Take it, Maddie," he grunted, driving deep.

I took it, holding tight, pushing my face into his neck, he kept pounding into me as my climax shook through me and I held on.

Then he sank his teeth into my earlobe, the nip of pain radiating down and becoming something else altogether before he released it and groaned in my ear.

I held his weight, absorbed his warmth, his strength, as mine left me and his left him.

Then I felt him kiss the side of my neck.

Down, pulling out slowly, he kissed my shoulder.

Down again, he kissed my chest.

And down, he kissed my midriff.

And down yet again, where he kissed my belly.

Lifting his head, he caught my eyes and slid back up. He touched his mouth to mine, lifted slightly away, and reached to the nightstand.

He brought a cloth back and his eyes came back to mine as he gently pressed it between my legs, cleaning him away, before he tossed it to the floor at the side of the bed.

His arms going around me, he took me with him as he rolled and lifted to blow out one lamp, doing the same with the other.

Finally, he settled us with me on top of him, taking my weight, hopefully absorbing my warmth, but also pulling the covers up high over us.

I pressed my face into his neck as I wrapped my arms around him as best I could.

"Happy?" I whispered.

"Absolutely," he whispered back.

"Hold tight to that, baby." I kept whispering, and his arms went super tight around me.

And against his skin, I smiled.

30
THE PLAN IS IN PLACE

"Oh my goodness," Élan breathed. "Is that the Black Prince?"

I didn't answer at first. I was too busy staring at the man and woman standing at the top of the steps of an a-freaking-*mazing* palace that was in an a-freaking-mazing city at the base of some, you guessed it, a-*freaking*-mazing mountains.

I knew the woman was Cora, the Gracious.

I also knew the man was Prince Noctorno of Hawkvale, ruler of Bellebryn, known as the Black Prince. I'd seen his pen and ink pictures in the papers from the Vale too.

They just did not do him justice.

In any way.

And staring at him as I drove our sleigh closer to the steps (or more to the point, the horses moved there without much direction from me seeing as I wasn't paying attention), I was wondering if all this craziness wasn't about Frey commanding dragons and such, Lahn being mighty and such, Tor sharing his soul with his wife (and such), and Apollo commanding the wolves.

I was thinking those witch bitches were jealous because our men were *hot.*

Seriously.

I fought to find my voice and said, "I think he is, honey bunch."

"*Wow,*" she replied.

She could say that again.

I pulled her closer as I started paying attention and guided our sleigh to a stop. This I was able to do after I tore my eyes off the tall drink of hot water that was the Black Prince. I then looked to the other person on the steps with Tor and Cora.

She was a woman with very straight posture, her eyes aimed down the length of her nose, wearing a cloak made of dark-brown pelts so lustrous, they were almost (almost) as fabulous as Élan's hair.

A woman who took regal to extremes.

A woman who had to be Finnie's mother (kind of, she was the other Sjofn's mother, but she'd claimed Finnie).

Queen Aurora.

I no sooner stopped the sleigh when Finnie dumped Viktor right in my lap, put a hand to the side of the sleigh and threw her legs over it.

She then raced up the steps, and even as the Queen of Lunwyn stared down her nose at her and didn't move a muscle, Finnie didn't hesitate to throw herself in the woman's arms.

I watched the queen roll her eyes to the chilly blue skies.

I also watched her arms close tight around her adopted daughter.

How sweet.

I could watch no more because Apollo filled my vision and he did this to reach in the sleigh and lift Élan over the side.

She giggled when he did this for no apparent reason other than it afforded her the opportunity to giggle.

I smiled when she did for no reason except I thought she was cute.

I moved Viktor to my hip as I stood and the fur blankets dropped away from my lap.

Apollo opened the door to the sleigh and Frey was there.

He reached for his son and I handed him over.

He took hold with a murmured, "My gratitude, Maddie," then turned and sauntered up the steps.

I exited the sleigh at the same time Apollo called, "Chris!"

Chris had dismounted and was moving our way. I felt Apollo's hand clasp mine and bring it up. He smoothed it around the inside of his elbow, and I moved closer to him as he took Élan's hand.

To my utter delight—delight that meant my head whipped around and tipped back so I could aim my beam of happiness to Apollo—Chris took his place beside me.

Taking in my smile, Apollo's lips twitched, and he turned his attention to the palace.

Thus, we all moved to the steps.

And when we did, Apollo murmured, "This pleases me."

It pleased me too.

Big time.

"What, Papa?" Chris asked.

"That Maddie will be meeting Prince Noctorno in a normal fashion, not in the throes of a needed rescue."

I wasn't beaming at that. I turned a glare in his direction.

He grinned down at me.

Chris burst out laughing.

I instantly quit glaring.

Apollo tucked me closer to his side and turned his attention to the steps, leading us up.

I wished they had cameras in this world so I could have a picture of our progression. I really, *really* did.

Alas, they didn't.

So I committed the moment to memory.

"Aurora is our queen, Maddie," Apollo said quietly. "You curtsy."

"Okeydokey," I mumbled in reply and that got my hand tucked deeper into his side.

"Remember, my precious girl, you curtsy too," Apollo instructed his daughter.

"All right!" she chirped.

He stopped us two steps down from Queen Aurora and I could feel Lahn and Circe trailing us. We waited while she leaned in and touched her lips to her grandson's cheek then Frey moved his family from Aurora toward Cora and Tor and Apollo guided us up the last steps.

He let me and his daughter go and swept into a deep bow.

I did my best to drop into a curtsy.

"Rise," she murmured practically the instant we all got into position, something I thought was nice considering a curtsy wasn't the most comfortable position I'd ever held.

We all straightened and I felt Chris get closer to me.

My heart swelled.

"You are well, my general?" Aurora asked Apollo.

"I am, your grace," he replied and tipped his chin down to one side then the other. "You know my children, Christophe and Élan."

She looked to the kids, murmuring, "Of course." Then louder, "I'm pleased to see you both."

"Same here!" Élan squeaked.

Aurora dipped her head to her then to Chris, who said nothing, and finally her eyes came to me.

"This is Madeleine, Lady Ulfr," Apollo stated, his hand in mine pulling both of them up to press tight to the side of his chest.

"Madeleine, Lady Ulfr," she said softly, eyeing me. Then she looked to Apollo. "Heartfelt congratulations, Apollo."

He inclined his head.

She turned to me and I took it as good that her lips curled up slightly at the ends.

I didn't know what to say, so I winged it. "It's a pleasure to meet you, your highness."

"Knowing Apollo since his youth," her gaze swept him, me, Christophe and Élan, before settling back on me and it could not be missed her eyes were exceptionally astute, "I can assure you the pleasure is mine."

Okay, she was a little aloof, but she was definitely nice.

I smiled at her.

The ends of her lips tipped up another millimeter.

Apollo moved us away and Circe and Lahn moved in behind us.

I wanted to watch how they met the queen since I didn't suspect Lahn bowed to anybody but seeing as Apollo was guiding us to Tor and Cora, I focused on that instead.

When we stopped, as they, too, were royalty, I dipped down into another curtsy.

"Oh, we don't get into that kind of thing," Cora said the instant I did.

"*She* doesn't," Tor muttered, and it sounded exasperated.

I straightened out of my curtsy to see Tor and Apollo shaking hands. But I only caught a glimpse because Cora was yanking me into her arms.

She swayed me a bit side to side, saying in my ear, "*So* cool to finally meet you. The people here are awesome, but it's good to have friends from home."

Okay, being duped by the other Cora?

Total idiot.

I knew the real Cora approximately a nanosecond and this chick was the bomb.

I hugged her back. We let each other go. Apollo presented me and his children to Tor. Tor did not give me a hug, but he did give a gallant bow to Élan (which, unsurprisingly, made her giggle). Then Apollo guided us to where Frey, Finnie and Viktor were standing so Lahn and Circe could say hello to Cora and Tor.

Queen Aurora didn't allow them much time before she called, "Let us get out of the cold. I have refreshments and something special prepared for the children."

She said this as she swept majestically to the front doors where two servants in weird uniforms of leather shorts, wool tights, boots, sweaters and slanted cloaks jumped to open them before she even had to hesitate a moment to await entry.

We were barely in when three women swooped down on Finnie. As other servants moved amongst the rest of us divesting us of our cloaks and gloves, they hugged, exclaimed and gabbled like girls.

Aurora allowed this for all of thirty seconds before she ordered, "Sjofn, the girls are here to take care of the children. Adult refreshments are awaiting us in the drawing room."

It was Finnie's turn to roll her eyes, but Frey handed off Viktor, Circe and Lahn gave over Isis and Tunahn and Apollo bent to Chris and Élan.

"Go, make sure those maids take good care of our wee princes and princess," he urged.

Chris nodded formally, his chest puffing out, clearly feeling this was an important assignment.

Élan jumped forward to give her father a loud kiss on the cheek before she skipped off toward the waiting women.

Apollo turned me Queen Aurora's way and I saw she had her arm extended to something. I found that something was a someone when Finnie came forward, latched on to it and leaned heavily into her mother.

They led.

Frey behind them, Apollo and I behind Frey, the rest behind us, we followed.

Thus, I was in the position to hear Aurora say to Finnie, "*Must* you wear breeches when you come to Fyngaard?"

And thus, I was also in the position to hear Finnie reply, "*You* traipse after a toddler in a long dress."

"My dear, you are not the first woman of Lunwyn in this generation or dozens before who managed to raise a child wearing a gown. In fact, I achieved this same feat."

"You had servants," Finnie retorted.

"You could too, if you installed your family at the Winter Palace where the future king of Lunwyn *should* be raised rather than sailing off into the sunset."

"Okay, *you* convince Frey not to sail off into a hundred sunsets," Finnie returned.

We entered an extraordinary room that seemed entirely made of dark intricately carved wood, including the wood around the blue velvet padding of the furniture, as Aurora retorted, "Your husband would anchor himself to a block of granite should you ask."

"No, I wouldn't," Frey entered the conversation. "So, wife, do not ask."

Finnie threw a smile over her shoulder but did not unlatch from her mother. "I'd never do that, husband."

He made no reply because he probably knew this.

I had to admit, I found it beautiful the way Princess Sjofn (who was not really Princess Sjofn) was with Queen Aurora.

I wasn't privy to the entirety of the story that led to them being that way. I just knew the Sjofn of this world chose to leave it. This was for some reason considered a traitorous act and thus she could not return or she'd be hanged (a little gruesome, but then again, a lot of this world was).

Being in love with her man, Finnie never wanted to go. And anyway, she'd never done anything traitorous, questionable or otherwise, in fact, the opposite. So she took the other Sjofn's place.

I knew Finnie had grown close to the king before he passed and was obviously close to the queen. Very close. Even if they weren't blood.

And I was happy she had that. It was sweet.

I hadn't asked after Ilsa's parents, my mother and father of this world, and Apollo rarely mentioned them. However, if they knew of my existence, the way they lost their daughter, it would be doubtful they'd welcome me with open arms.

But it was a moot point. They'd both passed since Ilsa's death. They'd lived to see their only child leave this world far too young, and then they both went.

When I'd learned this additional sadness, I didn't dwell on it.

And I didn't dwell on it now.

Instead, I sat on a velvet cushion mostly because Apollo planted me there. He followed me down and sat close to my side. The others were doing the same around the four couches that faced each other in a square.

Once settled, I marveled at how warm it was in the room.

Then again, there were two massive fireplaces on each side of it, both of them blazing.

Although we were settling in, and the Winter Palace was the abode of the Winter Princess (meaning it was Finnie's), that didn't mean that Aurora didn't lord over that residence as well.

However, the way she was, I figured she just lorded over everything.

"*You* could cease this delay with bringing about my second grandchild," she said, turning her reproaches to Frey. "The longer you wait, the more spoiled Viktor will become."

Frey draped his arm around Finnie where they were on their couch, which was down from Aurora on the same couch, and drawled, "Fret not, my queen. I've seen to that and enjoyed the endeavor. Finnie's with child."

I gasped in delight as I felt Apollo come alert at my side.

But Finnie turned to Frey and slapped him on his stomach. "Are you crazy? You don't tell a grandmother she's going to be a grandmother like that!"

He turned unperturbed eyes to his wife. "How odd. I just did."

She glared at him.

I forged into the breach, saying, "Oh my God! That's so exciting!"

"Yes, indeed it is," Aurora said softly, her lips tipped up two whole millimeters more than I'd seen them when she'd smiled at me which I took to mean she was super happy. "Very exciting. Congratulations are in order. We must send away this tea and order champagne."

She looked about ready to move to do just that, but she didn't when Apollo called in a strangely tight voice, "Tor?"

I looked to Apollo then to the couch Cora and Tor were sitting on.

He had her tucked close to his side, as Apollo had me, and Frey had Finnie, and also (at a quick glance their way), Lahn had Circe.

And my glance was quick to Lahn and Circe because Cora looked stricken and Tor looked alert, and not Apollo's earlier my-cousin-just-suddenly-announced-(somewhat inappropriately)-he-was-going-to-be-a-dad-again alert.

And both their eyes were on Circe and Lahn.

I looked back to Circe and Lahn.

Lahn looked scary and not his usual hot guy scary. A hot guy *concerned* scary which was a whole lot worse.

Circe looked worried.

Uh-oh.

"Cora's with child," Apollo guessed quietly.

"Yes," Tor replied curtly. Then he clipped out, "Lahn?"

Everyone looked their way.

"My golden queen carries another warrior or princess," Lahn confirmed.

Uh-oh.

All eyes came to me.

Oh shit.

I threw out a hand. "I'm not—"

My hand suddenly dropped into my lap as I did the mental math.

Then I got freaked out and redid the mental math.

Then my entire body strung tight.

"Poppy?" Apollo called.

Before Brunskar.

My last period was before Brunskar.

How could that be?

Slowly, I turned my head to Apollo.

"Does pennyrium always work?" I whispered.

His eyes held mine, but they weren't entirely focused.

He was doing the mental math too.

He got the same result as I did, I knew this when he did something Apollo Beautiful.

His eyes warmed and his arm curled me so I was forced to twist into him. When I did, he pulled me close.

"You carry my child?" he whispered like he wanted the answer to be yes.

I wanted the answer to be yes too.

Only when Chris had accepted me, Apollo and I had been married, and no one was targeting anyone I cared about with extreme malice.

"I'm taking the powder," I whispered back.

He dipped his face closer and his voice lower (all for nothing, I was sure, I felt everyone's attention on us, but at that moment I didn't give a shit I was entering a discussion about my period in front of two queens, two princesses, a prince, a king and whatever Frey was).

"You have not had a cycle in some time, my dove."

"Does the powder always work?" I repeated.

"It is rare when it does not, but it's been known to happen."

I stared at him as my lungs seized.

Then I let out a huge breath, doing it chanting, "Oh crap, oh shit, oh crap."

He pulled me even closer. "My dove—"

Suddenly panicked, I fisted my fingers in his sweater and cried, "We have to go back to the other world!"

His head jerked and his eyes narrowed before he stated, "We will not."

I shook my head and pressed even closer. "We *have* to, Lo. If I'm knocked up, I need vitamins, and ultrasounds, and prenatal tests, and—"

He gave me a slight shake. "Calm yourself, dove."

"*You* calm yourself!" I nearly shouted. "I'm pregnant in a world with no epidurals!"

He probably had no stinking clue what I was talking about.

He also didn't ask.

He lifted a hand to cup my jaw, dipped his face close again and repeated in a sweet whisper, "Calm yourself, my dove."

I deep breathed.

He didn't.

He stated, sounding happy and proud, "You carry my child."

"We're not married," I replied.

"We'll rectify that," he returned immediately.

"Chris hasn't accepted me," I reminded him.

"He's getting there," he reminded me.

Then I gave it to him.

"I haven't done real great with this before, Lo," I stated quietly.

His thumb stroked my cheek as he replied, "Then, if you feel more comfortable carrying our child with the medicine you can receive in the other world, after we see to these troubles, we will all go there so you can have that, and we'll return when she's safely arrived."

He'd do that.

He'd so do that.

For me.

God.

I loved this man.

I didn't tell him that. I'd share it (again) later.

Instead, still whispering, I said, "She?"

He was still whispering too when he replied. "Your hair. Your freckles. Your spirit. Yes, my dove. *She*."

He wanted her to have my freckles.

Tears welled in my eyes so Apollo's smile was blurry.

Queen Aurora broke into our moment when she declared, "Now we *must* have champagne." I turned my blurry eyes to her as she went on, "Or sparkling cider for you, child, if you are like my Finnie and don't drink spirits while expecting."

While expecting.

I was expecting.

Huzzah!

I cleared the frog in my throat before I confirmed, "I don't."

"I don't either," Cora put in.

"Me either," Circe said.

"You know I don't," Finnie added.

"Odd," Aurora murmured as she rose from her place on the couch and headed to a velvet cord hanging in the corner.

I looked to Frey when he remarked, his gaze on Apollo, "Well done, cousin. You beat pennyrium."

Finnie rolled her eyes.

I snuggled into Apollo when I heard his chuckle.

"Um...as beautiful as it was witnessing that," Circe began, and I looked to her to see her gazing at me with soft eyes. "And it *was* beautiful, Maddie." She then looked among the couches. "I'm thinking this is more than a happy coincidence."

Lahn looked no less scary when he grunted, "I agree."

"The women are protected. The plan goes forward. This ends soon," Frey stated.

I turned to him, surprised. "What plan?" I asked, and Apollo's arm, already tight around me, tightened further so I tipped my head back to look at him.

"The dragons, elves, witches, wolves and conspirators all are in place," he informed me. "Tomorrow night, you attend a gale. Outside the enchantments on this palace, Helda will be drawn out and captured by Lavinia. The Circe of this world, now of the other one, will be brought back to this world on the morrow. She will be in the palace with Tor's witches, keeping watch over the four of you. With Helda's magic eliminated, which we suspect will weaken their defenses, at the same time Specter Isle will be attacked by dragons and invaded by elves and Valentine. Minerva, Baldur, Cora and Edith either perish by dragon fire or are dispatched another way. We will hold no trial. They will find justice where they stand. Except Helda, who harmed you. She will find justice at my hand."

Justice at Apollo's hand.

Helda was fucked.

"Um..." I mumbled.

"You and the other women are here because our enemies have been told you will be and we're certain they hold watch so they must see you to be. They have also been told you will be delivered to Helda," Apollo continued. "Obviously, you won't. Valentine and Lavinia will create soulless doppelgangers who will draw Helda from Specter Isle."

"Holy cow," I breathed.

"The plan is in place. This ends tomorrow night," he concluded.

As happy as I was at that thought, I had questions.

"Can you kill a she-god?"

"I cannot," he answered. "Lavinia and Valentine also may not have that power. And the elves do not take lives. But they can leach her power, return it to the earth, and once stripped, anyone can."

"You're sure?" I pressed.

It was Frey who answered that. "The elves are sure."

That sounded firm.

I looked to him and nodded.

Lahn stood, his focus locked on Queen Aurora. "I wish to see the witches and assess the defenses that guard *kah dahksahna*."

"We're having champagne," she replied.

His look changed.

Aurora saw it and processed it.

Thus, she wisely murmured, "We'll have champagne after you assess the defenses of the palace."

Lahn stalked to the door.

Aurora followed him.

Apollo gave me a squeeze that gained my attention.

When he caught my eyes, he said, "I'll be attending them. I wish to make sure all is in order."

I nodded.

He watched me do it then his eyes dropped to my mouth. A second later, his mouth was there but not for a kiss.

For him to say, "We celebrate later."

He was pretty happy, as was I, so I had a feeling our celebration was going to be a good one.

I shivered.

When I did, I saw his eyes smile.

Then he brushed his lips against mine, gave me another squeeze and managed to get in another brush of his lips against my temple as he straightened from the couch.

I looked around the room noting Frey and Tor had the same idea as Apollo for they were all on the move toward the door.

Within seconds, the women were alone in the room.

We all looked at each other.

Cora broke our silence.

"That's super sweet, Apollo being willing to take you back home so you can have your baby there."

It *was* super sweet.

Then again, Apollo was super sweet.

I grinned at her and replied, "Yes. That's his way."

Cora grinned back.

Finnie had leaned forward and was pouring tea as she called, "All right, ladies, it isn't the good stuff, but since we're all up the duff and we should mark that occasion, it'll have to do."

She put down the elegant silver teapot and lifted a china cup.

Cora, Circe and I leaned forward, claimed our own cups and raised them after we did.

Finnie's eyes came to me. "To the dream team."

Circe and I raised our cups another inch and repeated, "To the dream team."

"What's this?" Cora murmured, but still took a sip as the rest of us giggled.

After she stopped giggling, Finnie explained.

As she did, my eyes wandered beyond her to the fire blazing in its enormous grate at her back. I held my cup in one hand but pressed the other to my belly.

I then brought the cup back to my lips and whispered to myself, "To the dream team."

I smiled.

I hoped.

I sent a prayer to the heavens.

Then I took a sip.

~

Apollo

APOLLO STOOD at the window in the formal sitting room at the front of the Winter Palace, impatient to get to his Maddie.

It was late. Dinner had been consumed. The children were in bed. Tomorrow was the hunt. Tomorrow evening the gale. Tomorrow night, it would be done.

They had planned for everything.

Absolutely everything.

Except one thing.

He heard the door open behind him and drew in an annoyed breath when the green witch glided in.

It was annoyed for he'd called for her over half an hour before and now she was gliding in as if wending her aimless way through a party.

She sent him a cat's smile.

He turned away from the window and crossed his arms on his chest.

"You called?" she asked, coming into the room and stopping by a chair.

"And you know why I did," he replied. "Have you seen him?"

She held his gaze but shook her head. "I have not."

Apollo tipped his head to the side. "Your demeanor suggests you have no concerns about this," he noted.

He didn't like that her eyes slid away. She raised a hand and studied her nails as she again spoke, but he couldn't help but think her nonchalance was a ruse.

"All is well planned," she told her nails.

"That does not answer my question," he returned, and she lifted her gaze to his, her brows arching.

"You asked a question?"

"Perhaps not. So I shall ask it now. Do you have no concerns about not being able to see the other me?"

Her gaze was again steady on his when she answered, "No. If you share with our *colombe* that he may be close."

He shook his head. "I do not wish to frighten Maddie with that information."

"I can understand that, *mon loup*. It is up to you whether you choose to frighten her or prepare her."

Apollo felt his jaw get hard.

"It's my opinion she must know," Valentine continued.

It would be Maddie's opinion as well.

Bloody hell.

"You've made your decision?" she asked, studying him closely.

"I'll tell her."

She seemed to relax which was something else he did not like.

"Alas, this puts a pall on a happy day," she murmured.

It bloody well did.

He didn't reply.

She tipped her head to the side, a small smile playing about her mouth. "Do you wish to know what she carries?"

Apollo felt his chest get tight.

"You know?"

"Of course, *chéri*."

"Do you know if our child will come to us healthy and strong?"

She shook her head. "I can sense what the sex is of the child she carries, but I do not have the sight, Apollo." Another small smile. "You could ask Meeta."

He would do this.

Later.

After they had prevailed against their foes.

He declared, "I wish a daughter."

Her eyes went half-mast before she whispered, "Then luck shines on you, *mon loup*."

He felt his chest tighten.

Maddie carried his daughter.

Their daughter.

Gods, he hoped she had red hair and freckles.

But he'd take her as she came, just as long as she came, leaving her mother well and happy, arriving on this earth the same way.

Valentine took him out of his thoughts when she asked, "Is that all you needed?"

"Yes," he replied.

She dipped her chin, and said, "Then I will leave you. Sleep well, *chéri*."

He inclined his head and watched as she glided to the door and out of it.

He stared at the door for some time.

Then he left the room and moved through the Palace, three destinations to achieve before he joined Maddie in her chambers.

The first took him to the door of servants' quarters.

The first maid he saw, he asked her to bring him Meeta.

"Of course, Lord Apollo," she muttered and moved quickly away.

Apollo stood at the door, still impatient.

But unlike Valentine, Meeta didn't make him wait.

"My lord," she greeted, still fully dressed and this was likely due to the fact she intended to traverse the halls to find Ruben's room. Indeed, he was lucky she wasn't already there.

"Meeta," he replied. "I call on you only briefly then I'll leave you to the rest of your evening."

She didn't wait for him to ask.

She answered. "I do not see her."

Apollo felt his brows draw together. "At all?"

"No," she answered.

"You explained you could lock on her," he reminded her.

"I explained I can pinpoint it if I sense something." She shook her head. "However, I sense nothing."

"So all is well," he remarked.

"All is never well, wolf," she said softly. "And I must admit, I am not privy to your plans but it is not lost on me we all journey here together under heavy guard with the protection of powerful witches, so I knew before you mentioned it that something was stirring. In knowing this, I was concerned that I could see nothing at all. But Miss Maddie seems most content. Perhaps it's simply that there is nothing to see."

By the gods, he hoped she was right.

"You'll notify me if that changes," he ordered.

"Most definitely," she returned.

"I'll bid goodnight to you then, Meeta."

"And to you," she replied on an inclination of her head.

He turned away, moved back into the house and up the steps.

His second destination was his daughter's room. He made certain there was fresh fuel on the fire, the covers were high, and she was tucked in before he brushed a kiss on her temple and left her.

His third destination was his son's room. He went through the same motions as with Élan and exited his room.

This took him to his final destination.

He entered Maddie's room and found her curled in a chair by the fire, a soft cream throw on her lap, her shawl on her shoulders, her body tipped to the side toward a lit lamp. She had a large sheaf of papers in her hands and her head was bent to them, her attention so acute on what she was reading, she didn't look his way. Not even after the sound of the door catching could be heard.

"Dove?" he called, moving her way, and her body gave a soft jerk before her head came up.

When she saw him and her expression changed, he stopped dead.

"I came into my room," she whispered then lifted the papers in her hands. "And this was on my pillow."

Apollo didn't look at the papers when the tears wet her eyes as the pink of emotion tinged her cheeks.

He was about to go to her when she declared, "Chris left me the story he's writing."

And again, his chest tightened.

By the gods.

"It's not done," she went on then visibly swallowed. "As it wouldn't be since it's about Loretta and Hans."

"He left it for you?" Apollo asked.

"On my pillow," she answered. "You have your own room, honey," she reminded him. "I don't think he's aware you sleep with me."

He did have his own room.

This meant his son left Madeleine a story.

Christophe would not let just anyone read his stories.

And he would never go out of his way to share one with someone unless that someone meant something to him.

No.

Unless that someone meant *a great deal* to him.

Maddie knew this and this was why her voice was croaky when she noted, "I think this is some serious progress."

Her understatement made him grin and finally move to her.

When he arrived, he plucked her out of her chair and sat in it, arranging her and her throw on his lap and curling his arms around her.

"Is it good?" he asked, but he knew the answer.

His son was a very talented writer.

He watched her draw in a deep breath, getting control of her emotions, before she nodded.

"Yes. Actually, it's great. He drew me in right away." She looked down to the papers she held in her hand. "Though, it's clear he wants Loretta to fall for Hans so I'm hoping he doesn't get disappointed."

"I hope so too," he murmured.

Her eyes came to him and they were filled with wonder.

"He left it for me, baby."

Apollo pulled her closer. "He did, poppy."

Her smile was shaky, but she pushed through it, and it finally lit in her eyes.

"Today is the best...day...*ever*," she whispered.

He'd had many better days than she, marrying a woman he loved, that woman bringing their two children into the world, Maddie sharing he had her love.

But he decided this day was definitely in the top five.

"I'm glad you think so, poppy," he replied gently.

This made what he had to tell her all the more frustrating.

But he had to tell her.

She would not only wish to know, she needed to know.

Preparing her and himself, Apollo gathered her ever closer and shared, "Alas, I have something to share that will bring darkness to this day."

Her eyes moved over his face as her lips muttered, "Great."

"First," he began, keeping her close, "I will preface what I have to say with reminding you of the fact that all efforts have been made to make you safe here, poppy. And you are."

"Okay," she said slowly when he stopped speaking.

"However, some weeks ago, Valentine reported that she has been keeping an eye on the me of the other world."

He felt her body tighten, therefore he swiftly gave her the rest.

"She is no longer able to see him. She does not understand why this is but has concluded that it is because he is in this world, protected by our foes, brought here to do ill."

After he gave her this news, her gaze drifted to his throat.

He opened his mouth to reassure her but didn't get a word out before she looked to him again.

"Figures," she stated calmly. "He's *such* a *dick*."

Apollo stared at her.

She continued speaking.

"So, I blew it with the other Cora, they're probably thinking that they can get to me through him since he's, like, a normal human being and can probably get through enchantments and the like. They figure I'll mistake him for you and then they'll get their wicked hands on me."

"I do not know their plans, dove. It is simply that *you* should know he might be here, and if he is, they have plans to use him. Thus, you must be alert."

"Well, whatever," she stated breezily, and Apollo blinked. "They're whacked if they think I can't tell the difference. I mean, seriously? First of all, he doesn't have a hand. And secondly, he's *so not you*."

Although her words pleased him—*greatly*—his eyes narrowed on her in surprise. "You're unconcerned?"

"Uh...in a million years, would you allow Pol to ever hurt me again?"

Gods.

"No." The word was firm, his voice was low, but yet again his chest was tight. "Not in a million years."

"So then," she shrugged, "whatever. Bring it on. Maybe you can cut his other hand off this time."

He stared at her.

Then he clasped her close and burst out laughing.

When he was done, she was grinning at him. She leaned in, touched her mouth to his smiling lips and pulled away to twist to the table by the chair. She carefully placed Christophe's story there and twisted back.

Then she reached behind her to curl her fingers around his wrist, pulling his arm from around her. Her hand slid over his so that she could press it deep to her stomach.

She did all this holding his eyes.

Once she had his hand in place, she said softly, "We have something to celebrate, baby."

They absolutely did.

She leaned in again and the distance was not vast, but Apollo met her half-way. He did this surging out of the chair, holding her to him.

He accepted her kiss as he walked her to the bed.

Once he had her in it, she accepted his kiss.

After she accepted it, he gave her a great deal more.

31

LOVE IS EVERYTHING

I tapped the feather of the quill to my lips, staring at the blank sheet of paper, totally at a loss.

"Maddie?"

At his call, my eyes went to Apollo.

"Hmm?"

He was fully dressed, prepared to take off on Torment and pump arrows into bunnies and deer in the hunt.

I was in my nightgown, robe and fur slippers, sitting at the writing desk in our room, trying not to think of my man off pumping arrows into bunnies and deer.

I watched him look to the desk then at me before he asked, "What are you doing?"

"Writing Chris a note," I answered and shifted my gaze to the paper.

Apollo's voice was getting closer as he noted, "Dove, he's just four doors down the hall." I looked back at him as he finished, "Why would you be writing him a note?"

"He didn't make a show of giving me his story, Lo," I explained. "I don't want to make him uncomfortable when I return it, but I *do* want to tell him how much I liked it. So I'm writing him a note."

He stopped by the desk and his face got soft as his lips murmured, "Ah."

It was at his "ah," which only Apollo could make sexy, belatedly, my eyes traveled over his lusciousness wearing his deep-green sweater and brown breeches, and I lost focus on my task.

I looked to his face and said, "We don't have trains, phones or scoop-shaped Fritos here, but I'm seeing a variety of pluses. Men on my...I mean, in the other world don't look hot when they go hunting."

Apollo ignored my remark about him looking hot and asked, "Scoop-shaped Fritos?"

"Corn chips that are awesome normally, but these ones are especially designed for dipping which increases their awesomeness exponentially mostly because I haven't yet met a dip I did not like," I replied.

His brows narrowed telling me that clearly didn't cut it as an explanation.

"Food," I said simply. "Food that I enjoy."

Upon my answer, he bent to me and offered quietly. "I'll give Valentine a diamond to bring some back for you."

Only Apollo would offer a diamond for Fritos.

Seriously.

My guy was the bomb.

"I'm not sure that's an equal trade," I shared.

"Anything my dove wants is worth whatever it takes to give it to her," he returned.

Seriously.

My guy was *the bomb*.

In that moment, sitting in my robe and nightgown, looking up at his beauty, carrying his child, knowing I'd soon have his name (well, a name I already had but the good one this time), I decided he needed to know that, so I told him, "You're the bomb."

His eyes lit with humor.

"I take it that's good," he remarked.

"You take it right," I replied.

He smiled.

I tipped my head back hoping he'd understand the invitation.

He did. Leaning further, he gave me a short, sweet, but thankfully wet kiss, the wet part being a touch of the tips of our tongues.

Delicious.

He pulled away an inch but kept hold of my eyes. "Anything you say to Christophe will be fine. Don't fret over it. Just be you."

Just be me.

Apollo thought that was enough.

And he taught me it was.

More than enough.

A beautiful lesson to learn.

"Okay," I whispered.

He lifted a hand to slide his fingers in the side of my hair and curled them around the back. Once positioned, he pulled my head down so he could touch his lips to the top of my hair.

He allowed me to tip my head back again and ordered, "Wish your betrothed luck in the hunt."

On a grin, not thinking of the unsuspecting deer and bunnies, I did as bid. "Good luck in the hunt."

He grinned back then his face got serious. "Do not leave this house, my dove."

Like I'd make that mistake again.

"I won't," I promised.

"Not much longer and all you'll need to worry about is preparations for our marriage celebration and decorating the nursery."

Happiness swept through me. So much of it, even though I was sitting, I had to lift my hand and curl it around his forearm to hold myself steady.

But all that had gone before understandably meant that happiness clouded.

This time, I didn't hold it in.

This time, I shared it immediately.

"Do you think I'll be able—?"

He cut me off with a firm, "Yes."

"This is...she is..." I swallowed. "She's ours, Apollo, we made her. And if something—"

He twisted his hand gently in my hair and took back half the inch that he went away.

"You and I, Madeleine, we have had more than our share of sadness and tragedy. Think on this, my poppy. It is an impossibility that we would find each other. But we did. And when we did, the odds were against us with who came before...for you and for me. We beat those odds. And to settle in your womb, this child beat pennyrium. Do you not think all this says that it is time we set the sadness and tragedy where it belongs and look ahead to a future that could do nothing but beam bright?"

Well, if he put it that way.

"Yes," I agreed.

"Yes," he repeated firmly. "You have proved time and again you can do anything. Keep yourself safe from grave danger. Find your way in a world all new to you. Win the affection of a boy burdened by grief. Witnessing you do all that, I believe in my heart, my poppy, that you can also do this."

Okay, I believed too since he put it that way.

"All right, honey," I replied.

"All right," he stated, took that last half an inch and touched his lips to mine. When he again moved back, he didn't go far. And I felt it in my belly in a warm way I'd never felt it before (and before I'd felt it in a *way* warm way), when he whispered, "I love you, my Madeleine."

I hoped my way was just as warm when I replied, "I love you too, baby." I grinned at him. "Now go show those cute bunnies and helpless deer who's boss."

His eyes crinkled and he again pulled me forward, this time to touch his mouth to my forehead before he let me go and started to move away.

"I'll see you this afternoon," he called.

"See you this afternoon," I called to his back.

He opened the door and stopped, turned to me and gave me a deep bow.

When he straightened, he winked.

I smiled.

The door closed.

I took in a deep breath and put my hand to my belly.

"A future that beams bright," I said to no one but did it still smiling.

Then it hit me, I turned to the paper and added ballpoint pens to the shopping list Apollo was going to pay for in diamonds because it took me ten back and forths to the inkpot to write:

Chris,

This was fabulous. Thank you for allowing me to read it. I couldn't put it down and can't wait to see the ending.

In more ways than one.

xx Maddie

~

I was strolling through the halls, giving myself a tour of all the fabulousness that was the Winter Palace, and being interrupted in this endeavor repeatedly seeing as there were a ton of people in Fyngaard for the Bitter Gales and it seemed the majority of them were staying at the palace.

I was also experiencing something strange. This was that, apparently, a number of them had seen me at the Drakkar gale in Brunskar, and further, word had spread about me pretty widely so not a lot of people were freaked at seeing me, the image of the departed Ilsa Ulfr, strolling the halls of their princess's regal residence.

Then again, it also appeared I'd been replaced.

They had new objects of fascination. These being knowing that Dax Lahn and his Dahksahna were attending. People I had met in passing at the Drakkar gale and people I'd never met before in my life stopped me to ask if I'd seen either of them.

It was obvious royalty from the Southlands didn't regularly hobnob with the aristocracy of the Northlands, so this was an event. But everyone was well aware of who Lahn and Circe were and the way many of them asked after them, I didn't like all that much.

They weren't celebrities.

They were clearly oddities.

I wasn't a big fan of this so I quickly learned not to make eye contact as I quickly decided to find Circe and fill her in so she wouldn't be blindsided by it, hoping that she hadn't already been.

Finding her was an easy task since the first servant I encountered knew exactly where she was and had actually been sent to find me to "Attend our Winter Princess, Cora, the Gracious, and the Golden Queen in the library."

I gave her a smile, a thanks and scooted to the library.

I found the doors guarded by Frey's men, Gunner and Stephan.

Since the palace was supposed to be safe, I wasn't sure that was good.

"Is everything okay?" I asked when I stopped at the doors.

"Finnie doesn't want to be disturbed. It's the Bitter Gales, and since she's off with Frey half the time, they now have their chance, so everyone wants her ear," Gunner answered. "We're here to make that stop."

"I see it's good having Raiders at your back," I noted.

"Always," Gunner agreed as Stephan moved to open the door for me.

"Thanks," I said as I moved in.

Stephan lifted his chin to me.

I walked in seeing six women standing at the window, Circe, Finnie, Cora and the three women who fell on Finnie when she arrived the day before.

"What's up?" I called, and all eyes came to me, but it was Finnie who spoke.

Waving her hand my way, she called, "Come here."

I moved through the vast space lined with books. It was warm, even though there was only one fireplace. Then again, that fireplace was shockingly huge, so it was definitely up for the task of heating that space.

I joined them at the windows just as Circe announced, "I think things are coming to a head."

I was thinking she was right because I was staring out the window at Loretta and Hans.

He was standing straight and removed, barely having tipped his chin down to catch her eyes.

She was leaned into him slightly, a beseeching posture, that was solidified by the look on her face which was definitely imploring.

At first glance, things did not appear to be going well for Loretta.

Stupid, *stupid* Hans.

"How long have they been at it?" I asked, pushing closer into the group so I could get closer to the window.

"I saw them and called for everyone," Circe replied. "At least twenty minutes."

Twenty minutes?

Oh crap.

Hans was making her work for it and I did not like that.

Suddenly, he moved as if to turn away and Loretta jumped to catch his hand.

He twisted it before she could latch on, and it took everything I had not to rap on the window and shout at him to stop being such a *man* and *listen.*

But I didn't need to.

Loretta instantly took a step back, disappointment washing through her features before she blanked them and jerked up her chin.

Her mouth moved, and unfortunately, try as I might (and it had been some weeks that I'd been trying), I could not read her lips.

Hans's back was to us so I couldn't see his expression. I could only see that when Loretta was done speaking, she was just plain *done.* I knew this when she instantly turned and started plodding through the snow.

Hans allowed her to take four steps before he went after her.

Okay. That was good.

He grabbed her hand.

Okay. That was better.

She twisted it free before he could catch it.

Okay. That was bad.

But in doing this, she had to turn his way.

He took advantage, catching her with an arm around her waist.

Now that was *excellent.*

"Go get her, tiger," Finnie whispered.

We watched Loretta lean away as Hans bent deep. He was obviously talking. She just as obviously wasn't hip on listening.

And then he quit talking and started kissing.

"All *right,*" Circe said softly.

Loretta didn't make him work for that. She didn't even protest a little.

She wrapped her arms around his shoulders and melted into his body.

He leaned in deeper, bending her over his arm.

"Nice," Cora remarked.

It sure looked it.

I just hoped it was.

Christophe was going to be pleased.

I was withholding judgment until...

Hans suddenly broke the kiss and straightened Loretta in his arms before he cupped her jaw in a tender manner that made Loretta's face get soft in a way that I liked very much.

Okay, it took approximately three seconds, but I'd stopped withholding judgment.

I smiled.

"Awesome," Cora said. "I wish I'd seen this whole thing from the beginning."

"Don't worry, we'll fill you in," Finnie assured her.

I was just about to suggest we give them some privacy by asking to be introduced to Finnie's friends when one of them asked, "What's that?"

My eyes went to her to see hers still at the window, so I looked that way, beyond Hans and Loretta.

Then my blood turned to ice because a sea of wolves was heading out of the forest behind the palace and into the clearing.

Not one.

Or five.

Or seven.

A sea.

That could not mean good things.

"Oh shit," I whispered.

"By the Gods!" another of Finnie's friends cried. "The skies!"

Pressing in with all the girls, I looked up to see the sky filled with meteors.

Yes.

Meteors!

Red, black and blue little missiles, hundreds of them, maybe thousands were raining down from the sky.

They exploded against what had been an invisible dome but now it was not. Now, with each missile strike, a burst of red, black and blue sparks shot out, and where they struck, a colored cloud of leafy or emerald-green spread.

But there were so many missiles, the green cloudbursts were blocking out the sun.

That was not good either.

"Shit," I snapped as I watched all this, taking in the wolves filling the space and Hans dragging Loretta toward the palace.

"This is not good," Circe whispered my thoughts out loud.

It absolutely was not.

We were under attack.

The dome was holding up, the wolves seeming to be forming a perimeter around the palace, my mind came unfrozen, and my thoughts centered on two things.

Therefore, I whirled.

As I turned, the doors burst open and Gunner and Stephan came in.

I ran across the library in order to run out.

Stephan caught me with an arm around my waist and I struggled against his hold as the room darkened further, the missiles hitting the enchanted dome so furiously, the clouds of protective magic blotted out the sun.

"You must stay together!" Stephan demanded, controlling my struggles with irritating ease.

I stopped suddenly and turned in his arm.

"Élan and Chris," was all I said.

"We are all safe in this palace," Stephan replied.

That might be so.

But I didn't fucking care.

"Until their father returns, I want them with me!" I snapped.

Stephan looked in my eyes and saw what I meant him to see. I knew this when he looked over my head. I twisted my neck to look at Gunner.

He jerked up his chin and moved swiftly out the doors.

I could feel the growing panic and confusion drifting in from the others of the palace when I saw Alek and Remi appear in the doors.

They looked to Stephan, and Remi ordered, "Close the drapes," before he grabbed one doorknob, Alek the other and they closed us in.

Stephan let me go and prowled to the windows.

"What should we do?" one of Finnie's friends asked.

"Nothing," Finnie answered. "Just stay calm."

I didn't stay calm, but I did it unmoving. I stood in the dark room, staring at the doors while Cora and Circe moved around lighting the lamps.

Seconds slid by and my panic escalated.

"Come on, get them here," I said to the door. "Get them here."

Cora got close, touched her hand to mine and urged, "Come and sit, Maddie."

I didn't take my eyes from the doors.

"Sit, Maddie," Finnie said from my other side. "Gunner will get them here."

I didn't move.

The doors opened and my heart leaped, but only for an instant.

Meeta was coming through.

I dashed to her.

"Élan and Chris," I said the instant I made it to her.

"I will go get them," she replied.

She turned to the doors that Alek and Remi had closed behind her only to find Stephan standing there.

"Stay here with your woman," Stephan ordered.

"My Maddie wants the children," Meeta replied.

"Stay—" Stephan started but didn't finish.

The doors opened again and Hans all but shoved Loretta through.

I was happy to see Loretta but, God!

Where were the kids?

Loretta rushed to Meeta and me. Her eyes were wild, and when she grabbed my hand, I felt hers shaking.

Feeling her fear, it cut through me. Belatedly but it did it.

I had survived bad shit. A terrible family. An abusive, criminal husband. Transportation to a whole different world.

And I was Captain Kirk. Kirk didn't freak. Kirk kept his shit together.

I needed to get my shit together.

I grabbed both Loretta and Meeta's hands and held tight.

"Just waiting for the kids to get here and all will be well," I told them. "We're protected."

"Yes," Meeta said on a squeeze of my hand, and I knew she squeezed Loretta's too. "Good magic will prevail."

Loretta licked her lips and held on tight.

I glanced around the room to see the others were holding their shit and I took a deep breath to hold mine.

That worked some.

So I did it again.

Not great.

But better.

The doors opened and Élan and Chris were ushered in by Gunner. I saw Laures and Draven out with Alek and Remi.

Laures caught my eyes and nodded.

Okay, the kids were here, the guys were out there, Laures seemed calm.

I was even better.

I nodded back.

Gunner closed the doors, joining us on our side.

Élan ran to me.

I let my girls go and crouched down just in time for her little body to hit mine.

I wrapped my arms tight around her.

"It's dark outside, Miss Maddie!" she cried, her little voice trembling with fear.

And we could just say the sensation was extreme when the ice in my blood immediately ran hot when fear washed out and anger washed in.

My attention went to Chris, and I held his sister tight to me as I said, "Everything's going to be fine. Your papa has made us safe. No one will get us."

Chris came our way, and he stopped close, putting his hand on his sister's back.

"It will be fine, Élan," he muttered, his gaze on mine.

I gave him a trembling smile.

His return smile was not trembling.

So like his dad.

Unfortunately, the next moment, we heard shrieks coming from the hall.

Élan pressed deeper and made a noise of fear from low in her throat.

At hearing her fear, I swallowed my growl and felt the women pressing closer around us.

"Perhaps we should go to the nursery." I heard Cora say quietly. "I'm not sure my Hayden will sleep through this and I don't want him to wake frightened."

"I agree," Finnie replied, but her voice was uncertain and worried, and her focus was on Stephan. "The nursery is higher ground and we should all be together."

"You stay here," Stephan replied. "It's a mistake to move you and Zahnin, Bain, Oleg, Quincy, Balthazar, Max, Annar, Ruben and Thad are guarding the children."

That was a lot of protection.

I just hoped it was enough.

One look at Finnie's face, which was still worried but no longer uncertain, I knew it was enough.

There was a thud that sounded like a body hitting the wall outside.

Damn it!

I jumped. Élan jumped in my arms. Murmurs filtered through the women around me. And Chris jerked to look at the door.

"We're safe," I whispered to Élan, smoothing my hand over her hair, hoping to God the boys outside were as well.

She pushed deep, whining, "I want Papa."

I did too.

"We'll be okay, honey bunch," I told her. "He'll be here soon."

I pulled her even closer as more shrieks came.

These were close and another body thumped. This time against the door.

Chris whirled to me, his eyes wide. The little boy coming out, he couldn't hide his fear.

And at that, fire burned through me.

Those fucking witch *bitches*.

The women got even closer, Cora putting a hand to Chris's shoulder and guiding him into our huddle.

"Miss Maddie," Meeta whispered.

"We're safe," I stated.

"Miss Maddie, give me the child." Meeta was still whispering.

Oh crap.

I tipped my head back to look at her.

I didn't like what I saw.

"No," I said softly.

She stared into my eyes.

"They blocked me," she said softly. "Their power directed on other things, I am no longer blocked."

She had been blocked.

She was no longer blocked.

She knew what was going to happen.

And she wanted Élan.

Okay.

Shit.

No.

Apollo's words pounded through my brain.

Do you not think all this says that it is time we set the sadness and tragedy where it belongs and look ahead to a future that could do nothing but beam bright?

I stared into Meeta's eyes.

Apparently, he was wrong.

Making my decision, I surged up, pushing Élan her way. "Go!" I cried and turned to Loretta. "Take Chris!"

Loretta instantly grabbed Chris.

"Maddie, it's oh—" Finnie started.

At the same time, Chris shouted, "I stay with Miss Maddie!"

It was then there came a deafening explosion, the force of which blew the windows and curtains in, shattered glass and shards of velvet blasting through the air.

I reached for Chris and shoved him to the floor as we all hit the deck.

When the glass settled, I lifted my head and my eyes found Meeta's.

"Take them now!" I yelled, rolling off Chris, coming to my feet and pulling him up with me, pure instinct prompting me to finish. "Take them to the wolves!"

Meeta rose, coming off of Élan who she'd thrown herself on, dragging the weight of the girl up in her arms and starting to run.

"I stay with Miss Maddie!" Chris shouted.

I looked to see Loretta was pulling him to the doors, but he was resisting her.

"Go with Loretta, Chris, please!" I shouted as the room started filling with mist.

Red mist.

Blue mist.

Black mist.

Bad mist.

All of it swirling around me, Cora, Finnie and Circe.

The men outside surged in, and I saw all of Apollo's men there and some of Frey's.

Shit!

"*Miss Maddie!*" Élan shrieked, stretching her arms my way as she and Meeta disappeared around the door.

In her place, another Circe raced in, trailed by Valentine.

They lifted their hands and gold and green sparks filled the room.

I felt my hand tagged and I looked right.

Cora had me.

I felt my other had tagged and I looked left.

Circe had me.

I looked in front of me.

Circe and Cora had Finnie.

"Shit, shit, *shit*," Finnie whispered right when the room faded away.

Apollo

APOLLO FOLLOWED Lahn into the stone room in the bowels of the Winter Palace, a room full of men.

And one woman.

The moment they hit it, Lahn turned to look over his shoulder at Apollo.

"Is this her?' he growled.

Apollo had no idea what he was asking and didn't care.

Maddie was gone. Knowing his children were under heavy guard of soldiers, witches and wolves, getting her back was the only thing on his mind.

Lahn decided to take his non-answer as answer and stalked directly to Franka Drakkar, who was cowering in the corner under Oleg and Laures.

He shoved the men aside and Apollo watched as he lifted the woman by her throat and threw her across the room.

She didn't even have time to scream.

Lahn followed her where she landed against the stone with a thud and he bent over, his face an inch from hers.

"*Betrayal*," he barked, "carries harsh punishment."

Frey, already in the room, got close to Lahn.

"For now, we need her alive," Frey said quietly, but his voice was tight, controlled. There was anger in his frame making it stiff and he was avoiding looking at Franka, likely for fear of what he himself would do if he looked at her.

"I did as you asked," Franka whispered, and Apollo forced his eyes to her.

Her gaze shifted from Lahn to Frey.

"I did as you asked!" she cried.

"Bring her to me."

All the men turned to see the other Circe and Valentine in the room, Tor having come in behind them.

Apollo moved until he was toe to toe, nose to nose with the witch, and he clipped, "You said they were safe."

"Bring the woman to me," she demanded then stepped leisurely to the side and turned her eyes to Frey. "Call your elves. We meet on Specter Isle."

Tor moved to her side, ordering, "Send us there now."

Valentine turned to him. "With the triad intact, their magic is too strong. I can't get you there. I can't get *me* there. And Lavinia has fallen to Helda."

Apollo's gut twisted at this news and Valentine kept talking.

"We will have to be clever. For the elves to do their work against our foes *and* for Lavinia, we will have to be swift. And we will have to have hope."

Apollo opened his mouth to speak but Valentine continued before he could utter a word.

"As I suspected, this is a battle of sisters and magic. Just sisters and magic. Both the same thing. Not all good. Not all evil. We shall see which side prevails. But you must trust in good for *our* side knows allies whose bonds are formed in ways that cannot be broken."

Apollo felt something unpleasant shift inside him and whispered, "You knew. You knew our plan would fail."

She looked to him. "I told you, *mon loup*, I do not have the sight."

He leaned into her and thundered, "*You knew!*"

She didn't respond to that.

She said, "Keep your wolves at the ready around the palace and bring the woman to me." Her eyes stayed locked to his. "Bring her to me, Apollo. To win, we need our own evil. There is only one thing more powerful than vengeance, and if you bring her to me, we will have both on our side."

Apollo held her gaze and clenched his jaw.

Then he stepped to the side and turned to Frey and Lahn.

"Give her Franka."

Frey didn't move. Lahn only moved to straighten away from the woman still on her back on the floor.

It was Achilles who shifted forward, helped Franka from the stone, and escorted her as any gentleman would do, as only Achilles would now do, to Valentine.

"Take hold of my arm," Valentine ordered her.

"I don't—" Franka started, shrinking away.

Valentine pinned her with her gaze.

"Do you seek vengeance?" she asked.

Franka hesitated before lifting her chin and answering, "Yes."

"Then take my arm," Valentine bid.

Franka wrapped her fingers around Valentine's arm.

Valentine looked to the other Circe. "Gather the children. If the choice is to be made, you know the only protection that will keep them safe. Your life for theirs."

The mood in the room, already dark, turned pitch.

Circe nodded.

Valentine lifted her hands.

Frey, Lahn and Tor gathered around Apollo.

"Bring them back," Apollo growled.

Valentine smiled a cat's smile.

"Oh *chéri*, have faith."

Gods, the woman was bloody infuriating.

The green mist formed.

Franka and Valentine disappeared.

But Valentine's final words could still be heard.

"Remember, love is everything."

Maddie

Holding tight, we'd been falling but we landed with a thud that buckled our knees, each and every one of us.

Recovering, I jerked my hands, pulling Cora and Circe closer. Obviously, they did the same for Finnie was just as close, we four forming a tight huddle.

"All right?" Finnie asked.

"All right," Cora whispered.

"Yeah," Circe said.

"Okay," I replied.

We looked at each other then we looked around.

"Fuck," Circe breathed.

She had that right.

We were in a mammoth room that had to be at least the size of a football field. It was entirely made of grayish-white blocks of stone.

There were two gigantic wooden doors behind Finnie. They were at least two stories tall and made of grayish-white wood with what looked like pewter hinges. It also looked like it'd take half a dozen men to open them.

And last, they were closed.

But that wasn't the bad part.

No.

The bad part was that we could see this beyond the glimmering, flickering, ethereal blue bars that formed a cage.

I glanced up, seeing the bars curved in at the top, making an enormous, magical birdcage.

Well, one thing was certain, Minerva had a thing for birds.

Cora shuffled closer, looking over her shoulder.

"Not good," she mumbled.

I scanned that way and went stone still.

This was because the cage was situated close to some steps leading up to a dais.

And on that dais was a large throne that looked to be made of gray-ish white branches that swept out and up, ending in lethal-looking thorns.

Sitting on that throne was Pol.

And last, snuggled in his lap was Cora, the Nasty.

Fuck.

We all turned toward them in unison, letting each other's hands go but tightening our huddle.

Cora, the Nasty was grinning down at us.

Pol was scowling down at me.

Fuck.

"Looks like those two found their perfect match," Cora muttered under her breath.

It was funny.

It was also true.

No one laughed, we just stayed close and watched the couple watching us.

Unfortunately, Pol moved.

He rose from the throne, lifting Cora with him. He put her to her feet and slung an arm around her shoulders, pulling her tight to his side.

She cuddled tighter, wrapping an arm around his waist.

And in that position, they moved down the steps toward our cage.

We stood still and watched them.

They kept coming.

I fought my teeth worrying my lip as Pol continued to approach, every move he made he did it with his focus glued to me.

They came to the glistening blue bars of the cage and I held my breath.

My stomach dropped when they walked right through.

The women shifted and did it shifting me so they could surround me.

But Pol didn't stop close.

He stopped five feet away, and the instant he did, Cora, the Nasty turned into him and curled both her arms around his middle.

Her eyes were aimed at Cora, the Awesome.

After I noticed this, I aimed my eyes back to Pol.

When I did, he lifted the arm that was around Cora's shoulders and waved his hand in the air.

I hadn't noticed it.

Then I did.

And I felt my lips part in terrified awe.

"Nice," he said low, his voice sinking into my skin and not in a good way. "Steel," he went on and my attention darted to the shining molten silver hand that moved like a normal hand but was absolutely *not.* "It's heavy," he continued then finished, "But it works."

The women pressed in closer around me.

"Yours," Cora, the Nasty put in at this point, and I tore my eyes from Pol to look at her and see she was still looking at Cora, the Cool. "Flawed," she carried on and cuddled deeper into Pol. "Mine is *perfect.*"

Pol curled his arm tight around her again.

I felt bile fill my throat.

We all jumped as we heard the loud creak of hinges fill the space. Then we looked over our shoulders to see the doors swinging backward.

In walked a round man wearing a red velvet cloak with black velvet breeches, exceptionally gleaming black boots and a shiny red silk shirt.

When he got closer, I noticed he also had mean, beady eyes.

He stopped outside the bars of the cage, peered in, his gaze moving straight to Circe.

Then it went to Pol.

"Is that one mine?" he asked.

"No," Pol answered. "Yours is coming."

The man looked back to Circe, and at the expression on his face, this time I had to swallow down the bile when he declared, "If I don't get her, I'll take this one."

"Baldur," Circe murmured low.

Fantastic.

"Watching them all these months," Cora, the Nasty stated, and we turned her way to see she'd disengaged from Pol and was prowling a circle around us. "They all seemed so brave." She stopped and tipped her head to the side, studying us. "Not so brave without swords at their back."

Again, my body froze except my eyes, which shot to Pol when he said, "Seems I'll finally get a kid outta you." My breath froze when he continued, "Me and Cora, we get to raise yours." He tipped his head Cora, the Righteous's way. "And hers."

Oh boy.

This was getting worse.

"Edith wants the ice," Baldur said, and we looked to him to see him staring at Finnie. "She wants it because she wants the dragons and elves. She'll be taking yours."

Oh God.

And worse.

"Yours just goes," Baldur went on, his gaze moving to Circe. "As do the other two you pushed out for that savage. For me to have the Southlands, the Golden Dynasty must fall."

I reached out, grabbed Circe's hand and her fingers tightened around mine the instant mine found hers.

"It's gonna be fuckin' cool, havin' the wolves," Pol said, and I looked to him to see he had moved to Cora, the Bitchy and claimed her again. "My woman, she just wants a place called Bellebryn. Likes the castle there. So that'll be hers."

I clenched my teeth so I wouldn't bite my lip and held his gaze, knowing he was not done.

And he wasn't.

"'Course, this means that not only does the blonde bitch's kids have to bite it, all of them do."

Shit, shit, *shit.*

"Viktor is the next Frey *and* Drakkar," Cora, the Terrible put in. "With him gone, and with the help of Minerva, the girl child you carry will make history being the first female to command the elves and dragons. We have you to thank for that, not being of this world, sharing the strength of your love for your husband with your female child. It makes not only the one you carry but the ones all of you carry immensely powerful."

There it was. Our coinciding pregnancies weren't a coincidence.

They knew this was going to happen and they planned to take away our babies.

"That's why your girl will command the wolves," Pol added my way. "Obviously, after we get rid of the boy."

My insides squeezed.

Chris.

"And your girl will take over the Northlands," Cora, the Bad told Cora, the Good. "We'll rule for her at first, of course. But Minerva has grand plans for her." She leaned in and smiled with saccharine sweetness. "*Grand* plans. She chose well with you and Prince Noctorno. She'll mold a powerful witch from the child you make." She leaned back and her eyes skimmed us all. "She'll mold powerful witches from *all* the girls you make."

"So you brought us here so you could steal our daughters?" Circe asked.

"She's a quick one," Pol murmured on a grin down at Cora, the Awful.

"It was Helda's idea," Baldur shared, and we looked to him. "Knowing it takes great magic to build love between the worlds. Magic greater than the dragons. Greater than the elves. Greater than anything. Magic the kind neither world has ever known. Minerva splitting the souls of Prince Noctorno and his bride gave her the idea. Then the stories came from the ice lands, the savage lands. Love forming legend. She knew if she could harness that magic, well..." He tipped his head to the side. "She also knew she couldn't do it alone. She approached Minerva, they recruited Edith, and of course they had to have those of us who wished to take care of the day-to-day tasks of ruling nations once they dispatched the mightiest of warriors, claimed their powerful daughters, and conquered the land." He walked forward, came through the bars, and tipped his head Cora and Pol's way. "That's what we get."

"So, essentially, to be a ruler the only quality you have to have is being foul?" Cora, the Bomb asked.

Baldur took no offense. I knew this when he smiled an oily smile.

"I see that you realize no harm will come to you for some months," he replied. "Still, bravado from a delectable morsel such as yourself is most enjoyable."

"Why do your witches not show themselves?" Circe asked.

"More bravado," Baldur murmured, his eyes moving over Circe in a way that made all of us get closer to her. "Don't think your magic will serve you here, my child. All magic save that of our mistresses is constricted. It won't work. Your green witch, when she arrives, will be rendered useless. Then she will be dispatched." His face lit with malicious glee when he finished, "You've woefully underestimated their power. Thinking something so immense could weaken under dragon fire. Understandable, most definitely, a dragon's blaze is immeasurable, and, of course, no one is more powerful than an elf." He leaned in, smiling big. "Except them."

This was not good.

It got worse when suddenly, four things penetrated the ceiling.

One was a shoot of black smoke.

It headed to the dais, formed a throne of what looked like a spray of black steel rods and sitting in it was a woman wearing a black dress cut in the fashion of the Vale. She had black hair and black eyes, alabaster skin and, surprisingly, a very pretty face.

And behind the throne, at the side, Derrik formed.

Derrik.

My heart stopped.

He glared at me.

What the fuck?

I thought he was off on some self-appointed mission for our side.

What was he doing here?

With *them*?

I wanted to think on it.

I couldn't think on it.

I had to look to the other side where there was a blaze of red falling.

It also headed to the dais, opposite the black and gray thrones.

It formed another throne that radiated red fire and in it sat a somewhat hefty woman wearing a dress of yellow, orange and red panels that looked like something a she-clown would wear (except way more scary than your average clown, of course).

She had a mass of ratted out, flame-red hair and she was, not unsurprisingly, not attractive at all.

Another was a flash of blue sparks.

It aimed and obliterated the gray throne in a flare of blue glimmers. In its place, it formed a see-through throne of what appeared to be crystals. In it hovered—not sat—a woman wearing a floating wispy blue dress, her white hair highlighted with electric blue streaks. And last, the pale skin of her face stretched over features that could not be described as anything other than birdlike.

Well there you go.

Her affinity to birds explained.

And last, a green spray that looked liquid rained from the ceiling. It fell straight to the foot of the dais, and when it landed, the prone body of Lavinia, the good witch of Lunwyn thumped lifeless on the stone.

Shit, shit.

Fuck.

"No," Finnie breathed, her voice choked with horror and sorrow.

"They are not here?"

The words sounded around us, not from a person, but the black witch (definitely Helda) and the red witch (by the process of elimination, Edith) looked to the blue witch (absolutely Minerva).

Thus, I guessed it was Minerva's disembodied voice that sounded around us.

No one answered her and I figured she was talking at least about Valentine because she had to see we were there.

Though no one answered her question, Pol spoke.

"I want her."

I looked to him to see he'd let Cora, the Unpleasant go and was pointing toward our huddle.

But I knew he meant me.

"Patience," the black witch Helda said. "Mere months and she will be yours to play with."

Okay, things looked pretty bad, but that shit was *not* going to happen.

Pol was moving their way, wearing a smile on his face I knew. A charming, handsome smile that, in the beginning, helped him get away with a lot of shit.

"I'll be gentle," he told them.

"Patience," Helda repeated.

Pol stopped and asked, "Do you think I'd do anything to fuck this gig?"

The witches looked down at him.

Finally, Helda lifted her hand and murmured, "Oh, very well."

Crap.

That was the only thought I had the time to have. I cried out in surprise as suddenly I was torn from the women. My body moving not on my own power, I shot across the space straight to Pol. I tried to twist and turn. I tried to do *anything* to stay away from him.

I could twist and I could turn, but nothing stopped me from slamming right into him.

His arms instantly curled tight around me.

Fabulous.

"What's this?" Cora, the Rotten asked, her voice pitched slightly higher.

"Just play," Pol answered her, but his focus was on me.

I struggled in his arms as I heard noises that would indicate Finnie, Circe and Cora were struggling as well. With what, I had no clue and I couldn't look.

I could only focus on getting away from Pol.

He had no problem holding me.

This was not magic. He'd always been stronger than me.

"You let him touch you," he whispered.

Here we go.

"Let me go, Pol," I whispered back, still struggling.

"Took his cock," he bit out. "Let him plant a baby inside of you."

I pushed against him, trying to find a way to get a kick in, but did not answer.

"Both my babies, gone. This one will come." He jerked his head to indicate the witches. "They've seen her."

I went still in his arms.

They'd seen my baby.

This one would come.

Something welled up inside me and it felt good.

Super-freaking-good.

Keep-myself-alive-at-all-costs and not-give-up good.

But I still had Pol to deal with.

"One of them gone," I snapped. "The other one you killed."

His eyes flashed, his arms tightened, and his face dipped to mine ignoring words that were heinous and flat-out true.

"Took his cock," he whispered.

"Yes," I hissed.

"Did you think of me when he was fucking you?" he asked.

I stared right into his eyes, lifted my chin and answered, "Not... fucking...*once*."

His arms got so tight, I feared for my ribs.

"His kid is out of you, all you got is me," he gritted. "They got plans. This is gonna be a bad day for you, baby. They get you. They'll get your girl. They're gonna take care of the rest. And that means that guy who you've been lettin' bang you, he's dust."

I couldn't believe that.

I wouldn't believe that.

Things did not look good.

But Apollo would find a way.

Frey would find a way.

Lahn would.

Tor would.

There was a way and they'd find it.

His hand came up, the steel one, and he touched my face with it.

It felt tremendously cold and very heavy against my skin, and suddenly all I could think was that it would cave in my skull if he landed it on me in anger.

Pol got so close all I could see were his eyes.

"I'll make you forget him."

"Fat chance," I shot back.

He smiled a smile that was not handsome or charming. "I'll find a way."

"What...is...*this*?" Cora, the Horrible asked from close and Pol looked to her.

"Back off a second, yeah?" he ordered.

"What is this?" she snapped.

Bad idea.

Pol didn't like it when someone didn't do as ordered.

"Back off," he snarled, his eyes now narrowed. When she didn't move, he continued. "Fuck, there's enough of me to go around."

I looked to her to see her eyes were slits and her back was ramrod straight.

"I do not share," she retorted.

"I say if you share or not," Pol returned.

She swung a hand toward the witches. "They gave you to *me*."

"No, babe, they gave *you* to *me*," he shot back.

"You aren't even of this world!" she cried.

"And you had no use except to dupe Ilsa," he replied. "Jesus, clue in."

"I am to be Queen of the Northlands," she declared.

"Queen to my king, woman." He shook his head. "So fuckin' worried you got your mascara on right, you couldn't run a schoolroom, much less a fuckin' continent. I know how to run an empire, bitch, and they know that. Now," he leaned both of us toward her, "back...the fuck...*off*."

She went for him in a way he had no choice but to let me go.

I heard a disembodied, "Such a *bother*."

But apparently Minerva nor her bitch friends felt like intervening.

Which was rather unfortunate for Cora, the Dreadful because she obviously hadn't gotten to the bad parts of Pol so she didn't know he didn't hold back.

So she could not know it was coming.

Therefore, after a short struggle, when his steel fist crashed into her head, it did, indeed, cave it in.

I stood frozen in shock as she dropped inert to the ground, blood pooling stark red across the grayish-white stone, blood that was coming from her head.

I waited, breathless.

She didn't twitch or even moan.

Holy cow.

He'd just killed her.

Right there.

He'd just killed her.

I backed up, bile again climbing up my throat.

"Maddie! The bars!" Finnie shouted right before a burst of electricity shot along my back and blue sparks sizzled around me.

I scuttled forward just as Pol whirled to me.

"Fuck! Look what you made me do!"

Seriously?

Seriously?

"Me?" I asked.

"You," he spat, starting to stalk toward me. "Christ, always lose my mind around you. Fuckin' crazy."

He *was* fucking crazy but not for the reasons he thought he was.

I couldn't share this. I was circling as he kept stalking and heard an obviously not torn up about the recent demise of Cora, The Nasty, Baldur call, "Please don't. This is most amusing."

Therefore, I knew one of the witches was going to intervene.

She didn't.

Pol kept stalking.

I kept circling.

They were probably amused too, and it was clear Pol was right.

Cora, the Dead was expendable.

I stared at Pol thinking this sucked.

It sucked!

How could life be so awesome, so full of promise, so beautiful, and here I was facing down my freaking ex confined by a magical cage in a whole other world?

I mean, really.

"Trust you to spoil it all when I'm finally happy," I snapped at Pol.

"Do not make me chase you, bitch," he clipped back.

"When Apollo gets here, he's totally going to cut off your steel hand, your other hand and conk you in the head with his sword again."

"Wake up, Ilsa, this shit is not gonna go good for you. The dude's probably already dead."

I could not believe that.

I would not believe that.

But just at the thought, my heart hurt.

"He'll save me," I hissed.

"Kiss him good-bye, babe," he returned.

"Come closer to us, Maddie," Circe called.

"I don't want him near you guys," I called back, still circling but doing it well away from the girls.

"Come closer, Maddie!" Finnie yelled.

"I don't—" I started.

"Come! Now!" Cora shouted.

I didn't know why I did it, but I ran their way.

The instant I got close, Circe clasped my hand and I noticed all of the women were holding hands in a circle.

Finnie grasped my other hand, and the second she did, Circe ordered, "Think about your man."

I had no idea why she wanted us to do that, but I did it.

It wasn't hard. It felt good. Beautiful. Calming. I pulled up a picture of Apollo, tall, strong, big, handsome, his cloak billowing out behind him, then falling forward, swaying around him, enveloping him in its embrace.

That cloak was totally badass.

So was my man.

On this thought, a charge shot through my hands and a ring burst out from our huddle colored in gold, ice blue, violet and poppy stripes. It sliced through Pol and Baldur, taking them off their feet.

Then the ring expanded, stretching tall, and the blue bars of the cage disintegrated.

Finally, it exploded and multi-colored sparks shot everywhere.

I guessed they were wrong about Circe's magic not working here.

Thank God.

"Now, run!" Circe shouted.

We ran toward the doors.

They closed with a loud crash.

Crap!

I skidded to a halt when my arm jerked because I was still holding Circe's hand and she'd gone down, tackled by Baldur.

She rolled him and Finnie grabbed on to his hair, yanking it back.

He howled.

"He was correct," the disembodied voice sounded. "This is *most* amusing."

Fucking witch *bitches*.

I couldn't think on them. Not yet.

I was about to help with the Baldur situation when I was pulled back with a forearm at my throat.

Pol's.

He jerked me two steps back, but I twisted in his hold, coming loose. I ducked and shuffled away.

He reached a steel hand to me but didn't get it close.

This was because Cora tackled him sideways.

Not prepared for her, they went to the ground, and I saw Pol getting ready to aim a blow of his steel fist to her head so I went for it. Lunging, I wrapped both hands around it and yanked it back.

Circe and Finnie must have dealt with Baldur because they showed, and Finnie aimed a kick of her boot to Pol's crotch.

Always a good choice.

Pol groaned, stopped struggling (and admittedly winning), and he curled up on his side, both hands cupping between his legs.

Cora ran to the doors, put her hand to the handle and it was immediately dwarfed by the large dangling circle.

This didn't faze her. She pushed.

I ran to her and pushed.

Finnie and Circe joined us and pushed.

"Use your magic!" Finnie shouted to Circe.

"That wasn't my magic," Circe replied.

"What was it?" Cora cried.

"*Our* magic," Circe answered.

"Where...is...*Valentine*?" Finnie asked on a grunt, pushing.

The voice sounding was actually shaking with humor when it stated, "*Most* amusing."

"Ugh!" I groaned then demanded, "We need to form another huddle, ladies!"

And when I did, suddenly we all fell forward when the doors swung open.

We righted ourselves and I stilled, staring at Franka Drakkar standing outside the doors.

She didn't look at a single one of us as she strolled right in.

Strolled.

Right.

In.

We didn't get the chance to make a break for it. The instant Franka passed the threshold, the doors slammed shut.

We all turned and watched as she slowly made her way across the expanse toward the witches.

"What the fuck?" I heard Finnie whisper.

"I'm not sure this is good," I whispered back.

"You know her?" Cora asked.

"Stay quiet and together," Circe cut in.

We again huddled.

"This is interesting," Helda said, her gaze cast down to Franka who stopped at the foot of the steps at the bottom of the dais. She tipped her head to the side. "You would have made a good ruler. But soon you will be nothing."

"You should have asked without taking my Antoine," Franka replied, and I had to hand it to her, she was good. Ice cold even in times like this. She sounded calm as could be.

"Antoine? Who's Antoine?" Finnie asked.

"Shh!" Cora shushed.

"Prepare," Circe warned.

Oh shit, I thought.

"This is your flaw. He was nothing. The lesson comes too late, but I shall give it to you regardless. You shouldn't waste energies caring about nothing," Helda said to Franka.

I could tell that wasn't the right thing to say with the way Franka's body language changed.

"So be it," Helda went on.

"Yes," Franka replied. "So be it."

And that was when it happened.

She moved, going into a crouch, twisting her torso around at the same time. Her arm extended, and from her hand, a shimmering wave of emerald green shot out.

At that moment, from the ceiling, a body fell.

Landing on his feet in a crouch at the foot of the dais was Tor, strangely wearing jeans, a chambray shirt, and brown boots.

He straightened out of the crouch pulling a gun (yes! A gun!) out of the back of his belt. He aimed it at Edith, who was coming out of her throne, and fired.

She fell back and down, hitting her throne which threw her forward. She rolled down the steps, trailing blood the entire way.

She barely came to a rest at the bottom before Tor turned his gun toward Helda.

But Derrik was on the move and he was moving swiftly. I sucked in a shocked breath when he took Helda's head in both hands, slammed it into the arm of her throne and let her go.

She slumped in the seat.

That was when Lavinia rose up in a shower of icy sparks that, when they dropped to the ground, up sprang miniature creatures, which immediately grew into not-miniature creatures with pointy Spock-like ears. They were also wearing little hats with feathers poking out.

And last, their bodies glowed ice blue.

Instantly, massive troll-like creatures and the bird-head men popped up by the dozens everywhere.

Fuck!

The creatures with hats didn't spare them even a glance. In unison, they threw up their hands and a wall of ice encased Minerva.

Just as they sprang up, the trolls and bird men all made popping sounds and disappeared.

Whoa.

Minerva had not risen from her chair, but seconds after the wall of ice surrounded her, she came out of it, floating high, her body arched back, and a blood-chilling shriek filled the air, making our group huddle closer when a bleed of liquid blue poured from her hovering body into the stone.

"On your knees!" Tor ordered, stalking our way, gun up, and my eyes flew to the side to see Pol up.

"I'm thinking that's not Tor," I mumbled.

"It isn't," Cora whispered. "It's Noc. Tor's twin from our world."

Apparently, Cora's guy's twin was a good guy.

Lucky her.

"Knees!" Noc shouted.

I looked back at Pol who was grinning.

Uh-oh.

"*Knees!*" Noc bellowed.

Pol dashed to the side.

Because he was an asshole, he did this toward me.

He didn't make it.

This was because a wall of man formed in front of me.

I had his back so I saw he was a man wearing a cloak.

A man carrying a sword.

A man who didn't hesitate using that sword.

He swung it out in a mighty arc and I heard a body hit the ground. A nanosecond later, I heard another, quieter thump that included a sickening roll.

"Okay," Cora murmured. "Gross."

Apollo turned to me.

I stared up into his furious jade eyes.

Jade eyes that were beautiful—furious, murderous, whatever, I did not care. I just loved those eyes. I would love those eyes forever as I would love the man who had them.

Not to mention, I was freaking beside myself I was looking into them right then.

So I ignored the bloodied sword (not to mention the drops of blood on his face and clothes) and ran into his arms.

Those arms closed around me.

I felt his lips at my ear and heard his deep voice say to me. "You are safe now, my dove."

I just *knew* he'd find a way.

I took in a long breath and held on tight as I let it go.

"I'm guessing you didn't take his other hand," I said quietly.

"You are correct. I did not."

Bye-bye, Pol.

I closed my eyes.

"It is done, Frey Drakkar."

I opened my eyes and looked to the side to see a pointy-eared man had his gaze aimed our way.

Apollo loosened his grip but didn't let me go. But I could look further around.

Frey was there. As was Lahn. As was Tor (the real one, or the *other* real one).

All was well.

I looked to the vaulted stone ceiling. *Thank you, God.*

"He is mine," Lahn grunted and stalked forward.

I should have known with the way he was stalking, but I didn't think. So I didn't look away and saw Lahn bend over a scuttling Baldur and raise him from the floor by his hair.

Luckily, his back was to us, but I still heard the unmistakable crack when Lahn's arms moved swiftly.

Then, with no ado whatsoever, Lahn dropped Baldur's lifeless body to the ground and turned, stalking back to his woman.

He'd broken Baldur's neck.

Bloodless, at least, but still.

Guh.

"I believe she is yours," Frey said, and my attention went back to him.

He was looking at Tor.

So I looked to Tor to see him nod, bend and kiss Cora on her forehead and then he moved to the thrones.

Lahn disengaged from Circe and fell in behind him. Frey disengaged from Finnie. And Apollo let me go.

They all moved toward the cage of ice.

The be-capped creatures that I figured were elves shifted back as they did.

Apollo was the first one to whip his sword around.

He went for a second pass and Frey pulled his sword out of the scabbard at his back.

Around they both went and Lahn unsheathed his.

Then they all rounded their swords as Tor walked up the steps.

They let fly.

I gasped as the swords struck the wall of ice and it shattered, blowing out. But suddenly, the shards arrested in the air in unison before they tinkled to the ground like harmless bits of crushed ice.

When they did, Minerva's body fell to her throne.

And when it did, Tor moved up the rest of the steps.

I watched her focus on him.

"This can't happen," she said, her voice no longer sounding all around but coming direct from her mouth, her face was stricken. "I'm a god."

"Gods have faith. Gods have loyalty. Gods have love," Tor replied. "You were never a god."

"But—"

That was her last word.

Tor swung his sword and Minerva's head flew to the side.

Okay, I could put up with some gruesome, I'd proved it.

But enough was enough.

I looked away.

I looked back when I heard, "I believe this one is for you."

When I looked back, I saw Valentine lounging casually against the black throne. Helda was still unconscious, slumped in it.

Derrik was not far from Valentine's side.

Apollo moved up the steps that way. I saw him look to Derrik before he turned to Valentine.

"We all go," he declared.

"Of course, *chéri*," she replied and lifted up her hands.

No sooner did she do that then the vast room filled with green mist.

She was a strange one, but it couldn't be said that Valentine wasn't something.

"Here we go again," Finnie muttered as the mist enveloped us.

The room faded away.

This time, we didn't fall.

But I cannot tell you how happy I was when the frozen tundra and snow-tufted pine trees formed around us.

Safe.

Alive.

Home.

I saw movement and turned that way as I felt the others shifting in around me.

The movement was Apollo. My view was from the back, and he was walking away, but I saw he was carrying something in his arms.

I didn't have a chance to see what it was before he thrust his arms forward and whatever he was carrying flew through the air and landed in the snow.

I saw it then.

A body in a black dress rolling through the snow.

I felt an arm go around my waist and looked right.

Finnie was there.

Another arm went around my waist and I looked left.

Cora was there.

Beyond Cora was Circe.

I slid my arms around the women at my sides.

The men (obviously save Apollo) closed in at our backs.

Valentine and Lavinia moved in toward Circe.

Franka, Derrik and Noc moved in next to Finnie.

My attention went to Apollo when I heard him give a sharp whistle and my breath caught in my lungs when the wolves slunk out of the woods.

Hundreds of them.

Maybe thousands.

I was right yesterday.

Helda was fucked.

He twisted to look at Valentine.

"Wake her," his deep voice growled.

"As you wish, *chéri*," Valentine replied then threw out her hand in an idle gesture.

The witch in the snow was pushing up on her arms, looking around.

But I didn't have much time to pay her attention.

Apollo was speaking.

"Justice be done," he stated, and without delay, turned his back to the witch, his cloak flying out behind him awesomely, and he sauntered our way.

The wolves also didn't delay.

As one, they pounced.

She got out one shriek.

Then nothing but growls, snarls and the sickening sound of moist tearing.

I swallowed.

Apollo, fortunately blocking my view of the carnage, walked right to me.

When he stopped in front of me, I drew in a deep breath and tipped my head back to gaze at him.

He was still pissed.

He again thought he'd lost me and he didn't like that much.

I had to do something about it.

I offered him part of what I had to offer him.

"Are the children okay?" I asked.

"Yes," he grunted.

"All of them?" I pushed.

"Yes," he repeated tersely.

"The guys? Are they all right?" I queried.

"Yes," he bit off.

Hmm.

It seemed all was okay and he was still pissed.

"All of them?" I pressed. "Frey's guys. Lahn's guys—"

"Yes, Maddie," he clipped out.

"Okay then, do you think there's time for me to put on my kickass dress and attend the gale? It'll be boring, what with no intrigue afoot, but I'm thinking I'd like to try my hand at dancing."

He stared down at me.

He did this for a while.

Then his hands shot out, grabbed hold of me and I slammed into his body as I watched him throw back his dark, handsome head and burst out laughing.

I wrapped my arms around him and smiled.

My job was done.

EPILOGUE
A BAG FILLED WITH HOPE

Needless to say, once the dome of protection went down and the Winter Palace was attacked by hewcrows and something called toil-roys (the troll-like creatures I saw on Specter Isle), and seeing as all the windows had been blown out and not all of them had yet been boarded up, pretty much everyone was freaked.

Thus, the Bitter Gales had been postponed.

This meant my kickass dress was still hanging in my room and I had my fingers wrapped around Apollo's arm as he guided us behind Tor and Cora, who were behind Circe and Lahn, who were following Frey and Finnie to a sitting room in the Winter Palace.

We entered, and Valentine and Lavinia were sitting next to each other on a couch. Derrik was standing beside the fireplace. Queen Aurora was sitting in a chair. Franka was in a corner, looking like she wanted to be anywhere but there. And Noc was standing at the boarded window, the other Circe not too far from him.

All eyes had come to us as we entered. Seeing as the room was huge, there was fortunately plenty of seating, so I was able to take a much needed load off when Apollo claimed a chair, seating me on the arm and curling his arm around my hips.

I wasn't sure who was in charge of the operation. I just knew when he spoke that Apollo was going to take charge of the debriefing.

"You first," he ordered, his voice curt, his eyes on Derrik.

"I infiltrated Specter Isle," Derrik replied.

"I could guess that part," Apollo returned.

Derrik turned more fully to Apollo and crossed his arms on his chest.

"It was not difficult to convince them there was a reason I was angry and would turn traitor," Derrik stated confusingly.

"I can imagine not. The question is, did you turn traitor?" Apollo inquired.

Derrik's face got hard. "Don't ask that, brother."

"Uh...just to say," I quickly put into this baffling exchange. "When the rescue mission commenced, Derrik was all over incapacitating Helda."

Derrik's face got soft as his eyes turned to me.

"Your purpose in doing this?" Apollo queried.

Derrik looked back to him. "Being with them, I could not know your plan and I could not get away to share theirs. All I knew was that both of you would have them. And I would be in the position to do something when they played out. I couldn't do much. But in the end, I was able to do something."

"This is true, *mon loup*," Valentine put in. "Our Noctorno of my world was sent there to dispatch Edith, as well as incapacitate Helda. This last was the difficult part that made it quite risky for him to go. However, you wanted her alive. I daresay those three didn't consider firearms entering the picture, or our handsome otherworld Noctorno. But I suspected it would not take long for them to recover from the death of Edith. The elves had to focus on resurrecting Lavinia so they could use her as the conduit to Specter Isle and then drain Minerva. It was most fortunate your man was there. It made things easier on us all."

Wow.

Lavinia had actually been dead.

And the elves resurrected her.

They *were* powerful.

Apollo turned his attention to Valentine. "Right, then, as you've explained that, it's clear you had this plan in place, a plan you did not share, when we already had a plan in place."

"You did, *chéri*, and it was a good one. I did not see it failing. And I did not wish to cause alarm by suggesting that it would. But you must admit, it is always wise to have a backup plan, no?"

I looked to Apollo's profile and saw a muscle jump in his cheek.

That meant it was wise, he just wasn't going to admit it out loud.

"Were you aware the witches could beat your enchantments and our women would be in danger?" Frey asked.

"Was I aware they were *that* in danger?" She shook her head. "No. Again, I did not see the protections on this palace beaten." Her eyes went languid when she stated, "I am rather good at what I do." Her lips tipped up. "But I did know they carried great power, so I asked Noctorno to be on call, just in case."

"Uh, just to say, no one calls me Noctorno," Noc stated, sounding irritated.

Valentine's lips tipped up further and she glanced his way.

"How did you do it?" I asked and Valentine looked to me. "They said you couldn't use your magic there. How did you?"

"You, *ma colombe*, and your sisters broke that enchantment," she answered. "This, I had hoped you would find your way to do. And you did."

"But I don't have magic," Cora remarked.

"I don't either," I said.

"Neither do I," Finnie added.

Valentine looked among us. "We women all have the capacity to carry magic. We just need the motivation. And love is a powerful motivation, don't you agree?"

Well, that couldn't be argued.

"Regardless," she went on, "Circe has magic and she was the channel to pull up yours. It was, as I'd hoped, quite powerful. Alas, I could not send your men or battalions of soldiers there, for even with their protections down, the triad was still at full strength, and someone might have been harmed in the ensuing fray. The instant they saw any of us, they would pull up defenses, vickrants, toilroys, etcetera. Therefore, once I could transport someone there, I sent someone they would not see as a threat, Franka, instilled with a spell to open a line for the elves to get to Lavinia as well as to create a diversion for," she glanced Noc's way, "*Noc* to arrive and finally make it safe for myself and the men to come, without the tedious bother of dealing with armies of creatures."

Tedious bother.

This woman was something else.

"So Franka has magic?" Finnie asked, looking Franka's way.

"She is, of course, a woman. A woman with her own motivation," Valentine murmured.

I was looking Franka's way too.

She was avoiding everyone's eyes.

Even so, I said, "Thank you."

Her head jerked and she focused on me.

"Thank you," I repeated. "That took a lot of courage and I...well, I appreciate it."

"I didn't do it for you," she stated coldly.

"Maybe not, but in the end, you still helped us and I'm still grateful," I returned.

Apollo's arm around me gave me a squeeze.

Franka's mouth got tight as she held my eyes for long moments before she looked away.

"Are you okay, Lavinia?" Finnie asked.

"It is not fun being dead," Lavinia replied, then she smiled a small smile. "But as I am no longer thus, and all is well in my Lunwyn again, I am fine."

"Are we done?" Valentine inquired into this exchange. "I'm sorely in need of a beverage."

"I am as well," Queen Aurora murmured, straightening from her chair. "Perhaps two of them. I'll call for a servant."

She moved and thus endeth the debrief.

Cora, followed by Tor, moved Noc's way.

Finnie went to Lavinia.

I got off the arm of the chair, grabbed Apollo's hand, pulled him out of the chair, and I headed us Derrik's way.

He looked only at me as we moved to him. I didn't know what this meant, but things needed to be said now so I decided to ask Apollo later.

For then, I just smiled at Derrik, and when I reached him, I let Apollo go, got close and moved in to give Derrik a hug.

His arms closed around me and I felt his jaw at the side of my head.

"That had to suck, hanging with them for so long," I noted and heard his chuckle as he gave me a squeeze and leaned a bit away without letting me go.

I tipped my head back to look up at him.

"It was not fun, but I am no longer *hanging with them*, so I am fine," he said.

"I'm glad," I whispered then finished with feeling, "And thank you."

"I would do anything for you, Maddie," he whispered back, and I felt my throat close because he'd proved that true.

His arms loosened and I shifted to his side as he looked to Apollo.

"And I would do anything for you," he declared.

The second he did, Apollo shot a hand out, curled it around the side of Derrik's neck and yanked him forward so they were nose to nose, eye to eye.

"My gratitude, my brother," Apollo stated.

I swallowed as my nose started to tingle.

They both looked into each other's eyes for some time, and I waited, watching and deep breathing.

Apollo finally let his friend go and I moved in quickly.

"Okay, I hate to interrupt the reunion," I started, giving Derrik an I-hope-you-understand grin then looking up to Apollo. "But I *really* want to see the kids."

"Then I will take you to them," Apollo replied immediately.

"And Meeta and Loretta," I added.

"I will find them for you as well."

"And then I have seriously got to eat," I finished.

He grinned down at me.

Then he bent to me and touched his mouth to mine.

After that, as was his way, Apollo did not delay in getting me everything I wanted.

~

A WEEK LATER, I stood in an antechamber of the Dwelling of the Gods, staring at the glittering bundle of delicate branches Finnie just shoved into my hands.

"Before you go in there and participate in *the* longest, *the* most boring wedding ceremony of all time...something borrowed," she said. "I carried that when I married Frey." She grinned. "Of course I had no clue who he was at the time, but it ended okay."

Yes. One could certainly say it ended okay.

I grinned back at her.

She moved away as Circe moved in.

"Something old," she said, grabbing my hand, lifting it palm up and pressing a golden feather there.

It looked like it came from the kickass headband of feathers she had wrapped around her forehead and mingling in her hair.

"It's from my first crown," she told me. "I ripped it up when I got angry at Lahn and took myself back to my world." She closed my hand around the feather. "He kept the pieces. Some of them are in the one I'm wearing now. Some of them are in a pouch he carries with him every day. He kept them even when the odds were against him in getting me back and *winning* me back." She tipped her head to the side. "So I figure, they represent hope. And, seriously, there isn't a day filled with more hope than a wedding day."

I could totally believe Lahn carried Circe's feathers with him every day but not in hopes of anything. That man wanted her back, he was going to find a way.

And he did.

Still, it was a total honor having one.

"Thank you," I whispered, lifting my other hand to curl it around hers.

She gave me a smile, squeezed my hands and moved away.

I tucked the feather into the sleeve of my glove as Cora moved in.

"Something new," she said, lifting my hand and leaving it suspended as she fastened on my wrist a bracelet made of delicate platinum links on which dangled tiny platinum charms she showed me by twisting it around my wrist.

As they came into view, the skin at my wrist began to tingle because I knew what each one meant.

The fang of a wolf. Apollo. A bow and arrow. Christophe. A tiny doll. Élan. And a miniature rattle. Our yet to arrive girl.

Cora curled her fingers around mine and I looked from the bracelet to her.

"You can add to that as life brings you bounty," she said.

"Thank you," I replied yet again, my voice husky.

She grinned at me.

I deep breathed so I wouldn't mess up my makeup.

"And something blue." We heard and I turned my head and blinked, seeing Valentine suddenly there.

She drew her elegant hand up, flicked it out and I felt cold at my neck.

"Holy crap," Circe whispered.

I had the chance to do nothing as Valentine got close, placed her hands on my shoulders and turned me, moving me forward toward a gilt-edged mirror, where she stopped me.

And I saw against my throat in place of the jewelry that had lain there, an exquisite, tiered necklace glittering ice blue with extraordinarily cut Sjofn diamonds from Lunwyn.

I also saw Valentine behind me and I watched as she bent her head so her mouth was close to my ear.

"Some time ago, a man filled with sorrow handed me a bag filled with hope. Those stones were in that bag," she told me quietly and my eyes dropped back down to the necklace. "He knew, as I knew and now you know, even as he paid for the chance to have it again that love is priceless, love is worth every battle fought, every wound endured. He knew, as you now know, *ma colombe,* that love is everything."

I lifted my hand and touched the stones with the tips of my fingers, but my eyes moved to hers in the mirror.

"You're giving this to me?" I asked.

"Oh no, *ma chérie,* they have always been yours. I'm just returning them to you."

Holy cow.

I shook my head. "But...it's your payment."

"I have learned, Madeleine, and I must admit it was against my will, but I have learned that there are many ways to be compensated." Her fingers tipped in blood red pressed into my shoulders. "Today, you bind yourself to a man who holds you precious. You walk to him carrying a child made from love. I played a small part in that. And that is the only payment I need."

I was *so totally* talking Apollo into giving her more diamonds to get my Fritos.

"I don't know what to say," I told her.

"Say nothing. Just be. And in being, be happy," she replied.

Okay. Until then, I wasn't sure she was my favorite person.

But now she'd hit the top ten.

I smiled at her in the mirror.

Her lips tipped up in return.

The door flew open and Loretta flew in. "The men are getting restless!" she cried.

Meeta strolled after her, her attention coming to me, and noted, "This is true. However, things can hardly get started without you and it is an exercise in character to learn to wait."

She wasn't wrong.

But I didn't want my man to wait, so I made a move and felt Valentine's hands fall from my shoulders.

"Time to get this show started," Finnie murmured, came to me and leaned in to finish in my ear, "Try not to fall asleep."

I grinned into her hair.

Apollo had explained the marriage ceremony of Lunwyn. I knew I was in for a lot of standing and a lot of hearing words no one in the room understood because the holy men of this place spoke in the ancient tongue.

I did not care.

When it was done, Apollo Ulfr (the good one) would officially be mine.

To get that, I'd stand for a year and listen to someone prattle on.

Luckily, I didn't have to do that.

Finnie grabbed my hand and gave it a squeeze before she leaned away and winked.

"See you at the post-nuptial festivities," Circe said, dashing forward when Finnie moved away and touching her cheek to mine.

"See you there," I replied.

She gave me another smile before moving away and Cora was there.

She touched her cheek to mine too and said, "Don't be happy. Be *ecstatically* happy. You've earned it."

She was *so* sweet.

"I will," I promised.

She moved away and they all gathered together, Valentine not giving me any words for which I was glad. She'd said enough. I was just holding up. I didn't need to break down. I wanted Apollo to marry the awesome me, not the puffy-eyed, mascara-streaked, red-faced me.

But before they exited, I studied them, thinking it was pretty freaking cool I was friends with two bona-fide princesses and a full-blown queen.

And just thinking it was pretty freaking cool I had so many friends.

Finnie in her ice-blue velvet gown with the kickass crown in her white hair that looked like diamonds formed into icicles.

Circe wearing a heavy silk sarong made of gold material held up by a belt made of gold disks. Her gold bandeau top could be seen because it was covered by a sheer skintight long-sleeved golden top. A heavy-looking gold necklace at her neck, deeply dropping gold chandelier earrings at her ears and what appeared to be hundreds of gold bangles at her wrists. Her crown of feathers glimmering at her forehead.

Cora wearing a royal-blue velvet dress in the fashion of Lunwyn, a heavy gold chain hanging low on her hips, the ends dripping down into massive sapphires, a tasteful, but fabulous gold crown mingled in her shining brunette updo.

The dream team.

My dream team.

Women who, like me, knew impossible, amazing, *fantastical* dreams could come true.

Dreams you would not dare to dream.

Dreams that we lived in every day.

I blew them a kiss.

They returned the gesture (all but Valentine) and moved through the door.

Loretta and Meeta rushed forward when they did, both putting their hands to me. Meeta's rising to my fiddle with my hair, Loretta's lowering to fidget with the skirt of my gown.

"What's this?" Meeta asked, leaning back, her eyes on my necklace. Then she looked to me. "This does not go with your gown Miss Maddie."

She was right.

It didn't.

My gown was the gown I was to wear to the Bitter Gales.

A gown that was now my wedding gown.

Ulfr-green satin, off-the-shoulder, but the low neckline and around my upper arms were fashioned in a wide luxurious line of black-brown mink. The hem and long train of my skirt had the same fur tracing it. My low-slung belt was also gold but fitted in every other link was an emerald and a topaz. I had half a dozen matching bejeweled combs holding up the intricate twists and curls of my hair and matching dangling earrings falling from my earlobes. And I had topaz evening gloves with thin tufts of mink at the ends.

The ice-blue diamonds didn't match.

And yet they were utterly perfect.

"It's from Apollo," I told Meeta.

It wasn't the exact truth.

But it was still true.

"Ah," she mumbled.

I smiled at her.

She caught my eyes and smiled back.

"There are two ladies who need to take their seats and the Head of a House who's growing rather impatient," a man's voice noted, and we all looked to the door to see Achilles had his head stuck in.

"Right! Must dash!" Loretta exclaimed, jumped forward, kissed me on the cheek and then darted out of the room.

"Until later, Miss Maddie," Meeta said calmly, leaned forward, touched her cheek to mine, leaned back as she caught my hands and gave them a squeeze before she let me go and sauntered out like she was taking an evening stroll.

Achilles had shifted out of their way to let them go but when they were gone, he joined me in the room.

"Ready, little bug?" he asked quietly.

"Ready, Lees," I replied quietly.

He offered his arm.

I moved forward and took it.

He guided me out of the antechamber and into the vestibule of the Dwelling of the Gods.

Draven, Hans, Alek, Remi, Gaston and Laures were all standing around, wearing the colors of their houses, waiting.

All except Derrik, who wasn't standing.

He was moving to me, smiling.

"And she makes a beautiful bride," he murmured when he arrived.

"Thanks, honey," I murmured back.

Apollo had since explained all that had gone down with him and Derrik. I was surprised, and it had to be said, a little sad to learn it. It was another miracle that both men got over it and now...

Well now...

He shifted to my side and offered his arm.

Now, he was ours again. Mine. Apollo's. And the House of Ulfr's.

I took in a deep breath, rearranged my bouquet of adela branches to rest against Achilles' elbow, and accepted it.

With Achilles on one side of me, Derrik on the other, they turned me to face the door.

Laures, Draven with Hans behind them moved into formation in front of us. Remi and Gaston, with Alek trailing, moved in behind us.

Laures jerked up his chin at the two young boys standing at the doors.

They opened them and my stomach dropped.

"All right?" Derrik asked, curling his fingers over mine at his elbow.

"Absolutely," I answered, gazing straight ahead.

The men moved.

I went with them.

At the front of the sanctuary were statues of the gods of this world and a man wearing white robes and a long multi-colored wrap draped around his neck that dangled down the front.

Also at the front was Apollo, wearing a well-tailored shirt of Ulfr green, an equally well-tailored brown jacket, exceptionally well-tailored brown breeches, highly-polished brown boots and a neck cloth.

I had a feeling, seeing him in that moment, I would have many times in my life where I was awed by his beauty.

But no time would be better than that.

We stopped at the end of the pews so we could turn right, the men could bow and I could curtsy to Queen Aurora who sat in the middle of the pew, Frey and Finnie, Circe and Lahn, Cora and Tor sharing the pew with her.

Christophe and Élan, though, sat at her sides.

When she bid us to rise, we did and I dipped my head to her, sent a smile along the entirety of the pew but I winked at Christophe and Élan.

Élan giggled and waved.

Christophe just tipped his chin to me.

We turned and the men led me to Apollo.

I only had eyes for him and he only had eyes for me.

In fact, when Laures, Draven and Hans cleared away and the man in white robes started speaking, Apollo didn't even look at him.

He also didn't look at him when the man stopped speaking and Apollo lifted his fist.

He continued to hold my eyes as Derrik let me go, Achilles moved me forward, lifted my hand, and curled my fingers around Apollo's fist.

He didn't even look away when the man in white robes said something and all Apollo's men called, "Yes!"

The man in white robes said more as I felt Apollo's men move away, and there I was, at his side, his head tipped down, mine tipped back, all so we could keep the contact Apollo would not break.

I had a feeling he liked my outfit.

Though, I had a stronger feeling he just liked me.

He finally looked away but only for an instant to gaze at my throat before his eyes returned to mine and I saw something flash in his.

"That's a becoming necklace," he noted on a low murmur.

"An early wedding present," I murmured back.

"And a pleasant surprise." He was still talking low.

He knew what it was.

"Indeed," I replied.

He grinned.

I took in that grin, those eyes, the feel of his hand under mine and I blurted, "I love you, Apollo Ulfr."

This time, his eyes didn't flash.

They blazed.

"And I love you, Madeleine Ulfr."

I shuffled closer.

Then I broke eye contact only to instigate a different kind.

I leaned into him, rested my head on his shoulder and turned my gaze to the man in the robes.

I saw the holy man nod to me, but I felt Apollo's lips touch my hair.

The man babbled on.

And on.

And on.

He even wandered around the statues doing it.

But I didn't fall asleep and I didn't get bored.

I might not have memorized every moment (because there were a lot of them, the Lunwynian wedding ceremony was *long*), but I definitely memorized what I was feeling.

And when the ceremony was finally done, my new husband turned me to him, wrapped his arms around me and dipped his lips to mine.

But before he could kiss me, I whispered, "Remember this kiss."

His eyes peering into mine, already warm, they turned sweet.

"Always," he replied.

And without delay, my husband gave me exactly what I wanted, in fact what he always gave me.

A kiss worth remembering.

Apollo

SIX MONTHS LATER, Apollo looked from the contract he was signing to the man sitting across from him at his desk.

"Is this all?" he asked.

"It is," Jeremiah answered.

Apollo nodded, lifted the paper and tossed it across the desk, murmuring, "Then enjoy the rest of your day."

"You as well," Jeremiah replied.

Apollo said nothing.

But he knew he would.

He straightened from his chair, dipped his chin at his secretary and sauntered out of the room.

He heard them the instant he opened the doors. Thus, he headed straight to the great room.

He got to the top of the steps and wasn't able to fully take in the room's occupants before Élan dashed to him, stopping only when she hit his body. The moment she did, she wrapped her arms around his hips and tipped her head back to catch his eyes.

"Maddie and me made cookies!" she cried.

"Is that so?" he asked softly, putting a hand to her thick hair.

"Sugar!" she stated excitedly.

"Are they good?" he asked.

"They are!" she exclaimed, then added excitedly. "And we rolled them in pretty colored sugar crystals so they're all blue and pink and green!"

"I can't wait to try one," he told her.

"It's safe now," she replied authoritatively. "But Chris has a burnt tongue. Maddie told him to wait until they cooled, but he didn't listen." She grinned. "He still said they were yummy."

Apollo smiled in his daughter's eyes and slid his hand to her cheek where he brushed it affectionately with his finger.

She let him go but only to move to his side and take his hand.

That was when Apollo fully saw all that was happening in the great room.

And that was when Apollo went completely still.

This was because the fire was burning merrily in its grate. A soft snow was falling outside the windows. Laures, Alek, Draven, Derrik, Remi and Gaston were lingering around chairs and a table that had been arranged in the center of the space. Off to the side, up the steps and almost hidden around a corner, Hans and Loretta were in each other's arms, faces close, attention absolutely not focused on what was happening twenty feet away. And Meeta was sitting in a chair, eyes on the action in the center of the room.

And the action was Achilles sitting opposite Madeleine, a game of ricken set up on a table between them, Christophe sitting in a chair pulled close to Maddie's side.

His Maddie had her eyes to the board but her hand resting on her rounded belly.

Achilles made a move. Christophe and Maddie studied the board, then Chris leaned deep, hanging over the side of his chair to whisper into Maddie's ear.

Maddie looked to him. "You're sure?" she asked.

Christophe nodded.

She leaned in and whispered in his boy's ear.

When she pulled away, Apollo saw his son grin at his wife. "That's better."

She turned back to the board, her lips curled up, and made her move.

"Bloody hell," Achilles muttered.

Remi hooted, "Get out of that one, Lees."

Achilles looked to Christophe and Madeleine. "You two are a formidable pair."

Maddie grinned at Achilles before she turned and lifted her hand, palm facing Chris.

His son lifted his hand and smacked it.

And Apollo's chest expanded so sharply, he thought it would burst.

Because there she was. His dove. His Maddie. His wife.

In a warm, safe place where she was always welcome because it was her home, surrounded by love, making memories of laughter and happy times.

And there was his son, right next to her.

A formidable pair.

Suddenly, she turned to him, smiled and called, "There you are."

Apollo didn't move.

For in her eyes he saw nothing. No darkness. No despair.

He'd mined those depths and nothing but light shined through.

He'd given that to her.

It had been the most important mission of his life.

And he'd bested it.

He swallowed past the thick in his throat and called back, "Indeed."

It was then he felt his daughter tugging at his hand.

He let her lead him to his family.

He pulled up a chair on Maddie's other side and allowed his daughter to crawl into his lap.

When she did, he wrapped his arms around her.

And then he watched Christophe and Madeleine beat Achilles at ricken.

Directly after, sitting in the heart of his familial home, his wife and children safe, close and happy, with great contentment, Apollo Ulfr listened to his family's laughter ringing in the air.

~

Maddie

I WAS SITTING on the sofa, reading a letter from Finnie.

Or I was trying to. She'd written it on the deck of Frey's ship so the salty sea air had made the letters bleed.

But I got the jist of it and the jist of it was that apparently, dads with sons stopped being idiot dads when they had daughters.

Or at least they weren't idiot dads with their daughters.

I could tell by Finnie's stories of how Frey was with their Alyssa.

Added proof were the stories I read through Circe's letters of how Lahn was with Andromeda (then again, he wasn't an idiot dad with Isis either, just Tunahn).

And last, from what I'd learned through Cora's letters of how Tor was with their little Dara.

I was grinning as I was nearing the end of Finnie's tales of Frey turning from idiot dad to an overprotective one when I felt movement in the room.

I looked up to see Élan entering.

She walked directly to me, threw herself on the sofa beside me and crossed her arms on her little girl chest.

I knew what that meant.

"I take it the carriage is ready," I remarked.

She tipped her head back to aim her jade eyes to me. "Do I have to go back, Maddie?" she asked on a pout.

"I'm afraid you do, honey bunch. School is important."

She aimed her eyes in front of her and kept pouting. "I don't know why you stay all the way out here in the country when Papa has a house right in Benies."

I didn't know either. Except that it was peaceful here. And I suspected my husband, as any soldier would in a time without war, needed peace.

"Maybe I can talk your father into moving there for a couple of weeks so you and Chris can come home after school rather than staying there," I offered. "And on the weekends, we can go shopping, and have a pastry in a café, and maybe he'll take us for dinner at *Le Pont de L'eau*."

Her head shot back, and I again got her eyes. "Would you?"

"Anything for you," I replied, and it was absolutely no lie.

Her face lit.

My sweet Élan's face lit often, but I suspected this time it was because she knew what I said was true.

A voice came from the door.

"Hurry up," Chris called. "The carriage is waiting."

Élan started pouting again, but I put the letter aside and got up from the couch, grabbing her hand and tugging her up with me.

We walked hand in hand to the door as Christophe watched, his eyes aimed to our clasped hands.

He never missed anything. Not Chris. He was ever watchful.

As any good soldier or writer would need to be.

He moved out of the door when we arrived. He then fell in step on the other side of me as we made our way to the front door.

I thought I would get used to it, the contentment, the calm that came from the absolute understanding that I had everything.

Walking to the door with Chris and Élan, marveling at the sweet sensation of having them in my life and having them accept me in theirs, I knew I'd never get used to it.

And I knew why.

Because it got better when Chris opened the door and my husband, standing on the steps waiting for us, the sun shining on his dark hair, his green shirt opened at the collar, his brown breeches fitting him way to well, turned our way.

His warm, contented eyes slid through me before he looked to his kids.

"Ready?" he asked.

"I'm ready," Chris answered.

"I'm never ready to go back to school," Élan groused.

"We'll see you at the week's end, precious girl," Apollo told her. "Now, give Maddie a kiss and let us be away."

Élan let my hand go but only to turn to me and give me both of her arms.

I bent to her and gave her mine as well as a kiss on the cheek.

She touched her lips to mine before she let me go and dragged her feet as she walked to her father. Her step lightened when he lifted a hand to her and she reached out to take it.

Chris turned and looked up at me. "Until the week's end, Maddie."

I lifted a hand and again marveled at the sensation of how beautiful it was when he allowed me to bend to him and cup his jaw.

"Look after your sister," I told him softly.

"I will," he replied.

I gave him a smile.

He smiled back.

I marveled at the sensation that caused too.

I dropped my hand and Chris turned, sauntering with his father's grace to the carriage Élan had already entered.

I moved to Apollo, put a hand on his stomach and tipped my head back.

He took the invitation and dropped his to touch his mouth to mine.

"I'll return in a few hours, my dove," he said there.

"See you then, baby."

He grinned against my lips.

I returned the favor.

Then he brushed his mouth to mine before he moved away, and I watched him mount his horse.

I stood on the steps of our country house in Fleuridia, the first place I'd known in this world, and waved as the carriage rolled away, Apollo riding at its side.

My husband didn't wave back but he bowed his head to me.

Élan, however, hung out the carriage window and waved frantically.

I stood where I was until they were out of sight.

Since the view was long, this took some time.

But I had hours to kill before my man returned, so I took it. And I enjoyed the vision before me. The colors so vivid they hurt the eyes. The memory that here was where I left a life not worth living behind and was given a life that was worth dying for.

When they were gone, I moved back into the house thinking I should write Finnie a letter. Or Cora. Or Circe.

However, I didn't go to my writing desk.

I went to the stairs, thinking it would be nice when Loretta returned from her honeymoon with Hans. I missed her. I was happy for her, but I missed her.

I then turned to thinking it would be nice when Meeta returned from her vacation sex-a-thon with Ruben.

He'd asked for her hand.

She said she didn't want to leave me.

He said he couldn't leave Frey.

They were at a stalemate, working it out at Ruben's house in Houllebec in Lunwyn. This meant, even if she left to journey to me in Fleuridia, I wouldn't see her for months.

And I hoped in those months she'd decide to give in to Ruben.

Her friendship and loyalty meant a lot to me (not to mention, she was a master at doing good hair).

But love.

Love was everything.

On this thought, I entered the room and made my quiet way to the exceptionally girlie crib with its frilly green bedclothes, the mobile hanging low over it made of padded gray wolves.

I looked down into the crib and blinked.

In it was Valentine, my daughter, with her little frizz of auburn hair and tiny nose across which danced freckles.

Though, if she opened her sleepy eyes, I would see their pure translucent jade green.

That was not what surprised me.

What surprised me was at the end of her crib was a bag of scoop-shaped Fritos, a box of ballpoint pens, a pouch made of emerald green satin, and an envelope with my name written on it.

I reached in and grabbed the envelope.

Tearing it open, I slid out the letter, the words written in green ink.

Ma Colombe,

Your wolf wished you to have these so here they are.

What's in the pouch, however, is a gift from me.

I dash this to you for things don't ever stay boring, fortunately. Love is in the air, and with it comes its tribulations.

This time, we shall see if a woman from there can settle into life with a man from here.

I do believe our Noctorno of this world will have his work cut out for him.

But in the end, I've no doubt he'll succeed.

With a little bit of meddling.

My namesake is, of course, beautiful, chérie.

As ever, I wish you happiness,

Valentine

. . .

Smiling to myself, I slid the letter back into the envelope, removed the goodies from Valentine's crib and set them aside. Then I touched the soft pink skin of my baby girl's cheek.

The pregnancy was not without its normal dramas. The delivery wasn't short. It thankfully wasn't long. And it happened in this world by my choice.

And my choice was, this was my world, and I didn't want to leave it.

And there she was.

Proof that the future beamed bright.

In fact, I was standing by the crib of my sleeping daughter, and I was blinded by it.

Even so, I could stand there for days.

But I didn't.

I moved to the green pouch Valentine had left. I nabbed it, shoved my fingers in the opening and pulled it wide.

Instantly, a glow emanated from the bag.

I stared at the glow a moment before I dipped my nose close and took in a breath.

Peppermint, with hints of vanilla and licorice.

It was then, I smiled.

~

Apollo fell to his back, taking me with him.

I was breathing heavily, my hand moving over his slick skin, my eyes moving across the room.

There we were in the mirrors Apollo had fitted to the doors of the wide wardrobe—Apollo on his back, his long, strong, muscled body stretched out on the bed, me straddling him, my forehead in his neck, my naked torso pressed to his, our bodies connected. My skin appeared creamy in contrast to the olive tone of his.

We looked amazing.

My eyes slid to the two empty china teacups sitting on our nightstand, but they went back to the mirror when I felt his touch.

I watched his hand glide lazily over the cheek of my behind. Watching it, feeling it, I lifted my head and slid up his chest so I had his eyes.

There it was. That look. The first look he'd ever given me.

Minus one thing.

He was staring at me with tenderness.

But no pain.

I gave him that.

Me.

Warmth that had not one thing to do with adela tea surged though me, and I dropped my mouth to his.

"More?" I whispered.

"You up for it?" he whispered back.

I felt my lips smile. Then I saw the same in his eyes, but I also saw more.

Tenderness.

Satisfaction.

Happiness.

Love.

I gave him that.

Me.

"Absolutely," I murmured, pressed into him and finished, "Always."

He slanted his head, his arms curved around me, his mouth took mine and he rolled me to my back.

Then, just like Apollo, he gave me more.

He did it right then.

And he did it again, in nine months, when our son Aether was born.

The End

GLOSSARY OF PARALLEL UNIVERSE

PLACES, SEAS, REGIONS IN THE KRISTEN ASHLEY'S FANTASYLAND SERIES

Bellebryn—(place) Small, peaceful, city-sized princedom located in the Northlands and fully within the boundaries of Hawkvale and the Green Sea (west)

Fleuridia—(place) Somewhat advanced, peaceful nation located in the Northlands; boundaries to Hawkvale (north and west) and the Marhac Sea (south)

Green Sea—(body of water) Ocean-like body of water with coastlines abutting Bellebryn, Hawkvale, Lunwyn and Middleland

Hawkvale—(place) Somewhat advanced, peaceful nation located in the Northlands; boundaries with Middleland (north), Fleuridia (south and east) and the Green Sea (west) and Marhac Sea (south)

Keenhak—(place) Primitive, warring nation located in the Southlands; boundaries with Korwahk (north) and Maroo (west)

Korwahk—(place) Primitive, warring nation located in the Southlands; boundaries with the Marhac Sea (north) and the nations of Keenhak (southeast) and Maroo (southwest)

Korwahn—(place) Large capital city of Korwahk

Lunwyn—(place) Somewhat advanced, peaceful nation in the farthest reaches of the Northlands; boundaries to Middleland (south), the Green Sea (west) and the Winter Sea (north)

Marhac Sea—(large body of water) Separates Korwahk and Hawkvale and Fleuridia

Maroo—(place) Primitive, warring nation located in the Southlands; boundaries to Korwahk (north) and Keenhak (east)

Middleland—(place) Somewhat advanced nation with tyrant king located in the Northlands; boundaries to Hawkvale (south), Fleuridia (south), Lunwyn (north) and the Green Sea (west)

[The] Northlands—(region) The region north of the equator on the alternate earth

[The] Southlands—(region) The region south of the equator on the alternate earth

Winter Sea—(large body of water) Arctic body of water that forms the northern coast of Lunwyn, filled with large glaciers

KEEP READING FOR MORE FANTASYLAND

Midnight Soul

Against his will, Noctorno Hawthorne, an undercover vice cop, finds himself embroiled in magic, mayhem and parallel universes. Too late, he meets an amazing woman only to find she's destined for his identical twin in another world.

And things aren't going great there.

Noc is recruited to help save that world.

What he doesn't know is his destined love resides there.

Franka Drakkar wears a mask. A mask she never takes off to protect herself in a world of malice, intrigue and danger.

When Franka meets Noc and he discovers her secrets, convinced she carries a midnight soul, having shielded herself from forming bonds with anyone, she struggles with accepting his tenderness and care.

When Noc meets Franka, over wine and whiskey, her mask slips and Noc knows it's her—only her—and he has to find a way to get her to come home with him.

And then make her want to stay.

Keep reading for more Midnight Soul.

MIDNIGHT SOUL
CHAPTER ONE

Wouldn't Even Blink

Franka

...I watched as he sauntered right in front of me to the chair accompanying mine, threw his lengthy frame in it and reached for the wine at the table that separated our seats.

He also reached for the extra glass.

These were seats, I shall add, that were turned at corners to each other with a small, round table in between, so my knee was nearly touching his.

He poured.

It was on the tip of my tongue to share that I had not invited him to attend me.

Alas, I became distracted by his long fingers, and the words died in my mouth.

"That shit was whacked," Noctorno declared, easing back in his chair, lifting the red wine to finely-molded male lips while I watched. "Glad it's done," he finished before he drew in a sip.

With some effort I refused to acknowledge, I turned my eyes back to the fire.

"Franka, right?" he asked my name.

"Correct," I answered, thinking that one of the other universe women claimed by men in this one should have shared with this man, princely or not, that as a member of the guard he was well beyond his station *tossing* his (long, powerful) body in a chair, *helping himself* to *my* wine and *introducing* himself *to me* with a, "Franka, right?"

Inexcusable.

Perhaps this was how they did it in his world.

It was not how we did it in mine.

I was of the House of Drakkar. I was aristocracy. My cousin, Frey Drakkar was *The* Frey, *The* Drakkar. He commanded elves *and* dragons. He was married to the Ice Princess of my snowy country (even though she actually wasn't the *real* princess, she was from a parallel universe, I had no earthly idea what had become of the real Princess Sjofn, but everyone seemed to be disregarding that so I had no choice but to do so as well, and frankly I'd never liked the woman much anyway, her replacement, however, was quite spirited).

Not to mention, my cousin, Frey, had already sired the future king on her, for Adele's sake!

I was, however, not going to offer myself up for etiquette lessons to this man.

I would sip my wine and hope he'd get the indication I wished no company through my manner. If he didn't, I would leave (though, I couldn't figure out how to do that and take the other bottle of wine with me without this appearing undignified).

As I turned this quandary in my brain, he said in that gentle voice, "Hay," again, but he added at the end, for some unknown reason and for the second time in the short period he'd been addressing me, "babe."

I turned to him and informed him condescendingly, "You speak strangely."

That got another twitch of his head before he asked, "Pardon?"

"Hay. Babe," I said. "What do these words mean?"

"You...uh, don't have the words 'hey' and 'babe' in this world?"

I lifted my chin a smidge.

"Of course we do. Hay is fed to horses. And babes are wee. Newborns. I simply don't understand why you utter them to me."

He grinned.

My heart squeezed, the pain so immense it was a wonder I didn't double over, fall to the floor, dead before I hit.

So handsome. That light in his striking eyes.

My Antoine had been handsome.

But when he'd smiled...

"Not saying 'hay,'" Noctorno told me. "I'm saying 'hey,' with an e. It's how people say hello, greet each other in my world."

I battled the pain, hid the severity of the fight and nodded my head once.

"And 'babe?'" I prompted, though I shouldn't have. Engaging in discourse would not get him to leave.

"It's what guys call chicks in my world."

I drew up a brow.

He watched it go and his striking eyes lit brighter.

"Chicks?" I asked, ignoring the amused light in his eyes.

"Girls. Women."

"Girls and women?" I asked.

"Well, you wouldn't call a girl-girl, like a little kid, a babe or a chick. You'd call women that."

"So it's an endearment," I deduced, thinking that I might, indeed, expend the effort to have a word with one of the women in this world who were of his world to share with him a few important things.

Precisely that he shouldn't be referring to anyone he barely knew, and certainly not his superior, with an endearment.

"That, though chick is more slang," he shared.

"In other words, in your world, you refer to the female gender with words indicating to said female every time you use them that you think they're as vulnerable and weak as a newborn child or the like, but that of a species of fowl."

Without hesitation, his mirth surged forth, filling the room, warming it, drawing me out of my mood, away from the events of that day, of the last months, of the loss of the only man I'd ever loved, and silently I watched and listened.

I gave no indication I enjoyed it.

But I enjoyed it.

He controlled his joviality but didn't stop smiling or watching me as he asked, "What do you call dudes here?"

"Dudes?" I responded to his query with a query.

"Men," he explained, still smiling. "Guys."

"We call them men or gentlemen."

"No, I mean endearments or slang."

"*I*, personally, *do not* engage in uttering *slang*."

He studied me like I was a highly entertaining jester who'd come to court before he inquired, "Okay, what do you call a man you're in with?"

"In with?"

"Who means something to you. Your guy. Your man," he stated.

I looked to the fire again, feeling my face freeze.

The instant I did, he bit off, "*Fuck*." There was a slight pause before, "Babe... Franka, Tor told me about the shit that went down...fuck." I felt strong fingers curl around my wrist, a wrist I was resting on the arm of the chair, before he finished, "That was stupid. I'm so sorry."

With a delicate twist, I freed myself from his touch, lifted my wineglass to my lips, and before I took a sip I murmured, "It's nothing."

"Bullshit."

This odd word made my gaze move back to him.

"I beg your pardon?" I snapped.

"Bullshit," he repeated.

"I don't understand this word."

Though I had a feeling I did.

There was no smile on his face. No humor in his eyes. He was regarding me closely again, but this time I was prepared and didn't shift in my seat.

"You're full of it," he explained. "You're not giving me the entire truth. You're saying something to get past something you don't want to be talking about."

"And if I did this, considering what we both know I'm moving us past, it's customary to allow the awkward moment to *pass*."

He leaned slightly toward me. "You're in here all alone, drinkin' wine by yourself, lookin' like the world just ended. And I get why you'd feel that way. I don't understand, when all the others are so tight, why you aren't tight with them. But that's not my business. All I know is, you put your ass on the line today to save four women's lives and the life of every being in this universe. It took courage to do that, babe. You suffered a big loss losing your man and I'm sorry for that. But at least for tonight you should be proud of what you did for your country, for four good women and the men who love them, for the memory of the man you lost. It's time to celebrate. The good side won and *you*," he pointed a finger at me (insufferably *rude*!), "were a part of that."

Again, on the tip of my tongue, words hovered to share precisely, in a calculated way, how I knew he had celebrated with Circe.

Those words did not drop off my tongue.

They vanished completely as I simply turned my attention back to the fire.

"And that kinda situation does not say wine," he carried on. "It says whiskey, vodka, or better yet, tequila."

I could not argue with that (regardless of the fact I had no idea what tequila was).

"To that, I heartily agree," I declared, deigning again to glance at him and wishing I hadn't, for his smile had returned, making me further wish I could snatch my words back.

"I'll go find something," he announced, putting his hands to the arms of the chair in order to heft his big frame out of it, and I felt my brows draw together as, once he was up, it seemed he was moving toward the door.

"You simply have to pull the cord and demand it of a servant," I explained.

He was now standing, staring down at me, appearing bemused.

By the powers of Adele, if she reigned in his realm, she gave him more than his fair share of *everything*.

He even looked delectable bemused!

I really had to leave as quickly as I could without giving anything away.

"Uh...what?" he asked.

I gestured indolently with a hand to the cord in the corner of the room. "Pull the cord. A bell sounds..." I didn't have the information of where it sounded as I didn't concern myself with such matters, and continued with, "somewhere. A servant comes. We tell him we want whiskey. He brings it."

His lips quirked.

I drew in an annoyed breath for that was delectable too.

"Right," he muttered and began to stride toward the cord.

I twisted in my chair and called to his back, "When they arrive, share with them more fuel needs to be added to the fire."

He stopped and turned back to me while I was speaking.

When I was done, he looked to the fire and then back to me.

"Babe, there's a pile of logs right there," he stated.

"Indeed, there are," I agreed, though I hadn't concerned myself with that matter either and had no idea if he spoke truth.

"So I can put more *fuel* on the fire."

By Adele, he again looked amused.

I needed to find a way to exit this situation with all due haste.

"If you wish to dirty your hands..." I left it at that but added a slight shrug.

He shook his head, his mouth again quirking, and he turned back to the cord.

Fine.

He would order whiskey.

I would imbibe a bit (or perhaps more than a bit). Then I'd find a way to purloin the extra bottle of wine and the glass and remove myself to my rooms.

This was my plan.

As Franka Drakkar of the House of Drakkar, I was very good with plans, making them and executing them to their fullest.

However, that night, not for the first time, I would not succeed.

Midnight Soul is available now.

ABOUT THE AUTHOR

Kristen Ashley is the *New York Times* bestselling author of over eighty romance novels including the *Rock Chick, Colorado Mountain, Dream Man, Chaos, Unfinished Heroes, The 'Burg, Magdalene, Fantasyland, The Three, Ghost and Reincarnation, The Rising, Dream Team, Moonlight and Motor Oil, River Rain, Wild West MC, Misted Pines* and *Honey* series along with several standalone novels. She's a hybrid author, publishing titles both independently and traditionally, her books have been translated in fourteen languages and she's sold over five million books.

Kristen's novel, *Law Man*, won the *RT Book Reviews* Reviewer's Choice Award for best Romantic Suspense, her independently published title *Hold On* was nominated for *RT Book Reviews* best Independent Contemporary Romance and her traditionally published title *Breathe* was nominated for best Contemporary Romance. Kristen's titles *Motorcycle Man, The Will,* and *Ride Steady* (which won the Reader's Choice award from *Romance Reviews*) all made the final rounds for Goodreads Choice Awards in the Romance category.

Kristen, born in Gary and raised in Brownsburg, Indiana, is a fourth-generation graduate of Purdue University. Since, she's lived in Denver, the West Country of England, and she now resides in Phoenix. She worked as a charity executive for eighteen years prior to beginning her independent publishing career. She now writes full-time.

Although romance is her genre, the prevailing themes running through all of Kristen's novels are friendship, family and a strong sisterhood. To this end, and as a way to thank her readers for their support, Kristen has created the Rock Chick Nation, a series of programs that are designed to give back to her readers and promote a strong female community.

The mission of the Rock Chick Nation is to live your best life, be true to your true self, recognize your beauty, and take your sister's back whether they're at your side as friends and family or if they're thousands of miles away and you don't know who they are.

The programs of the RC Nation include Rock Chick Rendezvous, weekends Kristen organizes full of parties and get-togethers to bring the sisterhood together, Rock Chick Recharges, evenings Kristen arranges for women who have been nominated to receive a special night, and Rock Chick Rewards, an ongoing program that raises funds for nonprofit women's organizations Kristen's readers nominate. Kristen's Rock Chick Rewards have donated hundreds of thousands of dollars to charity and this number continues to rise.

You can read more about Kristen, her titles and the Rock Chick Nation at KristenAshley.net.

facebook.com/kristenashleybooks
twitter.com/KristenAshley68
instagram.com/kristenashleybooks
pinterest.com/KristenAshleyBooks
goodreads.com/kristenashleybooks
bookbub.com/authors/kristen-ashley

Also by Kristen Ashley

Rock Chick Series:

Rock Chick

Rock Chick Rescue

Rock Chick Redemption

Rock Chick Renegade

Rock Chick Revenge

Rock Chick Reckoning

Rock Chick Regret

Rock Chick Revolution

Rock Chick Reawakening

Rock Chick Reborn

The 'Burg Series:

For You

At Peace

Golden Trail

Games of the Heart

The Promise

Hold On

The Chaos Series:

Own the Wind

Fire Inside

Ride Steady

Walk Through Fire

A Christmas to Remember

Rough Ride

Wild Like the Wind

Free

Wild Fire

Wild Wind

The Colorado Mountain Series:

The Gamble

Sweet Dreams

Lady Luck

Breathe

Jagged

Kaleidoscope

Bounty

Dream Man Series:

Mystery Man

Wild Man

Law Man

Motorcycle Man

Quiet Man

Dream Team Series:

Dream Maker

Dream Chaser

Dream Bites Cookbook

Dream Spinner

Dream Keeper

The Fantasyland Series:

Wildest Dreams

The Golden Dynasty

Fantastical

Broken Dove

Midnight Soul

Gossamer in the Darkness

Ghosts and Reincarnation Series:

Sommersgate House

Lacybourne Manor

Penmort Castle

Fairytale Come Alive

Lucky Stars

The Honey Series:

The Deep End

The Farthest Edge

The Greatest Risk

The Magdalene Series:

The Will

Soaring

The Time in Between

Mathilda, SuperWitch:

Mathilda's Book of Shadows

Mathilda The Rise of the Dark Lord

Misted Pines Series

The Girl in the Mist

The Girl in the Woods

Moonlight and Motor Oil Series:

The Hookup

The Slow Burn

The Rising Series:

The Beginning of Everything

The Plan Commences

The Dawn of the End

The Rising

The River Rain Series:

After the Climb

After the Climb Special Edition

Chasing Serenity

Taking the Leap

Making the Match

The Three Series:

Until the Sun Falls from the Sky

With Everything I Am

Wild and Free

The Unfinished Hero Series:

Knight

Creed

Raid

Deacon

Sebring

Wild West MC Series:

Still Standing

Smoke and Steel

Other Titles by Kristen Ashley:

Heaven and Hell

Play It Safe

Three Wishes

Complicated

Loose Ends

Fast Lane

Perfect Together (Summer 2023)